THE LARION SENATORS

The Eldarn Sequence Book 3

Also by Robert Scott and Jay Gordon from Gollancz:

The Hickory Staff
Lessek's Key

THE LARION SENATORS

The Eldarn Sequence Book 3

Robert Scott
and Jay Gordon

The right of Robert Scott and Jay Gordon to be identified as the authors of
this work has been asserted by them in accordance with the
Copyright, Designs and Patents Act 1988.

First published in Great Britain in 2007 by
Gollancz
An imprint of the Orion Publishing Group
Orion House, 5 Upper St Martin's Lane, London WC2H 9EA
An Hachette Livre UK Company

This edition published in 2008 by Gollancz

A CIP catalogue record for this book is available
from the British Library

ISBN 978 0 57508 2 823

5 7 9 10 8 6 4

Typeset by Input Data Services Ltd, Frome

Printed and bound in the UK by
CPI Mackays, Chatham ME5 8TD

www.orionbooks.co.uk

The Orion Publishing Group's policy is to use papers that are natural,
renewable and recyclable products and made from wood grown in
sustainable forests. The logging and manufacturing processes are expected to
conform to the environmental regulations of the country of origin.

ACKNOWLEDGEMENTS

When Jay Gordon died in November 2005, this book was a stack of scribbled notes and character sketches all dangling from a brittle skeleton of plot questions left unanswered at the end of *Lessek's Key*. Over the past eighteen months, Jo Fletcher and I have endeavoured to stay as true to those early notes as possible, wrapping up Steven and Mark's adventures in Eldarn without jeopardising that original version or losing sight of Jay's hopes for Act III. For readers unfamiliar with Amyotrophic Lateral Sclerosis (ALS), it is a cruel disease, and it robbed Jay of everything but his imagination. Even in his last days, he was thinking of Steven, Mark, Garec and Brexan, picturing them in their struggle to free the people of Eldarn. *The Larion Senators* is a story Jay dreamed of telling for most of his life: a traditional, epic fantasy tale – like so many he had read and loved. He was a computer programmer by trade, but a reader and a fantasy junkie at heart. The Eldarn books are a testament to Jay's enthusiasm for this genre.

I owe thanks to many people who helped bring the Eldarn story to a close. Gillian Redfearn, Simon Spanton, Ian Drury and others at Victor Gollancz and Orion Books who made it possible for Jo to drag, heave and haul these manuscripts through the editorial and production phases, somehow meeting deadlines despite my incurable need to take one last look at the proofs, again and again. Thanks to Taryn, Gena & Ian and Pam, for combing early chapters for inconsistencies or loose threads. And thanks, as ever, to Uncle G. for correcting my math and to Deena & Kat for reminding me of so many things about calculus I had sublimated years ago.

I owe a debt of gratitude to Kage, Mom and Dad, Susan Gordon, Aunt Burma, the administrators and teachers at Bull Run, and especially Aunt Chrissy for taking on the mantle of US marketing and sales – direct from the trunk of her car. Thanks to Steve Van Bakel for taking a risk on my short fiction, and to Sam and Hadley who were patient while 'Dad was typing'.

Finally, thanks again to Jo Fletcher, who championed this project from the beginning and made the Eldarn Sequence possible.

For Kage, Hadley and Sam,
with all my love.

CONTENTS

BOOK IV: *The Fold*

EPILOGUE: *Crossroads*

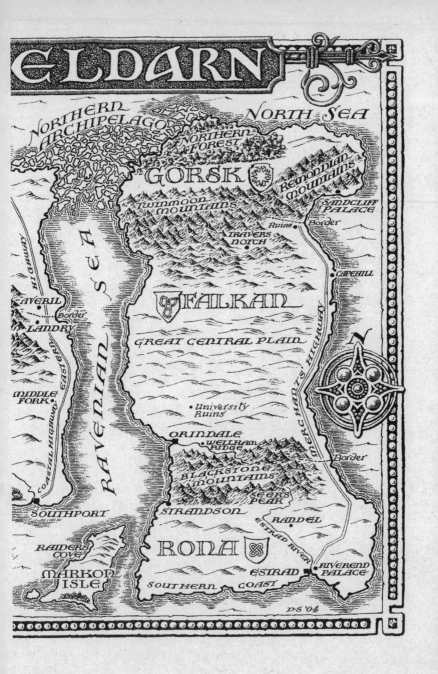

INTRODUCTION

Lessek

SANDCLIFF PALACE

Second Age, First Era, Twinmoon 2,829

Lessek paused long enough to cough up a mouthful of viscous phlegm; he spat into the mud beside the tower wall and wiped his face dry. They were coming; he could feel them close behind him now. His side burned with a runner's stitch, a pain he hadn't felt in almost a thousand Twinmoons. The Larion brother mumbled a spell, coughed again and waited – *it's taking too long* – for the sting to fade. His feet were bleeding, his boots forgotten in his bedchamber; his hands and face were marked with a cobweb of glass and bramble scratches, and his fever had returned.

Flu. *Influenza.* That's what Francesco Antonelli had called it, an infection: a sinister and calculating virus, and to date the Larion Senate's most reprehensible – if inadvertent – contribution to Eldarni culture. He didn't know which of them had contracted it, or who had brought it back, but that was irrelevant. It was here.

And thousands had died.

Tonight, they were coming; it was time to atone.

The first pursuers appeared as shadows from around the southwest corner of the keep. They had no torches, yet they were visible enough in the backlighting of the southern Twinmoon. The full Twinmoon was still a night or two away, but the winds had picked up noticeably since Lessek had gone to bed an aven earlier. The Larion founder used the howling gale and crashing surf to mask his retreat. He supposed he could kill them, conjure some spell to eviscerate the entire mob, but that would do nothing to exonerate him, or to redeem the Larion brotherhood in the eyes of their true appraisers: the Eldarni people. His only real choice was to flee, to reach the tower and to escape back to Italy for a cure. Besides, his own brother was with them, and Evete was there, too. He wouldn't risk either of them.

Just run, he thought. *It's not far now.*

Magic quieted the ache in Lessek's side and he ran for the north tower. The spiral stairs would be cold and unforgiving this evening but with the tribesmen, Harbach, that meddlesome businessman, and Gaorg – *and don't forget Evete, how* could *she side with them?* – running him to ground, Lessek used another incantation to quicken his stride, lowered his head and sprinted the last fifty paces to the tower entrance. *I hope they haven't posted a guard.*

He shouted the spell to unlock the wooden door and watched through the half-light as it swung open to welcome him, the master of the house.

Metal hinges. Do you see that, Harbach? The rest of you? Metal hinges. I brought back metallurgy unlike anything you'd ever seen – and what did you do? You forged weapons. Selfish bastards.

For the tenth time since leaping through the window of his bed-chamber, Lessek thanked the gods of the Northern Forest that he had remembered to take the keystone. It had been lying on the nightstand, beside a basin of cold water and a stump of paraffin taper. Picking it up had been second nature; he'd been half asleep, still lost in the heady slumber that accompanied his weakening symptoms, for he had been getting better, no question. Lessek patted the pocket of his nightshirt and felt it there, irregular and nondescript: a rock.

I'll take it with me, he thought, *that, and the book. They'll be begging for me to return. Antonelli will know what to do; I'll find him. He'll be in Roma, his civitate Dei.*

He made it across the threshold, spinning around when an alarm, faint behind his fever, clamoured in his head. *Arrow!* He cast quickly, flailing with one hand as he incinerated the shaft in midair. The spell was a simple one, slow, but effective; he hoped he wouldn't be forced to summon anything of consequence before escaping across the Fold. The mob behind him had grown to perhaps twenty or twenty-five. There were senators with them, too. A handful carried torches, and sporadic light fell over the group, illuminating some while masking others in darkness. It left his pursuers, his friends, colleagues and family, looking nefarious and deformed.

Would they kill him? Lessek couldn't imagine they would, but Harbach was there, and at the very least, the merchant wanted to see the Larion leader banished from Sandcliff and a new director appointed in his stead. That alone was enough reason to flee, for the moment anyway.

With a spell Lessek slammed the tower door closed behind him, but as the ponderous echo resonated up the stairwell, he heard a voice from somewhere in the midst of Harbach's mob, shouting, 'No, please! Don't shoot him. Don't shoot!' It was Evete, and at that, Lessek felt a surge of adrenalin, energy his magic had failed to provide over the last few days.

Perhaps she is with me still. He started up the steps two at a time, emboldened by love and a sense that there was hope yet for his vision.

Then he fell. Landing hard, he felt blood seep from a gash above his left eye. He pressed on it, regained his feet and kept moving. When he heard the tower gate breached, he wasn't surprised; the spell securing the door was known to almost all the senators. Any one of them could have called it. *It was Gaorg; you know it was.* Lessek wiped his eye clear again and ran on, his bloody feet slipping on the smooth stones.

By the time he reached the spell chamber, he was gasping for breath. He had tried twice to cry a spell that would strengthen his lungs, something to keep them full. But the fever, the fall from his chamber window, the cuts, gashes and bruises and especially the long sprint up the dizzying stairway had left him starved of air, too weak to mumble the words. Whatever adrenalin he had felt when Evete shouted for him had ebbed in a bloody trail along the stairs, and now Harbach's men were only a few steps behind.

Get the book.

Lessek moved hurriedly into the room, sidled past the spell table and started towards the scroll library, his private office.

An arrow, undetected this time, cut the air above his shoulder and glanced off the wall. As it clattered down the steps Lessek stumbled, then used what strength he had left to slam the chamber door, locking most of the mob in the stairwell for a few precious moments. The archer, a tribesman, from the cut of his tunic, looked as though he had seen a ghost. He was alone in the Larion spell chamber with the great one, Lessek himself, bloodied, raging and dangerous. The bowman dropped to his knees. In a tribal dialect Lessek had encountered a few times on trips south of the Blackstones, he begged for his life.

The Larion Senator considered knocking the bowman senseless but decided not to waste the time.

Get the book.

He drew a far portal from its place above the spell table and cast it across the floor.

Behind him, the door clicked open; there was no time to reach the scroll library or the spell book. *Gaorg, you horsecock. When I get back, I'll flay you alive.*

'There he is!' It was Harbach. 'Don't let him escape! Gaorg, do something!'

Lessek called a spell he had used on hundreds of occasions to bring a far portal across the Fold with him, a doorway home. Like picking up the keystone, calling this spell was second nature, but mid-verse, the Larion founder coughed, a feverish hack, wet with infection and phlegm. His last few syllables were lost in a guttural rasping fit and when Lessek disappeared from the spell chamber, the far portal remained behind. Green and yellow flecks of Larion energy danced in the air above the intricately woven tapestry until Gaorg Belsac, Lessek's own brother, folded a corner with his boot. The Larion spell chamber fell silent.

In one hand, Gaorg held a small grey stone, a piece of granite that had tumbled from his brother's pocket when Lessek slipped on the spiral stairs.

'Get started,' Harbach panted. His hands on his knees, the old merchant looked to be only a breath or two from a massive heart seizure. 'Do it now.'

Gaorg stared numbly at Lessek's keystone.

'You said you could work the spell.' Harbach turned to Evete and the others. 'Out of here! All of you. Now!'

Evete pushed past two bowmen and a scared-looking Larion apprentice. 'Don't do it, Gaorg,' she whispered.

'Get her out of here!' Harbach shouted, and the archers wrestled Lessek Belsac's lover towards the stairwell.

'Gaorg!' she cried.

Harbach ushered them into the stairwell, then slammed the chamber door. He leaned over the spell table with an air of complacent corruption.

Lessek's brother hadn't moved; the portal still lay crumpled at his feet.

'Get started,' Harbach said, examining a cracked fingernail, 'and secure your place in Eldarni history. You've been in his shadow too long, my friend.'

Gaorg Belsac woke from his reverie. 'Very well,' he said.

SCHÖNBRUNN PALACE, VIENNA

October, 1870

Saben Wald, valet to the Falkan prince Tenner Wynne of Orindale, the renowned doctor, stepped into the massive rectangular clearing as the sun coloured the gardens. To the north, a palace big enough to rival Riverend glowed yellow and ivory in the early light. Dry leaves blew about Saben's feet and tumbled across the now-empty flower beds. To the south, an unexpected hill jutted abruptly from the gardens. A switchback path carved into its side led to a collection of marble columns, arches and ghostly white statues of horses, raptors and powerful-looking men, gods maybe. The artisans who shaped them must have been amongst the most talented in this foreign world; Saben marvelled at the idea that such beauty could be left outside, exposed to wind and weather.

'What is this place?' he muttered to himself, a wary hand on his dagger.

A doorway opened in a low building adjacent to the palace; a group of men emerged. Dressed as they were, smoking, and carrying shovels, picks and wooden buckets, they had to be groundsmen. They were certainly not the estate's landlords – at this aven, anyone that wealthy would be still abed.

Saben backed beneath the trees. He hadn't been seen.

'What is it?' Regona Carvic asked, worried. She had been a scullery maid in Riverend Palace; now she carried Prince Danmark's child, Rona's heir and Eldarn's future monarch, and she would not put the baby in harm's way by being too stubborn to listen to those trying to help her. The sepia-skinned servant peeked into the clearing, watched the men disappear inside the palace gates and then glanced at the hilltop and the elaborate fountains and stonework of the now sunlit marble edifice.

'I don't know,' Saben said, worried, 'but we can't stay here.'

'That palace,' Regona started, 'perhaps if we—'

'No,' he cut her off. 'We have to find somewhere safe to hide while we learn more about where we are.'

'It's cold, nothing like Estrad.'

'This isn't Rona,' he said, urging her gently backwards, deeper beneath the foliage. 'That palace, those carvings, even the way the flower beds are laid out: none of this is Eldarni.'

Before this, Regona had never travelled further than Rona's South Coast; she would have to take Saben's assessment on faith.

Saben's head felt like it was cracking open. *They should have sent a soldier*, he thought again. He didn't belong here. That man, the horseman – he had to be a Larion sorcerer – he was the one who had sent them away. Riverend was burning and he and Regona had watched as the mysterious man waved to Prince Danmark ... and then Danmark had stood up straight, looked around for a moment – which was curious, because Saben had heard rumours the young prince was blind – and then leaped to his death. It had to have been the work of a Larion magician. And that tapestry – as soon as Saben had unrolled it he knew they were not on their way to Randel, and they would not be staying with the merchant Weslox Thervan.

The horseman had told him Tenner's plans had been jeopardised by an enemy named Nerak. Saben had never heard of Nerak, but the horseman appeared to know everything: where they were going, with whom they were supposed to hide, even how they had planned to get away.

Do not touch me, the stranger had said. Why not? What *was* it about that man? He didn't show his face, and he told them only what he had apparently decided was absolutely necessary. So why did they comply? Saben shuddered: what if *he* were the enemy, this Nerak? The horseman said Nerak was inside Riverend Palace, destroying everything, murdering everyone, Prince Tenner included. They had a narrow window of opportunity to use the tapestry hidden in the abandoned farmhouse. But if the rider knew so much about what was happening in Estrad and why Nerak was bringing death to Riverend, why had he sent them here alone?

Stories had spread through Estrad like a prairie fire: the Larion Senate had fallen, and the senators were all dead – but was that all but one? Or was the horseman someone else entirely?

Do not touch me.

Had he really been there?

Saben tried to recall if the dark rider had physically touched

8

anything, and had concluded the answer was no: not the dilapidated fence, nor the leather strap holding the door closed, nor even the tapestry tucked inside the empty fireplace.

Take her hand, and step onto it, that was all he had said, and they had obeyed him – and now where were they? He wondered what had happened to the tapestry; it hadn't come with them. How were they expected to get back?

'Where can we hide?' Regona's voice broke into his thoughts. 'We haven't seen a village yet, just these grounds, that palace, and that ... whatever it is there on the hill.'

Something screamed in the brush behind them and Regona shrieked.

Saben felt his heart thud. He had to fight the urge to bolt across the clearing, pound on the palace gates and beg for protection.

'What was that?' Regona whispered.

'Some kind of animal,' Saben said, 'maybe a wild bird or a monkey.'

A roar, throaty and unmistakable, split the morning. It was answered by another scream, and then a trumpet.

'Wild cats? Grettans? Elephants?' Regona was shaking. 'Isn't it too cold for elephants here?'

'We can't wait around to find out,' Saben said, taking her hand. 'Come on. We'll sneak along the edge of the gardens and see if we can get around that hill. Anything as large as that palace is bound to have a village nearby.' He looked at her. The young woman was beautiful; he wasn't surprised Tenner had chosen her to carry Eldarn's heir. He would fight, and die if necessary, to protect her and her baby – but would he be up to the task? They hadn't taken three steps in this world and already he'd carelessly ventured into the open, almost being seen, and roused the breakfast interests of a grettan, or whatever the beast was. Why hadn't he brought a broadsword, or a bow, or a rapier, even?

'Come with me,' he said again. 'We'll go east, away from whatever's making those noises.'

'No.' Regona's face had changed and she looked strangely determined. 'Not east, that's not the way.'

'You heard what's back there; you can't possibly want to—'

'No!' Her voice rose.

'Where then?' he asked, trying not to lose his temper. 'Which way do we go?'

Ringing the gardens were watchlights, lanterns that burned without sign of wood or thatch for fuel. Each was housed in a glass container and perched on a thin metal pole. Light fell in radiant waves down on the fallow flower gardens, and as it mingled with the morning sun it was lost.

'Regona,' he asked again, most gently this time, 'where would you have us go?'

Without speaking, she raised one hand and pointed west, through the palace grounds and past whatever creatures lurked in the remaining shadows.

'That way? Past the grettans and whatever was screaming at us?' Saben held her hand loosely. 'Why that way?'

'I don't know how, but I know that's the way: west.'

'All right. We'll find a place to hide for now and scout out the area once we're away from here.'

'It will be that direction tomorrow, and for many days, Twinmoons maybe,' she said.

Saben was sceptical, but he didn't push her further. Her mind was obviously made up and in the end, one direction was as good as any other.

BOOK I

The Larion Spell Table

WRAITHS

Jacrys awakened, and listened carefully. There were others in the chamber: Pace, and someone with a familiar accent, a lilt in his voice that was not unpleasant. It was the one leading the Orindale hunt for Sallax Farro. *What's his name?*

He could hear them talking.

'About twenty-five days now, almost a Moon,' said one.

'Querlis?' came the reply.

'Every day, but progress is slow. The only healer in the barracks that night was a lieutenant from Averil, a farmer's son who knew something about horses and pigs. He helped us stabilise him until the general's healer could get back on the *Medera*.'

'En route to Rona by then, I'm sure.'

'Yes sir, he was.'

'How bad?'

'Lung punctured and collapsed. Thankfully, the general's healer had enough magic to clot the blood and inflate the lung. Otherwise we would have lost him.'

'And Oaklen left his healer here?'

'Not the only one in the division, sir, but yes. He ordered me to remain behind as well ... wants Jacrys healed, said something about the prince.'

'Word of him?'

'Nothing.'

'Dead.'

'Perhaps.'

The voices drifted too far away for him to hear any more so he turned to his own body. He tuned his senses to the hollow cavity inside his ribs. The pain was gone; it had been astonishing. He tried to fill his lungs, but failed. Time passed, and he tried again. Still no good. He was breathing, but not well. *Twenty-five days, almost a Moon.* That seemed significant, but he couldn't home in on why, exactly;

answers eluded him, sneaking away behind shadowy folds of confusion. After a while he didn't care.

More time passed, and the voices, Pace and the other, the lilting one, returned.

'Is he coherent?'

'When he wakes, he tries to talk. He seems concerned that the girl got away.'

'Carderic, right?'

'Yes, sir. Brexan Carderic, a deserter. She had been posted along the Forbidden Forest outside Estrad. She disappeared the morning Jacrys ordered the siege on Riverend Palace.'

'Must have known they were hiding something there.'

'Yes, sir.'

'And she was with this partisan, what's his name again?'

'Sallax Farro, sir, Sallax of Estrad, one of their leaders.'

'But he was killed?'

'Yes, sir. The girl escaped. She stripped half naked and pretended to be a whore. She walked right out of the barracks.'

Did you now? Good show, Brexan, good show, indeed. You've become an adequate spy after all. Jacrys surveyed the room through one slitted eye. The chamber was blurry and indistinct. He could see the two men, little more than smears of black and gold: Colonel Pace and Captain Someone, the one from the searches. *Good news about Sallax, though. That rutting horsecock needed to die.* Jacrys let the knowledge seep through the paralysis and fatigue holding him hostage. It felt good to know the traitorous partisan was gone. *As for you, Brexan Carderic, if I see you again, my succulent little morsel, I'll gut you and mount your insides on the wall of my dining room.*

His eye fell shut; the hushed conversation, somewhere on the other side of the room, faded once again. Dreaming, Jacrys felt the bedding wrap him in a gentle embrace, a comforting, woman's touch, perhaps even Brexan's. She was a beautiful girl. *And if I don't see you again, my dear, well, then goodbye.*

'Oh, and Thadrake?'

'Yes, sir?'

Somewhere out beyond the coverlet's billowy embrace, Jacrys heard them pushing their way into his dreams. *That's his name, Captain Thadrake.*

'What news do you have on the murders?'

'We believe it was Sallax all along, sir ... killed a Seron with a knife, did it one-handed ... same description as the assailant who

14

had been haunting the waterfront . . .' Thadrake's voice tumbled back over itself in layers of sound, until, unable to decipher any more, Jacrys let go. *Twenty-five days, that's a long time. I've been here a long time.* Jacrys heard footsteps; that would be Colonel Pace leaving the chamber. Thadrake remained behind, but the Malakasian spy didn't care. *It's time*, he thought before spiralling back into oblivion. *It's time to go home.*

'I still don't understand.' Kellin Mora stood near the water's edge. Her cloak covered underclothes, tunic and overtunic, making her look like a wrinkled beige bag topped off with a thin-faced blonde-haired head.

Steven Taylor, wiry, pale and tired-looking, waded calf-deep in the river, his boots and socks in a heap beside the fallen pine he'd been sitting on.

Kellin was still wary of the power she had witnessed Steven wielding against the Malakasian girl, Bellan – or Nerak, or Prince Malagon, or whoever that had been – and she felt a pang of distrust for the foreigner. She wished she was back in Traver's Notch, with Gita Kamrec and the rest of the Falkan Resistance. Covert strikes, guerrilla attacks, hoarding silver and weapons: she understood these things. Battling wraiths, bone-collecting river monsters and possessed Larion sorcerers was unfamiliar and frightening, and she remained hesitant to trust this man completely, despite Brand Krug's apparent complacency with their current assignment. Only her loyalty to Gita and Falkan kept her from sneaking back home.

'Which part don't you understand?' Garec Haile, the good-looking bowman from Estrad, joined her near the river. He liked Kellin and welcomed her company.

'Most of it, I suppose,' Kellin said. 'If that little girl was Prince Malagon—'

'It wasn't,' Garec interrupted. 'It was Bellan, Malagon's daughter. Prince Malagon's body was dropped in—'

'South Carolina,' Steven interjected without looking back. He gazed across the river, choosing landmarks on the opposite shoreline and lining them up with a rocky cliff above and behind them. The cliff face was dotted with pine trees clinging to the craggy granite. 'Probably in Charleston Harbour, near Folly Beach. I know that doesn't mean much to you, Kellin, but rest assured, it's a long night's travel from here.'

'Wherever here is,' Garec mumbled.

'Have a little faith.' Steven turned and smiled at them. 'This is it. Don't you remember that hill? It looks like my grandfather's nose. That's a hard mountain to forget.'

'That's quite a grandfather you have,' Kellin said.

'Yeah, well, he wasn't much of an underwear model, but he could drink his own weight in Milwaukee beer and he could read cigarette ashes in my grandmother's ashtray. That has to count for something.' Steven turned back to the river.

'I thought it was tea leaves,' Gilmour said.

'It should be, but old Grandpop never liked tea, and my grandmother smoked enough to kill the neighbour's dog. So it gave us all something to do between dinner and dessert.'

Kellin raised an eyebrow at Garec, who shrugged. She returned to the previous conversation. 'So, Prince Malagon's body lies abandoned in your world?'

'Right,' Garec answered for his friend. 'Nerak, the Larion Senator who had been controlling Prince Malagon, had not been to Steven's world in a thousand Twinmoons. So when he arrived, he dropped Malagon's body and probably took the first person he found.'

'Why?'

'A head full of updated knowledge,' Garec said.

'He can read your thoughts?'

'Only from the inside, Kellin.'

'So Malagon was inside his own daughter?'

'Nope,' Steven said, 'that was Nerak.'

'Oh, yes, right. Sorry,' she said, 'I get them confused.'

'It's easy to do.'

'So, Nerak returned here to Eldarn and took Bellan's body?'

'Right again.' Steven wandered through the water, which crept above his bare knees to dampen his rolled-up leggings. 'Ah, crap. Now I have to dry these again.'

'You'll never get the wrinkles out,' Garec teased.

'Wait,' Kellin interrupted, 'don't change the subject again! How did he get back here, without a portal and without a body?'

Steven hunched noticeably, as if the wind was blowing cold in his face. 'He could have used anyone to make the trip back here, Kellin. And as for how he returned, I'm worried that he might have killed a friend of mine, a woman whose daughter I—'

'He didn't.' Gilmour cut him off. 'Nerak returned here because I opened the way for him.'

'How?' Brand was cooking venison steaks on a flat rock beside the campfire. 'How did you manage it without a portal?'

'I made a mistake.' Gilmour glanced towards his pack and the collection of Lessek's spells wrapped inside. 'I opened a book I had no business reading. It let Nerak pinpoint my location and make the journey home; I'm sure of it. Hannah's mother probably never encountered him at all.'

'Let's hope,' Steven said.

'But didn't you kill him, Steven?' Kellin asked. 'I saw you pick up that girl and throw her inside that boulder. She vanished; didn't she? Is she . . . or *he* . . . dead now?'

'It wasn't exactly into the boulder, Kellin,' Steven explained. 'It was through a rip, an opening that you weren't able to see. I threw her . . . *him*, if you prefer . . . inside, and he doesn't have the power to get back out.'

'So Nerak is dead,' Kellin said.

'Essentially.' Steven sighted along his finger between a clump of trees and the tip of his grandfather's nose.

'Then why are we still here? We've been riding these past few days as if someone is chasing us. Mark's gone; we didn't even look for him, and we've been hurrying through the forest trying to find this cliff, hill, stone table, whatever it is, and I don't understand why.' Kellin avoided looking at Brand. She was a Resistance fighter; she'd fought Prince Malagon's soldiers and shown her allegiance. Hearing her voice rising as she pleaded for understanding was embarrassing; she cleared her throat nosily to cover her anxiety.

Steven's smile faded. 'We're still here, Kellin, because we were guilty of exactly the same offence that allowed me to dispose of Nerak for ever. We focused on the wrong thing; we believed something that wasn't true, just like Nerak.'

The others, including Gilmour, were listening intently. The battle in the glen had been four days ago, and no one had yet endeavoured to explain what had happened, or why.

'What did you— What did *we* have wrong?' Kellin asked.

'Nerak believed he was powerful, much more powerful than he turned out to be. He actually used a spell to convince himself that he was the greatest Larion sorcerer that Eldarn had ever known. He removed the part of himself that understood who he really was, almost physically tore it out of his mind, and he hid that knowledge in a friend's walking stick, an old length of whittled hickory, that I found – that found me – on the other side of these mountains. The evil that Nerak released from the Fold took him, and it believed what it found

17

inside Nerak's head, because it didn't have any reason not to. What Nerak believed about himself was the truth to him, as real to him as – as this river is to us.'

'So he lied to this evil creature?'

'It was the evil's mistake to take Nerak's beliefs as truth.'

'Where is our mistake then?' Kellin hadn't yet made any connection.

'We did the same thing Nerak did,' Steven said. 'We focused on the wrong things.' He looked over at Gilmour. 'We spent two Twinmoons worrying about Nerak, when Nerak wasn't the one threatening Eldarn. We should have been worrying about the evil that had possessed him – it had possessed Prince Marek and the Whitward family all those Twinmoons ago. When I cast Nerak into the Fold, I permitted that evil to break its connection with a tired Larion Senator and to establish a link with—' He paused.

'With Mark Jenkins,' Kellin whispered.

'We focused on the wrong things,' Steven muttered. 'We believed Nerak was at the root of Eldarn's peril. We forgot that in all the time Nerak worked at Sandcliff Palace, researching, learning, teaching, Eldarn was never at risk. It wasn't until the evil slipped free from the spell table that Eldarn's future was put in jeopardy.'

'Then how can you just—?'

'Just what, Kellin?' Steven wheeled on her, sending concentric ripples out across the smooth surface of the water. 'How can I eat, sleep, make jokes with you and Garec, stand here like a goddamned fool looking for an ancient relic we aren't even certain will work even *if* we manage to get it out of the water? How can I do all those things?'

Kellin wanted to back down, to apologise, but the soldier in her took over. Now she did look over at Brand briefly, before saying, 'Yes, Steven. How can you do all those things when the real root of your problems, Eldarn's problems, is wandering around back there in the body of your roommate?'

Steven hesitated; Kellin hoped it was because some part of the foreign sorcerer was impressed with how she had stood her ground.

Finally, he said, 'We hurried up here, because Mark is coming, probably with whatever forces he is able to organise at Wellham Ridge. That may not be too many, and I'm sure Gilmour and I can take care of them, but I would rather not engage them at all, because I don't want to risk losing the spell table – which might just save us –

and I don't want to risk a confrontation with Mark, because I might inadvertently kill him.'

'Mark's dead,' Kellin said, 'isn't he?'

Steven shook his head. 'No.'

'Are you sure?'

'When Nerak took possession of people, both here and in my world, he killed them. He forcibly entered their bodies, took their minds, memories, thoughts and knowledge, and then allowed them to die. He did it to Gabriel O'Reilly; he did it to Myrna Kessler, and he did it to countless others. But when the evil that took Nerak came to Eldarn, it kept him alive. Granted, it abandoned his body, because moving about as a spirit let him take others, hundreds of others, that night and over the Twinmoons, but they worked as a team. Nerak was alive all that time.'

'How do you know that?' Gilmour wanted to believe there was still hope for Mark, but he too was sceptical.

'Because he was there in the glen,' Steven said. 'He wasn't propped up by anything; there was no evil puppet master pulling his strings. That was Nerak. Bellan was dead and long gone. Hell, we might have battled her sorry soul right there amongst those bone-collectors, but Nerak was alive and well when I tossed him into Neverland.'

'So Mark *is* alive.' Garec started up the shoreline. A steely grey day was reluctantly giving way to darkness.

'I'd bet on it,' Steven said. 'That night at Sandcliff, the evil force that consumed Nerak had just burst free from the spell table. It took Nerak and learned that it had hit the jackpot. *Ka-blam!* First shot, and it wins big: Eldarn's greatest magical mind. But what of all the others, all the Larion Senators living and working in the palace? Why not join with Nerak and grab a few others, fifty, two hundred, who cares?' Gilmour was looking sick, so Steven backed off somewhat. 'The being, the essence of things evil, whatever it is that took Mark didn't have anyone else to take. We're all still here, still alive. There were just a few farms between Meyers' Vale and Wellham Ridge. Does he need a plough-hand? No. He needs Mark. Mark knows us; he knows *me*. He knows our plans; he knows where we've been and where we hope to go, Gita, Capehill, the lot. Granted, the creature can get all that and still kill him, but I'm betting he's alive.'

'And what better prize, if Mark truly is Eldarn's king, Rona's heir?' Garec said. 'First, evil takes Nerak and discovers the greatest sorcerer in the five lands. Then it takes Mark and discovers a long-lost monarch.'

'Two for two,' Steven said.

'But is Mark truly Rona's heir?' Brand asked.

'It doesn't matter,' Garec said. 'Mark believes it. It's truth inside his head.'

'Will evil make that mistake twice?'

'Probably not,' Steven shrugged, 'but Mark is still a trophy catch. He knows everything about us.'

'Rutting whores. I hadn't thought of that.' Brand stood, ignoring his steaks.

'And you won't fight him?' Kellin pressed.

'Not yet, no,' Steven said, 'not until I have a better idea how to separate him from the evil holding him captive.'

'He's taken Lessek's key too,' Garec reminded them.

'True,' Steven said, 'but as long as we have the spell table, the key won't do him any good.'

'Why don't we blast it to fish bait with one of your spells?' Garec asked.

Steven cocked an eyebrow at Gilmour. 'What do you say? We certainly don't need it.'

Gilmour sat on his haunches beside the fire, carved a strip from one of the steaks and said, 'That one'll have to be mine, Brand. Sorry, I couldn't wait. He finished his mouthful and added, 'Actually, we may still need the table.'

'Why?' Garec said. 'We needed it to fight Nerak. He's dead or gone or something.'

'We believed we needed it to battle Nerak, but we also needed it to seal the Fold.' He popped another strip of meat into his mouth. 'Rutting hot, Brand, hot!' He fanned his mouth, then added, 'Unless Steven thinks he can close the Fold without the Larion magic, of course.'

Kellin said, 'Can you do that?'

Steven shook his head. 'I don't know.'

Garec changed the subject. 'It's snowing up there.' He pointed towards the Blackstone peaks in the distance. 'We may get hit before morning; we should think about finding some decent shelter and gathering a more significant stack of firewood.'

'I'll get on it,' Kellin said, glad to have something to do. Before leaving she asked, 'Steven, isn't that water cold?'

He chuckled. 'I suppose it is, but I'm warming it up a bit. It's a little experiment I wanted to try before diving in tomorrow morning.'

'Warming it up?'

'It's not much, just the water right here.'

'Isn't it moving?'

'That's the tricky part,' Steven said. 'At least it's not moving too quickly; I wouldn't want to try this in a stretch of rapids.'

Gilmour smiled like a proud parent. He said, 'You're sure this is the place?'

Steven nodded, 'Yup. Old Grandpop's nose was straight across from that clump of trees over there. I remember them because they were all aflame when we came through last time.'

'On fire?' Brand asked.

'Red,' Steven said, 'they're maples. They stood out like a bloody sore against all that green.'

'Very well, then,' Gilmour said. 'Tomorrow, we'll go in.'

A northerly breeze brushed the evergreen forest with a flurry of snow. A break in the cloud cover allowed the occasional beam of pale moonlight to reach Meyers' Vale; with a storm blowing off the mountains, even that little light would soon vanish. Eldarn's twin moons looked distant, almost insignificant. Though their light was faint tonight, it brightened the riverbank just enough for Steven to watch clouds of snow whirling their way north towards Wellham Ridge. Behind him, the others slept, chatted softly or stared into the fire.

The darkness beneath the trees lining the riverbank was depthless. Steven was glad they were in camp this evening; he would not have enjoyed travelling through the woods along the river. The tree trunks were cloned columns marked with the blackened vestiges of autumn sap, and the branches started high enough for him to wander about beneath the overhead confusion of prickly boughs. Something was there, lurking behind the willowy clouds of swirling snow, under the evergreen canopy.

Steven watched and waited.

Reinforcement clouds scudded north from the Blackstones and the moonlight went out. Steven stood at his post, turning periodically to chuckle at a joke one of the others made as they sat beside the fire. No one asked why he was there; they were content to leave him alone with his thoughts, even Gilmour.

Something in Steven's gut warned him. It felt like something slipping slightly off-centre again and again, until he was forced to stop and listen. They were coming. He had known that, but it wasn't magic; rather, the sense that something had been left undone, the stove left on, or the ironing board left upright in the guest bedroom . . .

He caught the flavour of a familiar smell, something tangy and unpleasant on the breeze, like over-ripe garbage: the stench of old melon rinds and rancid chicken fat, the pungent aroma of decay.

Steven wrinkled his nose and peered beneath the trees. The figures came in as indistinct grey mist, as if a handful of moonbeams had broken free and gone exploring. The wraiths were taking shape now, and that too was as familiar as the odour of decaying meat and honeydew. He had been right.

'Gabriel, Lahp,' Steven said. 'Ms . . .' He thought of Myrna as he raised the tone of his voice slightly; she'd taught him to do that when he had forgotten a customer's name. *Better to let them fill in the blank, than to fumble around for five minutes and end up filing the transaction in the wrong account.* She had always laughed at his attempts.

He tried again, this time more directly. 'I'm sorry, I don't know your name, Ms—'

'Can you send me back?' The woman's reply resonated between his ears as the memory of her living form took shape enough for Steven to recall the young mother, travelling alone with her baby.

Steven shrugged, then felt sorry for such an offhanded gesture. She regarded him with disdain: in her mind, this was entirely his fault. 'I'm sorry, I don't mean to sound selfish, but I don't . . . I guess I haven't thought about whether I can send you back.'

'Think about it now.' She wasn't pleased.

'I'm sorry,' he said again, 'but I'm afraid that if I tried, I might only get you as far as the Fold, and I don't want to leave you trapped in there.'

'How did *you* get here?'

Without thinking, Steven said, 'Mark and I both came through—' He interrupted himself. 'That might work. We have one of the far portals here. You could try slipping through. Granted, it might drop you anywhere on Earth, but you don't mind . . . I mean, at least it would get you back.'

'Then you don't know.'

'No.' Steven looked down. Despite everything he had achieved, and everything he had sacrificed, he couldn't look her in the face. She was right: her death, her baby's death: they were his responsibility. He didn't know what she believed, whether she thought she might ascend to heaven and join the child there, or whether she just wanted to get back so that she could haunt the graveyard where her family had interred the bodies. He had sworn to be compassionate, but at that moment he just felt selfish. 'I truly think the portal will take you back,' he said.

'That isn't good enough for me, Steven Taylor.' She slipped soundlessly beneath the pines, disappearing in a whirling cloud of dusty snow.

Steven watched her go, frowning. 'I'm sorry,' he whispered.

The wraith that had been Lahp came forward. Even in his ghostly form, the big Seron warrior still ambled awkwardly, as if carrying around that much muscle was difficult even after death.

'Lahp.' Steven smiled.

'Lahp tak Sten.' The big Malakasian touched Steven's shoulder with one gossamer hand and he felt the icy chill on his skin, colder than the wintry night.

'You don't have to thank me, Lahp,' Steven said. 'You saved my life.'

'Lahp tak Sten,' the Seron repeated, billowing his facial features into a crooked smile.

'Where will you go?'

'Forest,' Lahp said, gesturing over his shoulder as if the journey would take only a moment or two.

'Right,' Steven nodded, 'the Northern Forest. I wish you well, Lahp. I may see you there before my work in Eldarn is done.'

Lahp raised a translucent eyebrow. 'Lahp hep Sten?'

'No,' Steven replied, 'you've done enough, Lahp. Have a good journey.'

Like the woman from Charleston, the Seron warrior seemed to turn inside out before he flitted silently northwards through the trees.

Only Gabriel O'Reilly remained.

'It's good to see you again, Gabriel,' Steven said. Behind him, the chatter around the campfire quieted to a whisper. His friends were listening in.

'And you, too, Steven.' Gabriel looked as he had when Steven first saw him, clad in his nineteenth-century bank manager's uniform, complete with frilly shirt, braces and a belt buckle embossed with the letters *B.I.S.*

'What happened?'

Like the South Carolina woman and the Seron warrior, Gabriel's voice echoed in Steven's mind. 'I fought the almor. It had been hunting Versen and Brexan. When the battle ended, I—'

Steven cut him off, saying excitedly, 'Versen's alive?'

Gabriel nodded. 'He was when I last saw him, but he and Brexan were about to face a fierce-looking Seron, a killer.'

'Brexan? Who's that?'

'A woman, a soldier from Malakasia; she was travelling with Versen. They were both drowning in the Ravenian Sea when I found them; Versen's life had just about ebbed away when I arrived.'

'When did this happen?' Steven was anxious to hear the rest of the strange tale.

'It was shortly after I led Mark Jenkins to the trapper's cabin at the southern end of this valley.'

Heartened by this news, Steven asked, 'How did Nerak capture you again?'

The wraith grimaced. 'William Higgins.'

Steven started. 'The miner? But how is—? Oh, right ... Nerak took him in 1870.'

'Before opening the accounts at my bank – *your* bank as well, I suppose.'

'You were pulled back into the Fold?' Steven wasn't sure how to ask what he wanted to know.

'A small group of wraiths, led by William Higgins and working under Nerak's orders, found me crossing Falkan and, yes, they dragged me back into their ranks. When Nerak finally reached me, I was powerless once again. But you set me free; you set us all free there in the glen beside the river.'

'When I threw Nerak into the Fold.'

'When you refused to cast us back into the Fold, Steven, that's when it happened. You freed me – and Lahp and the woman.'

Steven said, 'We have a far portal here, Gabriel. You should try to go home. She should—' He broke off and looked towards the trees, but the woman was gone. 'She should try as well. I can't guarantee anything, but I'd bet you can make it back.'

'I'm staying with you.' Gabriel took him by the forearm and again Steven felt the odd convection of cold and colder pressing through the Gore-tex of Howard's old coat.

'You don't have to,' he said, touched by Gabriel's offer. 'You've been trapped, enslaved for so long. Why don't you—?'

'That is exactly the reason why I don't wish to return home, not yet.' O'Reilly loomed over him, swelling for a moment with anger or pride, Steven couldn't tell which, before shrinking back to his former size. 'I'll help you, Steven, and then we'll go home together.'

Steven gave up. 'The evil that was controlling Nerak now has Mark.'

'I know.'

'Can you free him?'

'No.'

Steven sighed. 'I had to ask.'

'Have you seen him?'

'No,' Steven replied. 'My guess is that he's in Wellham Ridge, organising a force to come find us, or maybe to find the spell table.'

'I will find him, Steven.'

'Be careful, Gabriel.'

'I will try to delay him, if possible, and when this is done, we will go home together.'

'Yes,' Steven nodded, 'you, me, Hannah and Mark.'

'I look forward to it.' Gabriel glanced beyond Steven's shoulder to where Garec, Kellin and Gilmour were watching the interchange. Brand slept. Raising one ghostly-white hand, the former bank manager waved to them.

'Farewell, Gabriel,' Garec said quietly. 'We will see you again, soon.'

The wraith looked back at Steven for a moment, then faded into the flurries of snow tumbling along the riverbank.

Mark Jenkins approached the barracks from a side street. Sheltered from view by a lumber cart that had stopped along the thoroughfare, he turned the corner, surprising the sentry posted outside.

'Move along, Southie,' the man warned. 'There's no need for you to be lingerin' here.'

'What did you call me?' Mark growled. The soldier was a private, a conscripted grunt; Mark needed someone of higher rank, a colonel or a general at least.

'I said move along.' The sentry, a broad-shouldered man with two days' stubble and a weary, hungover look about him, rested a hand on his dagger, clearly a warning.

'Do you know it was 1619 when the first slave ship arrived in Virginia? Did you know that? Of course you didn't. 1619. Astonishing really, that only twelve years separated the establishment of the first real settlement in the American colonies and the oppression of African slaves in the west. Twelve years, and I have to stand here now and listen to that kind of bullshit from you, you inbred lump of stinking pigshit.' Mark spoke a mixture of English and Eldarni

Common, but the bleary-eyed private deciphered enough of the rant to understand the arrogant South Coaster was being less than respectful.

'Ruttin' horsecock,' the guard growled, but as he shoved the man away, Mark took him through a moist, filthy sore he opened on the soldier's wrist.

Mark felt himself being sucked through a dank, cramped canal as he invaded the sentry's body. He felt suddenly nauseous as two hundred and seventy-five Twinmoons of emotions, memories, hopes and failures washed over him all at once and he thought he might vomit right there on the street. He wanted to collapse into the mud and rest for a few hours. He felt the soldier dying, falling away, and tried to accompany him, to slip past the presence, that creature of smoke and steam that had taken him in the forest four days earlier only to crush his will and press him into submission.

Not you! the voice thundered inside his head, *their* head. *Let him go; we have what we need from this one.*

Mark watched his own body collapse to the plank walkway outside the Malakasian Army barracks. He watched himself strip off the jacket Steven had stolen from Howard's closet, watched himself check the pocket for Lessek's key and finally watched himself remove his gloves and slip them onto his new hands, his pale, white Malakasian hands, the left one dripping a malign mixture of pus and blood. Mark wiped it on his favourite red sweater.

Let's go, he heard himself say. *We need to find the commanding officer. Where is he?* The dead soldier's memories merged with his own; vertigo gripped his guts with a talon. He needed to throw up.

Upstairs. She's upstairs. The guard's recollections provided the answer.

A she? A colonel? A general?

I don't know if there are any generals left over here except for General Oaklen. Major Tavon is in charge of the battalion here in the South. She's the senior officer here.

Mark kicked open the barracks door. A soldier, a lieutenant by his uniform, was crossing the foyer. He looked irritated when he saw the private. 'And where do you think you're going, Stark?' he shouted. 'You're on duty until the end of the dinner aven. Do I need to remind you—?'

'Eat shit,' Mark said, and hit him in the throat; his strength was unfathomable. The officer's neck snapped, cracking audibly a moment before he sprawled in a clumsy pile of limbs.

Why? Mark tried to speak, to *think* his outrage, but the creature of smoke and steam pressed him back against the walls of darkness. Mark's throat closed, his eyes bulged and he felt something inside himself rupture. The pain was instantaneous and unbearable.

I'll take what I need from you when I need it. The voice was terrifying, that of a monstrous god capable of torturing him for all eternity. *Until then, keep still.*

Mark screamed; nothing came out. He tried to weep, to call for his mother, his father, anyone at all, but nothing changed. No thoughts breached the shallow well of his own mind. He forgot things the moment he dredged them up from his memory. There was no hope, no comfort; there was not even the relative relief that might come from an anguished cry or a desperate scream. There was only the realisation that he was trapped, frozen inside a stone slab.

Mark took the stairs three at a time and kicked open the door to Major Tavon's private office. Tearing free from its hinges, it crashed across the room, upsetting a table strewn with maps of southern Falkan and the Blackstone Mountains.

Major Tavon, a thin, grey-haired woman of about four hundred and fifty Twinmoons, sat behind her desk, her feet propped up, a goblet of wine in one hand and a finger corkscrewing so far up her nose that Mark thought she might be trying to scratch an itch in her sinuses.

'Good day, Major,' Mark said.

Major Tavon spilled her wine as she hurriedly wiped her finger on her trousers. She looked aghast for a moment, and then flew into a rage. 'Stark! You great, stupid horsecock! What in the name of all things unholy do you think you're doing? I swear to all the gods of the Northern Forest, I will have you wiping the backside of every flatulent cavalry horse from here to Pellia for this interruption!'

'Do shut up, you irritating old bitch,' Mark said as he leaned on the woman's desk. 'I need a battalion, just for a few days.'

'A what? A what? You're done, Stark! Life as you know it is over!' She was still screaming when Private Stark fell dead on the floor of her office.

Lieutenant Blackford, Major Tavon's personal assistant, burst into the room, flanked by two soldiers brandishing short swords. He skidded to a stop when he saw the major calmly tugging a pair of worn leather gloves onto her hands. 'Major? Are you all right?' he asked breathlessly.

'Yes, I'm fine,' she said coolly. 'Nothing to worry about at all, Lieutenant.' She knelt beside Private Stark's body, took something from the pocket of a brightly coloured tunic he had been carrying and secreted it inside her own tunic. 'Would you have the men dispose of this, please?' She kicked at the body.

The young officer was dumbstruck. 'Uh, yes ma'am,' he murmured, wondering what was going on.

'Oh, and Kranst is dead, too. You'll find him downstairs.'

'Ma'am?'

'And I almost forgot.' Major Tavon smiled. 'Out front there is a young man, a South Coaster, in a red tunic. Please see to it that the bodies are incinerated out back, down near the stream. Get some of the others to help you, and be quick about it. We need to get word to Hershaw and Denne; I require an infantry battalion. I want the captains in Wellham Ridge and prepared to march south as soon as possible.'

'Ma'am?'

'Within two days, three at the most, understood?' Major Tavon righted her goblet, refilled it and gulped down the wine with a flourish. 'Lieutenant?'

'Yes, ma'am?' Blackford was still staring at Stark's body.

'Do you understand?'

An innate sense of self-preservation slapped Blackford hard across the face. He blinked several times and nodded yes.

'Good. I am going to write two despatches. I need riders ready to take them north; I want them gone within the aven. One is to the garrison commander at Traver's Notch, the other to the ranking officer at Capehill; there is to be a Resistance attack on Capehill within the Moon, and I want our forces prepared for the insurrectionists, should they still be in the city when the attack comes.'

'But Major, how could—?' Glancing at Stark's body, Blackford decided not to ask anything else. 'I will make the preparations, ma'am.'

'Excellent. I will be at the tavern on the corner. Tell me when it is done.'

'Yes, ma'am.' Blackford snapped to attention as Major Tavon left the room. When she was gone, he asked aloud, '*Still in the city* when the attack comes? I wonder what that means—' He looked again at the dead body and hurried to do his commanding officer's bidding.

PREPARATIONS

Steven rolled over. It had grown colder overnight; a little snow continued to fall in the river valley, but the bulk of the storm had passed them by. He longed for the comforting red glow of his bedside clock and squinted in the hope of making out the hands on Howard's old wristwatch. No luck. A few embers still burned in the campfire; Steven poked the remaining coals to life with a stick and leaned over to see what time it was at home. Ten-thirty. *Well, that's no help, is it?*

When the end of the twig caught fire, its glow brightened the meagre shelter they had constructed. Though little more than a few stacked trunks and a roof of interlocking boughs, the lean-to gave Steven the illusion of safety and comfort. Warmed by the firelight, it felt more like a cave than a stack of firewood. He gently urged the rest of the twig into flames. Adding a log and a bit of magic, he rekindled the small fire Brand had built before retiring for the night.

The glow reflected twin diamond glints in Kellin's eyes; she was awake.

'Good morning,' Steven whispered, checking to see if he had roused the others as well.

Kellin nodded and forced a smile.

'I don't know what aven it is.' He tried to shrug nonchalantly, but came off looking as though he had a tic.

'Pre-dawn,' Kellin whispered back. She reached for her overtunic. Without her cloak, Kellin was like the rest of them: too thin, and marked with a map of pink scar tissue, in her case across her arms and hands. Her body was like Brand's, hard from too many Twinmoons of rationed food, forced marches and guerrilla warfare. With her overtunic and cloak on, the lean, wiry warrior reverted to the cold, frumpy woman who had joined them in Traver's Notch.

'You should go back to sleep,' Steven said quietly. 'We don't need to get started yet.'

Kellin swallowed, summoned her courage and said, 'I'm afraid of you.'

Steven sat up, genuinely surprised. 'Why?'

'Watching you kill that little girl was ... unnerving,' Kellin whispered. 'I know it wasn't really a little girl, but it's been difficult to forget the look on her face when you cast her away.'

'Nerak was terrified, beaten, and he knew it. He knew where he was going and he had no recourse but to beg. The fact that he did it from inside his own daughter's dead body just reinforces what kind of a monster he really was. I don't want to kill anyone, Kellin, I really don't. I want to save Mark, find Hannah and go home, but I can't do that until I'm sure that things here are set right. I've been given a gift, and I admit that I don't know why. The staff's magic ... my magic ... is a critical component of your fight. But it isn't anything to fear, because I'm not someone to fear.'

Kellin wasn't convinced. 'It may take me some time. Nothing in my life prepared me for what happened in that clearing.'

'Me neither, Kellin.'

She sighed, then moved a pot of snowmelt onto the coals. 'Tecan?'

'Please,' Steven said. 'We haven't had coffee since Sandcliff. That's too bad; I bet I could convince Mark to break free if I could just brew up a pot. He's an addict; I'd be catering to his one real weakness.'

Kellin ignored his attempt at a joke. 'What will you do today?'

'Swim down there, try to unravel the spell protecting that underwater moraine, move some rocks and boulders around and hopefully retrieve the spell table without killing myself in the process.' He pulled a pouch of tecan leaves from his pack and tossed them over to her. 'How about you? Any plans for the day?'

Kellin's smile was genuine this time. Beneath the crusty exterior of a hardened partisan lurked an attractive young woman. 'I understand there is a wonderful hot springs spa near here. I thought I'd go and enjoy a relaxing day in the sun.'

'Ah, great. Well, bring me back a margarita, no salt.' Steven wanted her to trust him, but if she didn't, it would change nothing. He had his goals and couldn't stop to worry about every Resistance fighter who found him frightening.

'You think you're ready for this today?' She sprinkled several pinches of the dark leaves into the boiling water.

'Oh, sure,' Steven joked, 'they're always better with salt, but that stuff is so bad for you.'

'You know what I mean.'

'I hope I am.' He pulled on his jacket and quietly zipped it up. 'The difficult part will be unravelling the tendrils of Nerak's spell. I haven't done that before and I don't really know how it works.'

'Can't you just create a stronger spell to cancel the existing one?'

'I wish it were that easy, but I'm afraid I'd destroy the table or kill myself – all of us – in the process. From what little I understand about magic, the most powerful spells actually *change* what is real. They alter reality, and then allow time and space and Twinmoons to go on as if nothing had happened. The magic is still there, churning away, but the world keeps going on as if nothing's different. Reality isn't suspended momentarily – although there are spells that do that too. Instead, what is real is shifted, and then permitted to fill its own niche in who we are and where we are and what we're doing.' He broke a small stick and handed Kellin half. When she raised her eyebrows, he made a stirring motion with one finger.

'Oh, right.' She stirred the bubbling mixture, and said, 'I won't pretend I have any idea what you're talking about. How will you know what to do when you get down there?'

Steven said, 'I've been lucky so far.'

'Lucky?'

'The magic has shown me what to do.' He mulled over this another moment, then added, 'Actually, it has shown me what *not* to do, what's *not* important. Figuring out what *is* important has been my job. So, yes, I've been lucky.'

'And skilled,' Gilmour rolled over and rubbed his hands above the flames. 'Don't let him fool you, Kellin. He's been very deft at figuring out what needs to be done.'

'I don't know about this one, though,' Steven said.

'Because you're distracted by the water and the cold and the possibility of drowning,' Gilmour said.

'Well,' Steven chuckled, 'it's hard to get past those, my friend.'

'Nonsense.' The teacher in Gilmour took over. 'Don't think about it as an underwater moraine in an icy river.'

'That's easy for you to say.' Steven smiled over at Kellin. 'You're not the one going down there, Gilmour.'

'You must think of it as a pile of rocks on the shore, someplace warm and dry. Deal with the cold and the air first; then forget them. You said yourself: the most powerful spells change what's real. Change the water temperature; change your lungs and then get busy working on the moraine. You need to unravel the spell inside the rocks and the riverbed; that's what we're doing here. The rest of it is extraneous detail.' Gilmour handed Kellin his goblet and she filled it. 'Thank you,' he said. 'Think of it like the doorway to Prince Malagon's cabin on the *Prince Marek*. Remember that spell?'

'What I remember is that I couldn't unravel a damned thing, so I blasted it to matchsticks with the hickory staff.'

Gilmour looked disappointed. 'Right. So you did.'

Kellin said, 'I still don't understand what you mean by unravelling the magic. I thought you said once reality was changed, it was changed for ever.'

Gilmour said, 'Yes, it does change. But as Steven also said, the magic is still there, still churning away – like a diverted stream, it's a layer of refocused energy in our existential plane. As long as a wily sorcerer can get at it, he – or she – can change it again, change it back, even *paint the goddamned thing yellow* if he wants to.'

'Yellow?' Kellin said.

'Insider joke,' Steven said.

Gilmour went on, 'So all Steven has to do is find that place where Nerak's magic comes together, where all the scattered threads have been woven into something new. In this case it's something dangerous. It's probably somewhere near the base of the thing, especially if he cast a spell on the rocks and the riverbed simultaneously. Then, the rest of it becomes—'

'Geometry,' Steven finished his friend's thought, 'the mathematics of untying knots, imploding old buildings or folding paper into complex shapes. It's all just one turn, one brick, one fold at a time.'

'Exactly.' Gilmour handed back his goblet for a refill. 'So, Kellin, there you have it. That's all our young friend here has to do today.'

Steven smirked. 'Again, that's easy for you to say. You're not going down there.'

Gilmour frowned. 'Of course I am. Don't be silly; I wouldn't miss this for anything.'

'But the cold, and the water, and the rest of it,' Steven said, 'are you really up for all that, all those *extraneous* details?'

'I don't think so,' Gilmour admitted, 'but I'm certain that you are.'

It was one o'clock by Howard's watch, some time after dawn in Eldarn, when Steven sat on the fallen pine to remove his boots and socks once again. The river rolled inexorably through Meyers' Vale.

'Ready?' he said to Gilmour.

Gilmour had already stripped to the waist and was standing bare-foot in the dusting of snow that had fallen overnight. He looked unfazed, as comfortable as if he were on a tropical beach. 'I suppose I am,' he said, turning his arms in great spiralling loops like an Olympic swimmer warming up. Gilmour's body was an emaciated, bandy-legged leather sack, ribs pressing out against the paper-thin skin of his chest. The fisherman Caddoc Weston, whose body Gilmour now wore, had spent many Twinmoons hauling nets on the Ravenian Sea, and that time had toughened the old man's flesh into something near-impenetrable, otherwise Steven was sure that Gilmour would have frozen, cracked and collapsed into a pile of jagged pieces right there beside the river.

'Don't warm me up right away,' Gilmour said. 'I want to see if I can still handle a Winter Festival swim.'

Garec laughed. 'And if you can't?'

'I guess you'll have to gaff me and sell me at the fish market in Orindale.'

'With all that meat on you?' Garec said. 'A half-bucket of eddy fish and a slimy eel are worth enough copper Mareks to buy a round of beers. For you we'd be lucky to get enough for a loaf of day-old bread.'

'Trust me, I've got it where it counts, Garec,' Gilmour crowed, puffing out his narrow chest.

Brand and Kellin laughed at that.

Garec, lightening the mood in the cold grey of another sunless winter morning, looked around and asked, 'Where? In a box under your bed? Because from where we're standing, it doesn't look like that old fisherman left you with much – or is that just a wrinkle that won't iron out?'

'And what would I do with more than a handful, Garec?'

Preparing for an equally hearty dose of ribbing himself, Steven pulled off his jacket and started concentrating on a spell to warm air and water. 'So, size is an issue here, too, huh? Christ. A guy falls through a magic portal into a mystical world, and it still comes down to the size of the packet under the godforsaken Christmas tree.'

Garec roared with laughter, nearly slipping on an icy rock and tumbling into the shallows. Brand and Kellin joined in as Gilmour struck several ridiculous poses, his leggings sagging over his bony backside.

Steven focused his will; his skin tautened into gooseflesh, and he felt the familiar sensation of something charged moving through his body. The air began to thicken; the pines, the Blackstones and the snowy riverbank all blurred into a distant, waxy backdrop.

Gilmour stopped his posturing and moved to stand beside him. 'Is it working?' he asked softly.

As Steven nodded, the others quieted as well and Gilmour asked, 'How close do you need me?'

'Until I get it right, stay here beside me, please.'

'Get it right?' Gilmour put a hand on Steven's shoulder. 'My boy, if I don't get in that water soon, the heat out here is going to leave me senseless.'

'You can feel it?' Steven wished he had thought to bring along the hickory staff. Somehow having it in his hands gave him confidence; it helped him to feel that magic was tangible. His battle with Nerak had taught him he didn't need it, but for the first time since defeating the fallen sorcerer, Steven missed the wooden staff.

'You're doing fine. Let's go.' Gilmour waded in, gave a quick wave to the others and dived beneath the surface.

Steven stripped off his own tunic and jeans. Standing in his boxers, he turned to Garec and said, 'I don't know how long this will take.'

'We're not going anywhere. Take your time. Give a shout if you need anything.'

'I will. Watch out for bone-collectors. There were one or two we didn't kill back there, and this spell might alert them.'

Kellin's face was grim. Steven wished she would smile again; it had been good to hear her laughing with Garec.

'We'll be back,' he said, his voice deep and accented. Even though he knew they wouldn't get the joke, he smiled.

'Good luck,' Kellin, Garec and Brand called.

Steven let the spell burgeon and as it enveloped him, stronger now, almost malleable, he cast it out. It found Gilmour paddling in the shallows and wrapped the old man in its embrace. *One down. Get it started and it will go on for ever, like the Twinmoons, the fountains at Sandcliff. One down.*

He dived into the steely-grey, forbidding water, ignoring the chunks of ice from somewhere upstream. The river was as warm as a summer pond. Beneath the surface, it was clear and clean, untainted by industrial pollution, soil erosion or acid rain. Like the forests high in the Blackstone Mountains, this river was perfect to American eyes. Steven and Mark would have had to trek deep into the national forest above Estes Park to find anything similarly unspoiled; Clear Creek, the crystal stream dancing its roundabout way through Idaho Springs, was oily and foul by comparison.

Steven held his breath while he called up the magic; it was ready now, waiting at his fingertips. He reached out for Gilmour, whose toothy grin assured him it was working fine. At first the air that filled his lungs was cold, a painful shock after the torrid folds of their mystical blanket. A quick adjustment, and the air filling and refilling his chest was positively balmy.

That's better, he thought, then gestured, *let's swim*.

Gilmour grabbed his forearm. *Wait a moment*.

Steven raised his shoulders dramatically, asking why, then his vision, blurry despite the flawless clarity of the mountain water, sharpened itself little by little until he could see as clearly as if he were wearing a scuba mask.

Holy shit, he thought, *that's an impressive bit of sorcery*. He grinned and gave Gilmour the thumbs-up. An inquisitive look from Gilmour meant he had no idea what that meant, so he patted him enthusiastically on the back instead and swam towards the centre of the river, careful not to touch the muddy bed.

It wasn't long before he spotted it, in the distance. He had been right; halfway between the fiery maples and the granite cliff face above the opposite bank was the rocky moraine. The pagan altar seemed larger than it had on Steven's last visit, and he wondered if somehow Nerak's spell included a bit of fine print, a clause ensuring increased fortification of the spell table's fortress over time.

Hoyt wept. Outside, dawn was unfurling a grey flag over Pellia. It would be another day without sunshine, another icy day spent ducking the Palace Guard, and quietly mourning Churn. His breathing was laboured but soft, his sobs muffled by his woollen blanket.

Hoyt didn't want Hannah to see him like this. For five days he had managed not to fall apart, weeping and raging that his best friend had been left, dead, outside Prince Malagon's haunted keep, but this morning, Hoyt broke down. Every night he had been tormented by dreams of Churn playing that absurd rock-paper-scissors game with Hannah, then slipping off the buttress. Last night had been the worst yet. Churn had tried to tell him something, and in his nightmare, he couldn't understand. Just before he fell, the Pragan giant had looked over Hannah's shoulder – *had he really done that?* – and mouthed something to Hoyt, standing safe on the snowy balcony. And try as he might, Hoyt couldn't make out what Churn was trying to say.

Now the reality of Churn being fired upon, all those arrows piercing his back, falling, the big man falling to the greensward below and being left for those Malakasian monsters to rip apart – *rutting whores*, *those things probably* ate *him* – was more than Hoyt could bear. And he wept for his friend.

Hannah Sorenson, oblivious to Hoyt's suffering, stripped to her underwear and washed using the basin of tepid water in the corner of the room. While Hoyt still slept she planned to dress and find breakfast for both of them. Alen and Milla were in a smaller room across the hall, the little girl sleeping on the mattress while Alen curled up in a nest of blankets on the wooden floor. All through their flight from Welstar Palace, their journey using the small boat they 'borrowed' and subsequent passage north on a civilian barge they encountered, Alen had not left Milla's side. There was no sound from their chamber now, and Hannah assumed they were both still asleep.

She would find breakfast: tecan, warm bread, cheese, fruit, maybe even some meat. Hoyt needed nourishment. He hadn't been well since they had arrived in the capital city and Hannah was worried. The young thief was as taut as a piece of piano wire, tightening a bit each day. He looked drawn and haggard, worn to the nub, stretched near to breaking-point, Hannah thought. She hoped sleep and a good breakfast might help him find some peace.

Hoyt watched Hannah in the half-light, stifling his tears. She didn't know he was awake, hadn't heard him crying. For the past two Twinmoons they had spent many nights together, elbowing one another playfully out of the way as they shared rooms, blankets, wine and food and firelight. They had been on a mission, working their way north: Hoyt working for the Resistance, Hannah seeking a way home. For all he liked the foreign girl, Hoyt hadn't really *noticed* her before now. She certainly hadn't noticed him.

Hannah was striking, standing in her underclothes, those little pants she refused to discard for the bigger, more comfortable Eldarni underclothes. Her firm, rounded breasts were rosy, even in the dim light. The hard buttons of her nipples were like twin copper Mareks. The skin of her back, disappearing beneath that thin band of clinging material, was smooth, perfect. Her stomach was flat, too flat, for she was so thin now after long days walking, riding and eating whatever they could forage along the trail . . .

Hoyt had seen her strip to those little shorts countless times before, but it hadn't meant anything – they'd lived, travelled and worked together for two Twinmoons, and trapped in one another's company, it was unavoidable.

This morning, it was different. Hoyt wanted her. This morning he needed her.

He felt his stomach knot itself up and he came out in a cold sweat. He feared he might be sick right there in the bed as the candlelight shone on the firmly delineated muscles of Hannah's legs that shifted when she bent to wash her feet. *Gods take me*, Hoyt thought, *just take me now.* He coughed, and stifled it, and closed his eyes. Then, sliding one hand below the waist of his own underclothes, Hoyt let grief take him, and as he gave in to his need, he wept as he stroked himself, slowly at first, and then quicker. He watched Hannah wash herself, an intimate act he would have turned away from a Moon ago. *She thinks you're asleep, you rutting horsecock*, he thought. *Turn your back; this isn't your private show.*

But he didn't; he couldn't. Like a voyeur, he was unable to tear his gaze away from the supple perfection of her candlelit body.

Now Hannah heard something and whirled around, grabbing up her tunic and clutching it close about her body. She strained to see him through the gloom. 'Hoyt? Are you all right?' she asked, trying to decipher the strange noises.

He didn't answer as he sobbed in despair, embarrassment and lust. He couldn't stop watching her and wishing that she might somehow forgive him; he couldn't stop weeping for Churn, for leaving his friend there at the mercy of those diseased creatures, and he couldn't stop himself as he brought himself to fever pitch, pulling faster and faster beneath the blankets.

Hannah crossed to the bed, becoming indistinct as her body blocked out the grey streaks of dawn slipping between the drapes. He couldn't make out the look on her face. It had been surprise when she caught him watching; was it anger now? Probably.

'Hey.' Her voice was soft, an unnecessary whisper. She reached for his shoulder, felt it moving, saw him crying in the darkness. 'Oh, Hoyt, I'm so sorry.'

'Please,' Hoyt said, burying his face in the pillow.

Hannah dropped her tunic and stepped out of her underwear. 'Hoyt,' she whispered, drawing back his blankets.

'No,' he wept, 'please, don't.'

'Yes,' Hannah said quietly, 'it's all right.'

He pushed his fingertips through her hair and down the ridges of her back. She tugged down his underclothes as his hands stroked her back. He felt the smooth, muscular curve of her backside and gripped her, guiding her onto him. He held his breath . . .

Hannah took him in one hand, firm but gentle, and drew him into her, engulfing him in her moist, warm embrace.

Hoyt thrust his hips up in desperation as, still sobbing, he came with a shriek, a cry that was lost somewhere in the gulf between despair and joy. Hannah ground her hips down into him, over him, thrusting *for* him until Hoyt was through.

Later, their arms and legs entwined beneath the blankets, Hoyt finally whispered, 'I'm sorry, Hannah. I'm so sorry.'

'Don't be,' she said. 'We've been to Hell and back, Hoyt. If we can take comfort from strangers, we ought to be able to take it from friends.'

'I hate thinking about what those creatures might have done to him.'

Hannah felt her own tears well behind her eyes. 'Then let's not think about it.'

'Can we ... stay here a bit longer?' He swallowed dryly. He was embarrassed to ask but he would have been happy to have the world come to an end at that moment.

'Hold me now,' Hannah whispered in his ear. 'Go back to sleep. Later, we'll eat too much and try to forget where we are.'

'I don't want to forget.'

'Hush now. Go to sleep.'

To his surprise, Hoyt did, drifting off into peaceful slumber for the first time since Churn fell.

Hannah held him, lying awake as morning crept into their chamber and the candle burned itself out on the bedside table.

THE RIVER SNARE

It was difficult for Steven to overcome his natural buoyancy to maintain his position in the current. He'd been trapped down here once
before, and he didn't relish the idea of another wrestling match with
Nerak's watchdog spell. To make their excavation even more difficult,
Steven found that he couldn't stop himself from continually checking
over his shoulder in case one of the bone-collecting creatures might
be coming upriver to tear him and Gilmour to bloody tatters. He
appreciated what Gilmour had done for his underwater vision. Being
able to see clearly, despite the turbid clouds of silt they were kicking
up, helped him feel slightly more confident: at least if one of the
cthulhoid monsters did materialise, he or Gilmour would spot it
coming.

Steven circled the rock formation until he found the jagged cave-
like opening he and Garec had nearly been dragged into the previous
autumn. He waved at Gilmour to get his attention, then indicated
this was the place.

He felt an ominous sense of foreboding as he hovered before the
inky-black crevice. With a thought he increased the water temperature around them, but even that did little to mitigate the cold
emptiness of the cave. There were no fish swimming past, not even
the ungainly, crippled creatures that had been lurking about last time.
A glance across the riverbed confirmed that there were no plants
either; nothing grew within eyeshot of the crooked pile of rocks and
fallen trees. The moraine was powerful, so compelling that Steven
had once knelt before it, awed by its perfectly random majesty. He
realised now that it was something more than just a glorious piece of
sculpture. There was evil here, and the closer the two magicians
swam to the obsidian breach in the rocky wall, the more Steven
understood that they needed to be extremely careful or they would
die.

Then Gilmour swam about twenty yards out from the cave and

plunged one of his hands into the riverbed, startling Steven so badly that he nearly lost control of the spells protecting them. In a moment the old sorcerer was trapped.

Steven nearly inhaled a lungful of water as he shouted, 'Gilmour!' What came out was a garbled mouthful of bubbles and vowels.

Gilmour was gesturing. Steven watched him tug fruitlessly against the riverbed a time or two, then he grinned, a sinister smile, as if everything was working out according to some maniacal plan.

Steven shrugged as if to say, *I have no idea what you're doing.*

Gilmour pointed to himself, made a twirling motion in front of his face and then pointed at Steven, who looked blank. He repeated the gesture: pointed to himself, twirled two fingers near his mouth and then pointed to Steven.

You're telling me. You're telling me what? You're telling . . . you're teaching me! You're teaching me? What are you teaching me? How can this be teaching me anything other than how to commit suicide? Christ, what timing . . .

Reading his mind, Gilmour gestured again: motioning downwards with his free palm – *calm down* – and pointing to his head – *and think.*

Okay. Okay. All right. I must know what to do. He wouldn't have done this if I didn't know how to get him out of here. I must know . . . I must have done this already. Okay, I get it; I've done this before. When? Where?

And then Steven remembered: Sandcliff Palace, with the almor. The magic hadn't come to him until he needed it. He had been nervous and frightened – *I'm nervous now!* – and the magic he needed to find and kill the demon hadn't emerged until he had placed himself in a position of need. He had been so worried, so confused as to which magic to use, his own fledgling power or that of the hickory staff, that he had not been focused on what was most important: finding and killing the creature. *He's right*, Steven thought. *The lunatic sonofabitch is right again.* The magic had come to him when he cleared his mind and stepped into the snow; it would work again.

You're focusing on the wrong things, he told himself. *You're worried about the bone-collectors, you're frightened of the cave; it's the almor all over again. Get into the snow, Steven. The magic will come when you step off the landing and into the snow.*

Steven managed a shaky grin and plunged his own hand into the silty mud. Before he could think about retrieving it, he was trapped as well.

Mimicking Steven's earlier gesture, Gilmour smiled and gave a thumbs-up.

Steven shot him an incredulous smirk. *Oh, yeah, sure. This makes perfect sense, you crazy old bastard. I'll call you from Hell and let you know how things worked out.*

But despite his troubling lack of confidence, Steven's own magic swelled in a gust of protective power. There was no need for them to be concerned with air or warmth; Steven's initial spells went on without interruption. Now there was only the riverbed and the moraine, the burial ground for the Larion Senate's most powerful tool. Steven watched as the thin strip of mud separating the rocky cave and the underwater altar came into crisp focus.

He felt Nerak's old spell.

It was there in the mud, running back and forth between his wrist and the cave. A connection had been established, a linking of two powers, the magic to hold them fast and . . .

They started to move.

. . . the magic to drag them beneath the rocks.

Holy Christ, Steven thought, *gotta work quick, gotta figure this out—*

Just as it had when he had been trapped here with Garec, the underwater moraine began reeling the two sorcerers in, dragging them immutably towards the narrow breach in its foundation. They would soon become a permanent addition; Steven wondered in horror how many others they might find buried inside.

He fought to keep his head.

This is no different than finding and killing that almor. The magic is here; it knows we're in deep shit. I just have to get the right variables together to dismantle Nerak's old spells. Right? That sounded easier this morning, while I was still wrapped in my blankets by the fire.

There are two. What connects them? He thought it strange that both times the moraine hadn't begun to haul him inside immediately; it had been several seconds, maybe even a minute, after he had been trapped by the mud. *They're working in tandem?* he asked himself. *It doesn't matter where I put my hand or my foot, the riverbed has to find me first, before the rocks drag me in to die? The communication between them takes some time – why?*

They continued their languid journey across the river bottom.

That's it! Steven looked over at Gilmour, who was engrossed in his own deductions. *It's a web, a net, there is no spot on which to land; one could step anywhere near the thing, and it would eventually suck you in. That's it. That right hand doesn't know what the left hand . . .*

A brilliant light flashed, blinding Steven and derailing his analysis. Gilmour had summoned a ball of fire so hot that it burned despite being twenty feet below the surface of the water. It was spherical and pulsing with fury, almost breathing; Steven recoiled from it as far as his imprisoned wrist would allow. With a gesture, Gilmour sent the fireball slamming into the cave. For a moment, the inside of the moraine was illuminated, but the fire was so incandescent that all Steven could make out was that the great stone edifice was hollow where it met the riverbed. An instant later the ball exploded. The concussion reverberated in a nauseating shockwave that pushed Steven downstream, nearly dislocating his shoulder as his full weight bore down against the bones and muscles of his wrist.

Goddamnit, Gilmour! he shouted, *you're going to break my arm!*

He grimaced, a nonverbal apology: *it was worth a try.*

Steven shut his eyes until the clouds of silt cleared, then went back to feeling the connection between the moraine and the riverbed. He sent tendrils of his own magic into the mud, not waves of rage and fury, as he had with the hickory staff, but silent scouts searching for the place where the spells crossed. He was concentrating so hard on his work that he failed to see that he and Gilmour were moving more quickly towards the rock formation. The attack had triggered a response, a retaliatory measure that promised to bury both of them in a few seconds.

Look harder, Steven urged himself, *there's no time.* He sent more seekers along the path of the mystical bands holding him down. *It has to be there, or maybe just outside the cave?*

There was nothing but the same taut, fibrous web; the spider was hiding. *Hiding, but where? There's no place to hide down here. Where would the origin of this thing be?*

He pressed his thoughts through the mud, beyond the cave entrance, into the void between the rocky proscenia. *It has to be here. There has to be a change; the wiry bands, the manacles, the web: something has to shift. It wouldn't just hold us for ever, it would have to—*

There it was. Buried inside the cave, a few inches, perhaps a foot deep in the mud, the spell changed. Reflexively, Steven jerked his own magic back, for the slightest touch of that place was like pressing a sore, an open wound on Eldarn itself. It was circular and deep, neither liquid nor solid, but some home-grown combination of both: a fatty membrane, coated in Larion mucus, thin enough to slip through into unimaginable horrors below. That's where the spell table would be. It wasn't just buried under some rocks; Lessek's greatest invention had been secreted inside a makeshift, homicidal gullet.

To retrieve the spell table, he and Gilmour would have to be swallowed.

Steven's mind reeled from the contact and he began to panic. His thoughts started tumbling and he lost precious moments thinking what the vortex of black mysticism might do to him if he failed to free himself in the next few seconds. It was valuable time wasted; he braced his bare feet against the outer edges of the cave.

Do it the old-fashioned way: tug like hell and scream.

A hand took his waist. It was Gilmour, holding on. The old man sent another fireball careening into the cave entrance, a desperate attempt to fracture Nerak's posthumous magic. Gilmour knew it wouldn't work, but he had been counting on Steven's power to save them, and it hadn't.

The force of the blast knocked Steven's feet free and he slid wrist-first inside the rock formation. Darkness swept over him. He closed his eyes, ignoring it. The darkness didn't matter; what mattered was breaking the connection between the power sources. *Break it!* he ordered himself. *You can do it; just cut the thread.*

He imagined chainsaws, circular saws, butchers' knives and great laser-sharpened meat cleavers, but nothing worked. *It won't break. I can't do it, the web won't break; the spider's too strong. The web is too . . .* The web! *It's a web, that's why it took time to find us. You knew that three minutes ago, dumb fuck! Tangle it, don't break it!* With what could only be seconds to spare, Steven cast his magic into the mud inside and around the moraine. He imagined hundreds of hands and feet pressing themselves into the riverbed, slapping it, digging holes in it, walking back and forth, even dancing across it. Through the skin on his wrist, he felt the impact of a veritable brigade of heavy-booted soldiers marching up the river, stomping their feet, digging their hands wrist-deep into the silt, as if some priceless treasure had been buried there and was free for the taking a fistful at a time.

Their progress slowed, then stopped. *It's working.*

Steven, calmer now, looked down at his own hand and thought of an illusion he and Mark had seen at a carnival. A third-rate magician in a hand-me-down tuxedo and his flat-chested hippy assistant had performed a traditional set, nothing spectacular or novel, and halfway through the show Steven was thinking of bailing out when the magician reached suddenly for a cleaver and, chopping down dramatically, severed his own hand. It was masterful: a spray of arterial blood, an unnerving scream and a hand with a gold wedding ring lying palm-up in a crimson puddle of blood on a wooden stage. Mark had yelped and spilled his bucket of popcorn. Before anyone could move, the lights went out and the curtain came down, protecting the integrity of the illusion for all time.

They'd been three or four drinks into the evening and Mark had wanted to believe that the magician had gone insane, lost his mind right then and there. 'What could be more real?' he'd said as they made their way back to the beer tent. 'What could be more real than actually cutting it off?'

'Not cutting it off,' Steven had answered. 'Who in the audience knows what it's like to actually lose a hand? Probably no one, right?'

'So?'

'So if no one knows, then chopping off his hand can look, sound, smell and feel like whatever this guy wants it to. Who are we to argue?'

Mark hadn't been convinced. 'If you're right, then the beer guys ought to be cutting him in at the end of the night, because half the audience is lining up for a stabilising drink right now.'

What does it mean to chop off a hand? Does anyone know? Did Nerak know? He looked down through the darkness. He felt for the hand he could see with his mind; he imagined it had been lost in a childhood accident, a car wreck, a disease, maybe a shark attack. He imagined getting dressed, shaving, brushing his teeth, reading a newspaper, typing at the computer, all with one hand. He tied his shoes, phoned his sister, ate a lobster, folded his Visa bill ...

When the riverbed released him, Steven kicked wildly against the walls of the cave and clawed his way back into the light. He broke free with a cry and swam a good distance away before realising that he was alone; Gilmour was still trapped inside.

Shit! Oh shit! He turned in a turbid cloud of silt and swam back as fast as he could—

The explosions knocked him backwards and he covered his ears as he tumbled downriver. These were different, no flash of a white-hot fireball but more traditional explosions, like the bombs that had levelled Dresden or blew up the bridge on the River Kwai. Steven felt like his head had caved in; he was sure his sinuses had filled with blood, which might even be spilling from his ears.

Finally he was able to grab a submerged tree trunk to stop his downstream fall and, pulling and kicking as hard as he could, he started back against the current, watching for any sign of the old man, blood, torn cloth, or even body parts, through the almost impenetrable cloud of mud stirred up by Gilmour's attempts to free himself.

By the time he reached the moraine, the water had cleared again to its crystalline clarity. And Steven's worst fears were realised: the cave at the base of the rock formation had collapsed.

The storm blew in diagonally through the forests of southern Falkan, a howling, ceaseless roar that rolled and bounced off the slopes of the Blackstone Mountains. Lieutenant Blackford did a quick mental calculation and shook his head. *It's not enough.* He entered the barracks and made for Captain Hershaw, who was sitting behind Lieutenant Kranst's old desk, worrying over a goblet of tecan.

'Six days?' Hershaw asked.

Blackford nodded.

'Why?'

'I don't know. Could we be invaded from the south?'

'Over the Blackstones, in the dead of winter? Sure, Lieutenant, that happens here all the time.' Captain Hershaw frowned. 'She's lost her mind.'

'I've got to go and tell her we won't be ready.'

'Don't do that.' Hershaw stood, looking alarmed. 'She'll kill you too.'

'I have to,' the lieutenant said. 'We'll lose men, unnecessarily, if we attempt this before spring.'

Hershaw said, 'Good luck, then.'

'You want to come with me?'

'Rutters, no!' He grimaced. 'I don't think you should go anywhere near her, either. Wait for Pace; he'll clear this up.'

Lieutenant Blackford folded a sheaf of parchment under his arm and started up the stairs to Major Tavon's private office. 'Major?' he called, approaching from the outer hall.

'Yes, Lieutenant?' Tavon smiled, but it was a glassy, distant look, devoid of any real emotion. Something about her had gone tragically awry in the past three days, and Blackford hoped her illness – that's what it had to be, some kind of crippling mental illness – had not done any irretrievable damage; maybe an Orindale healer might be able to cure their battalion commander. He and Captain Hershaw had already dispatched a rider to the capital to bring Colonel Pace and a team of healers as quickly as possible. Three officers and two soldiers were already dead, their bodies reduced to ash, and Blackford trembled every time he was forced to enter this room – but he was the only one man enough to actually do it. Everyone else, including Hershaw and Denne, who ought to be reporting to her, were unwilling even to come up the stairs.

'We don't have enough supplies – horses, food, blankets or wagons – to make a six-day forced march.' He froze, waiting for the major's wrath to explode. Sweat trickled under his collar.

'Get more.' Tavon perused a map she had spread across her desk.

'Yes, ma'am.' Blackford turned to leave, then said, 'Uh, Major?'

Tavon looked up. 'What is it, Lieutenant?'

'I'm not certain where we'll find supplies enough for the entire battalion for that length of time.'

'Then we will make the journey in fewer days. We'll run the men day and night.'

'Yes, ma'am, but—'

'Lieutenant,' Tavon cut him off. 'I am not stupid.'

'No, ma'am. Of course not, ma'am.' Blackford kept his eyes on his boots.

'I know that you have been keeping this battalion running smoothly and well-supplied for the past thirty-five Twinmoons.'

'Yes, ma'am. Thank you, ma'am.' His hands shook, and he clasped them together behind his back.

'So I am not going to kill you, Lieutenant,' Major Tavon clarified, as if it had been obvious all along. 'Naked and drunk you're still worth more to me than any dozen of these rutters.'

Lieutenant Blackford had no idea what a *dozen* might be; he promised himself he would ask Hershaw when he escaped the office. 'Thank you, ma'am,' he muttered. He could think of nothing else to say.

'So I want you to figure this out, Lieutenant. You have until the dinner aven tonight. We'll march south after everyone has eaten.' Tavon returned to her map.

'That's just it, ma'am,' Blackford said. 'There isn't enough food. We have daily shipments from Orindale, but we have never had the entire battalion stationed in Wellham Ridge at the same time, so we haven't ever stockpiled that much food, that many blankets, tent shelters, boots, uniforms, any of it.'

Major Tavon glared at him. 'Mark me, Lieutenant Blackford. I don't give a pinch of pigeon shit if half the men expire from hunger, cold or even herpes between here and Meyers' Vale. It is your job to locate supplies and resources for this battalion. You have done an admirable job of it in the past, and that is why you are still standing here breathing. Take what you require from Wellham Ridge itself. Break into civilian homes, requisition their blankets, food, carts, horses, even trainers, if that's what you need, but have this battalion ready to move by the dinner aven!'

Blackford trembled as he saluted and agreed, 'Yes, ma'am. We'll be ready.' He backed towards the door, then turned smartly on his heel and hurried out. On the landing, he paused to look out the window. The storm was gaining strength.

THE MORAINE

The magic hadn't left him; it was there waiting for him when Steven called it back to his fingertips. He stood on the riverbed, ignoring the possibility that he might once again become ensnared by the subterranean spell; somehow he knew that it wouldn't reach out for him now; the moraine had caved in on itself and so there was no need for the web to gather up passers-by. The spell table and Gilmour were all but lost.

Steven was warm and he was still breathing, despite having been submerged for over half an hour. *Get the spells going and they will go on for ever, like the Twinmoons, or the fountains at Sandcliff.* Nerak had certainly put these spells in motion, and they had gone on for Twinmoons – but he and Gilmour had beaten one of them. He didn't know if they had succeeded in unravelling the magic, but nothing was reaching out to drag him into the moraine, so he was content to believe that it could be done: the magic could be turned, diverted like a stream, or even dismantled.

He was seething now, but he waited just long enough for his anger to take a more definite shape. Once he could envisage his rage focused to a point, he ascended the mound of rocks, boulders and fallen trees. With the magic rumbling beneath his skin, he began to dig.

It might have taken nature a hundred thousand Twinmoons to gather such a heap, or maybe Nerak piled them there over the course of a few days, but Steven needed only a minute or two to cast half of them across the riverbed, finding unexpected reserves of energy and strength. As angry as he was at Nerak – and the riverbed – he hardly noticed that he was chucking eight- and nine-hundred-pound boulders downstream as easily as pebbles. Those too heavy to move, rocks as large as a car, he shattered into manageable sections. He dug, pulled, heaved, tossed and dragged the moraine into pieces until the once-majestic, beautifully flawed piece of sculpture had all but vanished.

When the silty bed beneath the moraine came into view, Steven paused long enough to locate the stone that had fallen over the swirling membranous spell. Gilmour would be down there, beneath that rock, if not already inside the putrid gullet. He shifted the stone, then hesitated as a pang of doubt hit him. It was the same fear that had trapped him on his porch as he sat all night long trying to summon the courage to follow Mark into Eldarn. Reaching into the mud now might mean losing his arm, losing his mind, maybe – who knew what lurked beneath?

The river snare, Nerak's watchdog, was enormously powerful. Anyone bold and confident enough to breach the moraine's defences would most likely have the magical power to retrieve the spell table, so Nerak struck at the one common denominator all future sorcerers would share: they would all – including Steven Taylor – be susceptible to losing confidence.

Steven knelt as close to the spell's centre as he dared and cast his thoughts down inside that cauldron of hopelessness and death to search for Gilmour. *Do it!* he told himself. *You'll never save him just kneeling here – dive in!* He looked around the riverbed, hoping some alternative might present itself, and finally, when nothing did, he channelled the magic into his fingers and hands and dived headfirst into the centre of the swirling spell.

His fingertips entered the mud first, piercing the grim membrane and sending an icy shock through his body, a feeling of abject despair, suffering, ultimate loss. Now elbow-deep, Steven felt himself gripped by a paralysis that left his spine frozen and his legs twitching helplessly with involuntary spasms. Unable to pull back, he felt hope draining through his fingers, pooling beneath him and washing away in the current. *This is it*, he thought. *We underestimated him . . .*

When his hands hit bedrock, Steven felt the bones in two fingers snap and his left ring finger folded in against his palm in a grave dislocation. The pain was astonishing, but his efforts to withdraw his arms from the riverbed were futile. He was trapped up to his elbows, and he could get no sense of what had happened to Gilmour, or how he might extricate the spell table from its prison. Fighting to mute the waves of panic washing over him, Steven closed his eyes. He forced himself to ignore the pain in his hands, to forget everything except bringing back that mystical energy to save his life.

It was several seconds before Steven wondered how Gilmour could have disappeared inside the malevolent circle while he was trapped outside. Somewhere in some momentarily out-of-reach place in his mind, Steven knew there was no bedrock eight inches beneath the mud, yet cogent thought eluded him as his will weakened. He scratched with an intact fingertip at the granite floor. *It's rock*, he thought. *How in hell did Gilmour disappear into rock?*

As his vision faded, he wondered vaguely if the spells keeping him alive beneath the water would continue after he passed out.

That's when the bedrock pushed back.

The upwards movement, gentle at first, pressed on Steven's shattered finger and a bolt of pain brought him enough to his senses that he was able to shake his head to clear his vision. He pressed his hands flat against the shifting granite floor and mud slipped away from his forearms, tumbling in tiny avalanches that caught the current and spiralled away towards Orindale.

Something was pushing him free.

A faint wellspring of hope arose and Steven's own magic responded, slithering back into his hands, healing his bones and searching for some means of escape. Something familiar brushed his fingertips and disappeared. Steven remembered a game he played as a kid: you reached inside a bag and used touch to identify various objects. *Bring it back*, he thought, *I was good at that game – I always figured out the balled-up masking tape, the peeled grape* . . .

He was wrist-deep now, almost free. He cast tendrils of power into the riverbed, past the weakening membrane and into the bedrock beneath his hands. *There it is*, he thought. But the sensation was gone again . . . *What is this?* His right hand came free, then his left, and he pushed himself up and away from the river bottom, watching as the mud began to shift.

Frustrated at being beaten by the riverbed a second time, Steven moved a little closer to the surface and watched, uncertain what to do next, as he saw what had been the genesis of Nerak's spell break through the silt. It looked like a puddle of heavy oil spilled on the riverbed. It pulsed, shifting its shape slightly as it was forced upwards into the water, flapping like a fish tossed onto dry ground. *Christ, what is that thing?* he wondered. Having failed to free himself, Steven dared not venture any closer to the sentient-seeming membrane, now apparently struggling for its life. Instead, he waited, and saw the riverbed quaking more violently as it fought to expel something else, something bigger, in an agitated parody of birth.

Suddenly Steven understood what had found his fingertips inside the membrane: Gilmour – it was his Larion magic that had felt familiar, a faint tickling that had held his hand for an instant while it pushed back against the oily, black gullet Nerak had left waiting as a trap so many Twinmoons before.

Gilmour, Steven thought, *where are you? Tell me what to do; I'm afraid of that thing, whatever it is. Gilmour!*

The microcosmic earthquake continued, and all the while the sifting mud and silt took on an ever more defined shape, almost crowning, like a baby's head, as whatever it was pressed its way through the muck.

Finally the current carried away a layer of mire from the subterranean womb and Steven dived for the bottom, careful to avoid the inky membrane.

It was the table.

He knelt beside it, convinced that Gilmour was somehow beneath the great stone tablet, pushing with all his Larion strength. Steven summoned his own magic, wrapped it about the table, felt it grip like a dockside loading net, and heaved. The sensation that greeted him was at once familiar and refreshing. It *was* Gilmour; Steven recognised his friend's energy, the rippling waves of venerable power. Together, the two sorcerers hauled Lessek's spell table from the mud and let it come gently to rest on the riverbed.

Steven strained to find Gilmour through the muck and dark mud that washed away in waves as the river scoured the granite artefact clean.

There he was, emerging from beneath the table, looking like a swamp creature from a Saturday morning movie.

Gilmour Stow of Estrad scraped several inches of riverbed from his face, scrubbed another half pound from his hair, wiped his hand over his eyes and looked over at his young apprentice. He was beaming like a devilish child.

Steven grinned back and gestured towards the surface.

When Steven emerged into the wintry morning air, Gilmour was already shouting and hooting.

'You pimply-faced old horsecock!' He waved one fist at the sky, and screamed, 'I beat you, I beat you, you bucket of rancid demonpiss!'

'Gilmour?' Steven was confused. 'Beat who? Nerak? He's not here, is he?' Panic threatened to take him again, and Gilmour calmed down enough to assure Steven that they were alone in the river.

'No, no, my boy. Of course not. Nerak is right where you left him, screaming a silent scream for ever as the Fold swallows him into nothingness.'

'Then what are you talking about? Where were you? I thought for sure you were dead—'

Gilmour patted him reassuringly on the shoulder. 'I did, too, Steven, especially when you managed to free yourself but I was still stuck there.'

Despite the chill, Steven felt his face flush. 'Sorry about that; I wasn't thinking straight.'

'Oh, don't be. You probably saved my life.' Gilmour grinned again. 'Great gods of the Northern Forest, I could use a beer or six.'

'I still don't understand—'

'Because you weren't there.' He did another little victory dance.

'Under the riverbed?' Steven was getting increasingly bemused.

'At Sandcliff!' Gilmour raised his hands in a gesture that said *I'll start over.* 'No, Steven, you weren't at Sandcliff Palace fifteen hundred Twinmoons ago.'

'That saved you?'

'Sure did – and it would have saved you too. When you broke free and kicked clear of the cave, I thought I was done. I could sense that there was a nasty trap in the muck, but I didn't know what kind of spell it was, but you were clear, so I decided to blast the grettanshit out of the place, maybe throw it off enough to break myself loose. Instead, the whole moraine caved in on me, and there was no place to go but inside.'

'Inside that oily thing?'

'Right. And I knew it was a vicious bastard, but I didn't know what it would do to me, so all I could do was hope against hope that something would come to me when I got sucked inside.'

'What was in there?'

'Oh, that's immaterial.' Gilmour waved the question away; he was enjoying his moment of triumph. 'I'll tell you in a moment, but that's entirely beside the point. I was saved the moment that slimy, black-hearted puddle reached out for me.'

Steven ran his hands over his head, smoothing down his matted hair. 'How? I was lost the moment it touched me. I couldn't think, couldn't move, couldn't do anything.'

'You were hopeless.'

'Helpless, yes.'

Gilmour wagged a finger back and forth through the air, 'No, *hopeless* – the trap was designed to grab hold of you and drain you of all hope.'

'Jesus Christ.' Steven shuddered.

'Had you been at Sandcliff Palace fifteen hundred Twinmoons ago, you would have learned that the greatest sin any Larion Senator could commit was that of hopelessness.'

Steven pursed his lips, then said, 'There are some faiths in my world who teach the same thing.'

'Hopelessness was the one fault for which there was no excuse and no forgiveness: we were the world's greatest hope, the world's teachers, researchers, scientists and leaders. If responsibility for Eldarn's general welfare rested anywhere, it rested with us. Hopelessness was the worst thing a Larion Senator could feel. So Nerak left a spell here that would leave any Larion Senators who came looking for Lessek's spell table feeling hopeless, and they would die not only knowing they had failed, but, worse than that, as a cruel added bonus, they would die experiencing the one feeling Larion Senators worked to avoid at all costs.'

'Ironic little bastard, wasn't he?' Steven said.

'He certainly was.'

'I'm glad I killed him.'

'So am I,' Gilmour chuckled.

'But—' Steven interjected, 'I still don't know how you survived it.'

'You saved me.'

'You keep saying that, Gilmour, but I was out of the game. This was not my finest hour by a couple of touchdowns.'

'It's like I said, when you kicked clear of the cave, I brought the whole place down. It was all I could think to do. When the walls collapsed, the rutting rocks came smashing down on me. I think I've got two or three broken bones to mend when we get back to shore.' Gilmour felt along his collarbone with two fingers, checking for a fracture. 'Anyway, the riverbed didn't let me go. I was heading into that black circle, going in nose-first—' He winced and checked the opposite clavicle. 'I didn't do anything but hope, Steven. I hoped and I wished and I willed that someone – preferably you – would come along and save my life.'

'And in fact *you* did.'

'What happened to your magic when you reached inside the circle?' he asked suddenly.

'It disappeared,' Steven said.

'Did it?' Gilmour looked genuinely surprised.

'No,' Steven corrected him, 'it was still there, but it had faded to such a tiny little point that I couldn't reach out and get it. I didn't even try until you shifted my broken fingers and the pain slapped me out of that daze.'

'Exactly,' Gilmour said, 'the magic was still there, but you had lost hope of using it to save yourself – or me, for that matter.'

'Jesus, that's a nasty one.'

'It is,' Gilmour said, 'but there's one guaranteed way to slip past it.'

'Have hope?'

'Have *nothing* but hope,' Gilmour clarified. 'If you have hope *and* the Orindale Chainball Team . . .'

'You're screwed,' Steven finished.

'Interesting way of putting it, but yes.'

'Have nothing but hope,' Steven said.

'That's right.'

Steven's face changed. All at once angry, he glared at his friend and said, 'I'll be right back.'

'Where are you going?' Gilmour said. 'You have other plans? I think Garec has his eye on Kellin, so I wouldn't pursue that possibility.' He was obviously still pleased with himself for outwitting his old nemesis.

'It's still down there.' Steven dived for the riverbed, mustering all the hope he could summon. The end this time would be different. He knew how it felt to have nothing *but* hope; it had been a staple since the moment his best friend disappeared through the far portal in their living room. Now he would use that to his advantage.

The two sorcerers took a break to dry out and warm up. Brand built a bonfire, and both men, despite having been artificially warmed all morning, sat as near to the flames as they could. Steven and Gilmour answered question after question until Steven threw up his hands and begged a half-aven to rest.

'So where's the table now?' Garec asked as Steven unrolled his blankets.

Steven pointed. 'Just over there in the shallows. We'll haul it up here after I've had a bit of a sleep.'

'Why'd you leave it?' Kellin asked.

'It's a big table, it's heavy and cumbersome,' Gilmour said. 'Getting it out was one spell. Out of the water it'll be an entirely different animal.'

'It will be heavier,' Garec said.

'A great deal heavier,' Steven agreed.

'And you don't have a spell for that?' Kellin asked. Remembering what Gilmour had said, Steven noticed that she and Garec had been sitting next to each other through the midday meal. They stood beside one another now, looking comfortable together.

'Sure we do,' Steven said. 'It's just different, and it takes a bit of concentration.' He rested his head on his pack. 'We'll get it done ... later.' He yawned and closed his eyes.

'Did you destroy that last spell?' Garec asked.

Steven sat up again. 'Did the gods send you here to keep me awake, Garec?'

The Ronan laughed and agreed, 'They might have, yes.'

'I didn't destroy it,' Steven said, lying back and pulling his blankets tight beneath his chin.

'But Gilmour said—'

'*I* didn't destroy it,' Steven interrupted, 'but a weak-willed, terrified bank manager from Idaho Springs did.'

Garec looked quizzical.

Steven smirked. 'It was about the easiest spell I've cast since I got here. No kidding. It just fell off my fingertips and tore the thing to ribbons.'

Garec said, 'Nothing but hope.'

'I know that song, my friend.'

'Sleep well, Steven.'

'Watch for Mark. I probably shouldn't be resting at all, but I'm afraid I'll screw up royally if I do too much while I'm wiped out.'

Gilmour sat on a folded blanket, his back resting against a pine trunk and his feet propped on a flat rock.

'How are you?' Garec asked.

Gilmour shrugged. 'Not bad, I suppose.'

'Did you ...' Garec awkwardly mimed what he couldn't find the words to describe.

'I did all right,' Gilmour said, nibbling at a piece of venison. 'I couldn't get free from the riverbed or untangle the web, but I managed a few decent explosions and I did outwit Nerak's hopelessness trap, so all in all, I'm pleased.'

'You have the spell table, and you're sitting here intact,' Brand said. 'By my reckoning, that's a successful morning.'

'I couldn't agree more,' Gilmour said. 'I think I've reached a new phase in my life – one I could never have predicted. I thought I had to be a great magician, on par with Nerak, to win this battle, but I don't.' He grimaced comically. 'At least I *think* I don't.'

Garec smiled. Regardless of how his life's work might be evolving, there were things about Gilmour that would never change, especially his propensity for engaging life from a comfortable sitting position. Now, with Lessek's spell table successfully excavated and waiting in the shallows, Gilmour was stretched out languidly beside the fire and Garec waited to see one of the old man's ubiquitous tobacco pipes appear suddenly in his bony fingers. 'So what's your charge then?'

'To teach, to mentor. It was always my role, from my first Twinmoons at Sandcliff when I knew I would never be a great sorcerer. I lost sight of that over the last few hundred Twinmoons. With only me and Kantu left, I thought I had to be as powerful as Nerak to beat him.'

'But you weren't?' Kellin asked.

'Great gods, no,' Gilmour replied, 'even if Steven's claims about Nerak are true, that he was just a hack, a weakling who lied to himself about how good he was, the old bastard was still too powerful for me. The last few Twinmoons have been the worst. I've tried spells that have failed; I've been terrified to open that spell book. I've come face to face with my own weaknesses, and all these things have distracted me from what I was really supposed to be doing.'

'Guiding him?' Garec motioned towards Steven.

'Exactly,' Gilmour said, then brightened. 'And what I'm discovering is a new appreciation for everything I had before.'

'I don't understand,' Brand said.

'I did a lot of work over the last thousand Twinmoons, and before Sandcliff fell I amassed a great deal of knowledge, and a not-insignificant grasp of Larion magic. But recently, especially since Port Denis was destroyed, I've been honing skills I knew I lacked and never took the time to stop and appreciate the overall package of who I had become.'

'You were focusing on the wrong things,' Garec said, echoing Steven's own realisation.

'But now that I've had a chance to clear my head, I feel as though I've regained my perspective, and some of my strength is returning. I felt it for a while at Sandcliff, especially that first day when we battled the acid clouds and the almor. It was as if everything I needed to know was hidden behind a gossamer-thin curtain; I was so close to clarity there that I could taste it on my tongue like spring rain, but then Nerak arrived and I got distracted again.'

'He wasn't playing fair, either, Gilmour,' Garec said, 'using Pikan and that sword, and using poor old Harren's brittle bones to attack us ... it's no wonder you were a bit off-centre.'

'So what was different today?' Kellin asked.

'Today, I stayed inside myself, I trusted that if I showed Steven how to find the right magic, he would free us and find the table. When that didn't happen, I tried not to panic.'

'Did it work?'

'Actually, it did.' Gilmour finally produced a pipe and began smoking. 'I trusted what I knew, rather than what magic I *wished* I had with me. Even after I was drawn beneath the river, I kept my wits, tapped my strength and managed to bring the table back out.'

'So you were stronger than the hopelessness snare,' Kellin said.

'No, I was smarter,' Gilmour corrected her. 'In the end, my wits are what saved me.'

'What was down there?' Brand asked.

Gilmour puffed at his pipe. The embers glowed red a moment before a wisp of sweet Falkan smoke escaped. 'It was a chamber of sorts, about chest-deep with water. The ceiling – the riverbed – was a dark blanket, just out of reach. I never realised how noisy a river is until I spent those few moments beneath this one. The whole place echoed with the sound of perpetual motion. It was black as pitch, damp, smelling of mould and decay – and guarded by five or six of those bone-collecting creatures we faced in the glen.'

'Rutting whores,' Garec exclaimed, 'how'd you handle so many?'

Gilmour shook his head. 'I didn't. They were all dead, just hulking masses of stinking rotten flesh. It looked like they'd been feeding on each other, until the last one, a big bastard with about ten-thousand of those nasty pincers, died of its wounds – I'm guessing from its final battle. The humidity down there made it even worse, like wandering about in a big city's sewage.'

'I wonder why they killed one another?' Kellin mused.

'There wouldn't have been enough food in that chamber – not even in this whole stretch of the river – to keep even one of those beasts alive for very long,' Gilmour said. 'Nerak most likely had them guarding the new Larion spell chamber for a few days at a time in turn, replacing each other when it was time to feed. When Nerak decided to retrieve the spell table on his own, he probably called off the rest of the monsters and forced those inside to remain where they were. They were probably killing and eating one another after a couple of days. I'm sure it didn't take long.'

'And when we arrived in Meyers' Vale—' Garec started.

'Or when Nerak received word that we were coming this way,' Gilmour added.

'Who could have told him?' Garec interrupted.

'His men would have alerted the southern occupation officers when we gave that mounted battalion outside Orindale the slip.'

'Oh, right.' Garec winced and avoided looking at Kellin. 'I've tried to forget that day.'

Kellin wrapped an arm around the bowman's shoulders; Garec allowed himself to be drawn in, snuggling beside her.

'No matter,' Gilmour said. 'When we started south along the river, Nerak marshalled the rest of the bone-collectors to meet us in the glen. By that time, if this bunch wasn't already dead, any hope of getting replacements was lost.'

'How did you get the table out?' Brand asked.

'That was an old spell,' Gilmour admitted. 'Any Larion sorcerer could have cast it. One of our duties was the loading and unloading of barges at docks half an aven's ride from Sandcliff. Often we'd have to endure nasty stinging rain showers – even in summer, the weather in Gorsk can be positively petulant. Anyway, when it was rainy, the duty, however coveted on nice days, was delegated and re-delegated down to the greenest sorcerer on the campus. So even the most wet-nosed of beginners quickly learned the spells that helped the lifting, moving, shipping and shifting of heavy cargoes.'

'So you hefted it up and pressed it through the mud of the ceiling? The riverbed?' Garec asked.

Gilmour nodded. 'Just as if I was unloading a pallet of lumber from a Ronan schooner.'

'But the hopelessness snare . . .' Kellin began.

'I was trapped beneath the river in a death chamber full of decomposing bone-collectors. For all I knew, Steven had failed, and I would have to spend several days, Twinmoons even, eating rancid meat and waiting for our young friend over there to figure out the river trap and come down to retrieve me. For lack of a better option, I employed a beginner's spell to help get the table up and into the mud. And when I encountered the hopelessness snare a second time, to say that all I had left was hope would be to understate my condition significantly.'

'Then Steven destroyed the snare,' Kellin said.

'Right again. I outwitted it to save my life. Once he figured it out, he eviscerated it, literally ripped it apart from the inside out.'

Brand blew a low whistle through pursed lips.

'I couldn't have said it better myself. There is enormous power in that young man, enormous power.'

Garec glanced at Steven, asleep on the opposite side of the fire. 'Why don't you rest for a while, Gilmour? The three of us can work on fortifying that cart, and you two can ... do whatever it is you need to do when Steven wakes up.'

Stretching his feet even closer to the flames, Gilmour refilled his pipe, smiled contentedly and said, 'If you insist, Garec.'

MONTHS AND TWINMOONS

Gabriel O'Reilly moved undetected through the Malakasian ranks, flitting between rocks and trees in his search for Mark Jenkins. It was obvious the dark-skinned foreigner might look less conspicuous than he had in the Blackstones, when he had been wearing a bright red pullover and a pair of unusual leather boots, but Gabriel was still hopeful.

The infantry battalion stationed at Wellham Ridge did have several soldiers with dark skin, natives of the Ronan South Coast whose families had emigrated to Malakasia generations earlier. Gabriel passed as close to these few as he dared, careful not to make contact for fear of alerting them to his presence. The soldiers were weary and footsore, and it looked like most had been marching about as long as they physically could without a break. Some moved as if in a trance, mumbling strange sounds, barely able to lift their feet. There was a nervous lieutenant and an angry captain, both on horseback.

A rank of horse-drawn wagons loaded with all manner of engineering equipment, shovels, picks, heavy digging tools, pulleys and great coils of rope passed next. Even the horses looked tired out by the forced march. A soldier, a corporal, Gabriel thought, sat astride a splintery wooden bench in one of the wagons, loosely holding the reins and staring south along the trail through slitted eyes, seeing little, allowing the horses to meander down the path at their own pace.

Something – someone – *was pushing these men southwards*, Gabriel thought, *but which one was it? Which one was Mark Jenkins?*

A second company followed the wagons and Gabriel searched their ranks, coming as close as he dared to the dark-skinned soldiers but still finding nothing but angry, sick or terrified conscripts on the march into an unknown engagement with an unknown foe. There were two more tired lieutenants and another irritated captain, but no one Gabriel could sense in command of the battalion, no one obviously hell-bent on moving such a large force south into the foothills so quickly, with neither adequate provisions nor rest.

As the last of the soldiers passed him, Gabriel considered actually searching within their ranks; so many were nearly crippled with fatigue that he was sure he could move right through them and no one would be any the wiser . . .

Then she was there, materialising as if from behind a mystical cloak, a woman, the markings of a major on her sleeve, sitting astride a roan horse, and Gabriel cursed himself for a fool: he had been searching for a man.

'Lovely to see you again, Mr O'Reilly,' Major Tavon said.

'I saved your life in that storm, Mark.'

'You shouldn't have.'

'You wanted to go home.'

'And you were going to come with us,' she said as the last squad disappeared over a snowy rise, 'back home, after one hundred and thirty-five years.'

'Come with me now, Mark.'

'You were going to Heaven to see your God.'

'Our God.'

'Not any more, O'Reilly.' Her nostrils flared. 'And this time, I want you to stay dead.'

Gabriel tried to flee over the river, to let his spectral body fade to fog, but he was too slow. Mark had him. Reaching out, the major – *of course it was the major, stupid* – caught him in midair, his mystical grip as strong as a blacksmith's vice. Gabriel dived for the protection of the earth, hoping to bury himself in the frost and frozen mud of the riverbank, but Mark wouldn't allow it.

Holding fast to the wraith, the major said, 'You have been a troublesome fellow, Gabriel, troublesome indeed. But not any more.'

The former bank manager and erstwhile Union Army soldier watched as the forest itself began to melt. The colours, green, brown and white, ran together like a child's drawing left out in the rain, and a dark cleft opened behind the major's horse. Gabriel had seen it before and the realisation was quick to sink in: this time it would be for ever.

A recalcitrant Mark tried to rise up, to scream, but the presence keeping him inside Major Tavon's body cried, 'Shut up, you! Gods, but you are annoying! I expected more from you, more toughness, more resilience.'

'Don't,' Mark pleaded, 'stop this – he's never harmed anyone.'

'Shut up!' Mark felt the hand again, that invisible weight pressing against his chest, against the major's chest, stopping his air and leaving him gasping.

It's killing itself, Mark thought. *Jesus Christ, it's willing to kill itself to make a point.*

'I'm not doing anything to him,' the voice boomed, 'you are, Mark Jenkins. I can't do anything, I can't harm one forgotten hair on his translucent head without you. So before you start assigning blame, remember, you represent half of this marriage, my friend.'

'No,' Mark wheezed, the pain in his chest too great. He saw exploding points of yellow light and then fell back into the space he had been allotted, his arms and legs paralysed, his senses dulled and his breathing jagged.

He watched through Major Tavon's eyes as Gabriel O'Reilly disappeared inside what Mark guessed was one of the tears Steven had seen at the Idaho Springs Landfill. Mark hadn't been able to see them before. He could now.

'Blackford!' Major Tavon screamed along the ragged line of Malakasian soldiers.

The lieutenant hurried to her side. One of the sergeants in Captain Hershaw's company had built a small fire and was brewing tecan and preparing a hasty meal for the officers. Blackford gulped his tecan, scalding his mouth and throat, and hustled to the front of the line despite aching feet, blisters and a throbbing twinge in his lower back.

As dawn approached the major had agreed to a much-needed break. The battalion had marched nonstop since the previous evening and the men were in sore need of rest. They had arrived at the glen where, unbeknownst to them, Steven, Gilmour and Nerak had battled to the death just a few days earlier. Major Tavon rode down to the riverside and stared as if expecting Bellan Whitward to peek out from behind the field of boulders. The ravages of Steven's fire had been covered by new snow, likewise the chitinous remains of the dead bone-collectors.

'We've made it here in a day and two nights,' she said to Lieutenant Blackford.

'I am impressed. You can tell the soldiers that.'

'Thank you, ma'am. I'm sure they'll be pleased to hear it.'

'They are to have a full aven's rest. My orders are to drink plenty of water – the river is clean enough – and have them eat their fill.'

The major herself had not rested since their departure from Wellham Ridge. She had twice dismounted to allow her horse to feed, but other than that, she had been in the saddle the entire time. 'Feed them now, and have them go directly to sleep. I want to make twenty, perhaps twenty-five miles, before the dinner aven tonight.'

Like *dozen*, Blackford had no idea what a *mile* might be, but he didn't question the officer, who had been saying indecipherable things for the past five days now. Lieutenant Blackford had resigned himself to the fact that made-up words must be another symptom of the major's illness.

'And have Captain Hershaw and Captain Denne ride up here for their orders,' Major Tavon went on, oblivious to the lieutenant's train of thought. 'I want Denne here along the river and Hershaw's men fanned out to our west. They won't cross the river, but they might try to move out towards the Ravenian Sea. The terrain that way is unforgiving, but eventually it would bring them closer to Orindale and potential escape.'

'Er, who, ma'am?'

'Some old friends of mine.' Tavon glanced back towards the river. 'And Blackford, bring me some of that tecan.'

'Tecan?'

'Yes, lieutenant, you reek of it. I like mine with an extra pinch of leaves right in the goblet. Like they serve it at the Café du Monde.'

Major Tavon discussed the day's march with Captain Denne and Captain Hershaw, the ranking officers after her.

'It will be more difficult going, but I still think we can make twenty miles with your men fanned out to the west,' she announced.

Captain Hershaw, a young man considered a bit of a rising star in the Falkan occupation forces, did not presume to correct the major. He had lost seventeen soldiers to fatigue, injury and illness since leaving Wellham Ridge, soldiers he had been forced to leave behind because the major would not hear of providing an escort to safety. He hoped they would survive the journey on their own; at least the snow had stopped and the trail behind them was clear.

It had been three days since they'd sent riders to fetch Colonel Pace and he expected the colonel to have arrived in Wellham Ridge by the time the battalion returned from this fool's errand. The colonel would address Major Tavon's unconventional behaviour and brutality, so until then he would keep his mouth shut.

'I'd like your soldiers in a line, two-deep, running out from the river, maybe five hundred paces through the forest, longer if you can keep them all headed south at roughly the same clip,' the major went on, pointing.

'Yes, ma'am,' Hershaw answered smartly. It was a ridiculous order, but he would ensure his men complied as best they could. Marching all day spread out in a line five hundred paces long would guarantee that by nightfall, he and his lieutenants would spend a half-aven retrieving everyone who had been lost or had fallen behind. No matter; they would weather this temporary storm, and Colonel Pace would reward him for it.

Tavon went on, 'And you, Captain Denne, will remain here along the river.'

'Why?' Denne, a career soldier with more than two hundred Twin-moons' service, was incredulous. 'Why stretch Hershaw all the way out into the forest while my men remain bunched up here?'

A momentary look of irritation clouded Major Tavon's face. She didn't appreciate having her strategies questioned, even by a seasoned officer. 'Because, Captain, we are tracking an extremely crafty and resourceful prey, a Larion Senator and a young sorcerer of tremendous ability.'

'Two men?' Denne said. 'We've run the entire battalion down here for two men?'

'Two very powerful men, Captain. And while I expect they will stick to the river, they probably know we are coming and might try to sneak off to the west and work their way around us. They are hauling a large and cumbersome cargo so their progress will be extremely slow, but I do not wish to lose them because I failed to dispatch at least a token force to keep an eye on western routes around our line.'

'You're mad,' Denne said.

'Captain, don't—' Hershaw interrupted, but Denne ignored him.

'You've lost your mind; you realise that?' Denne gripped his saddle horn with trembling fingers. 'We've lost men coming out here. Our position north of Wellham Ridge is compromised. Our soldiers are collapsing with fatigue, and for what? For two men – one a *Larion Senator*? – hauling a wagon loaded with a cargo so large and heavy that we could take them with a squad, never mind an entire battalion?' Denne's voice rose as he continued, 'Please, Major Tavon, I'm begging you to turn us back to the Ridge. You need to see a healer, a team of healers.' He glanced at Hershaw and Blackford for support, but finding none, he pressed on. 'People are dying, Major, *our* people, and more will die if we march all day today!'

The spell struck Captain Denne in the chest, ripping through layers of leather and cloth to his flesh, crushing his ribs, perforating his lungs and tearing his heart free with an audible ripping sound. Blood splashed Captain Hershaw's face, but it was not the steaming fluid that caused him to shudder, but the unholy sound of whatever Major Tavon had called upon to eviscerate Captain Denne going about its work. He had never heard anything at all like the sound of his colleague, his *friend*, being torn to pieces in front of him.

Captain Denne, his body torn apart, pumping out blood, gurgled incoherently and tumbled from the saddle.

'*Captain* Blackford,' the major said, emphasising the field promotion, 'see to it that your men are ready to accompany me along the river. Captain Hershaw's soldiers will fan out, two-deep, to our right and make their way through the forest today.'

'Yes, ma'am.' The newly minted Captain Blackford was quaking too furiously to hide it.

Major Tavon didn't seem to care. 'Very good.' She looked down at Captain Denne's carcass. Blood had bubbled up between his lips and one eye was half open. 'I'm glad to see I can still do that.'

Captain Hershaw swallowed hard. This was no illness; Major Tavon was a demon, possessed by something evil, perhaps from Welstar Palace. He had never been there himself, but he had heard the legends. Clearing his throat, he asked, 'Might I be excused, ma'am? I have preparations to make.'

'Of course, Captain, of course,' Major Tavon said. 'I'll see you for dinner tonight.'

Hershaw's mind was blank. Should he run? Should he order the major taken under arrest? Should he direct his soldiers to sneak away during the day, to circle back and meet him in Wellham Ridge? He needed time to think, but she wasn't giving him any. He swallowed again, wiped Denne's blood from his face and said, 'Very good, ma'am.'

'One last thing,' she added. 'If you should come upon these two men, I want you to keep them alive for me. They can be broken, battered, missing limbs and crying for mercy, but I do need to speak with them before they die. Is that understood, gentlemen?

Blackford and Hershaw answered in unison, 'Yes, ma'am.'

As he accompanied a trembling Blackford back through the lines of sleeping soldiers, Captain Hershaw overhead Major Tavon say, 'I'm going to find you, Steven.'

*

'Where were the moons last night?' Garec asked.

'I don't know,' Steven said. 'They were in the north two nights ago. The clouds were heavy, though, and I didn't see them for more than a moment.'

'I haven't noticed either,' Kellin said.

'So we don't know how long it's been?' Garec said.

Steven said, 'We can figure it out.'

'All right. We left Traver's Notch the same day Gita sent a rider to Capehill to get that magician, the one Gilmour is going to knock senseless.'

'Stalwick,' Gilmour added.

'That's him,' Garec said, 'and then we were ... what? Fifteen days crossing the plains? It was so rutting cold out there, I can't remember. Was it fifteen days before we ran into that cavalry battalion?'

'I think so,' Gilmour said, 'then two in Wellham Ridge, three days to reach the glen, four more days to get here and one day to excavate the spell table.'

'That's twenty-five days,' Steven said. 'That should be enough time for Stalwick to get back to Traver's Notch, right?'

'Assuming they found him,' Garec cautioned.

'We have to take that chance,' Steven said. 'We have to contact Gita and get her marching on Capehill – we need the distraction to get the spell table out of here and hidden somewhere Mark will never think to look for it.'

'Wellham Ridge?' Kellin asked.

'How about Orindale?' Garec said.

'I was thinking more like South Dakota or Paraguay or New Zealand.'

'Ah,' Garec said, '*your* side of town.'

'Exactly,' Steven turned to Gilmour, 'and why not? We have the portals; we have that book. All Mark has is the keystone. If we get rid of the table, he's screwed.' Steven sounded childishly hopeful.

'I wouldn't go that far,' Gilmour said.

'But it would at least allow us to focus on Mark,' Steven clarified. 'Except for whatever damage he'd be doing with the occupation army – and I'll grant that could be significant – he won't be able to open the Fold. Evil's ascendancy will be delayed, possibly for ever.'

'He will come for us,' Gilmour said, 'for us, for the portals, and for our knowledge of where the table is hidden.'

'Exactly. He'd be where we need him to be. We're the only ones who have a chance of standing against him, and if he's pursuing us, we'll know where he is and what he's doing. Gita can occupy the military in the east for a while, hopefully long enough for us to face Mark on our terms.'

Gilmour nodded slowly. 'By now the forces called in to secure Orindale will be back on their normal patrols. Gita will face a relatively small force when they march on Capehill. She might just take the city.'

'That would certainly agitate things over here,' Garec said. 'It'd buy us time and a much-needed distraction to get rid of this table.'

Brand interrupted, 'But if Mark has infiltrated the occupation army, would he not have sent word to Capehill that Gita's planning an assault?'

'Probably,' Steven said, 'but it's a long ride up there, so we may still have time to warn Gita that her cover's blown.'

Gilmour agreed. 'Right. And I don't want to contact Stalwick until enough time has passed for Gita to get him into Traver's Notch. Knocking him senseless on a Capehill street won't do anyone any good.'

Kellin asked, 'Steven, when will Hannah's mother open her portal again?'

'At seven a.m. on February twelfth,' he said. 'It'll be open for fifteen minutes.'

'Grand,' Garec sighed, 'and when is that?'

Steven started calculating.

'While he's thinking, what do we do with the table until *febrerry-twelf*?' Brand asked.

'We find a barn, someplace out of the way, and hide the table there,' Gilmour suggested. 'It's too cold to keep it here, and with Mark coming for us we can't hide out here in the Vale; we'll be found.'

'Or we'll freeze to death,' Kellin added.

'That, too,' Gilmour said. 'There were a few farms between Wellham Ridge and the glen where we faced down Nerak. If one of those farmers would permit us to hide this in a barn, we can stay cosy, eat well and get caught up on our sleep while we wait around for Mrs Sorenson.'

'Won't Mark search every farm south of the foothills?' Kellin asked.

'Probably,' Gilmour said, 'but he knows that Gita is marching on Capehill so he might dispatch most of the Wellham Ridge battalion to assist in the north.'

'That would leave him searching for us by himself,' Garec said.

'Just as Steven wants it,' Brand said.

'So, when do you plan to clobber this Stalwick fellow?' Garec asked.

Brand said, 'I do wish I could be there to see that one.'

'You know him?'

'Gods, yes,' Kellin said. 'He is, without hesitation, the worst Resistance fighter I have ever seen in my life. He remains the only soldier I've ever seen who I wished would defect and fight for the other side, because that would increase our chances of victory severalfold.'

'Well then, I will delight in contacting him,' Gilmour said.

'Make it hurt,' Brand added with an uncharacteristic smile.

'I think I've got it,' Steven interrupted. 'It isn't exactly right, but all this time I've been calculating based on a twenty-four-hour day in Colorado and a twenty-hour day here in Eldarn. I think I'm off by just a bit; I'd tell you exactly how much, but for that I either need a bit of paper or a calculator. At the moment, I have neither; so, you'll just have to bear with me and accept the error margin. Agreed?'

Kellin shook her head, bemused. 'What's an hour?'

'Actually, Kellin,' Steven smiled, 'it doesn't really matter. Consider it one twenty-fourth of a day in my world or about one twentieth of a day here in Eldarn.'

'Good enough,' she said, 'go on.'

'When I left Colorado, it was at dawn on a Friday morning, October seventeenth. To my recollection, Mark and I were in Eldarn for sixty-six days before I fell back through the portal into Charleston Harbour. Now, if a day in Eldarn is twenty hours long, then I would take the sixty-six days we spent travelling through Rona and Falkan and multiply it by point eight three, or five-sixths, to get the amount of time that elapsed in Colorado while we were gone.'

'You're losing me,' Garec confessed.

'I'll go slower,' Steven said.

'Thanks. My mother dropped me when I was a kid. Maths and I have never seen eye to eye.'

'So what I'm saying is that sixty-six days in Eldarn equals fifty-five days in Colorado. So I should have arrived in Charleston exactly seven weeks and six days later. Right?'

Garec shrugged. 'Your lips are moving, Steven, but I just hear noise.'

Gilmour said, 'Steven, you should have arrived in Charleston on a Thursday in December.'

'Top marks, Gilmour,' Steven said, 'Thursday, December eleventh, to be precise.'

'But you didn't,' Brand guessed.

'No, I didn't,' Steven said. 'I arrived on Tuesday, the ninth, and returned here to the fjord north of Orindale on Friday, the twelfth.' He grimaced as he remembered the dreadful tragedy at Charleston Airport and his sleepless three-day race to the Idaho Springs Landfill and Lessek's key.

'All right,' Gilmour said, 'so, you're off by forty-eight hours, give or take a few. Over sixty-six days, that's less than an hour a day. Who cares?'

'We all will if we choose the wrong date to bring this table over to Jennifer Sorenson, and she hasn't begun opening and closing the far portal yet.'

'That might drop us anywhere, right?' Garec asked.

'The bottom of the ocean, the top of a mountain glacier, anywhere.' Steven grimaced. 'Not helpful.'

'All of a sudden, you have my undivided attention.'

Gilmour looked confused. 'What does your first trip have to do with when Jennifer Sorenson will open her portal tapestry?'

'When I left Denver on Friday, the twelfth, Jennifer agreed to open the portal at seven a.m. and p.m. every day and keep it open for fifteen minutes, but she wasn't going to begin for two months.'

'Two months? Why?'

'Because I figured we would need that much time to find Hannah in Praga.'

'I don't understand any of what you're saying, Steven,' Brand interrupted. 'How does this tell us when we can get rid of this table?'

'Sorry, Brand,' Steven said, 'it's a little complicated. Since I came back to Eldarn, I think about seventy days have elapsed – I'm a bit fuzzy on our time at Sandcliff Palace.'

'It wasn't the most gripping holiday I've ever taken either,' Garec said.

'Anyway,' Steven went on, 'seventy days here is the equivalent to fifty-eight days in Colorado.' He'd missed his maths quandaries.

'Give or take,' Gilmour clarified.

'So February twelfth is sixty-two Colorado days since I last saw Jennifer Sorenson.'

Garec sat up, finally grasping Steven's problem. 'That means we have to wait four days before Jennifer opens the portal?'

'We should wait six or even seven days,' Gilmour said. 'Remember, you were off by a couple of days last time.'

'True, but then again, maybe I miscounted the days we were

travelling. Some of our time in the Blackstones is more than a little hazy in my memory.'

'All the more reason to be cautious.' Gilmour was convinced he was right. 'The last thing I want to do is to drag this thing through the jungles of Siam just because you made a maths error.'

'Uh, Gilmour?' Steven said.

'What?'

'Siam isn't really there any more.'

'What in the rutting world have you done with it?' Gilmour feigned shock and horror.

'We call it Thailand now.'

'What kind of rutting name is that?' he huffed. 'I enjoyed Siam, wonderful cuisine.'

'Sorry.'

Brand said, 'So we find a barn, hide out for six days and then take this thing across the Fold?'

'Yup.'

'Very well,' Brand said, 'I think it's time to alert Gita. With luck, they can be marching on Capehill in six days – and even if Mark has sent riders north, they won't reach Traver's Notch until well after the army has begun moving.' He looked down at his boots.

Gilmour read his mind. 'Feel free to go, Brand. Seeing us to Wellham Ridge and then through Meyers' Vale was courageous; both you and Kellin have done more than we should have asked.'

'I don't even know how many of my company made it back to Traver's Notch,' Brand said quietly.

Steven gestured towards Kellin. 'You two ought to be able to get back without any trouble. Travelling as a couple, you can pass yourselves off as almost anyone. The work we have yet to do here is all voodoo anyway; Gilmour and I can handle it.'

Brand pressed his lips into another rare smile. 'Thank you. But I feel as though Gita would want us to remain with you two, at least until the table is safe. With Mark Jenkins almost certainly coming south to find you, I worry—'

'You can bring nothing to bear against Mark,' Steven interrupted. 'Our best option is to avoid him until Gilmour and I can figure out how to divorce him from the spirit holding him hostage.'

'I'm sorry.'

'Don't be,' Steven said, 'it's not your fault. Gilmour's right: you and Kellin have done far more than Gita expected of you, of that, I'm certain. You belong with your comrades. Go to them.'

Garec had been staring out between the trees, watching the river wind its way towards Orindale. He looked over at Kellin; she avoided his gaze.

Gilmour broke the tension. 'There is one more thing you can do for us, Brand.'

'What's that?' Kellin was happy to have something to say.

'Find us a farm. We can't be carting this table back and forth across the valley. Ride ahead; watch for Malakasian scouts; I'm sure they're out there.'

'Unless it's Mark travelling alone,' Garec said.

'Great gods, if you encounter him, don't engage him, no matter what he might say or do, no matter how innocent he seems,' Gilmour said in a rush. 'Turn and flee; get back to us as quickly as you can – in fact, stay off this path. We'll move into the forest as well. It'll be more difficult, but riding along this river is inviting trouble.'

'Very well,' Brand said, looking at Kellin. The Falkan woman didn't appear to share Brand's enthusiasm for the assignment, but she nodded regardless. From what Steven had told her, coming close enough to hear what Mark might have to say, innocent or not, would mean death for them both.

'Find us a farm,' Gilmour said, 'then ride for Capehill. You'll be there in ten, maybe twelve, days with hard riding and a fair wind.'

'This time of year you never can predict the storms across the plains; they can be merciless.' Garec caught Kellin's eye and blushed. He silently chided himself for a fool; this was no time for childhood crushes.

'Can you give us a few days? Perhaps three or four?' Brand asked. 'Let us find a farm tomorrow, a suitable place for you to secrete the table until the path across the Fold is clear. Then, give us a couple days to ride; I'd like to be north of Wellham Ridge before you knock Stalwick senseless. Maybe if Gita is delayed, even a few days, and we ride hard, we can reach our lines before they engage at Capehill.'

'I will wait until the day Steven, Garec and I plan to open the portal and escort the spell table into Colorado,' Gilmour said. 'That gives you six days. You understand that I don't want to wait longer than that for fear that we may find ourselves across the Fold for more than just an aven or two.'

'I hadn't thought of that.' Garec looked nervously back and forth between Steven and Gilmour. It was apparent that he had not considered making the trip.

'Ah, Garec, you'll love it,' Steven said. 'I'll take you for Thai food.'

'Thadrake?' Jacrys wheezed. He blinked to clear his blurry vision, but it didn't help. He rubbed his eyes, then closed them and pressed down hard; he saw bursts of yellow, red and gold. Afterward, he could see well enough to discern that night had fallen and someone was moving about in the corner of the room, maybe folding blankets. The master spy was afraid that in addition to stabbing him through the lung, barely missing his heart, Sallax, that horsecock from Estrad, had hit him hard enough to leave his vision permanently out of focus. Remembering the fight in Carpello's warehouse, the way Brexan had distracted him while Sallax tried to crush his skull with a table leg, Jacrys seethed. 'I'm glad you're dead, you bastard rutter,' he muttered.

'I'm sorry, sir?' The voice was male, a soldier, probably. Jacrys guessed he had been straightening up the room.

'Where's Thadrake?'

'The captain, sir? Uh, he's downstairs, sir, eating a bit of supper.'

Jacrys took a deep breath. It wasn't much; he guessed something less than half his left lung inflated, and that was with painful effort. When he inhaled, his breath made a sound like air being blown through a hollow tree. Breathing out was even worse, wet and rattling, like wagon wheels rolling over loose gravel.

'Get him now,' he managed. Three words without panting. Gods . . .

'Would you like some broth, sir? Maybe some soft bread?'

'Wine or beer,' Jacrys murmured, 'I don't care which.'

Jacrys let his body relax as the soldier hurried to do his bidding. He concentrated on his breathing – *in through a hollow tree and out over loose gravel, hollow tree, loose gravel*, again and again – until he fell asleep.

'Sir?' Captain Thadrake was young and trim and looked good in his uniform. He'd been ingratiating himself to Colonel Pace, perhaps even to General Oaklen – it wouldn't be long before Captain Thadrake became Commander Thadrake, or even Major Thadrake. If he kept from making any big mistakes or from getting himself, or his company, into any trouble, he might end up serving Prince Malagon as an Eastland colonel. *That's a no-win appointment*, Jacrys thought.

'Wine?' Jacrys licked his split and swollen lips.

The captain bent to help him drink. 'Take your time, sir. I've got plenty.'

Jacrys drank, revelling in the familiar flavour. It wasn't the best he'd ever tasted, but given the circumstances, it was a drink worthy of the gods. 'Am I dying?' he asked. He wasn't one to hide from the bald truth. He stared up at the good-looking captain.

'No sir; you're a gods-rutting mess, sir, but you'll live.' He offered more wine, but Jacrys shook his head. 'Two partisans broke in here, hoping to kill you,' Thadrake continued. 'They started a fire in the encampment, sneaked past the overnight watch, killed Hendrick, my assistant, and then stabbed you, sir. It was—'

'Sallax and Brexan,' Jacrys interrupted, wheezing. 'I saw them here.'

'Yes, sir.'

'More, please.'

Thadrake was surprised to hear the Malakasian spy, usually a disagreeable bastard, say "please". He held the goblet against Jacrys' lips.

'Malagon?'

'No one has seen him, sir, not since the late-autumn Twinmoon. That's about ninety days now, sir. There are all manner of rumours going about the city, but the only credible ones suggest that he's gone into hiding, that he drowned on the *Prince Marek* the night it went down, or that he was blown up and the locals took his body as some kind of twisted prize. I don't like thinking that one, sir, but it might have happened.'

Jacrys nodded. It would take too much effort to explain to the ambitious Captain Thadrake how little he cared.

'And I've just heard from a lieutenant who supervises shipments down at the wharf that word is coming in that Bellan Whitward has gone missing as well.'

Jacrys breathed – *hollow tree, loose gravel* – and said, 'So no one's home at Welstar Palace? That's interesting.' His last words were lost behind an especially wet and noisy breath.

'Correct, sir. There's no one watching the store, so to speak.'

'Oaklen?'

'Gone east with the bulk of the division brought up here for the blockade. I think he's going with them to Estrad, at least into Rona, to meet with the officers down there.'

'And Pace?' Jacrys was growing weary; even the few words he had managed were tiring him out.

'The colonel was called away in a hurry, sir, some trouble in Wellham Ridge. One of his majors, Nell Tavon – do you know her, sir? She's Malagon's soldier to the core – has had some kind of breakdown. She's run up into the hills with most of the Ridge battalion. Denne and Hershaw are the two captains. I don't know much about Denne; he's a bit older, but Hershaw and I trained together back in Averil Twinmoons ago. They managed to get a rider out with an urgent message to Colonel Pace. He mustered a guard and left as quickly as possible.'

Jacrys could not have cared less.

Thadrake held up the goblet. 'More wine, sir?'

Jacrys nodded. *Yes, Captain, keep it coming. I want to sleep tonight, not the drug-induced sleep of querlis, but the deep slumber of a good wine drunk.* He swallowed deeply several times until Thadrake cut him off.

'Whoa there, sir. This doesn't mix well with the querlis.' He set the goblet aside. 'We'll never get you up tomorrow.'

'Brexan?'

'No sign of her, sir. She just disappeared. If she'd been running with Sallax, then I guess she knows all the places along the waterfront where he was hiding.' He shifted the bedside candle, throwing a bit more light onto Jacrys' face. 'I found them in a tavern I had been searching with a squad of Seron warriors from the blockade; Sallax was posing as a simpleton, and Brexan had been pretending to whore for the scullery staff. We overlooked them a couple times; Sallax was surprisingly convincing as an addled idiot. I guess there really was something wrong with him. Brexan must have known what she was doing to get the two of them into the barracks and all the way up here to your bedside without alerting anyone. We're blanketing the waterfront with surprise searches. We haven't found anything yet, but we will.'

No you won't, you fool, Jacrys thought.

'Are you sure you don't want any food, sir?' He produced a bowl of broth and a chunk of fresh bread. 'I might be able to find a pastry or two in the city, even at this aven. I know you like those, sir.'

Jacrys braced himself, inhaled through his discomfort and said, 'I want to go home.'

'Home, sir?'

'Tell Pace; tell Oaklen, you're taking me home.'

'To . . . Malakasia, sir?'

Jacrys nodded.

Thadrake tried to hide his enthusiasm. He hadn't been home in nearly twenty Twinmoons, and while being stationed here at Oaklen's command post was good for his career, escorting the prince's personal espionage agent back home to retire, to die – *to dance with a malodorous fat man from Port Denis, who cares?* – would be a way to remain in Oaklen's good graces, to serve the prince's personal staff and to get back home for a Twinmoon or two. He would be packed and ready within the aven. 'Shall I charter a boat, sir, or would you rather take a naval cutter?'

'Private—' Jacrys was fading. One eye fluttered shut, while the other found Thadrake. 'Carpello's yacht.'

'Very good, sir. I'll take care of that tomorrow and report back when it's arranged.' Thadrake paused. 'Of course, I'll have to check with General Oaklen's healer as to when you can be moved.'

Jacrys managed a half-shake of his head. 'Bring him,' he whispered.

'Bring him, sir?' Thadrake beamed. 'Yes, sir.'

'And send riders.'

Captain Thadrake leaned in close to make out what his patient was saying. 'Riders to Colonel Pace and General Oaklen?' He couldn't just leave; he had to ask. Pace and Oaklen needed to know, and grant their permission. His mind raced. 'Where should I tell them we're headed, sir? They'll want to know where we've gone.'

'Pellia,' Jacrys whispered. 'I have a safe house over the wharf in Pellia. I'll stay there.'

'Pellia.' Thadrake waited for Jacrys to drift off, then gulped the rest of the wine. 'Very well, sir,' he said to the gaunt, sickly form lying asleep in the middle of the chamber, 'I'll tell them you've ordered us back to your home in Pellia. I'll make the arrangements tomorrow, sir.'

Jacrys didn't hear him; he was already lost in the brilliant dreams that followed closely on the heels of querlis leaves and wine. Brexan Carderic and he were on the narrow strip of sand that passed for a beach outside Pellia during the summer Twinmoon. Across the inlet from the city, the beach could be accessed via private ferries, usually little more than floating flotsam manned by entrepreneurial vagrants. Jacrys had paddled across the river in his father's rowboat, dodging genuine barges, Malakasian naval ships and fishing trawlers to reach the ribbon of sand. Even now, two hundred Twinmoons and an almost-mortal wound later, Jacrys still dreamed of the beach, where a hundred million tiny seashells lay upon the sand in a jumbled, glittering mosaic of beige, white and black. It was the most beautiful place that Jacrys Marseth had ever seen, and he was there now, back home with Brexan. She had won his respect, proving herself a talented spy, even if not quite a killer. He dreamed of breathing deeply again, of smelling the salt, the tide and the sea air. Breathing with the lungs of his childhood, he quietly inhaled the very essence of Brexan, touching her, feeling her body respond to his gentle caresses, and then cutting her open and watching as her lovely face twisted itself into a mask of terror.

A CARNIVAL TRICK

Garec was hungry. Dinner was still half an aven away, but though his stomach growled like distant thunder, he didn't bother complaining: he knew Steven and Gilmour would ignore him. The two sorcerers had been guiding, pushing, pulling, heaving and periodically casting all manner of creative spells to move the Larion spell table north through the forest beside the river. They were three hundred paces off the path, far enough east to hunker down and hide while any Malakasian scouts passed along the riverbank, he hoped. Truth be told, Garec would have been more comfortable if they were another two hundred paces into the forest, but progress would be slower and they would risk having the cart tumble over and having to excavate the granite artefact from yet another shallow grave.

Tuning his ears to the forest, Garec ignored the magicians' banter and listened for riders approaching. Kellin and Brand had been gone since dawn and he was growing anxious. He was especially hoping to hear Kellin galloping back to find them.

His stomach growled again.

'Are you keeping something from us, Garec?' Steven guided the carthorses around a crowded patch of saplings. His own horse was tethered to the rear slats.

'Me?' Garec's face reddened. He was too hungry to be teased about his attraction to Kellin and decided not to take it gracefully. 'Why?'

'Your stomach,' Steven said. 'Has some woodland creature snack disagreed with you? Or are you just hungry?'

Garec smiled, relieved. 'I could eat a woodland creature, if that's what you're wondering. I swear I'll kill the first edible thing I see.'

'We'll take a break soon,' Gilmour said. 'This has been much more difficult than I'd guessed. I for one could use a cup of tecan.'

'Beer for me,' Garec said.

'Oh, sure,' Steven joked, 'I'll just pop into the nearest pub.'

Garec said, 'I'll get a fire going.'

'In the lee of that boulder over there, please,' Gilmour warned, 'and a small one at that. Mark has had plenty of time to get to Wellham Ridge and begin making his way back here.'

Garec looped his reins around a low branch. 'How do you know he's gone to Wellham Ridge?'

'I think we would have seen him by now if he hadn't. He has the key; he'll want the table. My guess is that he's marshalling some local ruffians, mercenaries perhaps, interested in a few pieces of silver. He'll bring them along either to kill us, to distract us while he kills everyone – them included – or to help him excavate and transport the table if we have failed to do so already.'

'That's a grim list of options,' Garec said.

'He's not coming alone,' Steven said. 'He knows us too well. He knows what we can do. Together, Gilmour and I would be too formidable. While one of us locked horns with him, the other might blast the spell table into rubble; Mark's too smart to risk that.' He considered the wooden cart. 'My bet is that he's coming with a huge force, enough to overwhelm us all, even you and me, Gilmour.'

'Because he knows you won't engage in wholesale slaughter,' Garec finished.

'Right,' Steven said.

Gilmour dismounted and rummaged through his pack for the tecan leaves. 'Let's hope we don't have to face him then.'

Garec looked hopeful at that, an option he had forgotten existed. 'I'll get the fire going.'

'A small one, Garec,' Gilmour repeated, 'just enough to heat the water, and no smoke.'

'We don't need a fire; I'll heat the water,' Steven said. 'You two take a break.'

'Wait,' Garec warned.

'If you want to warm up a bit, go—'

'Quiet,' he said harshly, then, 'listen.'

'I hear them,' Gilmour said. 'Steven, cloak the cart.'

'Got it. Mom's old blanket.' Steven closed his eyes in concentration. Time slowed. The air thickened to a paste and the forest of green and brown melted into a waxy curtain. Draping the small company, their horses and Brand's stolen cart, Steven said, 'Done. We're hidden.'

'Excellent,' Gilmour whispered, dropping to one knee and peering back towards the river. 'They'll be along in a moment.'

Garec crossed to Gilmour's side and considered nocking an arrow.

He placed his hand palm-down in a frozen footprint the old man had left in the snow. Nothing, not the slightest vibration; the riders were close now, but not making much noise, no pounding the earth in great numbers. He wouldn't need his bow . . . not yet, anyway.

'There aren't many,' Gilmour whispered.

'No,' Garec agreed, 'a handful at the most.'

'Let's hope it's Brand and Kellin.'

When the Falkan partisans came into view, Garec was both relieved and alarmed. Seeing Kellin safe, obviously uninjured, lifted a stony weight from his chest; he was glad to see her and wondered briefly if it would be inappropriate to hug her when she slipped from the saddle.

Garec's amorous musings faded quickly, as he saw how hard Kellin and Brand were riding. The Falkan soldiers had loosed their reins and were frantically galloping, guiding the horses south. Chasing one another along the winding path would have been dangerous at half their speed; Garec looked away, afraid he might see one of the mounts slip on an icy patch or even shatter a limb on an exposed root or a snow-covered rock.

'Something's wrong,' he whispered.

'Yes,' Gilmour said, and cupping his hands over his mouth, he murmured a spell and whispered, 'Brand, Kellin,' across three hundred paces of empty forest.

As if they had been struck, Kellin and Brand reined in and searched the woods, patting the frothing animals gently, thanking them for what had obviously been a harrowing flight.

Their voices came in garbled snatches of adrenalin-charged conversation:

'*Hear that?*'

'*. . . over there?*'

'*Don't see—*'

'*. . . keep going . . .*'

'*. . . just the wind.*'

Gilmour cupped his hands and whispered again, 'Brand, Kellin.'

Garec barely heard his raspy whisper from less than two paces away. How they heard him from the riverbank was astonishing.

'Here,' Gilmour said into his cupped hands, 'east of you, three hundred paces.'

The Falkans turned as one, peering through the late-day shadows; even from this distance, Garec could see them looking perplexed.

'Let them see me, Steven,' Gilmour said.

'All right,' Steven answered, 'just wave an arm or something.'

Gilmour did, and suddenly Brand pointed in their direction.

All Garec's fears were realised when instead of coming at a gentle trot they plunged into the trees at a gallop. They were still a hundred paces out when Garec heard Brand shouting. 'Mount up! Get in the saddle now!'

'What is it?' Gilmour said as Steven let the cloaking spell dissipate; Brand reined in, a little surprised at suddenly discovering Garec, the foreigner and the spell table all secreted amongst the trees.

'How did you—? Never mind. It's an infantry company, at least one, maybe more – there were several mounted officers, so it might be an entire battalion.'

'How far?' Steven asked.

'An aven, maybe less,' Kellin said. 'They're coming south along the west bank.'

The Larion spell table was balanced on one side, leaning against the slat rails of the little cart. There was nowhere to go, nowhere to hide it, not within an aven.

A battalion.

Garec's hands were clammy; he wiped them on his leggings and looked up at Kellin. She was pale, obviously nervous. He shot her a half-hearted smile; she grimaced back at him. 'Don't worry,' he whispered. 'There's good news too.'

'What's that?'

'We can't fight a battalion,' he said.

Kellin frowned. 'How is that good news?'

'All we can do is run.'

Steven rinsed his mouth with snow and spat it out. 'We can't leave the table here,' he said.

Garec brightened. 'Let's drop it back in the river. You two hauled it out with no trouble at all. We can come back for it after we slip past Mark and the soldiers.'

'He'll know right where it is,' Gilmour said. 'He has Lessek's key; when Mark gets closer, he'll sense the table, no matter where we put it. It will knock his legs out from under him.'

'Like hitting a speed bump,' Steven agreed.

'Then let him have it,' Garec said.

Brand said, 'Kellin, check him for a pulse, please.'

'No, I'm serious. Let him have it. He's got at least a company of soldiers working for him. Let *him* haul it back to Wellham Ridge.'

Steven stared, then smiled. 'And then we steal it.'

'Exactly.'

'It's too risky,' Gilmour said. 'He has the key; he might clear a space right here and begin using the table against us.'

'Then we destroy it,' Steven said.

'We won't be able to seal the Fold without it.'

'We might,' Steven argued, wishing he had more time to experiment with his own magic. He had been able to cast spells that took form when his magic worked in tandem with knowledge he had of his environment, or the quandary at hand. A college physiology class had saved Garec's life in Orindale, a rudimentary knowledge of chemistry destroyed the acid clouds above Sandcliff Palace and a childhood memory of a loosely woven blanket had hidden them from Nerak outside Traver's Notch. 'We might just be able to do it, Gilmour.'

'The maths and compassion thing?' Garec asked.

'Yes,' Steven said. 'I know it can work.'

'And if it can't?'

'At least he won't be able to release his evil master,' Steven argued. 'Eldarn will be saved. And afterwards we can find some way to destroy the evil controlling Mark.'

'Without killing him,' Kellin said.

Brand shrugged slightly; Mark's survival was immaterial to him. Garec was glad Steven had been looking the other way.

Gilmour closed his eyes. The air was damp and cold, like a wet cloak. He thought of the lump of folded cloth lashed to the back of his saddle. Lessek's spell book was hidden there, protected. *The ash dream*. Nerak had used the book to reach across the Fold. Could Mark use it to usher an unthinkable evil into Eldarn? It was too great a risk. 'No, we can't destroy it yet,' he said.

'Why?' Steven said. He cleared his throat, trying to control the tone of his voice. It would do no one's confidence any good to hear him whining in fear. 'He can't open the Fold without it, Gilmour.'

'I think he can.' The Larion sorcerer pointed at his horse.

'What? The book?'

'Can you open the Fold, Steven?' Garec asked. 'Isn't that where you tossed Nerak?'

'It is,' Steven said, 'but I need more time, I need more practice. I need some frigging paper, a decent pen and a couple of days to think it through. If Eldarn's fate boils down to a fistfight here in the woods, ankle-deep in the snow, we're going to lose. I'm not going to kill my friend; it's my fault he's here at all.'

'But that's not what—' Garec began.

Steven interrupted, 'We can win, Garec, I know we can. But I've no idea at all what that book's about. If there's something the rest of us need to know, Gilmour, the clock's ticking. As for Nerak, if he could have used that book to open the Fold, I'm betting he would have done it Twinmoons ago. He wouldn't have hidden the table; he wouldn't have hidden Lessek's key, and he wouldn't have committed himself so diligently to running us all over Eldarn. I know it's a gamble, but we have to assume the book is secondary to Mark's goals. We can't have come this far just to change gears now. The book may be powerful; it may be cruel or beautiful or as pernicious as a bad case of crabs, but we have to focus on the table, because we *know* that can ruin us.'

'We can't destroy it.' Gilmour was adamant. 'We would be cutting off our own hands.'

Like a cheap vaudeville magician, Steven thought.

'So what do we do?' Brand asked. 'We can't roll this cart fast enough to escape, and if we can't destroy the table, we have to stand and fight.'

'Against a whole battalion?' Kellin looked as if she might tumble from the saddle after all.

'What option do we have?' Brand asked. 'Gilmour needs the table. Steven claims we don't. What should we do? We're not sorcerers. If Mark gets it, he'll use it, and we'll all be dead; Eldarn will be lost. If he waits to use it in Wellham Ridge or even Orindale, we might be able to steal it back from him – especially after the soldiers return to their normal duties. But there are no guarantees he'll wait.' Brand looked at Gilmour. 'Is that right? Have I missed anything?'

'That's it, and we're wasting time standing here, my friends.'

'So we fight,' Brand said. 'A battalion of soldiers can't stand against these two. Even if you don't want to kill them, Steven, you can—'

'Drop trees on them, catch the forest on fire, bring the river down on them, flood the whole rutting place,' Garec suggested.

'Vivid imagination, Garec,' Steven said wryly.

'I'd make a great magician.'

'And we'll run south with the table,' Brand said, 'while you delay the soldiers here.'

'West,' Kellin corrected, 'no one would expect that.'

'How far west can we go?' Garec asked. 'We're backed up against the foothills right now.'

'Exactly,' Kellin said. 'It might be slower and harder, but with all the horses working, we'll be hidden in the hills before they get here.'

'Unless they have scouts spread out to the west,' Garec said.

'I hadn't thought of that,' Kellin said. 'If even one of them sees us, we're lost. We'd never manage to escape uphill.'

'Then we cross the river.' Garec gestured east through the trees.

'No,' Steven said.

'No, what?'

Steven ignored them. Turning to the wagon, he allowed the magic to seep from his body, covering him like a bank of fog over a lakeside village. He reached between the wagon slats and pressed his palms against the spell table.

Gilmour whispered, 'What are you doing?'

The rear slats slid aside and the table began rolling backwards, its carved pedestal feet turning a sluggish orbit around a tiny slot into which Steven imagined Mark would fit Lessek's key. The inky granite shone dully in the muted winter light, solid now, impenetrable, but with the forbidding potential to transform into a swirling cauldron of magic and sorcery.

'Garec and Kellin are right, Steven,' Gilmour said. 'We should stand and fight while they get as far from here as possible.'

Steven ignored his friend and focused on his spell, guiding the massive stone artefact out of the cart. He ran his palms over the smoothly polished stone, then reached his fingers into the mal-shaped slot reserved for Lessek's keystone. With a grimace, he released the magic he had dammed up behind his will and watched as the spell table broke into three ragged shards.

'Good rutting whores!' Gilmour shouted. 'I thought I told you—!' The old man fell to his knees. 'After all this time, Steven, have you lost your mind?'

'Outstanding!' Steven crowed.

'What in the name of the great gods of the Northern Forest has come over you?' Gilmour choked. 'What's wrong with you?'

The others stood frozen, gripped by the realisation that something powerful and dangerous was unfolding before them. No one spoke.

'If it fools you, Gilmour, there's a chance it'll fool Mark.'

Taken aback, the Larion sorcerer wiped his eyes and whispered, 'If it fools me? If *what* fools me?'

'Come, see for yourself.' Steven gestured and Gilmour warily approached the broken pieces, hope returning a breath at a time.

Reaching out to grasp one of the jagged shards, he asked, 'What did you do?'

'I cut off my own hand,' Steven replied simply, 'for the second time since we came looking for this thing.'

Garec gasped, almost unaware he'd been holding his breath from the moment the spell table had shattered. 'It's an illusion? A visual trick?'

Steven nodded. 'Mark won't be expecting it. He knows me too well. He knows how I've been struggling with this power, and how Gilmour has been working with me on magic's ability to truly change what's real, to truly change the nature of something at its most fundamental level. So—' he smirked again, '—I've thrown him a curveball. We'll see if it works.'

'A curveball?' Kellin asked herself, then went on quickly, 'But won't the key still draw him to this place?'

'Yes,' Gilmour answered.

'So we have to hope he doesn't touch it,' Brand said. 'If he's in the saddle, he might see that it's broken and just keep going.'

'Chasing us, most likely,' Garec said.

'Grand,' Kellin echoed.

'Can you mask the power emanating from it, Steven?' Garec waved his hands about, trying to explain what he meant. 'Can you camouflage the magic coming off the thing as if it really is sitting here useless?'

Steven said, 'I don't think so.'

'Then this is a rutting gamble.'

'I don't know what else to do,' Steven admitted. 'At least this looks like we took the last option available to us: we broke the table to save Eldarn.'

A palpable silence fell over them. No one was comfortable leaving the artefact for Mark, but Steven's ruse was the only thing they could think of. If it worked, and if they survived long enough, they still had a chance to spirit the table away through the far portal.

Brand was first to speak. 'So we hide in the hills, wait for Mark to either just pass along the river or to discover the table. We hope he leaves it here, assuming it's broken and useless, and then we return to haul it north to the nearest farm with a barn.'

'That about sums it up, yes,' Steven said, 'unless anyone has a better idea.'

Garec screwed up his face, racking his mind for anything more promising. Crossing the river was too dangerous, and would take too long. Standing to fight was suicidal. The two sorcerers could ride north to face Mark, but scouts would be bound to discover them while they lugged the table into the foothills. And even if Steven and Gilmour managed to turn the bulk of Mark's battalion, it needed only one squad of armed Malakasians to easily overtake the partisans as they fled. Garec was deadly with a bow, and he would probably kill most of any squad coming for them, but it just took one soldier to escape alive and the force that followed them would be enormous.

'What if we open the portal now?' he asked finally.

Steven frowned. 'That could be our wisest choice, Garec. With the table, book and far portal gone, there would be no way for Mark to follow us.'

'But—'

'But there are massive oceans, vast ice floes and sprawling deserts in my world. When I crossed the Fold from Orindale, I found myself twenty paces deep in the sea, five hundred paces offshore – and I considered myself lucky.'

'The table might sink,' Kellin said, 'but you two could haul it back out, couldn't you?'

'The oceans in my world reach depths of over twenty thousand paces, Kellin,' Steven explained, 'and there's enormous water pressure – down there it would crush us to jelly.'

Garec laughed, a nervous chuckle. 'It was just a thought,' he said. 'Let's go with this instead.'

Brand agreed. 'If Mark sees through the charade and begins using the table here in the forest, we'll draw our weapons and charge. It'll be our only hope, but we'll have to try and kill him. If he waits, if he hauls the table back to Wellham Ridge or even into Orindale, we'll be able to steal it back.'

'Done,' Steven said. He wasn't willing to fight Mark to the death, but he needed to get the company moving again. 'Let's go.'

Garec looked around. 'We'll leave the wagon here; it looks more convincing that way.'

'Fine,' Gilmour said, 'and we'll ride west, so mount up, quickly now.'

Kellin asked, 'How will we know if Mark starts using the table?'

'We'll know,' Gilmour said.

SNAKES

A line of Malakasian soldiers appeared in the distance, spread thin and picking their way between the trees, over fallen trunks, and around mounds of blown snow. The line looked ragged and undisciplined, like hunters driving deer. Some were only a few hundred paces off; others, those with an especially unforgiving path through the underbrush, were further away, but there was no mistaking them. However weary they appeared, they were Malakasian soldiers, and they represented an insurmountable barrier, blocking the road north and closing quickly.

Garec was first to spot them. Motioning for the others to dismount and quiet their horses, he whispered, 'Steven, can you—?'

'Done.'

'It's a company, sixty, seventy-five men,' Garec said. 'The line reaches all the way to the river.'

'Where the rest of them are coming south in a rank,' Kellin added.

'Stay down,' Gilmour said. 'We want them to pass by.'

'Should we move off the back slope of this hill?' Brand whispered.

'Too late now,' Gilmour replied. 'Just stay down; they'll pass. We're well hidden.'

Beneath the protection of Steven's magical blanket, the forested foothills were a quiet haven. Garec was anxious that he might be called upon to kill again, but in the shimmering embrace of the spell he barely heard the soldiers as they closed to within a few paces. He rested his head on folded forearms. The diagonal pressure of his rosewood bow was comforting. The sun streamed through a momentary break in the clouds, colouring the forest gold and brightening the ridged wrinkles in Garec's cloak. He watched the shadows as he listened for the telltale sounds of the soldiers moving away.

' . . . *Denne's rutting bastards get the easy path*—'

'*Denne's dead.*'

'*Tavon's gone mad.*'

'Shut your mouth about her; I'm warning you.'

'. . . no one out here—'

'Forced marches—'

'. . . all too sick, anyway—'

The voices faded and the sounds of crunching snow and snapping branches were soon lost as well. Garec lifted his head and watched the last of the line pick their uncomfortable way through the drifts and tangled brush. He glanced at Steven and whispered, 'That should do it.'

Steven gestured with one hand and Garec felt the old blanket dissipate, leaving the winter chill to move back in almost immediately, reminding them all that despite the sun's momentary appearance, the day was damp and cold.

'That was too close for me,' Kellin said, wishing they had been another thousand paces west. 'What if one of the horses had whinnied?'

'They wouldn't have.' Gilmour sounded certain. 'Steven's refined that spell.'

'I guess he did,' Garec said. 'I almost fell asleep.'

'I did a bit,' Steven admitted. 'I was worried about the horses too, so I intensified it some. If you almost dozed off, that means it was working.'

'You didn't make the sun come out, did you?' Kellin took a wary step backwards.

'No,' Steven laughed, 'that was just good timing.'

'Where to now?' Brand was already back in the saddle; his horse was pawing nervously at the snow, ready, like its master, to get moving again.

'The first farm we come across,' Gilmour said. 'Something else: I'm worried that we came upon these fellows with no warning from Gabriel O'Reilly.'

'Probably not good news,' Steven agreed.

'We'll post a sentry near the river,' Gilmour went on, 'and wait for Mark to bring the battalion back into Wellham Ridge. When he does, Steven and I will return for the spell table. We'll have five days to retrieve it so we can join Mrs Sorenson right on schedule.'

'And if Mark doesn't come back by then?' Brand asked.

'Then we'll take the far portal to the table,' Steven said. 'At the right time, we'll open the port there and push the table through to Colorado.' He scratched at his whiskers and added, 'or wherever she is these days.'

'That's assuming Mark leaves the artefact in the forest,' Kellin reminded them.

'Let's try not to think about that possibility.' Garec mounted up.

'Good idea,' Steven agreed and started north along the ridge.

'Captain Hershaw! Captain Hershaw!' the soldiers milling around the broken pieces of the Larion spell table called.

Hershaw, freezing cold and nearly dropping from the saddle with fatigue, rode through the trees. He winced when a sapling slapped him across the cheek. His eyes filled with tears and he cursed, a string of incendiary obscenity that he hoped would reach all the way to Welstar Palace to Prince Malagon's own ear. 'What is it?' he finally managed through clenched teeth.

'Sir!' A flushed and trembling private with damp, matted hair snapped to attention. The others with him mimicked the gesture. 'Sir, we found something, sir.'

Hershaw felt a nauseating wave of fear as he looked down on the shattered remains of the spell table. He sucked up several deep breaths and waited for his stomach to calm. Finally, he said, 'Good work, boys. Have Sergeant Vanner find Lieutenant— excuse me, *Captain* Blackford. He'll be out near the river. Ask him to join me here immediately.'

'Yes sir!' The private saluted and hurried off.

'The rest of you—'

'Sir!' they answered in unison.

'—bring Sergeant Bota to me, and get your squad prepared. I want you to make a fire, prepare some tecan and eat what stores you can find.' Hershaw checked the trail of broken snow leading west into the foothills. 'They're riding, but from the looks of those tracks, they aren't moving very quickly. Be ready to travel in a quarter-aven; Bota will accompany you.'

'Yes, sir.' The soldiers moved away, gathering what dry wood they could find.

Hershaw watched Major Tavon and Captain Blackford approach from the river. The major was grinning unpleasantly. Alone beside the fractured spell table, Hershaw flashed back to Denne, his colleague, his *friend*, and the massive injuries dealt him by their frail-looking commander.

Major Tavon drew alongside. Ignoring both men, she growled, a frustrated sigh that rattled disconcertingly at the back of her throat.

'Steven,' she whispered, 'I am going to gut you, Steven!'

Neither Hershaw nor Blackford dared to breathe; both awaited imminent death.

'Blackford!' Major Tavon's voice was like a demon's, an otherworldly rumble that seeped into Captain Hershaw's bones. He was glad the major had chosen Blackford first, but he didn't fool himself into believing he was at all safe in the woman's company.

'Ma'am?' It was all Blackford could manage to squeak out.

'Make camp near the river, rope up those pieces and drag them over there. I will examine them after the dinner aven.'

'Yes, ma'am.' Given a reprieve, Blackford scrambled to dismount, rooted in his saddlebags and withdrew a coil of slim but strong rope.

Major Tavon turned to Hershaw. 'Captain, you've ordered them followed?'

Hershaw swallowed hard. 'Yes, ma'am. Sergeant Bota's squad will be ready to march in a quarter-aven.'

'Excellent. Be certain Bota knows not to engage them. I simply wish to know where they are.'

'Understood, ma'am.' Captain Hershaw looked forward to escaping back to the relative protection of his company, but as he wrenched his horse's head around, he saw Blackford, hurrying to affix the looped end of his rope to one of the granite shards, slip in the snow.

Blackford reached out with his free hand to break his fall, embarrassed to have tripped so clumsily in front of his fellow officers, Major Tavon especially, but before his outstretched hand came to rest on the ground, he struck something hard and sharp that wrenched his head back and left a bloody gash on his forehead.

'Rutting horsecocks!' Captain Blackford shouted, pressing a hand to his forehead. 'What in the Northern Forest was that? I broke my whoring—'

'Silence!' Major Tavon roared as Blackford moaned, blood pouring freely through the fingers he held pressed to the wound. 'Captain Hershaw?' Major Tavon's tone was suddenly pleasant, the most pleasant it had been since Wellham Ridge. She appeared to be positively *amused* at Blackford's unfortunate accident. 'Captain Hershaw, reach over carefully and touch that section of the table.'

He didn't understand the order, but he complied immediately, regardless.

'It's not there,' Blackford moaned.

'Shut up!' Tavon barked again without looking at him. Her eyes were fixed on Captain Hershaw as he reached for the fractured stone – but he couldn't touch it.

Instead, his hand came to rest on something cold, flat, polished, almost, but curiously hidden from view. 'I can't reach it, ma'am,' he said, desperately hoping this wouldn't infuriate the major once again.

Tavon laughed, an inane, maniacal giggle. 'Of course you can't, Captain, of course you can't!' She waved a hand over the broken pieces and watched as they righted themselves, pulled themselves together and healed their own wounds. 'Nice try, Steven,' she shouted to the forest, 'that was a nice try!'

Hershaw assisted Captain Blackford, whose face was covered with blood. He pinched the gash closed, shouting for a battalion healer: the wound would need stitches.

Beside them, Major Tavon ran her hands lovingly over the polished stone. Mumbling to herself, she withdrew what appeared to be a small rock, a little piece of granite that might have come from the same quarry as the table itself. She reached towards the centre of the table and the only place that had not healed itself, an irregular slot that was not polished as smooth as opaline glass.

Hershaw strained to hear what Major Tavon was saying, wishing Blackford would shut up; he caught only a snippet: '—see where you are, Steven—' but it meant nothing. Who *Steven* was, he had not the faintest idea.

The lights came on and Mark cried out, 'Christ, thank fucking Christ!' He was elbow-deep in lukewarm water, still dry, but propped up on his hands in some lunatic drill sergeant's idea of a push-up. His chest, stomach and legs rested on marshy ground and he tried to pull himself backwards far enough to extricate himself from the water before his arms gave out and he fell face-down. He could see vines, clumps of cordgrass and thick patches of brown bulrushes, shadowed black beneath the tangled canopy. He could hear the distant rustle of animals moving about, things at home in place like this.

Somewhere in front of him he could see sky the colour of aquamarine. It was noisy there, but clear, not humid and dank like here around the pond. Between him and that flawless sky the ground rose. Up the hill to his left was where the brightest of the light came from – not the sunlight, not the light from the perfect blue sky, but the *other* light, the light reaching him now. Someone was there, working; Mark couldn't see who.

His hands brushed against something solid and familiar, something manmade, with right angles. This was no pond, though it was solid and filled with water – a marble pond in a swamp? He slid back on his stomach until he could feel the edge. It was stone as well, a rectangular bit of thin stone edging a trough with a shallow draft and a short beam. He pushed himself out of the water, his sleeves shedding rotting algae and decaying bulrushes, and saw the first of the creatures struggle by. They were like great tadpoles, brownish-green, but elongated, as if stuck in metamorphosis. Most of them didn't look comfortable in the water, and many were crippled by bulbous tumours on their narrow heads and slimy necks, yet on they swam, muscular tails slogging back and forth through the muck like giant mutant sperm. One peered at him blindly through a ruined eyeball. A tumour had taken root behind it and Mark could smell the stench of death and decomposition as the tumours grew and rotted at the same time.

He slid further away from the marble trough, afraid the eyeball might burst like a bubble and splatter him with oozing tadpole slime.

A moment later, he understood why the tumour-riddled black-eyed tadpole sperm things had been swimming so ardently: they were trying to escape.

The first of the snakes slithered past, a scaled coil of diamond-patterned mercury. This was more than just a snake, even more than a prehistoric reptile: this monster was aware, a creature of cunning, capable of inflicting pain and suffering purely for pain and suffering's sake. It paused long enough to look at Mark, its forked tongue flicking in and out, then resumed its leisurely pursuit of the tadpoles, followed by the rest of the snakes. Some swam like the first; others slithered along the marble edge of the stone trough. One, with a body as thick as Mark's forearm, slid soundlessly over his outstretched legs, which were paralysed with fear. None of them bit him. They were going somewhere, together.

Then the lights went out again.

Steven, can you hear me?

Steven reined in and shook his head as if to clear it. He looked around for Gilmour. 'I just thought I heard something,' he said.

Garec grinned. 'Hearing things? You know what that's a sign of?'

'What?' Steven smirked.

'You can't keep playing with that thing,' Garec laughed. 'The urges will pass; you just need to concentrate on something else.'

Brand and Kellin chuckled, but Gilmour tensed suddenly.

'What is it?' Steven asked.

Steven?

'Who is that?' He looked behind him, unnerved.

'It's him,' Gilmour said suddenly.

Not out there, Steven . . . in here.

Mark?

Hello! I was impressed with your bit of trickery; the table looked such a mess. You almost fooled me.

Mark, he pleaded, *you've got to fight this thing; you've got to—*

Shut up! said the phantom voice in his head and Steven felt an icy hand grip his throat. It squeezed with inhuman strength for a moment – and then was gone.

Steven?

He rubbed the feeling back into his neck, and cast his thoughts back inside his mind. *What do you want?*

Do you know where the phrase 'Stygian darkness' comes from?

Of course, Mark . . . He used his friend's name, hoping to reach his roommate across whatever layers of evil and hatred held him captive. *It comes from the absolute darkness associated with the rivers Acheron and Styx, the legendary waters flowing through Hades.*

Of course you know, Mark whispered. *I knew you would.*

Where are you?

I've been there. Did you know that?

No one has been there, Mark. Please, meet me; I want to talk to you.

I've been there. It's— There was a sense of anticipation in Steven's mind, but it wasn't his. *It's unpleasant.*

Where are you, Mark? Let's meet; I need to talk—

Touching, Mark interrupted him, *but you have other plans, Steven.*

I do?

Yes. You're going to spend some time in the Stygian darkness.

Mark, please, I don't want to fight you. I don't want to—

Goodbye, Steven.

Garec shouted out as Steven fell, landing with a crunching thud on the unbroken snow. His eyes rolled back into his head; his breathing shallowed to raspy gulps and his arms and legs jerked in twitching, catatonic spasms.

'Pissing demons!' Garec yelled. 'Gilmour, get down here!'

'He's having some kind of attack,' Kellin said, wringing her hands in fear.

'It's a seizure,' Brand said.

'It's Mark,' Gilmour spat, 'the horsecock's hit him somehow.'

'Somehow?' Garec knelt beside Steven, but he, like Kellin, had no idea what to do.

'It's the table,' Gilmour whispered. 'Nerak couldn't have done this unaided.'

'Rutters!' Kellin swore. 'So the illusion didn't work.'

'What can we do for him?' Garec said. 'He could die – he's barely breathing!'

'Make him comfortable,' Gilmour ordered, trying to unlash a blanket from his saddle. 'I'll think of something.' He searched his memory, sorting through files of common-phrase spells memorised over hundreds of Twinmoons: healing spells, deception spells, distraction spells – anything that might break Steven's connection with Mark and the spell table. One knot must have got wet; it was frozen solid, and Gilmour, frustrated, drew his knife and slashed at the ropes, crying, 'I can't rutting think!'

That's too bad.

Mark! Gilmour hustled his consciousness into a hastily constructed, well-lighted cordoned-off section of his mind and hoped Mark wouldn't be able to follow.

See how they run, see how they run! Mark sang like an insane five-year-old. *You can't hide in here, Gilmour.*

What have you done to him, Mark? You know he didn't want to kill you. You know what kind of man he is . . .

Kill me? Mark was incredulous.

I might not show you as much compassion, however.

Oh please, old man, don't make threats. Mark lowered his voice to a whisper and added ominously, *I already know what frightens you, Gilmour.*

Gilmour's second blanket began to move, twitching in time to Steven's spastic jerks as the book wrapped within the blanket writhed furiously. Clenching his teeth, the old sorcerer focused on the layers of wool folded over the leatherbound tome. Not wanting to touch it yet, he used his knife to slash the remaining bits of rope and nudged the book into the snow.

It lay still.

Gilmour tossed the first blanket to Garec and said, 'Make him comfortable.' Then he leaned over, took one end of the blanket between two fingers and tugged. The first snake bit him through his boots. It was a long, heavy-bodied creature, a mythic serpent not of this world, with fangs full of a toxin powerful enough to kill a grettan. It encircled Gilmour's calf, biting him again and again.

Six, seven, eight of the creatures, ancient, and utterly alien to Eldarn, appeared now, slithering from the pages of the leather spell book. Their taste for human blood, denied for Ages, was maddening, and insatiable. They hissed wildly as they slipped into Gilmour's boots, up his leggings and beneath his tunic, sliding their fangs into his tender flesh wherever they could, biting, and biting again.

Gilmour's vision blurred; he thought he heard Kellin shriek in terror, but his friends were far away, insubstantial, fading into the night. One of the snakes lost purchase on his shoulder and tumbled off the snowy ridge; it had been pierced through with an arrow. *Garec, the old man thought as his consciousness folded in, only Garec could have made that shot.*

Then Gilmour fell backwards into the snow.

THE SCRAMBLE

'Whoring rutters!' Brexan Carderic cursed as she examined the fresh burn across her palm. 'How anyone can survive working in a kitchen is a gods-rutting mystery to me.' The erstwhile Malakasian soldier shoved chunks of wood into the belly of Nedra Daubert's old stove, then kicked the cast-iron door shut with a noisy clang. 'Demonpiss,' she swore, 'that'll bring her running.'

It was still early, before dawn, and Brexan had hoped that Nedra would sleep another half an aven at least, but her crashing about the kitchen was bound to have Nedra investigating what drunken louts had invaded the Topgallant Boarding House.

After her failed attempt to kill Jacrys, Brexan had limped back to the Topgallant, cold, wet with blood, and utterly distraught over the death of Sallax Farro. She had cried herself to sleep in her old room, that same room in which she and Sallax had interrogated the traitor Carpello Jax, the same man who had raped Sallax's sister Brynne … until Nedra had clubbed him with a piece of this very same firewood.

Brexan had slept the sleep of the truly exhausted, out cold all that night and the whole of the following day. When she finally came to, she had remained in her bed, staring hopelessly up at the smoke-stained ceiling. She had no idea what to do next. With Sallax gone, Brexan had expected vivid visions of her dead lover Versen to return – those near-tangible memories had kept her company during her time alone in Orindale, but they had vanished when she found Sallax and they began planning their revenge on Carpello and the spy Jacrys.

Lying in bed, she had waited for Versen, attractively dishevelled and smelling of woodsmoke and wild herbs, to appear in her mind's eye … but he never returned. Instead, Nedra Daubert came to her. She had not needed to ask where Sallax had gone. The bloodstains on Brexan's tunic and cloak and the clanging alarm bells were evidence enough that their foray into the Malakasian fortress had not been successful.

Nedra had sat on the edge of Brexan's bed, stared out across the salt marsh, and said, 'You ought to stay on here a while.'

Brexan rolled over to face the wall. She didn't want Nedra to see her come apart. 'They'll be looking for me,' she whispered.

'You've been on the marsh?' Brexan had nodded slightly and Nedra patted her on the shoulder and said, 'You'll slip out there when they come; no one would look for you out there.'

'But they—'

'We'll know when they're coming.' Nedra rubbed a hand gently over Brexan's back. 'There's nothing happens in this area that goes unnoticed. You've seen how quickly the board fills when word gets out that we're planning a bisque aven. We'll know when they're coming, so don't you worry about that.'

'I'll be worried about you.'

'Nonsense,' Nedra had said with a little laugh. 'I'm three hundred and ninety-nine Twinmoons old, give or take a Twinmoon ... I've been around longer than the mud in the marsh. I don't need anyone worrying about me. Besides, I could use some help around here.'

Brexan had rolled over, wiped her eyes and said, 'You don't need any help.'

'Well then, maybe I need the company.'

Brexan had felt her throat close, and she had pressed her lips together hard to keep the tears at bay. Finally, she had whispered, 'I need it too.' And that was sorted.

Now Brexan grabbed a potholder and lifted the lid off a bubbling pan of seafood stew – her own recipe. Sadly, it smelled like something left outside to die. Grimacing, she scattered a large pinch of dried herbs into the mixture. She sniffed again and, still not satisfied, dumped in a great spoonful of seasoning and stirred the contents hopefully. There was no noticeable improvement and Brexan wondered if perhaps she had been sold bad fish. Granted, she'd seen it pulled from the sea, but as she wrinkled her nose, she wondered if it were possible for fish to contract some sort of pernicious infection that made them stink mercilessly when cooked up with winter vegetables.

Her efforts to cast blame on anything other than her own ineptitude were interrupted by the smell of something burning. She had forgotten the pastry. Nedra's desserts were as pleasant on the eye as they were on the palate. Brexan's vision for her own sweetmeats had included a highly polished serving tray, a stately procession from the kitchen into the dining room, a smattering of applause as she unveiled her creation and a chorus of congratulations from patrons witnessing the advent of her career as a culinary master. Now Brexan was afraid to open the stove, from which smoke was seeping, in case the air caused what was left of her melt-in-the-mouth masterpiece to burst into flames. That would surely awaken Nedra, if not the entire neighbourhood.

Brexan sighed, then jumped as a voice behind her said, 'Mmm! What smells so good?'

She whirled around, using her body to hide as much of the disaster area as possible. 'You're not supposed to be awake yet.'

'I might have slept a little later, but with all the shattering and banging, I thought for certain we were under attack,' Nedra said merrily.

'I'm . . . cooking.' Brexan looked at the stinky stew on the stovetop, the smoking remains of her tart in the oven and the butcher's block, littered with flour, fish-blood and the remnants of what appeared to be an entire basket of winter vegetables. She smiled nervously and added, 'A few things.'

'I see,' Nedra said dryly. 'Do you need any help?'

'No, no,' she said as she clumsily tried to move the iron pot, burning her hand once again. 'I'm fine, I've got it.'

'Are you sure? Because from the subtle aroma creeping through the rest of the house, it smells more like a serious case of something very nasty indeed!' Nedra grinned.

Brexan gave up. 'I'm just no good at this! I was trying to work out a few things that I could make for your four-hundredth Twinmoon party.'

Nedra looked surprised. 'Am I having a four-hundredth Twinmoon party?'

'You weren't supposed to know,' Brexan confessed. 'Some of the regulars are helping me plan it, but I figured I had to get some practice in, otherwise I might ruin everything, and we'd be stuck eating—' she cast the stove a look of disgust, '—well, something foul.'

Nedra laughed. 'I have an idea. For the next Twinmoon, which I might, grudgingly, admit might *possibly* be my four-hundredth, gods-rut-a-whore, if you collect the ingredients, I will take care of the cooking.'

'But Nedra—'

She went on, ignoring Brexan's protest, 'I'll get everything started and you can spend all day in here stirring the pot. Come the dinner aven, I will be *genuinely* surprised that you have cooked, that I have friends in this city, and especially, that I have lived this long. Deal?'

Brexan frowned. Given the smoke-filled room and the increasingly smelly pot, she would most likely not get a better offer in the next few days. 'All right,' she said, plainly dejected, 'but I'm choosing the wine, and I'll not hear another word on the subject.'

Nedra snorted with laughter – which helped keep her from smelling the noxious brew. 'For now, please, draw a bucket of water and extinguish whatever it is you've set aflame in my oven.'

Brexan spun back to the stove, as if remembering her pastry shells for the first time that morning. 'Rutting dogs,' she spat, 'I'll be setting the whole house on fire.'

'And Brexan, take whatever it is in that pot and dump it below the high water mark, please. I don't want the occupation forces thinking we're burning dead bodies.'

'They won't,' Brexan giggled. 'Burning bodies don't smell this bad.'

Later that day a fogbank crept over the marsh. The icy cloud swallowed everything in its path as it rolled up over the Falkan shoreline and froze solid. Brexan sat outside the Topgallant, watching as the waterline disappeared into the grey haze. The whole of the northern district was wrapped in a heavy, grey blanket and no one ventured out save for the few neighbourhood strays sniffing through the streets for scraps of food. The city was nearly silent.

Brexan breathed deep, tasting the tang of salt and low tide at the back of her throat. She listened. From somewhere on the harbour, bells began to ring. The fishing boats were still out on the water, bringing in the day's catch, and they rang bells or shouted, or whistled, each distinctive noise alerting others to their whereabouts, so the harbourmaster could pinpoint exactly where they were and what anchorage they had chosen to weather the fog.

It was the bells that Brexan found unsettling.

Searching the fogbank for any visible sign of the fishing fleet, she felt an invisible fist close over her heart. Wondering if this was what one felt in the moments before a heart seizure, she took another deep breath and tried to calm down. *It's just nerves*, she thought. *You need to get hold of yourself, relax.*

The bells rang again, some high-pitched and clear, others clanking like cast-iron pots. Brexan shuddered, recalling Jacrys and the bell rope. He had stared at it, though he was bleeding like a stuck pig, spitting vermilion bubbles through blue lips; that horsecock had seen the bell rope and had somehow – *how?* – dragged himself across the room to it. She and Sallax had left him for dead, stabbed in the heart, one lung punctured – and yet still he had managed to pull that gods-be-damned bell rope, and as she had escaped from the barracks, Brexan had heard it clanging above the din, rousing an entire platoon and reminding her that Jacrys, despite being so badly wounded, was still alive.

The fog was a swirling cauldron of milky-white stew. *Just one boat, for all the gods' sake; let me see one whoring boat.*

She could see nothing through the gloom.

Brexan knew the bells were some distance away. She had sat here coaxing Sallax back to sanity, morning after morning, watching the fishermen come and go, from the deep waters offshore to the harbour, headed for the southern wharf, if they were heavy vessels with big hauls, or to the northern wharf if they were smaller boats hoping to offload their catches to the locals. Today they seemed closer, just off the marsh where she had discovered the cleanly picked remains of Brynne Farro. They rang out more clearly in the fog; they had to, of course. They were never normally this loud, this intrusive, never usually so reminiscent of so many painful things.

It's fishermen, Brexan told herself, *just fishermen. Jacrys is dead. He couldn't possibly have survived. Let it all go now. Plan the party; get refocused. It's all right for you to let it go. Nedra's party; what a time everyone will have. Forgive yourself and move on.*

She was lost. Forsaking Malakasia and her commitment – her *oath* – to the army had been a decision made in a moment of anger. Jacrys was a cold-blooded murderer; he had killed those people in Estrad and he had murdered Lieutenant Bronfio outside Riverend Palace, and for those acts, he needed to be brought to justice. But she had deserted. She had stripped off her uniform and left her platoon without permission. She had fallen in love with the enemy, a partisan, and taken up arms against Malakasia – she had erased nearly two hundred Twinmoons of her life. She had no home to go back to now, no proud parents to boast of her army career. She had no skills, save perhaps for espionage; she couldn't even make a decent stew. What did she have to show for two hundred Twinmoons of life? Nedra Daubert and the Topgallant Boarding House. Versen's memory – sometimes, not when she truly needed him. The Eastern Resistance? Try as she might, Brexan was embarrassed to admit that she still couldn't find them, no matter how hard she looked. She laughed, if only to keep from crying.

Out on the harbour, voices exchanged their melodic foreign cries and bells rang out, alerting any captain brave enough or idiotic enough to attempt navigation under such conditions.

Brexan buried her face in her hands.

Jacrys was alive.

You need to be the one to kill him.

She wiped her eyes on her sleeve, pulled her cloak tight around herself and went back inside.

On the harbour, the bells continued ringing.

Inside, Nedra was pouring out tecan. 'Drink,' she said. 'You'll get sick sitting out there, and I'll be left to plan my own old-lady party.'

'You're not an old lady, Nedra.' Brexan blew across the top of the goblet and sipped.

'Then why are we celebrating my getting older? I don't need a party.'

Brexan started crying again. 'I guess I do,' she murmured through her tears.

Nedra wrapped an arm around her shoulders. 'Then we'll organise a great, drunken, sloppy Twinmoon fest for an old woman as she clings to life by a greying hair.'

'A grey hair,' Brexan corrected, a sob turning into a hiccough. 'There's no *greying* about them. I want to have music.'

'Yes, of course, bring in the occupation army band; those old imperial songs always help me move my bowels – and at my age, a good bowel movement can mean the difference between a fine day and a rutting waste of sunshine.'

Brexan couldn't help but laugh through her tears. 'I don't know what I'm going to do.'

'You don't need to know, Brexan. You'll learn, hopefully earlier than I ever did, that if you go a few Twinmoons without a compass, eh, it's no great loss. I'm telling you that my worst days, my toughest struggles were invariably what led to the next wonderful turn in my life. But you can't force anything. So you're not a spy, or a killer. Who cares? I certainly don't. I like you better knowing you're not a killer. I sleep better at night.'

'But what Jacrys did was—'

'Jacrys will pay for his actions one day, and maybe you'll be there to see it happen and maybe you won't.'

'I would like—'

'And maybe you won't,' Nedra repeated. '*I* would like that even more. Don't allow a wicked man to dictate who you become. Pursuing him across Eldarn is not a healthy undertaking for anyone, not even for the best of reasons.'

'But I have to tell them what I know. I have to tell *someone* about Carpello and his shipments.'

Nedra sighed deeply. 'That's true; you do.'

'But I don't know where to find the Falkan Resistance; it's as if anyone who knows anything about them has been sworn to secrecy, or has no idea where they've gone. I can't even find a pocket of disgruntled old men.'

'Tell me about it,' Nedra said. 'Finding a pocket of old men in this city, disgruntled or not, has been my goal for quite a while.'

Brexan laughed. 'You old slut.'

'*Ageing* slut, my dear. I'm an ageing slut; I'm not old yet.' Nedra finished her tecan. 'You'll find them. There's a wonderful vein of gossip running right along our street, as reliable as the tides. Some of it is nonsense, pure grettan shit, but you'll hear something, catch a word here or a gesture there, and you'll reconnect with your friends; I'm sure of it. But you can't *make* it happen.'

'You sound like—'

'Like your mother? Good. I think I would like your mother.' Nedra started towards the stairs. 'There's tecan on the stove. Try not to set it on fire. I'm going to rest for an aven or two while you plan my surprise party.'

Hannah watched through the window of the Wayfarer Inn as the young Ronan pissed in the street. He was a South Coaster (she thought there must be something pejorative about that term), and couldn't have been more than four years old – twenty-eight Twin-moons, younger than Milla – but there he was, leggings down, tunic pulled up over his stomach, leaning back dramatically as he splashed the cobblestones. A pair of elderly Malakasian women hurried past, silver-haired clones, cloaks flapping, carrying canvas bags of vegetables, flour and smoked meat. They scurried behind the boy, all but snarling their disgust, but he didn't care. He finished relieving himself with a flourish, adjusted his clothing and watched them move away.

Hannah poked her head out the front room door. 'Hey, cheeky, you ought to do that inside; you're going to catch pneumonia.' She deliberately used English, and loudly enough to be heard by the frowning women. *Don't like foreigners, girls? Well, I'll show you foreign.*

The boy, confused, took off down the road, disappearing into the crowded marketplace.

Hannah smirked. Lingering a moment with the door open, she watched her breath cloud in the wintry air. It was a perfect day in

Pellia, with cobalt-blue skies and a breeze from the north, cold but fresh. The sun didn't hang around long during this Twinmoon, but there was something about the northern air that made sunny days brilliant. From their new base – Alen insisted they change inns periodically – she could see right into the waterfront market, a bustling hive of stores and wooden carts used as stalls. The market was convenient for supplies and, even better, for information.

Hannah hoped they might stay on at this inn for a while. The rooms were comfortable, the food good and plentiful, and the proximity to the sea a refreshing change from the forests, swamps and fields they had called home for the past two Twinmoons. She silently promised to get Hoyt out today; some fresh air would do him good.

'You shouldn't hold the door open like that,' a curt voice interrupted Hannah's thoughts.

'Oh, right, sorry,' she said, allowing it to close softly behind her. 'Sorry.' She turned to see a teenage girl in an apron carrying a tray loaded with dirty trenchers and goblets. The girl was rail-thin; her dirty-blonde hair was tied in a ponytail and tucked inside her tunic.

'It's just that you were letting in a draught,' the girl explained. 'My father complains all the time about how hard it is to keep this place warm. I thought—'

'No, no,' Hannah interrupted, holding up her hands in surrender. 'You're right; my mother says exactly the same thing back home.'

The girl adjusted her tray, holding it now with two hands. 'I'm Erynn. My father calls me Rinny.' She scowled.

Hannah smiled. 'It's nice to meet you, Erynn – but shouldn't you be in school today?'

'Yes, but I've got to work. My mother had to go to Treven – my grandda's sick; he's old. I'm only ninety-three Twinmoons, seven more to go before I'm done with school, but I think my father's going to pay to send me back for another fifteen Twinmoons. But what's the point? I mean, I'm just going to end up working here, right? What do I need all that schooling for, anyway?' She glanced disdainfully at the dirty trenchers.

'Erynn, you should go to school for as long as they'll let you stay. If your father's prepared to pay for you to stay on, then do, for as long as possible,' Hannah said emphatically.

'But why would I? All my friends—'

Hannah interrupted again, saying, 'Trust me, Erynn, this is absolutely the right thing to do.'

Erynn had dull hazel eyes, and bags were forming beneath them;

Twinmoons working in the smoky front room had not been kind. She tilted her head to one side, considering Hannah. 'You're not from Pellia, are you?'

'No,' Hannah said. 'And, sorry, I'm rude. My name is Hannah Sorenson. I'm from Praga.'

'What's that language you speak?'

Hannah hesitated. 'Oh, that's . . . well, that's a dialect from— Well, from Southwest Praga, pretty far from here.'

'I'd like to go there,' Erynn said dreamily, 'and to Rona, too, someplace warm – but I have to finish school first.'

'That's the really smart thing to do,' Hannah repeated. 'We've been travelling a long time to get here.'

'I know,' Erynn smiled, shifting the tray again, obviously wanting to stay and chat with the woman. She was attractive, even though she was old. 'I heard you talking with that man over there. I didn't mean to listen in; my father gets angry, but sometimes you can't help overhearing things.' She nodded to where Hoyt and Alen were sitting together, watching Milla finishing her meal. She whispered, 'He's cute; don't you think so?'

Hannah laughed. Erynn had to be talking about Hoyt. 'Uh, I hadn't really thought about it, but yes, I suppose he is cute.'

'How old is he? You two haven't stood the tides together, have you? Uh, I mean, he's not—'

'No, he's not,' Hannah assured. Calculating quickly, she figured Erynn was about thirteen. She wasn't surprised that Hoyt's wiry frame and ruddy, unkempt good looks had captured the girl's attention.

'I want to stand the tides with someone someday. And I'll wear a shorter dress. I've seen some of the women when they stand the tides and their dresses are all wet for the rest of the day. Lots of couples stand the tides over on the little beach across the inlet; we see them sometimes. The women wear long dresses, and the bottom bits get all soaked. I'm not going to do it that way.'

Hannah guessed standing the tides was the Eldarni equivalent of marriage. She wasn't surprised that a thirteen-year-old was pre-occupied with the details; she recalled, with some embarrassment, paging through bridal magazines when *she* was that age – after all, it was never too early to find the perfect dress.

'I need to get back to work,' Erynn said, struggling with the tray. She blushed. 'You won't say anything to him, will you?'

'Of course not,' Hannah promised. 'I was thirteen once, too.'

'Thirteen?' The girl sounded aghast. 'I'm ninety-three last Twin-moon!'

'Right, sorry, ninety-three,' Hannah said. 'Don't worry, Erynn, I won't say a word.'

'It has to be that bark,' Hoyt said, scooping up a fingerful of potato.

'Mine,' Milla said, wrapping a protective arm around her trencher.

'Then try to get more in your mouth, and less on your face, your tunic and, great lords, in your hair!' Hoyt chided her with a laugh.

Milla giggled. 'Like p'tatoes.'

'I can see that, Pepperweed.' Hoyt brushed the girl's hair away from her face. He turned to Alen and asked, 'What else, in your experience, could turn an ordinary soldier, or even one of those Seron things, into whatever that was we saw outside Welstar Palace? Can you think of anything? Alen, those were monsters! Blind, horrible creatures, able to ignore obvious pain – they were diseased, they had open sores, pox, fever – rutters, I saw evidence of four or five serious pandemics eating away at that group. Normal solders don't just stand around and fester like that, no matter how disciplined. It *has* to be the bark.'

Alen looked around the front room. The young girl who had been serving them was talking with Hannah. 'I think you're right, Hoyt. Why else would Nerak need so much of it? But given the dreams or visions that we experienced, I don't know how he's controlling them. With you the bark responded a bit differently, didn't it ... you were able to take orders, and you appeared to hear what we were asking you to do.'

Hoyt remembered waking from his dream of Ramella, the sexy thief from Landry and finding that he had stacked several days' worth of firewood. 'That's right, but with the rest of you, in the forest of ghosts, you were inconsolable, certainly uncontrollable. It was all I could do to get you moving. The army outside Welstar Palace is different; they're staring into space, waiting. They don't appear to be hungry or thirsty. Gods, I'd wager some of them die right there on their feet.'

'And the others eat the cadavers,' Alen interjected, watching Milla devour a mountain of potatoes covered in gravy. 'There must be more to it,' he said finally. 'The spell must harness the raw power of that bark, or ...' He drifted off.

'Or what?'

'Or he's mixing it with something else. Either way, I think you're right. He's harvesting so much of the bark and leaves that it must be for that army.'

'We can't just sit here knowing this. We have to *do* something,' Hoyt said.

'What we have to do is to take Milla home,' Alen countered.

'Hurray!' Milla shouted, a bit of potato falling from her lips. 'On a boat?'

'On a big boat, Pepperweed.' Hoyt smiled and wiped her face with a cloth, then checked over his shoulder to make sure they were still alone. He whispered, 'Think about it, Alen. We haven't heard anything from Gilmour in how long? Almost a Moon? He was on his way to the Blackstones to find the spell table – well, where is he? What if he failed and Nerak killed him and everyone with him? He told you himself that Nerak was in the Eastlands.' He didn't want to upset Hannah with talk of Steven's death, but that possibility remained very real. Perhaps surprisingly, there had been no awkwardness between them since their morning together, but Hoyt worried she would misunderstand or get angry if she heard him talking about Steven being lost.

Alen said, 'I should try to contact him again, but if Fantus is dead, I will have to return to Falkan.'

'Why? We're here. Think of what we can do here.'

'And think of what we *cannot* do,' Alen said. 'The city is overrun with Palace Guardsmen, all of them looking to retrieve our little friend, and you saw that army. What are we going to do? Shoot arrows at them? Call them nasty names? No, if Gilmour is dead, we'll have to find the spell table and Lessek's key. It's the only way. Gods, but I wish Pikan was here; she knew how to operate that thing.'

Hoyt smiled. 'You've come a long way from the man who wanted to march into Welstar Palace and commit suicide.'

Alen elbowed Milla playfully in the ribs. 'Well, I've been entrusted with something important. I've waited a long time for this charge; now the least I can do is see it through.'

'I'll offer you a deal, my friend.' Hoyt leaned back in his chair. 'You attempt to contact Gilmour, and I will find us passage to Orindale. The Twinmoon is coming and everything that floats will be making a run for the Northeast Channel. If he has the spell table, we'll take young Milla home, or to Sandcliff, or wherever it is you plan to take her, and I will come along quietly. If he doesn't have the spell table, we'll stay here and pick off a few of the Guard, or maybe disrupt the shipping industry a bit. Churn and I were top-notch at disrupting the shipping industry. I got good marks in school for *disrupting* things.'

'You still don't understand, Hoyt,' Alen said, '*without* the spell table, we're lost, and *with* the spell table, there's no need for us to be here.'

'But you said yourself, the Palace Home Guard have come into the city and the prince's army is stationed up there along the river. Why would we be anyplace else?' Hoyt argued.

'With the spell table, we can bring a firestorm down on them. Rutters, Hoyt, with the spell table, we could tear open the foundation of the hillside and drop the lot of them into an abyss.'

Hoyt nodded. 'All right, then. Sign me up for that.'

Hannah rejoined them, sliding into her chair. 'Holy shit, boys— Um, sorry Milla, that's not a nice word, I shouldn't use such words. But have you two been sleeping?'

'What?' Alen raised an eyebrow.

'Look at her; she's a mess.' She picked bits of potato from Milla's hair and head. Hannah couldn't imagine how she managed to get potato behind her ear.

'Pepperweed?' Hoyt shrugged and tweaked the girl's nose. 'It's just a bit of potato.'

'Love p'tatoes!' Milla shrieked.

'See? She loves potatoes.'

Erynn appeared with an empty tray, cleared the trenchers and wiped down the table. 'Can I get you anything else?' she asked, trying not to stare at Hoyt.

'Yes, thank you, Erynn,' Hannah said. 'This one needs a bath.'

'It's three Mareks,' she said. 'There's a big tub at the back of the scullery. You can pull the curtain across. I'll let my father know he needs to heat the water for you.'

'Three Mareks?' Hoyt was incredulous. 'For three Mareks, I'm getting in, too.'

'Age before beauty,' Alen said, 'and I want the warm water.'

'Not fair,' Hoyt said, 'you could heat it your—' He cut himself off, suddenly aware that Erynn was still at the table. Hoyt didn't notice that the girl was blushing too furiously to make sense of anything she might have overheard. He smiled at her and said, 'Thanks. Please do ask your father to fill the tub for us. We'll be down shortly.'

Almost ready to expire from embarrassment, Erynn croaked a weak, 'Yes, sir,' and hurried back to the kitchen.

The Wayfarer's scullery didn't have a stone foundation like the rest of the building; it had been added onto the back of the kitchen, a long rectangular room with a sloped ceiling. The flagstone floor was littered with stacks of firewood, rusty serving trays and stewpots, even a rickety wheelbarrow laden with old tools. There were several massive tubs, two of which were affixed to the wall on either side of the kitchen door. One, Hannah guessed, would be filled with hot soapy water – a hole had been cut in the kitchen wall big enough to accommodate buckets. The second tub was for clean water, after every trencher, bowl and goblet had at least a token dunking before returning to general circulation. A third tub, easily as large as the other two combined, rested against the back wall, doubling as laundry and bath; one hot bucketful for every two cold buckets, and the water would stay warm long enough for dirty travellers to dive in, scrub briefly, and then dash, shivering and swaddled in blankets, to the fireplace in the front room.

Two empty braziers meant the scullery was clear of smoke, but freezing cold. The tub, filled for three Mareks by the innkeeper, steamed like a volcanic fissure.

'Holy gods, but it's cold in here,' Hannah said, shivering as she helped Milla out of her tunic. 'Come on, sweetie, we'll be really fast.'

'But I want to swim,' Milla said, ignoring the cold and climbing over the side of the washtub. 'Oooh,' she said, crouching low in the water, 'it's warm.'

'Grand,' Hannah said, 'but when you come out, you're going to freeze solid. So let's get you clean and out of here.'

Milla sighed impatiently and glanced at the twin braziers. In an instant, both burst into cheery, crackling flame.

'Yikes!' Hannah said, smiling. 'That's a good one.'

'Uh huh,' Milla dunked her head beneath the water, 'but wait until you see me swim.' She backed to one side of the trough, curled like a spring and then kicked hard for the other side, paddling her hands and kicking her feet all the way. The entire journey took less than two seconds, but for Milla, the washtub was a snake-infested jungle pool and the journey took hours. "Did you see that, Hannah?" she cried excitedly, 'did you see me swim?'

'I did, sweetie.' Hannah was trying to wash whatever parts of the little girl would stay still for more than a moment at a time. 'What do you call that?'

'Mama calls it the scramble; she taught me before I went to live with Rabeth and Prince Nerak.' Milla kicked off the wall again, splashing water over the side of the tub.

'Whoa, easy there!' Hannah laughed. 'You know, my mom taught me that one too, but we call it the doggie paddle. And it works better if you cup your hands.'

'Like this?' Milla held up one hand, fingers splayed.

'No, sweetie, like this.' Hannah demonstrated. 'You see how I can pull the water along? That makes you go faster, with less effort.'

'I'm already fast.'

'And I'm cold, so we need to hustle a bit if we—' Hannah took advantage of Milla's momentary stillness to scrub her face and neck.

'I'll fix it,' Milla said and gestured again at the braziers. The flames in both leaped a bit higher, growing more intense. 'That should make it warmer.'

Bemused, Hannah shook her head. 'Where did you learn that?'

'Rabeth thinks he taught me, but I could just do it for ever. I used to make fires for Mama all the time.' Milla returned to her laps. 'Watch this.'

'That's better!' Hannah said. 'Good, just like I showed you, the scramble.'

'I like doggie paddle better.' Milla kicked her way across the washtub. 'I like dogs.'

Thinking back on how surprised she was to discover that Branag's poor wolfhound had tracked her – on Milla's orders – all the way from Southport, Hannah sighed. 'I remember, sweetie.'

Later, all clean and dry, her bare feet dancing on the scullery flagstones, Milla shivered. 'It's cold now.'

'Let's get you out to the front room and you can get warm by the fire while I get your dry clothes.'

'Should I heat the water for Hoyt?' Milla asked. 'He's been sad since Churn fell. Maybe the bath will be fun for him, too.'

Hannah swallowed hard. 'I'm sure he'd like that.'

Staring down at the washtub, Milla pressed her lips together and knitted her brow. She looked like a child who was angry with her doll and was about to give it a thorough scolding.

Hannah watched in mute amazement as the water started bubbling, then cried, 'Oh, Milla, sweetie, stop now – you don't want to cook him, do you?' She hugged the enchanting little magician close.

'Do you think it's too hot?'

'Nah,' Hannah laughed. 'Hoyt will figure it out.'

'Someone call my name?' Hoyt appeared through the kitchen door; like Milla, he started dancing as soon as his bare feet hit the flagstones. 'Yeow! It's cold in here. At least you lit the braziers – thanks for that.'

'Don't mention it,' Hannah said, collecting Milla and her blankets. 'Enjoy your bath.'

The two women were barely through the kitchen doorway, smiling conspiratorially, when they heard Hoyt cry, 'Gods of the Northern Forest, that's hot!' And then a moment later, 'Hannah!'

That night, Hannah lay in bed, waiting for Hoyt. A candle burned by the bedside; she watched its shadow flicker and dance on the ceiling.

Alen had found the Wayfarer and paid for two rooms, one for him and Milla and one for Hoyt and Hannah. They hadn't told Alen about their lovemaking; neither wanted it to be a source of discomfort between them, nor did they feel the cathartic encounter merited mentioning to the Larion Senator. Yet Hannah was beginning to worry. When alone, Hoyt avoided making eye contact with her, and their conversations had grown strained. Hannah wanted to say something, to clear the air. It might be weeks before they reached Orindale, weeks before she was reunited with Steven, and she didn't want to spend her last few weeks in Eldarn enduring awkward moments of strained silence with Hoyt, someone she thought of as a true friend.

Hannah waited, trying out different icebreakers in her mind, but when Hoyt finally joined her, she was so surprised to find the young thief dressed, still in his boots, and carrying a small canvas pack that she forgot all her prepared speeches and blurted, 'Well, I know things have been a bit awkward between us, but a pack? You aren't moving out on me, are you?'

Hoyt grinned. 'Awkward? Between us? Since when?' He set the pack on the edge of the bed. 'You mean since you fell off that cliff, and I had to put your busted head back together?'

'No,' Hannah giggled, then, embarrassed, pulled her blankets up to hide her face. 'And it wasn't my head; it was my shoulder.'

'Oh, yes, right. Well, then, you must mean it's been awkward since I taught you that song about the sailor's wife with the wooden leg, and you sang it until that barman told you to be quiet.'

Hannah pointed at him defiantly, but, still grinning, said, 'Hey, I taught *you* that song, cousin. And as for that night, well, I blame Malakasian beer. Good lord, but what do they put in that stuff? Seaweed?'

'Then you must mean that things have been awkward since you made me keep my head beneath the blankets in that pine grove so you could pee beside the fire, because it was too cold to go and look for someplace private?'

Hannah buried her face in the pillows and howled. 'All right! All right! I give up. Sanctuary! Sanctuary!'

Hoyt kneeled beside her bed and, suddenly serious, said, 'Are we all right?'

'All right? Hoyt, I'd be dead six or seven times over without you. I'd be dead and mad and raving like a lunatic on bad fennaroot.'

'So, you're not angry about . . . well, that morning?'

Hannah took his face in her hands. 'No, Hoyt. I'm not angry, and I'm not sorry, and if I ever find Steven again, I'll find some way to . . . oh, fuck it, to let it go, Hoyt. Look where we are. I have no regrets.'

'Neither do I.'

'Good,' Hannah laughed again, then stopped herself short. 'But where *are* you going?'

'Alen says we're short of silver. I'm going out for some. I'll be back before dawn.'

'Do you think that's smart? I mean— Well, that could be dangerous. We have enough, surely – we can cut back on our expenses. Is it really that much to make the trip to Orindale?' She sat up in bed and lectured him like a concerned spouse.

'Hannah, Hannah, Hannah,' Hoyt said, his face reddening again. 'Please, Hannah, one sympathy jump for a depressed friend does not make you my keeper.' He tried to keep a straight face, but cracked a smile when Hannah's mouth fell open.

'Why, you miserable—' The rest of Hannah's rebuke was lost as she shouted obscenities into her pillow.

'Nice talk,' Hoyt said, 'do you kiss your mother with that foul mouth?' Laughing, he started towards the door. 'I'll be back.'

Hannah collected herself long enough to say, 'If you insist on going to work tonight, remember the jewellery rule.'

Hoyt grimaced. 'I shudder to ask.'

Holding one bare arm above the blankets, Hannah said, 'If I can lift my wrist, it is *not* large enough.'

'It?'

'My diamonds.'

'Diamonds?'

'Well, whatever passes for precious stones here in Eldarn. God, you do *have* precious stones, don't you?'

'All right.' Hoyt smiled, opening the hallway door. 'If you can lift your wrist, it isn't large enough. Got it.'

'Be careful,' Hannah said.

'Always. See you in the morning.'

THE MAGELLAN TOUR

Steven woke from a dizzying dream to the smell of a long-distance bike ride.

It had been Mark's idea, one night at Owen's Pub after he'd finished the most recent of several-too-many beers and eaten about half a dozen too many of Owen's spicy burn-your-arse-and-cry-for-your-mama buffalo wings, and he'd named it the Magellan Tour, a circum-navigation of the Denver metro area. He raised his mug and announced, not quite soberly, 'Tomorrow, Steven Taylor, we round the Horn.'

'Why don't I like the sound of that?' Steven replied, grinning.

'Because, my good fellow, you are not a visionary.'

Howard Griffin had been there too; it was a rare occasion that the bank manager wasn't with them at Owen's. He noisily finished sucking the sauce from a chicken leg and said, 'I understand the winds this time of year are favourable.'

'Oh do you?' Steven raised an eyebrow.

'Yes, I do.' Howard raised his own mug before adding, 'Of course, I have no idea what we're talking about.'

'A circumnavigation,' Mark cried.

'Of what?'

'Or whom?' Howard raised an eyebrow too, mocking Steven.

'Dirty old man,' Mark chided, 'of our great, sprawling city of Denver, Colorado, where else?'

'We're going for a drive?' Steven smiled. 'All right; I'm in.'

'Not a drive, Steven, a bicycle ride,' Mark declaimed, as if an-nouncing they were about to take part in the Olympics. 'Tomorrow, we set forth where no man has gone before.' He lifted his glass and drank deeply. 'Although I'm certain hundreds of adventuresome and resilient *women* have already made the trip, but that won't mitigate our great pioneer achievement one iota.'

'What is an iota, anyway?' Howard sounded puzzled.

'Don't interrupt!' Mark ordered, and went on, 'Think about it. We'll park down by Chatfield Reservoir – the car'll be all right there overnight—'

'Overnight?' Howard interrupted, 'optimistic, aren't we?'

'Don't interrupt! We ride east through Highlands Ranch to Jordan Road. Granted, we'll need to pick our way north on the prairie, but from there, we can take Tower all the way up to the 120. We'll take 85 into Brighton and cut across Route 7 to Lafayette. There's a hotel off the service road where we can pass out, and then we'll be up and into Boulder for breakfast—'

'Boulder?' Steven said, 'Mark, that's not a circle, that's a bloody great oval!'

'Hear me out,' Mark said, ill-advisedly reaching for another hot wing, 'so breakfast in Boulder and then we come south along the Hogback on 93. We stop in Golden where I buy you a gigantic slice of blueberry pie at the drugstore—'

'Best pie in the world,' Howard pointed out.

'It is,' Mark agreed, 'but don't interrupt! Then it's down past Red Rocks into Morrison and back to our car.' Mark raised his hands as if to say *see, nothing to it at all?*

'Why?' Steven asked. 'It's got to be a hundred and fifty miles, and you want to do it on mountain bikes?'

'Because it's there.' Mark waved to Gerry, the bartender, and held aloft the empty beer pitcher. 'We will be there at the advent of a great and timeless tradition for cyclists in the Denver area: the Magellan Tour.'

Steven grimaced. 'All right. Never let it be said that Steven Taylor ever turned his back on the great unknown.'

'Oh, Christ,' Howard groaned, 'there are convenience stores, shopping centres, motels and fast food restaurants along the entire route. You'll both have cell phones with you, and the roads are paved, the whole way.'

Mark frowned. 'We understand your lack of vision, Howard, but if you buy this next pitcher, we won't hold it against you.'

'Thanks for that, Sir Edmund,' Howard said, 'but you two should probably start drinking water now, lots and lots of water.'

'And we will!' shouted Mark, 'for what is beer if not mostly water! Another pitcher, for we have a great adventure to prepare for!'

The first Magellan Tour had gone nearly as Mark – however drunk he might have been that night – had envisioned, and after that there were numerous other Magellan Tours, mostly on the heels of a long night at the pub or a particularly difficult week at work. Steven participated in all of them, gamely accompanying his roommate, sometimes with other friends, on the two-day ride.

But what Steven recalled most vividly from that first journey was the smell of onions. It was late autumn and most of the crops had been harvested, but one farmer near Brighton had left a field of onions to rot – maybe he failed to find a buyer, maybe he wanted the rotting vegetables to replenish something crucial in his soil for the following year, but whatever the reason, the aroma of rotting onions had been overpowering pedalling through Brighton, forcing Steven to the side of the road where he'd emptied his stomach, rinsed out his mouth with what was left of his water and limped the last few miles to their hotel, praying for a westerly wind before morning.

Awake now, slowly bringing his surroundings into focus, Steven smelled onions again, and his stomach clenched and he threw up what little he had left in his body. He rolled on his side, his head lolling until it struck the musty wooden floor. He shook off the last remnants of the dream and wondered how long he had been unconscious. The taste of vomit in his mouth made him gag again and he spat at the floor, trying to get rid of the saliva. He breathed deeply and stared up at the ceiling.

There's a ceiling. That's good.

'Where are we?' he asked anyone listening.

Footsteps thunked across the floor; Steven felt them. 'It stinks in here,' he whispered, breathing hard, 'just like Brighton.'

'Where?' Garec crouched beside him, holding a wineskin and a section of folded cloth. 'Let me wipe your face. You're sweating.'

'I puked.' Steven turned his head again and spat another mouthful of discoloured fluid onto the floor.

'If that means you emptied your stomach, then yes, you did. But no matter, we'll clean it up.'

'Where are we?' He struggled to lift his head; Garec helped him sit up. 'It smells like Brighton, like onions, rotten onions.'

'Well, I don't know where Brighton is, but what you're smelling is pepperweed. There's a whole bin of it there by the doors. It's rotting, stinks like a grettan's nightmare, but you'll get used to it after a while. Pepperweed is strong, like onions but much more popular. A good cook would say it's more useful in the kitchen, more flexible than onions. You had some in Traver's Notch, at the Bowman, remember? The roots in that stew?'

'Please, Garec, don't remind me of that stew. I'll be hurling again.'

Garec laughed. 'Right. Sorry. It is good to see you awake, though. How are you feeling?'

'Like the foul end of a buffalo herd.' Steven dragged his hands through his hair. 'How long have I been out of it?'

Brand and Kellin joined them, kneeling beside the confused foreigner. 'Four days,' said Brand.

'Holy shit! Four days? Where are we? Is this a barn? Did we get to a farm?'

'We did,' Kellin said, putting a hand on his shoulder. 'You had a seizure, a gods-rutting horrible seizure. It went on for so long, Steven, we thought you were going to die.'

'I might have,' he said. 'Where's Gilmour?'

Kellin winced.

Brand said, 'We lost him. There was nothing we could do.'

'He'll be along,' Garec assured. He tried to sound convincing, and hoped he was right.

'You keep saying that, Garec, but I watched those snakes. They killed him.' Kellin was visibly upset.

Garec took her hand. 'I know what you saw, Kellin, but he'll be back. We've lost Gilmour before. Trust me; the last time I burned his body on a pyre myself, and the old bastard still came back. It'll take more than a nest of – well, whatever they were – to kill Gilmour.' Garec hoped the others couldn't read the doubt in his face. The snakes had been hideous, otherworldly monsters and he was afraid that perhaps Mark had summoned them because they were powerful enough to kill even a Larion Senator.

'He's right.' Steven tried to stand, felt dizzy and gave up. 'What was it? Snakes?'

'It was Mark,' Garec said. 'He's working the table. He hit you with that seizure and then set a pack of unholy snakes on Gilmour.'

'They came out of that book,' Kellin said.

Steven nodded. 'That's Mark. He knows that book scared the dog-piss out of Gilmour on the way to Traver's Notch. He used it against him, I'm sure.' Steven looked around the barn. 'Where's the body?'

'Back through the woods, about two days' journey from here.'

Steven looked surprised. 'You left him?'

'There was nothing we could do,' Brand said. 'The serpents were all over him. Garec managed to shoot a few of them, but the others were all coiled around his arms, his neck; they were even inside his tunic!'

Steven drank; his body was aching from dehydration. He still had no memory of the seizure. 'Has Mark gone north?'

'Yesterday,' Brand said. 'He'll be at Wellham Ridge by tomorrow. The table is intact; Mark has it loaded on a wagon. His soldiers look bad, though, beaten by the forced march.'

'They must be,' Kellin said. 'Look at the ground they've covered in so little time. He must be pushing them day and night.'

'Did you see him?' Steven asked.

'No, nor Gabriel either,' Brand said. 'I was well hidden and didn't want to risk going any closer. With you unconscious, the last thing we needed was to be chased back here.'

'Good thinking,' Steven said, and then to Garec, 'He must be one of the officers.'

'Right. There'd be no other way for him to take command of such a force in so little time.'

'So he'll take the table back to the barracks, probably to the commanding officer's private quarters.'

'It's a good guess. So ... we follow them tomorrow?'

'I'm afraid so,' Steven said. 'I need to eat. I might be able to whip up a spell to sort myself out, but I'm certainly not up for a fight right now.'

'That's fine,' Garec said. 'Staying here will give Gilmour another night to catch up as well.'

Kellin looked sceptical, but said nothing more.

'Where's the farmer?' Steven asked. 'Who's our host?'

'No idea,' Brand said. 'There's no one here, no one we can find, anyway.'

'Some of these farmers work winter crops in Rona,' Kellin said. 'They might be on the other side of the Blackstones for the season.'

Steven wrinkled his nose again. 'I suppose they must be somewhere else. No one would be able to live with that stench all winter.'

'Good point,' Garec said. 'So we're in no hurry. You rest. We'll wait another day for Gilmour, and if he shows up, terrific, and if not, we'll work our way carefully into Wellham Ridge and wait for an opportunity to steal the spell table.'

Steven was not looking forward to facing his roommate. If his seizure and Gilmour's disappearance were any indication of what Mark was able to do with the Larion artefact, the battle would be deadly dangerous for all of them. Disheartened, he said, 'Fine. I suppose that's our only option right now.'

'He's shown a willingness to insert the key and start calling up magic from inside that thing. Those snakes he threw at Gilmour were like nothing I've ever seen in Eldarn,' Garec said quietly.

'So we don't have the luxury of time,' Steven finished Garec's thought.

'Or a lot of discretion,' Brand added. 'Without Gilmour to contact Gita, the Resistance attack on Capehill will be a tragic failure. It's been too many days already.'

'Not yet,' Kellin assured. 'Even the fastest riders won't have made it north yet. There's still a bit of time, but if Gilmour is coming back on his own, we need him to hurry.'

Brand said, 'If you can kill Mark, Steven, you have to do it.'

Steven didn't answer.

Two avens later, while wayward streaks of sunlight dappled the farm in orange, a Malakasian soldier approached from across a field between the barn and the woods near the river.

'Someone's coming,' Garec warned, turning from the blurry, blown-glass window.

'Is it him?' Kellin asked.

'Yes.' Steven sounded certain.

'I don't know,' Garec said. He nocked an arrow and moved towards the sheet of heavy canvas that hung between the storage bins and a wagon-sized loading dock. He pulled back on a corner and stepped out so the lone soldier could see that he was armed. 'That's far enough!' he shouted.

The others heard the man say, 'Garec?'

'Who are you?' Garec called. 'If you know me, you know I can drop you from here. So don't come any closer.'

'Of course I know you, you great, blazing rutter,' the soldier said, his hands in the air. 'I also know you prefer trout to steak, although God knows why. I know you are one hundred and ninety-six Twin-moons old and that you think Steven's coffee tastes like burned dirt.'

'Gilmour?'

No one inside the barn heard his reply.

Kellin whispered, 'What's happening? What did he say?'

Garec pushed his head back beneath the cloth. 'He's showing me his wrist. It's a mess, all bloody.'

'He had to kill one of them,' Steven said. 'It's him, Garec.'

'How do you know? Gilmour's never had that hole in his wrist before. Demonpiss, it's awful-looking, even from here.'

'It's him,' Steven said again, peering out the wrinkled glass window. 'He's only ever taken his hosts in the moment right after they've died;

that's why he's been an elderly man most of the time. It looks like he found Mark's battalion and picked off one of the soldiers.'

'So he abandoned that other body?' Kellin shuddered at the thought.

'Exactly,' Steven said. 'That's probably why he's been delayed.'

Garec frowned, disappeared outside the canvas flap again, and shouted, 'When days in Rona grow balmy—'

Gilmour's response was faint but enthusiastic, 'Drink Falkan wine after Twinmoon – but you, Garec, you prefer beer, because you are an uncultured heathen.'

Kellin smiled. 'He does seem to know you, Garec.'

He poked his head back inside and muttered, 'Wine gives me a headache.' Then, in a shout, he added, 'Come on inside, Gilmour.'

When the Larion sorcerer slipped past the canvas, Steven laughed. 'You look good.'

The muscular young soldier shot him a bright grin marred by three seriously crooked teeth. Gilmour's new body was tall and lean, with broad shoulders and a strong jaw. He had a head of shoulder-length, pin-straight hair, bright eyes and a nose that had been broken and poorly set at least twice. The bloody wound on his wrist was the only sign that he had been killed by the spirit of a disembodied Larion Senator. It was clotted with dried blood, but it was festering.

'Well, I'd never done this before,' he admitted, 'so I figured I'd use someone healthy. I found the battalion near the river and sneaked this fellow into the undergrowth two nights ago. It was dark, and the officers were pushing them north so quickly that no one really looked for me. They're all so rutting tired, I think I could have slipped away with a squad and no one would have been any the wiser.' He winced. 'What is that smell anyway? Onions?'

Steven frowned.

Garec said, 'Pepperweed. There's a whole bin of it rotting over there.'

'Good God, but that stinks. It smells like—'

Brighton, Steven thought.

'It smells like the compost heap out behind the Bowman Inn. You remember that place, Garec? Rotting pepperweed. God.'

'Well, we won't be here long,' Brand said.

'Right,' Gilmour said, 'at the rate they were moving that table, they'll be in Wellham Ridge in a few days.'

'Tomorrow, most likely,' Kellin said. 'They passed by here yesterday.'

'Then we need to strike them soon,' Gilmour said. 'The soldiers are falling down with fatigue, and the officers are just leaving them to die or to drag themselves back on their own. Some are dragging their weaker mates along, but none of them are strong enough for a real fight.'

Steven shook his head. 'Neither am I, Gilmour.'

'That's right, my boy. How are you? What was it, a seizure? Some sort of attack? Any permanent damage that you can sense?'

'No, but I feel like a warm barrel of pigshit.' He looked depressed. 'I'm not up for much of a fight.'

'Tomorrow?'

'Another night of rest and some decent food would do me good.' Steven didn't try to hide the fact that he was pale, weak and tired.

'Very good.' Gilmour smiled. 'Tomorrow, then. What do we have to eat? Something more than those onions, I hope.'

'We've got a bit,' Kellin said, 'but not much, I'm afraid.'

'Garec, any chance you and Kellin can find some game out along the edge of these fields? Brand and I will raid that farmhouse for any dry stores.'

Kellin said, 'We did that already; there were some pickled vegetables and a few jars of preserves.'

'Any flour?'

'No.'

'Rutters.' Gilmour shook his head and his hair swept over his shoulder. 'We'll have to make do with what we have, but I promise I'll buy everyone as much hot food as they can eat the moment we reach Wellham Ridge. By the way, why aren't we hiding in the farmhouse?'

'You'll see when you go inside,' Kellin said. 'This is much more comfortable.'

Brand added, 'We figured soldiers would search there first, maybe giving us a few extra moments to mount a defence here in the barn. And Kellin's right; whoever farms this land left more than just rotting pepperweed in there.'

'Meat?'

'Meat, chamber pots, an assortment of disagreeable, albeit unidentifiable, heaps of something covered with burlap sacks . . .'

'Nothing you'd spread on a crust of bread, Gilmour.'

'I see. Is there a fireplace?'

Kellin said, 'Yes, that they do have.'

'It would be good for Steven to spend the night beside a real fire.

It's draughty in here with only that tarp hanging over there.'

'I'll be fine,' Steven said.

'You rest, leave dinner to us. Before we go, I'll get a fire going, a big one.'

'Don't burn down the building!'

'Don't worry,' Gilmour assured him, 'we need you back in shape, and quickly, so rest now, and sleep if you can.'

'He's right,' Garec said. 'You don't look very healthy, Steven.'

'What do you expect with that stench in here?'

'Trust me, Steven, it's worse in the farmhouse,' Kellin said.

'No arguments,' Gilmour said. 'Take a nap; we'll be back with dinner.' He motioned with one hand and stoked their small fire into a crackling blaze. 'That'll burn all night now,' he said and gestured for the others to join him outside.

Steven furrowed his brow but wrapped himself back into his blankets, thumped his pack into a makeshift pillow and closed his eyes. It was not long before he was sleeping again.

Later, fed and resting comfortably, Steven dreamed again. He and Mark were biking north on Tower Road, the old two-lane stretch that ran out past the airport. It was the first Magellan Tour, and there wasn't much of a hard shoulder along Tower, so cyclists were regularly pushed off the road by the passing trucks hauling shipments out to the mail and cargo jets that used Denver Airport. Mark had called this 'getting buzzed', and they'd perfected their protection manoeuvre pretty quickly. Steven had a small mirror affixed to his helmet, so he rode behind, watchful for trucks hugging the shoulder too closely. When one approached without giving them a wide enough berth, Steven would shout, 'We're getting buzzed!' and he and Mark would bail out, turning onto the hardscrabble where the vast rolling prairie pressed up against the northbound lane.

No matter how many trucks rumbled by en route to the freight terminals, they were always uncomfortably aware that any one could have flattened them both to jelly. Now, in his dream, Steven saw in the small circular mirror a massive, eighteen-wheeled beast lumbering towards them. It was a heavy-bodied semi, something prehistoric and clumsy, dragging an open trailer with slat sides. A northerly wind carried the aroma of foetid onions, rotten vegetables bound via Fed-Ex to ports unknown: somewhere, eye-wateringly rank onions had some value. The truck driver, hugging the right shoulder, gave no sign that he saw the two cyclists.

'We're getting buzzed,' Steven shouted.

'What's that smell?'

'Mark!' he shouted again, louder this time. The rumble of the truck's engine was deafening; it was too close. In the tiny mirror, the grille and twin headlights looked like the maniacal grin of a homicidal creature bent on running them down. As if to terrorise them further, the driver pressed down on the monster's air horn. Steven felt the blast tickle the hairs on the back of his neck. His eyes blurred with the foul stench of decomposing onions and he screamed at Mark as he pulled off the road and into a clump of dry chaparral, 'Mark! Bail out, Mark!'

Mark gave no sign that he heard, and Steven watched in horror as the great truck bore down on his friend. At the last second, he turned away, closed his eyes and screamed.

The magic woke him. It was at his fingertips, ready for battle, ready to blast the vegetable truck to scrap metal. Instead, Steven rolled onto his back and released the spell into Gilmour's chest. The Larion Senator's new body, the young Malakasian with the crooked teeth, bent nose and bloody wrist, was looming over him, a short knife drawn and poised to strike. The others slept on beside the fire.

'No!' Steven screamed as the magic crashed into Gilmour, shattering his bones and crushing his organs. It was as if the Malakasian soldier had been hit by a lumbering truck loaded to the brink with rotten vegetables, onions or pepperweed ...

Gilmour was thrown back, his body turning a lazy half-somersault in the firelight. One foot smashed through a wooden gate near the vegetable storage bins and the impact flipped his body back over itself and his head thudded hard against a support beam. Something cracked, his skull or his neck, and his body finally tumbled to rest inside one of the larger bins along the far wall.

Garec and the others were on their feet.

'Steven,' Garec cried, 'what did you do?'

Steven was breathing hard, the magic still coursing through his veins, invigorating and charging him for another attack. He stared at Garec, his eyes wide in disbelief.

'You killed him,' Garec said, hustling towards the vegetable bin.

'Don't!' Steven finally managed.

'But—'

'*It's not Gilmour!*'

'What?' Garec looked at him as if he had gone mad.

'It's not him, Garec.' Steven repeated. 'It's Mark, or sent from Mark, anyway. It's not Gilmour.'

Garec moved back into the firelight and knelt beside Steven.

'Get me some water, will you?' Steven held his head in his hands. 'That was too close.'

Kellin brought a water-filled wineskin and Steven drank deeply before emptying the rest over his head, trying to calm down enough to explain.

'How do you . . .' Brand ventured.

'It was the things he said, what he did,' Steven said at last. 'He mentioned onions today, twice, even after Garec had told him it was pepperweed. Gilmour wouldn't have done that; he wouldn't have thought of onions first, like I did.'

'That's it?' Brand was incredulous. 'Rutters, Steven, you killed him over a reference to onions? We *do* have onions in Eldarn, you know that!'

'There was more. He said "God" twice. Not "gods", but "God", singular. Gilmour doesn't do that. A singular god is our God, not your gods of the Northern Forest.'

'That's still pretty thin.' Garec was looking back and forth between Steven and the storage bin as if expecting Gilmour to heave his broken form from the dirty floor like Harren Bonn had done in the spell chamber at Sandcliff Palace.

'Then he told me to take a nap.' Steven shook his head. 'It was too much; that's just not a phrase Gilmour uses. Taking naps, as if they're tangible, you know, as if they come in a carry-case, that's one of our sayings as well. It had to be Mark.'

Kellin drew her sword. 'Is he here?'

'I don't think so,' Steven said. 'And there was something else. Did you see the wound on his wrist? It wasn't right; it was a fake. I mean, it was ugly and bloody, but it wasn't full of pus and dripping with all that stinking infected shit like the others.'

'What others?' Brand asked.

'I caught a glimpse of Malagon's when we were on the *Prince Marek*, only for a moment, but it was an unholy mess. Then there was a dead security guard in the bank lobby; the cops had covered him with a blanket but I had a chance to get a look at him. And finally, I saw Bellan's. She'd been wearing gloves, but I saw where Nerak had forcibly entered her body, when she reached up to hit me with the hickory staff, just for a moment. So I've seen enough to know that the wound on this guy's wrist was bullshit.'

'So he's not here?' Kellin still wasn't convinced. She stood facing the vegetable bin, brandishing her sword.

'No,' Steven said, 'if he had been here, that wound would have been real. That was a decoy, just something to throw us off long enough for him to kill me.'

'Demonpiss,' Brand whispered.

'How did he know all that about me?' Garec asked.

'You and Mark have spent a lot of time together,' Steven explained. 'He didn't say anything earth-shattering, did he? He didn't mention anything from your youth.'

'So what do we do now?' Brand asked. 'He obviously knows where we are.'

'Maybe not,' Garec said. 'Maybe he sent out a whole company of those things, each armed with just enough information to lull us into a false sense of security. He's not stupid. Of course he would check all the farms in the area.'

'Farms, caves, lean-tos, everything,' Steven agreed.

'So there could be others,' Kellin said. 'How will we know if the real Gilmour comes back?'

Steven looked to Garec. 'You need to think of something only Gilmour would know, something he would never have shared with Mark. When he gets here—'

'*If* he gets here,' Kellin interrupted, still unconvinced.

'*When* he gets here, we'll ask him.'

'We can't stay here,' Brand said. 'We'll post a watch for the rest of the night, but at first light, we need to move north.'

'Agreed,' Garec said. 'I'll take the first watch.'

'What do we do with . . . well, whatever it was over there?' Kellin motioned towards the bin where the soldier's body had fallen.

'Leave him,' Brand said. 'It can't smell any worse in here.'

Garec smirked. 'It might improve things, actually.'

Hoyt ducked into the stable as a soldier passed, her gilded black uniform glinting in the torchlight. The main road running south from Pellia to the Welstar Palace encampment was dotted on both sides by merchants' homes and ranches. The farm houses, while similar in size and grandeur to the homes of shipping magnates or industrial executives, were easy to spot, for they were invariably flanked by barns or stables and had a patchwork of fenced-in fields. This was an expensive area and those who owned property here were all in business with the Malakasian military. Supplying goods to

Welstar Palace was lucrative enough; supplying the Welstar encampment *and* shipping goods to other regions of Eldarn would put Pellia's largest companies amongst the wealthiest in the land, rich and powerful enough to rival even the massive export companies of Falkan.

This is where Hoyt chose to hunt.

He could hear animals in the night: sheep bleating, cows lowing, horses nickering and pulling at mangers of hay. This district south of the city was redolent with the scents of manure, winter hay, woodsmoke and the faint tang of burned blood: there was a slaughterhouse somewhere further along the road. Hoyt was wondering why shipping and industry tycoons would choose to live alongside smelly farms and noisy animals when it struck him that these were the smells of silver, great piles of silver. The fancy carriages, the elaborate stained-glass windows, the houses built of brick or stone: they all screamed out *I have sold myself to Prince Malagon, and this is what I have reaped.*

Tonight, Hoyt planned on some reaping of his own. He had been out the last few evenings, and had acquired mostly copper, mixed with a few silver Mareks, mostly from lazy tavern owners, and once, a ship's captain who'd returned to his cabin drunk and slept like the dead. But to Hoyt, stealing from the hard-working people of Pellia was wrong. *Granted*, he thought, hidden behind the stable wall, *Churn and I used to fleece most of Southport, regardless of whose silver it was; that never mattered to us.* But things had changed. Hoyt had seen too much ever to steal from the common people of Eldarn again. That sort of robbery left him feeling hollow. Tonight would be different.

These people, the whole rotten district, deserved to be stripped of every penny they had made from shipping food, weapons, clothing – anything at all – to that gods-forsaken army.

The farmhouse across the road from the stables was a grand, two-storey edifice, with multiple brick chimneys, a stained-glass atrium, a slate roof, and a side entrance for servants. Smoke billowed from three chimneys, but the only windows illuminated this late at night were the upstairs corner rooms, front and back, on the north side. Hoyt waited until the soldier was out of sight, then, patting a curious plough horse gently on the nose, he slipped into the shadow of a tree by the road.

In through the servants' entrance, down the main hall and out the back, he thought, now focused intently on the upstairs windows, watching for a candle flicker or a moving shadow. *The silver will be in the office; all these places have an office, some private sanctum for the master of the house to gaze out over his domain, rutting stuffed-shirt horsecocks, all of 'em.*

He crouched another moment. *Then it's either out the same way, or through the back entrance and into the fields. Two means of escape, and both of them away from the main route downstairs and out the front door. Perfect.*

When he was certain there was no movement behind the windows, Hoyt crept into the street. For a moment, he was exposed: a dark figure moving warily into the farmyard. The frozen road and snowy fields were a stark, moonlit backdrop against which Hoyt was suddenly conspicuous. The stables and the lone linden tree provided the only cover between the farmhouse and a stone wall marking the property line, but that was three hundred paces to the northeast.

Hoyt was halfway across the farmyard and nearly beneath the sheltered overhang of the servants' recessed entryway when he heard wagons on the road. He had an instant to make his decision – hide beside the farmhouse or scurry back to the stables? With the wagons still out of sight in the darkness, Hoyt turned and fled across the road, running low to the ground, trying to look like a farm dog, or maybe a fox out for a late-night hunt. He tumbled to a stop beside the linden tree, then crept back inside the stables.

'Well, that wasn't exactly how I had planned it, was it?' he whispered to the old plough horse. 'But still, better to be in here with you then over there if the whole household woke up to see what rutting fools are driving south at this aven.' He brushed snow and mud from his tunic, wiped his face on his cloak and peeked out the stable door. 'Who do you suppose it is?' Hoyt asked the horse, keeping his face in the shadows.

The wagons came slowly into focus, massive slatted wooden carts emerging from the darkness. They were covered with canvas, and hauled along by teams of horses or oxen. Wooden axles squeaked, and Hoyt flashed back to the forest of ghosts and the platoons of Seron warriors harvesting the bark. They had been driving similar wagons, hauling shipments of bark through the Great Pragan Range, north to Treven and the Welstar-bound barges.

These carts – twelve of them – looked the same. Each was guarded by a squad of Seron warriors, not like the harvesters, staring vacuously into space, but real Seron killers, snarling, angry beasts that would tear Hoyt to pieces in a heartbeat if they found him huddled in the stables.

'Holy rutting Pragans,' Hoyt whispered, 'it's more bark; it has to be. But how—? Why are they bringing it from the north? There's nothing between here and the sea, no forests, nothing but the city.' He ducked back inside, found a corner in an empty stall and curled up in his cloak. He had seen enough; there was no reason to risk capture, either from the road or from the farmhouse, where, he was certain, the entire family would be awake, their noses pressed against the windows by now.

With his forehead on his knees, Hoyt sat listening to the creak and clatter of the wagons fading along the road. A quarter of an aven later, cold and tired, he considered returning to the Wayfarer. He badly wanted to sneak into his room, and maybe slip into bed beside Hannah. *Let her warm you up? You think she'd be willing again? Maybe just once?*

In the farmhouse windows candles had appeared and Hoyt could see shadows moving about.

'I'll give them this much,' he whispered to the horse, 'they're certainly early risers.' He pulled his hood up, patted the old horse a final time and slipped outside, trying not to think about Hannah. As he hurried towards the stone wall, he said to himself, 'Let's see if the neighbours are still asleep.'

WELLHAM RIDGE

Wellham Ridge, while playing host to the largest infantry battalion along the northern Blackstones, was a comparatively small town. Mud streets, most quite narrow, intersected in a muck-and-sludge cobweb separating the residential outskirts from the commercial centre. One cobblestone street, an avenue running west from the common towards the river, delineated the town's lone affluent district, where half-timbered stone buildings with slate roofs, flower gardens and well-pruned trees lined the thoroughfare. Most housed businesses – mining and assay offices, a textile shop, a dairy, a grain wholesaler – and there were several prosperous-looking inns catering to merchants, officers of the occupation army, and the few wealthy travellers still moving in or out of Orindale. Much of Wellham Ridge, including its one cobblestone boulevard, lay in a great flood plain spilling north from Meyers' Vale. It was a damp region, especially here along the river, and the Twinmoons had been hard on the town, judging by the sinking, cracking and sagging foundations, even amongst the most expensive properties.

Fine horses, leather tack and livery polished despite the season, clip-clopped along the street, while pedestrians walked on wooden walkways on either side of the cobbled road. The sun was out. It hadn't made more than a cursory appearance in days and Garec sat on the wooden sidewalk enjoying the relative warmth. Steven and Brand had gone inside to secure lodgings for the night. Garec, content to wait, turned his face to the sky, closed his eyes and breathed deeply of the moment's grace.

'Tired?' Kellin stepped in front of him, blocking the light.

Garec opened his eyes. 'You're in my sun.'

'Sorry,' she said and stepped aside.

'No, I'm not too tired. I'm just enjoying the heat.' He gestured towards the worn planks next to him. 'There's plenty; have a seat.'

Kellin shrugged off her cloak and folded it into a square cushion.

Sitting as close as their packs allowed, she reached over, hesitated, her outstretched hand hanging in the space between them, and finally placed it gently between his shoulder blades.

Garec turned his thoughts inwards, trying to focus his mind's eye on the place where her fingers came in contact with the heavy folds of his cloak. He found them, five tiny spots, islands of gentle pressure. The sun on his face and Kellin's hand resting softly on his back: this was the best he had felt in Twinmoons.

'You should do that more often,' he said, unconcerned that he might blush in the face of the gods.

'I'm not doing anything.' Kellin didn't remove her hand.

'You have no idea.'

'It's been a hard road for you.' It wasn't a question.

'I can't imagine it's been easy for you, either.'

'No, I suppose not.' Kellin pressed harder, wanting him to feel her touch. 'You're a legend in Falkan; did you know that?'

'It's nonsense,' Garec said.

'You're the greatest bowman in Eldarn.'

'I'm inhuman; I hate myself for it. I regret every shaft I've ever fired, every one.' He leaned into her, trying to slip his shoulder under her arm.

'Hopefully, we'll soon see an end to all this.' She didn't sound convinced, but it was something to divert the conversation from Garec's self-loathing.

'We?'

His response surprised her. Kellin wrapped her arm around him, resting her chin on his shoulder and whispered, 'You know what I meant . . . I meant we, as in we, us, *Eldarn* will soon see an end to this struggle.' She nibbled his ear; it was simply too close to leave alone.

'Oh, that "we". That's disappointing. I like the other "we" better.' Garec turned his head far enough to kiss her. Her mouth was soft, moist and sweet. He might have stayed there, sitting in the sun, tasting those lips for the rest of the Twinmoon, had they not been interrupted by a throaty, guttural cough behind them.

'Ahem.' Brand coughed again, louder this time.

Kellin pulled back. 'Brand,' she said as she stood up, retrieved her cloak and cast it over one arm. 'You have the timing of a summer snowstorm.'

The stony-faced partisan leader wasn't amused. 'I don't think I've ever seen a summer snowstorm, Kellin, and I might say the same about you two.'

Garec cleared his throat, and swallowed a muffled, 'Sorry, Brand.'

Kellin was not about to back down. 'Well if you ever took the time to—'

Garec took her hand, interrupting her, and asked, 'Did you get rooms?'

'Yes, Steven's carrying more silver than a Grayslip prince. He could buy the building, never mind rent a couple of rooms.'

Garec chuckled. 'He stole it in Estrad. It must have been someone's life savings.'

'We'll live well while we're here,' Brand said. 'He's still in there, talking with the cook about dinner. I think he's hoping for something elaborate that just isn't going to happen in a Wellham Ridge kitchen, no matter how expensive the lodgings.'

'Maybe he wants to celebrate,' Garec said.

'Celebrate?' Kellin asked. 'What have we got to celebrate?'

'You don't know how far Steven came to fight Nerak. He deserves a night off.'

'Well, he's not going to get one,' Brand said. 'Every day we drag our feet is another day that Gita and the Resistance remain an easy target outside Traver's Notch. We need to contact Stalwick to move the battalion south and to engage the forces at Capehill. Who knows what Mark has done? He might have sent word to Orindale. Half the occupation forces in Falkan could be marching on Traver's Notch right now.'

Garec shrugged. He didn't want to seem callous, but there was little they could do without Gilmour. Steven could attempt to contact Stalwick, but there was no telling the foreign sorcerer would be successful. 'How much time do you figure we have?'

'Riding day and night, a tough cavalry messenger could be in the Notch in fifteen days, even less to Capehill.'

'That leaves us ... what, six? Seven?'

'About that,' Brand said, 'but that assumes Gita can get her men moving at a moment's notice. It takes a while to get an infantry battalion going, especially during this Twinmoon. And they'll be vulnerable on their way into Capehill. If it's snowing up there, it could take them another five, maybe six days to get that far southeast.'

'That's a long time to be exposed.' Kellin licked her lip absentmindedly, hoping to taste Garec's memory. 'Can Steven do it?'

'Who knows?' Brand said with a shrug, 'but he's agreed to try tonight, once things have quieted down. He'll need to concentrate, but he doesn't really know what he's looking for.'

'Sometimes the magic seems to show him what to do.' Garec tried to sound reassuring.

'Let's hope.'

A Malakasian soldier, walking alone, paused to look them over, then he turned and hurried towards the centre of town and the grassy common. He stopped several times to look back. The soldier's odd behaviour and sudden haste worried Garec.

'Demonpiss, we shouldn't have stood around out here,' he said through clenched teeth. 'We should have kept our wits— it's this rutting sunshine.'

'Why?' Kellin said. 'Who knows us? None of these soldiers have ever seen us before.'

'We don't know that,' Garec said, 'and we don't know what Mark is capable of. Maybe he implanted our images in the minds of every soldier from here to Pellia.'

'I'll take care of it,' Brand said.

'We'll all go,' Garec said. 'Brand, take the north side of the street. Kellin, you stroll down the other side. I'll go behind those buildings on the south side. He's got to be heading for the barracks, but if he realises we're following him he'll turn south and try to find the rest of his company.' Garec looked towards the inn, hoping Steven would appear, but there was no time to waste. They'd have to trust that he would wait in the front room. 'Everyone armed?'

Kellin felt unobtrusively beneath her cloak and nodded. 'Where's your bow?' she asked.

'In the stable with the horses.'

'Why, for rutting sake? You can carry it here; this isn't Orindale.'

'I didn't want to be recognised,' Garec replied. 'I've got my knife, though.'

'All right, let's go. Try to get him cornered someplace out of sight. If you can't, and you have to hit him in the open, make it quick and deadly. Keep moving; don't stop to admire your work. Use the crowds to get away. We'll meet back here in half an aven.' Brand started towards the common.

Kellin and Garec exchanged a glance before following. They agreed – without needing to speak – to retrieve what they had momentarily lost after the day's business had been completed.

The soldier they followed was short, a little on the chubby side, and slow. He hurried to the end of the cobblestoned street and turned south towards the barracks. He checked several times, hoping to find one of the partisan criminals trailing him, but even with no one in sight he didn't slow down; these partisans were famous for their cunning, especially the Ronan bowman – the *Bringer of Death*. He smirked at the stories of Garec Haile *actually disappearing*, before reappearing in a blinding flash and firing arrows more quickly than anyone in the five lands. Garec was a ghost.

Still, the Malakasian smiled, enjoying the first sun Wellham Ridge had seen in days. He crossed a muddy street, his boots making comical slurping sounds in the muck, stepped onto the opposite walkway, slipped between two buildings and down an alley behind a row of businesses near the encampment. He ignored the handful of soldiers he passed ... they might have saved his life; even against the *Bringer of Death* there would be some safety in sheer numbers.

Kellin followed, using the crowds as cover. She watched the pudgy soldier cross a dirt street and disappear into an alley. *Rutting stupid bastard*, she thought. *Maybe he'll pull a knife and stab himself too.*

She was curious about why he'd ignored a group of fellow soldiers. She pulled her hood up and looked down at her boots as she hurried past them. Several of the men watched her go by, but there was nothing suspicious in their glances; they were young soldiers with an aven or two of free time and they'd watch any attractive woman.

In the alley, Kellin saw the solider exit the opposite end and turn west, *right to Garec*. She didn't want Garec to have another murder on his conscience if it was at all possible, so she speeded up a little, hoping to catch the Malakasian – she thought he might see Garec, understand that he had been cornered and flee back towards the alley.

Kellin looked back only once; she didn't know where Brand had gone but assumed he was nearby, perhaps one alleyway further east.

As she turned the corner, she drew her knife, just in case the chubby fellow attacked suddenly. Several paces further on, Kellin knew something had gone wrong.

Garec walked towards her. There was no way the soldier could have slipped past him. He looked at Kellin and shrugged.

'I don't know,' she whispered. 'He was here, coming this way. I didn't lose sight of him for more than two breaths. You didn't see him?'

'No.' Garec searched the street in the opposite direction, worried that perhaps the stout little fellow had somehow secreted himself inside a building, or maybe behind a stack of crates. 'I didn't see anyone. Are you sure he came this way?'

Kellin nodded. As she turned, Brand was there, his knife drawn as he came at a slow jog around a muddy bend.

'What is this?' Brand said, too loudly, unconcerned that he might be overheard. 'Kellin, didn't you have him?'

'I did,' she said.

'It appears you didn't.'

'Brand, I am telling you, he was right in front of me—'

'Maybe if you'd have had your heads on straight, the two of you, you wouldn't have lost him.'

Kellin's face reddened. 'You know, Brand, you can keep your—'

Garec interrupted the fight. 'We didn't lose anyone, Brand; he's right here. He must have some magic, a cloaking spell or something. Maybe he slipped by me, but he can't have simply disappeared.'

'Mark could.' Kellin's words stopped them dead. For a moment, nothing happened; no one moved.

Finally, Garec drew his knife and motioned for the others to come closer. 'Here,' he said, 'stay together, watch your wrists. Cry out, even if you get an itch on your wrist.'

They moved together, standing back to back, knives drawn, waiting. They all leaped noticeably when the soldier cried from above, '"*Ducdame, ducdame, ducdame.*" 'Tis a Greek invocation, to call fools into a circle. *As You Like It.* That was always my favourite; the dramas were so god-rutting serious, everyone dying all over the stage. The comedies really were his best works.' The Malakasian soldier was leaning out of an upper-level window, his cherubic face flushed with amusement.

'Mark, you dog-rutter, you're not going to fool us this time.' Brand's voice was a growl; he couldn't care less whether Steven's friend lived or not. 'Why don't you come down and I'll gut you right here in the street?'

'Wrong guess, Brand. It's me.' The soldier held out his hands. With his sleeves rolled up, he turned his arms over, exposing his wrists. There were no wounds on them.

'It's a trick,' Kellin said. 'How do we know it's you?'

'Because I led you here instead of killing you in front of that inn, because I sneaked up here instead of engaging you in a secluded back street where I could easily have killed you all, because I have no injuries to my wrists, and because I am happy to answer whatever question it is that I'm sure you've encouraged Garec to dream up to ensure it really is me and not some incarnation of Mark Jenkins.' The soldier smiled at them and asked, 'May I come down now?'

'Not yet,' Garec warned. 'Why did you lead us here?'

'Because it would not have done any of us any good to be seen chatting amiably on the side of the busiest street in Wellham Ridge. I made certain you saw me, made certain you thought I was heading towards the barracks and then made certain I found a place quiet enough for us to talk. If I had been able to secure a decent outfit before running into you, I'd have approached you on the street and encouraged you to quiz me all day, but instead – and preferably, I might add – I ran into you soon after arriving. I will find a decent change of clothing before dinner tonight, especially if you plan to eat in that tavern, because I'm quite sure it will be much better than the fare they'll be serving at the barracks.'

'Why not wait for Steven?'

'That wasn't my choice; you did that.'

'Why don't you have a wound on your wrist? If you're really Gilmour in there, why don't you have the hole in your arm?'

'Because, Garec, and I wish you would credit me with a touch more consideration than you apparently do, I am a Larion Senator, and Larion Senators do not kill people to find a host. Mark is disguised as a Malakasian officer; I'm guessing the major who led that battalion into the forest looking for the table, because she is the ranking officer here in Wellham Ridge, and because she is the only officer who did not remove her gloves the entire time they were on their forced march. She pushed her troops too hard, too many nights following too many days of marching through snow and several died. I think many were sick before they left Wellham Ridge in the first place. This fellow was certainly in poor health. He was left behind by his squad, and I waited around for a few days for him to begin his journey to the Northern Forest. I've been on foot ever since, coming here as quickly as my short, chubby little legs could carry me.'

'Why did you abandon the fisherman's body?' Garec had sheathed his knife; he wanted desperately to believe that Gilmour had found them again.

'I retreated inside myself,' the soldier began. He considered his words for a moment, then went on, 'Yes, I think that's the best way to put it: I hid inside Caddoc Weston's body, running further and further into the recesses of his mind until the adder poison had spread so thoroughly throughout his system that I had to flee. Those snakes were not from this world – they weren't from Steven's world either – so my guess is that Mark called them from the spell table, like Nerak used to summon the almor, calling them from the fringe worlds, the

Fold's margins, what Steven might call Hell. If I had been given all day to prepare, I might have generated some spell to neutralise their venom, but they came at me so quickly, I had nothing, nothing but hope.'

'What did you say?' Kellin asked the solider.

'Nothing but hope. It seems to be a recent habit of mine, saving myself from hopelessness by having no resources left but hope. But I'm not complaining; I am a hopeful person. I always have been.'

Kellin nudged Garec in the ribs. 'Ask him.'

Garec had heard enough as well. 'Tell me, whoever you are, when I turned one hundred and fifty Twinmoons, Brynne and Sallax had a party for me at Greentree Tavern. It was simultaneously a great day and a wretched day. Why?'

The soldier looked down from the second-floor window. Staring at Garec, he hoisted himself over the windowsill and dropped gently into the mud beside the partisans. Kellin and Brand flinched; Garec remained frozen in place.

Garec felt unnerved having a stranger gaze at him with such ardent emotion. He blinked hard, then asked the red-cheeked Malakasian, 'Well?'

'It was a great day, Garec, because so many of your friends and family were there to usher you into real adulthood – Sallax, Versen, Brynne, Namont, Jerond, Mika, oh, and so many more. We drank and revelled and carried on, and it was wonderful. There was music and beer, great food and dancing. We played absurd drinking games and sang bawdy songs. It was one of the best parties I have ever been to, because your friends and family loved you, and you knew it. You had grown up so quickly, done so much killing, dealt in so much death, that having you turn one hundred and fifty Twinmoons amongst friends was as much a celebration for them as it was for you.'

'But—'

Gilmour held up a hand to stop Garec. 'It was all perfect – but there was *one* wrinkle, wasn't there?'

'Tell us, Gilmour.' Garec surprised himself when he used his old friend's name, but he shook his head; the test wasn't over yet.

'Capina.'

Garec swallowed hard.

'Capina was an easy target, Garec. I'm sorry. It's been almost fifty Twinmoons and I've never told you that. I am truly sorry. I cannot think of that day without feeling embarrassment, both for myself and for Versen, Sallax, Brynne, all of us.'

'My true friends,' Garec said.

'No one loves you like we do.'

'But—' Garec was looking down at his boots now.

'But she did, didn't she?'

Garec didn't respond.

'We were drunk, all of us, me included, and I don't know why, it just happened. We had known you so well, for so long, it felt like we could get away with it, because you knew how much we cared about you, how much we valued your friendship.' The Malakasian soldier approached slowly, stopping just a few paces in front of them. 'She broke it off that night, didn't she?'

Garec nodded.

'And although you joked about it then, and you still joke about it now, I think you were heartbroken. I know she was. We were merciless. It was embarrassing, and by the time I realised how personally she was taking our jibes, the damage had been done. We left her feeling that she would never be one of us, no matter how much she loved you, and that is tragic, Garec, because she was good for you. You would have been happy with her, instead of . . .'

'Instead of what?'

'Instead of being miserable with us. You could have settled down, moved back to the farm and had four children by now. Instead, you became—'

'The *Bringer of Death*.'

'Sallax never should have started that.' Gilmour took Garec in his arms. 'He had no idea what he was saying, and someday, Garec, when this business is through, I'll tell you why.'

'You know something I don't know, Gilmour?'

'I know a great many things, yes, and one of them is how sorry I am about that night. We don't get many chances at love, not real chances, anyway. We allow plenty of emotions to masquerade as love, but most are just interlopers, busybody intruders playing with us.' Gilmour leaned in close to Garec's ear and whispered, 'And what hurts most about that night is the fact that you don't believe you've ever been anything but a killer, and you lost your chance at a normal life when Capina disappeared. But I know better. From where I'm standing, Garec, you've never been a killer. Someday, you'll understand.'

'I hope so,' Garec whispered.

'You will.'

'We have to contact Stalwick.'

Gilmour released him, wiped his sleeve across his face and looked at Brand and Kellin. 'Very well,' he said, 'let's find me some clothes. I am a deserter, after all.'

'You're dead,' Kellin clarified.

Gilmour laughed. 'True, but the Malakasian Army is known for its strict adherence to policy. Even dead, I'll draw all manner of disagreeable attention if I stay in this uniform. We'll find me some clothes, meet Steven and contact Stalwick.'

'Good,' Brand said, relief evident in his voice. He mentally tallied the days left for Gita and the Resistance forces to escape Traver's Notch.

'What about the spell table?' Garec asked.

'It left Wellham Ridge this morning, on a barge bound for Orindale.'

'Why? Where's he taking it?'

'From what I can gather, Mark is bound for Pellia; there's a northern Twinmoon coming, and the tides should be high enough for him to run up the Ravenian Sea and through the archipelago.'

'Why Pellia?' Kellin asked.

'He's heading for Welstar Palace,' Garec said.

Gilmour nodded.

THE BRIG-SLOOP

'I'm not talking about new tits, you great blazing idiot, I'm talking about different tits, temporary tits.' Marrin Stonnel was drunk – and why not? There was nothing to do, nothing critical, anyway, other than some cleaning and a patch-up job or two, but the others could take care of that. He was better with tar and lumber than the rest of them, even though he was the youngest, next to Pel Wandrell. No one knew what they'd hit on the run up from Strandson, but whatever it was, Marrin planned to have the leaks patched and tarred inside two days.

'Do we have to call them tits?' Sera Moslip asked, puffing on her hand-carved wooden pipe. It had taken several Twinmoons to fashion, but it drew almost perfectly. 'I mean, I'm no fancy woman from the big city or nothing, but even so . . .' She grimaced, displaying tobacco-stained, crooked teeth.

Marrin gulped his beer, wiped the foam from his upper lip and explained, 'We have to call 'em tits, and I'll tell you why: because we're not talking about *breasts*, or *bosoms*, or *glandular organs*. We're talking about tits: grip 'em, hold 'em, suck 'em tits, playthings designed by the gods to reduce men to babbling prehistoric critters at the mere mention, and worse – gods willing – when we catch sight of one . . . and it don't even need to be a pair to get us going; it's the promise of both of 'em out in the open air that drives us so rutting mad.' He took another drink and pointed out, 'But you're changing the subject. I was talking to the captain.'

'Right, sorry,' Sera said through a mouthful of billowy smoke, her sarcasm as thick in the air. 'Please, do go on.'

'Now, Captain,' Marrin began.

'Wait,' Doren Ford interrupted, 'are we really having this conversation?'

'Of course. Why?' Marrin looked surprised.

'I am not going to have sex with another woman while we're in

Orindale and my wife is in Southport, Marrin; it's just not going to happen.'

'But you see, Captain, you're coming at it from the wrong tack.'

'Am I?' The current conversation notwithstanding, Captain Ford liked these two; they were the closest thing he had to a first and second mate on the *Morning Star*, his weatherbeaten and currently a little leaky old brig-sloop. With nothing to haul back home to Southport, he'd ordered them to oversee the repairs while he met with business contacts in Orindale to find a westbound cargo to see them all through the Twinmoon: firewood, textiles, winter vegetables – anything to bring in a few copper Mareks. They were moored on the mudflats north of Orindale, just south of the salt marsh. It was too expensive to pay for mooring off the southern wharf, even during the winter Twinmoon, especially as he wasn't unloading anything lucrative. And this far north, the inns were cheaper and less crowded; he preferred it that way.

'Take your wife,' Marrin insisted, pressing on with his argument.

'I don't like where this is going,' the captain said warningly. He crossed his arms, trying not to look unsettled when they came to rest on top of his paunch. *I need to cut back on the pastries*, he thought in passing.

'Hear me out, hear me out,' the young sailor protested, motioning for another beer. 'Your wife is near-on perfect, wouldn't you say?'

Captain Ford nodded.

'I mean, her tits have got to have been formed by a randy god, and that backside – rutting whores, but that backside was carved from marble by a Pragan master. She may be the most beautiful woman in the Westlands, sincerely.'

'And?' Captain Ford twirled a finger as if to say, *So get to the part where I smack the shit out of you.*

'And . . . and I would never suggest that you do anything to violate the holy bond that you and your wife consummated when you stood the tides together, but don't you ever want just a different look, a different taste? I'm not saying you'd have better; you probably wouldn't – again, that being my own, personal and entirely qualitative opinion – but don't you ever want a different shape or flavour, just for an aven or two?'

'No,' Ford said dismissively.

'Good for you, Captain!' Sera frowned at Marrin, one yellowed, chipped tooth peeking out beside the curved stem of her pipe.

'Well, then you're a madman, Captain, a gods-rutting madman. I love you, I do, I'll not deny it, and may I grow old and never serve on a different ship than our own little stewpot out there, but you are a madman, and I just hope you find a healer somewhere to help you overcome this tragic affliction.'

'Who *are* you?' Sera said, taking a swing at Marrin's head.

'I'm a man,' Marrin replied, 'an honest man who understands what men need.'

'And get it from you, will they?'

'No,' he grinned, 'that's not what I meant, you seagoing whore. What I meant was— Well …' He looked around the room. The captain had taken rooms for himself, Sera and Marrin here, rather than them sleeping aboard the *Morning Star*. The rest of the crew had politely turned down the captain's offer and found their own lodgings near the northern wharf, where Tubbs and Kanthil knew a generous barman. Marrin figured young Pel for a goner but wished him good luck as he tagged along with the more experienced sailors.

'Over there, her,' Marrin pointed towards the bar, 'just take a look at her.'

'Great gods, Marrin, she's got to be four hundred Twinmoons old!' Sera was appalled.

'No, not her, you drunken wench, the other one; look, her!'

Brexan Carderic emerged from the kitchen balancing trenchers of fresh jemma fillets, potatoes, several loaves of bread and a small bowl of gravy.

'Her?' the captain asked.

'Right, her,' Marrin said. 'Now, she's not your wife by a healthy margin, but look at her. Look at that taut body. Look at the way her hair falls about her face when she walks; can't you just imagine that hair all spread out over the pillows while you looked down at those pert little twins from above?'

The captain sighed. 'What you don't understand, Marrin, is that when my wife and I stood the tides together, we agreed not to look at other people in that way, and if you don't understand that, then you're not ready to get married.'

'Thank the gods of the Northern Forest for that,' Marrin said with a heartfelt sigh. Sera shook her head and shrugged.

Captain Ford watched Brexan move through the tables, almost dancing as she sidestepped, spun and slipped around and between the other patrons. She looked up and caught him watching her. Seemingly amused, she smiled; Ford couldn't help but grin back. He reached for his beer, meaning to finish it off, but feeling the swell of his stomach beneath his shirt, decided on a sip instead.

When she finally reached their table, Brexan doled out the trenchers and the bread then carefully put the gravy bowl in the centre where everyone could reach it. Laughing to herself, she said, 'Well, that was tricky. I'm glad you didn't order the soup.'

'This looks delicious,' Captain Ford complimented her. 'Did you make it?'

Brexan laughed out loud and covered her face with both hands as if embarrassed. 'Sorry,' she giggled, 'but, *ahem*, no – you'd know it was mine if all the locals were lined up outside with buckets while women and children leaped to safety from the upstairs windows.'

He smiled back. 'Please give my thanks to the cook, in that case.'

'And bring three more beers,' Marrin cut in.

'You must be thirsty,' Brexan said.

'I am a lot of things.' The inebriated sailor tried to guess her age; he figured she couldn't be over two hundred Twinmoons, close enough to his own age for a sexual foray to be entirely acceptable.

Brexan glanced at Ford, who sighed and said, 'We let him out of the basement from time to time; it seems like the humane thing to do.'

'I understand,' Brexan said. 'I used to work with— well, a group of men, and—' Realising her mistake, Brexan tried to back away from discussion of her time in the Malakasian Army, 'Well, they were ... You know—' She decided to stop digging any further and hoped they'd put it down to shyness.

'See that?' Marrin was smug. 'She's speechless.'

Sera winced. 'Please, if you know what's best for you, run, run fast!'

'Let me ask you something,' Marrin said to Brexan, who nodded slowly.

'Are you attached to any man right now? Are you married, or into anything serious?'

Brexan thought of Versen, and while she expected to feel sadness – memories of him usually brought on her depression – she surprised herself by smiling. 'Yes, I suppose I am. Why?'

'Excellent, truly.' Marrin finished his beer. 'Of course, I don't want this to interfere with you bringing me drinks until my friend here is checking me for a heartbeat.'

'I understand.'

'Outstanding.' Marrin thought for a moment, then asked, 'When he's not around, do you ever think about other men, you know, in *that* way?'

Brexan didn't hesitate. 'Of course I do – but *not* about you.'

'Aha! See, I told you, Ford, you old— What was that?' Marrin sat up ramrod-straight, looking as if he had been slapped.

'I said, yes, but not about you, sorry.'

Sera laughed and clapped, spilling a bit of burning pipe tobacco into her lap. 'You are without doubt the best scullery-maid in the whole of the Eastlands; I don't doubt it. Please take the rest of the night off and stay here with us. Ford will pay you; just keep going like you're going. This is better entertainment than we'd ever find in town.'

'I'd love to, honestly,' Brexan replied, 'but Nedra is on her own tonight, and as you can see, we're rather busy.'

'You have truly glorious tits, my dear,' Marrin said.

Captain Ford finally lost his temper and reached over and cuffed the young sailor hard around the head, but so enamoured was he that the boy didn't appear to notice.

Brexan didn't miss a step. 'They're all right, I suppose, although they do look much better when you've had more to drink. So let me get those beers, before I have to drag you out back and smack the piss out of you.'

Ford and Sera nearly collapsed with hysterical laughter as Marrin watched the fiery young woman move towards the bar.

'Do you think she'd marry me?' he asked.

'Well, now that you've made such an impression,' Sera replied, 'I don't see how she could turn you down.'

'Good,' he said, 'I'll ask her when she comes back. We could stand the tides tomorrow; you two could be witnesses.'

'Sadly, Marrin, I have other plans tomorrow,' Ford said, deciding to ignore his paunch for the night and dive into the potatoes.

'Work, work, work,' Marrin said, 'Captain, you ought to think about what I said.'

'What? All that drivel about tits?'

Marrin raised a finger to make his point. 'First, yes, of course, and second, you should never use the word drivel when talking about my advice on the opposite sex.'

Sera interrupted, 'Marrin, *you* don't have an opposite sex.'

'No one likes you,' he shot back, then to Ford, added, 'that girl, our own tavern girl, right here in Orindale . . . think about it, Captain. I saw the way she was looking at you.'

'Yes,' Ford agreed, 'like a fat old uncle here with his two unruly children.'

Marrin mumbled, 'He has such little faith in my teachings. It's sad, really.'

'Eat your dinner, Marrin.' Sera tapped out her pipe.

'But he could have her, Sera,' Marrin insisted. 'You could, Captain.'

Ford looked at the bar where Brexan was delivering food and drink to Nella Barkson's extended family. 'Her?' he said. 'Somehow I doubt it, Marrin.'

The following morning, Captain Ford went down to breakfast alone. Not surprisingly, Marrin and Sera had decided to sleep in.

Brexan brought a flagon of hot tecan over to him. 'Good morning. Bread and cheese?'

'Please,' Captain Ford said, then thought of his weight. 'No cheese, just a bit of fruit, if you have it. I'm away from home too much; I get to eating things I shouldn't.'

'You look healthy enough to me,' Brexan said.

'I've the poor lighting in here to thank for that! And good morning too, by the way. I'm sorry about my friend last night. When he drinks, he thinks he's funny and we usually end up wiping the floor with him; it's never pretty. He was rude, and I hope he apologises when he comes down.' Ford kept his eyes locked on the girl's; he was not about to get caught sneaking a look at her body.

'Oh, don't worry about that,' Brexan said. 'Working in a place like this, I hear it all. Is that your ship out on the flats?'

'You're asking because it's low tide.' He'd been captain of the *Morning Star* for almost half his life, and the old boat didn't merit a second glance when afloat, but when listing dangerously to port on a mudflat, it made quite a conversation piece.

'Well, I guess so, yes,' Brexan flushed. 'Do you always leave it like that?'

'Nope,' Ford inhaled the aroma then sipped his tecan, 'just when I'm watching the Mareks. It doesn't cost anything to anchor up here.'

Brexan looked out of the front window. The port gunwale was nearly resting on the mud; had the sails not been tightly reefed, they would have been stained the colour of mud by now. 'I can't imagine why.'

Ford laughed. 'I guess you're right. Who would pay for that? But when the tide comes in, she'll be back on her feet, ready to go. She doesn't draft much; she's small, even for a brig-sloop. So we won't even need to kedge off; there's plenty of tide up here.' He tried not to feel embarrassed at the condition of his ship, keel-naked in the mud. He was her captain; he knew what he was doing.

'Where are you going next?'

'Southport, if I can find anything to transport.'

Brexan's brow furrowed. 'You're here without a cargo?'

'No, we delivered a load of lumber to a builder in Strandson, but we didn't have a return shipment. I decided to make the run on the off-chance we'd find something here. I know a few people; I'll see if I can't underbid someone. Like I said, she's not very big, so we don't get a lot of heavy commercial business, nothing from Malakasia is what I mean. Mostly, we make the run between Orindale and Southport; it's not very exciting, but the scenery is good.'

'Nothing to ship, betting on low bids, that sounds like a risky way to make a living, Captain—?'

'Ford, Doren Ford.' He rolled up his tunic sleeves, revealing strong forearms, tanned like leather and tufted with greying hair.

'Nice to meet you, Captain Ford. I'm glad you chose the Topgallant. Nedra keeps a nice place here, and she's the best cook you'll find north of the city.'

'If last night's dinner is any indication, you're not exaggerating.'

'And from here,' Brexan chuckled, 'you can certainly keep an eye on your boat.'

'Again, you're not joking—?' It was his turn to wait.

'Brexan Carderic.'

'Been working here long, Brexan Carderic?' he asked. He let his gaze follow the crooked line of Brexan's jaw. He figured she'd either had a difficult birth and a doula who had pressed too hard on one side of her head, or that young serving woman had sustained quite a nasty blow to her cheek. Either way, Ford was transfixed by the irregularity; it was strangely endearing.

She put a stack of dirty trenchers on a nearby table and struggled to tie her hair back with a bit of rawhide. 'No, about a Twinmoon actually, which reminds me, if you and your crew are here through the next Moon – it's only a few days now – you can join us for the party.'

'Party?'

'Nedra's turning . . .' She hesitated, checking towards the kitchen. 'Let's just say she's getting older.' She lowered her voice and whispered, 'She might be ancient, but she can still hear like a woodland predator.'

'Got it – if we're still here, I trust you'll give me some idea of what to buy for her.'

'Men!' Brexan said. 'Nedra just wants a man, but I understand they sometimes have them on a discount rack at a place just off the southern wharf.'

'I'll see what I can do.' Captain Ford smiled. 'Thanks for breakfast.' He watched her go until visions of his own wife, frowning, one arm cocked dangerously on her hip, distracted him. 'Ah, Marrin,' he murmured into his trencher, 'it'll be a double shift for you today, my boy. I'll teach you to get my thoughts wandering so.'

BOOK II

Orindale

STALWICK REES

'Stalwick, go and help someone else, please,' Sharr Becklen said as politely as he could. 'I've got this on my own, really.'

'But I can help with the folds,' Stalwick started. 'I've done these before. Do you remember when we attacked that caravan on the Merchants' Highway? What was it, fifteen, maybe sixteen Twinmoons ago? Were you there, Sharr? I think you were— Anyway, do you remember when we attacked that caravan, and Gita was so furious that the one driver was her uncle's friend's daughter's betrothed? The driver with the red hat? You remember him, Sharr, don't you? Or was it a beige hat? I don't . . . never mind, never mind. Anyway, when we hit that caravan, Sharr, and we spent those two nights in that ditch beside that field? It was a pepperweed field. Do you remember, Sharr? Because I was there, and I kept the fires going – I'm good with fires, I mean, that's one of the things I can do pretty well. Anyway— Oh, it *was* a red hat, I can see it clearly now! And Gita was fuming, I don't know why, I mean, everyone's got to make a living, so he's a driver, so what? Does every driver ask what he's hauling, I mean, when they're getting paid well, do they always ask? Anyway, anyway, Sharr, that day, after we hit that caravan, I helped with the tents, Sharr, and I was good with the folds— Do you remember Timmon? Of course you do, of course you do . . . He's dead now, isn't he? Bone-collectors, or some kind of monsters in a cavern, rutting dogs, I tell you, rutting dogs, but anyway, Timmon was there, and his company was there, and they were packing things up that day. I mean some of us were hurt, but I wasn't, and Timmon wasn't, so some of us who weren't hurt, we took care of packing things up, and I helped Timmon that day, because I'm good with folds, Sharr— Sharr?'

Sharr stood up from kneeling, folding canvas tents into tight bundles. It was sleeting in Traver's Notch, and that stinging, freezing downpour had soaked the tents through; they'd all need to be unrolled to dry out as soon as the weather cleared, otherwise the cloth would sprout fungus and start rotting through. Trying to prepare for travel or combat in the rain was unavoidable, and Gita had ordered the entire Resistance force – almost regiment-sized, if they were part of a proper army – to be ready to march on Capehill at a moment's notice. Platoons, companies, squads of farmers, merchants, woodsmen, sailors, even, were all scattered throughout the surrounding foothills, all disguised as miners and spread out so they wouldn't attract notice from passing occupation patrols. Every group, no matter their size, had a cache of mining implements to help with the ruse, and some of the soldiers were actually working the lode shafts outside Traver's Notch when not drilling, each hoping to tap a rich vein before the assault on Capehill.

The order had come that morning: prepare to move southeast right away. And an extra order for Sharr Becklen: keep a close eye on Stalwick Rees of Capehill.

Sharr cursed, scraped the mud from his knees and glared at his annoying countryman. Gita had made it clear that Stalwick was not to be left alone at any time, and any changes in his behaviour, any seizures or fits, were to be reported to her immediately. Inexplicably, Stalwick had grown attached to the burly Capehill fisherman, and Gita had encouraged the pairing, telling Sharr, 'It'll be good for you! You two have so much in common; I imagine your new friendship will last a lifetime.'

Standing in the sleet, his clothes clinging to him like wet laundry, Sharr thought that even for one as old as he had managed to become, a lifetime of friendship with Stalwick Rees would leave anyone contemplating suicide. He scratched at his grey-streaked beard, considering his charge.

Stalwick was tall and lean, with blotchy skin and hair that looked permanently matted to the top of his head. His vision was poor and he had nervous tics and idiosyncratic gestures that left everyone around him on edge. He was interminably clumsy, and more than one dinner companion had discovered the challenge of eating beside him – Kellin Mora now automatically moved her goblet out of his reach the moment he came near, although even that didn't always save her from having its contents spilled on her food. But they all put up with Stalwick, for he had a few uncanny abilities that made him an asset to the Falkan Resistance. He could make a fire anywhere; Sharr had heard that his campfires managed to burn even through the torrential rains that blew through Falkan in the early spring. He didn't quite believe it, though he had also heard that a log from one

146

of Stalwick's fires had remained alight even after it had accidentally been kicked into a pond.

In addition to kindling his resilient flames, Stalwick periodically foretold the future – not the distant future, Ages and Eras yet to come, but the immediate future, the next aven, or the following day. What was troublesome about Stalwick's clairvoyance was that he himself rarely knew he was seeing anything at all; he'd say something odd, leaving those around him to try to work out what he was prophesying. 'I'm looking forward to the fish tonight,' or 'The mud will be thick tomorrow,' might be followed with 'I've never sailed on a schooner before.' Later, Stalwick's family and Resistance colleagues – now plagued with anxiety about what might happen – would discover that a relative who had been fishing near a mud flat had dropped by to share the day's catch and was keen to talk about the schooner he'd seen passing by on the horizon. Sharr found Stalwick's ability to capture glimpses of the future infuriating; he tried to ignore the periodic babble, pretending not to hear.

'Did you hear me, Sharr? Did you? I said, "what".' Stalwick tied a length of bailing twine about the rolled canvas tent, but Sharr stopped him, gripping him too tightly by the shoulder. 'Ow, stop that, stop it, Sharr. That hurts, don't you know? That hurts.'

'Sorry, Stalwick,' Sharr sighed. 'It's just that these tents have to be ready to go. We may be leaving for Capehill at any moment, and if we don't have tents loaded into the wagons, half of us will be without shelter. Do you understand?'

Stalwick nodded excitedly; Sharr was making his point for him. 'That's why I'm saying you need to let me help, Sharr, you do! I can do this, watch me.'

'No, Stalwick.' Sharr gripped his shoulder again, less forcefully this time. 'I'll finish these, but why don't you go and get us some beer, or some tecan. Someone around here must have some brewing; see if you can find us a couple of goblets.'

Stalwick beamed. 'I will, Sharr. I can do that. I know, there was a guy ... I think his name is Daran or Deren, I can't remember, but anyway, anyway, he knows a woman from the second company – that group from the plains – who fights like an unchained nightmare, I guess, but anyway, she makes tecan for them. I don't know why none of the rest of them can make their own, or maybe she's just especially good at it, but anyway, anyway, she makes it, and it's drop-dead good tecan, the best in the whole battalion. And well, you know, the second company is camped on the other side of the stream. So, it's not far. It's really not, I mean, I can be over there and back in a breath or two, so it won't even get cold, and if it does, well, then I'll make a fire. I'm good with fires. I mean, I'm good with folds, too, but you know, fires are something I am good at too.'

Sharr sighed again, a long, slow exhalation to purge the lingering feelings of homicidal rage. 'Thank you, Stalwick,' he said, and forced a smile. 'Some tecan would be wonderful. I could use a warming-up. I'll be here.'

'Good, Sharr, good. I'll be back. I'll get as much as I can— Well, I'll get two goblets, anyway, but if there's more, I'll get more. I mean, that'll save us a trip later. You know? I mean, the second company is close, but who wants to cross the stream, especially today, more than once if you don't have to. You know?'

'Go on, Stalwick, and when you get back, we'll make a fire.'

Despite the bone-deep chill, Stalwick's face flushed a warm red and he looked as though he might expire from pure unchecked enthusiasm. 'I'll start one, Sharr. If you want a fire, I'll get a blaze going that they'll be able to see in Pellia. We'll be the warmest, driest squad in the whole company, maybe the whole battalion. I'll do that, ho, ho, will I ever!'

'Good. Thank you, Stalwick,' Sharr repeated. 'I'll be here when you get back.' He turned back to the tents until he was sure Stalwick had left. He felt the tension leave his shoulders as he relaxed into the welcome silence. He really didn't mind the sleet; he'd had a lifetime fishing the deep trenches off the coast of Capehill. He missed the steely-grey, freezing cold days, even when it had been utterly miserable, for fishing the North Sea had been glorious in its unpredictability. Hand-lining for summer jemma-fish, the giants that had not yet begun the season's migration; that was lucrative fishing. But it was the nets that Sharr missed; hauling them along the trenches and canyons was like reaching into a wizard's chest and withdrawing a handful of whatever magic might be secreted inside. Sometimes it was schools of hullen, tough little fish he could sell on the wharf for a copper or two a basket. On other days, they'd haul up a shark, a fat-bodied monster, stuffed to bursting on jemma and too slow even to get out of its own way. Sharr sometimes looped a line around their tails and dragged them for half an aven – there was no reason to bring a live shark on board, stuffed full or not, and dragging them backwards drowned them. Most tried to fight it, engaging in a titanic tug-of-war while intrepid archers would take turns firing, but eventually, the sharks always succumbed. His crew loved these fights especially; Sharr found the whole ritual gruesome. He always heaved a sigh of relief when the sharks died.

He recalled another day that had begun with frigid sleet, when he and his crew had hauled up a giant tapen, its tentacles coiling and grasping as the creature fought for its life in the unforgiving sea air. They didn't know quite what to do with it, but they weren't willing to cut it away and lose a valuable net, so Sharr and his men had beaten it, gaffed it, shot it full of arrows, even stabbed it with a makeshift harpoon fashioned out of a fillet knife lashed to a docking pole. When finally the beast quieted, they hauled it aboard, assuming it was dead.

No sooner had the tapen struck the deck, than it found new reserves of energy, a monster dose of will. It rolled across the deck, its powerful limbs crushing or shattering anything it could grip on to – Sharr himself was injured when his feet were yanked out from under him and he went down, his head striking the starboard gunwale. He was lying there with his head bleeding, watching as the monster fought to the death, his crew battling to kill it before it tore out the transom and sent them all to the bottom, and he had smiled. He would not have traded places with anyone that day.

Now, folding tents mechanically, the erstwhile fisherman glanced down the hill only to see the tapen once again – it wasn't a giant this time, nor was it threatening his life or his boat, but it was there just the same: lying in the mud, halfway to the stream, legs and arms flailing in the air.

'Stalwick!' Sharr roared, running down the slope. He slipped, tumbling out of control, then dizzily regained his feet. Others heard his cry and ran to see what had befallen the irksome soldier. Within moments, Stalwick had half the squad standing over him in the freezing rain.

'Brand's coming,' Stalwick panted, his eyes rolling white and his limbs twitching in an ungainly dance, 'March on Capehill, now. Malakasians know. Capehill now. Malakasians know. Brand is coming!' Something wet ran from Stalwick's nose, sticky phlegm the colour of spoiled milk, bubbling from one nostril as his convulsions subsided. He lay in the mud, his gaze focused on something half a world away.

'Let's get him up,' Sharr said. 'Get one of those tents back up and find some dry clothes or blankets.' A few of the men hustled off. 'And bring Gita,' he continued, 'quickly! Tell her to get over here now.

One of you stay with me; we have to listen to everything he says. We can't miss a word.'

Although Sharr remained by Stalwick's side all day, he didn't speak again until the following morning. As he stared out at nothing, he looked as though he had been kicked by a horse.

Raskin rode hard as the sun rose behind her. She was less than a day from Traver's Notch now, and she promised herself as soon as she had found the officer in charge and reported the loss of her entire squad to a grettan pack the previous Moon, she would find a tavern – the one she'd visited before, The Bowman – and get drunk. How long she would stay drunk was yet to be determined, but it certainly wouldn't be less than three to five comatose days.

Staying alone at the border camp had been difficult, but Raskin hadn't wanted to abandon her position, not when she was all that remained of her squad. She didn't patrol; that would have been pointless – the first band of border runners she stumbled upon would have flayed her and left her for the grettans. Instead, she stayed in her tent, tended her horse and periodically went in search of firewood. She had plenty of food, enough to last through the Twinmoon, but somehow being warm and dry was no real comfort. Twilight came early in Gorsk during the winter Twinmoons, and Raskin sat up most nights, listening to the sounds of the forest with her blankets clutched nervously beneath her chin. She cried frequently during the long periods of darkness.

Denny, Mox, Maia, even Sergeant Greson with his homemade mittens, they all visited during the Moon she waited alone in camp. Sometimes they came all at once, whole, healthy and laughing. Other nights, they came to her one at a time, haunted, broken and bleeding. Mox was the worst. He had been torn to pieces by the first attack, and whatever remained of him the following day had been scattered when the grettans returned. When Mox visited Raskin's tent, he came with pieces missing: one leg chewed off below the knee, both hands, part of an arm and half his throat. He never spoke; she worried that if he had, his voice would have been little more than a raspy gurgle. Raskin felt guilty about it, but in the end she was glad her old friend never said anything.

Occasionally she was visited by the Ronan, Garec Haile. He had saved her life. He knew the grettans were coming; he'd told her to get back to her horse. Had she not been in the saddle, ready to ride, Raskin would have died with the rest of the squad, but as it was, she barely managed to outrun the one grettan that pursued her down the draw and into the river. She had no idea where Garec was now, him and the South Coaster, the fennaroot smugglers working with Rodler of Capehill. She didn't care.

One Moon. She had promised herself she would stay in camp for one Moon, following procedures, until someone arrived with orders or until one of their platoon mates came west from the border station for a visit.

No one did.

Before he'd died, Sergeant Greson had mentioned strange goings-on, and a curious lack of communication from Capehill. Raskin wasn't sure, but she feared that perhaps she had heard nothing from the major because somehow the southern occupation had been jeopardised, perhaps even beaten by a surprise attack from the Falkan Resistance. Her fears were fuelled on this, her first trip out of the mountains; she had set off for the border station less than a day's ride away, but when she reined in alongside the wooden gates spanning the Merchants' Highway, she knew something was wrong. The second squad in her platoon, the one that staffed the border crossing, was missing.

She was alone, a full Twinmoon's travel from home.

Capehill was too far, alone, so avoiding the main routes into Falkan, Raskin turned towards Traver's Notch, conscious that she was fair game for any number of human predators. Whilst her chances of encountering other Malakasian soldiers along the Merchants' Highway were good, her unwarranted fear that they had all been killed or pushed south continued to bother her all the way down the Remondian foothills.

Now, nearing the canyon leading into the Notch, Raskin began to breathe easier. Had she been travelling with the squad, they would have come into town from the northeast, through the mining encampments and over the ridge. There were several decent roads over those hills, kept open even during the worst Moons of winter. But she was riding alone and didn't want to come too close to the mining camps for fear that she might disappear for other reasons entirely. So she dropped down from the foothills, entered the forest south of the Notch and picked her way west towards the main avenue running into town. Behind her, the sun rose and for the first time in the past Moon, it felt warm.

Raskin had done her duty; she had stood her post a Moon longer than most soldiers alone in the northern mountains, and she felt a sense of pride in having held out that long. With the sun on her shoulders, she could feel the memory of them all fading into the bright yellow glow, even Mox. She turned once to see if they were following, those ghostly apparitions that had kept her company in the dark avens, but they were gone, Garec Haile too.

Raskin crested a short rise and saw the miners moving towards her. She had no option but to ride through them. There was no one coming behind her, no serendipitous band of occupation infantry closing the gap.

'Well, rutting horsecocks,' she sighed. 'I made it this far, and now I'm ruined.'

The rising sun was in their eyes, and several of the men pulled hat brims down in an effort to see more clearly. A few pointed, gesturing in her direction, and in a moment Raskin knew that despite the shovels, picks and coils of rope, these were not miners. 'Demonshit!' she cried, turning her horse into the sun, 'what are they doing out here, anyway? Someone serving breakfast?'

They were Resistance fighters. All her worst nightmares had come true: the southern forces had been overrun. Raskin was on her own.

'Look at that,' Stalwick said, 'who's that? Who's that, Sharr? That's a soldier. What's he doing out here? Oh no, oh no; we're in trouble, we're in trouble, Sharr. He saw us, he knows, he does; I'm sure of it. Look! Oh no, look, Sharr, look, he's turning towards Capehill. He knows!'

'Would you shut up for one godswhoring moment, please, Stalwick?' Sharr fought the urge to slap the man. 'Can anyone see him? Is it a soldier?' He squinted into the sun.

They all tried to make out the mounted silhouette against the dawn.

'That's a soldier, Sharr, I know, I saw a whole column of them one time outside Cape—'

'Shut up, Stalwick!' Sharr pointed at a farmer from the plains. 'Give me your bow, Sal, quickly.'

He sighted along the arrow. It was hard to see; the sun was blinding, its rays refracting through a hundred million glints of overnight frost. On any other morning, he would have found it beautiful, but right now it was a deadly nuisance. He fought to get a clear shot at the fleeing occupation soldier. 'He's alone,' he muttered, 'and if we can drop him, no one will be any wiser.' He closed his eyes but could still see red behind his lids, his own blood, lit from across the heavens.

He's just like one of those sharks, just a fat old dogfish, fighting for his life, trying to drag the whole trawler out to sea.

Sharr aimed, blinked and released the arrow with a muted *thunk*. The others strained to follow as the shaft arced into the brilliance.

Raskin rode directly into the morning sun, chanting, *Blind them; blind the bastards!* like a mantra. She spurred her mount into a gallop; there was no sense masquerading as anything other than terrified. It was a long shot, but a skilled bowman could make it. She held her breath and counted the horse's steps. *A few more, maybe ten more, and I'll be out of the fire, at least for now.* She didn't know what she might discover on the road to Capehill, but from the look of the miners walking southeast – *marching, Raskin; they're marching* – away from the mountains, Traver's Notch was no longer safe for her.

Sharr's arrow took the Malakasian soldier in the leg. Sharr couldn't see if it hit the thigh or the calf, but from its angle of descent, he knew he had missed anything vital.

When the rider screamed, Stalwick winced, visibly taken aback by the unnerving cry. 'It was a woman, Sharr,' he whispered. 'You shot a woman. That was a woman, not a soldier.'

'It wasn't.' Sharr's hands shook. *It was just a shark, a big, slow, stupid fish. That's all.* 'It was a soldier; I don't care whether it was a man or a woman. If he ... or she ... gets away, we'll have a long and unpleasant walk into Capehill.' Sharr had already nocked another arrow and was taking aim at the disappearing rider, a hazy shadow now. It was an impossible shot, a wasted arrow, but Sharr released it anyway.

It was almost half an aven later before they came upon Raskin's body. She had ridden surprisingly far with an arrow in her leg and another in her right lung. Sharr couldn't tell if her tumble from the saddle had pushed the arrowhead into an artery, or if the woman had bled out before falling.

Standing over the body, Sharr realised that were he to survive the coming Twinmoon and get to sea again, he had roped and drowned his last shark.

THE MEDERA

Gilmour watched from above as the folded wrinkles of the Twinmoon Foothills gradually smoothed, trowel-flat, into the frozen Falkan Plain. This far north the arable midsection of the Eastlands, a tapestry of green, gold and earthen brown during warmer Twinmoons, was now a vast carpet of white. Free from the cold he knew he would find were he truly suspended several thousand paces over Falkan, Gilmour nestled deeper into his blankets, deeper into his spell, and turned his gaze west towards the Ravenian Sea and the busy streets of Pellia. He enjoyed the journey.

Finding Stalwick Rees had not been difficult; Gilmour had searched in the hills above Traver's Notch until he felt a dim flicker of rippling energy slogging through a curtain of freezing rain. He had been as gentle as he could from this distance, but Stalwick still went down as if he had been clubbed.

Realising that he might kill the boy, Gilmour had remained inside his mind for only a moment; his message was brief: *March on Capehill now. The Malakasians know of the attack. Brand is coming soon.*

Finding Kantu would be more challenging; Gilmour hoped he would succeed before growing too weary and needing to sleep. While Stalwick was a faint but distinct beacon in the forested hills north of Traver's Notch, Kantu would be a bright light, a veritable signal-fire amongst the crowds in the Malakasian capital – *if* Kantu was still in Pellia, and *if* he was still alive.

Gilmour felt himself soar over the Ravenian Sea. Moving quickly now, outdistancing even the trade breezes along the narrow waterway, he honed in on a great throbbing rift in the ambient energy above the waves, a pulsing rhythm he could feel against his flesh, even this imagined flesh. It had to be Kantu; Gilmour grinned. With Nerak lost inside the Fold, there was no one but Mark Jenkins who would radiate such power, but Mark was still close by. Gilmour felt lucky that he had stumbled upon Kantu while the magician was working a bit of sorcery; finding his old friend mid-spell made the evening's work a bit easier.

He's on a ship. I'll catch him there. We'll meet in Orindale.

But when Gilmour closed in on the schooner, he realised that he had been wrong – it was easy to locate; its power resonated out and up in concentric waves of energy that nearly sent Gilmour spiralling into the water – but it wasn't Kantu. And it wasn't heading south to Orindale; the schooner and whoever or whatever it carried was sailing north towards the archipelago, and the few navigable passages to Pellia.

What is *that?* Gilmour considered breaching the ship's hull and finding out what was secreted inside, but he pressed on; Kantu might already know what was being shipped. If his old colleague had heeded Gilmour's advice and avoided Welstar Palace – *avoided killing himself* – he might still be in Pellia, or one of the towns or villages lining the river between the palace and the capital city. Gilmour noted the schooner's position and heading, then shifted the locus of his tired consciousness towards Pellia.

Above the city, he felt certain again that he had located Kantu. A steady mystical force, surprisingly strong, drew him towards a comfortable-looking inn, a cosy place a few streets off the east bank of the Welstar River.

There he is, Gilmour thought. *That looks a nice enough place. He won't mind spending the next Moon there. The way he sleeps, he won't notice much of it passing, anyway.* Gilmour dropped from the skies, imagining he could smell the tang of the wharf, the myriad chimneys spewing woodsmoke into the windless morning and the mouth-watering flavour of kneaded dough rising above the hearth.

Kantu. Kantu, wake up. He nudged the silent form with his mind.

He's sleeping, someone answered from the corner of the room, someone sitting on a second bed, looking out of the window towards the river.

Gilmour reeled as if he had been thumped in the chest by a god. Tumbling backwards out of the guestroom, he turned head-over-heels through the air, fighting to regain control over his transcendental self.

In Wellham Ridge, he stirred for a moment, pulled his blankets up and groaned.

The unfamiliar presence followed. *Where are you going?* It was an innocent question. *Who are you?* There was no anger in the voice, merely curiosity.

Gilmour wondered how anyone outside himself or Kantu would be able to communicate this way. There was no one left in Eldarn who knew this spell; not even Steven could perform it.

How are you doing this? he asked, wary, ready to freefall back into Wellham Ridge if necessary. *Who is this?*

Milla. Who are you? How did you find us?

Milla. Gilmour's mind raced. It hadn't been Kantu; he hadn't found his old friend. Kantu had been there; Gilmour could feel him now, a presence beneath an old quilt. Instead, he had found *Milla* – but *who* was Milla? Someone powerful, that was obvious, for her strength eclipsed Kantu's, buried inside the guestroom.

Milla?

Yes? Hello again.

Hello. May I ask who you are?

I told you already, silly. I'm Milla. Alen calls me Pepperweed, but my real name is Milla. There was a brief silence. *Are you Fantus? Or are you Prince Nerak? You don't sound like him.*

Sound? Who was this person? There was no sound here. This was only flat, toneless communication. A few Senators could manage a bit of inflection, even a laugh from time to time, but Gilmour hadn't been trying for anything more than clarity. Milla. Wracking his memory, he couldn't call her up. She spoke like a child. He guessed she might be someone Kantu had met on his journey through Malakasia, a prodigy he had discovered in Pellia, or perhaps even— He cast his thoughts back to her. *Milla?*

What?

It's Fantus.

I knew it, really. You don't sound like Prince Nerak. He always sounds mad. I don't like it when he talks to me.

I don't either. Can you tell me how old you are?

I'm thirty-one Twinmoons, but another one is coming pretty soon.

Gilmour tried to laugh. It didn't work. *I know, just a few more days. Well, I was trying to find Kantu . . . Alen . . . but he's asleep.*

He sleeps a lot.

I know he does, my dear. He's a boring old grettan, isn't he?

He's nice. He just gets tired. Hoyt and Hannah play with me when Alen sleeps.

Hannah, Gilmour thought, good news. He was weakening and felt himself slipping back towards Falkan. He wouldn't be able to keep this up much longer.

Milla interrupted his thoughts. *Do you need help?*

What's that? He was fading, falling fast.

Help, silly. Here, I can help you.

Gilmour felt an invisible band snake around his waist, hug him close and keep him from tumbling backwards over the Ravenian Sea. Milla was powerful. *Good lords, my dear, but that is an interesting spell.*

Something that sounded like enormous pride reached him across their gossamer lines of communication. *I learned that one from Prince Nerak! But he didn't know I figured it out. Sometimes he liked to talk too long.*

Yes, he was full of gret— He was full of fun chatter, wasn't he? Gilmour felt for the band, wondering whether he would be powerful enough to break it were the child to become angry or hostile. *Milla, I need to tell Alen something, but I'm too tired to wake him up now. I've been doing this for a long time, and I need rest, too.*

I can tell him something for you.

Will you remember? Of course she would, he thought. There was nothing this little girl couldn't do.

I can remember lots of things. Mama used to say I was one of the smartest girls on the whole North Shore.

You're from Orindale?

I don't know. We lived by the water. I can't remember the name.

I thought you said you could remember lots of things.

Milla laughed; there was no mistaking it this time. *You tricked me, silly.* The band tightened, and Gilmour tried to remain calm. There was no need to hold his breath. He was perfectly safe; he hoped. Then Milla's grip loosened – it was a hug, that's all, a mystical hug imbued with more energy and focused magical power than Gilmour had ever seen in a novice sorcerer, never mind one less than fifty Twinmoons old.

All right, I trust you. Can you tell him to stay in Pellia, right where you are? Tell him that Fantus is coming in the next Moon. Will you remember that?

Of course. He could almost see a smug, pouting toddler with a mop of tousled unruly hair looking back at him in disbelief. *That's not hard.*

Tell it back to me, then.

Milla sighed. There was no doubt about it, either. It was a sigh, an impossible sigh, just like her impossible laughter. Larion Senators worked for Twinmoons to be able to do what this little girl had accomplished twice in one spell, never mind her ability to reach up and grasp Gilmour's essence out of the sky.

I'll tell him that we have to wait here, right at this place, because Fantus . . . that's you . . . is coming in the next Moon.

Excellent work, Pepperweed.

Are you going to call me that, too?

Do you want me to?

Yeah, I guess so.

Well then, Pepperweed, you should call me Gilmour.

That's a funny name.

Yes, I suppose it is.

Do you have to go now?

Sorry, but I do. I'm not very good at this, and I will need to sleep for a long time to get my strength back.

Will you come talk to me another day?

Why don't I come and see you in person?

Milla laughed again, a twinkling of delicate chimes rising from the boarding house to find him hovering outside. *That would be nice.*

And Milla—

What?

Will you tell Hannah that Steven is coming, too?

I guess so.

Thank you, my dear.

Goodbye Fan— uh, Gilmour.

Goodbye, Pepperweed.

When she released him, Gilmour felt the extent of his fatigue. Nauseous, he closed his eyes, hoped he wouldn't vomit and tumbled all the way from Pellia to Wellham Ridge.

Erynn brought drinks: beer for everyone, milk for Milla. On her way back to the Wayfarer's kitchen, she paused to talk with a young soldier, a boy, no more than fifteen or twenty Twinmoons her senior, and looking like a child playing at dressing up in his father's infantry uniform. He was alone, eating a bowl of stew with a loaf of bread and a tankard of beer. Hoyt watched as he reached out, surreptitiously, to touch the scullery girl's hand. Erynn turned towards the bar, saw her father, and shifted her tray, effectively pulling herself out of range. The boy slid forward on his chair, said something Hoyt couldn't hear, smiled, and then shrugged. She checked her father again, frowned, and hurried back to the kitchen, calling out food orders. In her handmade tunic and soiled apron she looked to Hoyt like a girl condemned to being plain for life. The avens, the smoke, the scullery basins and the nimble-fingered drunks had already left irreparable marks.

'She needs to be careful of that one,' Hoyt said.

'What's that?' Hannah asked.

'Erynn.' Hoyt nodded towards the soldier. 'That boy over there is practically bursting out of that uniform for her. Gods, look at him in that carnival suit. I have boots older than he is. He looks like he spent all morning . . . polishing himself!'

'Hoyt,' Alen grimaced, 'not in front of Milla.'

'What?' Hoyt smirked guiltily. 'I'm just saying he looks like he spent a lot of time shining up that uniform.'

'I'll talk with her,' Hannah promised, 'but can we get back to it?' She had been reeling from Milla's announcement that Gilmour had contacted her that morning. Conflicting feelings of joy and frustration threatened to drive Hannah mad: she wanted more information, now, about how and when the Ronans would arrive. Had Steven asked about her? Was he happy? Healthy? Looking forward to seeing her again? Alen was especially stunned, because he had slept through the entire conversation, never sensing even a flicker of his former colleague's presence.

'Get back to what?' Hoyt said. 'We know they're coming, but we don't know when or how, whether they'll come overland or via the Northeast Channel. My guess is that it'll be by sea from Orindale: there's going to be a barrel of traffic through that passage with the Twinmoon looming. Anyone could sign on to almost anything that floats, and as long as they can get through the blockade, they'll arrive in Pellia without a wrinkle.'

'He's right,' Alen said, 'but it worries me that Fantus—'

'Gilmour,' Milla interrupted, sipping her milk.

'Sorry, Gilmour, that he didn't say anything about the table or the key.'

'Don't let it bother you, Alen,' Hoyt said. 'If they have it, they'll figure out how to get it here. If they don't, then there must be some good reason for them to make the trip up the Ravenian Sea. Either way, this isn't going to be a social call; he's up to something, and we need to stay here until he arrives.'

Milla pouted, her eyes welling with tears.

'What's the matter, sweetie?' Hannah whispered.

'Alen said we were going to see my mama.'

'Oh, we are, sweetie,' Hannah assured. 'We are. I promise. Alen promises. We just have to wait a bit longer; some special friends are coming here to meet us first.'

Milla perked up. 'Gilmour, right? I talked to him; he's funny. I thought he was going to fall backwards, but he didn't; I caught him.'

'You did what, Pepperweed?' Alen asked.

Milla shrugged and tilted her goblet, trying to catch the last drops of milk on her tongue. 'I had to catch him; he was going to fall.'

Alen's brow furrowed. *I had to catch him?*

Hannah said, 'So this means we can stop looking for a transport south?'

'Right.' Alen waved to Erynn, who was back talking with the young soldier.

'Oh, good,' Hoyt sighed. 'That schooner captain was driving me strange-to-silly with his blather about a Falkan plot to rig the chain-ball championships next Twinmoon – I'd have drowned myself in the bilge by the time we reached Orindale.'

Milla giggled, echoing, 'Strange-to-silly.'

'So?' Hannah asked, 'What do we do? Just wait?'

Erynn came up behind them, her ubiquitous serving tray held at the ready.

Hoyt, not noticing the girl there, said simply, 'No, we don't just wait. We bury them, as many as we can without getting caught. And I suggest we start with the horsecocks running shipments along that highway.'

'We can't risk Milla,' Alen said. Mention of terrorism had him immediately on edge, worried about the child prodigy.

'No risks,' Hoyt assured. 'She'll be here; she'll be fine. It'll be just you and me.'

Erynn cleared her throat. 'Are you ready for some food this aven? Or can I bring you more beer?'

Hoyt and Alen exchanged a nervous glance. Hannah, smiling sweetly, said, 'Another three beers, please, Erynn, and another milk for our driver here.'

'All right,' Erynn said, glancing sheepishly at Hoyt. 'I'll be right back.'

Hoyt forced a smile, blushing.

Hannah rescued him. 'And Erynn, maybe later, when you're done for the night, you and I can talk a bit.'

'Really?' Erynn's eyes widened. 'I'd love that – what about? Just ... I mean we can just—'

Hannah pointedly looked over at the young soldier and smiled.

'Oh,' Erynn said, 'oh, yes. All right, I'll be done after the dinner aven.'

'I'll be here,' Hannah said, giving the girl a reassuring squeeze on the forearm.

Alen frowned. 'Do you think she heard us?' he asked after she'd hurried back to the kitchen.

'Of course she did.' Hoyt, mimicking Milla, tipped his goblet to catch the last of his beer.

'What do we do?'

'We do nothing,' Hannah said. 'I'll take care of this.'

Later, in Alen's room, Hoyt sat on the edge of Milla's bed, watching as the girl twirled a finger at her stuffed dog. Bits of old straw spilled from seams in its neck, hips and stomach, making the animal look like a bag of hay that had been run over by a logger's cart. Despite its fractures and dislocations, the toy jumped and danced, flipping over, sitting up, and occasionally extinguishing and relighting the candles on the room's small table.

Hoyt said, 'That's quite a dog you have there, Pepperweed.'

Milla, showing off, made the stuffed animal execute a full flip with a twist. 'I taught him all these tricks.'

'I can see that, but you know, Pepperweed, you can't have him doing those tricks outside this room.'

'I know,' Milla sighed. 'But if I had a *real* puppy—'

Hoyt picked her up and tossed her backwards into the pillows; Milla shrieked, and her dog leaped all the way to the ceiling. 'If you had a real puppy, you could teach him great tricks. I'm sure he would be the talk of the marketplace: Milla and her Wonderdog . . .' Hoyt paused.

'Resta!' she giggled.

'Milla and Resta the Wonderdog!' Hoyt bowed in mock deference. 'People would come from the corners of the known lands to watch as Resta did . . . what?'

'Wrote his name.'

'Wrote his name!' Hoyt laughed.

'And sang funny songs.'

'And sang funny songs!'

'But didn't chase cats or bite or growl or anything mean like that.'

'Of course not,' Hoyt said, tucking Milla into her blankets and blowing out her bedside candle. 'Maybe when we get to Falkan, we'll go looking for Resta together.'

'Mama says dogs cost too much.'

'Well, you let Hoyt worry about that.' He kissed her forehead. 'You know, I like pepperweed with gansel eggs and baked potatoes.'

'Good night, Hoyt.'

'Good night, Pepperweed.'

Alen joined them, said good night, and brushed two fingers gently over the girl's hairline. Milla's eyes fluttered a moment; she sighed through her nose and fell asleep.

'You going out tonight?' Alen asked.

'Just to the waterfront. I need to ask a few questions, do a bit of eavesdropping, find out about whatever's heading south next.'

'More bark?'

'I hope so, but I don't honestly care. We'll hit whatever they're shipping.'

Alen pulled a leather pouch from his tunic. 'You need bribes?'

'No. After my last visit to the southern highway, I'm a wealthy man.'

'All right, but be discreet.'

'Naturally.' Hoyt checked his sleeve for the surgical scalpel he carried. It was tarnished now and had a few deep scratches along the blade, scars from their brief tenure in the Welstar Palace prison. Hoyt's fingertips had healed but his nails would be Twinmoons growing back.

'How do you want to hit them?' Whilst he knew he was expected to bring Larion magic to bear against Prince Malagon's wagon-trains, Alen wasn't actually sure what a terrorist raid looked like.

'I think fire is best,' Hoyt said. 'It creates confusion, disables wagons, terrifies the horses or oxen, and, if we're lucky—'

'Incinerates the enchanted bark,' Alen said.

'It doesn't do onions, flour or greenroot a lot of good either.' Hoyt was in his element. This was a measure of vengeance for Churn. 'Can you conjure up a pretty resilient flame?'

'I'm sure I can figure something that'll impress them.'

'It mustn't be totally impervious to their efforts; I don't want them to realise they're up against Larion sorcery.'

'Right. They'll triple the guard if they think we have magic.'

'Or use the river as their only supply line.' Hoyt tucked Milla's stuffed dog into bed beside her. 'We can't attack one of those barges, not by ourselves.'

'So, fire then.'

'Fire.'

'Good luck tonight.'

'I'll update you over breakfast.' Hoyt left, quietly moving down the back stairs.

Alen sat on the edge of his own bed, watching Milla's tiny chest rise and fall. She clutched the stuffed dog, silent now, protectively under one arm, giving the animal some much needed rest before its morning caelisthenics.

This is why I'm here, Alen reminded himself. Beset by the lassitude of so many Twinmoons hiding in Middle Fork, he hoped the feelings of hopelessness would rub off before Fantus arrived. It had been easy to marshal his enthusiasm for an assault on Welstar Palace: rage was an ardent motivator, and suicide had an endpoint, a built-in expiration. He hadn't had to keep up his anger for very long.

This was different. Caring for a child prodigy was not what he expected to be doing a Twinmoon after leaving Middle Fork. Were he and Fantus to succeed, Milla would be one of the most powerful sorcerers in a new generation of Larion Senators. It would rest with him to see her safely home, and then through her training.

And what about you, Fantus? Alen thought. *Are you well rested? Ready to be burdened with these responsibilities again? And why are you bringing the key and the table to Malakasia? Do you not know how dangerous that is?*

Alen wanted a drink, perhaps a whole bucket of drinks.

'Not tonight,' he muttered to the window. He watched for some sign of Hoyt in the shadows but knew he wouldn't find anything. 'Not tonight, and perhaps not for a long time.'

He sat back on his mattress and watched Milla sleep. 'I do have hope, though,' he whispered to the sleeping girl. 'I suppose that counts for something. Although sometimes I fear that *all* I have is hope.'

Alen waved the tapers dark and fell into his pillows. Drifting off, he thought, *Nothing but hope*.

'So what's the name of this river, anyway?' Steven asked anyone who might know. Unlike the others, he couldn't rest. Knowing Hannah was alive, safe and waiting for him in Pellia had Steven pacing the deck like a nervous prom date. The old wooden barge, as big as a floating parking lot, crawled towards Orindale, not covering much more than a few knots an hour. But even if it had been racing, it couldn't move fast enough for Steven.

Gilmour sat with his back braced against the starboard gunwale; he was still tired from his attempt to contact Kantu and his long-distance conversation with the child prodigy Milla. He wondered where Kantu had discovered her – Welstar Palace, perhaps. He opened his eyes long enough to tell Steven, 'This is the Medera River, at least north of the foothills and west of Wellham Ridge. Up in Meyers' Vale and beyond, I'm not sure it has a name.'

'Medera,' Kellin said. 'Wasn't she Prince Draven's mother?' Brand Krug had ridden north for Traver's Notch; Kellin elected to remain behind, ostensibly to offer what meagre protection she could to the sorcerers.

'Grandmother,' Gilmour corrected, opening his eyes now. 'Medera was Remond and Ravena's youngest, their only daughter. Markon and Glasson were her older brothers.'

'Our Markon, the one from Riverend?' Steven asked.

'No, Markon I, his grandfather, Remond's oldest son. He lived at Riverend Palace, ruling Eldarn when King Remond died. Glasson and Medera lived in Orindale when they were old enough to take up the reins of leadership, but it didn't last.'

'What happened?' Steven asked.

Garec said, 'I know this one. They had a war, a bloody mess. It started in the Eastlands but then spilled over into Praga and Malakasia. Right?'

'That's right, Garec,' Gilmour answered. 'Medera actually left Orindale and moved into Welstar Palace when the war began. No one ever thought to change the name of the river, I suppose.'

Steven laughed softly. 'So she was Draven's grandmother.'

'Correct,' Gilmour said. 'Medera had Nora, Draven's mother.'

'And Draven had Marek,' Garec said. 'At least, that's what the history books say.'

'Right,' Steven said, 'I remember: Draven's wife was the one who had the affair that produced Prince Marek.'

'The bastard dictator,' Kellin said.

Garec shrugged. 'If you believe rumours – I mean, once Nerak got hold of him, it didn't matter any more.'

'Good point, Garec.' Gilmour rolled gracelessly onto one hip to reach his pack. He rooted around for a loaf of bread and tore off a generous handful. Chewing, he said, 'Glasson stayed in Orindale. He had Detria, who eventually ruled in Praga, and Remond II, who took over Falkan when Glasson died. That all happened after the war.'

'So Remond was Tenner and Anaria's father?' Steven was trying to build the Grayslip family tree in his mind, glad of the distraction.

'Sorry, wrong,' Gilmour said, tearing off another mouthful of bread. 'Tenner and Anaria were Elana's children, Remond the Second's older sister, Glasson's middle child.'

'But she didn't rule Falkan,' Garec said.

'No, she was dough-headed; Remond took the Falkan throne soon after Glasson's death.'

'She was what?' Steven asked.

'Dough-headed,' Gilmour explained. 'How would you say it in English? An idiot, a lunatic, right?'

Steven shook his head. 'It's been a long time since you've visited, Gilmour. You really need to come back with me for a while.' He looked around. 'Where are we anyway? We didn't come this way last time.'

'We were in the woods south of here,' Garec said. 'I'm guessing we're another day or two out of Orindale at this rate.'

'Do you think Mark will still be there?' Kellin asked.

'Impossible to say,' Gilmour said. 'I think he'll sail on the first outgoing tide. He'll have no difficulty securing a ship and a crew; he will just need to ensure his captain knows the passages through the Northern Archipelago. Then he can stow the spell table and be safely on his way to Pellia.'

'The ship won't take him to Welstar Palace?' Steven asked.

'Too many shallows in the Welstar River,' Gilmour said. 'He'll have to offload it to a barge or a river-runner. There's quite a fleet of them.' He gestured around the deck. 'Like this one, they run with a shallow draft, even when loaded to the slats.'

'Then that may be a chance for us to take him, when they're transferring the table,' Steven said. 'He certainly can't use it at that time so he'll be vulnerable.'

'We could do that here in Orindale too,' Garec ventured.

'I don't know that we'll make it before he leaves, but if we find the right captain, we might make up valuable time as we head north.'

'That's true,' Garec said. 'We ought to hire a fast boat.'

'*You* ought to,' Gilmour said. 'Steven and I won't be coming all the way into Orindale.'

'What?' Steven was taken aback. 'Why?'

A gentle wave moved upriver and lifted the barge before moving on towards Wellham Ridge.

Garec said, 'I don't understand, Gilmour. Where are you going?'

'We'll make our way north along the coast. When we reach the fjord, we'll take that old boat Mark rigged for us and sail out to its western end, right where it meets the ocean. Ten days from now, we'll sail offshore and join you and Kellin en route to Pellia.'

As comfortable as Steven was hiking, biking and climbing amongst the craggy peaks of the Rocky Mountains back home, the thought of sailing a single-masted wooden catboat out into the shipping lanes off the coast of Eldarn's largest port made his stomach clench. 'Shit, Gilmour,' he said, 'I wish you'd given me a bit of warning.'

'I hadn't decided before this morning,' the sorcerer explained. 'While I was trying to find Kantu I saw something strange. There was a schooner carrying something that rippled with mystical energy, like a Twinmoon celebration at Sandcliff Palace. It clobbered me as I came by, almost knocked me out of my own spell.'

'Was it Mark?' Garec asked.

'No, it was too far north.'

Kellin swallowed dryly. Despite her growing familiarity with Steven and Gilmour's special abilities, she didn't like the thought that that there were insidious magics hunting for them. She asked, 'So Garec and I will hire a ship?'

'That's right,' Gilmour said.

'What do you know about ships?' she asked the bowman.

'Not a rutting thing.' Garec grinned. 'You?'

'Less, I'm afraid.'

'Grand,' Garec smiled, 'then we're the perfect pair for this charge. But Gilmour, you need to give us more than ten days. What if we don't find anyone setting sail right away? What if we can't get past the blockade? What if it takes us too long to get there? You and Steven could be capsized in a storm or blown halfway to Raiders Cove.'

'Can't we take your ship?' Kellin asked. 'Can all of us fit? Or is it too small?'

'In Mark's boat, we'd be fish food in a matter of avens,' Gilmour said sadly.

Steven blanched. 'I don't like this at all, Gilmour. Why are we doing this?'

'Because Mark will be watching for us,' he said matter-of-factly. 'He knows we didn't die in Meyers' Vale, and he knows it will only be a matter of time before we come after him. Every customs official, every dockside informant, every Malakasian sympathiser on that wharf will be looking for us, not to mention almors, wraiths, acid clouds or slimy bacterial infections he might leave waiting in the shadows. No, going into Orindale is a mistake for us.'

'But not for us?' Kellin asked.

'No. Mark will track Steven and me, just like I tracked that schooner yesterday. He will search for our mystical energy – he can almost certainly sense the far portal we carry.'

The bow rose again, higher this time, and fell into the following trough with a splash.

'What was that?' Kellin asked.

'Tide must be coming in,' Garec guessed.

'Sending waves this far upriver?' Steven said.

'What else could it be?'

Kellin returned to the discussion. 'All right, so it will be more difficult for Mark to spot us.'

'You can blend in much easier,' Gilmour agreed.

'Fine, but you still haven't answered Garec's questions.' Kellin sidled a few steps closer to Garec. She wanted to reach out for him, but fought the urge. 'What about the blockade, the customs officers, the informants? How can Garec and I find an honest captain willing to undertake an outlaw journey against the crown? None of them will do it. It's a one-shot agreement: they take us to Pellia and they never work for the Malakasian Army again. Who would take us?'

Gilmour passed the rest of his loaf around. Then he said, 'You forget, Kellin, that I have a new head, full of army knowledge. While this chubby young fellow didn't spend much time in Orindale, he did know that the blockade around the city had broken up, so getting to the wharf ought to be quite easy; you might even decide to stay right on this barge – our captain seems happy with the fare, and he hasn't given us a second glance all day. Also, I'll remind you that in a deft display of self-preservation, our good friend Steven Taylor stole some sorry slob's life savings back in Estrad.'

'Hey, Mark found it,' Steven broke it. 'I gave the guy a couple of ballpoint pens. It was a fair trade!' He smiled. 'Well, maybe not immediately, until he invents the ballpoint himself. Perhaps we did come out on the upper end of that one.'

'It's a gods-rutting fortune, Steven, and you're finally going to get to spend it buying safe passage to Pellia.'

'With my money?'

'Your stolen money, yes,' Kellin said. 'Pellia is a long way.'

'But you're not buying safe passage to Pellia,' Gilmour interrupted.

'Demonpiss,' Garec said, 'make up your mind.'

'You are buying safe passage to Averil.'

'Averil?' Kellin said, surprised. 'But that's nearly a Moon's walk from Pellia.'

Garec grinned, finally understanding. 'We're not going to Averil, Kellin.'

'Well, where in the gods-rutting ... oh, I see. We get him out to sea; we pick up these two, and we renegotiate our destination.'

'Renegotiate.' Gilmour was pleased. 'I like that way of putting it. Yes, I do.' He dug in his pack for a pipe and a tin of Falkan tobacco.

Steven said, 'You are a nefarious old man, Gilmour.'

'I am not!' He lit his pipe with a gesture and a ring of smoke encircled his head. 'This fellow was less than two hundred Twinmoons old. I'm as young as you.'

Kellin frowned. Something wasn't right.

'What's the matter?' Now Garec did put his arm around her.

'It doesn't make sense.'

'What doesn't, my dear?' Gilmour puffed while he spoke.

'Why go to all the trouble of finding your boat and sailing the length of the fjord if all you're going to do is join us on whatever vessel we hire for the trip?'

'Because I'm betting that whatever I encountered on the Ravenian Sea yesterday is not the only shipment making its way north.'

'I get it,' Garec said. 'Mark might look for you two, but what he'll find is—'

'Just another ship radiating magic,' Kellin finished Garec's thought.

'Exactly.'

'Like I said, Gilmour, you are a nefarious old—'

'Young.'

'Young man.'

Garec laughed. 'All right. I understand, but either way, I think you should give us twelve days. There's no telling how long it will take us to find a ship and a willing captain.'

'Fine,' Steven said, 'we'll make it twelve days, off the mouth of that fjord where I found you when I came back from Denver.'

Garec glanced at Kellin. 'That will give us a little time to look for Versen.'

'And maybe Sallax,' Steven added.

'Right. We might get luck—'

'Wait,' Gilmour cut him off. He stared west, his eyes focused on nothing.

Steven felt the magic gurgle to life; something was coming.

'What is it?' Kellin looked nervous but moved away from Garec, making more room to fight if necessary.

'It's Mark,' Steven said.

Gilmour nodded. 'The table's open. Brace yourselves.'

THE HARBOUR

Major Tavon didn't look tired, though she had been awake for days, but spry, well-rested and cheery. However, her uniform, unchanged in as many days, was filthy, accompanying what Captain Blackford assumed was the breakdown in Tavon's mind. Her shirt was untucked, her leather belt and boots mottled with mud and neglect, and she looked as though she had been beaten up by a gang of dockers. It was clear that the once-excellent soldier had been taken over by a destructive force that had driven her to retrieve the stone artefact, whatever it was, and see it safely to Orindale. *If we're even staying in Orindale*, Captain Blackford thought.

Major Tavon stood outside the boxy living-quarters stacked on the aft end of the westbound barge like so many discarded crates. She was standing a silent vigil; she hadn't moved from her place in front of the centremost wooden door. She had instructed Blackford, Hershaw and the single platoon of soldiers accompanying them to make fast the granite relic for their journey downstream.

Colonel Pace had come as quickly as he could to Wellham Ridge. When news reached him that the major had murdered several men and then taken the battalion into the foothills without orders or any communication with any senior officers, he had mustered a company of soldiers, including one squad of the disgusting but brutally effective Seron warriors, and made the trip east in hopes of quelling the unrest.

Major Tavon had killed him with a glance. Like Captain Denne, Colonel Pace's body was left looking as though he had been torn open by wild animals. One look from her had quelled the company commander accompanying Pace. Even the Seron seemed to know better than to mobilise against the wiry little woman. With Pace dead and Captains Hershaw and Blackford standing by, it didn't take the colonel's Orindale security force long to understand that if they crossed this woman, they would die.

Before leaving Wellham Ridge, Major Tavon had appointed the

company commander, a captain from Averil named Regic, battalion commander, promoting him to major in an impromptu and illegal ceremony. She then ordered him to take what remained of her battered and footsore battalion along with his own platoons and march them all to Orindale's southern wharf. When the newly appointed officer asked why, Tavon silenced him with a glare. 'You will find out when you arrive, Major.'

'Er, ma'am . . . you do understand that by taking the entire battalion to Orindale I am essentially abandoning our position in southern Falkan.' Major Regic looked as though he would rather have been lashed to a torture-rack than be standing here before this foul-smelling, possessed woman.

'It is of no matter any more, Regic,' Major Tavon replied. 'It's time for this occupation force to move on.' She turned to leave.

'To move on, ma'am?' Regic said hesitantly.

'To move on,' Tavon repeated, then shouted for Captain Blackford, who was never far away. 'Come with me,' she told him. 'We need to get messages to Rona as quickly as possible. We'll need riders, six of our best—'

'We don't have many left in any condition . . .' His voice died away as he blanched and beads of sweat broke out along his hairline: he had interrupted her.

Tavon stopped, stood ramrod-straight and said, 'I hope you realise what will happen if you ever do that to me again, Captain.'

Blackford swallowed; it seemed to take avens for his throat to open far enough to speak. 'Yes, ma'am.'

'Good. I don't care what condition they're in. I want them ready to ride for Rona. This far east it seems a shame to wait until we're in the capital.'

'Good point, ma'am.'

'Now, if you and Major Regic are through second-guessing me, I would like to get our cargo loaded on the first barge ready. Bring Captain Hershaw and one platoon of our healthiest soldiers.'

'Yes, ma'am.' The captain saluted. After her dough-headed forced march into the foothills, he knew without checking that there was not a full platoon of healthy soldiers left in the battalion. No matter; he and Hershaw would scrape together the strongest of the lot and encourage the major to grant them some much-needed rest on their journey downriver.

Now, standing a post on the barge Tavon had chosen to carry her precious cargo safely into Orindale Harbour, Captain Blackford watched large clumpy snowflakes fall on the Falkan capital in one of the coastal city's rare snowstorms. The flakes dusted Major Tavon's head and shoulders; she didn't bother to brush them off. Blackford marvelled at how whatever it was that had purloined his commander's body could stand so still for so long, staring out at nothing, perhaps seeing nothing, even ignoring the snowflakes that clung to her lashes and melted into her eyes. Tavon didn't blink.

The barge passed through the city towards the harbour. Blackford and Hershaw huddled in one of the shack-like cabins. It was clear the major did not plan to remain in the capital very long. Before dispatching riders east towards the Merchants' Highway and the Ronan border, Blackford had sneaked a look at one of Tavon's hastily scribbled messages: using Prince Malagon and General Oaklen's names, she had ordered the entire occupation army in the Eastlands back to Pellia as soon as ships could be commandeered and safe passage ensured. With a northern Twinmoon coming, tides would be high in the archipelago. If the army was needed in Malakasia, there would be no better time to order them all home than now.

Given the inanity of Tavon's dispatches, Captain Blackford was determined to be as far from the major as luck and determination could get him before word of her exploits reached the officers in Orindale. General Oaklen, wherever he was this Twinmoon, would not appreciate any field commander using his name to direct entire divisions home to Pellia. Blackford guessed that the general had made his way back into Orindale; he might even be staying at the old imperial palace just off the river. He certainly wasn't within screaming range of any of the messages Major Tavon had sent to Rona. She had run rampant over the battalion while they trudged through the snowy drifts south of Wellham Ridge. Here in the capital, with an entire palace full of Malakasian officers hunkered down for the winter Twinmoon, circumstances would be different; surely she wouldn't be able to engage in random murders without drawing attention? He couldn't guess what Tavon had planned for the barge or the stone table, but he was pretty sure that things were about to get much worse.

Puffy snowflakes fell about his face as he stood in silence, waiting for his commanding officer to direct him once again. He watched the city snowscape roll by. The barge was passing through rows and rows of trenches dug hastily two Twinmoons earlier, a blockade of the entire city by every available soldier in the southern divisions.

Blackford's own trench had been several hundred paces north of the Medera, hidden now by the snow.

Then came the imperial palace, a grand old edifice with its sprawling gardens – lying fallow under trampled snow – stretching out towards the wharf and the commercial districts. One wing had been destroyed recently in a freak explosion; Blackford had heard the blast from his trench. Now he could see boarded-up windows and one collapsed wall, the stones of which had been piled into a heap. On through a well-to-do neighbourhood; he wondered what people did to afford such homes, especially in an occupied nation. On his lieutenant's wages – Blackford didn't expect ever to see one Marek of a captain's pay – he would not have been able to purchase even a quarter of such a home. Slate roofs, stone walls, multiple chimneys; who were these people? Business owners? Ship captains? They certainly weren't soldiers. Most of them had probably worked out some kind of lucrative, symbiotic agreement with the occupation—

Tavon was gone.

Captain Blackford rushed aft and knocked on one of the dilapidated doors. 'Hershaw,' he hissed, 'wake up, get out here.'

He ran to a corporal standing watch. 'You there,' he said to the startled soldier who'd jumped to rigid attention, 'where is the major?'

'Sorry, sir. If she's not back there, where she's been for the past two days, sir, I don't know, sir.'

'Rutting whores,' Blackford muttered, leaving the corporal looking confused. He went back to rapping on Hershaw's cabin. 'Captain, I need you out here right away,' he called again.

Nervous, uncertain, needing an outlet for his anxiety, Blackford started pacing and swearing. Wringing his hands, he mumbled to himself, 'Rutting demonpissing ... opening the whoring thing again ... dead out here ... godswhoring cold—'

On the riverbank above him, a heap of large barrels stood in haphazard arrangement outside a waterfront alehouse, a big wooden place with a sloping roof, and plenty of raucous noise coming from within. It looked, sounded and smelled like a lonely soldier's spiritual redemption, and Blackford found himself longing for a tankard of ale, maybe two. That would set him right. He watched a boy, probably no more than seventy-five Twinmoons, hurrying out of a side-door to scoop a bucketful of what looked to be sawdust from the closest of the wooden containers. *That's for the floor, gods love 'em, to soak up the blood and piss.* He looked again for Hershaw, although for what, other than helping him calm down, he couldn't say. *There'll be blood on this floor soon enough*, he thought to himself. *No sawdust here to soak it up, though.*

They were about to pass under the massive arched bridge separating Orindale's northern wharf and its fine taverns, expensive apartments and fancy businesses from the southern wharf, where the many tarred and scarred wooden fingers of the town pier reached out into deep water. Compared with the northern wharf it was a dingy, colourless place, yet this was where Orindale's heart beat the strongest.

When Hershaw finally emerged, Blackford nearly ran him down. 'She's gone,' he barked.

Hershaw blanched. 'Gone? What do you mean she's gone?'

'I think she's in there.' Blackford nodded towards the ramshackle cabin that housed the mysterious stone table.

'Oh, gods-rut-a-whore.' Hershaw ran his fingers through sleep-tousled hair and started straightening his crumpled uniform. 'What do we do?'

'I don't know. Wait? Take cover? Swim for shore?'

The corporal Blackford had startled remained at his post, but he was staring at the two nervous officers, obviously straining to hear what was being said. His superiors were not instilling him with much confidence.

The barge passed beneath the stone bridge and, moving quickly with the current, slipped out the inlet and into the harbour.

With the corporal watching, Hershaw tried to project an air of quiet confidence and leadership; instead, he looked like someone with bad stomach cramps, trying his best to stand upright.

Blackford said, 'Let's send him.'

'Who?'

'Him.' He nodded towards the anxious sentry.

'Send him where?'

'The imperial palace, the old Barstag place. It's not far from here. He could sound the alarm, rally the whole division, tell the whole story, General Oaklen's dispatches, Pace's murder, all of it. But we need to act quickly—'

The barge moved towards a group of mooring buoys several hundred paces offshore; it would be too far to swim in this weather. They had either to convince the corporal to slip over the side right away, or one of them would have to go themselves.

Hershaw pressed his lips together in a tight smile, made eye-contact with the soldier and waved him over—

It was too late. A low resonating humming sound began behind them, coming from the major's quarters. Blackford and Hershaw braced themselves for something terrible, but even so, they both jumped when the first ship, a Malakasian schooner moored nearby, began to break apart.

Mark slogged through the muck, stepping over exposed roots and fallen trees, all the while trying to get to the centre of the marble trough, to the bridge. He hadn't noticed the bridge last time; he had been distracted by the tadpoles with their tumours, and the snakes chasing them down. But the bridge was there, lit by the glow coming from the top of the shallow rise. It spanned the marble trough, a short arch also made of marble, a miniature version of something he might have seen in Venice, the *Ponte de Rialto* . . . but Mark decided to cross there, nevertheless. He didn't want to be back in that water again.

Why have a bridge if I don't need to use it? Mark thought, and wasn't surprised when someone answered; it sounded like him.

Now you're thinking. Why don't you come up here with me?

He stopped near the edge of the nightmarish koi pond. It was longer than he remembered and lined on both sides by rows of marble columns. *Shaker, baker, candlestick-maker columns? Neo-classical. That's it. Neo-classical columns, the ones like they have in front of the Capitol Building in DC, hell, they're all over DC, marble bones holding the place up.*

That's not the right place, Mark.

Blow me; I'm busy.

The bridge was a trap; it had to be. He could jump this trough. It wasn't more than four or five feet across. Hell, he could step over it, step through it. He'd already been elbow-deep in the thing, and as long as there were none of those snakes – he was fairly sure the crippled tadpole sperm were no threat – he'd be fine.

I didn't put the bridge there, Mark. You did.

I did?

I don't give a shit if you get across. I'm fine over here by myself.

You sound like me. Why do you sound like me?

Blow me; I'm busy.

'Fucker,' Mark said aloud. 'Where are you? Why don't you leave the lights on in here, and I'll come kick the shit out of you, just for fun. Huh?'

The lights dimmed and Mark heard something slither through the slime. Panic gripped him; his voice changed and he begged, 'No! No, leave them on.'

It does get friendly in here when it's dark, doesn't it?

Something crawled from his boot onto the skin of his lower leg; it had too many of its own legs to count. Mark swatted it away and felt it crunch beneath his palm. 'Screw it,' he said, 'I'll take the bridge.'

Good choice.

He pushed on until he reached the marble trough then hugging the perimeter, he walked on the stone coping. It was solid and clean, free of marshy debris, and it made for faster going. He just had to be careful he didn't step off and slip into that putrid water. He shivered at thought of it.

The tadpoles were there, not fleeing this time but lazing in the pool. Fat bulbous tumours still disfigured them. *There mustn't be any snakes around*, Mark thought.

You want snakes?

No.

The others had a job to do for you.

For me?

For me.

They're gone?

We have a few snakes left in here if you need one.

Mark squinted through the gloom. Whoever was talking to him – *thinking to me* – had to be the one working on top of the rise. If he could just get over the bridge, he could run up there, hit him, just a couple of quick cathartic shots to the head, and then make for the clearing. That sky meant safety; somehow he knew it did.

He slipped and fell, hitting his head on one of the columns. The marble was wet in places, and treacherous. He wouldn't make that mistake again.

Rolling over, he used the column to regain his feet, but something gripped his right ankle, a whorl of snarled root protruding through the muck. Mark tugged his lower leg, trying to extricate himself. It was hot here, and humid, hard to breathe. His clothes were soaked through with sweat and clung to his flesh like a peelable second skin. He was covered head to toe in marsh muck and shit … and he reached for the root, pulled hard and slipped his boot free.

A coral snake – *those are poisonous!* – slipped from behind the root and up onto the back of his hand. Mark, covered almost entirely in goose pimples, screeched and jerked back reflexively. The rainbow-coloured serpent went on its way, slipping over the root, across the marble ledge and into the trough.

Told you we had a few more.

Fuck you.

I'm not the one doing this to you, Mark. I was happy with you in the dark. I have what I need, and I'll call you when I need you again.

The lights began to dim. Before they faded all the way to black, Mark checked the length of the rectangular koi pond. It *was* marble, narrow, shallow, and lined as far as he could see with neo-classical columns. Where had he seen these columns before? The Capitol Building. Those were the ones that flared up in his memory, anyway.

Wrong again. The voice was fading with the lights. *That's not the right place, Mark,* it said, echoing its earlier admonition.

Well, where then?

The column was cold. Real marble had a way of staying cold, no matter where you put it. *The marble columns of Hell would be nice and cool, a good place to rest while enjoying a cold drink, whatever they're serving down there.* He tried to memorise the lie of the land between himself and the bridge. *If I can follow the columns, I'll get there. I'll cross in the dark. That'll surprise him, the bastard. I'll cross in the dark and the next time he turns on the lights, I'll be there.*

There were eight or nine columns between Mark and the bridge. They were each about twenty feet apart. *One hundred and sixty feet. I can make that. Just stay on the edge, I can make it.*

He remembered the coral snake. *That one'll bite you. The others wouldn't, but that one will. That's the one I have to watch.* Mark used the dying light to check for the colourful serpent. It was there, keeping pace with him in the water. It would know if he moved. He hugged the column; it felt good against his face. He had to stay put. The snake would bite him – *more than once, too. It'll go on for a while* – if he tried to reach the bridge in the darkness.

Night closed in.

Where had he seen these columns?

The Capitol? New Orleans? Europe? They were all over Europe. The Gloriette. What the hell is a Gloriette?

Now you're thinking.

It was dark again; the coral snake slithered onto the edge of the marble trough and waited between Mark's boots.

'Over the side! Over the side!' Gilmour shouted, shoving Garec and Kellin towards the rail where the barge's first mate had tethered their horses. 'Just cut the reins, *cut them!*' he yelled, checking to be sure the spell book and far portal were safely lashed to his saddle.

'What is it?' Steven followed the others. The magic was bubbling over, preparing for battle.

Gilmour ignored him. 'Lead the horses to that shore. We'll go north, find cover and dry out. But be quick now, quick. You have to get as far into the shallows as possible. Don't look; just head for shore.' The riverbank was no more than sixty or seventy paces off, but to Gilmour the relative safety of dry land seemed a Moon's travel away.

'Gilmour!' Steven shouted, 'what is it? What's he doing? What's coming for us?'

'I was too tired, too rutting tired from yesterday, from chatting too long with Milla,' he lamented. 'I didn't feel it – I *should* have, when those waves rolled past.'

'The waves?'

Gilmour tried to untie his horse's reins, then, frustrated, cast a noisy blast that blast through the starboard gunwale. 'Just ride off the deck and into the water. But stay with your horse. They'll be able to move through the shallows and up the riverbank faster than we will.'

Garec held his own horse by the bridle, trying to keep it steady after Gilmour's explosion. 'They won't step into the river, Gilmour. They know how cold it is.'

'I'll help them,' he said, his hand already glowing red. 'Now, go.' Gilmour slapped Kellin's horse, sending a bolt of Larion lightning into the animal's hindquarter, and with a loud whinny, the horse, with Kellin in tow, plunged through the broken slats and into the frigid waters of the Medera River.

'You do have a way with women,' Garec said with a wry grin.

'No time to chat,' Gilmour replied, and slapped Garec's horse with a similar charge.

Still confused, Steven said, 'It's too cold. Why are we doing this? Let's stand and fight here, where it's dry.'

Gilmour took him by both shoulders and shoved him towards his horse. 'Mount up. Stay in the saddle, just hang on. She'll get to shore; you just hang on.'

'Gilmour, what—?'

The old Larion Senator pointed downriver.

Steven gaped at the wall of water coming towards them. 'Oh my dear Christ.' It was massive, nearly eighty feet high, an unstoppable nightmare dragging all manner of debris: broken bits of lumber, cracked spars trailing torn sails, wooden doors, fence-posts, and scores of uprooted trees. What remained of a ship, wrenched in two, rode the crest of the rogue flood. There were carcasses, too: cows, a horse, most of a pig, and too many people. Steven set his jaw and looked away. Reaching shore was pointless; they would need to be at least a hundred feet higher to avoid being swept all the way back to Wellham Ridge. He knew they wouldn't make it; the barge would be reduced to splinters.

Somewhere near the bow he heard a scream and then a splash. It was followed a moment later by two others. The crew was abandoning ship.

'Go, go!' Gilmour shouted, smacking Steven's horse into the river behind Kellin and Garec. 'Stay with her, hold on as long as you can.' He checked a final time for the spell book and far portal, then spurred his own horse as, with a deafening roar, the floodtide ploughed its way towards Wellham Ridge.

The barge was lifted up and tumbled head over heels before it finally shattered in a prolonged ripping crack, like so many brittle bones snapping beneath the weight of a hundred thousand tons of water.

'Alen?' Milla touched him gently on the shoulder. 'Alen? Are you awake?'

Cramped and stiff as a corpse, Alen Jasper opened one eye, swallowed dryly and groaned, 'I am now, Pepperweed. What's wrong? You need the pot? There's a clean one under the—'

'Something's happening,' the little girl cut him off.

Alen propped himself up and rubbed his eyes. Yawning, he asked, 'What's the matter?'

'The people are in trouble. Should I try to help them?'

'What are you—?' Alen sat up, found a goblet beside the bed and drained whatever had been inside.

'The people, they're far away, but they're in trouble from the water.'

Now Alen felt it begin, quietly at first, like the low hum of a familiar tune. He shrugged off his irritability and focused his attention inward. 'What is it, Pepperweed? Can you tell where it's coming from?'

'Far away, back where Gilmour fell when I let him go,' she whispered.

Alen tried to hone in on the monstrously powerful magic, but it was distant, half a world away. 'You're right, Milla,' he said finally. 'It's coming right from where Fantu— um, Gilmour said he was going.'

'Should I try to help them?' she asked again.

'Do you think you can?' He let the distant drone fade, knowing the shockwaves would reach him in a moment, like huge ripples churning a mill pond.

'I can try.'

Orindale Harbour was the busiest port in Eldarn, even during the coldest winter Twinmoon. Moorings were rented by the Moon when necessary, but most captains paid for a few days' anchorage at a time. Cargoes were loaded, offloaded, speculated on, bought and sold, day and night, in all weathers and at all tides. The northern wharf was tucked into a crooked semi-circle of a cove, a natural jetty of topsoil and rocks rolled or dragged across southern Falkan by the river over the ages. The southern wharf was larger, if more sparsely populated, and it dominated the lower part of the waterfront, a sprawling testament to the city's industrial growth.

On the day that Mark Jenkins sailed into the harbour, thinly disguised as Major Nell Tavon of Malagon Whitward's occupation army, absent without leave and in command of a missing platoon, there were thirty-two merchant and naval vessels docked, moored or making their way into the harbour on the inbound tide. Hundreds more small barges, skiffs, ketches and transport vessels worked the harbour as well, but Mark was interested only in the fat ones, the fancy sailing ships rigged for the gusty headwinds that blew along the Ravenian Sea. A scattering of naval vessels monitored the passage of merchant ships to and from the wharf; Mark didn't give these a second glance.

With the spell table opened, his first target was a Malakasian schooner, which started breaking apart audibly. When the mainmast snapped, it was loud enough that Captain Blackford covered his ears and he was still holding his head when the thick post crashed through the foredeck, bringing down the main and topsails in a tangle of canvas and rigging. The hull opened and the sea poured in, but by that time Blackford had been distracted by the devastation in other quarters and when he briefly looked back to the schooner, it was already gone, the few crew members who had escaped rowing towards shore in an overfilled launch boat Mark had overlooked – but before they reached the wharf, he'd spotted it and set the small boat aflame. A couple of sailors managed to swim the last few paces to shore, but that was all.

A Pragan galleon, crammed to bursting with textiles, tanned leather, mortar sand and quarried stone was also on fire. Her crew had been watching the schooner snap in two when their own vessel started to burn. Their screams filled the air as they tried to reach the sides and jump over. The flames, oddly resistant, quickly engulfed the galleon, and once the rigging went up and the fore, main and mizzen masts were burning, the firelight lit the whole harbour. Heat radiated across the water and the sailors working Major Tavon's barge felt it warm their faces. The fire was a beacon, and could be seen from anywhere in the city, a harbinger of grim events yet to come.

As the news spread, the city of Orindale turned out in force to watch as frigates, barges, two more galleons, a massive carrack and a handful of sleek schooners were all sent to the bottom, ripped in half, punctured, blown to splintered bits or simply set ablaze and burned to the waterline. One sloop, a single-masted vessel from Strandson, was lifted from the water and those watching from the relative safety of the wharf talked for Twinmoons about seeing its keel clear the surface as it rolled lazily to port then back to starboard before wrenching itself in two, snapping like a handful of kindling and disappearing beneath the waves. Two barges were swept clean of their cargo by rogue waves and then broken into flotsam. The bits that remained afloat caught fire, looking like a string of macabre lanterns floating upstream.

A Falkan carrack, one of the largest ships currently making its stately way into the harbour, came about hastily, despite the tide, and endeavoured to tack into the open sea. Onlookers cheered – it was a local ship, after all – and when the captain ordered the top and main sails set, the waterfront erupted with an ovation Blackford could hear halfway across the harbour.

'Stop cheering!' he shouted, 'don't you understand? You'll make it worse! Stop cheering!'

The cheering did stop when the carrack exploded. It was almost to the horizon, almost into the currents – almost free – when the proud giant simply blew apart. The concussion was massive, throwing Blackford and his men to the deck as the shockwaves passed by. He had never seen such a disaster, had never heard such an explosion – nothing in Eldarn exploded like that! This was the work of a god.

All manner of vessels set out on a mercy mission in hopes of rescuing the hundreds of sailors, soldiers and merchant seamen now drifting amongst the floating debris, though many had already drowned; either they couldn't swim or they had succumbed to the cold.

Fathers and mothers, fat merchants, aged grandparents and children barely old enough to grasp an oar all rowed, hauled lines, gripped tillers and tied great loops into heavy rescue lines, a flotilla of venerable, chipped, rotting and battered family boats, making their way into the harbour to save what lives they could. Even the soldiers, the Malakasian brutes who periodically beat them, or hanged them for no reason on the common near the imperial palace, even they did not deserve to die like this.

Mark attacked them all, using five-foot waves to wipe the sea clean of the determined but irritating little boats. The more seaworthy craft, those that rode the five-foot swells, he set on fire or snapped into splinters. There was howling from everywhere as people burned to death, drowned or succumbed to hypothermia: everyone cried for mercy in the same miserable language.

When it was over, the galleon burned brightest, a signal fire warning all craft away from this place. With the chill snaking into their bones, many of the spectators, their lust for carnage sated, realised with a catch in their throats that perhaps the gods weren't done with them yet; perhaps the devastation they had witnessed was just the beginning; perhaps the city itself was next. There was a moment of stunned silence, broken only by the crackle and snap of the flames and the piercing cries of the injured and dying, then panic blew through the crowd like a fogbank and, pushing, pulling, shoving, punching and kicking, the people of Orindale turned and fled as one.

Captain Hershaw offered a hand to Captain Blackford, still lying on the barge's deck. They were both in shock, mute in disbelief.

'Why?' Blackford finally managed.

Hershaw gestured towards the southern wharf. Three ships remained intact, tied to a deepwater pier and facing north, as if they knew somehow that they would survive the morning. These were frigates, giants, capable of carrying massive cargoes to anywhere in Eldarn.

Hershaw said, 'I don't think she wants to be followed.'

'So we're going home in those?'

'Not just us.'

Blackford tried for a moment to figure out who might be joining them when he heard a change in the low humming coming from Major Tavon's quarters. It was slight but unmistakable as the pitch ratcheted up a tone or two, resonating with an extra pinch of mystical intensity.

He looked at Hershaw. 'Rutters! She's not yet done!'

As if hearing him, the harbour itself rose up. Swelling first in the middle, a hummock of smooth water bubbling up from below, it grew into a rounded hill, higher than the tallest buildings along the waterfront. Burning ships tumbled off its slopes and were extinguished in the waves. Bits of jetsam and floating debris slipped down its sides and scuttled across the surface. Still the hill grew until it was a tremendous liquid dome, dwarfing the waterfront like an alpine range.

'Great rutting whores,' Blackford said, 'she's going to destroy the city!'

'Let's go,' Hershaw said, drawing his sword.

'She'll kill us both,' Blackford argued, 'we can't—'

'We have to.'

Trembling, Blackford followed, hoping he would get the chance to run Tavon through, especially if she was distracted, even for an instant, by the stone table. *Or by killing Hershaw.*

But before they had reached her, she struck, and the blast ripped the door from its leather hinges and sent much of it ripping through Captain Hershaw's body in jagged splinters. He was dead before he stopped tumbling, somewhere amidships.

'Blackford!' Tavon screamed.

He approached warily. His face and arms were bleeding, and he feared he would spend the next aven picking splinters out of his skin, but he was still here, still alive. 'Yes, ma'am,' he said politely.

'I want you to watch this, Blackford.' Tavon was elbow-deep in what looked like a waist-high circular pool. Blackford knew better, though. It was the stone table, transformed somehow by magic into a fluid, unending cauldron of energy and power. He watched the colours change, flickering from hue to hue as the major's wiry arms pulled and pressed spells and charms about inside. There was an animal, something that looked like a tadpole, and then a snake, and a hideous-looking fellow with a grim countenance, if that was possible. There was a creature Blackford guessed was an almor and then a blurry and indistinct image of a man, a South Coaster hiding in a stone temple with a rainbow-coloured serpent coiled at his feet.

'Why are you doing this?' he whispered. 'Please, Major, enough.'

'Oh, shut up, Blackford, your breath stinks. It'd stop my watch if I hadn't given it to that Ronan slut.' The pool changed again; this time, Blackford could see the outline of the Orindale waterfront. The northern and southern wharfs were on either side of the inlet. He saw the Medera and the stone bridge arching above it, connecting everything in the Falkan capital. The bridge looked different, though: cleaner, whiter, as if it had been carved from pristine marble. When the centre of the table rose up in an aquamarine hummock, Blackford understood what he was about to witness.

'Please, Major,' he repeated, shaking.

'Watch this, Captain.' She released her hold on the hill of magical energy she had called up beneath the waters of Orindale Harbour and, as the tiny hillock of blue careened through the imagined inlet and across the waterfront Blackford could see lining the circular edge of the stone table, he heard the deafening roar of the actual harbour rushing east to swallow the wharf and flood the Medera from Orindale to Wellham Ridge. Inside the spell table, Blackford saw the waters crash over the stone bridge, collapsing it like a bit of folded paper. Without looking towards the city, he knew that the bridge spanning the Medera had fallen as well. There had been hundreds of people on that bridge. They'd be dead now; there was no way they could have survived. Hearing the fading thunder as the great floodtide rolled east into Falkan, Blackford tasted something tangy and metallic in his throat. The dead would number in the thousands.

'Captain.'

'Yes, ma'am?' He was crying and didn't care. He wiped his nose with his sleeve. No matter. He hadn't changed his uniform since they had ventured into the foothills.

'I want you to seize those three frigates and get them prepared for a journey north.' She pointed towards the ships still tethered to the wharf. They bobbed gently in the small swells that skidded along the shore in the aftermath of the mammoth tide.

'No, ma'am.' Blackford swallowed, coughed and said, 'Kill me now, ma'am.'

Tavon laughed: a hearty, belly-laugh that chilled Blackford's blood. 'Oh, but that is funny, Captain.' She withdrew her hands from the pool, waved them over the surface and waited while the depthless cauldron congealed and then froze into solid granite. Still laughing, she picked a small bit of stone from its centre and slipped it into her uniform pocket. 'No, really, Blackford. I want you to get those ships ready. Pay the captains, kill them; I don't care, but I want them ready to sail by high tide, three days from now.' Major Tavon chuckled then mimicked him, 'Kill me now, ma'am.'

'Yes, please.' His hands were shaking and he laced his fingers together in hopes of appearing brave.

'You're a coward, Blackford, a whimpering baby. You don't want to die any more than I want to kill you. I need you. When I'm through needing you, if you've done what I ask, you'll enjoy a long life. At that time, whether you're a coward or a hero, I don't give a shit. I'll be going home. So, stop dicking around making jokes and get those boats ready to go.'

Blackford took a breath and tried, unsuccessfully, to compose himself. 'To where, ma'am?'

'Ah, finally a cogent response. Good. To Pellia. I want as many soldiers as we can muster, including your former colleagues from Wellham Ridge, on board, well fed and ready to hit the road in three days. Got it?'

'Hit the road, ma'am?'

'Right, skedaddle, bug out, take off, hit the highway, jet back to Kansas with Toto. Know what I mean?'

'Yes, ma'am. To Pellia.'

'Excellent, Blackford. Now, get us south to one of those open piers. I want you to scare us up some beer and maybe a burger.'

Blackford backed away. 'Yes, ma'am. Whatever you like, ma'am.' He kept eye contact with her, not because he wanted her to see that he had summoned every bit of his courage to stand there with Captain Hershaw's body spilling blood all over the deck, but rather because he did not want to be caught looking at her pocket. *The stone. Don't look down, or she'll know. But you've got to get that stone.*

Orindale Harbour was a ruin. The waterfront had sustained massive damage, and apart from the three frigates Blackford had been ordered to commandeer and the few naval ships that had almost miraculously escaped the devastation, there was not another seaworthy vessel in sight.

Jacrys' skin tightened into gooseflesh. *Something's wrong.* He didn't have much magic, just a few spells he learned from the failed carnival conjurer-turned-fennaroot addict, a lodger beneath the brothel where he had worked as a boy, but he knew enough to sense that something significant was occurring. Rolling over the Ravenian Sea like summer thunder, the distant spells penetrated the weary spy's bones. Someone powerful was painting with a broad brush.

'Malagon,' he whispered. 'So you're not dead after all.' He rested against the bulkhead. 'Unless,' he mused, 'it's someone else.'

As he did every time he woke, Jacrys tried to draw a full breath. It was the benchmark against which he charted his recovery. General Oaklen's healer, an elderly man named— named some rutting thing the injured spy couldn't recall; Jacrys had been so thoroughly smothered by the mind-numbing power of his querlis poultice that he couldn't remember much more than sleeping, ordering Captain Thadrake to confiscate Carpello's yacht, and enlisting the services of ... Mirron. That was it: Mirron Something, one of General Oaklen's healers. Otherwise, the only recent memories were recollections of how well he had managed to breathe the previous day, and of Brexan Carderic, the partisan spy haunting his dreams.

He breathed in now, his lungs filling with smoke from the wood Mirron had left burning in the brazier. Jacrys coughed; pain stabbed through his chest like a rapier.

'Pissing demons,' he choked, 'pissing motherwhoring demons.' He could barely speak; his voice was a whisper, barely audible above the sounds of Carpello Jax's private yacht, a sleek, twin-masted ketch the bloated Orindale merchant almost never used. Carpello had struggled with sea travel.

'Mirron,' Jacrys wheezed. He sucked in a stabilising lungful then cried, 'Mirron!'

The healer ducked in from the companionway and saw Jacrys fighting to sit upright. 'No, no, no, sir,' he pleaded, 'you must lie back down. Look at you; you're all sweating and flushed. What were you trying to do, sing?'

Mirron Something was an army officer, but he was more a fixture in the division than a legitimate rung in the military hierarchy. He was over four hundred and twenty Twinmoons old, and he couldn't remember the last order he had given that anyone had actually followed. He was alarmingly tall and thin, with a head of unkempt lank white hair; he looked rather like a wall torch that had grown tired of standing about in a boring sconce.

'Breathe, you worthless lump of grettanshit, I was trying to *breathe*,' Jacrys growled. Worn out with the effort of summoning the healer, he let his head fall back into the pillows and ignored Mirron rambling on about torn scar tissue, internal bleeding and allowing his lung to heal fully before shouting. Jacrys concentrated on his respiration. *In, hollow tree . . . easy . . . out, loose gravel . . . easy. And again.* Slowly, he regained control. 'I wish to go up on deck.'

'No sir, you mustn't,' Mirron said, agitated. 'You need more rest, another Moon at the very least. Every time you tear that scar tissue, you end up all the way back at the beginning of this journey – shouting, standing up, walking around, all these things put you at risk. You may already be bleeding again in your lung—'

'I don't care,' Jacrys snarled through gritted teeth. Sweat dripped from his face onto the coverlet that stank of smoke, spilled broth and pungent bodily fluids – even his berth revolted him.

'Here,' Mirron said as he reached into a leather pouch, 'let me give you another application of querlis.'

'No, not that. It's like getting hit in the head with a club. Trust me on that, I know.' He pushed Mirron's hands away. 'I want to go on deck. I want to breathe something other than the gods-rutting smoke you've got billowing in here. I want to stand up and I want real food.'

'As your healer, I must tell you tha—'

'You're my subordinate, and I am giving you an order,' Jacrys whispered. 'If you can't follow it, get Captain Thadrake in here, and I will have you in irons for the remainder of our journey.' It was an empty threat and Jacrys knew it; Carpello might have left a cupboard-full of silk tunics in the main cabin, but there were no manacles on his yacht.

'Very well.' Mirron poked his head into the companionway and shouted for the captain, who arrived a moment later. 'He'd like to stand up, go on deck and eat solid food,' the healer said. 'It may kill him.'

Looking at Jacrys, Captain Thadrake said, 'You could die. Do you understand that, sir?'

'Of course I understand,' Jacrys whispered, 'and I can assure you I'm not planning on dancing. I just want fresh air.'

'All right,' Thadrake said, 'we'll see you on deck.'

Mirron said, 'I reiterate: he could die.' And then to Jacrys, 'Sir, you could die.'

Jacrys nodded.

The captain said, 'Listen, Mirron, if he dies, we'll toss his body over the side and make for Southport, or better yet, Estrad Village. I'll buy the jemma-steaks and you buy the beer.'

Jacrys coughed back a rare bout of genuine laughter. Clutching his chest, he wheezed, 'That's the spirit, Captain.'

'See you on deck, sir,' Thadrake repeated, and was gone.

Once outside, he felt energised, refreshed by the icy cold. He stood at the starboard rail, almost hoping for a wave to splash him in the face. They had come far north, through the Narrows, and were closing in on the archipelago. With any luck, they would ride the Twinmoon tides through the Northeast Channel and into Pellia. Memories of his youth intruded as he stood there. Below, in his berth, only pain and anger kept him company – *and the girl, don't forget her. She's been with you all along* – but out here, Jacrys found himself wrapped in a sense of homecoming.

Watching the waves, he remembered his father, and evenings kneading bread dough beside the hearth. His mother had died when he was young, and he had grown up with only his father to look after him – but that was fine; he had no regrets. It had been so long since he had been in Pellia that he wondered if his father was even alive, and if they would find anything to say to one another. Would he even recognise his father if they met in the street? 'It's worth a try,' he murmured to himself. They were approaching the Northeast Channel; it wouldn't be long now.

'Feeling better?'

Jacrys jumped. In his melancholic, injured state he had permitted someone to sneak up behind him. Perhaps his decision to retire had come at exactly the right moment. Smiling, he said, 'Captain Ellis?'

Wenra Ellis joined him at the rail. Middle-aged, wiry and obviously tough, Captain Ellis had run Carpello's yacht for nearly thirty Twin-moons. The sandy-haired sailor had skin like tanned hide, but she was not unattractive; still, Jacrys seriously doubted that Carpello had ever managed to bed this woman. He enjoyed a good fight in bed, but Carpello also enjoyed winning, and Jacrys didn't think Captain Ellis was the type of woman to tolerate that sort of nonsense.

'Going home?' she asked him.

He nodded. 'I grew up just south of the city, on the west bank. It was a nice old place. My father did a lot to make it comfortable for us.'

'Is that where you're bound?' She checked the main sheet and automatically tugged on a ratline.

Jacrys said, 'Eventually, maybe.'

'Is he still there?'

'I don't know.'

'I don't know who you are, or what you do for General Oaklen,' Captain Ellis began, 'but I'm impressed that you've been assigned a healer and a company commander just to see you home.'

There was no longer any point in hiding who he was, Jacrys thought. 'I was a spy for Prince Malagon and his officers, a good one,' he whispered. 'Recently I killed a powerful partisan, Gilmour Stow, who was rumoured to be a Larion Senator – though I don't know if I believe that, because when I stabbed him, he just died. No magic, no great blinding light, nothing. But I'm sick, I'm tired, and I'm hurt. And more than anything I want to go home.'

'A spy?' She sounded a little surprised, and maybe a little impressed.

'I'm out of shape,' Jacrys explained. 'I've been hit too many times, climbed too many icy mountains, stabbed too many sleeping partisans. Just now, you came up behind me, and I had no idea you were there. Five Twinmoons ago, I would have gutted you before you'd even realised I'd heard you.'

Captain Ellis backed away a step, her forehead creased. 'I'll be careful next time.' She forced a chuckle.

'Not to worry,' Jacrys said, 'all I want now is to go home.' *That isn't true, you liar. More than anything, you want Brexan Carderic: you covet her, you who have never coveted anything. You want to feel her, to taste the salty tang of her sweat as it runs across her skin, to taste her blood as it splashes over her breasts. And you want to kill her, and that's what's different: you've never wanted to kill anyone before, not Steven Taylor, not even Gilmour Stow. You want to kill Brexan Carderic.*

'Well, sir,' she said, 'going home can be a cathartic experience for any of us. Perhaps you'll find the rejuvenation you need to get back to work.'

'I hope not.' He stared out across the waves. The winter sun, cool but bright, shone in blinding glints off the water.

'Looking for redemption?'

'There is no redemption for me.'

'Just peace and quiet then?'

'A place to regroup, to decide what comes next, and especially to let go of a few things.'

'I know that feeling,' she said a wry laugh.

'You do?' It was Jacrys' turn to be surprised.

'I work for a Falkan traitor, a man who beats and molests young women. It's no secret: Carpello Jax is a monster. Do you know how many nights he's slept in the main stateroom while I've been up here, considering what an enormous favour I could do for Eldarn if I just slipped in and slit his throat?'

'Many?'

'None.'

'None?' Jacrys smirked. 'Let me guess: because you have learned how to let go of a few things.'

'Exactly.'

'So how do you look at yourself in the mirror, Captain?'

'I don't,' she said simply. 'I've never been what anyone would call pretty—'

'Now, I wouldn't—'

'So,' she cut him off, 'I've never had any need for mirrors. If I need to get a look at myself, I do my job well and then try to catch a clear glimpse of my face reflected in the silver that fat son-of-a-whore pays me to take care of his little boat.'

'That sounds like overly simple cynicism, Captain Ellis.' Jacrys gripped the rail with both hands. The talking was wearing him down.

'Overly simple cynicism, Jacrys?' Captain Ellis laughed. 'You have many mirrors in your house?'

He was beaten – but he felt a bit better. The truth was doing him good. 'No, I suppose I don't.'

Captain Ellis changed the subject. 'You don't look good. You're too pale; you ought to have some water, maybe some fruit. I've got tempines in my personal stores.'

Jacrys managed a smile of thanks. 'I am hungry, a little.'

'You want to go back below, lie down for a while?'

'No. I'd rather stand here a bit longer and then maybe try to eat something, maybe drink a beer.'

She nodded laconically; Jacrys guessed that Captain Ellis wouldn't waste a great deal of energy flailing about out of control. 'Very well,' she said, walking away, 'suit yourself.'

'Captain?' Jacrys called, and fell victim to another coughing spasm. Something came loose in his chest, something lumpy, tasting like salt. Whatever it was threatened to make him retch, and he swallowed: he didn't want to think that he was bleeding internally, and he especially didn't want to be spitting blood in front of Captain Ellis. Bleeding into his lungs was bad enough; having Ellis see it, somehow, would be worse.

'Are you all right?' she called, hurrying back. 'Let me get Mirron. Where is he?'

'No!' Jacrys wheezed, 'no, I'm fine, I just need a minute.'

She guided him towards the forward hatch and helped him sit, then offered him water.

Jacrys ignored her, asking instead, 'Captain, have you ever coveted anything? Anyone?'

Surprised, Captain Ellis tilted her head for a moment, considered the sea rushing by and said, 'Just this, I guess, the chance to feel this degree of freedom, to earn my silver doing my job, rather than peddling something – bread, wine, my tits and backside – you know.'

'I understand.' As another who had revelled in his job, Jacrys felt an unexpectedly strong kinship with the Falkan sailor.

'Why?' she asked, 'what is it you covet?'

Again Jacrys surprised himself by being truthful. 'A woman.'

Captain Ellis laughed. 'Isn't that always the way it goes?'

'Not like that,' he interrupted, 'she beat me – she was a beginner, a clumsy pawn in a dangerous game and I could have killed her several times over. Probably should have, now that I think about it. But oddly, I didn't. And in the end, she sneaked into the most secure barracks in the Eastlands. I have no clue as to why. It was essentially suicide, even to try, but she knew my personal password, killed my guard and stabbed me in the chest before leaving me for dead.'

'She broke in just to kill you?' the captain asked. 'What did you ever do to her?'

'I killed her commanding officer.' Jacrys frowned. 'He was just a platoon lieutenant, a nobody.'

'Maybe she was in love with him – was it a him?'

'Yes, and maybe you're right, maybe it was love.'

'So, you covet killing this woman? This clumsy traitor-spy who tempted death just to kill you and avenge her platoon commander?'

'I do.' Jacrys shifted on the hatch, trying for a comfortable position.

'Why?'

'I don't know why,' Jacrys said, 'and if you don't mind me speaking plainly, it's more than that, because I don't know if I want to screw her like a whore, or just kill her and open her up to see if what's inside is really flesh and bone.'

'You realise, Jacrys, that we can sail this little boat all the way across the North Sea and back again, but you aren't going to find any redemption, any peace, any quiet, anything at all, until you deal with this irritating little fixation of yours.' She absentmindedly tugged her tunic straps tight and pushed her hair more securely beneath her hood. 'There is no rest for those of us who covet.'

Jacrys smiled, then, afraid his teeth might be coated with blood, pressed his lips together. 'I know, but maybe I deserve it. A measure of unrest might help me remember who I have allowed myself to become.'

'A measure of unrest does that to all of us, Jacrys.' Captain Ellis patted him on the knee. 'I'll send Thadrake; he'll help you find something to eat.'

'Thank you, Captain,' Jacrys said. 'I hope I haven't frightened you, or made you feel uneasy. That wasn't my intention.'

'I'll be fine.'

'Perhaps we can talk again later?'

'You just get busy healing.'

'I think I already have,' Jacrys whispered.

WRECKAGE

Steven watched Kellin's horse reach the riverbank. She was shivering, blue with cold, and caught in the numbing throes of a panic attack, but she sat tall in the saddle, seemingly immune. Her soaking cloak dripped river-water, leaving a trail through the patchy snow. Her wet hair was matted against her head.

Garec followed a few paces behind Kellin, still in deep water. He had slipped off the saddle and was furiously trying to regain his seat, using his reins to tug and clawed his way astride the nervous horse. He'd managed to regain the saddle, however ungainly, when the shivering duo clambered onto dry land.

Steven clung to his own reins, his knuckles white with the effort, and tried hard not to look upriver. Unimaginable devastation was coming, but watching that wall of water and debris roll down on them would only distract him from his goal: reaching the riverbank.

But the need to know was unbearable, and Steven glanced west. There it was, a roiling, tumbling mountain of water, littered with corpses, rigging, bits of boats of all sorts, and pieces of houses, farms, barns, stables, whatever it had managed to scoop up on its way across Falkan. There was a deafening roar, like a perpetual thunderclap. Steven gripped the saddle-horn – the reins were no longer up to the challenge – and regretted ever looking back.

I'll never make it. None of us will.

He felt the magic around him, warming the water to a comfortable bathtub temperature as it had in Meyers' Vale. He tried to project some of that energy into the swirling current around Gilmour's horse, but he couldn't tell if it was effective; he was too distracted by the incoming tide and the thunder. Whilst he wouldn't die of hypothermia, Steven didn't have much hope that his power would be able to stave off the wave.

He leaned over and urged his horse, 'Just a couple more feet, sweetie. C'mon, you can make it; swim, girl, swim!'

When the flood finally reached him, it didn't strike with the force he'd been expecting. It didn't shatter his bones, or break over him like an ocean wave, *like one of those waves out at that beach Mark's always talking about, Jones Beach*. Instead, Steven felt himself lifted, gently at first, and carried on a burgeoning swell. It felt strangely like a roller-coaster ascent, slow and steady to start with, then careening downhill, unchecked. First he could see the top of the riverbank, then the tops of the trees in the distance, the naked branches stark against the slate grey of winter. He was still on his horse, still facing north and still swimming along in the warm-as-a-bath current, when he saw the wave swallow Garec and Kellin and their horses, all disappearing without even a splash. The world pitched perilously as he heard Gilmour shout something, then everything was brown, turbid, cold, and tumbling wildly, both in his mind and in reality.

Steven held his breath, summoned the magic and let it burst forth, a flailing explosion of self-preservation, but he had no idea if it helped at all, because he kept rolling, lost somewhere beneath the surface.

He tried to swim, but it was pointless. The wave was carrying him at better than forty miles an hour. He felt his horse slip from between his legs and go spinning off. For a few moments he gave up and let himself be carried. The muddy water reminded him strangely of the riverscapes of his life in Colorado; it was always the same, no matter which river, no matter what time of year: light brown, almost beige near the surface, giving way to murky brown, then black in the depths, and whether he was swimming, leaping from a rope swing or tumbling from a raft in whitewater, the underside of all rivers was the same, and this one, however huge and deadly, was no different.

Then he was hit—

A log, or maybe a heavy beam struck his leg just below the knee. He was sure it was broken, a compound fracture, skin and muscles shredded, the knee hyper-extended ... he screamed, but he kept tumbling east towards Wellham Ridge.

Tibia and fibula again, he thought. *I can't believe I broke those fuckers again.*

His lungs burned, and he grasped his magic and filled them. *Thank Christ for that spell.* He wouldn't drown, not yet, anyway. Something hit him in the small of his back, not a bone-breaker this time, but a puncture by something thin and sharp. He cried out, swallowed a mouthful of muddy water and reached back to feel for the injury, but he couldn't find it. Instead he clamped his mouth shut, biting his tongue when something hit him in the back of his head. *That was a rock*. His shoulder scraped against something rough, the ground perhaps; then he was following his feet, upside down but moving fast towards the surface and the lighter-coloured water. A foot broke free of the river; he could feel it jutting into the air, as dissociated from himself as the spinning bits of flotsam and jetsam pelting him from all sides.

Steven twisted onto his stomach, lifted his head and managed a real breath, then another. He managed to avoid being crushed by a skeleton of logs still lashed together, maybe the frame for a thatched roof, ripped from the top of a Falkan farmhouse.

Then he was beneath the surface again, tumbling backwards and waiting for the impact that would knock him senseless. Part of him continued to kick and thrash, fighting a madman's battle, while the rest of him floated, fluid and graceful, watching the devastation unfold and witnessing the carnage in its wake. He didn't know if the magic was somehow granting him a welcome feeling of distance from the nightmarish cyclone in the centre of the wave but he did summon enough clarity to regret that he had come so close to finding Hannah, only to die at his best friend's hand.

He stretched out, arching his back and trying to knife through the water like a human surfboard. It was surprisingly effective, and in that moment's grace, he folded his hands over his face, covering his head while waiting for the lights to shut off.

They didn't. The tea colour of the surface water – bright enough to give him hope that he might kick hard with his good leg and get free – began to dim. He wasn't sinking; the surfboard strategy was keeping him afloat, but it *was* growing dimmer ... something was coming down on him. Steven didn't know whether it was the crest of the wave, finally breaking, or part of the sailing vessel he had seen somersaulting along the watery ridge moments before, but it was large enough to cast a shadow over everything around him. If it was the ship, he would be broken, but if it was the wave itself, he would be dragged along the riverbed and his skin peeled away in an Eldarni version of what Mark liked to call macadam rash.

Gambling that the ship might not crush him to pieces in deeper water, Steven tried to bend his body into a makeshift rudder, to catch the current and force himself towards the bottom, and perhaps to safety. It didn't work. The current was too unpredictable for him to do anything more than ride it out. He continued to slam into branches and rocks, felt stones and dirt pelt him in a hundred places at once: his face, hands, neck and back, as he waited for five tons of Falkan schooner to come slamming down on him from above.

He rolled into a ball, tucked his head down, filled his lungs and waited, wondering in a desultory manner if Garec and Kellin had survived, and if he would ever find Gilmour again.

It was some time later when he awakened.

What's broken?

The world came into focus, as light and colour emerged from behind the curtain of hazy grey and blurry black. Eldarn repositioned itself around, under, above and beside Steven Taylor. He was lying in a shallow puddle of mud and cold river water. Fearing to exacerbate his injuries, he didn't move.

Tibia and fibula, broken; they must be. Head hurts. What's the head, anyway? Cranium. That's it, your pointy little head, dummy. That feels broken, too, maybe a hairline crack. Shoulder's badly scraped . . . a pound of flesh? Take two; they're small . . . but intact, and my back's all right.

He snaked a hand down his thigh. *I can't have broken this leg twice in four months; I just can't.* He pulled his hand back. *Later. Check it later.*

Now, what hurts?

That one was easy: everything.

Take your time; let's see what you remember. What hurts? Ulna, radius, coccyx . . . that's your arse, for everyone in the cheap seats, thank you very much . . . both clavicles, ribs on the left, ribs on the right, and the knee bone, the patella, feels like it is connected to the shoulder bone, which feels like it's still connected to the grille of a passing garbage truck. That's it. That's all I know, good for probably a D+ on your average biology exam.

Lying still, he tried to focus on anything but the fact that he might have rebroken his leg. Without lifting his head, he endeavoured to take in as much of Eldarn as he could from his current vantage point beside what remained of the Medera River.

He could see a rock, as big a small truck, resting on the razed, muddy ground as if it had been deposited there by a fast-moving glacier. There were countless uprooted trees, lying in myriad ungainly positions throughout the clearing as if they'd been tossed about. *If this was a clearing. It was probably a forest until five minutes ago.*

The smell of decay found him, tickling the back of his throat. He didn't want to vomit; he breathed heavily through his mouth for a few seconds, until he was more accustomed to the aroma of upside-down river. It was like autumn, the smell of death and decomposition, but autumn had a way of being delicate about it, of mixing its scents with more pleasant aromas: mulled wine, ripe fruit, mown hay, and wood smoke. This was just the opposite: the hegemonic smell of shit and rotting earth.

Mud and silt coated everything, as if the world had been hastily slathered in a quick coat of something muck-brown, foetid. It was cold now, despite the lingering effects of his warming spell, and he knew he would either need to concentrate enough to recast the magic, or get to his feet and find someplace to dry out.

He could hear the river trickling by somewhere behind him. He guessed he was facing north, lying perhaps two hundred feet from the riverbank. The sustained thunder had passed, even its echoes, and Steven closed his eyes and listened for a moment to the rhythmic babble as the Medera rediscovered its former self and wound its more familiar route towards Orindale. There was no sign of Garec, Kellin or Gilmour, no sign of any of the horses, and no sound of anyone shouting for help . . . just the river, and the same light breeze he had felt that morning.

Steven closed his eyes. Despite the cold, he might have slept for a few minutes, until the *slurp*, *drag* and *slurp* sounds of something large and broken being dragged through the mud finally roused him. He rolled, with surprising ease, onto his back and lifted his head. It took a moment for everything to make sense; the land looked like it had been bombed. Then, across the mudscape, he saw the grettan, a big female – not nearly as large as the creature that had attacked him in the Blackstones, but a muscular and dangerous animal, nevertheless. She had sustained a serious injury to her back during the floodtide and was dragging her hind legs, grunting as if in pain. The creature's fur was matted, covered with mud. She bared her teeth with each step, but it was more a show of pain than any real hostility.

'You planning to eat me?' Steven pushed himself up. 'Huh? Eat me and then rest somewhere while you heal?'

The grettan growled something threatening; she hadn't expected Steven to be alive, never mind capable of mounting a defence.

'I have bad news for you, sister,' Steven said. 'You're screwed. That's not going to get better; you've got maybe a day or two left, and I wouldn't recommend any dancing in your condition. So what happened, Dorothy? Someone drop a house on you? I think they dropped a ship on me.' Steven focused his thoughts inward and brought the magic forth in a tightly woven spell. He thought about just stinging her, driving her off somewhere to die on her own, but that would take time. If there were healthy grettans about, the end for her would be ugly. Instead, he decided to finish her here. 'Sorry about this, my dear, but it's for the best.'

He lashed out at a spot between the grettan's forelegs. The spell slammed into the creature, ripping her apart in a hailstorm of bloody fur and sinew. Steven watched as the animal's tongue lolled from what was left of its mouth, poking its pink tip into the mud.

'Nicely done.'

Gilmour. Sonofabitch.

'I'm glad to see you're feeling up to a bit of magic. You must be relatively whole, and if you're not entirely ready for the winter chain-ball tournaments, you're at least strong enough to sit up and work a spell or two. That's a relief.' He pointed towards the grettan's remains. 'She was planning on an early lunch, wasn't she?'

Dragging a leg himself, a bloody piece of cloth over one eye, Gilmour, masquerading for the moment as a Malakasian soldier, made his way across the mud.

'You've got nine lives, old man.'

'Pissing demons, I've got more than nine, Steven. I must've used nine up since I met you.'

'I'll try to take that as a compliment.'

'Are you broken and battered?'

'Am I?' Steven shrugged. 'The verdict isn't in on that yet, but so far, I think I need a new head, new leg, new arse, a new set of tyres and a couple of gallons of paint.'

'Oh, good. Is that all? I was worried.' He sat with a sustained groan. 'Actually, I think there's a place just up the road where we can get all those things.'

Steven suppressed a chuckle. 'Don't make me laugh; my ribs hurt.'

'Sorry.'

'How about you?'

'Cuts, scrapes, abrasions in embarrassing places and some damage to my hip, but I'm betting you can fix that.'

'I'll need a box of Band-Aids and a couple of quarts of hydrogen peroxide. Any broken bones?'

'A dislocated finger, but I took care of that before I came to find you.' Gilmour held up the swollen knuckle. 'Let me see your leg.'

Steven indicated his calf, the same leg that had been nearly bitten off in the Blackstones, the same leg that had tripped him up in the landfill outside Idaho Springs, where Lessek's key had been buried. 'It's numb. The cold helps.' He ran his hands along either side of his knee and down. 'Actually, it doesn't feel ...' He stopped, then tried to bend it. It complied, with only a twinge of muscle cramp. 'Holy shit!' he cried, looking enormously surprised.

Gilmour smiled. 'You used the magic?'

'No, not here, not since I woke up here – oh, I did! It was right as the wave was swallowing me up; I just let fly with whatever I had inside me. I called it up and it blasted out into the water. I didn't think it did—'

Gilmour finished his thought. 'It did. That's good. It kept you relatively safe.'

'I don't feel relatively safe.' He rubbed one of several lumps that had welled up on the back of his head.

'Imagine where you would be right now without it,' Gilmour said.

'You're right,' Steven agreed, 'my leg would have been broken, at the very least, and I suppose I would have ended up drowning ... oh, shit, what about Garec and Kellin?'

'I haven't seen them,' Gilmour said quietly.

Ignoring his aches and pains, Steven pulled himself to his feet, then helped Gilmour. 'We need to look for them; they could be lying anywhere, injured badly, dying—'

'We'll look for a day or two,' Gilmour sighed, 'but then we'll have to move on. We can't forget where we're going, or why.'

Steven grudgingly agreed. 'We keep to our schedule: twelve days from now, we need to be on the Ravenian Sea, off the mouth of that fjord. I watched them get swept up by the wave, but they were much further north than I was; they might have tumbled around for a bit and come out just fine.'

Gilmour didn't seem hopeful. 'We'll attempt a crossing in Mark's skiff if they'll don't manage to meet us with a vessel.'

'But that will mean using—'

'I know.'

'But he'll sense us coming—'

'I know.' Gilmour frowned. 'There's nothing else we can do.'

'Shit.' Steven opened his tunic and checked his shoulder. It was deeply scraped and bloody, but once clean, it would heal over.

'You saw the remains of that schooner riding the wave before it crashed over us?' Gilmour asked. 'It was too big for this river, certainly this far east.'

Steven paled. 'You mean it came all the way from Orindale? But that would mean that Mark ...'

'Right again,' Gilmour said. 'Even if Garec and Kellin reach the city, they may not find much in the way of seagoing transportation available.'

Steven wiped his eyes and swept the wet hair off his forehead. 'So it may be just you and me. Where's the spell book and the portal?'

'I hope they're still tied to my saddle. I caught a whiff of them from over there.' He pointed, then added, 'I don't think it's very far. I was on my way when I stumbled on you and your ladyfriend.'

'All right,' Steven said, 'let's go.'

'First,' Gilmour said, grabbing hold of him, 'I need you to think about fixing my hip.'

'I don't know anything about hips, Gilmour.'

'Sure you do,' he replied, 'you fixed Garec's lung, didn't you? You kept your own bones from breaking.'

Steven was confused. 'But they were moments of— well, heightened emotion, really. I just took what I knew about physiology and infused it with—'

'Exactly,' Gilmour said. 'Where do you think new spells come from? Why do you think we spent all that time in your world? Collected all those books? Sponsored research and medical teams from Sandcliff for all those Twinmoons?'

'I don't understand.'

'Think about the magic you've done, the crafty spells, not the bombastic stuff.'

'Yes, I remember, "Explosions aren't magic".'

'Good. You've been paying attention. But think about how you managed to heal Garec, to neutralise the acid-cloud, to find and defeat the almor, to keep yourself warm beneath the water, to keep yourself free from the need for oxygen for so long. There is a common denominator for all those spells, Steven.'

'What's that? Knowledge?'

'Of course. The knowledge and experience you have of anything, human lungs for example, impacts the power you bring. It's how we used to generate common phrase spells, the complex spells called via a series of common phrases in their incantations. Those spells weren't constructed because their incantations were similar; their incantations were derived because their etiologies, their origins and impacts overlapped: they had common effects, because they were based on overlapping fields of knowledge or research.'

'But I've tried to operate out of compassion . . .'

'And your magic is powerful when you're compassionate,' Gilmour assured him, 'far more powerful than anything I've ever seen, and

I've been at this for some Twinmoons. Remember what happened when you handed the hickory staff to Nerak; even I doubted you.'

Steven sighed. 'All right, I'll try it. Let me see your hip.'

'That's the spirit, my boy. Fix me up; I might have a race to run later today.'

'Wait a moment.' Steven looked up at his friend. 'Why don't you fix it?'

'I don't know how to.'

'Bullshit.'

'Maybe.' Gilmour smiled. 'I want to see you do it. You're the sorcerer, Steven. I'm just an old teacher, and we still don't know if Mark can detect your power. Nerak certainly couldn't.'

'Grand, a physiology test.'

'Don't think about it that way.'

'How should I think about it? As a Larion magic test? At least I passed physiology!'

Gilmour laughed and Steven scolded him to hold still. He examined the injury, then asked, 'So Nerak was the one who put all the common phrase spells together?'

'Many of them, yes.'

'I would have thought it was Lessek who did that.'

'Well, Lessek built the foundations which Nerak – all of us – were able to build on, that's true, and Lessek summoned and created magic. He called all the magic in the known universe into the spell table; it was an impressive and powerful feat. What Nerak did was to refine and enrich the Larion magic, to expand it through research and knowledge – just like you're doing now.'

'And he did it through common phrase spells?'

'Amongst other things, yes.'

'The same spells he eventually used to destroy the Larion Senate?' Steven felt around Gilmour's hip joint with his fingertips.

'Some of them, yes. But for a long time, Nerak's resources went beyond hatred and destruction. He was a powerful asset to the Senate. How's it going?'

Steven said, 'You dislocated the joint, similar to your finger, but this joint is much bigger and a dislocation here involves a good deal more tissue damage. The bones are back where they belong; that probably happened when you were tumbling about, it popped out and then popped right back in. But the damage is to the muscles and connective tissue holding the whole works together. You can't play sports for twenty years and not see a few of these, so you're in luck this time. Just don't come to me with a case of lung cancer or anything.'

'Not to worry.'

'The way you smoke, you might surprise yourself.'

'Just heal me so we can be on our way, please.' As he felt the familiar tingle and itch of magic at work beneath his skin he closed his eyes and tried to remain still.

Steven went back to his previous subject. 'So how long before the fall of the Larion Senate was Nerak generating the spells that eventually became his undoing?'

Gilmour stared at a spot in the distance. He answered quietly, 'I have no idea, Steven, but I fear it was a long time.'

'So he might have found critical bits of what he needed while visiting Earth?'

'I'm almost certain he did.'

'And he might have experimented with spells to desecrate or destroy long before he brought them to bear against his own brother-hood?'

'Again, I'm sure he did.'

'Why didn't he kill you earlier?'

'He didn't kill me at all; I'm standing here right now.'

Steven laughed, and a bit of magic slipped from his finger to lance through Gilmour's thigh. As he winced, Steven apologised. 'Sorry, sorry. I was distracted. Sorry.'

He went on, 'What I meant was why – if you and Kantu were the only real threats to him and his work – why didn't Nerak arrange for your death and then take over the Senate at his leisure?'

Gilmour drew a breath as if to respond, then he paused and, as if thinking to himself, said, 'Honestly? I don't know. But your question has some merit; why wouldn't he have tried to kill me? I was his equal; he couldn't do anything radical, new, dangerous or different without consulting me. Perhaps he did try. I don't know.'

'Hmm,' Steven said. 'All right. How's that?'

Gilmour tested the leg. 'Much better, thanks.'

'Don't mention it, just leave your insurance card with my recep-tionist on your way out, and don't take more than one lollipop.'

'Agreed.' Gilmour stretched, and started across the mud.

Steven brushed as much of the filth from his clothes as he could and joined him. After a few paces in shared silence, he asked, 'So where is Lessek now?'

'He's dead.'

'Is that why we only get to see him in dreams and memories?'

'And on Seer's Peak,' Gilmour added.

'How'd he die?'

Again Gilmour paused. 'I don't know. It's my understanding that in the earliest Twinmoons of the Larion Senate, there were not as many regulations and policies governing the transport of foreign objects and substances back and forth through the far portals.'

'Ah, drug-runners, even way back then. The Coast Guard must have had a hell of a time tracking them down.'

'Not drugs so much as trinkets, innovations, a few get-rich schemes.'

'What's that have to do with Lessek?'

'Well, this is all legend, mind you, but we have been led to believe that a Senator, perhaps Lessek himself, came back through the portal with something deadly.'

Steven slowed, his boots sinking to the heels in silt. 'What was it? A weapon? Poison? Explosives?'

'A virus.'

'No shit,' Steven frowned. 'An unfamiliar viral infection with nothing in your immune system to battle it, I bet you lost thousands.'

'And Lessek was killed.'

'He died in disgrace? After all that he did for Eldarn?' He looked at Gilmour, who shrugged. 'But since then history has recalled his greatness and elevated him back to an appropriate position in Eldarni memory?'

'It has,' Gilmour agreed, 'but what good is that to Lessek now?'

'Just press down on it, rutting whores!' Kellin said. 'I'll stitch it up, but we have to stop the bleeding.'

'It's not stopping, Kellin.' Garec tried not to sound nervous. With his chin pressed against his chest and both hands pushing down on a broad flap of scalp that had been peeled back over part of his skull, it was difficult to do. 'It's been bleeding like this since I landed here.'

'Just keep pressure on it; I need a moment to get some clean thread. If we use dirty thread, it'll get infected, and we'll just have to rip it out and start again.'

'Fine, that's fine with me.' He took a deep breath. He could feel the blood running over his head, behind his ears, down the back of his neck, along his cheeks and even across his forehead into his eyes, and he could smell it too. 'Demonshit, Kellin, just stitch it up with anything you've got. We'll let it clot and then do it with clean thread tomorrow.'

'You'll be all right.'

'I'm going to bleed to death!'

'You'll be all right.' Her hands shook as she rifled through her pack. Her horse was dead, his head crushed against a tree on the riverbank, but her saddlebags and pack were still lashed to the corpse. Her ribs flared with pain and one collarbone throbbed as she searched for a clean needle and a length of sturdy thread, preferably a piece that hadn't been stained brown with filthy river water so she could stitch up Garec's scalp – *it's going to be a lot of stitches, great rutting Pragans!* – and then see to her own injuries. From the way one arm was dangling numb and useless at her side, she feared she had broken her collarbone. As soon as her adrenalin waned it would start hurting; she knew that much. And the pain in her ribs could only mean that she had cracked at least one, if not more.

'I've got it!' she called and hustled back. 'Now, I need you to let go for a moment. I've got to lift it up and make sure everything is cleaned out of there. If there's any dirt left, it'll get infected and you'll be dead before we can get you to a healer. Do you understand?'

Garec whimpered a little. Now he was frightened.

Kellin took both Garec's hands in her own, squeezed them tightly and guided them gently into his lap. 'It'll just take a moment, then we'll get to stitching it up.'

'Grand,' Garec said. 'It's just that … it's just a lot of blood, Kellin.'

'It's not that much,' she lied; he looked as though someone had emptied a bucket of blood over his head, and the wound was still bleeding. She took a calming breath and wiped his forehead with the cleanest cloth she'd been able to find. 'I don't want you to worry; you'll be in one piece again in no time.'

A hoarse cough followed by a prolonged wet wheeze reached them from somewhere in the underbrush. The sound was unmistakable: a death rattle.

'What was that?' Kellin asked.

'I'm guessing that was my horse,' Garec said sadly. 'She took a branch in the chest; I guess it went into her lungs. It was just a matter of time.'

'Great grettan shit,' Kellin muttered.

'No matter,' Garec said, his voice wavering. 'If I pass out – I'm about to; I can feel it coming – I want you to bind my head, tie it up tight, then go find a horse. With all this devastation, there'll be plenty of them running about – I'd think a lot of the farms around here will have been destroyed, buildings damaged, topsoil stripped ... find a horse, Kellin, and get us to Orindale. Are you hurt?'

'Shut it, Garec,' she ordered. 'I know what I'm doing, but I need you to shut yourself up right quick; I'm trying to work.'

'Find a horse, Kellin,' Garec's voice was weaker now, a whisper. 'Bring my bow and quivers and Steven's silver ...' His head slumped forward; his hands slipped from his lap into the mud.

Kellin was horribly nervous, working alone and against time. She tried to relax and focus on her work, muttering to herself, 'There's no need to rush, no need to hurry. He's fine; he's sleeping, that's all. It's better this way, he won't be complaining and squirming around. Just clean the wound and sew it up. You have to find a horse and then clean water, but first things first – how does it go? Well begun and ... some rutting thing.' She peeled back Garec's scalp to expose the layer of bloody muscle beneath.

The bleeding was astonishing, even for a head wound, but when she'd finished cleaning it, she couldn't find see any evidence that the skull had been cracked. She'd never seen anything like this before, and had nothing with which to compare it. Were any major blood vessels severed? *Were* there any there? Yes, at least one, across the top of the head – but would the bleeding be even worse if an important vein or artery had been cut? Would it close up on its own, or should she try to cauterise it somehow, maybe in some sort of makeshift branding ceremony? But she didn't even know where it was, never mind how to cauterise it. She supposed she could heat up an iron and singe the spots that were bleeding the worst, but she had no dry tinder, nothing to burn and no iron to hand for the task.

She sighed. 'Forget it,' she told herself, 'just stitch him up and run like mad for Orindale. Keep him full of water and, hopefully, he'll sleep the whole way.'

She rinsed the wound several times with the cleanest water she had been able to find, then, trying to keep the flap of skin in place by leaning on it with her numb arm, she stitched the wound closed as quickly and carefully as she could. Garec twitched and groaned each time she pushed the needle through his flesh, but she closed her ears to his cries and concentrated on making her stitches as small and neat as possible, thanking the gods of the Northern Forest it was the other arm that was damaged.

Several stitches along, Kellin realised that she was closing the half-moon tear crookedly. 'Mother of a whore—!' she growled, and thought about pulling out of the thread and beginning again. Garec moved restlessly. 'No, toss it all,' she decided, 'I'll just squish a bit of it up there in a small wrinkle. He'll never notice.' And pulling a tiny pinch of skin into a small fold, she aligned the rest of the injury perfectly and finished the job with deft alacrity, despite shaking hands.

A quarter-aven later, Kellin had managed to get Garec to drink nearly half a water-skin. It wasn't the cleanest of water, and she was pretty sure he'd suffer for it later, but right now it was more important to get as much water into Garec's body as possible. She prayed to the gods of the Northern Forest that she wasn't killing him – dehydration and disease had accounted for more casualties than any war ever could.

Garec half-awakened, enough to repeat his orders to find a horse and get them both to Orindale.

Kellin promised she would, but they needed rest first. She wrapped him in their cloaks, though they were still soaking wet, and tried to drag him up the bank, but it was no use; her ribs and collarbone protested too much. The pain was overwhelming, and Kellin fell in the muck, weeping quietly, shivering and wishing that Steven and Gilmour would find them somehow. As wary as she had been of the two sorcerers and their fantastic abilities, she longed for one of Steven's campfires right now.

But they were alone and injured. They'd have to do this themselves. 'We're farmers,' she rehearsed, 'farmers from outside the city. We were hurt badly when the wave came through. Can you help us, please?'

She found a spare tunic in her pack and with her good hand clumsily tied a loop in the end of each sleeve. She pulled the sleeves around herself from behind, then tucked a short stick through the loops and twisted it, tighter and tighter, until she cried out, screaming from the pain in her shoulder.

'We're farmers!' she shouted, cranking the stick another half turn and pulling the tunic splint close around her injured arm and ribs. 'We're farmers from outside the city. We were hurt when the wave came through, hurt badly. Can you help us, please?' She tucked one end of the stick into her leggings. Her shoulder was immobile and her ribs braced; it wasn't perfect, but it would do for now.

Kellin rested her forehead in the mud. The cold felt good on her face. 'Just a moment's rest,' she said. 'I need a moment; then I'll find a horse. I promise.'

It was nearly dark when she woke; at least an aven had passed.

Shivering and confused, she sat up with a start. Garec was sleeping, but he looked as if he had been cast deep beneath the shadow of death. She wondered if he had already started the lonely journey to the Northern Forest.

In between the mud and dried blood Garec's skin was pasty-white. He was shivering as well, and an inhuman humming sound came from the back of his throat: death's drone. Kellin shook him, slapped him hard, then shouted his name, trying to call him back from the forest path.

Garec murmured, opened his eyes briefly and then slumped back into unconsciousness. He wouldn't live through the aven, not like this, wet and unsheltered.

'I've got to make a fire,' Kellin said out loud. 'I need flint and tinder, and something dry.' She looked around. Everything was wet. 'North, away from the river, it'll be dry there.' She ground her teeth together until her jaw hurt. 'Stay awake, you bastard,' she murmured as she staggered into the brush. 'Stay awake. Make a fire.'

Garec had a flint in his pack. She had heard his horse – *I hope it was his horse* – die in the bushes off to her left. If she could get the flint, and find some dry wood outside the waves' wreckage area, she might be able to light a small fire and warm herself for a few stolen moments, and then she'd come back for Garec. 'But he'll have to wake up,' she whispered. 'He'll have to help me; I'll never be able to drag him that far. But first things first . . .'

She found the horse, and Garec had been right: it had a splintered branch protruding from its chest. The flint was in the saddlebag, but it was another twenty-five paces before Kellin reached a dry area of the forest. If she was glad for anything, Kellin thought, it was that the flood had thrown them north. They hadn't been inside that roiling nightmare very long; had it cast them south, or carried them further east, they would both be dead already.

Igniting the fire took longer than she had planned, but she finally captured a small spark in the handful of dry tinder she had scraped together, then generously heaped winter brush on the determined little flame. 'Who cares?' she said, 'I'd be happy to have the whole rutting forest on fire. You need to find us, Steven? Well, that'll be easy; just look for the big orange glow in the sky.' Kellin laughed for the first time all day, then winced. 'All right, no laughing,' she told herself firmly, a smile still on her face.

With a hearty blaze crackling, Kellin added several logs. She knew it would take time to drag Garec – *if he's still alive* – through the forest, so she was trying to ensure there'd be at least some smouldering coals when she returned. She stood close to the flames, feeling the heat on her face and watching tendrils of steam rise from her clothing. She captured the feeling and secured it inside her mind: a warm place, a summer place, where no one ever found themselves washed two hundred paces through the woods by a rogue wave as big as a small mountain. Then she went back for Garec.

She was feeling better for a bit of heat and moved faster, determined to find reserves of strength to heave the Ronan bowman back to the campfire, but once outside its peripheral glow, she felt the chill creep back into her bones. Her clothes were still wet and her skin rose in dimpled gooseflesh. She started shivering, great quaking spasms. She couldn't do this . . .

When the mule brayed, Kellin pissed her leggings. She couldn't see anything, and hadn't heard it moving through the brush. She thanked the gods that the animal was not a squad of armed Mala-kasians; they would have had her gutted, sewn up and gutted again before she'd even realised they were there. If she hadn't been so cold and in so much pain, it would have been hideously embarrassing – but there was no one to witness her discomposure, so she tried to recover herself and hurried to find the animal, lost but otherwise healthy, munching bits of brown vegetation poking through the patches of snow as it wandered in the general direction of home.

'Well, aren't you a surprise?' Kellin said, hoping to sweet-talk the mule into carrying her and Garec to the nearest healer's doorstep. 'Would you like an apple?' The mule didn't answer; it didn't appear to care one whit that Kellin was there at all. 'No? How about a crate of apples?' she said softly, approaching the animal. 'Come on, we have a little job tonight, and then Kellin will get you all the dry grass and thistles you can eat, agreed?'

The mule was wearing a rope bridle and had the remains of a pink ribbon tied into its mane: it was obviously a child's pet.

'What's your name?' she asked as she took hold of the bridle; the mule didn't care, and when she tugged, surprisingly, the mule com-plied without complaint, plodding happily alongside her until they found Garec, looking worse, barely breathing, still wrapped in the damp cloaks.

'Mule,' Kellin said, patting the animal gently, 'I need you to wait right here while I help Garec up. Will you do that?'

Again, nothing.

'Fine, I didn't expect you to answer,' she told it. 'You're not much of a conversationalist; I can respect that in a beast of burden, but I need you to understand that if you run off, I'm going to find you, kill you, eat you and then make a nice pair of winter pants out of your miserable hide. Understand?'

The mule twitched an ear. Kellin knelt in the mud and pressed her cheek against Garec's forehead. Panic struck hard: he was too cold.

'Oh, no, no, no, please no,' she cried, shaking again. She moved her hands back and forth between Garec's hands, cold and stiff in his lap, and his ivory face, marked with a roadmap of dried blood. She put her cheek near his mouth, felt nothing and moved closer, pressed her skin against his lips, blue-black in the moonlight. Still nothing.

Kellin blamed the cold: she was too cold to feel his breath. He was breathing; of course he was. She was simply too cold to feel it. She rocked back on her haunches, hoping something would come to her. She was too cold, too tired and too injured to lift him herself; as determined as she wanted to be, Garec was too heavy, a deadweight. 'Think, think, think of something. Think,' she chanted, rocking back and forth, 'it's too cold. I can't believe it's come to this . . .'

The rope bridle.

Kellin slashed through one end of the mule's reins and hastily tugged the free end across Garec's chest and beneath his armpits. He didn't stir at all; there was no sign that he was still alive. Now Kellin longed to see a bit of blood seep from the wound on his head, just a few drops, that was all, just to confirm that his heart was still beating.

With the rope knotted as tightly as she could with one functional hand, Kellin took hold of the bridle and tugged the mule towards the fire. After a moment, the animal followed docilely, dragging Garec through the hardening mud.

At the campfire, Kellin threw her arms around the mule's neck and buried her face in its musty fur. The beast nuzzled the crook of her arm and offered a derisive snort that said, 'Touching, but how about my apples?' She managed a faint grin and set about untying Garec, making sure to link the rope around a tree when she was done.

She managed to untangle their wet cloaks and spread them over low-hanging branches, as near to the fire as she could get them without setting them alight. They started steaming almost immediately as she pushed Garec close to the fire.

She spent a few moments gathering a big pile of logs, then returned and sat herself, cradling Garec's head in her lap, willing the heat to restore him to her, whole and unharmed, save for the crooked needlework ringing his scalp.

'Rest on me,' she whispered, tossing another log onto the fire. 'I'll stay awake and keep the fire going; you rest on me.' Her ribs blazed; the shattered ends of her collarbone scraped against one another and a cold sweat chilled her face. She was sick, exhausted, but she had done it; she had done everything she could to save him. Whether or not he lived through the night was now up to the gods. She stroked his face, then massaged his legs and arms as well as she could with just one hand, willing his blood to start circulating into his extremities.

Rocking him this way in her lap, she passed the night and saw dawn begin to whiten the eastern sky. Shortly before sun-up, Kellin finally fell asleep, Garec's head resting across her thighs.

THE WAGON TRAIN

Brexan waved to Marrin, Sera and those members of the *Morning
Star*'s crew she could see from the porch at the Topgallant. Captain
Ford was missing; Brexan assumed he had gone into the city to make
arrangements for whatever cargo he and his crew would ship back to
Praga. In just a few days he had gone from being almost destitute,
struggling with the uncertainty of securing any business at all, to
being one of the few men left in Orindale with a seaworthy vessel.
More than once in the past three days Brexan had heard Ford com-
plain that the *Morning Star*, his chubby little twin-masted brig-sloop,
was too small; right now he was wishing he had invested in a larger
vessel: a bark, maybe, or a fat galleon. But even so, he could ship
almost anything anywhere, and he had been getting offers every day
to carry sundry cargoes all over Eldarn. Captain Ford could name his
price; Orindale's merchants would pay.

Anchoring on the flats near the marsh might have been humili-
ating, but it had been the wisest move the captain had made since
sailing north. When the mysterious power had broken, sunk or burned
the rest of the merchant fleet to the waterline, the *Morning Star* had
been safely out of sight around the northern point. With her leaks
patched and tarred and her stores replenished, the *Morning Star*
waited only for her captain to make a deal, then he and the crew
would bring her south to the quay, take on whatever they were
hauling and sail on the next falling tide.

But Captain Ford wasn't fooling himself into thinking he had a
monopoly on Eldarn's largest economic centre. Ships were coming
from Pellia, Strandson, Southport, Averil and Landry; there were
plenty of vessels plying the Ravenian Sea and as word spread of the
recent devastation, all of them would see Orindale as a goldmine, a
chance for lucrative long-term contracts for five, ten, maybe even
twenty times what they would have been worth in the past.

Captain Ford seemed to be a wise and experienced seaman; he

wouldn't drag his feet now. Brexan had enjoyed having him, Sera, even Marrin, staying at the Topgallant for the past few days, and she wondered if he and the *Morning Star* would be back at the boarding house in the coming Twinmoons.

Brexan had yet to see the devastation, she'd heard plenty about it, and she got the feeling that her life was about to go back into motion; the pendulum marking the passage of her time here in Orindale had begun swinging the other way. She pulled her cloak closed as she crossed the jetty and entered the northern wharf. She felt the wind bite at her face and hands. It was always windier down here than up near the marsh. Sheltered by the city and the stubby peninsula jutting into the harbour, Nedra's cove was rarely windy, and almost never as cold as the Falkan capital. Though winter at the Topgallant had been marked by chilly rain, periodic snow showers and plenty of fog, the frigid winds here reminded Brexan that spring was still a Twinmoon away. She sucked in a breath, felt it chill her lungs and hurried towards the city centre. Right now, shopping was the most important item on her agenda.

Brexan had invited the entire neighbourhood, including Nella Barkson's extended family and the crew of the *Morning Star*, to Nedra's four-hundred-Twinmoon party, at least twelve people more than she had originally figured, and the way the Barksons and the sailors ate and drank, she was going to need more supplies – another barrel of beer, at least, another gansel, more bread, and more fish stew. She wouldn't be able to carry everything on her shopping list, but she might get lucky and run into Captain Ford along the wharf and maybe she could persuade him to lug a box or two of provisions back, perhaps in exchange for free beer that night.

She watched as three massive frigates, rigged with an impossible tangle of ropes and sheets, made their way north from the harbour. Loaded to bursting, they plunged north through the whitecaps under full sail. They all flew Malakasian colours. *Heading home to Pellia, I'd wager. I wonder how they survived. Maybe the mess down here isn't as bad as everyone claims. Things do tend to get inflated a bit by the time they reach Nedra's cove*, she thought.

Another hundred paces south, with the frigates nearly out of sight on the northern horizon, Brexan realised that no one had exaggerated the details of the mysterious attack on Orindale's merchant fleet. Like so many others in the past few days, Brexan stared in disbelief.

The ships that were moored along the quay and off the offshore buoys were gone. There was nothing left. A few naval vessels plied the waves, but there was nothing to patrol. A handful of small civilian boats scurried between the derelict ships and bits of wreckage that remained tied to offshore moorings, while scavengers and legal salvage companies picked over what remained of the massive merchant vessels, collecting bits of metal, a few salvageable lengths of rope, even some miraculously unburned planks and beams, but otherwise, the harbour was empty, devoid of its usual bustle.

Something fluttered through Brexan's memory; she whirled around, peering into the distance where grey water met grey sky in a perfect demarcation of the end of the world. She could just make out the last of the frigates, making way towards Pellia, as Carpello Jax's final confession came back to her: *It's wood, processed wood, but not lumber. Bark and shavings, leaves and roots. I don't know what he wants with it, but he wants as much as I can ship. He pays anything I ask.*

'Is that what they're hauling?' she whispered to herself.

She watched until the topmasts disappeared over the horizon. Carpello was dead; she had stood with Sallax and Nedra as his body was washed away on the outgoing tide. Could the evil merchant have something to do with those frigates? Were they carrying the last of Carpello's shipments of bark and roots? It seemed unlikely, but Brexan couldn't discount the possibility that Carpello's fading stench was somehow all over the devastation of Orindale Harbour.

She pressed on, taking in the rest of the city's scars. Not all the destruction had been directed at the shipping industry; the wharf had fallen victim as well, and the bridge, Orindale's signature edifice, had collapsed, blocking the river and leaving barges stacked up behind like logs in a jam. Even the abandoned barrels Sallax had hidden in, stacked behind the down-at-heel waterfront alehouse, had been washed away.

'Great rutting lords,' Brexan murmured. 'What could have done this?'

She asked the question of no one, but she feared that she had a good idea what might have wreaked such havoc: Nerak.

'They're here,' she said, and felt something inside her shift and click back into place. She ignored the guilt, forcing thoughts of Nedra from her mind. She had been fooling herself, thinking she might live out her days as a scullery-maid; *this* was what she needed to do. If Steven and Garec were nearby, then that horsecock Jacrys wouldn't be far away. They were here; Brexan could feel them on the breeze, that same breeze that somehow never reached the Topgallant Boarding House. 'It's just a matter of time now,' she said, lowering her shoulder into the wind and heading for the fish market.

Two avens later, Orindale slipped from day into night. For a few moments, the entire city was caught on that narrow horizon between shadow and light. Everything was the same colour, a monochromatic grey, the colour of winter. Brexan had bought some things for Nedra's celebration, but she'd deliberately left a few items off her list: she needed an excuse to come back the following day. Sitting in a tavern, she sipped at her wine and nibbled a pastry. She watched the traffic move along the quay, searching for anyone with a longbow – so few people did; it was begging for trouble in the capital to tote weapons around – or carrying a wooden staff. As darkness enveloped the seaport, Brexan gave in, shouldered her canvas satchels and made her way back to the Topgallant to help Nedra with the evening meals.

She would be back.

Brexan found them the following day; she knew she would. She almost stumbled over Garec Haile before recognising him. He was standing amongst a crowd waiting to cross the makeshift bridge across the Medera, a pontoon of wooden barges lashed together. While the remains of the great stone span dammed the river, the barge captains were unloading their cargoes beside the barracks at the old imperial palace. The floating bridge was open to foot and wagon traffic, but the river was essentially closed, empty downstream barges were tied up to anything left standing on the north and south banks, and commerce in the capital city was at a virtual standstill.

Today, with northerly winds raking the coastline again, pedestrian traffic was slow. The crowds of cloaked and hooded travellers waited impatiently for their turn to cross, and in the press of people moving back and forth, several had already fallen in and had to be fished out by unemployed stevedores on temporary assignment as lifeguards.

Brexan looked at the man for a long time, making sure she was right before finally approaching. Excited, she ignored the woman on his arm, and said 'Are you Garec Haile?'

'No,' the man replied in a whisper, clearly ill, 'you're mistaking me for someone else.'

Brexan's sudden enthusiasm vanished; she had been so sure she was about to fulfil a promise to Versen, and to be within shouting distance of another to Sallax. She sighed deeply and, crestfallen, was about to turn away when she looked at him again. *That's Garec; it has to be.* As he started over the first barge, she caught up with him and said, 'Please – Versen wanted me to find you. I promised I would.'

The man turned quickly; his hood fell back. He had been gravely injured and looked mere moments from collapsing. His head was wrapped in cloth bandages, the remnants of a querlis poultice poking out from beneath. His skin was sickly-white and his face was deeply lined: too little food; too many Twinmoons running, hiding and fighting.

'Who are you?' He stared into her face. It was unsettling: unarmed, obviously injured and weak, yet he left her feeling as though he could kill her with a glance. The *Bringer of Death*, that's what Versen and Sallax had called him; from the look in his eyes, Brexan could see they hadn't been exaggerating.

'My name is Brexan Carderic,' she said, 'and I'm a friend—'

'Brexan,' Garec interrupted, his features softening. 'Gabriel O'Reilly mentioned you. You know of Versen?'

'I do,' she said, 'and Sallax Farro of Estrad.'

'Sallax?' Garec shook his head. 'That's not possible.'

'It's true.'

'Take me to them, then. Where are they?'

'I can't. I wish—' Brexan stepped out of the line of people crossing the pontoon barges. 'I can't take you to them, but I can tell you what happened.'

Garec noticed the sudden strain on her face. 'Both dead?' he said softly. When she nodded, he asked, 'Were you with them?'

'Yes, I was.' Brexan's eyes fill with tears; she hardly noticed when Garec took her arm.

He looked around the wharf, then gestured at a makeshift tavern, its windows shattered and door hanging by a leather hinge, near the pontoon. 'Let's go. I want to know everything.'

The first of the wagons rumbled south, an unexpected Seron escort in tow. There were three others following, each filled to the slats with canvas bags, sewn shut and stamped with a Ronan customs seal. A schooner had arrived from Orindale two days prior, and for a flagon of wine and a few slivers of fennaroot, two of her crew – merchant seamen, not navy sailors – were willing to describe her cargo in detail: winter wheat, four hundred crates of it, already ground to flour and en route to Welstar Palace.

Hoyt closed his eyes and thought of Churn; he'd have enjoyed this. Face-down in a frozen ditch by the side of a Malakasian highway in the middle of the night, Churn would have found it impossible to keep still. Hoyt imagined him signing, *Is it cold over there? It's cold over here!* or perhaps, *Tell me again why we didn't become farmers*, and giggling under his breath. Hannah had told him that Churn spoke in his final moments astride the flying buttress, but Hoyt would always remember his friend signing with nimble fingers.

His own fingers were stiff with cold and his face was numb. He'd left his cloak at the Wayfarer, foregoing the bulky wrap for a second wool tunic and a neck muffler that made him look like an elderly woman with a chest cold. He hadn't anticipated Seron; neither had Alen, wherever he was now. *It's just wheat*, Hoyt thought, *so why the escort? It doesn't make sense, unless they're starving and they need the wheat as much as they need armour, enchanted tree bark and weapons.* With the second wagon passing, Hoyt stopped thinking about why there was a Seron platoon less than ten paces away and instead tried to focus on becoming as invisible as possible. *We'll hit the next shipment,* he thought. *There'll be another, something less protected. The traffic in the harbour never stops; another schooner will dock soon enough.* Huddling in the frozen mud in the ditch, Hoyt willed Alen to read his thoughts and stand down.

Then the fire arrows struck.

Hoyt didn't see the first barrage of flaming shafts as they arched through the night; he was hiding his face and hoping his body would be mistaken for a particularly dark shadow, or maybe a piece of rotting wood. But he did risk a glance at the second salvo, and in the moment before panic took hold, Hoyt was proud of Alen. The old Larion magician did not disappoint. Seemingly scores of flaming arrows streamed through the darkness. Some embedded themselves in the wagons or the stacks of canvas satchels; others struck Seron soldiers, wagon drivers and Malakasian guards, igniting their cloaks and sending them screaming into the surrounding fields. From where Hoyt crouched, it looked like a whole company of bowmen had attacked the wagon train, and those Seron warriors not running burning into the night drew their blades and charged what they imagined to be the firing line. The wagon train was, at least for the moment, unprotected.

Alen, you crazy bastard! Hoyt thought, drawing his scalpel and snaking up the ditch. *All right, let's go!*

He hurried behind a burning wagon to reach one whose cargo had not yet caught fire. The driver was fighting to keep his team of horses calm, trying to lead them around the blaze blocking the roadway. As Hoyt slipped past, the driver reached for him, grabbing a handful of his scarf, and Hoyt rounded on him, slashing tendons in the man's wrist to render his hand useless. The fight was one-sided and quick, but as Hoyt ran, he heard the driver shouting, 'They're here! Come back! They're already here, you fools!'

'Not long now,' Hoyt muttered, quickening his pace. At the rear of the wagon, he tore off a piece of burning wood and tossed it into the bed, scorching the bags of wheat. *Two down*, Hoyt thought, and dived into the ditch to avoid being trampled by the horses pulling the third cart. The driver was dead, slumped sideways and crackling like a campfire. The horses, spooked by the conflagration, galloped wildly across the ditch and into an adjacent field. The cart, smouldering here and there with outbreaks of yellow flame, failed to negotiate the ditch, crashed over and spilled its load. The reins snapped and the team took off eastwards. Hoyt watched as what was left of the wagon caught fire, brightening the Pellia night. 'Three down,' he said, checking for Seron as he made his way towards the last cart in the convoy. He had still not spotted Alen but knew his friend was all right, because salvos of fireballs continued to rain down intermittently, occasionally coming close enough to Hoyt to leave him swearing. The fireballs looked and sounded like arrows as they flew overhead, a simple ruse, but convincing enough to buy Hoyt another moment or two to ensure the final wagon was well on its way to ash. *Then I'm getting out of here*, he told himself.

The Seron were coming back. Any normal guard, having found no one in the fields, might return warily until they knew what strange enchantments were upon them . . . but these weren't normal soldiers. The Seron charged the wagon convoy as wildly and with the same recklessness that they had attacked the invisible enemy line. *Demon-piss, out of time!* Hoyt thought, and risked calling, 'Alen!' No one answered, and the din from the injured and the dying went on unabated.

Hoyt dived for the last cart. One of the slat sides had caught alight, and he planned to do as before, break off a bit and chuck it into the wagon bed, then to flee as fast as he could. He pounded on the end of a burning slat, trying to keep from watching the Seron soldiers as they ran, barking and grunting, across the frozen field. 'Come on, come on,' he muttered as he pulled, 'I've no time for this. I need to get going—'

Then he saw Alen, lying in a heap, hidden by dancing, fire-lit shadows. It looked to Hoyt like he had fallen into the cart and struck his head, *or maybe broken his rutting neck*. There was no time to think.

Hoyt climbed over the burning side, scorching himself as he dropped onto the soft canvas bags.

'Alen,' he whispered, 'come on, Alen, wake up.' He shook the old magician, praying his friend would open his eyes. Outside, the Seron had returned and were now searching the area for terrorists. Some shouted orders; others ran here and there, chasing down every flicker and moving shadow. One soldier climbed the cart where Hoyt and Alen were hiding and used a muscular paw to wrench the burning slats free without so much as a grimace.

Hoyt had already moved, dragging the canvas satchels over him until he and Alen were buried. 'We'll sneak out when you come around,' he whispered, 'until then, stay low ... and ... and I'll have the venison ...'

'I'll have the venison,' Hoyt said, 'and a flagon of wine, something decent, not the cat's piss you were pushing in here last night.'

'Right away, sir,' the waiter said as he disappeared behind the bar.

'Thirty volumes!' Hoyt said to himself, 'and state-of-the-art works, too. I can't imagine where Alen managed to get them all.' He considered how he might transport the outlawed books back to Southport. Smuggling a bit of fennaroot or a few weapons was a challenge; this, however, would be a significant undertaking. He'd stolen a wheelbarrow, but that wouldn't be enough. He'd have to—

'Good evening.' A woman, attractive but dangerous-looking, took the seat beside him.

'Not tonight,' Hoyt said. 'Go and find someone else.' He had more important things to attend to than hungry prostitutes on the prowl.

The woman motioned to the barman. 'I'll have the same, and another flagon of that too, please.'

Hoyt took a drink. 'I'm sorry, maybe you didn't hear me. I'm not interested. And I am not buying you dinner.'

She tossed a worn leather pouch onto the table. It chimed with the telltale *clink* of silver Mareks. 'I'm not a prostitute; so relax. I can pay my own way. I was just looking for someone interesting with whom to have dinner.'

'Hoyt,' Milla tugged his sleeve. 'Hoyt, you need to come with me.' She was dressed in her overnight tunic and held her straw dog by one dislocated leg.

'What? Milla?' Hoyt was confused. This wasn't right, this was not how things had happened ... *had to* happen. 'Milla, what are you doing here?'

The woman, Ramella – *how do I know her name?* – went on, seemingly oblivious to the little girl beside the table, 'That looks delicious. How is it?'

'The best venison I've eaten in Middle Fork,' Hoyt lied.

'Hoyt,' Milla insisted, 'the Seron are coming; they'll find you. You can't stay here.'

Hoyt tore his gaze away from Ramella, the seductive thief from Landry. He whispered to Milla, 'Why don't you go up to bed? I'll be up in a while, and I'll come and say good night to you then.'

'Sorry, Hoyt,' Milla said, 'but you need to come with me now.' Something bit him hard on the ankle.

'Holy rutting horsecocks!' Hoyt shouted, standing suddenly, spilling the wine and upending his food. He gripped his leg, stemming the flow of blood, then remembered himself. 'Sorry, sweetie, Hoyt said a few bad words there, huh? You won't tell Hannah, will you?' *Who's Hannah?* he thought. *I don't know anyone named Hannah . . . not yet.*

'Of course not, silly,' Milla laughed, 'and sorry about the puppy, but I need you to pay attention, or you'll die in here. You'll get stuck for ever like the ones at the palace.'

He nodded dumbly. He had no idea what the girl meant, but somehow he was aware that her words had significant meaning for him. Tentatively, he checked beneath the table, understanding before he did that he would find Branag's wolfhound, the same dog that tracked them – *will track us* – from Southport to the Welstar docks. The wolfhound was there, his tongue lolling, in good spirits, healthy, young, well-fed, and with a shiny coat, not the tattered, trail-worn hunter that had been dying when it finally caught up with them. 'Ramella,' Hoyt said, 'I'm sorry, but I have to go.'

The sultry woman ignored him, carrying on with their conversation as if Hoyt's input meant nothing. 'Do you want to know what my vices are?' she asked.

Hoyt shook his head. 'This is impossible. This happened already, so long ago.' He turned to Milla. 'Long before you were even born, Pepperweed.'

'I know,' she said, stealing a chunk of bread from Ramella's platter, then dipping it into the stranger's gravy. 'Can we go now?' Ramella didn't notice.

'Yes.' Hoyt took her hand. 'How? Do you know how to get us back?' He'd begun to put the pieces together.

'Of course.' Milla spoke through a mouthful of food. 'That tastes good.'

'Yes, it did,' Hoyt agreed. 'All right, Pepperweed, take me back – but not back to the inn, I have to get Alen.'

'He's coming back, too. I already talked to him. He's waiting for you. He was in someplace else, Durram or somewhere. I don't know where that is, but the lady with him was very sad. They had to leave the baby behind. Alen was sad, too.'

'But the Seron, and the Malakasian guards – how can we—?'

'I'll scare them off for you,' Milla said, stealing another piece of gravy-dipped bread. 'But they won't stay away for long so you two have to hurry.'

'What a negative outlook on human emotion,' Ramella went on, now staring into the space left empty when Hoyt rose to follow the little girl back to reality.

'How are you doing this?' Hoyt asked. 'How is this possible?'

'Some things I can just do,' Milla said. With that, Hoyt felt a band wrap around his chest. It tightened, hardening to iron and threatening to suffocate him.

'Not too tight, Pepperweed,' he warned.

'Sorry,' Milla grinned, her hair an endearing scribble.

'Is this how you kept Gilmour from falling?'

'Uh huh,' the little magician said smugly, proud of her work.

'Good job.' Hoyt stroked her curls, and said, 'Let's go.'

'One moment, I have to chase the Seron away first.'

On the highway south of Pellia, with three wagons in flames, most of their cargo lost and more than a few of their number dead or dying in the fire, Prince Malagon's Seron warriors were undeterred; no one fled, no one wept and no one dallied over the bodies of fallen comrades. They formed ranks around the final wagon, salvaged what they could from the burning carts and resumed their journey towards Welstar Palace. When the aerial firestorm slowed, they conducted a search of the fields, but they found no sign of terrorist archers, no Resistance army, and no reason to dig in or to return to Pellia.

Their lieutenant, a big female with a grisly burn on her forearm, climbed to the driver's bench and barked orders at what remained of her platoon. The others fell in step and the wagon rolled on, quickly leaving the fiery devastation behind. Soon the burning wagons – and bodies – were little more than flickering lights in the distance.

The woman checked the perimeter, checked the sentry lines,

checked the squad assigned to the wagon itself, and then settled on the bench beside the driver. 'Welstar,' she growled.

The driver, shook out the reins and the team started off while the last of the Seron took up their positions. He shouted at those Malakasians in his way; they had emerged from their homes, still in their nightclothes, to view the carnage. *This bunch ought to get back inside*, he thought, *they don't know what these Seron might do*. 'Go on now!' he cried, 'back to bed with you all!'

A few complied, but others, possibly unaware they were risking death, continued to watch the Seron monsters, some snarling with smouldering rage, as they marched towards Malagon's legendary keep.

When the first of the dogs howled, he squinted into the darkness. 'Now that's a big dog,' he said. 'A herder, that one, and with a bull's set of pipes on him, too.'

The Seron lieutenant ignored him as she bound the wound on her arm with a strip of cloth torn from a blanket beneath the bench.

'You know, you ought to—' the driver began.

'Welstar!' the Seron repeated, cutting him off.

'All right, all right. I'll shut up, but you're going to get some kind of nasty infec—'

Another dog howled, this one from across the highway, a lingering wail, an unnatural sound sustained too long in a shrill, threatening cry. It was answered almost immediately by a macabre echo, this from the south, somewhere ahead of the wagon team.

'Now that's not something you hear every day,' he said shakily, but a withering glance from the lieutenant silenced him again.

She stood and shouted a quick string of orders to her platoon: *Stand fast! Don't be drawn into the fields*.

The howls and barks came from all around them now. Some were low and resonant, rumbling deep in broad, powerful chests; others were like screams, pitched high and wailing, dangerous even from far away. 'I don't like this,' the driver said, trying unsuccessfully to quieten the horses. He peered left and right, trying to move only his eyes, as if sitting still might keep danger from spotting him.

Something moved, low and fast, just out of sight, crunching through frost and brittle cornstalks.

'Oi! What's that then?' He jumped, and cried out, 'Rutting whores, there must be fifty of them – gods, but I wish they'd stop yelping so. What could have them so fired—?'

'Shutap!' The lieutenant cuffed him on the temple, nearly

knocking him from the bench. She grunted more orders to her platoon: *Look sharp! Be ready!*

A dog appeared in the highway, its eyes glowing red, even in the dim light of the torches carried by the Malakasian guards. It was a wolfhound, the biggest the driver had ever seen. Its mane bristled as it growled through clenched teeth, its jowls dripping froth.

'Great whoring—' The driver drew his sword and twisted the reins around his free wrist as the wolfhound charged the horses, snarling and biting at their forelegs. The lieutenant gestured to a Seron guard, urging him forward to kill the animal, but before he could comply, the roiling din of barking, growling, yelping and shrieking choked to a sudden, unnerving silence. Only the dog attacking the horse team continued to bark.

The lieutenant shouted down at the soldier, 'Ahat dog! Ahat!' Her voice carried over the snowy field like a thunderclap.

The Seron came abreast of the rearing horses. The driver tried to calm the animals, keeping a steady grip on the reins, as the Seron moved in for the kill, raising his knife and then leaping for the dog.

As if the Seron's action was a cue, wolfhounds similar to their leader attacked from all sides, materialising out of the darkness. One sprang onto the attacking Seron's back, biting first at his neck and then at the hand holding the knife. Another, an ebony copy of the first two, used the struggling Seron as a springboard, leaping from his back onto the first horse in the wagon team. It snarled at the driver, then sank its fangs into the horse's neck. The animal screamed, reared in terror, kicked the Seron warrior in the head and then bolted, dragging its teammates and the cart through the ditch into the cornfield.

'Whoring mothers!' the driver shouted, slashing at a dog trying to climb the side of the wagon. The animal fell away, its jaws snapping audibly, and the frightened driver hauled back on the reins until the wagon crashed through a plough rut and he was jounced from the bench, landing with a bone-jarring thud in the frozen soil. He dropped his sword but kept a grip on the reins, which was a mistake, for no amount of tugging slowed the horses and he was dragged halfway across the field until he finally let go and fell face-down in the snow.

Back on the road, what remained of the Seron platoon was engaged in an epic battle with a seemingly endless number of inky-black wolfhounds. For every dog they slashed, stabbed or clubbed to death, another appeared, hurtling out of the darkness like a phantom. They stood their ground, hacking and stabbing to all points of the compass;

any that fell were soon covered with snarling beasts; three and four at a time climbed onto the fallen warriors, snapping at arms, necks, ankles and faces, until the Seron, exhausted or dead, finally lay still.

As the wagon thundered across the cornfield Hoyt pushed his way through the canvas bags, then cleared several more for Alen.

'What just happened?' he shouted. 'What was that?'

'Milla,' Alen said, checking his forearm.

'You hurt?'

'Her dog, that cursed hound bit me.'

'Me too.' Hoyt pulled his boot halfway off, exposing his lower leg. 'It hurt like a motherhumper, but look: no blood. None on you either.'

'We'll worry about it later. For now, let's get the blazes out of here.'

'Fine by me,' Hoyt said and started up the side of the cart, climbing the slats. 'We're going to have to jump. It'll hurt.'

'No worse than staying around to see what the Seron plan to do with us.'

'Good point,' Hoyt said. 'I think most of them are back there. Milla's sent some kind of— Ah!' he screamed as the Seron lieutenant stabbed him in the shoulder. She had been aiming for his neck, but a lucky jolt as the cart bounced over uneven ground sent her blow wide of the mark. Alen shouted as Hoyt tumbled backwards and fell beside him, neither in any position to defend themselves. Alen fired a spell, a wild blast, hoping to get lucky and kill the angry warrior, but he missed, and blew out the upper slats instead.

'Rutters, that hurts!' Hoyt tried to roll away from the knife-wielding soldier. 'Look out, Alen! Get back!'

'Over here!' Alen tugged Hoyt's good arm, looking for a safe corner, but there wasn't space enough in the wagon bed. The Seron woman adjusted her grip and sprang towards them.

The wolfhound hit her in mid-air, driving into her from the abandoned driver's bench. It clamped its jaws around her forearm, the bones snapping with a sickening crack, and the two creatures slammed into the side of the cart, each more furious than the other.

It was a fight to the death, but neither Alen nor Hoyt planned on staying around to see the end. 'This way,' Alen said, raising his hands at the wooden tailgate. An explosion rocked the night and the end of the cart was blown away, scattered across the cornfield in splinters. 'Now, jump!' he cried, grabbed Hoyt by the elbow and shoved.

When he landed, Hoyt tore the wound in his shoulder more deeply. *Whose idea was this?* he thought, lying on the freezing ground, resilient stalks poking him in the back. Nearby, he heard Alen groan. 'You all right?' he wheezed.

'Fine,' Alen chuckled. 'Never better, really. I'm actually thinking I would like a bit of corn about now.'

'Stop it.' Hoyt hugged his sides. 'Don't make me laugh.'

Alen knelt beside him. 'Whoring virgins, you're a mess. That shoulder's going to need some stitching.'

'I'll be all right.' Hoyt sat up. 'Let's get out of here. Those dogs were a nice trick, but they won't keep the Seron away all night.'

'You think they were real?'

'They seemed real enough to me,' Hoyt said. 'Remind me to take Milla shopping tomorrow for whatever her little heart desires.'

'I hope they were apparitions, you know, fighting the Seron from within, figments of our collective imagination,' Alen said, helping Hoyt to his feet. 'If they weren't, the city is going to be a tough place to live.'

'A highway full of dead soldiers?'

'Not exactly how we had things planned.'

'It was bark.'

'I know.'

'But it was different this time.'

'I know.'

VERSEN AND SALLAX

The southern edge of the Falkan plain rolled beneath them as Gilmour and Steven, riding in tandem, encouraged the horse just a bit further before stopping to camp for the night. They were in no hurry to reach the fjord; they had eight days yet to arrive at their rendezvous point – if Garec and Kellin even survived the flood tide – and there was ample time to locate Mark's boat, sail west and, on the appointed day, make for open water. Gilmour had assisted the stolen skiff with a Larion tailwind when he, Garec and Mark had navigated the twists and turns of the great granite cleft the previous Twinmoon, so he was sure he and Steven would be able to do the same on the return journey. A hearty northerly wind freshening behind them made him wonder if he could come up with a spell to turn periodic gusts westwards behind the skiff; it would be a tricky manoeuvre, but with nine days to reach the open sea, they would have time to experiment.

'I think this poor horse has had just about as much of us as he can take for one day,' Gilmour said. 'There's a place not far from here where we can tuck ourselves in for a couple of days, always assuming we don't run into any occupation soldiers in there.'

'A popular vacation spot, is it?' Steven asked wryly.

'Not really, but you never can tell where those rutters'll turn up.'

'I wonder why we haven't seen any since the Medera did her thing,' Steven mused.

'I've been thinking that as well, and I don't know.' Gilmour patted the horse, whispering, 'Not much further, my friend. We'll rest soon.' They had found the animal wandering along a hillside north of the river, Lessek's spell book and the far portal still tied safely to the saddle. Though battered and bruised, the animal had come through the devastation without serious injury, and after walking beside them for a day, it finally permitted the two sorcerers to ride.

'Don't the Malakasians patrol this area?' Stephen asked as they moved from a field lying fallow into a thick patch of cottonwoods lining a draw at the base of a gully. The gully separated the field and a rolling meadow that looked like it had been left for spring hay. There was a row of mature trees lining the draw-end of the meadow and Steven watched for the shallow stream he was sure they would cross before climbing into the dry, waist-high grass.

'Of course they patrol. We haven't used any major roads, but we also haven't been too deliberate about hiding ourselves either. I can't understand it, but if we get where we're going without running into an entire brigade of soldiers there enjoying a professional lecture on the finer points of sword sharpening, I'll be content to call it a great mountain of very good fortune.'

'Drunks' and children's luck,' Steven said.

'I'll drink to that.' The horse broke through the thin ice of the stream and they began their climb into the meadow.

'Do you think Mark's boat will still be there?' Gilmour didn't sound as confident as he had when he initially presented this course of action to the others.

'I don't see why not,' Steven said. 'It was well hidden, and any snowfall would only add to its camouflage. Who on earth would be sailing for pleasure during this Twinmoon, anyway?'

'Only fools,' Gilmour laughed.

'You and me, cousin,' Steven said, then asked, 'what if Kellin and Garec don't make it?' They had found no sign of the others after the flood waters receded.

'Then we attempt the crossing on our own.'

'You've been in the fennaroot again, haven't you, old man?'

'Not me, though there's no doubt my horse and I both could use a bit of root right now.'

'Your relationship with your horse is your own business, but I'll reiterate, in case you didn't hear me: cross the wide ocean, on our own, in that catboat?'

'Any other suggestions?'

'How about finding a clean, comfortable inn with a big fireplace, a well stocked bar and a squad of randy coeds next door?'

'A lovely thought, Steven, truly.' Gilmour sighed. 'If only we had that kind of time ...'

'Yeah, I know, but it's nice to dream,' Steven acquiesced. 'Fine, then, I'm going to figure on Garec and Kellin having survived the wave.'

'You and me both, cousin.'

'There's the spirit,' Steven laughed. 'I am worried, though – I saw the water swallow them, and then I never saw them again. Of course, I was preoccupied at the time.'

Gilmour changed the subject. 'Regardless, we have a few days, and I need to look for something the Larion Brotherhood misplaced long ago.'

'Why don't I like the sound of that?'

'Oh, this doesn't concern you. Just think of it as a learning experience.'

'That's what my stats professor called the two-by-three-way analysis of covariance; we all called it "that fucking nightmare".'

'Nonsense,' Gilmour said, 'an aven or two – in and out. We'll be back on the road before nightfall.'

'Where are we?' Stephen asked as they crested the highest point in the meadow. He looked across a patchwork of fields at a jumble of dilapidated buildings marring the pastoral landscape.

'At school.'

'So you were with him; he made it here to Orindale?' Garec sipped his tecan, considered it with a frown and motioned to the barman. 'A beer, please, a big one.'

Brexan waved at him too. 'Make that two, please.'

Kellin raised a hand. 'Three.'

It was still an aven early for the dinner crowds, so the front room of the alehouse they'd found was almost empty. Scarred wooden tables crowded the floor between the bar and the fireplace. Brexan drank what was left of her tecan, then turned to the beer before she replied, 'No, Versen never made it to Orindale. I lost him ... *we* lost him in a meadow near a stream south of the city. From what Gabriel told me, it was some time after you and Steven had battled the wraiths in the trapper's cabin.'

'Rutters,' Garec said, 'he lived that long? We were sure he had been killed at the base of Seer's Peak. When we came down from the heights, the camp had been torn to shreds by grettans and the Seron.'

Brexan grimaced. 'We were unfortunate enough to meet the Seron, and if I ever find their leader, a big horsecock named Lahp, I'm going to gut him and fry his heart.'

'Lahp?' Garec said, visibly surprised. 'You knew Lahp?'

'The whoring rutter broke my cheek. I'm looking forward to killing him.'

'He's dead.'

'Good.'

'Not really,' Garec said, 'although I can see how you would think that. But shortly after you left Seer's Peak, Lahp and the rest of his platoon were attacked by a pack of grettans sent by Prince Malagon to finish us off. Lahp was badly injured; Steven saved him, touched him somehow, and he helped us cross the Blackstones. He saved Steven's life more than once and died protecting us as well as he could from the wraiths.'

'That's— well, surprising,' Brexan admitted. 'I wouldn't have thought he had anything good in him at all.'

'It surprised all of us,' Garec said. 'So tell us what happened to Versen.'

'He died because I passed out. We were fighting a Seron, another ruthless big bastard called Haden. I left myself exposed and he shattered my cheek again. Versen had broken Haden's leg; he was twisting and punching it when I lost consciousness.' Brexan paused to take a breath; she didn't want to break down in front of Garec. She had no idea what he thought of her, a deserter-turned-partisan who failed to save either of his childhood friends; she wasn't about to cry in front of him.

Instead, it was Garec who started to cry, as tears filled his eyes and spilled down his cheeks. He sniffed loudly, then wiped his face. He pressed his lips together and swallowed hard. 'What happened to Haden?'

'I cut him.'

'Cut him?'

'Two hundred and thirty-six times, give or take. I wanted to remember the number exactly, but after a while they ran together.'

Garec nodded grimly. 'Good.'

Kellin, looking tired and wan, ran an ashen hand between Garec's shoulders. She let her fingers rest on his neck, toying with a lock of his hair. 'So you came into the city on your own?' she asked.

'I can't remember how long it took me to get here,' Brexan said, 'things were pretty blurry. They still are, when I think back on it. It's almost as though it happened Twinmoons and Twinmoons ago. But I made it here, and I was in the city less than an aven before I ran into Sallax.'

Garec said, 'We looked for him when we were here, but never found him.'

'I'm not surprised,' Brexan said. 'He was a mess, living like an animal behind and between the warehouses on the southern wharf. He was struggling badly with guilt and regret.'

'He had a painful realisation the day he left us,' Garec said softly.

'I know, and he wanted me to find you. It was the last thing he asked me, actually. He specifically mentioned you, Garec. He wanted me to find you and to tell you the truth about what had happened.'

Garec raised his eyebrows. 'Me? Not Gilmour?'

'Gilmour's dead.'

'No he isn't, Brexan, Gilmour's fine – well, he was the last time we saw him, anyway. We're on our way to meet him now.' The irony wasn't lost on any of them, and Garec spat a string of curses into his beer. 'If only Sallax had known.'

Brexan repeated, 'He wanted me to tell you the truth about him.'

'You don't have to.' Garec was crying again. 'I know the truth about him.'

Kellin pulled him to her and Garec buried his face in the nape of her neck.

Brexan felt horribly uncomfortable, an interloper with nothing but depressing news. She went across to the huge fireplace and threw a log onto the fire, giving them a moment alone together.

'How was he?' Garec finally asked.

Brexan took her seat. 'He struggled for a long time. He was sick with guilt, wild, almost out of his mind. I never knew for certain, but I think the wraiths in the Blackstones did something to him, forced him somehow to consider what he had done to Gilmour ... or at least think on what he believed he had done. It took a long time to get him back.'

'But you did?'

'For a while, yes,' Brexan said, then hesitated before adding, 'until he made another tragic discovery.'

'Brynne.' It wasn't a question.

Brexan held up her wrist; her tunic sleeve fell to reveal Mark Jenkins' old watch, still hanging where Sallax had strapped it while the fugitives huddled together in the empty barrel behind the seedy riverfront alehouse.

'And afterwards?' Garec asked, 'did he run off on you again?'

'No, but he did get cold, ruthless and deadly. We interrogated and killed – well, sort of killed – a merchant, Carpello Jax, who was shipping something nefarious from southern Rona to Welstar Palace through Pellia.'

'Why? Who cares what some merchant is shipping north?' Kellin asked. The beer had brought some colour back to her cheeks.

'It's something ugly, I don't know what, but Prince Malagon is willing to pay almost anything to get it by the shipload, some kind of tree bark or leaves.'

Garec and Kellin shared a knowing glance.

'What?' Brexan asked, 'you know something about it?'

Garec shook his head. 'I'm not sure. Gilmour detected a shipment moving north along the Ravenian Sea a few days ago. Maybe there's a connection, but either way, you don't have to worry about Prince Malagon any longer. He's dead; he's been dead for over a Twinmoon now.'

'And Nerak?'

'Dead, lost, cast away; I don't know how to describe it, but Steven did it, opened the Fold and tossed him in like a rubbish sack.'

'It was actually pretty cathartic to watch,' Kellin said, smiling. 'I'm sorry you weren't there. It sounds like you've had a difficult time.'

'Well, Sallax and I had a catharsis of our own.'

'This Carpello?'

'He was essentially responsible for Versen's death.' Brexan took a long draught of beer and motioned for another round.

'Then I'm glad you killed him,' Garec said, 'or sort of killed him ... whatever that means.'

'Oh, he's dead,' Brexan said, 'and we were there. We just didn't get to deliver the final blow.'

'Sorry. It sounds like you deserved that one.'

'Brynne deserved it more than I.'

'Brynne?' Garec frowned. 'Why Brynne?'

'Versen saw it right away. It took Sallax a bit longer, but he eventually realised it as well. Carpello Jax was the man who raped Brynne as a child.'

Garec's lip quivered and instead he twisted his face into a sneer, malevolent and deadly. He spoke through welling tears. 'I want to know how you did it.'

Brexan was happy to impart the details. Remembering Carpello's death was like recalling a pleasant experience. 'We clubbed him a few times, we beat him up and terrorised him until he was weeping like a baby. He shat his leggings, bled all over himself and finally summoned the courage to try and escape.'

'And?'

'And a friend of mine struck him with a piece of firewood. It didn't kill him, but slipping and falling headlong into the stone fireplace did.'

'What did you do with the body?'

Brexan didn't like the tone of Garec's question; she had a sudden and disturbing image of the *Bringer of Death* digging up a corpse and eating it, just to make *certain* it was dead. Shrugging off the image, she said, 'We set him adrift on the outgoing tide. It was just north of here, around the point, up near the marsh.'

Garec regained his composure. 'It ruined Brynne as a kid. I never knew her to have serious feelings for anyone until she met Mark Jenkins; she joked and played around with men who sometimes came by the tavern, but she wasn't able to show real affection for anyone. Maybe it was different because Mark was from somewhere else; he wasn't tainted by whatever she believed tarnished Eldarni men. Carpello Jax ... so that was his name. He turned her into a killer. We didn't know it at the time, but she was the first of us to fall; she did it with such grace and conviction, using a pair of knives – I wouldn't have wanted to fight her. She was the best, better even than Sallax, with a short blade.'

Recalling the deftness with which Sallax had killed the Seron, Brexan understood that Brynne must have been deadly. She changed the subject. 'How's your head?'

'Inside or outside?'

'Outside, I suppose.'

'Not bad,' he said, 'although I worry about Kellin's skill with a needle. I'm afraid I might end up with a few permanent wrinkles up there.'

'Rutting ingrate,' Kellin chided, then to Brexan said, 'He was passed out, bleeding everywhere. My horse was already dead, crushed against a tree; his died while I was tending to him, scared the dogpiss out of me. It barked, or shouted a horse curse, who knows? My fingers were cold, and I had two cracked ribs and a broken collarbone; so yes, I might have mis-stitched a time or two.'

'Demonpiss, broken bones?' Brexan said. 'Are you all right?'

'I'm fine,' Kellin replied. 'We saw a healer yesterday and went back for more querlis this morning.' Brexan hadn't noticed the heavy bandages holding Kellin's arm immobile against her ribs. 'I can feel it working, but it makes me so tired; I can barely stand up, never mind traipse all over Orindale looking for one of the six remaining captains who haven't committed suicide in the past three days.'

'You ought to rest,' Brexan said. 'Do you have a place to stay?'

'We found an inn a few streets east of here, about halfway between the wharf and the old imperial palace. Why? Where are you staying?'

'You should come with me. It's a comfortable place, up north, around the point. It's a quiet district off the salt marsh. Nedra keeps a quiet, clean inn, and she's the best cook I've known since I came east from Malakasia.'

'We have a few things in our room: my bow, some clothes and a bit of silver. We have about six days to find some transport heading north.'

'Where could you possibly need to get to?' Brexan asked. 'You two are a mess – sorry, but you are. You ought to spend a few days in bed, a Moon. Take some time; get healed up. You're in no condition to be travelling now.'

'Gods, but that sounds tempting,' Kellin sighed. 'And as much as I would like to spend a Moon in bed, with or without Garec—'

'*With*, please,' he interrupted, 'I mean, what else would you do with all that time? Rest? Sleep? Talk to yourself?' He smiled for the first time all day. Brexan thought he looked refreshingly boyish.

'You have other suggestions?' Kellin asked.

Garec slid an arm around her waist. 'I don't want to commit too early, but I'm sure I could come up with something.'

'Ahem,' Brexan flushed, 'sorry to interrupt you two, but where are Gilmour and Steven?'

Garec left his hand on Kellin's backside. There was comfort in touching her. 'We're not sure, but we're supposed to meet them in nine days off the coast of a narrow fjord about three days' journey north of here.'

'On the ocean?' Brexan nearly spat a mouthful of beer across the table. 'Have you not seen it outside? The northern Twinmoon is coming and has kicked up a nightmare wind; the tides are going to be high and running fast. Did you see those frigates this morning? They were damned near skipping across the surface of the harbour. They'll be in Pellia by the dinner aven at the rate they're going.'

'We have to try,' Garec said. 'And Steven and Gilmour have a way of encouraging things to work out in their favour.'

'How will they get to the meeting place?'

'In a boat, of course.'

'So if they have a boat already, why can't you all just sail in that?'

'It's too small, dangerously small, given the conditions,' Garec said. 'And if it's this bad in here, I can't imagine what it's like out on the sea. We'd capsize inside an aven.'

'But Gilmour and Steven are using this boat to sail offshore and ... what, wait around for you two?'

'We were hoping for good timing and quiet seas.'

'Why didn't they come into the city with you? You could have left together,' Brexan asked.

Kellin answered, 'Because some of their magic and a few of the artefacts they carry can be tracked from afar.'

'But with Nerak dead, who's—'

'Mark Jenkins,' Garec said. 'He was overwhelmed and taken, just like Nerak almost a thousand Twinmoons ago. Mark is trapped inside his own mind by the same minion of evil that held the Malakasian royal family hostage for more than five generations. It can certainly track Gilmour and it might be able to track Steven, but we don't know for certain. That's why Orindale Harbour was all but destroyed, and that's why the massive floodtide was sent up the Medera. Mark knew we were following downriver so he sent the flood to kill us, or at least to delay us until he could—'

'Could what?' Brexan was held transfixed.

'I don't know,' Garec said. 'Open the Fold, ensure evil's ascendancy in Eldarn, destroy the world, enslave us all, I don't know. But that's why we have to find a ship and that's why we have to meet Gilmour and Steven. We have to get to Pellia and then, perhaps, to Welstar Palace to find and deal with Mark Jenkins.'

'Deal with?' Brexan pressed.

'If I can get within two hundred paces of him, I'll kill him,' Garec said. 'That's why we need a ship.'

Kellin glanced out the front window towards the harbour.

'I don't think we're going to make it, though. There don't look to be too many heading north – or heading anywhere, for that matter. Other than those three frigates, that's been the extent of the traffic.'

'There isn't even anything to steal – not that Garec and I could crew the thing anyway. I'd be trapped on a yard-arm or strung up by a tangled rope within an aven,' Kellin added. 'We've plenty of silver, but not a clue about where to find boat or captain.'

Brexan finished her beer with a flourish. 'Then you certainly need to come with me.'

'You have a ship heading north?'

'Maybe,' she said, 'if we're not too late.'

'Then go,' Garec said, 'don't wait for us. We'll get our things; you go get us that boat. We need to leave in about six days.'

Brexan reached for her cloak then stopped. 'Us?'

Garec nodded. 'I want you to talk with Gilmour; it'll be good for him to hear what you have to say. He and Versen were close, but he and Sallax were like—'

'I know.' Brexan felt her heart speed up again; this was it, she was back in her element. She'd be sad to leave Nedra, but hopefully she would understand. *And I'll come back*, Brexan thought, *when this is all done. I'll come back and stay with her until the end.*

Kellin interrupted her thoughts, asking, 'Do you *want* to come with us?'

'More than anything,' Brexan said quickly, in case Garec changed his mind.

Garec took her hands. 'Good. You belong with us.'

'And now I have to hurry,' Brexan said. 'I'm at the Topgallant Inn, north of the point, at the end of Tapen Rise, near the marsh.'

'We'll be there.'

'And we'll find Gilmour?' Brexan felt reborn; she could have kissed them both.

'We will.'

'Oh, whoring rutters,' Brexan stopped. 'What if Ford and his crew won't take us?'

'We'll offer them all we have to get us to Averil,' Garec said.

'Averil?' Brexan stopped. 'It'll take you until spring to get to Pellia from there – and that's if you're allowed through. Prince Malagon didn't encourage unannounced guests.'

'We'll hire your captain to take us to Averil, and once we're at sea, we'll . . . well, you know—'

'We'll renegotiate our destination,' Kellin finished for him.

Garec smiled. 'There you have it.'

Brexan's stomach knotted at the unsettling feeling that she had allowed her enthusiasm to cloud her judgment. Captain Ford didn't strike her as one who would do well with liars or scheming partisans. She'd have to tell him the truth – but surely he'd understand the importance of their journey and take them all the way to Pellia. It wouldn't be a problem. She hoped.

Kellin read her hesitation. 'What's wrong?'

'Nothing – it's just that this captain isn't a fool. He's been working the Ravenian Sea for a long time, and I'm not sure how many trips he's made north of the archipelago.'

'We'll worry about that when we get there,' Garec said. 'If it's too bad, we'll put in to shore and make our way into Pellia on foot.'

'That might work,' Brexan murmured. 'I just worry that it may not be a very pleasant journey after we find Gilmour and *encourage* Captain Ford to take us through the Northeast Channel.'

'Pleasant?' Garec said. 'Brexan, when we get there I will personally explain to Captain Ford how little I care whether our journey is pleasant.' The boyish look on Garec's face had faded. The *Bringer of Death* was back.

KNOWLEDGE AND MAGIC

Mark shifted in his chair. Old Grünbaum had the worst chairs, the kind that connected to the desk with a curved bar of what was, at one time, polished silvery metal. Now, forty years later, those desk-chair connectors were corroded rust barely holding the shape, with exposed bolts on each end. Mark scraped his arm on a jagged corner and wondered if the school board knew about the condition of Herr Grünbaum's classroom furniture. *I'll have to ask Mom if my tetanus vaccination is up to date.* Even Gerry O'Donnell, Mark's curmudgeon of a calculus teacher, had new desks; the whole county had them, all except for Grünbaum, the venerable Kraut, here forty-one years and still teaching German I through V, the advanced placement class for the bright kids or the kids from Bakersfield, who had German or Jewish grandparents. Many of them knew a good bit of the guttural language long before coming to lessons in ninth grade. But the desks had to be some kind of retribution on the part of the Massapequa Public Schools Division, for four decades of Herr Gerrold Grünbaum's Teutonic dictation: *hören und sagen. Jetzt, fanger wir an . . . eins, zwei, drei, vier . . .* and all the time his sparklingly clean wingtips clicked in perfect rhythm on the scuffed tile floor.

This was German II, non-honours, a general education class for college-bound tenth graders, exceptional ninth graders and those who needed a spare foreign language credit. Save for a pair of Hungarian kids who spoke some German at home, the class was not a hotbed of talent. Mark was amongst the brightest in the room, and he periodically had to pinch himself – *or slice my goddamned arm open on the desk* – to stay awake.

Today, there was a snake on the floor, one of the colourful ones he and Steven had seen on the Discovery Channel, a coral snake: a nasty little bastard with plenty of the Crayola ringlets the tiresome narrator with his now-you-hear-it-now-you-don't British accent had called 'nature's way of saying danger'.

Steven had paraphrased: *Stay back, meathead, or I'll sting you where it hurts.*

That wasn't right; Mark wouldn't meet Steven Taylor for seven years.

The snake was coiled up and motionless, watching and waiting; Mark tried not to step on it – that would piss it off – while he shifted uncomfortably and tried to follow Herr Grünbaum's lesson.

Heute müßen wir . . . blah, blah, blah.

Somebody knock me senseless for the next twenty-two minutes.

Jody Calloway was sitting next to him. Mark wanted to check her pulse; she hadn't moved in ten minutes. *She might be dead, bored to death. And my mother said that was impossible.* He craned his neck to see if she was breathing or if there was a puddle of drool pooling on the desktop. *I'd get interviewed by the paper. They'd ask what happened, and I'd tell them she was fine, looking normal, chatting with friends, but then Old Grünbaum started in on the differences between Viennese and Bavarian German, but I wasn't really listening; I was trying to see if Jody was still alive because I thought it might be entertaining if she would, you know, move around a bit, maybe lean back once or twice before the end of the period. She's no dairy princess, but at least there's something there to see.*

On the board, Grünbaum had drawn one of his famous sketches. Mark's Uncle Dave had gone to Massapequa Heights as well, twenty-seven years earlier, and he'd had Grünbaum for German I and II. Even then, back in the sixties, the old bastard had been drawing bad sketches of castles, battlefields, rivers, and all manner of architectural styles: Gothic this and Baroque that; Mark wondered how he didn't manage to improve over time. *He's been drawing the same shit for four decades; you'd think he'd eventually get better,* he thought. *How many times do you have to draw the Stephansdom before it begins to look like a cathedral? Jesus, there he goes again.*

1742, Maria-Theresa von Hapsburg . . .

What did he say? How many *kids did she have – God Almighty, lady, read a book or take in a movie or something – just get off your back!*

She loved this muted yellow colour . . . used it for many of her architectural projects, including her summer home, the Palais Schönbrunn. Kyle, why don't you tell the class what that means, auf Englisch . . .

Good, good, on the hill south of the palace . . . the Gloriette, which members of the Hapsburg family used, amongst other things, for shade—

'What was that?' Mark said aloud, 'What did you say?' Without warning, he was back within himself, trapped inside the swamp with the marble-reflecting pool and the neo-classical columns. The lights flickered for a moment, flashing off the pool, then dimming into darkness. Outside the thick canopy of swamp foliage, the sky was blue. That's where he was going, across the bridge, over the reflecting pool, whatever it was, and then up that hill. Things would be different up there; he'd have more control.

At his feet, the coral snake shifted slightly, as if sensing a change in Mark Jenkins.

The Gloriette, in Vienna. That's where he had seen these columns and this odd, rectangular structure, like a stone building's skeleton with the skin peeled off. In tenth grade, he'd gone on the spring break trip to southern Germany with old Gerrold Grünbaum, and they had taken two days to visit Salzburg and Vienna. Jody Calloway had gone too. She and Mark had made out in the hotel that night after Billy Carruthers and Jamie Whatshisname had sneaked all those bottles of beer back inside Billy's raincoat – though they could have wrapped them in fluorescent paper and tied them with bows; Herr Grünbaum couldn't see a thing by that time. He had to have been well over eighty by the time he led that trip.

But this was the place, the Gloriette, Maria-Theresa von Hapsburg's private shady spot, overlooking her private zoo. Lovely.

Mark remembered Jody sneaking him behind one of these columns and kissing him hard, then leaving him to finish the tour looking like he was smuggling bananas in his jeans. He'd tried to grab a feel, but she'd been too fast, spinning away and rejoining her friends; she had been a track star, too damned fast for a horny, boob-grabbing sophomore.

Nice to see you've figured it out.

'Figured what out?' Mark took a wary step along the marble coping. If they were talking, he might be permitted to move closer to the bridge and safe passage across the dangerous water.

The Gloriette. It's a nice touch; don't you think? Although I prefer it there on the hill behind Schönbrunn. It's too humid in here.

'I don't get it,' Mark said. 'What's your point?'

Your trip to Vienna, my friend. Think back; think hard. You're focusing on the wrong things . . . again. Forget Jody Calloway's tits; they were never much to speak of, anyway.

Mark slid along the coping side of the nearest column, careful to avoid slipping into the water. It was dark, and he wasn't supposed to move when it was dark, but as long as they were talking, the snake might leave him alone. 'A detail? I'm supposed to remember some detail from a spring break trip when I was fifteen – and then what, I get to go free? Or maybe make it across this puddle? Fuck you, chief, I'll take my chances wi—'

The snake bit him, then bit him again.

Mark winced, wanting to run, but knowing it would be worse if he did. He shouted and swore, rooting around in the muck, waiting for his fingers to pass over the snake's slippery body.

It bit his wrist. Mark howled in shock more than pain, but at least now he had it. It tried to strike him and slither free at the same time, but Mark would have none of it. He slid his free hand along the wriggling body until he reached the tail, which he clenched it in his fist, then he spun the creature like a bolo, faster and faster, until he snapped the snake like a bullwhip against the column, breaking its bones and paralysing it. He repeated the action until he felt it go entirely limp. It splattered against the stone with a wet splashing sound.

Finally sure it was dead, Mark tossed it away. It landed with a rustle in a patch of ferns.

Mark couldn't feel the poison working, but he'd been bitten three times, and he was worried that he might die, if he *could* die in here. While the mutant tadpoles with their bulbous tumours and the monster serpents that had pursued them all seemed benign, he understood that the coral snake had been real – it was real enough to die, and therefore real enough for its venom to be deadly.

Happier now? The voice was amused. It laughed and said, *I'm not doing this to you, Mark.*

'Yes, right, I know, it's all me. I put the bridge there, I conjured up the snake, and I went back to high school for the Hapsburg family Gloriette.'

Exactly. And you're so worried about me, all the time, me, me, me and what's happening with me. You're focusing on the wrong things, Mark; you need to think back – it's your favourite way of solving problems, isn't it? I know it's how you figured out that worthless bastard Lessek was trying to tell you something about your family and Jones Beach and all that rubbish about your father and his beer. And I know it's how you alleviate stress. Well, Mark, here's a dilemma for you: I've been honest. I've told you that you're doing this to yourself, and I've said, at least once, that I preferred you in the dark, in the first room. You recall that room, don't you?

'Yes,' Mark said, feeling for the twin puncture marks on his wrist and trying to squeeze as much blood from them as possible, hoping he might also squeeze out a bit of the venom.

And you don't want to go back in there.

'No,' Mark said, 'it was worse in there.' He pulled up his jeans and tried to squeeze the bites on his leg as well. It was difficult to assess how well it was working so he decided to try tightening his belt around his calf as a sort of tourniquet; it might stem the flow of venom around his body, buying him a few valuable minutes in which to reach the top of the rise and the blue sky. Everything would be fine if he could just reach that clearing.

So I will be honest with you again. I cannot keep you in there if you choose to be out here. How do you like them mangos, my boy?

'It's apples, dickhead.'

You eat what you like, and leave me alone.

'So, what now?'

You deal with your new dilemma.

'And what's that? Vienna?' Mark tugged his belt a bit tighter; his wrist and lower leg throbbed. 'What am I supposed to remember?'

Not remember; infer.

'Oh, grand,' Mark said. 'And what happens in the interim, while I'm here in the dark, inside a four-hundred-year-old Austrian gazebo, *inferring* something from a trip I took fourteen years ago when all the German I could manage was "How is the soup today?" – are you going to send more snakes, or are you content to watch while the venom already in my blood kills me or drives me mad or makes me piss mango juice?'

That would be a neat trick.

'Again—'

Enough insults. It was irritated now. *You're forgetting again, Mark – great lords, but you didn't strike me as this stupid. I expected more from you, truly. You're as stupid as Nerak.*

'Well, I can be disappointing.'

Everything is coming from you. The only snakes, homicidal killers, venereal diseases, whatever, are those you bring in here. I have nothing to do with that.

Mark didn't know why, but he wanted to believe that was true. 'I won't invite any more snakes in here to bite me, and I won't give myself crabs, but if I do get bit again, I'm blaming you, sh—'

Now back to work.

The lights flickered again, just long enough for Mark to see the coral snake, its head torn open and its body twisted into knots, slithering out from beneath the ferns to resume its post between Mark's feet. When the lights faded again, Mark screamed.

'So what is this place?' Steven tethered Gilmour's horse to the sturdiest post left upright on the porch. He walked along the warped boards, looking uninterestedly through the broken windows. The packed earth of the road was now a strip of frozen mud and snow. 'It must have been someplace important to have a three-storey building. Although I don't suppose anyone has been here in a long time.' They were alone and hadn't encountered anyone riding down from the grassy meadow south of the village.

'Most of my life, anyway.' Gilmour leaned in through one of the windows, then backed out quickly, peeling invisible cobwebs off his face.

Steven wandered onto the road, knocking off an icicle as he passed. It slid across the mud. 'This is another university, isn't it? I get the same sort of feeling as the last one – although I'm pleased that there don't seem to be any acid-clouds or starving almor here. That definitely gets this place an extra star in the Barron's Guidebook to Eldarni Colleges.'

'Good guess.'

Steven continued, 'And judging by the general disrepair, I'd guess that this was one of the first schools our friend Prince Marek closed after meeting Nerak back in the day.'

Gilmour leaned against a post and blew a smoke ring. 'Marek Whitward was a pleasant young man, one of the nicest of the Remonds, and it was quite tragic about him and Nerak – but don't let me interrupt. Please, go on.'

'If this university is like those back home, I'd wager that stone building over there with the collapsed roof is the library – but I don't expect we'll find any books in there today.' He pointed to an even larger, sprawling structure, standing at the centre of what might once have been the university common.

'Correct again, Steven,' Gilmour said. 'Any surviving manuscripts would have been taken to Welstar Palace, or destroyed, but we haven't come here for books.'

'All right, you have my attention. Why then have we come out of our way to visit a derelict, abandoned and obviously off-limits former institution of higher education?'

The old Larion Senator wearing the chubby soldier's body smiled, the same boyish grin Steven had seen on both of Gilmour's previous hosts. 'I need to look for something, something that's been missing in Eldarn for some time.' He started towards a set of double wooden doors, one of which hung crookedly by a single hinge.

'In there?' Steven was sceptical.

'Come on,' Gilmour said, 'or wait here. This doesn't really concern you.'

'Oh, really? You meeting some woman? Because if you are, I can wait in the car. Or give me a couple of bucks, and I'll take in a movie down the street.'

'Trust me.' Gilmour ducked through the broken frame. The empty room was a hall of sorts, with several doors off it leading to unseen rear chambers and, Steven guessed, stairs to the upper floors. There was no furniture; it, along with most of the floorboards and panelling, had been stripped, probably stolen by intrepid builders from nearby farms. A thick layer of dust moved in the air, disturbed by their arrival.

'Lovely place you've got here.'

'Like it? I call it Minimalist Grime.'

'If I run into any homicidal maniacs looking for a quiet summer hideaway I'll send them to you.'

Gilmour reached the rear wall and tried one of the doors. 'This one's latched inside.' He moved to the next; that was blocked as well. 'Curse it all,' he said, 'I hate to do this.'

'What? Force the door? Stop joking, Gilmour, just blast the thing off its hinges and let's get going. Just try not to knock down the whole building.'

Gilmour stepped back and whispered a brief spell; the door collapsed into a pile of kindling. A tremendous cloud of choking dust arose, momentarily blinding them both.

Coughing, doubled over, Steven said, 'Oh yes, great idea – that's much better!' He pushed past Gilmour into the darkness beyond the ruined doorway, saying, 'Better let me go first – who knows what might be waiting for us now that we've rung the bell?' Two steps in and he disappeared into the dark.

'I'll get some lights on,' he said after a bit and reached above his head. A pleasant glow filled the chamber, a room larger than the entryway, with a high ceiling and a polished stone floor. 'It's a damned cavern,' Stephen said. 'This one room must take up most of the building.'

'I thought you might find it interesting,' Gilmour replied.

Without speaking, Steven waved his open hands towards the

ceiling, still invisible in the shadows above, and with each gesture, a fireball, glowing with a warm, bright light, leaped from his palm and floated off to brighten another corner of the massive chamber. There were several bulky, irregularly shaped structures arranged in a desultory pattern on the floor. 'What the hell?' he whispered, brightening the orbs with a nod. 'Gilmour, what is it?'

'This? I'm not sure; it looks like a pile of wreckage, probably dumped in here when they closed the school. What I need used to be stored along that rear corridor. Wait just a moment; I'll be right back.' He crossed to an antechamber behind the debris and slipped quietly inside.

Gilmour closed the door, cast a small flame toward the ceiling, and examined the gloomy storage closet. As expected, it was empty. He sat on the dusty floor, lit his pipe, and waited.

Steven circled the mountain of trash.

He called toward the corridor. 'Okay, well, then I'll just wait in here. That's fine. I don't mind cold, damp, dusty, creepy, *and* dilapidated. It's kind of like my first apartment, only bigger ... Gilmour?'

The debris was actually a stack of variously sized cogged gears, the smallest no larger than a bicycle tyre, the largest a huge wood-and-metal wheel with a circumference of half the cavernous chamber. It looked like the gears had been dropped, one atop the other, in an upside-down pyramid, smallest at the bottom. A polished metal rod was attached to a single cog on each gear.

'There's no rust,' Steven said to himself.

He knelt beside the largest wheel and ran a hand up the silvery metal spike. 'This might have been something once, but it's just a pile of rubbish now – this big one has got to weigh two tons, though. And those loose cables up there – what are they for? Hold on a minute, just a minute ... they'd have to be attached by—' He took another lap around the pile, muttering, 'Eight ... eight to thirty and thirty to sixty, but that can't be right ... one is to four, but then there's a switch, but there's no switch in here ...' He searched the walls, the ceiling and the pile of cogged wheels, looking for a missing piece that might bring his ruminations to a tidy conclusion.

Stephen lectured to the empty room. 'It wouldn't work on the walls, and the rods are vertical ... they don't interlink – the cogs are the wrong size – but they do turn in a pattern; so what's the denominator for the ratio? One to four to eight to thirty to sixty to— Christ in the jungle, that's not right: one to four has to be a mistake, unless—unless it's on the floor ... Sonofabitch!'

In the closet, Gilmour laughed silently into his fist, relit his pipe and leaned against the doorframe, listening. He gave it half an aven, then brushed the dust from his cloak, pocketed the pipe and reentered the chamber.

The cogged wheels were suspended, seemingly of their own volition, above a series of coloured tiles cemented into the floor. A matching set of tiles was affixed to the ceiling, just a short distance above the largest gear, which wobbled and wavered dangerously as it hovered above them, parallel to the floor.

'Good gods! ' Gilmour feigned surprise. 'What have you been up to?'

Now stripped to the waist, his lean frame shiny with sweat, Steven jumped, his apparent reverie broken. 'Shit, Gilmour, don't do that!'

'What is it?'

'You don't know?' He wiped his eyes on the back of his hand.

'I'm hanged if I have any idea.'

Steven gave a self-satisfied grin. 'Do you know what day it is?'

'Of course not.'

'When was the last time that you knew – for certain – what day it was?'

'I'd have to say it was about—'

'Nine hundred and eighty-two Twinmoons ago?' The excitement was plain in his voice.

'Give or take a handful of avens, yes.'

Steven focused his attention on the floor beneath the smallest wheel. 'What you need, Gilmour, is a mathematician, and more than that, you need a mathematician who can tell you what Twinmoon it was when a miner named William Higgins walked into the Bank of Idaho Springs, now known as the First National Bank of Idaho Springs, home of the lowest-interest small business loans on the Front Range, and opened a basic interest-bearing account with more than seventeen thousand dollars in refined silver.'

'And where would I find one of them, then?' the Larion Senator asked, smiling.

'It's a clock,' Steven broke in, too excited to banter any more, 'but it doesn't use a wound spring or a counterweight.'

'If you say so,' Gilmour said, sounding nonplussed.. 'Remember your telephones and calculators? I'm not one for higher-order maths quandaries.'

'Well, this is one of the best, my friend. Because this clock uses the rotation of the world, the actual movement of Eldarn through the heavens, to determine the Twinmoon. It even charts them, up there. See those couplings, and those wires?'

'Aha.'

'It uses magic – although I bet I could get it to work with an electromagnet – because these wheels look like interlocking gears, but they actually hang here, just like this, completely independent of Eldarn's rotation. They interact with one another, but they only interact with Eldarn on the aven.'

Steven interrupted himself, ignoring the gigantic ruined timepiece for a moment. 'Have you really lived the last thousand Twinmoons without knowing the exact time of day or the exact day of the Twinmoon?'

Gilmour shrugged. 'There are a few tally-fanatics out there who claim to have maintained an accurate count, but their sum totals all conflict with one another, so none have any real credibility.'

'How old are you?'

'Exactly how old? I don't know.'

Steven looked shocked, then said, 'Do you know the role that the mechanical clock plays in a culture? It's one of the first steps in socialisation, centralisation and industrialisation. Business, city life and urban development, education, medicine and research, they all hinge on people agreeing upon what time it is and what time things happen.'

'I know; I was there.'

'Why didn't you come back and start this thing up again?' Steven asked.

'I didn't know how.'

Steven smirked. 'I did.'

'Show me.'

'You see, if Eldarn has a north pole – and based on the construction of this clock, the orbit of your twin moons, the motion of your tides, the changing of your seasons, and a rack of other variables, we must assume that it does – anyway, if Eldarn has a north pole and you could suspend yourself above it for a full day with a writing instrument in your hand, what would you draw if you left its tip on the pole for eight avens?'

'A very small circle?' Gilmour guessed.

'Top marks, but an even better answer is a dot, a spot, a three-hundred-and-sixty-degree speck. The north pole, the south pole, too, for that matter, would rotate around the tip of your pencil, quill, whatever, forming a dot on the page.'

'All right, I'm with you so far,' Gilmour said.

'Now, imagine you're suspended above Eldarn's centre point, its widest point: the equator. What would you draw?'

'A huge circle?'

'Right, the biggest circle you could draw and still be in Eldarn, and everywhere in between the dot and the gargantuan circle fits in the ratio between the tiny and the massive.'

'Why don't you forge ahead without me?' Gilmour suggested, looking blank.

'That was the tough part,' Steven said, 'and, as luck would have it—'

'Good luck, or *our* luck?'

'Good luck, for once! So as *good* luck would have it, all the work here has been done: the ratio has been calculated, and the mechanism put into place. I just had to figure out how to get it all back where it belongs.' He cocked a hand on one hip and took in the strata of overlapping gears. To Gilmour, he looked like a grimy ditch-digger taking a break.

'And it all hinges on that little wheel, there on the floor? What is that? An aven?'

'Four, actually.'

'Why four?'

'These engineers were frigging brilliant – they knew how to measure avens exactly, and they did it every day, but they checked themselves twice during every four seasons, at the winter and summer solstices. You see, no one knows how long an aven is until someone measures it exactly. Whoever built this clock knew the longest day and longest night, and by using those lengths, dividing the full day by eight, and then knowing where this room was in relation to the pole and the equator – they knew exactly how far apart to space the cogs on this little wheel and the metal rods on this floor.'

'So they didn't measure an Eldarni day in eight avens?' Gilmour asked.

'Nope, they could be more accurate by measuring four avens and then repeating the process.'

'So the floor moves with Eldarn's rotation, but the wheels don't, and the metal rods in those tiles on the floor move the cogs in this small wheel, the aven wheel, and the aven wheel completes two revolutions in one day . . .'

'*And Bingo was his name-o!*' Steven did a little dance.

Gilmour frowned. 'And once each day, that rod sticking up there turns the next largest, the day wheel? And then the day wheel's vertical rod turns one cog on the Moon gear every thirty days and the Moon wheel turns a cog on the Twinmoon gear every second time it rotates, because there are two Moons in every Twinmoon.'

Steven quoted his Larion mentor, saying, 'You get it all started and it will go on for ever, like the Twinmoons.'

'What about Ages and Eras?' Gilmour asked.

'I don't have those figured yet, but I think they're calculated by the interaction of those cables up on the wall near the ceiling. That's a tough one, because Ages and Eras are specific to Eldarni time and I don't know anything about them – I was only able to figure the clock mechanism, because I have some knowledge of maths and . . .' Steven's voice trailed off. 'You old sonofabitch . . .'

'What?' Gilmour suppressed a grin.

Steven glanced at the door through which Gilmour had disappeared almost an aven earlier. His voice boomed to the rafters as he jogged towards it. 'You tricked me! You knew!'

'I have no idea what you're talking about.' Gilmour followed. 'Wait, Steven, wait! You shouldn't go in there. It could be dangerous.'

Ignoring him, Steven threw open the door and cast a small light inside the empty closet. A cloud of aromatic pipe smoke billowed out. 'Just as I thought: you did this on purpose.'

'I knew you could do it,' Gilmour beamed. 'Magic is about knowledge. You deciphered the timepiece. No one in Eldarn could have done that, Steven, not me, Kantu, not even Nerak.'

'Because I knew when William Higgins opened his account? It was October 1870; I'm not sure which day, but you could have come close, hell, even if you had guessed.'

'But I don't know the maths, all the calculating you've been doing, comparing your time to Eldarni time.'

'I've tried to account for as many unknowns as I can. I'm embarrassed to admit I don't know exactly how many minutes there are in an Eldarni day even after I've been here this long.'

'You've had a lot on your mind,' Gilmour excused him. 'What's your guess on the Twinmoon?'

Steven used his cloak to dry his sweat, then pulled his tunic on. 'Based on a starting date of October 15, 1870, and something just over twenty hours in an Eldarni day, which is damned close, I'd call this next Twinmoon, the northern Twinmoon, nine hundred and eighty-five Twinmoons since Higgins opened the account.'

'So be it,' Gilmour said. 'You used your knowledge and your magic together. That's how the Larion Senate worked. I wanted you to experience this without my coaching. This day, this exercise will make you more powerful, Steven. Now, set the clock.'

The magic began as a faint tingling. To Gilmour, Steven said, 'Eight thousand, seven hundred and sixty hours in a year. That's over four hundred and thirty-three days in an Eldarni year, more than seven Twinmoons. How many days until the next one?'

'I think eleven,' Gilmour said, 'eleven – or maybe twelve ...'

'Eleven.' Steven went back to his murmuring; the orb constellation grew brighter with the burgeoning magic. 'That's about fifty days in this Twinmoon so far. Fifty days. And we're just past the midday aven today.'

As if hearing him, the aven gear rotated halfway around, pivoting on each metal rod in turn. After passing over the fourth, the entire wheel spun around the rod and returned to its position over the first tile, ready to repeat the morning process. 'Look at that,' Steven said. 'I was right.'

'Yes, you were,' Gilmour whispered.

At the clock's centre, magic radiated between the tiles on the floor and the ones in the ceiling, a powerful current of energy. Steven revelled in it, sensing its response even to his most insignificant commands. This was how magic was supposed to feel, not flailing wild gestures or bombastic explosions, but careful, controlled and powerful – the very energy he had used to heal Garec's lung, and to locate the almor above Sandcliff Palace.

Now he used it to start time in Eldarn. This was precision, accuracy and skill, and coupled with compassion, Steven felt there was nothing he couldn't do. *This* is what the spell book had been trying to tell him; *this* was the power Lessek's key had used to trip him on his way into the landfill, and *this* was how he had managed to defeat Nerak in the glen below Meyers' Vale. The world around him blurred; it was all inconsequential. He was focusing on the right things: the gears, the cogs, and the rotation of the world itself. Looking towards the Moon wheel, he said, 'Eleven days until the next Twinmoon.' The gears complied, rotating until eleven cogs remained on the daily wheel and one bigger cog on the Moon wheel: it would rotate the Twinmoon gear once, and Eldarn would be back to marking her own time.

'In what Twinmoon did Sandcliff fall?' Steven called.

'Third Age, third Era, Twinmoon one hundred and sixty-one.'

'In eleven days, it will be the third Age, third Era and the one thousand, one hundred and forty-sixth Twinmoon of Eldarn.'

Gilmour was silent for a moment, then he surreptitiously wiped his eyes and whispered, 'It's been a long time.'

Beneath the clock, Steven sighed and felt the magic strengthen the bond between the tiles, ensuring the Eldarni timepiece would continue spinning along its inexorable path for ever. He said, 'They were in that pile when we arrived because they had dropped. They landed in a heap and sat there for almost a thousand Twinmoons.'

'I like to think there was enough magic left in here to know that eventually someone would get time started again; it was hopeful that one day you would show up.'

Steven pursed his lips. 'Perhaps.' He paused, then said, 'Thank you for an excellent workout ... and I think I understand much better what you were trying to tell me earlier.'

'Powerful feeling, isn't it?'

'I just wish I knew as much about other things as I know about maths. Look at what I did today.' He stood back, admiring the clock and wishing Hannah or Mark, even Howard Griffin, could have been there to see it.

'You know Mark Jenkins pretty well, don't you?'

Steven blanched. 'Yes,' he whispered.

'Then this may prove useful in another arena too.' .

'You must have been a good teacher, back in your prime.'

Gilmour forced a smile. 'I think I might have been.' He followed Steven out through the dusty antechamber and into the street. 'We should probably push on. With any luck we'll find a farm between now and nightfall.'

'I hate to leave this place,' Steven said, looking around. 'For once it feels like I've done something important, something permanent, and I'd like to be around it for a while.'

'Ridding Eldarn of Nerak was something important and permanent.'

'Yes, but this is tangible. I can go in there and look at it – and I earned this one, in countless maths classes, and countless hours studying the nature of numbers. This one was in my blood.'

'I understand entirely, my friend, but sadly, the stomach must rule the heart. If we want to eat, we need to get going. This was a good learning experience for you, and if we lost a day, well, we still have eight to reach the rendezvous.'

Steven looked embarrassed – he had forgotten. 'All right, let's go.'

'Actually,' Gilmour said, 'I want to see the library again, just out of curiosity.'

'Again? So you've been here before?' Steven followed him across the street.

'Long before your grandmother's grandmother was born. One of my former colleagues was in charge of keeping time for the Larion Senate and the Remond family. He was actually more a maths professor than a sorcerer.' He led the way up cracked stone steps to the library doors, which were still firmly on their hinges, unlike the clock room.

'A teacher instead of a magician,' Steven mused. 'Mark would have been proud of him.'

'Mark's a good teacher, I assume?'

'I've only seen him teach once,' Steven said, 'when I was guest-speaking on the Great Depression and its impact on the banking industry, but his students—'

There was a brief rustle and then a loud squeak, wood on wood, from one of the chambers off the main hallway. Holding up a hand for silence, Gilmour pointed to the dusty corridor, where scores of footprints ran the length of the hall and passed in and out of adjoining rooms.

'What do we do?' Steven whispered. 'I don't think they're soldiers.'

Gilmour nodded agreement, then whispered, 'Let's go.'

The door was shut but not latched. Gilmour looked at Steven, then knocked.

'Come in,' called a hesitant voice, surprising them both.

The room looked like it might once have been a reading room, or maybe a chamber for a small collection. There were six rectangular tables, several wooden benches and a smouldering brazier that lent a bit of warmth to the room. There were no tapestries for insulation, but a few threadbare rugs softened the floor. Fourteen people, men, women and a few young adults, no children, were seated around the tables. They were obviously not occupation soldiers. Some had stacks of paper and parchment; others appeared to be reading from crumbling books. A few were gathered around the brazier. They all wore woollen tunics over thick shirts; their shoes and boots were tattered, some worn quite through. Most had heavy cloaks draped over their shoulders, but even these outer garments looked torn, patched and patched again. They all stared, mute with terror, at the two strangers.

Finally an older man with a distinctive roadmap of bulging veins criss-crossing his wrists got up to greet them. He had a pinched nose in a narrow face, and his scraggly beard was flecked with grey. His eyes were sunken. To Steven he looked simultaneously wise and insane.

'Are you here for the class?' he asked, his voice cracking. He clasped his hands behind his back to hide their trembling.

'No,' Gilmour replied with a reassuring smile. Steven nodded to a few of the others, hoping to put them at ease as well. 'Who are you?'

The thin man made a faint gesture towards the assembled group. 'This is my class.'

'They're adults,' Gilmour said.

'Yes,' the outlaw professor confessed.

'That's good,' Steven interjected. 'You're a teacher?'

'I am.'

'You're teaching adults?'

'Teachers.'

'You're teaching teachers?' The magic warmed him, bubbling up with Steven's adrenalin. 'How many of you are there?'

'We have one hundred and twelve altogether,' the professor replied. 'We mean no harm,' he pleaded, 'we just want to be able to instruct—'

'No,' Steven interrupted.

The little man gave a reflexive jerk and shrank bank.

'No, no,' Steven said quickly, 'you misunderstand me. I think this is wonderful. It's a damnable shame that you have to meet here in squalor. That's what's wrong.'

A sigh of relief passed through the classroom.

The professor looked around. 'You're right, young man, but the neighbouring farms are not always safe. Patrols come through frequently, oftentimes just looking for food, but we cannot risk being discovered so we meet here.'

'But they must patrol the university as well, surely?' Gilmour asked.

'They're gone.'

'Gone?'

'The soldiers are all gone; most rode south towards Orindale a few days ago. Some looked to be heading for Wellham Ridge, but wherever they were bound, there are none left out this far.'

'That's impossible,' Gilmour said.

'It's true,' said a woman near the brazier. 'I saw them march past my farm. It had to be an entire brigade; they were making for Orindale.'

Steven leaned over one of the tables and was paging through a textbook. 'How old are these?'

The professor joined him. 'Nearly a thousand Twinmoons. I keep them in as good condition as I can, but they're falling to pieces. Time and overuse, there's nothing I can do.'

'There are no newer texts?' Steven asked.

Gilmour said, 'Everything printed since Prince Marek's takeover is nothing but—'

'The party line,' Steven felt growing anger meld with his magic in a flood of crimson and black. He wanted badly to find and kill Nerak all over again. To the professor he said, 'I want you to keep going. I don't want you to worry about the soldiers. I want you to keep teaching. I want you to find more students, more literate adults, and I want you to teach them economics and democracy, parliamentary government and language skills. Can you do that?'

'Yes, I suppose we can use what little—'

'Good,' Steven interrupted again. 'I want you to find them and teach them, and I want all of you to tell your students – I don't care if you're teaching in a barn, a wood or a university classroom – I want you to tell them all that they have to get ready. One more Twinmoon, that's all it will take.' His voice was rising, but Steven didn't care. 'I want you to tell them that in one Twinmoon Eldarn will be free, and a fair, compassionate, democratic prince will return to Riverend Palace. You need to get ready. Tell them. We'll need teachers, leaders, economists, business managers and—' he looked around the sparse, cold room, '—at least one mathematician.'

No one moved. Whatever relief they had felt at the discovery that Gilmour and Steven were friendly was dissipating: this was obviously a madman.

Steven went on, still too angry at what these people had suffered to lower his voice, 'Which one of you is a mathematician?'

A frightened woman near the wall hesitantly raised her hand. 'I am.'

'Good,' he said. 'That clock across the street, it's working again.'

This news shocked them all. A few of the rag-tag students looked as though they might bolt, dive out the windows.

Steven asked, 'Can you learn to read it?'

'Yes, sir,' she said, beginning to look less worried.

'Good,' he said, and then to the entire room, shouted, 'Tell them to get ready! If you're teachers, then you understand how important this moment is for Eldarn. One Twinmoon more. Then this world will be in your hands. If you know of outlaw classrooms elsewhere, in Praga or Rona or Gorsk, wherever they are, get word to them. I want it spreading like a prairie fire: Eldarn will be free in one Twinmoon.'

'Excuse me, sir.' The little professor with the pinched nose took Steven by the forearm and dropped it as quickly as if he'd been shocked with a bolt of electricity. His eyes widened and he backed a few steps towards the brazier.

'What is it, professor?'

'Sir, who *are* you?'

Steven looked at Gilmour and then grinned. 'We're the Larion Senators.'

BOOK III

The Crossing

THE EXODUS

Gita Kamrec shouted, 'What do you mean we don't know where they are? Bleeding whores, but I need Brand here! I can't get a decent piece of intelligence from this band of pissing—' She stormed along the path; her lieutenants avoided eye-contact with one another, each fearing that one of the others would roll their eyes or chuckle and that would be the end of them all. Gita might be small in stature, but she'd have them gutted and filleted for a Twinmoon festival in a heartbeat. Gita missed Brand Krug, her tough, level-headed commander. He was still not back from his foray south, escorting the Larion Senator, Gilmour Stow, and his company of freedom fighters into Wellham Ridge.

They knew he was coming, thanks to Stalwick Rees's fit. He had collapsed, repeating over and over again: Brand is on his way and the Malakasians know about the Capehill attack. Several of her men were concerned, but Gita would not be swayed: she had agreed with Gilmour that taking Capehill would give the Falkans a foothold in the east, and she meant to follow through. It was an easier target than Orindale; the capital had a full infantry division, even without counting the Seron companies. She would need at least one more regiment *and* to make it a surprise attack if she had any hope of taking Orindale. Winning Capehill would give the Resistance a place to call home, a base in which to muster an army and prepare for a bloody march westwards.

In spite of all Gita's planning, a problem had arisen. The Falkan Army, moving southeast as covertly as possible, had encountered no occupation forces. A battalion of partisans, travelling in small groups disguised as miners or farmers, had encountered just one Malakasian, a woman apparently separated from her unit. Sharr Becklen had killed her, a miracle shot into the rising sun. Apart from the woman, there had been no patrols, no soldiers away on leave, nothing. It was far, far too quiet. And that worried Gita.

Now, half an aven from Capehill, she wondered if she was marching her boys into a carefully baited snare. She had orchestrated what she believed to be one of the cleverest troop movements in the history of modern warfare, breaking her force up into its component parts and using everything from side roads to goat paths to move the squads and platoons – and she was certain no one, not even the country dwellers through whose land they were passing, had realised.

And now here they were, within striking distance, and no one could give her a cogent report on the Malakasian Army's whereabouts.

She stalked through their temporary camp, fuming. 'Tell me again!' she barked, trying to think fast.

'We just don't know where they are, ma'am,' said Markus Fillin, a lieutenant from the Central Plain, looking anywhere but at his commander.

'Is the city that big?' she mused aloud. 'Can they really be hiding a brigade down there? If Stalwick was right, they know we're coming, but *how much* do they know – do they know we're here now, that we were coming from Traver's Notch? Do they know how many soldiers we have, what we ate for breakfast this morning? Can *anyone* tell me *anything?*'

Her officers and advisors shook their heads and Gita shouted, 'Where is Sharr Becklen? He lives there, doesn't he? He must know where the flaming horsecocks are hiding – what's the most defensible position in the city?'

'The heights above the wharf, ma'am,' Markus interjected quickly. 'It's already been checked, but there's no one there, ma'am, not one single soldier. The locals say they were in the city as normal, until sometime this morning, when they all disappeared.'

There was a moment of heavy silence, broken only by the crackle and spit of the camp fires, then Gita was shouting again. 'An entire brigade of occupation soldiers does not just *disappear*, Lieutenant, do you understand? And I repeat: *where* is Sharr Becklen?'

'Here I am, ma'am.' Sharr himself came over the rise, as if summoned by Gita's cries.

'Oh, thank the gods,' Gita said. 'So what can you tell us?'

'I'll show you, ma'am.' He reached out, inviting the partisan leader to join him. 'It's just up here. I think you'll find this interesting.'

'Where are we going, Sharr?' Gita said. 'I have to tell you; I'm not amused by any of this.' She glared at her officers, then took Sharr's offered hand and allowed him to help her up the snowy embankment.

At the top she released him. 'Where are they dug in?' she asked.

'They aren't,' Sharr said.

'That's impossible.'

'Be that as it may, ma'am, but apart from a bunch of very nervous-looking fellows on the wharf, the Malakasian Army is gone.'

'Gone.'

'If you come a bit further up here, just up this next hill, I think I can show you where to find them, but we need to hurry, they've at least a two-aven head-start.'

Gita frowned. She was not one who appreciated surprises, not on the Twinmoon, not at festivals, not even after she stood the tides with Rove Kamrec, all those Twinmoons ago. 'Where are you taking me, Sharr?'

'Up there.' He pointed towards the rounded summit of a small hill they'd been using to watch the arriving groups of partisans forming up into an army. The gentle slopes around Capehill were teeming with Resistance fighters, every one of them awaiting Gita's word, and they would take the city.

She herself had expected to be fighting already; she had never dared hope they would make it all the way from Traver's Notch without a fight. Her orders had been simple: kill or take prisoner every Malakasian soldier you see. If by some stroke of profound luck Stalwick had been wrong and their attack was still a surprise, the last thing Gita wanted was for a Malakasian to escape and reach Capehill in time to warn them.

She looked behind her and called, 'Markus, come with us.'

The lieutenant hustled up the rise, his boots slipping in the snow. Markus Fillin was not thrilled to be in Capehill; he didn't suppose he was alone in that. It was hard to leave home and wage war in another part of one's own country. All his life, Markus had watched Malakasian troops on the Central Plains, as had his father and his grandfather when they were boys working in the family fields. Sometimes soldiers would come into the yard and buy food; other times – *most* times – they simply rode into the barn or the storehouse, or even broke into the canning cellar, and took what they wanted.

He wondered how many fit young men had left farms like his to start this war. He was uneasy at the thought that he had left his own home vulnerable when he joined the partisans, but he was needed in Capehill, and if Falkan were to be free, this battle needed to be fought and won.

Sharr helped Gita as she scrambled awkwardly up the icy slope to the relatively flat summit, then checked back for Markus. He made no move to assist the lieutenant.

The two sentries stopped talking and stood to attention when they realised who had joined them. 'Ma'am,' one of them said, echoed by the second.

'Good evening, boys,' Gita said, trying to mask her wheezing. She was tired, and her stomach hurt from the climb. 'Anything to report?'

The two shared a nervous look then shook their heads. 'No, ma'am,' said one.

'Everyone in place?'

'It's getting harder to see, ma'am,' he told her, 'but from here it looks like the third and eighth platoons are moving into position, south of the city.'

The second sentry added, 'Ma'am, we lost sight of Arden's company when they passed across that snowfield there in the north.'

'Captain Arden,' Sharr corrected softly.

'Sorry, sir, sorry, ma'am.' The sentry coughed, and repeated, '*Captain* Arden.'

Gita ignored his lapse. 'Good. My staff are here, their companies assembled behind these hills and in that grove to the southeast ... so we're in position. All we need now is the enemy – and we don't know where the enemy has gone.'

Markus winced. 'Ah, ma'am, if we—'

'Just a moment, Markus,' Gita interrupted, 'Sharr was going to show us something. What is it, Sharr? I know you wouldn't have had me haul my broken-down old body up here for nothing.'

Sharr grinned. Capehill lay sprawled at their feet, glittering firelight casting a shadowy glow on otherwise silent homes and businesses. From the hilltop, the city looked a natural target.

The harbour was different, however: something about it looked fundamentally *wrong*, though Gita wasn't sure what had changed. There was a veritable fleet of boats moored in the shallows and lashed to the docks, and even from this distance she could hear the faint chime of a hundred or more bridges as bells rang out the aven changes. It had grown dark and there was no colour; the boats all looked like hulks, floating shadows. Gita shook her head, trying to figure out what was different. 'What is it, Sharr? Where are they?' she asked.

The erstwhile fisherman pointed towards the horizon, darker in the east. 'You see that group of stars out there, just off the water?'

Gita sighted along Sharr's outstretched arm. Her vision wasn't what it had been two hundred Twinmoons earlier, but finally she focused on the low-lying constellation. 'What is that?' she asked, adding, 'I've never seen those before.'

'Demonpiss,' Markus whispered to himself.

'What? What is it? Someone tell me.' Gita was irritated now, feeling as if she'd been left out of a secret everyone else knew. Behind her, the two sentries stood a bit straighter.

'It's a squadron of ships, ma'am,' Sharr explained. 'They left with the tide about two avens ago. They're naval ships. There's a bark, two brig-sloops, square-rigged, and a frigate, a big fat bastard, that one.'

'And who in the names of the gods is on them?' Gita was still confused, and angry at her own ignorance. 'What do I care if—?' She cut herself short. 'That's it. This harbour,' she said. 'I *knew* there was something awry, but I couldn't figure it out. That's it; that's what's different.'

'Ma'am?' Now Sharr looked confused.

'The boats, Sharr. Markus, look at the boats. What do you see?' Gita didn't wait for them to reply. 'There're only fishing boats, no big merchant vessels, and no naval ships, only the trawlers and net-boats. See?' She waved an open hand at the wharf as if the answer was obvious. 'There's no accommodation at Capehill Harbour for big merchant ships because passage through the North Sea is essentially impossible – unless there's a northern Twinmoon and high tides in the archipelago – and anyway, very few merchant ships make the passage around the Ronan peninsula—'

'Because the Malakasian navy has it blockaded,' Markus finished up for her.

'No one knows why,' Gita went on, 'it's something to do with Estrad Village and the Forbidden Forest, but there haven't been big merchant ships around Ronan point in generations, so, in turn, Capehill rarely plays host to those size vessels.'

Markus scanned the small fishing boats, owned and operated by independent fishermen like Sharr. He said, 'So the only large vessels moored in this harbour would be—'

'The Malakasian navy,' Sharr interrupted, 'and there they go, ma'am. That little group of stars fading on the horizon are the watch-lights on every Malakasian ship in these waters. They loaded stores, took on water, and then boarded all the Malakasian soldiers in Capehill, except for a handful securing the wharf, and I'm guessing the next ship to round the point, perhaps one of those policing the Estrad Inlet, will be coming north to pick them up.'

'That's the group of nervous-looking men you mentioned earlier?' Gita asked, dazed.

'Right,' Sharr nodded. 'They're acting as if things are normal, they're still in command of the city, but there are maybe fifteen of them on the wharf, and they must know already that they're on tomorrow's lunch menu.'

'Why would they leave a squad behind like that?' Markus asked.

'Who knows?' Gita said. 'No room on the ships? Orders? Who's to say why these horsecocks do what they do, but Sharr's right; we'll carve those whoring bastards up and grill them for dinner – that'll be easy. What I don't understand is why did they leave? And where are they going?'

'North,' Sharr said.

Gita laughed. 'North? Is there some kind of armed insurrection going on in Gorsk that we don't know about? That's even more confusing – and it's gods-rutting reckless; they'll lose half their ships just trying to navigate the archipelago. If they're loaded to bursting and they actually didn't have room to take on fifteen extra men, they'll be scraping their hulls inside the next Moon.' She cocked an eyebrow at Sharr. 'How much draft do they need to make it through those islands?'

Sharr pulled his cloak closed against the evening chill. 'A lot less than they've got, unless they plan to go far to the north, out beyond anything we have on the charts.'

'Why?' Markus asked. 'Why did they leave?'

Gita looked at him. 'I honestly don't know, Markus.'

'Shall I give the order, ma'am?'

'No,' she said. 'Sharr, take a squad into the city. I want to be absolutely certain there's no one left, other than the lot at the harbour. Spread out, check everywhere, and be back here ready to report at dawn. If it's clear, we'll move at sunrise.'

Sharr nodded and hurried down the slope as Gita continued, 'Markus, get word to the officers to stand down until dawn.'

'Very well, ma'am.' He too rushed off into the night, leaving Gita standing with the sentries, looking down on the fires sparking into life here and there in the darkness below.

Brexan rolled over, shaking the wine-cobwebs from her head, wondering what aven it was and why she'd awakened—

Someone was knocking.

She squeezed open her eyes and yawned, then rasped, 'Come in.'

She cleared her throat, which was horribly dry and uncomfortable. 'Come in,' she said again, more clearly this time.

'The door's latched, Brexan,' a muffled voice whispered from the corridor.

She pushed back the coverlet, pulled a tunic over her head and padded across the floor. She let the door swing open while she used her bedside candle to light several more. Doren Ford emerged from the shadows.

'Captain Ford,' she said, obviously surprised. 'Uh, what are you—? Is everything all right?' She tried to smooth down her night-snarled hair, hoping to tame her curls before he noticed what an unco-operative nightmare they were. She self-consciously shoved as much hair behind her ears as she could.

'I'm fine.' Ford moved to the foot of her bed. 'Do you mind?'

'Uh, no, no, please, have a seat,' she stammered then, finding nothing useful to do standing up, sat down herself, keeping as much of the bed between them as possible without tumbling off. 'What can I do for you?' Her heart was thudding with anticipation; while she found the older man handsome, she certainly wasn't ready for sug-gestions like, *Strip naked and climb into bed with me!*

'I'm concerned about your friends,' Ford said. 'And I know I prom-ised safe passage to Averil with no questions asked, but I feel as though—'

'You can ask me,' she completed his sentence.

'Yes, I feel as though I can ask you.' He smiled. 'We don't know each other very well, but I have the sense that I can trust you – and I am not one who trusts many people, Brexan. I have the feeling that you'll tell me the truth if I ask.'

I won't – I can't, she thought wildly, hoping nothing showed on her face. *Please don't ask me,* please!

'I need to know who they are.'

'They're friends of mine from the city,' Brexan began, 'and they need to get to—'

'Stop that, please,' Captain Ford cut her off. 'They may be friends of yours, but I don't believe any of that story about picking up a cargo three days' north of here. Do you know what lies three days' north of here?'

She shook her head.

'Cliffs, lots of them, and deep water.' He pulled a pipe from his tunic, remembered where he was and put it back. 'I've picked up cargoes from other ships before; everyone has – it's standard when dealing with the Malakasian navy. So we sail north, tie up to an outlaw ship and load whatever it is your friend Garec doesn't want to tell me about. And a run to Averil wasn't what I had in mind; I was hoping for something that would get me back to Southport. But with the merchant fleet reduced to splinters and the docks here filling with unshipped cargoes, I can get to Averil and back and still load up for Southport before the southern Twinmoon. As word of what happened spreads, sailors are going to flock here from all over Eldarn. I've come to some agreements with a few wholesalers in the last couple of days. However . . .'

'However?' Brexan caught him glancing at her bare legs in the dim light. When he looked away she quietly drew the coverlet over them.

'However, Garec and Kellin have a great deal of silver, more money than I would make even in a long-term contract with an Orindale distributor. I know I can put them off for a Moon, if necessary, but I need to feel confident that nothing untoward is going to happen to my ship or my crew on this daisy-run Garec claims we'll have to Averil. So—'

So?' Brexan bit her lip. *Stop doing that to him.*

'What's the cargo?'

She watched the bedside candle flicker in the draft from the hallway. She wanted to tell him the truth. She wasn't quite sure why; maybe it had something to do with Nedra and the Topgallant Inn. Since Versen and Sallax had died, Brexan had been toying with the idea of a new life, an honest life, in which she always told the truth, and was rewarded through hard, honest work. Sitting here in the half-light, colluding with Captain Doren Ford: this was her old life again, and though she wasn't slicing him open or crushing his skull, still this felt underhanded to her; dirty, even.

She decided to start with the truth and see how long she could maintain it. 'The cargo is people, two men who couldn't come into Orindale.'

'Outlaws?' He hadn't been expecting this; transporting people was relatively easy, even if he was boarded and searched. People were easy to hide or disguise. Once, during the warm season, he had dropped a political outlaw in the Ravenian Sea when Sera Moslip spotted a Malakasian naval cruiser bearing down on them. After the search he'd ordered the *Morning Star* about and they had picked up their waterlogged guest, none the worse for an aven in the refreshingly warm water, and continued on to the Estrad River. 'Well, why didn't Garec say so? People aren't a problem; we've done that before. Who are these fellows? Criminals? Political idealists? Partisans?'

'They are—' Brexan searched for the right words. 'They are powerful men.'

'Really? With the Resistance?' He didn't care for politics, but for what Garec and Kellin were willing to pay, he would make the run – the daisy-run – to Averil, drop these idealists in the shallows and be back to ship as much as he possibly could to Southport with the southern Twinmoon. With no loading or unloading to worry about, he might even make the run in record time, saving five or six days.

He felt better about the whole thing now. 'Brexan, I do apologise for waking you. I'm embarrassed that you—' He glanced where her naked legs had been.

'Don't worry about it, Captain Ford,' she said, ignoring the little voice that was nagging her to tell him he was really going to Pellia, and there was a chance he might not survive the trip.

The soft light of her candles illuminated the lines in his weather-beaten face. He reached out for one. 'Do you mind if I take this? I need to see my way back to my room. I didn't use one coming down here; I didn't want anyone to think—'

'That's fine,' Brexan said quickly. 'Good night, Captain.'

'Good night, and thank you again.' He started to pull the door closed, then Brexan hissed at him to wait.

'One last thing,' she murmured, taking a deep breath and steeling herself. 'Please be careful with these people. I know Garec doesn't look it, but he can be a dangerous young man.'

'Him? Nonsense,' Captain Ford smiled. 'I've been around a long time. I'll be fine.'

'Trust me, Captain. If things should take an unexpected turn, remember what I'm telling you. These are nice people, but they're also partisans, and very tough. They've been through a lot.'

'Garec's a boy; he could be my son,' he said. 'Good night, Brexan.'

As the door swung shut, Brexan whispered, 'His friends call him *Bringer of Death*.'

Ford hesitated. 'Really?'

'Really.'

'Then thank you,' he said, his smile fading. 'I'll keep that in mind.'

Brexan felt her insides clench. She was sitting astride a dangerous fence, and she didn't know on which side she might fall. *Tell him to flee*, she thought. *Come up with some excuse and get him out of this. He's a nice man, and you're going to get him killed.* She pulled the covers up to her chin and asked, 'When can we leave?'

263

'On the turning tide tomorrow, if you're ready.'

'We'll be ready.' She blew out the remaining candles and said, 'Good night, Captain Ford.'

In the front room, Garec and Kellin relaxed in great padded chairs by the fire, a mostly empty flagon of wine between them. The landlady had finished clearing up for the evening and had gone to bed an aven earlier. Garec stretched his legs towards the flames and said drowsily, 'Why are we still awake?'

Kellin swallowed. Her mouth was dry and tasted like stale wine. 'Because it's our first night together in a real boarding house.'

'So what do you call all those nights since the wave washed us almost all the way to the Northern Forest? Weren't those nights together in a boarding house?'

'Those nights of you shivering with fever and me nearly comatose from the effects of querlis, not knowing where we were, if we'd live through the night, or what we'd do if we did survive to see the sun rise?' Kellin asked. 'No, they don't count!'

'Good point.' Garec yawned, then blinked to clear his vision. 'What aven is it?'

'Middlenight, at the earliest.'

He stared into the fire. 'You don't think we're still awake because we don't know if Steven and Gilmour are alive, or if we've found a captain and crew to get us to Pellia, or if we have the resources, military or mystical, we'll need to exorcise whatever is holding Mark Jenkins hostage, to free him and send Steven, Hannah – wherever she is – and Mark home to Colorado while simultaneously liberating Eldarn for all time?'

Kellin smiled. She slid her chair close enough to reach him and slipped a hand under his tunic. Caressing the taut flesh beneath, she whispered, 'No, I don't think it's any of ... whatever it was you said just then.'

Garec, distracted now, took a swallow of wine to moisten his own throat and said huskily, 'So why are we still down here?'

She fumbled with leather ties; Garec made no move to stop her. Loosening the knots, she said, 'How's your head?'

'The wine and querlis help. How's your shoulder?'

'The same, I suppose.' Kellin ran her hand lower, feeling him begin to tremble. 'Have you ever ... in public?' she murmured softly.

'In a tavern?' Garec's eyes widened. 'No!'

'But you could be convinced?'

He closed his eyes and slid low in the chair. He wasn't sure he would make it all the way up to the room without embarrassing himself. He groaned softly and said, 'At this moment, I'm confident you could convince me of almost anything.'

'That's good,' Kellin said, releasing him long enough to use her one good arm to unfasten her own leggings. 'We'll head upstairs to continue our conversation, but I think we need to see to something else first.' She fumbled with her ties and cursed.

'I'll do that,' Garec interrupted. 'You busy yourself with something constructive, will you?'

Kellin laughed as he slid her leggings to the floor and ran his hands up her smooth thighs. 'Hm, no underclothes,' he said appreciatively, stroking her flanks.

She moaned in anticipation, pushed him back in his chair and pulled herself onto him. The chair creaked under their combined weight, but the lovers ignored it as they explored each other's bodies by the wavering firelight.

'I took them off when I went upstairs earlier,' she whispered provocatively. Her legs were too thin; she needed a Twinmoon resting and eating, but in Garec's eyes she was beautiful.

'Upstairs? But that was two avens ago,' Garec said, sounding shocked. 'You knew?'

'Of course I knew, you cracked-headed Ronan,' she cooed as she did something with her internal muscles that left him gasping.

He held his breath, hoping to hold off the inevitable, but it was no use. As Kellin moved her hips in a lithe, unexpected motion, Garec cupped her soft buttocks.

'Unlace my tunic,' Kellin breathed in his ear.

'I can't—' he gasped, but Kellin was inexorable.

'I want to feel you against my body,' she panted. 'I can't get the laces—'

Garec closed his eyes tight and sucked in a deep breath; he held it as long as he could before crying out, his body spasming with the power of his orgasm. He held her tightly to him as he came, and they stayed entwined together for several long moments.

Finally he croaked, 'Upstairs,' his voice hoarse with effort, 'upstairs, please.'

Kellin rested her forehead on his shoulder. 'Yes, upstairs, now. I want to feel you, all of you – and there's not enough space here to do everything I want you to do to me.' She licked his ear and he twitched again. She grinned devilishly, climbed off him and snatched up her leggings.

'Bring the wine,' she ordered, and made a dash – naked from the waist down – for the staircase at the back of the room.

Garec struggled out of the chair, looked around for his own leggings, which had somehow ended up tangled under her chair, and rescued them. Staggering slightly, he collected the flagon and followed Kellin up the stairs.

Marrin Stonnel knocked twice and poked his head around the door to the captain's cabin. 'Tide's turned, Captain,' he announced.

Ford was sitting behind a modest desk, writing in his log; he didn't look up. 'Are our passengers aboard?'

'Aye sir, she is,' Marrin said, then corrected himself. 'Sorry, *they* are, Captain.'

Ford pretended not to notice. 'Good, then we'll get underway. I'll be up in a moment, so up anchor and make ready.'

'Our course, Captain?'

'We'll be heading north once we hit deep water,' he said, his mind back on the log in front of him.

'North?'

Marrin's obvious shock made the captain look up. 'North, sailor, that's right. I'll be up in a moment to give you a heading, but in the meantime, get all hands on deck and make ready. And, Marrin, I don't like repeating myself.'

'Uh, Captain?'

'What is it?' Ford was about to lose his temper.

'Well, sir, I was just wondering— Last night, sir, you— I noticed you were gone for a stretch, sir, late last night, and I was wondering—'

'On deck, Marrin, at once!' Captain Ford roared. He had no idea how anyone knew he had left his room, but if that little piece of gossip was out, he'd have to prepare himself for days of rumour and innuendo. He sighed, then jumped a little as he realised Marrin was still there.

'I'm just saying, sir, that I think it would have been cathartic for you to bring closure to your relationship, sir,' he said.

'Marrin!' Captain Ford shouted as he rose from his seat, but the mate had already dashed away.

He closed his log and stowed it safely, laughing to himself. 'Closure,' he murmured as he made his way to the bridge.

*

There was a stiff breeze from the south and the *Morning Star* had already come about and was tugging at her anchor, raring to go. With the Twinmoon only days away, the tides pulled the Ravenian Sea towards the Northern Archipelago. In half an aven, when the slack water started to run, the little Pragan brig-sloop would dash north like a racehorse. With an empty hold she'd be skipping over the waves on a quick and lucrative journey to Averil.

It was the talk of the crew that the quiet Ronan, the one called Garec, was carrying a lifetime's savings in silver: easy work for easy silver, something that rarely happened to a merchant sailor. On any other ship, they might well sail into deep water, kill the passengers, pocket the silver and be back in Orindale for their next cargo, but Captain Ford would have none of that; he was no killer – and even if the thought had crossed his mind, Brexan's warning had set him slightly on edge. He didn't know who was waiting for Garec and Kellin in Averil, or if they had alerted anyone in Orindale to their travel plans. And he didn't know who the two strangers were – *powerful strangers* – that they were to pick up outside the city.

So given that degree of ambiguity, the captain had decided to transport these passengers as quickly as possible, and then start tacking for Orindale as soon as he had discharged his duty. Perhaps Brexan would decide to accompany them back; that would be fine with him.

No one was more excited about their current journey than Marrin, who had figured that with the *Morning Star* running empty, he and Sera had about thirty-eight fewer things to get done before making way. As far as he was concerned, this little jaunt was as near to a pleasure-cruise as he was going to get: a half-Moon at sea for no apparent reason. Lovely!

His enthusiasm was contagious as he fired off a series of ridiculous orders. 'Mr Tubbs,' he shouted, 'secure the for'ad hold!'

'We're not shipping anything in the for'ad hold, Mr Marrin!'

Some of the men laughed, while others shouted off-colour jokes.

'Common mistake, Mr Marrin; don't let it bother you!'

'Mr Tubbs,' Marrin laughed, 'secure the aft hold!'

'We're not shipping anything in the aft hold, Mr Marrin.' Olren Tubbsward, a grizzled mariner who'd been sailing for more Twinmoons than Marrin had been alive, chuckled as he pawled the capstan.

'Ah, Mr Tubbs, secure the main hold, stow the quartermaster's inventory and cast off the barges. Get moving, Mr Tubbs, this tide won't wait!'

Dropping everything, Tubbs snapped to mock attention. 'Aye, aye, sir,' Tubbs shouted and, to the amusement of the crew, took several steps before pausing and pointing a gnarled, arthritic finger at his temple. 'Uh, sir?'

'What is it, Mr Tubbs? Make it quick, sir, make it quick!' Marrin gripped the helm, doing his best impersonation of Doren Ford.

'Uh, sir, we're not shipping any cargo, sir. There are no ledgers; we don't have a quartermaster, and there are no barges to cast off.'

'Very well then, Mr Tubbs, nice work. Why don't you help yourself to a jigger or two from my private stores?' Marrin was lost in his performance, so engrossed in playing up the captain's idiosyncrasies for his appreciative audience that he didn't notice the sudden silence that had fallen over the crew.

'Do you really think that's wise, Mr Marrin?' the captain said. 'Beer at this aven?'

Marrin stammered apologies, slinking back from the helm, his face blazing red despite the cold. 'Sorry, sir, it's just— Um, Tubbs looked thirsty, sir.'

'Get us underway, please.' The captain had been a good sport, but now it was time to work. The crew of the *Morning Star* leaped into action, each to his or her appointed place, some scuttling up the rigging like monkeys, setting the sails, checking the lines; others manned the capstan whilst the day's first watch took up position as they came about for their run up the coast.

Captain Ford smiled. The *Morning Star* was his life, and he was happy to be back to sea. He felt the brig-sloop beneath his feet; he knew this ship inside out and could almost guide her through the water by touch alone. She was only a little larger than a naval pleasure-boat, but they were single-masted, with fore and aft rigging, while the *Morning Star* was square-rigged on both her fore and mains. She was sleeker even than the quickest of the Malakasian schooners, already fast, and running empty she'd make even quicker time. Ford wondered what the record was from Orindale to Averil. With a northern Twinmoon and an empty hold, whatever it was, the *Morning Star* stood a good change of beating it. *Or we might heel and swamp*, he thought, searching for Marrin in the rigging.

'Marrin,' he called.

The youth dropped to the deck.

'Did we take on additional ballast for this run? With no cargo, the Twinmoon and a northerly course, an unexpected gust could have us heeling to the scuppers.' He wasn't angry, not yet, but making good time was secondary to keeping the *Morning Star* afloat.

'We did, sir, just a bit. I thought you might want to hurry along so we didn't add much, just enough to compensate for drafting so high.' As Sera Moslip joined them, Marrin elbowed her in the ribs and said with a raucous laugh, 'The ballast, Captain, and whatever Sera's added to her backside. I know you always count on that for a bit of additional weight. That old Nedra could certainly cook, couldn't she?'

Sera, excited to be underway as well, pressed her lips into a thin smile before rearing back and slugging Marrin hard across the jaw. She shook an aching fist and muttered, 'Sorry, Captain.'

The crew roared as Marrin fell to the deck.

The captain didn't bother to hide his own grin. 'May the gods bless and keep you, Sera,' he muttered under his breath.

'Thank you, Captain,' she murmured back, equally quietly.

Marrin, bleeding from a split lip, pulled himself up and stood on trembling legs. He turned to the captain, embarrassed, and shouted, 'I do love this job!'

A roar of approval came from the sailors busying themselves on deck and in the rigging. The boy knew how to take his licks. It would be a fine sea day.

Garec laughed so hard his head hurt. He hooted and whistled and shouted Sera's name along with the crew, while Marrin pulled himself together. 'Did you see that, Kellin?' Garec said, clapping her on the back. 'That was beautiful; she's like Versen, no gods-rutting warning at all, just, *blam!* and you're on your backside waiting for the fog to lift. Oh, he would have loved this.'

Brexan, who had been quiet all morning, brightened. 'I wish you would do more of that,' she said.

'What?'

'Talk of him.' Brexan's face was half in shadow.

'Of Versen?' Garec said, looking a little surprised. 'All right, I'll talk of him all the way to Pelli— ah, Averil, if you like.' He searched her face, not sure what he expected to see. Brexan simply stared back at him. 'You got to know him well in a short period of time, didn't you?' he said finally.

'I don't know what's worse for me now,' she said, 'wanting what I had, keeping my little box of memories all tidy and neat, or wanting what you have, a lifetime of stories, highs and lows, good and bad. Do you know what I mean?'

'I do,' Kellin said. 'It's like my father – he died when I was young, and I never asked my mother about him. She told me some things, but I've always been content with what I remember of him. He's the only perfect person I've ever known. He probably had just as many flaws as the rest of us, but I'm not interested in knowing them.'

Garec felt the *Morning Star* creak as it rolled beneath them. He said, 'I don't know what to tell you, Brexan, but I've lost six close friends in the last two Twinmoons. Sallax, Versen and Brynne were the best friends I'd ever hoped to have.' Without looking at Kellin, he added, 'I am as alone as I can imagine, but like anyone, I find comfort where I can, from Kellin, from knowing my family is safe at home, working the farm, from feeling like we're nearing the end of a painfully long struggle ... and most especially from my memories of who they were – who they still *are* – in my mind.' He reached for Kellin, who took his hand. 'Did you know that Versen could eat his own weight in eddy-fish? Eddy-fish ... We lived a quarter-aven from the ocean, and all he ever wanted to eat were those fatty bottom-feeding river fish that any seventy-Twinmoon-old kid would throw back as worthless. We used to stay up late, drinking and singing, and sometime after the middlelight aven, when the rest of us were beginning to drift, he'd come charging in with rods and rigs, a couple of bottles of wine in his cloak, wanting to go night-fishing.'

Garec looked around the deck and smiled. 'I wish now that I had gone with him more often, but it was always humid and the bugs were bad down there. But Sallax often went, and they'd come back after dawn, hungover, and smelling like a warm case of death, and we'd all eat eddy-fish for breakfast. It was wonderful.'

'How did he prepare it?' Brexan was crying, but she was smiling through her tears.

Garec snorted, then, embarrassed, said, 'He always rolled them in something – ground sugarroot, pepperweed, greenroot, anything he could lay his hands on. We teased him about it, that all he was doing was trying to find the perfect mask for the flavour – eddy-fish tastes like day-old laundry water to most people. But actually, he had a way with them that made them edible – the sweet potatoes were the best.' He licked his lips, savouring the memory. 'It was his own invention. He'd fillet the fish, dunk the bits in egg, and then coat them in mashed-up sweet potatoes. Then he fried them ... gods, I can remember the smell! Those mornings everyone joined us for breakfast.'

'Sweet potato-wrapped eddy-fish, for breakfast?' Kellin made a face.

'And beer,' Garec added.

'Sounds wonderful,' Brexan said as she wiped her eyes. 'You'll have to make it for us one day.'

'I'll have a go at it, but I don't know where we're going to find eddy-fish out here.' He turned to watch Orindale fade off their stern.

Kellin pointed at Marrin, now climbing the rigging above the mainsail like a lemur. 'Punched out, and he can still crawl about up there. I'd have given up five or six times already.'

'Or bailed my stomach, for the gods and everyone to see,' Brexan agreed.

'We were lucky to find them,' Kellin said softly, 'and even more lucky to find you, Brexan.'

'They do seem to be a competent crew,' Garec mumbled.

'I hate lying to them,' Kellin said.

'So do I.' Brexan was glad for the chance to bare her soul a bit. 'I don't know how we'll convince them to make for Pellia.'

'*We* won't have to,' Garec said. 'Steven and Gilmour will take care of that.'

'It doesn't seem right,' Brexan said, pressing the point. 'These are good people.'

'This is bigger than us, Brexan,' Garec said. 'You know that. If a guilty conscience and the loss of their trust is all we have to suffer from here on in, then I'm all for it. Unfortunately, there's much, much worse waiting for us in Malakasia; trust me.' Garec blurred for a moment, his shadowy doppelgänger, the *Bringer of Death*, appearing, flickering and then fading like Orindale harbour. He had seen and suffered more than either of them knew; that much was apparent. If he could stay focused on their goal, surely they could too.

'Come on,' he said and started towards the helm. 'Let's see if we can help.'

A GIFT

The Wayfarer Inn wasn't one of Pellia's most popular watering holes, but it enjoyed a steady business letting out rooms to merchants, sailors and the occasional naval officer. The front room was comfortable, and warm even in the worst winter Twinmoons, and the bar was well-stocked with an interesting selection of wines and well-kept beer, and hearty food was always on offer. Yet the inn lacked the one thing that brought drinkers in droves: it lacked women. It was situated two streets away from the marketplace and four blocks from the waterfront, far enough from Pellia's shipping and market districts that young people ignored it. There was little tourist trade, even in summer, so the Wayfarer relied on its regulars, the dinner-aven crowds, and the letting of rooms to cover the Moon's overheads. It was a lean living for Erynn Kestral's family, but most Twinmoons the bills were paid, the firewood replenished, the larder restocked and the casks refilled.

Once or twice in every ten Twinmoons, Erynn's parents planned a Moon party, not on the Twinmoon itself – there were too many festivities planned by the waterfront and marketplace taverns, and the Wayfarer couldn't possibly compete with them – but a few days afterwards. Morgan Kestral liked to wait just long enough for Twinmoon hangovers to fade, wine shakes to subside and indigestion to pass. Then he and Illia would spread the news that they were slaughtering a pig, or a dozen fat gansels, and there'd be a few extra casks, from the Peeramyde Brewery in south Pellia.

The locals, many of whom worked in the marketplace or on the wharf, carried word of the party across the city and on the eve of the festivities, assuming Morgan and Illia's timing had been right, the district was abuzz with anticipation.

The street in front of the Wayfarer was clogged with hawkers and revellers. Musicians played for spare Mareks; prostitutes – men and women – worked the shadows and the street corners, and after dark, people dragged out wood, old furniture, once even a broken-down cart, and built a great bonfire on the cobblestones. The city guards would carry off anyone who flagrantly broke the law: stabbings, gang assaults and too-public negotiations for fennaroot were generally frowned on, but the mood was usually good and the party raged on until dawn.

When the street reopened the following morning and the debris was shovelled away, Morgan and Illia were exhausted, looking ten Twinmoons older, but the locals were happy and the Wayfarer's future was secured for a bit longer, thanks to the great pile of copper Mareks secreted under a floorboard in the Kestrals' bed chamber.

As a young girl, Erynn had envied the older children in her street on festival nights, for she was confined to her room upstairs, where she would sit for avens watching the partygoers, drinking and eating and dancing and groping one another, their voices growing louder and louder as the night wore on until the whole street was just one teeming, screaming mass of roiling pleasure. Watching from above, Erynn was entranced by this fundamental, basic kind of revelry. For her, it captured the essence of Pellia's dockers, fishermen and merchants. It was sexy and violent and fun and dangerous all at once, and the girl longed to be there, smelling, tasting and feeling the myriad sensations.

Now Erynn was old enough to work the party, and she was exhausted, constantly moving from the open fire-pit for trenchers of meat to the bar for fresh tankards. She was inside the Wayfarer just long enough to break into a sweat, then as she pushed her way between the partygoers outside, she felt the layer of moisture on her skin threaten to freeze and she realised she'd wake the following midday with a thundering cold. Already her throat felt sore – as did her budding breasts, which had been pinched and fondled so many times Erynn worried that they might not be there at all. Only the pain assured her that they were still attached. And her backside was so bruised that she might never sit down again. *I'll fall down*, she thought; *that's how I'll get some rest.*

Yet the heavy apron pocket full of coppers heartened her. With every new tray of beer or spitted pork, Erynn braced herself for another go at the crowd. *More copper*, she told herself, *just keep collecting their money.* She was careful to empty the coins out every third or fourth lap, in case she was robbed, or jounced so hard she tumbled over. Her legs ached so much that it wouldn't take much to knock her to her knees, and Erynn didn't want to risk losing a night's wages across the cobblestones if that happened.

And then there was Karel, the soldier. He was only a few Twinmoons older than she, but he was finished with school – the gratis Twinmoons, anyway – and had already enlisted in the army. He came around a lot, stopping in for a meal or tankard of beer, and he was always polite, greeting Erynn's parents and using a napkin while he ate. He wasn't attractive; with his wide eyes and a sloping forehead beneath a tangle of tiny curls, he looked a bit dough-headed, but Erynn liked him immensely, and had already decided to let him kiss her tonight – if he was still around when the party finally died. He had tried to kiss her already, in the shadows across the street, but Erynn had been in a hurry, and her tray had been full of dirty trenchers and half-empty tankards. She didn't want their first kiss to be over a filthy trencher filled with uneaten bread crusts and pig-fat and discarded pipe ashes.

And then there was Hoyt, who was older than her, old than Karel, even. Erynn thought the dashing, witty Pragan was gorgeous, even if he was a bit unkempt, and he set her heart thrumming. She had been smitten at first sight. Now she made a point of going via the fireplace and Hoyt's table, adding unnecessary distance to each hurried lap, but that didn't matter. Passing by the fire helped to banish the cold, and this way, she never had to go more than a few moments without seeing him. If this was how people were supposed to behave when they drank and told the truth and coveted one another, then Erynn Kestral wanted to be as near as possible to Hoyt Navarro in case he decided to join the fray and maybe even come looking for her.

Hoyt was in a sour mood. Grimacing into his beer, he kneaded his shoulder, trying to shift the pain. 'I don't know why it still hurts,' he grumbled. 'Alen stitched it neatly enough, it's been treated with querlis and I've kept it immobile. It ought to be feeling better by now.'

'You were stabbed,' Alen said, 'and by a nasty rutting Seron; that's going to take time to get over properly. Finish eating, then you can head back upstairs to bed. I don't like the idea of Milla alone up there, anyway.'

'She's all right,' Hannah said, peeling back Hoyt's collar to get a look at his stitches. 'She was sound asleep when I checked on her.'

'You need the rest, Hoyt.' Alen sounded determined.

'I guess you're right,' Hoyt said as he nibbled at a piece of pork.

Erynn had brought them great slices from the spitted animal roasting out back as soon as it was ready. Now she collected Alen's empty trencher and checked they all had drinks.

'That was some news about those terrorists, huh?' she asked anyone listening. Erynn didn't care who answered, as long as someone did, giving her a reason to linger.

'We hadn't heard much about it.' Hannah took the bait, although her aim was to divert the girl to another topic.

'Really?' Erynn sounded surprised. 'The whole city's talking about it. It was terrible, a whole squadron or something, a bunch of them anyway, shooting arrows, *flaming* arrows. And then they had dogs or wolves, or some kind of creatures trained to attack all together. It was horrible. I bet it was Ronans; my father says they're the worst of the foreigners.'

'Oh, does he?' Hoyt said, craning his neck to see her over his shoulder. 'Does he really?'

Erynn hesitated. 'Um, yes, well, not all the time, you know.' She glanced at his shoulder and the bulky bandage peeking out beneath his collar and blushed crimson. 'Um, I'll just get rid of this trencher.' She loaded it onto her tray and was gone.

'Does she have to keep doing that?' Hoyt frowned.

'What?' Hannah laughed, 'she's over the moon for you, Hoyt – give her a break; she's just a kid. Don't let your shoulder turn you into an old fart.'

'"Over the moon"?'

'Over the moon; you know, full of passion,' Hannah explained, 'she's intrigued by the mystique of an older man. Trust me; it's very common at that age.'

Hoyt smirked. 'So she ought to be after Alen, then. Good rutters, he's older than ... than the city!'

'Nonsense,' Alen interrupted, indignant, 'Pellia was here *days* before I was born.'

'Enjoy the attention while you can,' Hannah said. 'We'll be gone from here before too long.'

'It's just irritating, that's all.'

'It's adorable, and you're going to break her heart. There's nothing you can say or do, short of promising to take her away and marry her—'

'Stand the tides,' Alen corrected.

'Fine,' Hannah went on, 'short of *standing the tides* with her, nothing will ruin her memory of the handsome stranger who passed through her life and ignited the fires of ardent, youthful love.'

'Holy rutting whores, but do you make this stuff up for the theatre or something?' Hoyt drained his beer in a gulp.

'Just the voice of experience, brother, the voice of experience.'

'Well, I don't— Oh gods, here she comes again!'

Erynn danced between the tables. She paused in front of the fire, warming herself and trying hard not to look at their table. In a moment, she was on her way over again.

'Lords, but it's cold out there, and crowded. There's hundreds of them,' she said, trying again to extend her visit.

'You look tired,' Hannah said. 'Do you want to sit down for a bit?' Hoyt glared at her.

'I'd love to,' Erynn grinned, 'but there's too much to do. My mother and father would strap me silly if they caught me sitting down now.'

'At least make sure you get some rest when this is over,' Hannah said. 'And don't worry about the breakfast crowd. No one will be awake tomorrow, not after a night like this.'

Erynn wiped her forehead on her sleeve. 'How's your shoulder, Hoyt?'

'It's fine,' he murmured into his trencher.

'That must have been some fall you took, huh?'

'Yes, a real nasty tumble.' He didn't look up.

'Well,' Erynn was running out of excuses to stay. 'Can I get you anything else?'

'Another round, please,' Alen said, loading empty tankards onto her tray.

'Yes, and a moment's peace,' Hoyt said.

'What's that?' Erynn pretended she hadn't heard.

'A rutting moment's peace, please,' Hoyt repeated, although he already regretted saying it. He wouldn't look at Hannah, for fear that he might turn to stone.

Erynn didn't know what to do. Her hands shaking, she gripped the edges of her serving tray like a lifeline. Her lips quivered a moment, and she pressed them together, determined not to cry. 'Another round of beers, all right.'

Hoyt started, 'Erynn, I—' but the girl was already behind the bar.

'Smooth, dipshit,' Hannah muttered.

'Should I go after her?' Hoyt asked, frowning and tugging at his shoulder dressing.

'Don't worry about it,' Alen said. 'She'll be back; you can make amends then.'

None of them gave the girl a second glance as she took up a tray filled with tankards and hurried into the street.

Alen had just realised they were still waiting for their drinks when he noticed the young soldier standing in the doorway, staring them down. Erynn had been conspicuously absent since the awkward exchange with Hoyt, and now Alen realised why. 'Oh shit,' he said in English.

'What's that?' Hoyt asked.

'That's my kind of profanity,' Hannah laughed, then said, 'what's the matter?'

'Don't all look at once, but isn't that whatshisname over there by the door trying to stare us into submission? The one who's been chasing Erynn's skirt the past Moon?'

Hannah turned in her chair, ostensibly to order another drink. She caught Morgan's eye and motioned to him, then turned back to the others. 'Yes. His name's Karel, and he looks wicked pissed off about something.'

Hoyt understood. 'Oh great. That's just rutting great, just what I need: a lovesick boy angry with me because I managed to put his lovesick girlfriend's nose out of joint.'

'And he's with the Malakasian Army,' Alen's said.

'Yes, right, the baby corps.' Hoyt tried to laugh it off as nothing. He flushed bright red and, tugging at his collar, said, 'It's too hot in here; I'm going up.'

'Me too,' Alen said.

'Should I stay? Try and talk with her?' Hannah asked.

Alen dropped a few copper Mareks on the table. 'I think the damage is done. Let's go.'

They were all upstairs when the representatives of Prince Malagon's Welstar Palace Home Guard passed through the throng, checked the front room and then moved on towards the wharf. For a few moments, the whole of the street was silent, its collective breath held as the dangerous warriors, their black and gold leather shining even in torchlight, searched for someone. It was a cursory investigation, otherwise they might have tossed the rooms, interrogated the guests or beaten information out of the barman. Only after the soldiers had disappeared back into the city shadows did the revelry begin again.

Redrick Shen was high up in the rigging of the frigate *Bellan* when Mark Jenkins destroyed Orindale's merchant fleet, the stone bridge spanning the Medera River and most of the homes and businesses along the wharf. Like many of the *Bellan*'s crew, he had been transfixed by the carnage. The devastation had been awesome, and rather than flee – there was no reason to believe the *Bellan* would be spared – Redrick had remained aloft, clinging to the lines and riding the swells that followed the massive, unholy wave as it swallowed the centre of the city.

He was in the shrouds now, riding northerly winds towards the archipelago and the Northeast Channel. Flanking the *Bellan* to port were the *Souzett* and the *Welstar Prince*, both frigates, and jewels in the Parofex Shipping Company crown. Redrick didn't have any idea where Stahl Parofex was right now, but the *Bellan*, his flagship, and two other frigates had been impounded by the Malakasian Army, so maybe old Stahl was dangling from the end of a rope in the drawing room of his Orindale mansion. The ships were escorted by a handful of Malakasian naval schooners, another frigate, this one crewed by actual Malakasians, and three smaller, faster boats – two ketches and a sloop – commissioned for what purpose Redrick didn't know. But all together and from this height, the miniature fleet, all of them under full sail, made an impressive sight.

Redrick guessed the naval cruisers left in Orindale Harbour were Malakasia's token navy in southern waters, there to oversee the resumption of shipping and commerce in the Falkan capital again. Everything else that could still float was bound for Pellia, via the harrowing Northeast Channel.

Not many sailors wanted to spend much of a voyage aloft. The swells at that height, even on a quiet day, often had the heartiest of seamen hurling their stew; a gentle pitch or roll on deck could be a stomach-churning experience above the topsails. Yet Redrick spent most of the watch and much of his free time as far up in the *Bellan*'s rigging as he could, balancing effortlessly on his favourite perch, astride a spar rigged for a topgallant and a string of signal flags.

When he was one hundred and fourteen Twinmoons he left Rona's South Coast and shipped out on a cutter, working for an intrepid businessman hoping to lure seagoing commerce back into Estrad. The journey had been a disaster; they never made it beyond Markon Isle before pirates took the cutter, killed the businessman and drowned most of the crew in the waters off Southport. Redrick was spared, perhaps because of his youth, and forced to sign on with an outlaw schooner, running raids and ducking the Malakasian navy from Southport to Orindale. Over the course of thirty Twinmoons Redrick learned to sail, to screw, to fight and, when necessary, to kill. It was also where he had learned to be comfortable high above the foredeck; pirates weren't always the best company.

Nor did pirate careers last long. Many died young: ships were lost to the storms that tore up and down the Ravenian Sea, especially during the Twinmoon, and Malakasian naval officers were brutal and merciless. Redrick's luck couldn't last for ever, and when it ran out, he'd be captured and hanged by the navy like so many before him. One night he checked his pocketful of silver coins was safely stashed and his good seaboots were firmly tied to his belt, then Redrick slipped over the side and made for the lights of Southport Harbour. He swam as far as he could towards a Pragan vessel hauling nets offshore, eventually hailing the trawler through the darkness.

That had been almost fifty Twinmoons earlier, and now, ironically, here he was, sailing as a forced conscript for the Malakasian navy. The navy had seized the Parofex frigates, famous in shipping circles for the enormous loads they could carry, and when Captain Harwick argued, he had been killed – not just killed, but eviscerated – by the little woman who seemed to be in control of the entire Malakasian military operation in the Eastlands.

The woman had come aboard from a river barge, supervised the careful transfer of one slab of smooth granite, some kind of sculpture or something, Redrick didn't know what, and then retired to the captain's cabin with the great grey brick in tow. From there her orders were conveyed to the crew by an army officer who scurried about like a fennaroot addict.

Within a day, the battered and threadbare soldiers who'd come on board with their leader had been joined by what looked to be at least a regiment of tired infantry. They had come on a forced march from Wellham Ridge, and most looked as if they were about to collapse from fatigue and exposure. They were wet and cold and many had already fallen ill with lung infections. Those that had already died had been unceremoniously cast over the side.

Now the *Bellan*, the *Souzett* and the *Welstar Prince* made their way recklessly north, chasing the Twinmoon. All three were big ships with deep drafts and whether there would be enough tide remaining for them to reach the North Sea and make the run to the mouth of the Welstar River was a gamble. Yet it was plain to Redrick that as long as the small woman was in charge, they would bully their way through on piss and anger alone.

Redrick adjusted himself astride the spar, feet dangling above the decks as he ignored the footrope. He had found no reason to descend from the shrouds since Captain Harwick died. He didn't wish to go near that woman if he could help it. She was undoubtedly powerful, but there was something profoundly *wrong* about her; anyone who could tear open the captain's chest with a glance was someone to avoid, even if it meant spending the next Moon up here amongst the clouds.

The *Bellan* pitched hard to port as she was hit by a rogue wave, a big one that was bouncing back and forth between Falkan and Praga, regardless of the tide. The Narrows north of Orindale had towering cliffs on both sides. Passage through could be quick, especially with a following wind and the tide with you, but there were odd currents and unexplained swells that came and went, whipping the sea into a boil and disappearing just as quickly. Redrick, like many who ran cargo along the Ravenian Sea, could almost pinpoint their location on a chart based entirely on the way the ship was handling through the Narrows. Now he held on with one hand, his back braced against the foremast, watching the swells rolling into whitecaps below. A bit of bread he had been eating for breakfast slipped from his lap and tumbled into the water where it disappeared in the mêlée. 'Whoring Pragans,' Redrick murmured, 'this is getting rough. Might actually have to go back—'

He stopped dead, his words almost hanging in the air. The woman was on deck, still in her uniform, still without a cloak. She had climbed to the quarterdeck, spoken briefly with the fennaroot-mad officer and then turned to look directly at Redrick Shen, her hair blowing about her face.

The fennaroot addict glanced up, said something to the woman and then pointed at Redrick.

'Ah, rutting horsecocks,' he spat, 'let 'em come up here and get me.' He had a filleting knife in his belt, thin but deadly-sharp. 'Let him climb up here and bring me down himself.'

The fennaroot officer shouted something; Redrick ignored him. It was an excuse he had used countless times: 'Sorry, but it's too windy! I can't hear a thing!'

He changed his mind when he saw that the addict wasn't climbing the ratlines himself, but was sending Redrick's crewmates, his *friends*. 'Well, you won't be fighting 'em, not over this, leastways,' he muttered, and looked back towards the quarterdeck, where the woman was still staring at him. Redrick felt a tingling sensation, and a visceral certainty that her eyes were fixed on him and if he didn't hurry himself down there for whatever nightmarish task she had dreamed up for him, she would blast him out of the shrouds.

When he reached the deck, Captain Harwick's first and second mates, Harp and Spellver, were waiting with the Malakasian officers. Both looked haggard and weary, and both avoided looking at him. This was not going to end well. Redrick glanced east in hopes of catching sight of the Falkan coast. *Too far to swim*, he thought, *too cold, anyway*. He braced himself.

'Good morning, sailor,' the woman said politely. 'My name is Major Tavon.'

'Redrick Shen, ma'am,' he replied, his hopes rising. This was more courtesy than he'd expected.

'Remove your cloak and tunic, Redrick Shen,' she ordered.

He looked around. The wind was blowing winter up their backsides with a fury. 'Ma'am?'

'And stupid, I see,' Major Tavon said, ripping his tunic open with alarming strength.

Redrick tried to back away, but he couldn't; some strange power was keeping him immobile. He glared at Harp and Spellver, entreating them to help as the icy morning wormed its way inside his clothes and bit his flesh.

Major Tavon considered his naked chest for a moment, then to Harp she said, 'He'll do.' She turned back to Redrick. 'You'll do. Come with me.' As she started back towards the poop deck, she cried, 'Blackford!', and the fennaroot addict was there in an instant, looking every bit the major's personal slave. Up close, however, Redrick could see that his apparent obsequiousness hid fear.

The major told the officer she was not to be disturbed, then ordered Redrick to follow her as she walked along the companionway leading aft to Captain Harwick's cabin. Redrick, still gripped by the iron talon, followed reluctantly.

'Give 'er a good ride, Redrick,' one of the hands called.

'Take your time, boy,' another shouted. 'We'll keep this tub afloat for 'ee!'

'Don't touch nothing with teeth in it, Reddy.'

Is that what this is? Screwing? I've got to ride that old wagon? Demonpiss. He tried to step back, but found he couldn't move of his own volition. Panic threatened to overtake him.

'In here, sailor,' the major called, and closed the door behind him.

Redrick's body ignored the cold and began to sweat. 'Ma'am, I—'

'Shut the fuck up, shithead!'

He didn't understand her words, but her tone was clear enough. Redrick bit back a plea and stood quietly.

Smiling, the woman peeled off a glove, revealing a horribly infected injury on the back of her hand. 'Do you see this?' she asked rhetorically.

'Yes, ma'am,' Redrick said. 'I think that Mr Spellver would be a better person to help you with an injur—'

'Do you not understand shut the fuck up?' the woman screamed at him, spittle flying from her mouth.

Redrick cowered, and tried to explain, 'I don't speak that—'

She punched him, and the words disappeared. This was truly unfathomable: Redrick had been at sea most of his life, and he had been punched more often than he cared to admit – but no one had ever hit him as hard as this little Malakasian woman. He gasped for breath as he staggered up from the corner and checked to be sure nothing was broken. He fought the rage warming in his chest.

'I don't like this,' Major Tavon said, again showing him her bloody wrist. 'It stinks like a corpse.'

This time the South Coaster didn't say anything.

'So I am going to make you a gift, a token of my goodwill.' Her eyes flashed.

Redrick felt something inside himself slacken. He was giving up hope. 'Ma'am, I don't need a gift, I—'

Major Tavon laughed in his face and repeated, 'And stupid, too. I knew it.' She came a step closer and took him by the throat. 'I'm not *giving* you a gift, you simpleton, I am *making* a gift *of you*. I need you dead.'

An alarm blared inside Redrick's mind, but he could do nothing to defend himself. The woman was a monster, most likely one of those summoned from other worlds by Prince Malagon himself. She was stronger than anyone he had ever known, and she stared not at him, but *into* him, until the shadows in Captain Harwick's cabin swallowed them both.

It took only a moment and it was over.

Captain Blackford jumped when Redrick Shen kicked open the hatch to the aft cabins. The big Ronan was carrying something and Blackford shrieked like a frightened schoolgirl when he realised it was Major Tavon. The South Coaster crossed to the port gunwale and, with one muscular arm, tossed the body over the side. It bobbed about for a bit, the filthy remains of the black and gold uniform tunic puffing up with trapped air like a great demon jellyfish, then a wave broke over her and Major Tavon slid beneath the surface and was soon lost in the frigate's wake.

The soldiers and sailors on deck stood silent, expecting to be struck dead, simply for witnessing such an act. A few backed away, and one frightened corporal slipped through a forward hatch and shouted an unintelligible warning to the soldiers massed below. Then no one moved or spoke. The *Bellan* creaked and snapped in the wind as Redrick stalked back into Captain Harwick's cabin.

The hapless Captain Blackford nearly lost his breakfast when he heard the sailor's voice echo from the companionway, calling, 'Blackford!'

'Oh goddamnit!'

'What's the matter?' Gilmour pushed through the brush.

'It's nothing,' Steven said. 'I had forgotten about these two.' He was standing beside the partially decomposed, partially frozen remains of the two Seron warriors Mark had killed near the fjord early the previous Twinmoon. 'Christ, they look like roadkill someone's been keeping in the freezer.'

Gilmour wrinkled his nose. 'We should have burned the bodies.'

'Come on; you're not religious.' Steven stepped around the corpses, careful not to come in contact with them.

'No, I don't suppose I am, but we should have burned them, anyway. This way, who knows what diseases they might be spreading?'

'Don't touch them,' Steven warned, 'they may still be moist inside and then we'll have every hungry grettan in Falkan coming over for a midnight snack.'

'I wonder why they haven't been dragged off yet.' Gilmour bent over the bodies, looking for evidence that they had already been nibbled by scavengers.

'Nothing big enough down here to do it,' Steven said. 'When Mark killed them, it was still autumn; the grettans were in the mountains, except for the ones Prince Malagon sent south to find us. By the time the grettan packs came down to the Falkan plains, probably following the big herds, deer and elk, or whatever else you might have roaming around north of the border, these fellows were already frozen stiff.'

'No aroma.'

'Exactly,' Steven said, 'and that's also why we don't want to disturb them. Anything fluid left inside those skin cases will stink to high heaven, and we'll have all kinds of company in our little camp this evening.'

'I get your point,' Gilmour said, and crossed to the sailboat, which was also right where they had left it. He brushed a covering of fallen leaves off the bow and started to scoop more out from beneath the gunwales. There were a handful of empty beer cans inside as well; he tossed these into the brush beside the Seron corpses.

'And now you're a litterbug,' Steven joked wryly. 'Still, it looks seaworthy enough, doesn't it?' he added, peering at the hull. 'It's the sail I'm worried about. If we stowed it wet, it might have rotted a bit in the past Twinmoon.'

'Let's hope not.' Gilmour grabbed hold of the transom and began pulling. The wooden hull had frozen to the ground in several places, but a mumbled incantation melted the ice and soon Mark's little catboat was crunching and sliding over the smooth rocks and into the fjord, making Steven wince every time the hull grated over a stone.

'We never thought about tar or patch lumber,' he muttered. 'What if the damned thing leaks?'

'Then we will have a significantly more damp and chilly journey than we expected, I imagine.'

They reached the water's edge and Steven untied the bits of twine keeping the sail reefed and the dropped mast secure.

'What are you doing?' Gilmour asked. 'We still have two days.'

'We're going to take her out, just to see if she'll stay afloat.'

'Ah, excellent idea,' he said. 'I'll wait here. Enjoy yourself.'

'Funny, but no.'

Later, with the sailboat running west along the fjord, Steven fixed the main sheet, checked and re-checked the tiller, then moved forward on his hands and knees, inspecting every inch of the hull for cracks, leaks or patches of rot. Gilmour huddled in the stern, swaddled in his cloak, smoking, content to watch as the grey and black granite walls rolled by.

'Tell me about the archipelago,' Steven said at last. 'Do we stand any chance at all of reaching Pellia intact?'

'Of course we do,' Gilmour said, 'With a northern Twinmoon, the high tides will give us ample depth. The main route through the islands will be busy; a few days either side of this Twinmoon is the only time a heavy ship with a deep draft can reach Pellia, so there'll be plenty of traffic, merchant and navy. The rest of the time merchants make the long and more dangerous journey from Westport or Port Denis – when there *was* a Port Denis – and Northport, the closest major shipping centre to the Malakasian capital. Lots of small vessels move in and out of the archipelago any time they choose, but I do mean small – a tall person who knows the channels could just about walk from Pellia to Gorsk when the tides are low. Getting a big ship through there is dangerous, but luckily we're going at just the right time.'

'Assuming Garec and Kellin manage to hire us a boat,' Steven said, still on his knees.

'If they didn't, then as this little boat has almost no draft at all we'd sail through without a scrape.'

'Sure, if we don't freeze to death or capsize on the way. Mark and I were in Estrad for the southern Twinmoon. It was our first day in Eldarn and I remember the winds vividly. If the northern Twinmoon is anything like that, I really don't want to be out on the water in this bit of kindling.'

'I do understand,' Gilmour said, 'but given the circumstances, we might not have a choice.'

Steven sighed. 'So what's the main passage like?'

'Oh, it's not that tricky,' Gilmour said nonchalantly. 'The only captains who lose their ships in the archipelago are those in a great hurry to reach Pellia. They spot what they believe to be a deep passage west and run aground a few avens later. It's a maze of twists and turns in there, and many wrecks litter the shallows. There's no place for them to sink, so they break apart, leaving bits jutting up above the water. It's quite unnerving to see if you haven't been through before. They look like skeletons, some wearing sheets, all crippled by the wind and the rocks.'

A waft of pipe smoke drifted past Steven; it smelled sweet, familiar. Gilmour said, 'A safe, deep-water channel runs northeast during this Twinmoon, and if you know it, or you have a good chart, you can make it through, but it feels wrong because you have to run far east before you turn southwest and run downwind into Pellia.'

Steven watched the sail fill as they moved towards the next bend in the fjord's serpentine passage. 'If Mark left Orindale for Pellia, and with that wave he sent for us, we have to assume he did, but if he's travelling in a heavy ship with a deep draft, he'll have to take the long way through.'

'The *only* way through.' Gilmour punctuated this point with his pipe stem.

'The only way for a deep-drafting ship, a frigate or maybe a galleon, certainly. But what if we *did* make the run up there in this thing, could we take a short-cut?'

'In this? We could, but we'd never catch him. I can see where you're going, but a frigate or a galleon, they've enough sail on them to capture a typhoon. They might be bigger and heavier, but they're much too fast for us, even with our magic. We'd probably survive the crossing; I'm not worried about that. We have enough power between us to get there in one piece. But even conjuring up a Larion tailwind, we'd never overtake Mark.'

Steven looked downcast. 'I guess you're right. And if we use magic, we're just inviting him to crush us with another surprise from the bowels of that spell table. It was just a thought. I'd have liked to get there before he does.'

'Sorry.'

Steven crept aft, careful not to rock them; he didn't feel up to bailing icy seawater. 'I'll give Mark credit: he did a good job patching this tub together. There's not a leak or a bit of rot that I can find, and the sheet seems to be in good shape.'

'It'll be a shame to abandon it out there.'

Steven took a bit of the old cloth between his fingers. 'So you think they'll be there?'.

'I hope so.'

'Ever the optimist, Gilmour. That's a good trait.'

'I try.' Gilmour shifted the tiller and released the sheet, crying out, 'Jibing.'

'Ducking,' Steven replied, suiting actions to words.

'What's for dinner?' Gilmour set a course for their camp, re-fixed the sail and re-lit his pipe.

'Not a blessed thing,' Steven replied, 'unless you've got more than an unending supply of tobacco hidden in that cloak. Let's hope Garec and Kellin hired a ship with a five-star galley. We're going to need it.'

The Gloriette pool tilted, righted itself and then tilted the opposite way. Mark hung on to the marble column, expecting the ground beside the rectangular coping to do the same. It didn't. He listened to the water slam into the far end of the marble tub, then slosh right and bounce back out of the darkness. It went on that way for a while, as if someone had balanced the whole lot on a see-saw.

The screaming started as a faint wail in the distance and rose in volume and intensity, then broke. Mark knew it was human; the high-pitched cry was interrupted only by frantic gulping for breath, then the scream modulated from a piercing shriek to a staccato of noisy panting shouts.

Ah, welcome, Redrick. Nice to have you with us.

The lights came up, dim at first and then bright enough to see the remains of the coral snake coiled in the mud, the rectangular pool, still sloshing back and forth, the marble columns, the coping and the arched bridge leading up the marshy slope to freedom. Distracted by the light and the brief opportunity to take everything in, Mark ignored the familiar voice; he even ignored the screaming.

'Hello, jerkweed,' he said to the snake, 'how's your head, still crushed?'

The serpent sentry lifted what was left of its head and attempted to hiss at him. It was decomposing in the humidity. Mark kicked the rotting snake into the pool, though he knew the ghoulish creature would be back.

Mark?

He moved to the next column. The snake was swimming after him, though it was struggling; he had broken many of its bones. He listened out for anything approaching through the foliage, but all he could hear were the cries of another soul damned to Hell – *what did he say, Roderick? Rhetoric?* He tiptoed across the coping and dashed for the next column in line. The lights were still on, and the marble bridge was only three columns away. 'Three left,' he muttered, 'and then I'm coming for you.'

I've got you a present.

He wiped sweat from his face and checked his snakebites. The one he could see, on his wrist, was oozing a thick, pasty substance. He squeezed at the inflamed area around the punctures and frowned when a tablespoon of milky foulness spilled over the back of his hand. It had the consistency of hardening glue and smelled of summer gangrene, but once rid of the tapioca pus, the punctures ran freely with blood, cleansing themselves. Though he couldn't see as well, Mark endeavoured to repeat the procedure on his leg. He didn't feel sick or woozy or about to puke, nor did he feel his temperature rising, although any change would have been difficult to sense in this swampy heat.

Are you ignoring me?

'Yup.'

But I've brought you something.

'You mentioned that. It's not a cheeseburger and a couple of cold beers, is it? Because that's tops on my Christmas list these days. Otherwise, blow me.'

I'll show you.

A black man, stripped to the waist and screaming in unholy terror, floated by in the pool. It sounded like all his nightmares were being realised, everything that had ever frightened him: the dark, the creature that haunted the woods outside town, the rainbow-coloured snake in the grass, it was all here. Mark had no idea if their new resident was seeing and feeling the same things, but he didn't doubt that whatever held the sorry sod in its grip was unpleasant. He held fast to the third column from the bridge and watched the newcomer slip into the darkness of the other place. It was worse in there, like being trapped inside a stone.

So what do you think?

'I think you're a sick bastard,' he said, checking the brush in hopes of catching sight of whatever might be waiting for him. 'What did that guy ever do to you? Did he bang your wife? Steal your lunch money? What?'

I told you, Mark. He's a present.

'What do I want with him?'

Come on. I'll show you.

A feeling of mild vertigo set him spinning as Mark felt the cool marble become insubstantial and waxy. Worried he might get trapped by the wrists, he backed away, checking for the snake and feeling the world upend. He tumbled backwards into the damp mire, watching as the giant tumorous tadpoles swam hurriedly after the newcomer.

'Christ Almighty, they're going to eat him,' he shouted, and tried to roll into the pool, hoping to grab a few of the tadpoles and toss them into the swamp, where maybe they'd be eaten. But before he could move, the lights came up, brilliant yellow, and the air cooled.

He was lying on his bed. Steven was in the kitchen and the aroma of fresh coffee was snaking its way up the stairs. It was morning in the Rockies; the winter sun, unbearably bright at this time of day, had broken through the window to blind him. He revelled in the familiarity of things he knew by touch: the cool side of the pillow, the flannel blanket, the clean woollen socks, dry on his feet. Mark rolled over and pulled a bit of blanket between his knees; he didn't know how anyone slept with their knees knocking together. Outside the wind brushed the ponderosas, singing a song unmistakable to anyone who had ever been in the mountains. There was no more perfect place on Earth than the Colorado hills.

He tried to go back to sleep; his department chair could find someone to cover first period. What was it? The Stamp Act? Anyone could fake that – hell, the kids could read the chapter and talk about it on their own. No one would begrudge him a few extra minutes of sleep. Didn't they know what he'd been through, following Steven Taylor on a doomed quest to save a foreign world? Didn't that merit an extra two or three minutes of snooze?

But there were things out of place, even in the shambled disarray of his bedroom. He knew when something wasn't right. On the far wall, between the closet and his old poster of Roger Clemens, was a shelf. The clock, the paperbacks, the old baseball and the pocketknife all belonged up there, but that snake did not. It was slithering through the one-size-fits-all strap on the back of a Denver Broncos hat, its tiny orange rings matching the Bronco hue exactly. Its head had been crushed and its slippery skin was rotting away: it looked as though it had been run over by a car.

And the green sweatshirt on the wall, that might have been there before; Mark had gone to college in Fort Collins, but this looked too large for him – and it had been shot full of arrows. He tried to think of anyone from Fort Collins who might have been shot to death by an archer. A voice, thick with beer and stupidity, clamoured in his head and then was gone. *She's the one with the nigger coach from Idaho Springs. Oh, yeah, I hear great things about him too. He was tough in his day.*

'Who said that?' Mark sat up, wanting to be angry but still too groggy, a little behind the beat.

I told you I had a present for you.

'What? Do I get to stay here at home? Great, thank you. I'll remember you on your next birthday – do you wear sweaters, or should I get you a DVD?' He kicked back the covers, put his feet on the floor.

Alas, this is all temporary, but necessary for me to show you your gift.

'I can't have it back in the swamp?'

You can't see it in the swamp. You have it already.

'All right, I'll bite. At least it isn't hot in here.' Mark stood and stretched. His legs felt strange, as if he had spent two months on crutches. 'What do I have to do?'

Come over here to the mirror.

'Over here?' The idea that whoever was holding him hostage might be near the mirror intrigued him. He had to move a wooden longbow out of the way; he didn't remember owning one, but perhaps it was Steven's. He closed the closet door to see the mirror and noticed a quiver of homemade arrows stacked behind his fishing waders, next to an old pair of skis. He expected to see his captor in the mirror, protected behind some sort of Lewis Carroll force-field, and wondered what would happen if he just shattered the thing into a pile of jagged shards. 'Take that, Alice,' he said aloud.

What's that?

'Nothing. Now, what is it that you're so—'

It was him, but at the same time, *not* him. He was there, seeing his own eyes as they rolled up and down, checking the length and breadth of the mirror, searching for any sign of Mark Jenkins. When he looked up, his eyes – *the* eyes, *those* eyes – looked up. When he looked down, they followed suit. He raised a hand to his face and ran a finger across his cheek; the young, muscular black figure in the mirror did the same. 'Holy shit,' he said. 'Where am I? What did you do with me?'

With you? Your body, Mark, had a nasty, purulent sore. Major Tavon ordered it burned.

Mark fell forward and gripped the sides of the mirror. Bracing himself, he stared into the unfamiliar face. It was the man from the pool, the sorry bastard who had drifted past the row of marble columns and into the dark place. The tadpoles were snacking on him right now. 'So who is this? Who am I?'

His name was Redrick Shen. He was a sailor from Rona, a South-Coaster. I thought you might like to know that I had found a likely replacement: young, of dark skin, strong and healthy, and with no open sores on his hands.

It was true; Redrick Shen had been killed before being taken. Except for some painful-looking bruising on his neck and a swollen jaw, Mark could find nothing amiss. 'But why?' he asked, bemused.

Why what?

'What difference does it make? Did you think I wanted to be a black man? That being a black man would somehow make this easier for me than being a white woman? Are you fucking nuts? It isn't enough that you made me a black man, you dope – you want to make me happy, go find *me* and put me back inside *my* body.'

I can't do that, Mark. Major Tavon—

'I know. She had it burned.'

I hoped you'd be pleased.

Mark shook his head, the stranger's head. 'You still haven't answered my question. Why? What difference does it make what skin colour I wear now?'

Mark, you disappoint me. I thought you had it all worked out: Vienna, the Gloriette, that patch of sunshine you're trying so hard to reach.

He turned away from the mirror, checked the snake on the shelf and watched as his room began to change. The floor bowed and creaked, warping into the irregular rise and fall of a swampy riverbank. The walls cracked, the sheetrock popping and bursting as thick lengths of coiled, snakelike vine writhed into the room, covering the walls. Ferns crept up around his feet and he heard the sound of mud slurping and sloshing through the floorboards.

They were going back.

'Why did you bring me here? Why did I need to see this?' His feet were wet; he searched the room for whatever might transmogrify into the stone bridge or one of the last three columns.

I have plans for you, Mark Jenkins, big plans. I just thought you'd be more comfortable in something familiar.

The air was all at once heavy and dank with decay. As if welcoming him home, a deer-fly bit him on the neck and Mark slapped it dead, wiping the broken wings and gore on Redrick Shen's leggings. The lights were fading and he had not yet seen the coral snake. Maybe it was stuck in Colorado – it would freeze to death there at this time of year. Before being plunged into darkness, he made a cursory check of the ground cover, mud and ferns.

'Nothing there?' he said, and dived for the next column.

'Two to go, shithead,' Mark said as darkness fell.

A FOLLOWING SEA

Jacrys lifted his head, blew hard enough to clear a lock of hair from his face and considered the stairway. It might have gone on for ever. He had been up and down these same stairs countless times over the Twinmoons but had never before realised how steep and precarious the crooked slats nailed into sloping cross beams were. They could not be more than a breath or two away from collapse.

'I can't make it,' he wheezed. No one heard; the others were wrestling with bags and a heavy trunk. 'Thadrake,' Jacrys' voice rattled, 'Thadrake, I can't make it up there. All that time on Carpello's yacht and I never imagined I wouldn't be able to make it up the steps at my own safe house.'

'What's that, sir?' The young officer dropped the bags and walked into the foyer. Thadrake was back in uniform since negotiating their safe passage through the naval blockade early that morning. With his leather polished to a shine and his jacket brushed to within an inch of its life, he looked as if he expected to encounter Prince Malagon strolling along the quay at any moment.

Jacrys gripped the one handrail that looked sturdy enough to support his weight. 'I said, there's no way I can make it up these stairs. I never—'

'Mirron and I can—'

'Don't interrupt me when I am speaking!' Droplets of blood sprayed from Jacrys' lips and his head bobbed in time with his laboured breathing. He inhaled as deeply as he could, *hollow tree*, coughed a wet, throaty spasm, *loose gravel*, and said, 'Don't interrupt me, Captain. Remember your place.'

'Yes, sir.'

Mirron, General Oaklen's healer, joined them, and immediately spotted the blood. 'Good rutting lords, sir, you're bleeding again. I told you to stay in bed! I said going about on deck was a mistake – you have opened that wound again, sir, you have to—'

'Shut!' Jacrys whispered, then doubled over in a prolonged coughing fit. When he finally raised his head again, the front of his tunic was splattered with blood, and a trail of blood-stained saliva dripped from his lower lip. With an effort, he spat, then whispered, 'Just get me upstairs.'

Together Mirron and Thadrake helped Jacrys up the ramshackle staircase and into the small apartment. It was sparsely decorated, with a simple cot against the back wall, a small chest of drawers and a chair near a window overlooking the quay and twin wardrobes flanking the wooden doorframe. Inside one, Mirron found bedding, a rack of expensive clothes and a ceramic basin, which he placed on top of the chest of drawers. In the other, he discovered several shelves of outlawed books, science, history and even storybooks, all generations old, printed before Prince Marek closed the universities.

In a bedside table, Thadrake found several candles and a tinder pouch. He kindled a small fire in the tiny hearth and when it was burning nicely, he added a couple of logs from the woodpile next to the fireplace, just enough to warm the room.

All the while, Jacrys lay on the cot, staring out of the window towards the harbour. Finally, he tilted his head far enough to find Mirron, standing with his back pressed against one of the wardrobes. Unwilling to minister to the wounded spy without permission, Mirron waited for instructions.

Jacrys nodded at him and the healer crossed and knelt at his bedside.

Jacrys fought to lift his head from the pillow; he didn't want to give orders lying down, not any longer. 'Mirron . . . leave the querlis,' he managed, then, haltingly, 'You are relieved of duty. Find a transport back to Orindale. Tell Colonel Pace that I dismissed you.'

Mirron flushed, indignant, and started, 'But sir, you—'

'Don't argue,' Jacrys cut him off. 'I don't care what you have to say. You're dismissed.'

The elderly man stood stiffly, trying to preserve a measure of dignity, and said, 'Very well, sir. Good luck with your convalescence.'

Jacrys tried not to laugh. Mirron had been quite right: he had done this to himself. If he hoped to live through the next Twinmoon, he needed to proceed cautiously; laughing was banned. 'Thank you,' he whispered, 'although I think we both know there isn't going to be any convalescence.'

Mirron said nothing, just started for the door.

'Ah, Mirron,' Thadrake said, 'the querlis?'

The irritated healer stomped down the rickety stairs and into the crowds moving along the Pellia waterfront. Thadrake retrieved the bags, did some unpacking to avoid the uncomfortable silence in the small room, then added more wood to the fire.

'Leave it be,' Jacrys whispered.

'But sir, it's too cold—'

'It'll warm up when they stoke the ovens downstairs. They'll bake bread for this evening. It gets plenty warm in here when they do. If you make me a querlis poultice, I'll most likely sleep through the night. That should give you some time to look around a bit, perhaps find someone who can tell you about the goings-on here in the capital, or even at the palace. And I know you're not a healer, Captain, but I'm glad to be rid of that horsecock Mirron.'

'Me too, sir.'

'Excellent. Now, please look beneath the third plank from the left, there near the window.'

'This one?' Thadrake heard a hollow thud when he thumped the board with the toe of his boot. 'Something under here?'

'Silver, copper, some tobacco – although it's probably no good any more – and a bit of root.'

'Fennaroot?' Thadrake looked surprised. 'You don't seem like the kind of man who would use that stuff.'

'Not for me,' Jacrys rasped, shaking his head slightly, 'but it can be an excellent aid in interrogation.'

'Really?' Thadrake used his knife to pry up the length of old wood. 'I would have guessed that your methods of interrogation were a bit more ... well, rough.'

'There are many ways to conduct interrogations, Captain.'

'Yes, sir,' he said as he withdrew the contents of the hidden storage chamber. 'Did you want some of this root now, sir?'

'No, you blazing fool,' Jacrys murmured. 'I want you to take some of the silver and get us something to eat, some wine, the best you can find, more querlis and maybe a pair of willing young women.'

'That'd kill you,' Thadrake smirked.

'Ah, but what better way to start towards the Northern Forest?'

'How about much older, and in your sleep?'

'Good point.' Jacrys found to his surprise he was enjoying the banter. 'Forget the whores, but maybe bring back—'

'A pastry or two?' Thadrake risked the interruption. Pastries were one of Jacrys' weaknesses.

'Yes, please.' The spy rolled into his blankets and closed his eyes. 'I'll be here.'

'Yes, sir.' Thadrake pocketed a handful of copper Mareks – there was no need for silver.

'Thadrake?' Jacrys didn't bother opening his eyes. 'Nothing for the morrow. I take only bread and tecan in the mornings, understand?'

'Very good, sir.'

Later, with the remnants of their shared dinner on the table, Thadrake, still in uniform, sat near the window, watching a team of sailors and stevedores prepare a three-masted schooner tied up at the wharf. He swallowed a mouthful of wine, the finest he had tasted in his life, and propped his feet up on the chest.

Thinking Jacrys asleep, Thadrake poured another goblet and nibbled at what meat remained on the gansel leg. From the darkness behind him, the spy asked, 'What's happening out there?'

Thadrake jumped, spilling wine on his leggings. 'Rutters, you scared me.' He put his goblet on the table, mopped up the wine and moved to beside Jacrys' bed. 'Not much, sir,' he reported. 'The dockers are making that three-master ready to sail. Customs officers have already been on to check her hold. I expect they'll be pushing off shortly.'

Jacrys' breathing sounded worse. He wouldn't live much longer if he didn't get to a sorcerer with knowledge of the healing arts. There was too much blood pooling in his lung and attempting to cough it out would only exacerbate the injury and kill him more quickly. 'I'd like to see that,' he murmured.

'Would you?' Thadrake considered the cot. It was a simple wooden skeleton with leather straps to support the thin mattress. 'Hold on, sir.' He hefted the head of the small cot and dragged it to the window, then went to the wardrobe and collected the rest of the bedding to prop up Jacrys' head and shoulders, giving Jacrys an unimpeded view of the quay, the waterfront and the harbour beyond.

When he'd finished, he asked, 'Are you all right, sir?'

At first Jacrys didn't respond, and Thadrake was starting to fear he'd actually killed the spy. Finally, Jacrys made a sound that, a Twinmoon earlier, would have been a sigh of contentment but now sounded like something broken. 'Thank you, Captain,' he whispered.

Thadrake drained what was left in his goblet. 'I worry, sir, that perhaps you shouldn't be at the window for too long. It is quite draughty here.'

'I'll be fine right here,' Jacrys said. 'Good night, Captain.'

'Good night, sir.'

'And Captain,' Jacrys turned his head and found Thadrake in the candlelight and repeated, 'thank you.'

Within the aven, Jacrys was back on the slip of sand across the Welstar River. Brexan was with him.

Thadrake sat up until the candles burned out, finishing the wine as he watched the schooner push back from the pier and disappear into the night. Listening to the Malakasian spy struggling to breathe, even in his sleep, Thadrake eventually drifted off himself.

Garec stepped on deck and immediately regretted it. Roiling black clouds filled the sky with the promise of freezing rain. What would be a pleasant dusting of snow on the Falkan plains was a bone-chilling drenching for the passengers and crew of the *Morning Star*, and just to exacerbate the discomfort, the ship was running north under a steady Twinmoon wind, heeling over in a way that – to Garec – felt dangerously close to capsizing. He braced his boots on the canted deck, gripped the gunwale and made his way carefully towards the helm. *I will never get used to this*, he thought grimly. *Give me the mountains any Twinmoon; this is madness.*

Captain Ford was at the helm, looking absurdly happy with their tailwind and the following tide. 'Good morning,' he shouted over the din.

Garec grabbed the wheel to keep from falling. 'Do we have to be tipped quite so far over? Is this normal?'

'Perfectly normal,' the captain assured him. 'Just a bit of heel – we want to make good time; so I had Marrin and Tubbs haul the sheets in tight. We're rutting near flying before this wind. You don't feel it while you're asleep, because your hammock acts as a plumb: the ship rolls around you. It's not a good way to get your sea legs, though. You ought to sleep in a bulkhead bunk. By the time you wake up, you're already used to the swells.'

'Is that what you call these terrifying waves? *Swells?*' Garec sounded incredulous; it felt like a full-fledged flood tide to him.

'They're not the big ones.' He grinned and wiped the spray from his eyes. 'We're saving those for up north.'

'Oh, good,' Garec forced a smile, 'because I was worried that perhaps this would be too easy. I mean, we've had such a quiet and enjoyable journey so far.'

'I noticed your head. How is it? Getting better?'

'Sure, and if I don't drown when this boat rolls over, I'll probably have Kellin take the stitches out in the next day or two. Right now it itches more than anything.'

'I know the feeling.' Captain Ford made a slight adjustment to their course, forcing Garec to release the helm for a moment and trust his footing. 'I'm sure Tubbs or Sera have some tecan brewing if you want some. They'll be in the galley.'

'No thanks.' Garec swallowed hard. 'I don't think I could eat anything right now. I like to swim on an empty stomach.'

'The ship is fine,' the captain assured Garec with an avuncular smile. 'As a matter of fact, this is the way she likes to run, just like a horse; loose her reins and let her go.'

Garec thought of Renna, his much-loved mare. It was true; the fiery beast was never happier than when he let her have her head. 'Can I bring you some tecan?'

'No thanks, that's a port drink, a luxury. Out here we drink our own brew, something Sera dreamed up about fifteen Twinmoons ago. It's mostly rosehips; they grow all over southern Praga, right up to the waterline, too. They're easy to find and we dry them over a beam in the for'ard hold.' He smiled wryly. 'Marrin tried smoking them once, just for laughs. He looked like his face was on fire.'

Garec looked anxiously across the rolling sea to where waves were shattering against the granite cliffs of western Falkan. 'How much further?'

'At this rate?'

'Or a bit slower,' Garec said. 'Too many people hurry too much these days. It's not healthy.'

'We ought to be in sight of the fjord in about two avens, just after midday.'

'What? That's too early,' Garec cried. 'We're here too early; it needs to be late tonight, or tomorrow morning.'

'Sorry, my friend, a couple of avens and we're there.' He fixed his gaze on Garec, ignoring the ship for a moment. 'Unless you want to make a run in there.'

'Into the shallows?' Garec shouted over the wind. 'It looks rough.'

'It won't be the high point of your trip.'

'Is there a way to wait out here for them?'

'To stop? No. But we can reef the main, foremain and topsails. In this wind, the topgallants will keep us on course, but—'

'But what?' Garec was turning the colour of mould-cheese.

'You're going to feel every one of those swells; it'll be like riding on driftwood.' He hid a smile. Normally he would be angry at losing time with such a following sea, but he had agreed to take on additional passengers and that meant waiting.

'Fine.' Garec started for the galley. 'Thank you, Captain. I'll bring you some of your rosehip concoction.'

But the captain was already shouting, 'Into the shrouds! Let's go, all of you! Reef the main, fore and tops! I want to hit a wall! Let's get the brakes on!'

'Gilmour?' Steven was at the tiller, double-checking that the sail was lashed to a wooden cleat near the stern. Gilmour sat in the bow, leaning against the mast with his legs extended, his ankles crossed, utterly comfortable. Steven thought he looked like he was sunning himself in a poolside lounger. 'Do you remember when we talked about maybe crossing in this little catboat?' Gilmour opened one eye and Steven went on, 'I lied. I'm not going out there. It's insane.' They were at the mouth of the fjord, having enjoyed a pleasant, if chilly, run through the cleft in the Falkan cliffs. The swirling breezes inside the fjord had been tricky, and more than once Steven had cursed and changed course moments before splintering the sailboat against the sides, but compared with what lay before them, the fjord was a milk-run.

A narrow channel of deep water appeared to roll west to east with the rising tide, while the shallows on either side of the granite gates looked like they were closing in. Whitecaps were forming well out at sea, breaking, rolling and breaking again before reaching the cliffs in a noisy crash of spume and saltwater.

Steven was seriously thinking about turning back. 'This is insane,' he repeated. 'We won't make it beyond the breakwater.'

'Of course we will,' Gilmour said. He was irritatingly calm. 'Just keep the boat inside the channel there in the middle and we'll pass right through.'

'The channel? You mean that tightrope of deep water swelling up and rolling in here, Karl Wallenda?'

'Who?'

'Never mind,' Steven said, 'but look at how the wind's blowing; it's a frigging gale. Once we clear this southern cliff, we're either going to capsize or we're going to start hauling arse to Gorsk like we're being chased by the goddamned hound of the Baskervilles.'

'Just think about what has to happen. Use your knowledge; use your determination and make it happen.'

'This is too big, Gilmour. This is too much. I can't—'

'Yes, you can.' Gilmour sat up and looked at his apprentice. 'It's just wind and water, that's all.'

Steven watched the Ravenian Sea hurtle past the mouth of the fjord like traffic on a highway. Beyond the granite gates the scene was a seamless grey background for a dreary Expressionist painting; whitecaps and black storm clouds were the only things distinguishing sea from sky.

He thought about what he knew of physics and wave motion. The whitecaps crashing against the shore were not striking at right angles, but coming in on a diagonal tack, pushed by the wind and tide, and then they bounced, out of phase, back into the fray for another turn around the dance floor. If he could capture that breeze first, the reflected breeze off the cliffs, he would have a tailwind – granted, on an angle – but a powerful tailwind that would hopefully push Mark's toy sailboat far enough into the crosswind that they wouldn't find themselves splashed flat, like Wile E. Coyote, against the northern cliff face. With the fjord ending, there was no time to come up with another option.

'I think I've got it,' Steven said.

'Do you need my help?'

'Just keep your head down; try and stay dry.'

'No, I mean my *help*. Can I do anything?'

'No magic this time. I don't want to risk Mark sensing us.'

Gilmour sat up, genuinely surprised; he'd decided to risk a bit of magic to reach Garec and Kellin, and then belay it entirely until their arrival in Pellia. 'Really?' he whispered, shrugging out of his cloak and kicking off his boots. 'This ought to be interesting.'

Steven hauled the little sheet in and reached out to take hold of the boom himself. He held it steady, pointing directly east into the fjord.

The catboat slowed almost to a stop, her sail flapping, empty and ineffective.

'Steven?'

'Just wait for it, Gilmour, one more second ...' The little boat rode up one side of a huge swell, hung on its crest, hesitantly overcoming inertia, and then slid into the trough. Just enough of its snout peeked into the crosswind for the sail to fill with the tendrils of the northerly breeze.

At first, it was a gentle gust that tugged at the sheet and took up the slack in the rigging; the sail puffed out a bit, and Steven let go of the boom but clasped the rig line, keeping the sheet close and the bow pointed directly through the channel. 'This isn't bad,' he murmured, as much to convince himself as anything, 'we can do this.'

As the little skiff cleared the granite gates of the fjord, the full force of the crosswind slammed into them like a broadside cannonade. The sail, surprisingly tough, took the punch and held on. The boom ran out to starboard and the rig line tore through the flesh of Steven's palm, leaving a red stain on the last few inches of hemp.

'Holy shit!' Steven shouted, ignoring the blood and clamping his injured hand down on the rope. He hauled it back in as far as he dared and quickly made it fast to the tiller cleat. 'Mother of Christ, that hurt!' he yelled as they began to pitch hard to starboard; they were going over.

'Let it go, Steven!' Gilmour yelled, 'we're going to sink!'

'Get to port,' he called back, 'throw your weight against it. Get up on the gunwale; sit on the bastard if you have to!' Steven pressed his back and shoulders against the port rail himself, pushing the tiller as far to starboard as he could with one foot. He watched the rig line strain against the cleat and cursed himself for tying it off too soon. There was no way to reach the line and let the sheet out, even a few inches, to ease their starboard pitch. 'Come on baby,' he urged, 'come back, just an inch or two, you can do it!'

For a few seconds, the little sailboat balanced on a knife's edge. With the sheet filled to bursting, the tiller hard to starboard and all the ballast Steven and Gilmour could muster far to port, they waited, holding their breath and praying that they would right themselves.

'Stay over, Gilmour,' Steven cried, 'and pray to all the fucking saints in Christendom! Just another breath—'

They were being blown northwest, the deep fjord slipping away to the south and the rocky shallows off the northern gate closing fast.

'We're going to hit those rocks!' Gilmour cried.

Steven smiled despite his terror; this was exhilarating, and any thought of giving up and using magic to guide the little boat through the channel was lost in the excitement of the moment.

When the keel finally gave, correcting to port, Steven shouted, 'Woo hoo! What a ride, Gilmour! Goddamn, that was something!' He started for the cleat, wanting to let the sheet out, just a little, when they started to pitch back to starboard. 'Stay over, Gilmour,' he cried, 'straddle the rail if you have to!' He loosened the rig line and let the boom slide a bit further out; with the tiller still pressed to starboard, the keel righted and they slipped through the channel like quicksilver.

Gilmour stood in freezing ankle-deep water and looked questioningly at Steven. 'And for your next trick?' he asked, grinning.

Steven smiled and wiped his face. 'Get bailing. We don't want to swamp.' He too grinned, and when Gilmour looked quizzical, he added, 'It's just that I'm staggered at how often my maths obsession has saved our necks on this little vacation. Be glad I wasn't a poetry junkie!'

Gilmour started cupping handfuls of water and shovelling them over the side, but there was twice as much coming in. He growled, then stood up and shouted a quick spell. The bilge-water suddenly turned into a miniature tidal wave, rolled from stern to bow, and then up and over the gunwales into the sea.

'That's better,' Gilmour said, retaking his seat beside the mast. 'Tell me again why we didn't use magic to get through there.'

'Mark might find us, and anyway, I was too distracted by the physics of the whole thing.' Steven watched the water bailing itself over the side. 'Can he detect that?'

'No, it's a carnival trick. It would be like him finding a burning candle.' Gilmour pushed his matted hair away from his face and said, 'Distracted, huh? Weren't you distracted when the floodtide swallowed us in the river outside Wellham Ridge?'

'That was different; I was afraid of dying and the magic just burst out of me in an explosion of frantic self-preservation.'

'And you weren't – *aren't* – afraid of dying today?'

Steven smirked. 'Mathematics can be pretty distracting, Gilmour! Now hold on, we're about get clobbered again.'

'Do you want me up on the railing? I don't think I can get any wetter than I am right now.'

'No, this one shouldn't be that bad. We don't need the tailwind here; so I'll let the sheet out, come about, and then haul it in gently. We'll get kicked, but it won't be anything like that last one. You start watching for Garec and Kellin. They'll likely be the only ship out there – any captain would be near-on suicidal to be in this close today—'

They plunged into a deep trough, burying the bow beneath the waves. 'Shit and shit and shit,' Steven said, 'I didn't see that one coming. Keep bailing will you, or we're screwed running.'

'Got it,' Gilmour muttered, repeating his spell, but adding a lilting phrase to the end of his incantation, something he hadn't said before. The water, deeper this time, began receding almost immediately. 'That ought to keep us dry, but watch the bloody road, will you?'

'You sound like my mother,' Steven said. 'Anyway, as I was saying, a captain would have to be raving mad—'

'Or exceedingly well paid,' Gilmour finished.

'Exactly. So we'll signal the closest ship we see and hope to hell it isn't the Malakasian navy.'

'Or your roommate.'

'That would be awkward, too.' Steven checked the sheet, let go the boom and pulled the tiller slowly to port. As they came about, he hauled the sail in and caught the wind before the northerly swells overwhelmed their bailing spell. It was a clumsy tack, and the little boat jolted as Steven held fast, tearing a bit of fresh flesh from his already bloody palm. 'Sorry,' he said, 'I'll have to mix up another couple of gin and tonics after that one. I guess I'm rusty.'

'Rusty? At sailing a rickety skiff through a gale? I'm disappointed; I had such high hopes for you.'

'This isn't a gale; this is just . . . bumpy.' They were running north now, canting steeply to starboard but making way with alacrity. Steven let the sheet out a few inches more; he didn't want to be stuck out here having to make repairs, especially with the fjord fading behind them.

'Just watch for anything hull-up on the horizon,' he said. 'I trust you've thought up some creative way to signal them.'

'I'll handle it.' Gilmour dug in his tunic, withdrew his pipe and a pouch of dry tobacco.

'Does that stuff ever get wet?'

'Once, yes, some fourteen hundred Twinmoons ago. Southern Malakasia. It wasn't a good day.'

'There,' Sera said, pointing over the starboard cathead, 'd'you see it?'

'Pissing demons,' Marrin said, 'what is that? Fire?'

'That's them,' Garec said. 'Can we get in that close?'

Captain Ford watched the fireballs leap over the swells, climb as high as the Falkan cliffs and then explode in colourful pops. He didn't like it. For a moment he considered turning about, giving back the silver and making the near-impossible run to Orindale, close-hauled on the wind.

Garec said, 'It's just them, maybe a few satchels of extra clothing. Apart from a knife or two, neither of them carries any weapons.'

'So what is that?' Captain Ford was angry. 'What haven't you told me?' He searched the deck for Brexan. 'Who are these people?'

'We agreed, Captain Ford, that you were not going to ask any questions.'

'I understand that, but these aren't Resistance leaders, or soldiers. At least one of them has significant magic at his disposal.'

'He does,' Garec said.

'What are you doing in Averil?'

'None of your whoring business.' Garec wasn't about to be bullied. 'Suffice to say that we have engagements in Malakasia that don't concern you or your crew.'

'Magical engagements? Or are they transporting some sort of explosive? Because if I get one sniff of anything that might blow a hole in my ship, I'll cast the lot of you overboard.' Captain Ford glared at him, but Garec was unimpressed.

'Did you hear me?' he shouted again.

Marrin and Sera backed off a few paces, while staying near at hand, ready to assist the captain in any scuffle – not that either of them thought he would need help to subdue the younger, smaller man.

Garec lowered his voice to a whisper. 'And you'd be dead before you took two paces. Pay attention, because I don't have time to argue with you. I'll kill you, your crew, your dog if I have to, and I will take your ship and sail it anywhere I please. Now, I am happy to pay for your services, and I assure you that neither of my friends is carrying anything explosive. Both of them have a bit of magic they can summon from time to time, but nothing that represents a threat to you or your ship. The only threat you need to be concerned with is me.'

Captain Ford stopped, considering Garec's threat. He was not one to be bullied either, especially on his own ship and in front of his crew, and he silently cursed himself for agreeing to carry passengers, regardless of how much silver he stood to make. He had promised himself he would never get involved in politics, and apart from the occasional illegal passenger tucked behind a pallet of lumber or vegetables, he had never broken his vow. This was not going to end well. 'Listen, you snot-nosed little brat—'

'Pay attention!' Garec shouted again, then lowered his voice. Without averting his eyes, he looked at Captain Ford and said, 'You have one man working on the forecastle, one in the rigging. Sera and Marrin are flanking us, waiting for any sign from you that they should tackle me or heave me over the side. Tubbs is still below with Kellin and Brexan, and I promise you, Captain Ford—' his voice rose 'that I could kill all of them before you cried out a warning.'

Captain Ford laughed and took a menacing step forward. 'That's impossible, you pinch of grettan—'

'Not,' Garec interrupted, 'if I start with you.' Neither Captain Ford, Marrin nor Sera had seen the arrow appear in his hands, but he held it to the captain's throat, a makeshift skewer. Rotating it gently in his fingers, Garec ground the tip into the leathery flesh until a trickle of blood ran under his collar.

Captain Ford's hands were trembling. He tried to see Marrin and Sera, but he couldn't find them. Finally, he said, 'Stop.'

Garec lowered the shaft and said pleasantly, 'Let's go and get my friends. That's a little boat they're in, and I don't believe either of them wants to spend all day waiting for it to capsize.'

'Tell me who they are.' Captain Ford hadn't moved. 'Resistance leaders?'

'Yes, powerful ones.'

'Magicians?'

'Yes, powerful ones.'

Captain Ford felt the *Morning Star* beneath his feet and vowed to make the run to Averil in record time, even if it meant staying at the helm the entire trip. 'What do they do for the Resistance?'

'Espionage, mostly, no real military entanglements.'

'Brexan and Kellin?'

'The same, I guess.' Garec shrugged. 'Kellin was part of a military unit until she accompanied us south from Traver's Notch.'

Captain Ford nodded, swallowing something bitter. 'And you?'

'I kill.'

'Very well,' Captain Ford said. 'But I don't take orders on my ship, Garec Who Kills.'

'I have no interest in ordering you to do anything, Captain,' Garec smiled, 'and I am happy to take orders, swab decks, fillet fish, haul lines, polish brass, and dig ditches, just as soon as you stick to your end of our agreement and sail over there to collect my friends.'

Captain Ford turned away. 'Marrin, Sera.'

'Sir?' they replied in unison.

'Make your heading zero, six, five, and prepare to take on passengers.'

'Very good, Captain.' They were already moving away.

'Thank you, Captain, honestly,' Garec said. 'If it's any comfort, I don't enjoy my role with the Resistance. Not ever.'

'I don't find that especially comforting.'

'I don't suppose it is, but I am telling you the truth.'

Captain Ford dabbed at the wound in his neck. He held up a finger, looked at the blood, then wiped it on his cloak. 'That's fine, Garec. Let me just say that I hope it haunts you for a hundred lifetimes.'

'It already does.' Garec started below. 'I'm going for some tecan. Would you like some?'

Captain Ford was taken aback, but after a moment, he said, 'Some of the rosehip, if you would be so kind.'

'Right away.' Garec disappeared below.

Hannah saw Hoyt stumble, but he kept his feet and they continued running through the serpentine coils of Pellia's northeast district, a largely residential area with roads that looked they'd once been goat paths before being cobbled over when civilisation arrived.

'You all right?' Hannah wheezed.

Hoyt was pale and dripping sweat, too winded to answer as he half-ran and half-staggered through the twisting confusion of alleys. He was weak; his shoulder hadn't healed, despite his efforts with querlis and Alen's medicinal spells. He ran with his arm tucked against his ribs, making him look ungainly, disfigured. Hannah guessed the Seron who stabbed him had dipped her knife in something deadly, not magical, for Alen could disentangle even the worst magic a Seron could concoct. This must be bacterial. Hoyt's fever had been raging for days, and though querlis brought his temperature down at night, during the day he could barely stand by himself. He was running now on pure will.

Halfway across a junction of five roads, he stopped and bent over, trying to catch his breath. 'Do you see them?' he gasped.

'No.' Hannah put a hand on his shoulder. 'You should stop.'

'We can't, we have to catch up. Who knows what that horsecock will do with her?'

'Erynn won't let anything happen to her.'

'Erynn?' Hoyt looked up. 'She's the bloody nuisance who got us here in the first place. She's a ninety-Twinmooner; you think the Seron are going to listen when she asks them to please keep their hands off the little girl? No, Hannah, Erynn is in this as deep as the rest of us.'

Hannah turned a full circle, looking and listening. 'Which way?'

'Down there, across the northern neck?'

'No, we went there once already; it goes out to that little beach, and I bet this one does, too.' Hannah pointed to her left, along a westbound alley.

'That leaves these three.'

'Eenie, meenie, meinie, mo.' Hannah pointed east. 'Let's try this one.'

Hoyt wiped his eyes. 'Remind me never to learn that language of yours.'

'Come on.' She helped him up. 'The houses are too small along these others; I'm betting something as big as a warehouse is east of us, maybe even on the water.'

'I'm going to kill that docker when we get back.' Hoyt started running again. 'His directions were ganselshit.'

'Maybe Alen got lucky,' Hannah said, trying not to give in to her fear that it was already too late, that Milla was right now on her way upriver, bound for child slavery in the bowels of Welstar Palace.

'I hope so,' Hoyt said, 'because if Alen finds them, they're all dead.'

The cobblestone road narrowed, and Hannah's hopes fell: this was the wrong way. They'd have to double back all the way to the roundabout. There were too many ways to get lost in here.

'Hoyt, this can't be right,' she said sadly. 'We have to go back.' The buildings had closed in on either side; it was too narrow now even for two carts to pass.

'Wait,' Hoyt panted, 'look down there. Is it brighter, or am I dying?'

'Okay, we'll try it,' she said. Hoyt wouldn't make it all the way back to the intersection, not running, anyway.

The cobblestone street widened into a public marina with squat warehouses on either end. This was more an elaborate dry-dock and smokehouse than a storage facility, but they had guessed right. Wooden longboats and bulky trawlers were moored in the cove, their masts canted over like trees in a gale. Along the shore, dozens more were resting belly-up, waiting for shipwrights to patch them up in the spring so they'd be good for another season's work.

'There it is,' Hannah said, 'that one, over there, with the hole in it.' By hole, she meant the seaward access door, where those needing repairs or winter dry-docking could sail in and, using a clever system of pulleys and belts, have their longboats lifted from the water, later to join the others lined up and frozen outside.

'Here.' Hoyt handed her a hunting knife he had stolen in the last Moon.

'Terrific, another knife.'

'Just take it,' he said. 'And don't think about it, just slash anyone – any*thing* – that gets too close.'

'Fine,' she murmured to herself, 'super, "just slash", lovely. Can't

306

wait.' She followed him across the marina. 'Hey, how are we going to do this?'

'If it's just Erynn and whatshisname—'

'Karel.'

'If it's Erynn and Karel,' Hoyt said, 'we're going to scare the dogpiss out of them, take Milla, and threaten to turn them in for abduction.'

'And if there're Seron?'

'Then we're going to die.'

'Oh. Good.' Hannah considered the hunting knife. *Just slash.* 'Why don't we go and find Alen?'

'No time,' Hoyt said, and stumbled again. Hannah propped him up, holding him around the waist. 'If they take her out of here, we'll never get back inside Welstar Palace, certainly not into that slave chamber,' he pointed out grimly.

Inside the warehouse, Hannah nearly vomited at the unholy stench, a grim concoction of rotting fish guts, seagull guano and charred hickory. The facility obviously doubled as a smokehouse as well as a shipwright's dry-dock before the onset of winter. Bracing herself, she ushered Hoyt down a short hallway and into the main chamber where a wooden dock, about twenty feet across, lined three sides of a vast open workspace. The fourth side, while still protected beneath the cathedral-style roof, was open to the sea, and a twelve-foot drop separated the dock from the water below. The sea was comparatively still inside the dry-dock station, and it had actually frozen in places. The pylons were coated in a thin sheet of ice which reflected the late-day sun and brightened the inside of the warehouse. Across the open rectangle of sea water they could see Erynn and Karel standing next to a brazier. A heap at their feet could only be Milla, wrapped in a blanket from the inn. With one side open perpetually to the sea, and the chilly northern waters lapping about underfoot all day, Hannah could not imagine a colder place than this to work. For a brief moment she envied the smokers; at least they could huddle around their aromatic fires.

'Erynn!' Hannah shouted, her voice bouncing about the cavernous room. 'Erynn, what are you thinking? Do you know how much trouble you're in? How worried your parents are?'

'Leave us alone!' Erynn shouted, shocked that they had been discovered.

Hannah ignored her and started around the pier. 'Milla? Are you okay, sweetie?'

'It's cold in here,' Milla replied, 'but I'm all right.'

'We're coming to get you, Pepperweed,' Hoyt said.

'Stay there,' Karel warned, drawing his sword, but still looking like a child playing soldier in his father's clothes.

'And Karel, you stupid shit,' Hannah was too angry to stop, 'what's wrong with you? Are you so lovestruck, you ignorant little bastard, that you've lost your mind? What are you planning to do, hand her over to the army? Sell her to a seaman? I'll tell you this, Karel, you're in over your head. Officers don't take clandestine meetings in abandoned smokehouses. So do you know who's coming here? Do you have *any* idea what you've done?'

Still snarling and brandishing the blade, Karel puffed up his chest to respond, but Erynn cut him off. 'It's you, isn't it? You and Hoyt and Alen? You're not her parents, you're terrorists. I know it was you; I heard Hoyt saying he was going to bury them. He said it that night in the front room. I told you, I don't try to overhear things, but sometimes I do. And, anyway, I know it was you who attacked that wagon train. You killed those soldiers, and you burned all that wheat. There are people in Treven who needed that wheat, Hannah! My grandfather is there, and he needs that wheat. He's sick; you knew that. How could you be a terrorist?'

Hannah continued to make her way around the rectangular dock. 'Erynn, you have it all so wrong – that wasn't wheat, and it wasn't headed for Treven.'

'Liar!' Karel shouted. 'Don't listen to her, Erynn.'

'You're wrong, Karel,' Hoyt said, staggering beside Hannah. 'It wasn't wheat, but enchanted tree bark on its way to Welstar Palace, where it will be used in a monstrous spell. There are unimaginable horrors going on at the palace, and if you've got any bit of brain left in that empty head of yours, you'll try to avoid being stationed there, ever. Tell me you haven't heard rumours.'

Karel looked down at Milla. 'They're liars, Erynn. They'll say anything to get her back.'

'So what exactly are you planning to do?' Hannah asked, trying to sound concerned, friendly. 'You've kidnapped a little girl. How can you imagine this will end well for you?'

'They're just going to keep her until you tell the truth,' Erynn said. 'You have to turn yourselves in and tell them where the others are hiding.'

'"They're going to keep her"?' Hannah echoed. 'Who's *they*, Erynn?' Hannah and Hoyt were nearly all the way across the interior pier, rounding the final corner.

Erynn started to cry.

'Who are you waiting for? Who's meeting you here?' Hannah realised she and Hoyt been so desperate to rescue Milla that they had come through the building without checking their flank. She looked now, quickly, for other routes to the outside.

'We thought you would go quietly if you knew they had Milla,' Erynn tried to explain, 'otherwise you might have been hurt.'

'You're nothing but a pawn in their evil game, Erynn, and you too, Karel.' Hoyt sounded disgusted. 'They know Milla at Welstar Palace. They've been searching for her for the past Moon – surely you've seen them in their black and gold leathers? They're Malagon's personal police force. You think you're heroes; you're not. You've done nothing but endanger an innocent child, and you'd better pray to the gods of the Northern Forest Alen doesn't find you.'

Exactly on cue, three men emerged from the smokehouse. Their black and gold uniforms outshone even Karel's polished army leathers. Hannah had seen soldiers like these before, with their distinctive ceremonial capes; she flashed back to those chilling moments astride the flying buttress, hearing Churn call for her and then watching him slip away. 'Oh shit, Erynn, what did you do?' she said softly, despairingly.

'Are these the ones?' the tallest of the soldiers, a sergeant, by the markings on his sleeve, demanded of Karel.

Don't do it, you prick, Hannah thought, *please don't turn us in.*

'Yes, Sergeant; that's them,' the boy said, shaking. 'And there's another. He's here somewhere, here in the district, anyway. His name is Alen Jasper and he's from Middle Fork.'

'Disarm her, and take them into custody,' the sergeant ordered. 'If they resist, kill the sick one; keep the woman. She can explain herself to the captain.'

Hannah had forgotten the knife, which she was still holding loosely; Hoyt had his scalpel beneath his cloak but he was in no condition to wield it, especially against these two. When the soldiers started for her, Hannah smiled nervously and tossed the blade into the sea. She held her hands up in surrender.

'Wise decision, girlie,' one of the soldiers said. 'You're going to live through the day. How about that?'

Hoyt mimicked Hannah, lifting his cloak over his shoulders and raising his arms.

'Some terrorists, huh?' The soldier elbowed his squad mate.

'Deadly dangerous, eh?' He twisted Hannah's arm behind her back, ignoring her cry of pain, and ushered her towards Erynn and the others.

'You injured, son?' the second guard, a lean fellow with a rapier, asked Hoyt.

'Just my shoulder,' Hoyt replied, 'a stab wound, but I'll come quietly.'

'Then I'll lay off the arm, how's that?'

'Seems fair,' Hoyt said and fell in behind Hannah, the soldier following with his rapier drawn.

The sergeant crossed to Karel and Erynn. 'Surprisingly good work, soldier.'

'Thank you, sir.'

'Sergeant,' he corrected the boy.

'Sergeant, sorry, Sergeant.' Karel flushed.

'What's going to happen to Milla?' Erynn was still crying.

'She's going to Welstar Palace where she'll be enslaved by Prince Malagon,' Hoyt said. 'All thanks to you, Erynn.'

'Shut him up,' the sergeant ordered. The soldier guarding Hoyt stabbed him through his already injured shoulder.

'Ah, gods!' Hoyt screamed as he fell, hitting his head on the chilly planks as blood soaked his tunic.

'Hannah?' Milla said, trying to disappear inside her blankets. 'What's happening?'

'Don't worry, sweetie.' Hannah kept her voice calm, despite the pain in her elbow. Another inch and she was sure her arm would simply pop off.

Erynn stepped between the sergeant and the little girl. 'No,' she said, 'you can't have her until you tell me the truth. You have these two; why do you need to take—?'

The sergeant backhanded Erynn hard enough to knock her reeling. She stumbled to one side and Karel tried to catch her.

'Hey,' the boy shouted, 'keep your hands off her! We've done our duty!' He drew his sword, a toy compared to the array of weapons the Welstar guards carried.

'No!' Hannah screamed, but the boy was already staggering backwards, the sergeant's short blade hilt-deep in his chest.

The sergeant picked up Milla and rewrapped her protectively in the blanket. 'Come, my dear,' he said. 'We have a long trip home.'

Karel stumbled then collapsed. *Stupid bastard*, Hannah thought bitterly, *he never had a chance*.

The soldier holding Hannah's arm said, 'You, too, girlie. Let's go.'

'Let me help him, please,' she said, nodding towards Hoyt.

'He'll be all right,' the soldier said, then just stared at Hannah, a look of shock and confusion on his face. He released her arm as he cried out and fell, clutching his ankles.

Hoyt rolled onto his back after he'd used his scalpel to slash the guard's heel tendons. The man stood for a moment, then folded up, cursing, and tugging at his short-sword. The guard with the rapier tried to run Hoyt through, but the moment's distraction as he'd watched Karel die had allowed Hoyt to slice into the man's knee, straight through the ligaments.

Hoyt would have preferred to disable both legs, but he had lost the element of surprise and had no option now but to dive outside the rapier's range before attempting a second attack. He didn't know how he would deal with the sergeant; the man already had Milla in his arms and might kill her before Hoyt could get off the floor. He was dizzy, sweating with fever, and bleeding, but he had to stay lucid.

What would Churn do? he thought, but came up with nothing except: *Beat the grettanshit out of everyone.* That wasn't much of an option for the weary would-be surgeon.

'Stop!' the sergeant screamed, drawing his sword. He was still holding Milla, but he knew he could best Hoyt one-handed. He didn't give Hannah a passing glance as he hurried to assist his men.

'No,' a small voice interrupted imperiously, 'don't you hurt him.'

The sergeant felt pressure in his chest, but he ignored it. This fight would be over in two breaths. One of his men lay crippled, the other was bravely trying to attack while dragging a bloody leg.

'I said no!' The voice was angry this time, and the Malakasian felt an iron fist grip his heart. He gaped at the little girl in his arms. She had a tiny hand pressed flat against his chest and was pouting up at him, her bottom lip trembling in the cold.

He dropped his sword, ignoring his men as they fought on, determined to kill everyone in the warehouse, and stumbled around. He stared at the tiny girl, little more than a baby, frowning back at him and held her tightly – he had no other choice – as he staggered to his left and fell into the freezing waters of the North Sea.

'Milla!' Hannah shrieked. She turned to Hoyt, but he was already crawling to the pier's edge. The rapier-wielder, still armed and deadly despite his knee injury, thrust as Hoyt passed; he missed, but only by an inch or two. Hannah saw an opportunity and took it, shoving into the guard with her shoulder. As she crashed into him, they seemed to hang in mid-air, then went over the side and through the thin sheet of ice.

'Milla,' Hannah choked, and kicked away from the injured Malakasian. The cold hit her like a train; she would only have a few minutes before hypothermia set in. 'Milla! Sweetie, where are you?' she called urgently.

'I'm over here,' the little girl said, 'watch me, Hannah! Watch this.' She was swimming furiously, kicking and paddling with her determined little chin thrust out of the water. 'I'm doing the scramble!' she howled with pleasure, completely ignoring the dead body floating beside her. 'Watch me, Hannah, watch how well I'm doing.'

Certain her skin had already turned blue, Hannah turned to look at the second soldier. He'd managed to get to one of the slippery supporting pylons, but couldn't get a grip on the ice. He was shouting up to his comrade, the one with the severed Achilles tendon, but apart from calling down words of encouragement, the third Malakasian was able to offer little help.

Hannah paddled over to Milla, and wasn't surprised to find the water around the little girl was as warm as a summer bath. 'You are a great swimmer,' she said, and dropped a kiss on her head.

'We have to tell my Mama, and Alen,' Milla said excitedly, and then she remembered the sergeant. 'I'm sorry, Hannah,' she started to say, downcast, 'but he wanted to get Hoyt, and I thought—'

'Milla, it's fine, sweetie,' Hannah said, and kissed her again. 'Don't you think about it another moment, all right?'

'All right!' She looked around. 'Do we have to go now?'

'We should. How about we swim together to that wooden ladder outside the big doors?'

'All right,' Milla repeated as she started to paddle away. 'Do you think there are sharks?'

'No, sweetie, no sharks; it's too cold.'

'Good, because I'm afraid of sharks.'

'I'm afraid of sharks too,' Hannah told her, then shouted to the Malakasian guard who was screaming and tearing his fingernails on the pylon, 'Hey, hey! You want to live? You'd better come with us.'

'I can't— I can't do it . . . I need—'

'Shut up!' Hannah shouted, surprising herself. 'Get over here, the water's warmer.'

Hoyt was kneeling above her, watching through glazed eyes. 'You sure you want to do that?'

'We'll be fine. How are you?'

'Never better,' Hoyt murmured. 'I'm just going to lie down for a bit while you two climb out of there.'

'Stay awake, Hoyt,' Hannah shouted, then to Milla said, 'come on, Pepperweed. We've got to hurry.'

Captain Ford drank his third beer. It wasn't enough to get him drunk but it would soften up his corners a bit. He never got drunk before going to sleep; he needed to be able to get on deck in a hurry should the overnight watch cry out. He skewered a piece of Tubbs's jemma, simple but hearty fare, and with the schools running south, there were plenty for the taking. He never tired of watching the old sailor heave his ancient net over the rail. Tubbs would never allow anyone to help him, and sometimes he had a hard job of it to keep from being dragged overboard.

Save for two lamps the captain's cabin was dark. The *Morning Star*, riding the heavy, rhythmic swells towards Averil, rocked gently. Other than when he was at the helm, this was Captain Ford's favourite time at sea.

He thought of Kendra, back home, and wanted very badly to be with her. She wouldn't mind if he came into Southport with an empty hold; she knew the run from Strandson to Orindale had been a gamble, but she also knew that he had to take it. They had plenty of money to see them through the winter Twinmoon, even without an inbound shipment, but Captain Ford had his crew to think of. He needed to keep them working, earning enough that they wouldn't need to consider leaving the *Morning Star* for a bigger, more lucrative boat. He was happy with the brig-sloop; she was not the biggest of ships, but she was quick. His crew knew their jobs, got on well with one another, and were invariably ready for the next run. He was lucky; there wasn't much turnover of manpower on the *Morning Star*, so he rarely had to worry about new people getting used to the culture established over time and adventures together.

But this journey had put all of that in jeopardy. He had put everything in harm's way – his lifestyle, his crew, his ship, everything – for a bag of silver, and he felt sick to the stomach about it. He regretted ever letting Brexan talk him into delaying his Orindale contracts for this 'daisy-run' into Averil – daisy-run? He was shipping sorcerers, partisans, *killers* to Malakasia. What would Eastland partisans want with Averil? Were they planning to burn the city down? Poison the flour shipments, maybe sink a few galleons? Who knew what these people were capable of? He propped his elbows on the table and rested his forehead in his palms and sighed. 'But you brought them there, didn't you?' he said out loud. 'You rowed them to shore, even gave them a big, wet slathery kiss as they said farewell and began planting their explosives. So they all get killed, but not before they mention you and your boat during the interrogation. Then you get to spend the rest of your life shipping dirt to dirt farmers in Dirt Village for free, because no one in Eldarn will hire you. Or, even better, you get to run from the Malakasian navy until they finally corner you in some gods-forsaken cove at the arse-end of nowhere and burn your ship to the waterline. And all because Marrin Stonnel got you thinking about tits one night after one too many beers. And maybe it would have been different if she had just *walked* over to the table, but no, the place was crowded, and she almost danced her way to us. That's all there was too it: bad luck, bad timing and bad decisions.'

Captain Ford finished his beer, tried to steer his thoughts back to his wife, and considered opening a fourth bottle. Maybe it would help him sleep after all. He stabbed another mouthful and cursed, 'No, you bastard, no easy rest for you tonight.'

A knock at the door derailed his thoughts. 'Marrin,' he growled, 'bugger off—'

Brexan stepped inside. 'Sorry,' she said. 'I didn't know you were eating.'

'Of course they sent you,' he muttered.

'Of course who sent me? For what? Did I miss something?' she sounded genuinely confused.

'Have you not been huddled all day in the forward cabin with Garec, Kellin and those new fellows, the two young men we picked up this morning?'

'Yes, but—'

'So they sent you.' He reached into his crate for another beer. It was heavy, clumsy to ship in bottles, but he didn't care for fennaroot, and wine was a luxury, like tecan, a port drink. 'And I'm certain I know why they sent you. I've had my dose of Garec Haile and his esoteric brand of diplomacy. Does he kill everyone he meets, I wonder? So that wouldn't work; after all, I'm already in fear for my life, my crew and my ship. So you wouldn't get any further with me by sending Garec. But you're not stupid, are you? You know I've taken a fancy to you, call it a schoolboy crush, maybe, or a feeling of getting a bit older and losing a step and wanting badly to have it back. And ka-blam, you enter my life, bat your pretty eyes at me and ask me to ship your friends to Averil. Of course, I say yes. What else can I say? It's a huge amount of silver for almost no work, and I get to spend the better part of the next Moon watching you, Brexan, I watch you hauling lines, and mopping decks and even helping Tubbs dole out the evening crud for supper. I'm getting older, and I should know better, I *should have known better*, but I didn't, and now I'm here, waiting to see what bucket of grettanshit they've sent you in here to sell me.'

'No one sent me,' Brexan said. 'I came on my own.'

'An honest answer? Or are you just softening me up? That tunic isn't nearly as flattering as the one you were wearing when you asked me to take you on this little pleasure-cruise.'

'I didn't lie.'

'But you didn't tell the whole truth, did you?' Captain Ford leaned forward, then relaxed back into his chair. He had been taken for a fool; now he wanted to salvage what dignity he could. 'What's happening in Averil, Brexan?'

'I can't—'

'Or are we not really bound for Averil?' He saw her involuntary reaction and sighed. 'Rutting whores, that's it.' He poured the beer. 'You want one?'

'No, th—' She paused. 'Actually, yes, why not?'

'Have a seat,' he said politely. 'We can discuss our destination.'

'They meant to tell you,' she said. 'I was just coming to apologise. I didn't want you to think—'

'Well, I'm thinking it. So you can take what little conscience you think you have and toss it over the side. What do you do for the Resistance? I know you're not a scullery-maid. And was the old lady, Nedra, in this with you, or is she the reason you're trying to salvage your self-esteem?'

'I'm a . . . a spy, I suppose,' Brexan confessed, 'and yes, Nedra's one of the reasons I came to talk to you.'

He was shocked at her admission, but he wasn't sure what he meant to do about it. 'You must not be much of a spy; I don't know of many spies who go around admitting it's their job.'

Brexan half-grinned. 'No, I'm not a very good spy, but you should have seen me in the beginning. I was downright wretched.'

Captain Ford didn't join her in celebrating the thimbleful of honesty. 'So where are we bound?'

'Averil, if you insist. I can talk them into it. I know I can.' Garec's words came back to her: *If a guilty conscience and the loss of their trust is all we have to suffer from here on in, then I'm all for it. There's much, much worse waiting for us in Malakasia.*

'Don't do that.' Captain Ford was angry. 'Don't try to make amends now. *Where* are we bound?'

She hung her head, remembered Garec again, and forced herself to look the captain in the eye. 'Pellia,' she said quietly.

'Pellia!' Now he leapt to his feet again, shouting, 'Pellia? You're joking, aren't you? Why not just sail upriver to Welstar Palace? I can hear the Malakasians manning the blockade already – they have one, you know, a gods-whoring net as tight as my uncle's arsehole. "Where are you bound, Captain Ford?" "I'm bound for Pellia, sir." "What are you shipping, Captain Ford?" "Oh, nothing!".' He was raging as he spat out the little scenarios. 'And that's where the road ends, Brexan, in case you were wondering where and how your life would unfold over the next two hundred Twinmoons. Nope. It ends right at that exact moment. And not just yours, but mine, Garec's – well, thank the gods of the Northern Forest for that one – and the rest of us. We'll all be taken prisoner and escorted into the blackest, most foul-smelling nightmare of a pit you've ever imagined.'

'It's important,' Brexan said quietly.

'I knew you were going say that. *Of course*, you think it's important. You wouldn't be sitting here with your guilty heart bleeding all over my charts if you thought it was a "daisy-run". But let me share a secret with you: It's not important to me or my crew!'

'Actually, it is,' she said, trying not to sound as desperate as she was. 'Your life depends on it – all our lives depend on it. Without this trip, we will all die.'

'We're going to die up there anyway.'

'Not just us,' Brexan shouted, '*all* of us, every single person in Eldarn, *everyone*! That means your wife and family as well.'

Captain Ford lunged across the table and took her by the throat. 'Don't you dare mention my family, Brexan Carderic, not ever. Do you understand, spy?' He spat out the word as if it were an obscenity.

'They're all going to die,' she repeated, her eyes watering and her face flushing red. 'I'm sorry.'

Trembling, Ford let her go, gulped the rest of his beer and rooted in the crate for a fifth. 'Tell me—' His voice was shaking; he took a long swallow before continuing, 'Tell me how we're all going to die.'

Brexan fell into her seat, gulped a mouthful herself and rubbed feeling back into her neck. Wiping tears from her face, she said, 'The three frigates that shipped north from Orindale, you remember them?'

'Apart from the naval cruisers, they were the only ships in the harbour left untouched by the storm.'

'They're shipping a stolen Larion artefact, something with the power to open the Fold and usher into Eldarn an evil so destructive that we will all be killed in an instant, or, worse still, enslaved forever in a foul, never-ending nightmare.'

'Larion?' he said, disbelieving.

'It's true, and the two men we picked up this morning have the power to destroy it and kill the man who's stolen it. They can't defeat him if the artefact is in operation; they don't believe they could even get near it, but if we can arrive in Pellia before those frigates, Steven and Gilmour could be at the wharf when the stone table is transferred.'

'And kill the thief before he has an opportunity to begin using this artefact?'

'Exactly.'

'So your friends, these magicians, are on their way to Pellia to kill another sorcerer?'

'Yes.' Brexan didn't see any point in confusing the situation by telling him Steven was determined to save Mark Jenkins.

'And all we have to do is to reach Pellia and get through the blockade with no cargo and no reason for being there so that your boys can be on the wharf when three ships carrying what looks to be a whole division of Prince Malagon's soldiers pulls into port.'

'That's it.'

'Have you forgotten that they left before we did? They have a significant head-start.' Captain Ford had calmed enough to return to his supper and finished another mouthful before asking, 'How will we get past them? The Northeast Channel is a rutting highway this Twinmoon. We'll be held up just by the amount of traffic running through there, that's *if* we get there in time to catch the northern tides. And while we might be able to put on all sorts of sail and run the channel faster than most other ships heading north, bullying our way through the archipelago is just another way to draw the attention of the Malakasian navy. It won't fly, Brexan.'

'It will if you hug the coast and skip the Northeast Channel.'

Captain Ford laughed, a great burst of genuine disbelief. 'Oh, that's a much better option,' he said, almost choking. 'You'll avoid the edge of the blockade right enough, but Brexan, a rowboat can't get through that way. We'll be kedging off every mud flat and rock formation the gods saw fit to sprinkle along that coastline. Have you ever kedged off in a brig-sloop? I know it isn't a very big boat, but hauling it over a sandbar, even with the capstan and the anchor-line, you realise it's a touch heavy. And during this Twinmoon, the water is quite cold. So scurrying about out there in all that nasty mud, we're bound to catch a sniffle or two.' He shifted in his chair. 'You're talking about suicide.'

'I'm talking about the end of life in Eldarn as we know it,' she said, deadly serious.

If nothing else, she obviously believes wholeheartedly in what she was doing, he thought. 'You lied to me.'

'I'm sorry.'

'I liked you.'

'I hope you might again some day.'

'If I refuse, Garec will kill me and take the ship?'

'He probably won't kill you, but they will take the ship.'

'You lied to me.'

'You said that, and I'm sorry.'

Captain Ford sighed, letting his shoulders slump. He was tired and frightened. Considering Brexan in the lamplight, he said, 'I've never been anything but ... My wife and I are ...'

Brexan closed the door latch; it slipped noisily into place: warped wood on warped wood. Turning to him, she pursed her lips and unfastened her tunic belt.

'Don't,' he said. 'I don't need your sympathy, and as much as I might need your ... company, I don't want it. I want to—'

'What do you want?' she asked as she went on removing her clothes.

'I want you to go.'

'Are you sure?'

'Yes.' It was hard for him to say. 'You don't want this, and if you don't want this, I certainly don't want this.'

'Very well,' she said. 'Thank you.'

'You're going to die, Brexan. Don't thank me. I'd just as soon wear about, drop you with Nedra and make way, empty, for Southport and my family. This whole thing makes me want to run and hide.'

She buckled her tunic belt and finished her beer. 'There is no place to hide.'

Captain Ford closed his eyes; it was easier if he didn't have to look at her.

'And I'll make you a promise, not as a spy or a partisan or whatever you think I am, but as a scullery-maid and a friend of Nedra Daubert. I won't lie to you again. It isn't much, especially now, but I'll be straight with you, about anything you ask.'

'Do you find me attractive?' Captain Ford murmured, unsure why he had asked, but hoping that perhaps chasing his emotions into this business might not have been an old man's folly.

'Yes.'

'Do you want to sleep with me?'

Now Brexan sighed. 'No, but I will.'

'Very well then.' He ushered her to the door. 'Thank you. You can tell the others we'll make for Pellia.'

'Thank you, Captain.'

'Again, I don't want you—'

Marrin Stonnel crashed through the hatch, catching his foot on the doorframe and tumbling to the deck. 'Captain,' he cried, frantic, shaking.

'What is it, Marrin?' Captain Ford's demeanour changed in a heartbeat as he became again the man he had been before Brexan's unexpected visit.

'A ship, northwest of us, was running off the wind, but she must have caught sight of something, because she's just jibed to cut us off.'

'Horsecocks!' Captain Ford pushed past Brexan into the companionway, giving orders as he went. 'It's probably a naval cutter, or a schooner, maybe. If they're running full, it'll be a close race. Douse every flame, every light, and dump a bucket over the galley brazier.'

'The coals, Captain?'

'We're upwind, Marrin; we don't want them smelling smoke.' Ford paused at the hatch, briefly making eye-contact with Brexan. 'I want us in the dark, as dark as you can make it. And no smoking, no leftover food, nothing. Make our course due west; I want us running for the Pragan coast like a shadow. We'll heel to the bloody scuppers on this beam reach, but we need to be hull-down by dawn. With luck they'll think we doused the lights to make a run past them to the north. This wind is tempting; lots of captains would try it.'

'But we'll turn west?'

'Right,' Ford said, 'and even if they catch sight of us at sunrise, we'll come about and put on every bit of sheet we've got and make a sprint up the Pragan coast. Now I need to talk to these sorcerers.'

THE NAVAL CUTTER

Steven heard the hollow thud of someone running on deck. 'What's that?'

'Probably the captain,' Garec said.

'Captains don't run,' Gilmour said. 'It instils too much fear and excitement in the crew, makes them jumpy.'

'You don't know this one,' Garec said. 'He's not your ordinary merchant captain. With him, when it's time to run, he runs. Ouch!' He flinched as Kellin extricated another stitch.

The forward cabin was lit with all the candles they could find so Kellin could see what she was doing. She was just halfway through when Captain Ford barged in, pausing on the threshold to make sure none of his crew were within earshot. 'Are you two truly sorcerers?' he asked, a little out of breath.

Gilmour answered, 'I wouldn't say that we're sor—'

'No time for lies, my friend,' the captain interrupted. 'We've got a naval cutter, very fast, tacking to overtake us. We're quick, especially running empty, but we're not quick enough to get past them without a fight.'

Steven started, 'We can perhaps—'

'Let me finish,' he went on. 'I've ordered the ship about. We'll make a run for the Pragan coast.'

'West?' Garec asked, stopping Kellin as she started on the next stitch. There would be time for that later.

'It's a difficult tack, granted, and the wind will carry us northwest, but the cutter's on the same wind so even if he sets a course across our current heading, he'll be carried to the northeast, towards Falkan. So we put out all the watch-fires and run on a beam reach in the dark. My goal is to be hull-down on their horizon by morning. If we're lucky it'll be hazy. If we're blessed by the gods, there'll be fog.'

'So what do you need from us?' Garec said.

'How much power do you have? Are you truly sorcerers?' he asked.

'Time's wasting and I need to know. One of you ignited those fireballs in the sky this morning.'

Steven looked at Gilmour and shrugged. 'Captain Ford, both Gilmour and I could easily sink that ship from here if we chose to.'

He blanched. That was obviously more honesty – and more formidable power – than he had expected from them. 'Oh,' he murmured, 'well then—'

'But we can't.'

'Why not?' Ford asked, now completely bemused. 'Do you know what they'll do if they catch us running empty through the Narrows, obviously trying to escape?'

'Impound your ship?' Garec said.

'And lock us in the brig, at the very least, and that's if we're lucky. I could tell them we're making for Averil, but I don't have a cargo to pick up there, and I'm not about to admit that I'm shipping five passengers, none of whom are Malakasian and none of whom have any business links to anyone in Averil.'

'So you know,' Steven said.

'We'll discuss that *if* we live through the night, young man,' the captain said. 'Right now, we've other problems. Why can't you use magic? You used it this morning right enough.'

Gilmour asked, 'Were you in Orindale when the great floodtide devastated the city?'

'I didn't see it happen, but I've seen the aftermath.' He shuddered.

'The person – the *thing* – that caused all that devastation is watching for Steven and me right now. Every time we use our magic, he knows it. We're carrying a couple of things that give off a low hum of mystical energy, and I'm hoping that's not enough for him to hone in on. He's deadly dangerous, the most dangerous being ever to exist in Eldarn, and if Steven or I do *anything* to attract him, he will crush your ship to splinters and send us all to the bottom. I don't doubt that for one moment, Captain Ford.'

'But you used magic this morning—'

'Nothing more than a party trick, I'm afraid.' Gilmour sounded apologetic. 'Skilled youngsters can do it, even without training. The man hunting for us wouldn't give them a second glance.'

'Hunting you?' The captain was increasingly confused. 'I thought you were hunting him.'

'We are,' Steven said, 'but we have to be considerably more covert about it.'

'Well, that's just rutting great! A Malakasian cutter about to ram its bow right up my backside, and two sorcerers who can't do any magic because they've got to hide from a rutting demon!'

'It's much, much worse than a demon,' Garec said, unmoved by the captain's anxiety. 'What can we do?'

Ford leaned against the mainmast where it passed through the cabin, trying to regain his composure before returning to the helm. 'You can douse all these candles, and no smoking; you'd be amazed what carries on the breeze. Garec, will you go aft and make sure someone has extinguished the cooking fires? We'll need everyone on deck; this is a hard tack; we're turning broadside to the wind, rutting near broaching, and it's going to get rough. I would tell some of you to get some rest, but you probably won't sleep now, anyway. And on deck, you do whatever Sera, Marrin or I tell you, no questions, no hesitation. Got it?'

Garec smiled grimly. 'Absolutely.'

'Are you any good with that bow?'

'I've been known to hit my target, yes.'

'He's the best bowman in Eldarn,' Gilmour clarified.

'How close would they need to be for you to take out their officers and a few key members of the crew?'

'In this wind?' Garec considered the candles. 'Not very close.'

'Good,' Ford forced a smile. 'Then we'll do it the old-fashioned way.' To Steven and Gilmour, he said, 'Gentlemen, if either of you has a change of heart, I need to know right away.'

Both men nodded.

Captain Ford's voice changed. 'Very well. Douse those flames, and let's head west.' He was once again the wise, experienced captain of the *Morning Star*.

By middlenight the Malakasian cutter had corrected her course to due north. Captain Ford left Sera at the helm and came forward to where Garec and Steven were helping Marrin haul in a sheet that had come free.

'He's second-guessing you, sir,' Marrin said as the captain joined them.

'He's not stupid.'

'What's happening?' Steven asked, shrugging out of his cloak. It was damp now, and heavy; he could work better without it, though he'd need to be careful to warm himself. With the ship broaching in the swells the way it was, he didn't relish the idea of being below decks. He thought he might throw up if he spent too long in the cabin.

'He took the bait for about an aven. When we doused the lights, he thought we were trying to run past him in the dark, but now he's turned north again.'

'In case we try to slip by to the west?'

'Like I said, he's not stupid.' Captain Ford dried his face on a kerchief. 'He saw enough to know that we're not going to be able to bolt past him and be gone by dawn. This way he can run ahead of us and wait for sunrise.'

'When, theoretically, we'll either be off his starboard flank—' Marrin started.

'Or running west,' Steven finished.

'Either way,' the captain said, 'we can't get past him.'

'So even if we make it to the Pragan coast, we still give him ample opportunity to come west and cut us off.'

'Right again, Steven,' Marrin said. 'You should be a sailor.'

'So what do we do?'

'We either come north now, use the wind to get as far as possible and make ready for a fight at dawn, or we run for Praga and try to find an inlet or maybe a cleft in the cliffs to hide for a day or two.' He didn't sound thrilled with either option.

'Or we run right at him,' Marrin said. 'He won't be expecting that.'

'And do what? Offer him a beer?'

'Strafe him with fire arrows? Hit him with a few of those fireballs the old man was tossing about this morning? Maybe we could set his shrouds on fire,' Marrin suggested.

'In this weather?' The captain wasn't convinced. 'We'd maybe get his topgallants, but not the mains: they're too damp.'

'Let's think about this for a moment,' Steven said. He shouted for Gilmour, and as the boyish figure came within earshot, asked, 'The fire, *our* fire: can Mark sense it from here?'

Gilmour thought for a moment. 'It's a gamble; I certainly shouldn't do it, but we've been lucky with you before.'

'I'm worried that was just the staff, not me,' Steven said. 'What if—'

'Don't get started with the *what ifs*. He may or he may not. You did plenty without the staff that Nerak never noticed, and if Mark doesn't have the table opened, he shouldn't be able to sense anything that would have got past Nerak. Mark's only indestructible when he's using the table; the rest of the time he must be about as vulnerable as Nerak was.'

'Unless he's been drawing strength from the table's magic,' Steven suggested.

'That's true, but if there's no way past, we may have to risk it.'

Steven felt cold. He'd been trying to ignore it, but it seeped beneath his skin now, making him shiver. 'He'll kill us all, Gilmour.'

'That's already his plan. It's just that we're closer to the end now. All the edges are sharper from here on in.'

'It's an easy spell, I've done it—'

'—plenty of times, I know,' Gilmour said. 'That's not the issue. The problem is whether or not he'll feel it. I'm betting he won't, not the fire.'

'What fire are we talking about?' the captain asked.

'Larion fire,' Gilmour said, 'a tough, resilient flame that'll easily catch their ship alight; it'll set the sails, perhaps even the water around them on fire.'

'Great rutting gods of the Northern Forest,' Ford whispered.

'Larion like in Larion Senators?' Marrin laughed. 'Captain, I'm all for running up on them because we'll have surprise on our side, but I'm not counting on any Larion Senators to magically appear from out of one of my Nana's fairy tales and save the day for us.'

'Don't,' Steven asked softly, still staring at Gilmour, 'don't run up on them, Captain. I'm sorry. You're the master here and you give the orders, but please, I am begging you to keep to our current heading. Let's try to sneak past them tomorrow, and if we can't and they close on us, I promise you that I will help Garec fight them while you and the crew keep us on course.'

'You and Garec alone?' Marrin interjected, then realising what he had done, added, 'Sorry, Captain.'

There was silence for a moment while everyone considered their options, then Ford sighed and said, 'Very well then. Marrin, keep us on this heading. We'll get as far to the southwest as we can before we have to come about, but I want us running north by dawn, and by running, I mean as if grettans are at our backsides. Understand?'

'Aye, aye, Captain,' Marrin barked, and was gone, a hundred questions left answered.

Ford said, 'You and Garec can do this alone?'

Steven laid an arm across Garec's neck and smiled through chattering teeth. 'We can hit them when they are well out of range of normal archers, and if we need more help, Kellin and Brexan can shoot into their ranks. Kellin's shoulder is good enough for her to manage a few rounds if need be.'

'Tubbs and Sera can shoot,' Captain Ford said, 'though I'd rather keep them about their jobs.'

Steven's reassurance was cut off by Sera, who shouted from the bow, 'Captain, the cutter's dousing her fires.' As they all peered into the night, they saw the last of the cutter's own watch-fires blink out. Just before everything went black, Steven thought he noticed something odd about the angle of the cutter's bowsprit.

Captain Ford read his mind. 'Did I just see what I think I saw?' he asked.

'I'm afraid so,' Steven said.

'There's no way to tell,' Garec said, grasping for straws.

'No,' Gilmour said, 'they're right. It's as if he can see us!'

'Marrin!' the captain shouted, 'the cutter's gone covert, and she's coming this way.'

Marrin's voice reached them through the wind. 'Understood, sir.'

By dawn, it was apparent the captain of the naval cutter had either seen them, scented them or second-guessed them perfectly. With the first rays of light whitening the horizon, Captain Ford rubbed his bleary eyes and shouted for Marrin and Sera. The whole crew had worked all night, keeping the *Morning Star* running west, away from the cutter, and half an aven earlier, they had changed course and were now heading due north. The rest of the crew had been sent below to sleep.

'Is that her?' he asked, 'there, do you see her?'

Sera leaned over the rail, staring into the grey sky. Marrin jumped into the rigging, climbing towards the main spar for a better view. Sera was the first to pick it up.

'Aye, that's her, Captain.'

Marrin called down, 'Captain, I don't understand – how'd he do it? At this rate, we'll be ramming the horsecock before midday.'

Ford leaned against the helm. 'I don't know how they did it, Marrin, but we're going to stay on course and run past them just as fast as we can.'

'Captain,' Sera asked, 'won't he just tack to match our course?'

'Probably, and that's when we'll trust our new friends to slow them down.'

'Very good, Captain.' Sera didn't bother trying to mask her doubts.

'For now, I want you two to rest. Tubbs and Kanthil can take over for a while. Nothing's going to happen in the next aven, anyway.'

'You'll call us if he changes course, sir?' Marrin dropped nimbly to the deck, despite his fatigue.

'I will,' the captain lied. 'When you get below, see if Tubbs has any more rosehip brew going. I'm going to need a bucketful to get through this morning.' He watched with quiet pride as his tired sailors, loyal even in the face of questionable leadership, disappeared.

'They work hard,' Steven said, 'and it's obvious they're doing it for you.'

'Nonsense.' He shrugged the compliment off. 'They do it because they love this ship.' He changed the subject and said, 'Steven, come with me, would you? There's something I want to show you.' He called over to Garec, sitting in the stern checking the fletching on a handful of arrows. 'Garec, would you take the helm for a moment?'

Garec stumbled getting up and spilled his entire quiver. 'What? You want me to steer?' he stuttered, 'to— to drive? But Captain, I don't know how to— I mean, I'll kill every one of those bastards for you, but you can't let me drive – I can barely get my horse out of Madur's corral most mornings. And I'll be straight with you, Captain: I don't have enough silver to buy you a new boat.'

The captain laughed. 'It's really not that difficult, and I'll not be gone above a few moments,' he said. 'But let's have a lesson, to make sure you can manage.'

Once he was certain Garec could keep the *Morning Star* on her current heading, he led Steven into the bow and pointed to a number of fixed ropes. 'You see these standing lines?' he asked quietly.

'I think they're called stays, or standing rigging,' Steven said, 'at least, that's what we call them where I— well, I think that's right.'

'It is,' Captain Ford said, steadying himself against one, 'and they're just about the most important part of the ship – can you believe that? Right out here, where anyone could get a sword on them . . . They're keeping the mast up.' As he spoke, he pointed to the separate cables. 'These are the forestays, inner and outer, and those back there, just aft, are the mainstays, upper and lower.' He ran a hand lovingly along one. 'Now, the cutter will have some additional masts, but the ones I need you to remember are the fore, the main and the mizzenmast, and most especially, remember the mainmast.'

'What do I do?'

'If you can't get the shrouds to ignite – and I'm hoping you can because it's quick, and great at creating nervous tension—'

Steven chuckled. 'Nervous tension? All the way out here in the middle of bloody nowhere with the only thing between you and hell being a ship on fire, yeah, I suppose you could call that nervous tension.'

'They shit themselves, even the gods-rutting admirals,' he admitted. 'Anyway, if you can't get the shrouds to light, I want you to try and snap these lines. At first, it'll look like nothing much has happened, but in this wind, they won't be able to keep all those sheets on her, and that'll pull the masts down and cripple the cutter for a Twinmoon or more. She won't be able to pursue us any more; she'll have to limp into the nearest docks, at Landry, and we'll be able to outrun her.

'So this is what you need to remember: the forestays, mainstays and mizzenstays: Snap 'em, and they've got to run her into a wall. If they don't, the ship will tear itself apart beneath them.'

'Good. Thank you.'

'Good luck,' Captain Ford said. 'Now you and Garec should get some sleep. Gilmour, too.'

'He never sleeps,' Steven said, 'and we'll be all right.'

'Garec's that good?'

'I've never seen him miss.'

The sun was high and burning off the morning cloud cover when Garec joined Steven on deck. The two ships were rapidly closing on one another.

'Can't see anything yet,' Steven said, 'just that one fellow up there, in the bow. I can't decide if he's an archer or just some kind of lookout.'

'At this rate we'll soon be able to ask him face-to-face,' Garec said. He had both quivers on his back and held his bow loosely in one hand.

'Captain Ford seems to think they'll tack north and strafe our broadside until we heave to and let them board us.'

'Or they'll not be so polite,' Garec said, calm despite staring at an entire shipful of sailors and soldiers, all intent on killing him. His experience in the meadow near Meyers' Vale, standing in the face of a cavalry charge, was still fresh in his mind. 'They may decide to run in, get their hooks over our rails and come aboard uninvited.'

Steven ran his hand along the weathered railing. 'So it's up to us to discourage them.'

When they were within five hundred paces of the Malakasian cutter, they heard someone hailing them, ordering them to heave to.

'Here we go,' said Steven.

Garec nocked an arrow, considered the wind and the swells and aimed above the shouting Malakasian. 'Shall I deliver our reply?'

'Let me try first,' Steven said, 'and perhaps no one need get killed.' He flexed his wrist a few times, summoned a pair of glowing fiery orbs and sent them hurtling with surprising speed towards the man hailing them, the cutter's first officer, he presumed. The fireballs crashed into the side of the ship, blasting through the gunwale and knocking the sailor to the deck.

'Excellent shot!' Captain Ford shouted from the helm, 'now see if you can get their sheets to fire up.'

Steven repeated the gesture and six of the orbs, trailing fire like Larion meteorites, flew into the cutter's rigging. The bigger, faster ship came about suddenly, turning north to match the brig-sloop's own tack. This was clearly something the Malakasian captain had expected, though from the behaviour on board the cutter – the frantic shouted orders and general scurrying-about – it looked like Steven's attack forced their change in course earlier than they had planned.

'They're turning!' Gilmour called from amidships. 'Hit them again, Steven – two or three are catching fire; the others passed right through. Not so much speed on this next barrage perhaps.'

'I'd like to drive them off,' Steven admitted. 'The fewer we kill, the better.'

Garec shielded his eyes from the sun. 'You certainly scared the dog-snot out of that officer. He'll be changing his leggings pretty soon.'

The ships were on a parallel course now, the cutter some three hundred paces north of the *Morning Star*. They were well within range of skilled archers, but, a little surprisingly, the marines weren't lined up, ready to fire on the hostile Pragan boat. Garec himself was in position now to kill every officer on their quarterdeck. He waited for Steven to ask for help.

'This one should do the job,' Steven murmured, calling up more of the brilliant orbs.

Garec felt the heat on his face and turned away. 'Gods, but that's hot, Steven.'

'I'm hoping to finish this right—'

He dropped the fireballs into the sea, where, hissing and spitting, they sank towards the bottom. He barely managed to throw up the protective spell in time to ward off the Malakasian's counterattack, which struck with all the force of a bottled thunderclap against the brig-sloop's starboard bulkhead; Steven and Garec were sent sprawling at the impact.

'What the fuck was that?' Steven shouted as he rolled to his feet.

Garec spat a mouthful of blood onto the deck and said, 'But waiter, I didn't order this.'

'It's that fellow there,' Gilmour was pointing towards a lone figure standing in the stern of the cutter.

'It's the lookout, the one you spotted earlier,' Garec said.

'That's no lookout,' Steven said, 'they have their own magician, and he just got a punch in.'

'How are we still alive then?' Garec was crawling towards the rail, an arrow nocked and ready. It was obvious he meant to kill the enemy sorcerer with one shot.

Steven kept pace with him. 'It's a spell I used in the river, something that just blew out of me.'

'Oh well, thanks then,' Garec said. 'Why don't you just keep your head down while I send him to the Northern Forest?'

'We probably don't have to kill him,' Steven said.

'No,' Garec said, 'this one's all right. Call it a donation to the cause.' He knelt, took aim quickly and fired. The arrow arced cleanly across the sea, but burst into flames and disintegrated before it reached the enemy ship. Garec cursed. 'Sorry, Steven, looks like he's all yours.'

Steven waved at the Malakasian magician, trying to get his attention. The other seemed to understand that he was being challenged, and pointed back. 'That's right, you bastard, just you and me,' Steven muttered.

He turned to Gilmour and asked, 'Who is this guy?'

'No idea,' the Larion Senator said cheerfully. 'Probably someone who discovered skills as a child. A thousand Twinmoons ago he would have been recruited to study at Sandcliff Palace. Instead, now he's a dangerous young man. That last spell was most likely honed on trees and rocks as he was growing up.'

'I'd love to see his house,' Garec smirked, wiping twin blood trails from his nose. 'I'm sure it's a lovely place, apart from all the holes.'

Steven said, 'He's not all that powerful. I could pull his tongue out of his head from here if I wanted to ... I'm just not willing to risk doing anything so magically noisy.'

'Probably too late,' Gilmour admitted. 'The blow *he* struck at us was quite enough to hit Mark like a slap in the face. You might as well do whatever you like to end it quickly, and we'll pray to the gods that Mark doesn't have time to pinpoint where we are while you're cleaning up.'

'Maybe you're right,' Steven said. 'If I just— *What* did you say?'

'The spell he cast at us,' Gilmour said. 'Can't you feel it? It's still lingering in the air. I'm sure the ripples have gone all the way to Philadelphia by now.'

'Oh no,' Steven cried as his eyes widened, 'no!' He cupped his hands and shouted, 'You must stop what you're doing, right now! Stop it!'

The Malakasian shot them a broad grin and waved. He was joined by an officer who cried, 'Heave to! Strike your mains and tops! Prepare to be boarded!'

Captain Ford joined in now, shouting from the bridge, 'We left your sister and mother in Orindale – most entertaining girls, they were!'

'Heave to!'

'Heave yourself, you're not taking my ship!'

Steven, distracted by the exchange, failed to see the Malakasian gesture towards the Morning Star, but Gilmour shoved him and Garec to one side, threw up his hands and shouted a deflective incantation.

The sorcerer's second volley crashed through the gunwale, showering the deck with splinters and sending all three men tumbling once again.

'Red whoring rutters!' Garec cried, 'but I hate it when he does that!'

'Steven! Garec!' the captain screamed, 'will you kill that annoying little bastard or do I have to ram him? Look what he did to my ship! Kill him, Garec; kill him now!'

Steven was up again and firing back, sending a barrage of fireballs, one after another, slamming into the cutter's stern. Three explosions later, the stern rail was on fire and the officers, with their sorcerer, had retreated amidships. 'One down,' Steven murmured, 'and now for the stays.'

His next volley was aimed at the knots of heavy hempen cord and the wooden tackle and metal spikes bracing the cutter's masts. Without mystical protection, the stays were easy to hit and surprisingly easy to sever. When the hawsers snapped, the reports carried like gunshots.

The sound brought the Malakasian captain round. It took just a moment for him to realise that he was beaten and the captain and crew of the Morning Star heard him shouting orders to douse the fires and tack to safety.

The brief engagement was over.

On the quarterdeck, Captain Ford hooted wildly and danced like a drunken schoolboy. 'Outstanding!' he shouted at Sera, who took over at the helm and kept the *Morning Star* running north. As the gap quickly widened between them, Steven returned the captain's excited embrace, then ran for the stern.

Cupping his hands again, he screamed, 'Don't do it! You must stop now!'

But the Malakasian magician, enraged and embarrassed, leaped high, whirled his hands above his head and cast a destructive spell at the fast-moving brig-sloop.

Steven felt it coming, felt the air and the water around them almost flinch in anticipation, but the attack was easily deflected. Steven closed his eyes, concentrated, and felt the assault shatter, shards of magic spinning across the water. 'Don't,' he whispered, fearing it was too late. 'You don't understand.'

'What's the matter?' Brexan asked. She and Kellin, armed with longbows, had watched the exchange from the quarterdeck. With the danger apparently behind them, Kellin now propped hers against the rail and snaked her injured arm back into its sling.

'Hopefully nothing,' Steven said, turning to rejoin the others. 'We're free, and unless any other patrolling vessels we come across just happen to have a crewman who doubles as the ship's magician, we have a dead-certain way to convince them to give up the chase.'

'I heard those ropes snap,' Kellin said. 'They hold the masts up, don't they?'

'Not any more,' Steven laughed, looking around for Tubbs. 'What's for breakfast?'

'Whatever you wish,' Tubbs replied. 'I think this morning you've earned captain's honour.' He cocked an eyebrow at Captain Ford, who nodded.

'Oh God,' Steven sighed, '*anything* I want? I'd kill for a Western omelette, Cajun hot sauce on the side, black coffee, orange juice and a copy of the *Denver Post*.'

Tubbs' brow furrowed. 'You're really not from Orindale, are you, young man?'

Steven laughed. 'Not exactly, no. If you've got some fruit, I'll have that with some bread and tecan.'

'That I can do. I'll be right back.' Tubbs scurried off as the others turned back to their interrupted conversation.

'At least we know how they tracked us overnight,' Kellin said.

'True,' said Brexan. 'He probably knew where we were the whole time.'

Gilmour said, 'That was smart of you, Steven. You didn't use anything too resonant. That little bit of fire wasn't more than a couple of pebbles in a pond. We should be all right.'

'But it may be too late, anyway,' Steven said, 'not because of us, but because of him, the Malakasian. He was blasting away at us with a goddamned Howitzer. I'm worried that fool alerted Mark, hammering away like that.'

'You're right,' Gilmour said. 'We'll need to be prepared for anything, just i—'

'Captain!' Kanthil had been in the rigging all morning and now, gesticulating wildly astern, he was screaming, 'Great whoring gods, Captain, look at it!'

'Did they hit something?' Ford called, running to the stern.

'No,' Kanthil cried, distressed, 'it's just opened, like a hole in the ocean!'

Partisans and crew alike leaned on the aft rail and watched as the Ravenian Sea opened and swallowed the Malakasian cutter whole.

'Mother of Christ,' Steven whispered.

'That answers your question,' Gilmour said. 'He didn't pinpoint our position, but he found them.'

No one else spoke as the surface boiled white and choppy, then wrinkled back into soft swells. Nothing remained of the cutter; there were no survivors in the waves.

'Brace yourselves,' Kellin cried, looking nervously over the side. 'We could be next.'

Garec took her hand. It was cold and trembling. None of them had slept in two days. 'We'll be all right, won't we?'

Still staring at where the naval ship had been, Steven murmured, 'Yes, we should be fine. Mark figures he just killed us ... killed *me*. This ship was under attack by a powerful sorcerer with a penchant for big, showy attacks. That sorcerer was targeted and is now dead.'

'So Mark thinks that was us,' Garec said.

'That's right. Unless he sensed the orbs I was using, I guess he believes we're just a Malakasian ship. If the table had been open, he'd have felt my deflective spells and we'd be swallowed up too, so it must have been closed until he used it to drown them.'

'Nerak would have been able to sense the resonant spells that blazing idiot was hurling at us,' Steven went on, 'that's why I was trying to stop him. And Mark in turn felt them, found him, opened the table—'

'And ate him,' Garec finished.

'So what are you saying?' Captain Ford interrupted. 'Do I need to worry about my boat or not?'

'I don't think so, Captain,' Gilmour said, 'because it would have happened already, and because Steven didn't use any magic that Mark Jenkins would have been able to sense from this far away.'

'Very good,' he said. 'Well then, let's get some breakfast and then set the watch. We could all use a few avens' sleep.' He turned to Sera and ordered, 'Downwind run, sailor. Everyone else, come.' He smiled, even at Garec. 'Let's get below; Tubbs will have breakfast ready in a moment, I'm sure.'

As the others disappeared beneath the forward hatch, Gilmour motioned for Steven to join him in private.

'What is it?' Steven fought off a yawn.

'I cast the deflection over you and Garec when he sent that second blast at us.'

Steven stopped. 'Oh shit, oh shit, Gilmour, oh *shit*.'

'What do you think?'

'I don't know,' Steven said, suddenly lucid. The magic began swirling again, tumbling and folding over itself in the pit of his stomach, ready to continue the fight. 'But hold on: the air was full of noise and echoes, wasn't it?'

'True.'

'So maybe he didn't get it. Maybe we were too close to the other ship and maybe he thought it was just another ripple—' He was trying hard to convince himself that they were out of harm's way.

'We need to be wary.'

'I can see why you never sleep,' he said wryly, starting below.

'It does help from time to time. And seeing as how the last occasion that I decided to get some sleep, some rutting Malakasian spy—'

'Brexan says his name is Jacrys,' Steven interrupted.

'Fine, so the last time I slept, a spy called Jacrys came into camp and rammed a knife into my heart. Believe me, I'm happy to stay up late.'

Later, tucked together inside the *Morning Star*'s main cabin, the company, now all fed and in dry clothes, sat around a crate of beer donated by the captain, pleased with the outcome of the morning's encounter. Gilmour smoked ceaselessly, and after a while Kellin joined him for a pipe.

'I didn't know you smoked,' Garec said, surprised.

'I don't,' Kellin said, 'but Gilmour always smells so alluringly sweet, I thought I might try some.'

'So that you can smell alluringly sweet, too?' Garec asked.

'I'm a woman who knows what she wants, bowman,' she joked, winking over the pipe stem.

Gilmour passed a beer to Brexan, who had been content to sit quietly and watch the interplay. She still felt a bit of an outsider, despite her relationship with Versen and Sallax.

'Tell us about your journey, Brexan,' Gilmour said. 'Garec mentioned that you were at Riverend Palace, that morning so long ago. I guess you were on the wrong side when all this started, but I'm glad you've seen the error of your ways and joined us.'

Brexan gave him a thin-lipped smile. 'You looked a bit different back then, Gilmour.'

'That I did, my dear,' the youthful Malakasian replied. 'Over the Twinmoons, I've looked like a lot of things, some a good deal worse than this fellow.'

'I thought you were dead.'

'Everyone did. I still manage to get a few surprises out of this ageing spirit.' He thumped one temple with a knuckle.

'Sallax would have wanted to know you were alive; he wanted to see you, to apologise,' she said, sadly.

'It was Nerak,' Gilmour said, 'it wasn't Sallax's doing. I would have forgiven Sallax in a heartbeat.'

'I told him that.'

'Thank you; I hope he believed you.'

'He talked often about you, once he recovered. And from what I've seen recently, he and Versen were telling the truth,' she said.

'Those two always made up nice things about me,' Gilmour teased. 'Anything off-colour they might have spilled . . . well, that's different!'

'About you, too, Steven.' She told them all about how she had ended up in Orindale, working for Nedra Daubert. She told of first meeting Versen, of being beaten by Lahp and transported to Strandson, of Gabriel O'Reilly's rescue and of Versen's death in the meadow near the stream. She cried when she spoke of the big woodsman; Garec joined her. But then she was cold and economic in her description of Haden's torture. Gilmour was fascinated at how Sallax had found her, and once again he thanked Brexan for helping the big Ronan wrestle his emotional demons.

'In the end,' she said, 'it was really Brynne who helped him get the edge he needed to kill Carpello Jax, and to try to kill Jacrys Marseth.'

'How did she help?' Kellin asked.

'Knowing she was— well, lost to him, that helped Sallax find enough anger and rage to keep focused. He'd come a long way, but he was still prone to drifting a bit. His guilt was enormous, but the wraiths had twisted it into such a knot, Sallax struggled for a long time just to see through the hazy grey of everything plaguing him at once.' She took a long swallow of beer. 'After discovering that Brynne had died, so much of what had been haunting him didn't matter any longer. He wasn't able to banish it, but he did find the strength to push through it.'

'So he was back?' Garec asked. 'He was cured?'

'No,' Brexan said. 'He still referred to himself as "Sallax" sometimes, but he certainly found his skills again. I watched him kill a raging Seron with just a knife, a big bastard, stinking like shit and set on killing us both. Sallax's shoulder was damaged at the time; it was healing but still not strong enough for combat.'

'How'd he do it?' Garec asked.

'One-handed,' Brexan replied. 'It was unbelievable.'

Gilmour said, 'He was tough and single-minded; there's no question about that.'

'And then we captured Carpello Jax, the shipping magnate who assaulted Brynne all those Twinmoons ago.'

'And killed him?' Steven asked, no longer surprised that such things were considered fit topics for polite conversation over drinks.

'Essentially, yes.'

'Tell us about Carpello Jax,' Gilmour said. 'Garec mentioned shipments. Do you know what they were?'

'Something from Rona, bark or roots, leaves maybe. I don't remember very well, and Carpello wasn't articulating as clearly as he might have under other circumstances.' She closed her eyes, trying to recall the details of that morning at the Topgallant Inn. 'He did say that it came from the Forbidden Forest. You know, the one out beyond the Estrad River on the peninsula? My squad used to patrol there for Moons at a time.'

'Something magic?' Steven asked, 'Gilmour, maybe that's what you felt that day you were searching for Kantu?'

'It could be,' Gilmour said, then asked, 'Garec, how far out on the peninsula did you and Versen go?'

Garec thought for a bit. 'We never tried to get to the end; that would have been asking for trouble. We only ever went in far enough to hunt and fish. Sometimes we rode for half a day, but I don't remember ever going as far as the end. No one would try that; they'd have to be suicidal. It's probably been five generations since any significant number of Ronans were out on that point. The odd boat runs southeast from the inlet, chasing schools of fish, but too many have been burned to the waterline by the Malakasian navy. That's never been a secret to fishermen: stay out of those waters.'

Steven said, 'So, I wonder, did Prince Marek close that forest?'

'About the same time he was wrapping up his takeover and establishing his occupation force in Eldarn,' Gilmour said. 'We were always told it was because Riverend Palace was on the other side of the river, and it was some kind of retribution for King Remond and, in turn, Prince Markon establishing the seat of Eldarni government there. We figured he wanted Riverend to crumble.'

'It has,' Garec interjected.

'That's true,' Steven said, 'but could he have been using that land for something else?'

'Maybe growing whatever it is that Carpello Jax was shipping north to Pellia,' Brexan said. 'If it's trees, they've had almost a thousand Twinmoons to spread and mature out there.'

Gilmour's cherubic face was hidden behind billowy smoke. 'When did you kill this fellow, Brexan?'

'Nedra did it,' Brexan laughed, 'accidentally. But I suppose it was about a half Moon ago.'

'That was too early for him to have shipped whatever I sensed in that schooner heading north,' the old magician said. 'With him dead, do you think his shipments continued running?'

'I don't see why not,' Brexan said. 'No one knows he's dead. His employees may just think he's missing, and I overheard a pair of bakers talking about him, saying Carpello was involved with all kinds of women – several of whom might even believe themselves to be his wife. So it wouldn't surprise me if he frequently disappeared on business trips so he'd be away from the capital for Moons at a time.'

'All right,' Kellin said, 'so if we assume that his shipments are some kind of magic bark or leaves or roots, and that they are bound for Pellia, who cares? What are the Malakasian people doing with that much magic?'

'But they're not really bound for Pellia. That's just a stopover,' Brexan said. 'They're loaded onto barges and shipped upriver to Prince Malagon's palace. That much we did manage to beat out of Carpello before he died.'

'A whole schooner-full?' Steven said.

'Several,' Brexan corrected, 'many, even from what Carpello said.'

Gilmour paced around the small room, holding his pipe with one hand, swinging his beer bottle with the other. No one said anything; it was clear he was thinking.

Finally, he said, 'So Prince Marek closes Rona's southeast peninsula. The climate's right, so he plants something he knows he will need one day in the distant future, though he isn't sure exactly when. Over time, and subsequent Malakasian dictators, Nerak monitors the progress of his crop, whatever it is, and as he draws ever closer to his date with destiny and the Larion spell table, his trees take over much of the landmass south and east of Riverend Palace. A few poachers slip over the river to kill a deer every now and again, but anyone caught out that far is given a tag hanging in Greentree Square. The message about their necks is easy to read: KEEP OUT. And so for nearly a thousand Twinmoons, the peninsula is essentially the prince's personal garden.'

'Keep at it, Gilmour,' Steven said.

'Generations later, Prince Malagon finds the slimiest shipper he can and hires this fellow to oversee the transport of his harvested crop from Rona to Pellia and then upriver to Welstar Palace, where it's either stockpiled, or put to some other use. The slimy merchant makes a few trips to Estrad Village, to get a sense of the lie of the land, shipping demands, deep water anchorage off the inlet, and on one of these trips he brutally assaults a young girl at Greentree Tavern—'

'For which crime he is eventually beaten up and killed and left to drift on the outgoing tide,' Brexan added as a quiet interruption.

'And we thank you for that.' Gilmour raised his bottle to her. 'So what is it, and why did Prince Marek – *Nerak* – plant so much of it? Why did Prince Malagon – *Nerak* – harvest and ship so much of it? And, assuming what I encountered on that schooner was one of Carpello's shipments, how can something that powerful be in use here in Eldarn without me or Steven or even Kantu feeling it?'

'Those are the key unanswered questions.' Garec reached for another beer, then asked, 'Anyone else?'

A chorus of 'please' and 'just one more' broke Gilmour's concentration for a moment; when everyone had quietened again, the old magician was staring at Steven.

'I've never been inside Welstar Palace,' he said finally. 'I have no idea what Nerak might have been doing there, what preparations he was making for the advent of his dark master's reign. I should have gone. A thousand Twinmoons later, and I realise now that I should have gone up there and taken a look for myself.'

'Gilmour,' Steven started, 'you can't blame yourself for—'

'I've been there,' Brexan broke in. 'I was stationed there for a while before I came to Rona. But I can't tell you much about the palace; no one gets anywhere near it.'

'How about the army?' Gilmour asked. 'I understand it's massive.'

'Rutters, yes! The whole of the river valley on either bank is the army encampment. When I was there last, I'd wager there were nearly two hundred thousand soldiers on the grounds and in the hills above the river. The tents are a veritable city, and the barges running up and down the Welstar River are a wonder to watch. The river is the palace's own supply highway; a regiment of soldiers is assigned to oversee the depot along the road into Pellia and to work the docks on either bank.'

'Great dry-humping lords, why?' Garec asked.

'Versen asked that same question,' Brexan said. 'He was convinced Prince Malagon had gone insane – he said there was no need in Eldarn for an army that size, and unless Malagon planned to march through Praga and the Eastlands to kill everyone they encountered, there would be no reason to amass such a huge fighting force. Versen said any army that size, encamped for so long, would be riddled with disease. Ailments, afflictions and infections would spread like wildfire, and they'd lose more soldiers to sickness than they ever would to an enemy.'

'Two hundred thousand.' Steven whistled low. 'Why?'

'Could they be slaves?' Garec asked. 'Once the Fold is open and that thing, that essence of all things evil is released into Eldarn, could they be slaves, or maybe a source of energy? Maybe it needs souls, warm bodies, blood, who knows?'

'That may be,' Gilmour said. 'Apart from knowing it exists in there, we never knew anything about what it would do when it arrived.'

'Blood, souls and warm flesh,' Kellin repeated. 'Rutting whores!'

'But that still doesn't answer the question of the shipments,' Brexan reminded them. 'Unless the trees do something to fortify the soldiers.'

'Maybe they eat the trees,' Garec said.

'We won't know until we get there,' Gilmour said finally, definitively.

They spent a quiet moment looking at one another, wondering how many more of their own they would lose. Sallax and Versen had been brought back to life, if only for a moment, by a woman who refused to allow either of them to fade away entirely. Who would be the next to fall?

Garec said, 'Well, the Twinmoon is upon us. If we can get to Pellia and stop Mark before he reaches Welstar Palace, we might be able to use the table to stop the shipments, neutralise the effects of whatever Malagon has already managed to transport and perhaps even to eradicate or disband that army.'

'You think they'll go home quietly?' Brexan asked. 'Malagon's Home Guard are humourless individuals who take their role very seriously. It will take more than just us asking sweetly for them to pack up and head for home.'

Garec said, 'True; we'll probably have to fight them, and the Seron, but by that time we'll have the table.'

They drank in silence. There was nothing left to discuss: they would find Mark Jenkins or they would die.

Eldarn's twin moons, burnt-yellow and silvery-blue, drifted towards one another in the northern sky and as if in deference, the Ravenian Sea rushed through the Narrows to flood the archipelago that sprawled from Pellia to the wind-ravaged Gorskan coast. With the tide rising in Pellia, ships overladen with Malakasian lumber, textiles, quarried stone and sometimes even livestock set sails and tacked into a queue to pass through the naval blockade. Outbound ships were inspected at their mooring buoys, then given scarcely a passing glance as they made their way across the blockade and into deep waters. Prince Malagon's naval officers saved their scrutiny for incoming vessels. Ships were expected to heave to and submit to agents of the Harbourmaster, the Malakasian Customs Admiral and the prince's navy. Terrorists, while rare, were either transported to the wharf and hanged for a Twinmoon, or lashed to a quarry-stone and cast over the side to join the pile of decomposing freedom fighters on the muddy harbour bottom.

A gold-and-green-striped banner was run up when terrorists or Eastland partisans had been discovered hiding below decks, or stowed away inside a foreign merchant ship. The little flag was known informally as *Stripes*. At night, when it couldn't be seen, a lilting melody, *Stripes' invocation*, was piped across the water and a second watchlight was set – a lantern was hung from the bowsprit. *Stripes* was more than just military intelligence; it was also an invitation to an aven of distracting entertainment. Guilty merchant officers were arrested and shipped off to a Pellia prison, their vessels seized for bounty or, if old and battered and considered next to worthless, set alight. navy crews were allowed – if not encouraged – to watch the conflagration, and to provide a chorus of hoots and jeers as the guilty men and women, often beaten and bloody by now, were transferred to a Pellia-bound naval vessel. Malakasian navy officers, not normally a generous sort, would dole out beer or rum while their crew enjoyed the spectacle from afar.

On this night, with the twin moons precariously close to one another in the heavens and the southern waters rushing north, three Falkan frigates were escorted towards the narrow mouth of the only deep-water passage through the Northern Archipelago. Somewhere in the midst of all the atolls, islands, spits and sandbars that made up the archipelago they would encounter the convoy of textile, lumber and livestock boats sailing from Pellia Harbour. Assuming the helmsman on each of the lead vessels knew the twisty route well enough, northbound and southbound ships would pass safely, though close enough to hail one another without shouting. Should one of the captains make a mistake, running inside a key marker or placing too far across the channel on a difficult tack, the entire group of ships would be in danger of running aground.

Redrick Shen, the raider-turned-merchant-seaman, had been through the Northeast Channel before, but like most first-timers, he had spent much of the journey watching from beside the rail as the lethal rocks and unexpected sandbars passed within a few paces of the ship's hull. He might have glanced at a chart once, Twinmoons ago, but it had not been his responsibility to navigate the harrowing passage so he hadn't committed the sequence of geographical signposts to memory.

Now he watched as the twin moons sought one another in the northern sky. They were an awesome sight, the massive glowing orbs sitting low on the horizon, one smoky-yellow and the other glinty-silver, destined to kiss before dawn.

Around him, the officers and crew, ignoring the Twinmoon, backed away. No one wanted to be in Redrick's field of view when the demon sailor finally shifted his gaze from the heavens.

'Captain Blackford,' he said finally, 'are you familiar enough with the charts to see us through this Northeast Channel?'

'I'm sorry, sir, but I am not.' The captain winced, looking as if he expected his insides to boil out of his orifices, or his flesh to ripen into pus-filled sores at any moment.

There was a thin covering of ice on the main deck and coating the lines. It would melt after sunrise, but right now the *Bellan* glowed moonlit-silver, the colour of cold. Redrick's tunic was torn and his chest was bare, yet he wasn't troubled by the icy temperature – indeed, he appeared to be positively enjoying it. He sniffed and caught the aroma of something dank – a swamp, or a stretch of water that has stood too long in the sun. It was certainly not the smell of anything common to winter on the Ravenian Sea.

Eventually the demon sailor blinked and asked, 'What was I saying?'

'Uh, you were asking about the passage, sir.'

'Yes, very good,' Redrick looked distracted again. 'Check to see if any of these fellows knows how to see us through – and if they do claim to know the way, assure them that I will hold them personally accountable for every scrape and scratch we get while running north. If none of them feels up to that challenge, hail the *Souzett* and have their captain guide us through.'

'Right away, sir,' he said, trying not to let the pleasure of such a relatively simple assignment show in his voice.

Redrick stopped him again. 'Did you feel anything odd today, Blackford?'

'Odd? I'm sorry, sir, but I'm not sure what you mean by odd.'

'Today, when I finally managed to kill Steven bloody Taylor and that band of milksops he hangs about with. Did you sense something curious about that?'

'I don't— I can't—'

'Never mind, Blackford, never mind,' he broke in impatiently, staring north again. He pointed beyond the topsails. 'Those moons up there are actually worlds and worlds apart.'

'Yes, sir.' The hairs on Captain Blackford's forearms stood up; this sudden contemplative mood made him nervous.

'But from this far away, they look like they're about to butt heads. It's funny what a little distance can do to one's perspective, isn't it?'

'It is, sir.' Blackford ventured a bit further. 'Plenty of things appear different when examined from far away.'

Redrick's more common look of vacuous disengagement returned as he whispered, 'Yes, they do.'

'I'll make arrangements for the passage, sir,' Blackford said, sweating inside his cloak.

Redrick snapped his attention back to the frigate. 'Let me know when we enter the passage. I enjoyed that run last time.'

As Blackford backed away, he heard Redrick murmur, 'There was something odd about those spells … almost as if …' Redrick turned and strode into the aft companionway, leaving the moons to their rendezvous in private, still mumbling to himself, '—would look different up close—'

In the Viennese swamp, something large moved quickly past Mark. It didn't stop to consider him, as foreign as he was to this environment, but sloshed briefly in the pool at the dark end of the Gloriette, scurried through the bushes on the opposite side of the bridge and then splashed again in the water off to Mark's left. It was like spilled mercury, quick and insidious.

The entire swamp seemed to gasp when the shadow passed through. There had been evil in here before – the coral snake with its ruined head, the poisonous serpents, the tadpoles moving in that ungainly crawl to feed on Redrick Shen – but those things were the kind of evil one expected from a haunted swamp. This newcomer, already gone, was worse, for this would have been evil anywhere; there was no force of goodness strong enough to mitigate it. And Mark suddenly understood from where Nerak had summoned his almor hunters and his acid clouds.

'What was that?' he said, confident whatever it had been was gone already, the chill in its wake weakening.

That? Just a bit of insurance for me.

'Planning to take up bungee jumping?' Mark wanted the lights on; he needed to move between two more of the columns to reach the little bridge. It wasn't far and wouldn't be long, but he didn't want to risk the slippery coping in the dark; if he stepped in the water, the swamp's retaliation would be swift and terrifying.

Some things just look different from far away. Moons, mountains, and magic spells, especially.

'Where are you sending … whatever that was?'

I'm not sure, Mark, that's why I'm sending her. Perhaps she'll rid me of your irritating roommate, or maybe she'll just eat a crew of my own navy. Wouldn't that be ironic? Ah, well, you can't make an omelette without killing a few sailors, can you?

Mark didn't answer. Hugging the column, the same one Jody Calloway had pushed him up against when she grabbed his crotch on Herr Peterson's class trip, Mark closed his eyes and waited.

THE TAN-BAK

The tan-bak gripped the brig-sloop's hull with webbed fingers. The journey had been brief but exhausting. She had paused along the bottom to feed on soft-shelled booacore scuttling beneath rocks and clumps of seaweed. The miniature crustaceans had been tasty, but the tan-bak would need more sustenance to remain on the light side of the Fold. On a previous trip outside her obsidian prison she had fought with abandon, although she hadn't fed for days. Now, thousands of Twinmoons later, she was getting older and feeding was the only thing she intended to do this time.

Her webbing slipped on the slimy, barnacled planks of the old ship's belly so she abandoned the webs, sprouted a fistful of talons and dug in, heaving herself nimbly up the side. She glanced at the Twinmoon and her flesh dripped dry as she considered this curious place: wet below but dry and windy above. The tan-bak had come across images inside the Fold – mostly lost thoughts and drifting memories – but had never imagined how it would feel to swim in seawater.

Gills closed as puckered lungs opened. Pupils shrank and toes split into claws. As she clung to the starboard bulkhead, her smooth leathery skin reflected the moonlight. The tan-bak looked like the twisted offspring of a spider, a black-haired monkey and a lithe, sinewy woman. The appendages she had used to locate and reach the ship, now useless, had been reabsorbed into her malleable flesh, vanished like forgotten vestigial organs and replaced by fingers and toes, resilient bones and opposable thumbs.

Almost as an afterthought, the circular tympana she had used to hear the booacore fleeing across the sand ruptured and caved into the side of her head, forming primitive ears. That was better; there was less background noise. Now she heard them: breathing, snoring, rolling over in their blankets. One farted, another coughed. They were nestled together inside a cabin, somewhere below the forward mast, but there were others, just a few, above decks. One stood in the bow, the tendons in his joints creaking with the rolling swells. Another, a woman, waited at the helm; the tan-bak could smell her musty aroma.

She listened. There was another back there, a man, breathing in slow, barely audible sniffs through his nose.

Him she would take last.

The rest would be easy.

She would deploy a team of scouts below to locate hidden defences, weapons or magic she hadn't sensed while she dispatched the woman at the helm and the rickety sentry in the bow. She pinched one of her fingernails, a barbed talon, and wrenched it off. The pain was immediate and excruciating, and the tan-bak whined, biting back a scream. She had been too loud. She froze in place, listening for the woman or the forward watch.

At the helm, Sera cocked an ear towards the starboard rail and peered into the half-light. She waited, but heard nothing more. She made a mental note to warn Captain Ford that something might be coming loose somewhere below the scuppers.

Oily black blood from the torn finger dripped into the water and a moment later, the first of her assistants pushed through the meaty flesh, and crawled, trailing a length of sticky afterbirth, onto the brig-sloop's hull. Two more followed, then the tan-bak replaced her talon. The soft sucking sound as it reattached was lost in the wash of wind and water. The huntress gestured to her scouts and watched as three tiny spider-beetles, their exoskeletons black with demon blood, scuttled over the rail and crept across the main deck, searching for the cracks Captain Ford had meant to fill with tar just as soon as he and the *Morning Star*'s crew returned to Southport.

Before the evening's attack had ended, one of the tan-bak's scouts was dead, crushed underfoot. Another found a berth and a folded blanket, where it waited. The third, the most fortunate, had dropped through a hatch onto someone's shoulder, crawled under a forest of flaxen hair and, undetected, inserted itself into the twisting canal of a sleeping partisan's ear. An irritated scratch and a shift of the pillows was all the resistance the creature encountered.

Now the tan-bak, matching the ship's colour and texture perfectly, rubbed a healthy talon over the grainy wood. She straddled the gunwale and leaped into the rigging like a fugitive shadow, looked around and chose her target, then sprouted a mouthful of fangs and dived into the night.

Sera struggled to stay awake. *Run downwind* had been Captain Ford's final order an aven earlier; that had been his only order for days now: push north for the archipelago. Tubbs was in the bow, also standing the middle watch. The fire in the watch brazier winked periodically; so she knew he was still moving about, still awake. When the old sailor caught a whiff of her Pragan tobacco – she had no use for fancy Falkan leaves – he would wander back, purloin a pinch and then retake his position between the catheads. The two had stood the middle watch together for more Twinmoons than Sera could recall.

She was waiting for him to join her for a smoke when the tan-bak struck. The creature plunged a clawed fist wrist-deep into her chest and Sera, neither shouting nor releasing the wheel, looked down in amazement, as if witnessing a marvel of ancient magic. Her eyes, half-closed against the cold and wind, flew open as her jaw clamped shut, biting straight through the hand-carved pipe.

A yellowed tooth distracted the tan-bak, who tapped at it with a claw, thinking it might be a piece of something Sera had been chewing, or perhaps even one of the insect scouts, far out of position. With her hand still buried inside the woman's chest, the tan-bak plucked Sera's fingers from the *Morning Star*'s wheel, leaped back to the starboard rail and dumped the yellow-toothed woman over the side.

She heard the man approach before she saw him; his knees and ankles were so noisy, it was a wonder the old man could still get himself around the deck.

When Tubbs reached the quarterdeck, he found the wheel abandoned and the little ship beginning to spin with the wind and the current. He turned a quick circle. He couldn't call for Sera – Captain Ford had a special connection with the brig-sloop; like many captains, his sense of the *Morning Star* went beyond the merely tactile and he could sense the tug in a line, the draw on a sheet, the pressure against a plank in the hull, as if the ship was a living, breathing thing. If he called out, Tubbs knew Captain Ford would be dressed and on deck in two breaths. Instead, the old mariner took the helm, steadied it – changes in course were enough to keep Ford awake for a Moon – and continued his silent search for the ship's navigator.

*

The tan-bak was thrilled with the acrobatics she was able to perform on the shifting vessel. She dived from the shrouds, touched down on the rail, leaped for the main spar and tumbled out of the darkness to tear Tubbs's throat out with one vicious swipe. Before his body struck the deck she was on him, feeding. The blood was warm and salty, delicious, but the meat – ah, that was something inhabitants of the Fold dreamed about. And inside the Fold, there was ample time for dreaming.

The captain stirred. It didn't take much to wake him. He sat up and strained to hear anything out of the ordinary. A wave lifted the *Morning Star* ... it wasn't right. He had left orders for Sera to keep the old ship running before the wind and from the way his cabin rolled over that last swell, he could feel that they were at least a few points off their tailwind.

'What's wrong?' he asked the empty cabin. 'Why is my boat running sideways through the water? Is that odd to anyone but me?' He lit a candle in a hurricane glass and dressed quickly, then picked up the lantern and hurried into the companionway.

Steven bumped his head against the bulkhead. He rolled over, fluffed up the blanket he had folded into a pillow and drifted back to sleep.

When another wave rolled him into the wall, he sat up, careful not to knock himself senseless on the berth above. He yawned and tried to stand when a third swell rolled him back into his berth.

'Christ, who's driving this thing?' he muttered, finally rolling free of his tangled blankets.

'Ssh,' a voice whispered.

'Who's that?' Steven said, lighting the lantern beside the bed with a thought. 'Gilmour? What's wrong? It feels like we're going over in these waves.'

The Larion sorcerer was crouched near cabin door. In the lamp-light, his face was pale. 'I want you to stay here,' he whispered.

'Why? What is it?'

'I'll handle it,' he said firmly.

'No,' Steven insisted, 'we'll do it together, like everything else. You can't just leave me in the car like a first-grader. Is it Mark?'

'Not Mark,' Gilmour said. 'I'm worried that the watch are already dead.'

'What?' Steven's voice rose. 'Jesus, Gilmour, let's go – what are we waiting for?' He pushed past, tugged the door open and stepped into the companionway.

'Steven, please!' Gilmour hissed, but Steven was already halfway to the deck when the magic roared to life with such force he nearly lost his balance.

The phantom white shrouds, the black spider-web rigging and the masts scraping the night sky all melted into a watery curtain dangling from an overhead spar. He watched a rolling, tumbling cloud of red and black pass over his vision, and then everything was waxy, slippery and insubstantial.

'Holy shit,' Steven said, 'what's out here?' He tensed for whatever might be haunting the foredeck. In the distance, near the helm, the blurry backdrop was broken by a flickering candle, protected somehow from the wind. He guessed the light represented whatever had Gilmour so frightened. Ducking low, he crept silently astern.

The tan-bak didn't wait for the newcomer to reach the quarterdeck. She was surprised that anyone had sensed her arrival and understood there would be no time for her scouts to report back. No matter; they knew what to do in the event that they were unable to rejoin their mistress. Peering down from a topgallant spar, she chewed on a lump of the old man with the noisy joints. She flattened her back teeth to grind sinew and fat into masticated mush, then gave herself a make-shift oesophagus, just for the sheer thrill of feeling the meat pass down her throat. She bored a ragged flap-covered nostril in the centre of her face and inhaled with each bite; it was tastier with a bit of sea air.

When the two men appeared, the tan-bak wrapped a footrope around what was left of her meal, storing it for afterwards, then, diving for the topsail, she used the billowy sheet as a springboard to catapult herself into the fight. One of the newcomers looked young. Curious about the difference in flavour, the tan-bak decided to eat him too.

'Up there!' Steven screamed, an instinctive response to a half-glimpsed dark patch, a quick-moving blur that was somehow out of place. He lashed out with whatever he found on his fingertips, a wild, roundhouse punch.

The tan-bak had never been hit by anything before. The pain as the young man's magic ripped into her chest was wonderful. Thrown backwards over the stern, she careened in ungainly tumbles, splashed down and started to drown. The huntress willed her lungs closed, recalled her gills and webbing and swam in powerful lunging strokes after the fleeing ship.

'What the fuck was that?' Steven asked, shaking. 'Jesus, it just came out of the night. I thought we were—' He stopped; Gilmour was gone. 'Hey,' he said, 'where are you?'

'I'm in here,' Gilmour called from the companionway. Steven could hear Garec and the others inside. He wasn't surprised when the bowman appeared, armed and ready.

'What's happening?' Garec asked.

'I'm not sure,' Steven said. 'There was something, but it's gone. Gilmour? What're you doing? I thought you were— Yikes! What happened to you?'

Gilmour's nose was bleeding and he had a cut above his right eye. His left was closed and he was pressing against it with one hand.

'Christ, are you all right?' Steven helped him up. 'What happened?'

'You did.' Gilmour spat a mouthful of blood and a tooth onto the deck. He retrieved the tooth and held it up to his good eye. 'Ah, rutters. I need these teeth to last.' He turned to Steven. 'That was quite a shot you gave her.'

'Sorry.' Steven flushed. 'I didn't mean to clobber you too.'

'No worries, no worries,' Gilmour said. 'I'm glad you did it. She would have killed us both in a heartbeat. Come, we need to check on the others.'

Steven, Garec and Gilmour, now with Kellin and Brexan in tow, came nose to kneecaps with Captain Ford, who looked pale and frightened.

'Sera's missing,' he said, 'and I've found what's left of Tubbs.'

Gilmour sniffed at the air, then shouted, 'Everyone, get below, quickly!' He pushed Kellin, Brexan and Garec towards the corridor.

Garec resisted, saying, 'I can help. What is this?'

'She's nothing you'll even be able to see,' Gilmour said, trying to explain, 'and we don't have the time right now. Please, just get below and close that hatch. You too, Captain.'

'I'll give the orders on my ship,' he said forcefully as Gilmour tried to push him away.

'Captain Ford, I can promise you that you'll be as dead as Tubbs and Sera if you don't get below,' Gilmour cried. 'Just get back to your cabin and block the door – quickly!'

Marrin and Kanthil appeared through a forward hatch, asking, 'Captain? What can we do, sir?'

Gilmour whirled on the two sailors. 'Rutting gods, but is everyone on this damned tub awake?'

'So it seems,' the captain said wryly, trying to remain calm.

'Captain Ford, there is a monster, a starving otherworldly killer, haunting your ship right this moment. Now get below!' Gilmour ordered, 'and you two as well.' He waved a dismissive hand at Marrin and Kanthil, but neither moved; they didn't take orders from passengers.

Marrin said again, 'Captain?'

Ford sighed. 'Get below, and secure that hatch. I'll be at the helm. We'll find Sera, and we'll need to give Tubbs his rites. He's a rutting mess, and I don't want—'

He was cut off by a hiss, sharp and unnerving, from somewhere in the rigging.

'There!' Garec shouted, already firing.

'Do you see it?' Marrin shouted.

'No,' Garec said, still shooting. 'I heard it, out on the end of that crossbar, above the main sheet.'

'I see it,' Steven said, his voice toneless and flat. The magic was with him again. 'Get below. Everyone. You too, Gilmour. I'll do this by myself.'

The tan-bak dived for the deck; Steven lunged for the place he guessed the monster might land, but he wasn't quick enough: as the creature touched down, it lashed at him with a clawed finger, opening a bloody slit across his shoulder.

'Motherless son-of-a-bitch!' Steven shouted, rolling to the deck and blasting at the shadowy figure as it leaped from the starboard gunwale to the bowsprit to the topmain and then back to the deck. It was like a madman's carnival shooting gallery where the ducks, pigs and chickens all moved as unpredictably as lightning – and fired back. 'Get down!' Steven cried. 'Get your heads down, now!'

Garec had an arrow trained into the rigging, but he didn't fire – Gilmour had been right: it was too fast, too well-hidden. Running amidships, Steven cast a handful of fireballs into the night, illuminating the *Morning Star* as if it were midday.

How do you catch a shadow? he thought. *How can I kill a shadow? You can't kill a shadow . . . No, we can't kill it; we mustn't!*

Garec was behind him. 'There it is.' His bowstring thunked twice; twin shafts arched into the night.

'I've got it,' Gilmour said, rearing back for a thunderous blast.

Steven skidded to a stop and shouted, 'No, Gilmour, don't!'

His arms raised, the magic ablaze on his fingertips, Gilmour stared at his young apprentice.

'Don't! We have to keep it alive!' Steven cried. 'It's the only way to avoid him sending another, a frigging brigade of them. If you fire back, he'll know, and then . . . look out!'

The shadow dived. Gilmour ducked as the creature passed over his head and slashed open Kanthil's throat, then punctured ragged claw-marks down Marrin's chest.

Steven sent a volley after it, catching the creature's flank and sending it tumbling over the bowsprit into the sea. Ford rushed to his fallen men; a muffled curse confirmed that Kanthil lay dead.

It flies, it leaps around and swims like a fish. But just now it didn't have fins, gills or a tail. What can do that? How can it do all those things? Steven waited beneath the mainmast, ready to parry another attack; he hadn't killed it.

Gilmour said quietly, 'We can't capture it.'

'True, but if we kill it, or if you start blasting away, Mark will know he sank the wrong ship this morning. There's no way a navy crew could deal with that . . . whatever it is.'

'He must know already,' Gilmour said, keeping a wary eye out for their hunter. 'Why else would he have sent her?'

'Just to be sure,' Steven said. 'He showed us this morning how he would deal with our ship. The sea opened and swallowed them, right down to the frigging nuts. This thing . . . this is some kind of sick entertainment for him. If we kill it, he'll send us to the bottom for sure.'

Gilmour sighed. 'So I'm convinced, but what are we going to do?'

Steven ignored him, staring at a spot just starboard of the bowsprit, a plank in the weatherbeaten gunwale that had come into focus, separating itself from the blurry backdrop. *It flies, swims and jumps around like Olga Korbut. What flies, swims and leaps around like that? An insect? What can do all that?*

'Steven,' Gilmour asked again, 'how do we capture it?'

'*We* don't,' Steven said, standing in the bow, ignoring Marrin's curses and Kanthil's corpse. '*I* do.'

With another piercing hiss, the tan-bak burst from the sea, dragging a frothy trail of salt water like a rogue comet. Landing nimbly on the gunwale, her feet, webbed for swimming, transmogrified into clawed toes. She took Steven by the throat, gripping his neck with a thickly webbed paw.

'Perfect,' Steven choked.

The creature's head changed. Gill flaps, opening and closing with the breeze, folded flush and disappeared; a primitive nostril beneath a flap of slippery skin perforated the monster's face. Steven cringed when he smelled its breath, the aroma of old death, rotting corpses and disease. Bulbous black eyes rolled back, irritated by the brilliant false dawn, and when they reappeared they were gimlet, still bulging, but with smaller, almost human pupils. Finally the hand around Steven's throat began to morph. Talons grew as bones hardened and webbing dissolved.

So that's how you do it.

The monster hissed directly into Steven's face, taunting him for being stupid enough to come searching over the rail. Rows of needle-sharp spiny teeth flattened into molars, leaving it with an evolved mouthful of ripping and crushing jaws. It hissed again, its fist closing tighter around Steven's throat.

When the talons broke his skin, Steven struck with a fiery current. 'No you don't,' he said, grabbing the demon's wrist. 'I just needed you to stand still for a second – and now you're fucked.'

Paralysed, the tan-bak gaped, unable to kill the annoying creature and unable to break free. It couldn't change form, or breathe, nor could it summon the strength or the speed to retaliate. The tan-bak, one of the most dangerous and powerful creatures to haunt the Fold, was frozen in space and time – two of its favourite killing fields.

Gilmour had been watching. 'You all right?' he asked, sounding strained.

'Fine, you?'

'I'm afraid we lost Kanthil.'

'Sorry about that,' Steven said. 'It took me a bit of time to come up with this.'

'How are you holding her still like that?'

'Remember the almor, and how surprised I was that a demon would be made of actual, physical flesh? I was gambling that this thing would be the same. I figured that unless Mark dropped this sonofabitch right on the deck, it either flew here or swam here – but I don't see any fins, feathers or gills on it now, do you?'

'No,' Gilmour said, peering more closely at the demon.

'Exactly,' Steven went on. 'So judging from the way it was leaping about, and from how quickly it caught up with us after I kicked it off the ship, I guessed it must have some way of adjusting to its environment, and doing it in a hurry.' The monster was limp in Steven's hand. 'By the way, why do you keep calling it *her*?'

'It's a tan-bak,' Gilmour whispered.

'A what?' Garec had joined them, leaving the others to tend to Marrin.

'Tan-bak. It's a legend. Tan-bak and tan-bek are creatures that haunt the nether regions of the Fold. The tan-bak, the female, is the hunter.'

'So you've known about these things and you failed to mention them?' Steven said, sweating, but forcing a smile. 'I've been here over five months, Gilmour, and you're just mentioning them now?'

'Sorry.'

'I guess I was right, though,' Steven said. 'It was a lucky guess, but I figured if it was made of flesh, then I could paralyse it with a direct current.'

'How's that?' Garec came a bit closer, still holding his bow.

'As close as I can get to lightning,' Steven said. 'It's a way to paralyse muscle; I hoped it would work with any kind of muscle.'

'What do we do with it now? Can we kill it?'

'Actually, we can,' Steven said, 'but I'm betting Mark will know if we do, so we have to keep it alive, but also keep it from following us or attacking again later on.'

'Oh, grand,' Garec sighed. 'And I thought this would be a tough one.'

Gilmour raised an eyebrow. 'So?'

'This is another gamble, but if I'm right, this thing has an astonishingly advanced brain and nervous system. It can change its physical features with a thought, or just a few moments' exposure to a new environment. So we pith this bitch like a frog and we toss her over the side. She'll sprout gills without trying, and she'll float around out there for a few days, unable to think enough to grow webbing and swim, or even if she does grow webbing, she won't know what to do with it. She won't have any idea where she is or why her body is keeping itself alive. Eventually, she'll die of exposure or starvation, or something nasty will swim along and eat her on a cracker. Best of all, Mark will still be able to find her, feel her, track her and, hopefully, not have any clue that she's adrift on the tide without a brain.'

Garec smiled. 'You know, Steven, your whole compassion campaign has lost some of its lustre.'

'This is a monster,' Steven said, 'a killing machine. She doesn't get compassion.'

With one finger, he felt for the base of the tan-bak's skull and loosed a powerful arc of mystical current which lanced into the monster's brain, killing the stem and paralysing much of the cortex. The shape-shifter spasmed, then fell limp again in Steven's hands. He shut down the current and dumped the tan-bak's body onto the deck. It lay in a greasy heap as the others came over to watch.

'What now?' Garec said.

'Now we test it.' Steven conjured up a small fireball, no larger than a penlight, and guided the orb in front of the tan-bak's unnerving eyes. The pupils shrank away and Steven grinned coldly. 'Good,' he said. 'I think it worked. Gilmour, help me toss her over the side.'

Marrin grimaced as the two sorcerers disposed of the inanimate body. They watched her leathery flesh bob in the swells until she passed out of sight. Captain Ford, as if slapped, cried, 'Rutting Pragans, the helm!'

The spell was broken. Everyone moved at once.

Garec and Kellin took Kanthil's body below. Brexan, catching the captain looking at her worriedly, followed him aft and they both started shouting for Sera.

Gilmour climbed into the rigging to retrieve a large piece of Olren Tubbsward, the *Morning Star*'s veteran seaman.

Steven kept the lights burning long enough for the captain and his remaining crew to restore order and return the brig-sloop to her northerly course. Then, dousing the flames, he stepped alone into the bow and looked towards Pellia.

Behind him, the *Morning Star* found the wind and corrected her course as the much reduced crew followed Captain Ford's orders, hauling in sheets and belaying lines until the sails filled, the lines pulled taut and cracked and the brig-sloop groaned as if waking from a deep sleep.

Below, the tan-bak's tiny emissaries took shelter and waited.

CAPEHILL

Sharr Becklen huddled over one of Stalwick's inextinguishable fires, clutching his cloak tightly around him, and shivered. It was raining again this morning; he forced a smile at a bedraggled Markus Fillin and nodded towards the sky. 'Right on time.'

Markus ducked beneath the porous canvas tent that provided mean shelter at their guard post. He missed his family and worried about them often, especially during quiet moments, like this one. The rain, turning to sleet, wasn't helping. Markus was young and handsome, but today his hair hung about his face in dripping strands and he looked like a warmed-over cadaver. 'Lovely. This place goes from light grey to dark grey and back with the predictability of the tides. Bright and cheery, Sharr – and you live here?'

'All my life,' Sharr said, 'and most days, I'm on the water, hauling nets or traps.'

'In this? Markus rubbed his cramped fingers. 'You've got ice in your bones, old man.'

'Nah, it's only dismal during this Twinmoon. Be glad this isn't snow.'

'Hoorah!' Markus sniffed and asked, 'Where's our next meeting? Your friend, right? The harbourmaster's mate or something?'

'Assistant,' Sharr nodded. 'The harbourmaster is Malagon's man to the core, but this fellow, Lan Hernesto, a Pragan if you believe him, has been with us all along. He makes life a bit more livable for those of us working nets or long lines offshore.'

'Yes, well, he's late,' Markus said, 'and it's bloody cold out here. Tell me again why we aren't meeting these people inside someplace warm and dry, like a tavern, or a nice comfy cathouse?'

'Because we're standing a post, Markus. Come on; this is soldiering.'

'I thought we were officers.'

'We're Resistance, and that makes us full-on revolutionaries,' Sharr said. 'Call it Gita's progressive leadership style.'

'Progressive? I don't even know what that means.' Markus draped a blanket over a chair, then pulled the chair close to the fire. 'Need to keep these dry,' he mumbled, then said, 'I don't see her out here standing post.'

'Markus, do you know where the occupation brigade went?'

'No.'

'Do you know if there is a regiment of cavalry or a fleet of naval frigates coming here to slaughter us?'

'No.'

'Has anyone shown us anything that leads you to believe that we're going to live through the Twinmoon?'

'No.'

'Then come here next to the fire, warm up, stand your post, and wait for Len. Later, I'll take you down to the waterfront. I want to check on my trawler – with me gone this Twinmoon, it would be just like one of the wharf brats to stuff my scuppers full of rags. The old tub will be halfway to swamped in this rain.'

Markus crossed to the back wall where a lone figure drowsed contentedly on a cot. 'Forgive me, Sharr,' he said quietly.

'No. Wait!' he cried, but Markus ignored him.

Kicking one of the cot legs, he said, 'Wake up, Stalwick. Come on now. Time to clear out the cobwebs.'

Sharr groaned. 'Did you have to do that? I was enjoying the morning.'

'What? What is it, Markus? Sharr? What is it? I'm up. I am.' Stalwick was on his feet in a heartbeat, completely lucid and talking without pause. 'Is it an attack? What'd I miss?'

'It's nothing, Stalwick. I'm cold, is all, and I need you to stoke up our fire a bit.' He ushered the bandy-legged, unkempt figure towards the firepit. 'There might be something wrong with this one,' he explained. 'It's plenty bright, but there's not much heat.'

'Oh, I can fix that,' Stalwick went on without a breath, 'I can fix that right away, right away, I tell you.' He gestured over the fire, winced as if he had smelled something bad, then flicked his wrist with a flourish. The flames leaped to the tent's waterlogged ceiling.

'Whoa!' Sharr cried. 'Ease off a bit, Stalwick. You singed my whiskers, old man.'

'Sorry, Sharr, Markus, sorry.' Stalwick blushed. 'I just, you know, I just wanted it to be warm for you. But I guess that was a bit overdone, a bit, anyway.'

Sharr raised his hands in surrender. 'It's fine, good even, much

355

better this way. Can you just ... well, just keep the chatter to a low roar, all right? I'm trying to think.'

'Sure, of course, Sharr. Sure I can.' Stalwick paced around the tent's interior a couple of times, ostensibly looking for something productive to do. 'I'll just ... well, I'll just ... you know. I'll—'

'So,' Markus interrupted, 'where's our man, whatshisname?'

'Len Hernesto,' Sharr replied. 'He'll be here.'

Gita's Falkan Resistance forces, essentially a battalion with the dregs of a couple of companies that had wandered in over the past several days, still held Capehill. They hadn't lost a soldier, nor had they encountered an enemy. Unsurprisingly, the handful of Malakasian soldiers apparently left behind had gone missing, most likely in civilian clothes, and none of the locals they'd met so far had any clue as to where the rest of the Malakasians had sailed. Sharr hoped Len would be able to shed some light on the situation, on the condition of the import–export businesses still operating, and on the availability of food stores, in Capehill and on the Eastern Plains. Gita needed to know if there would be enough food to see Capehill and its new lodgers through the winter Twinmoon.

Sharr had met the harbourmaster's assistant in a local public house the previous evening. Unwilling to talk there, Len had offered to join Sharr and Markus after the dawn aven, but now he was late. Sharr tried not to worry as Stalwick carried on about whatever desultory topic had sparked his interest. Sharr had about given up trying to focus Stalwick's attention on anything.

As Len arrived, slogging through the sleet and mud, he heard: '—and that's how you tune a bellamir, Markus, but I guess you might have known that, coming from the Plains, right? I mean, lots of farmers are bellamir players, aren't they? What else is there to do at night? There's nothing else out there, I mean, no towns or cities to visit, so music makes sense, right? Music or chainball. Rutters, I bet you all play some chainball out there. Don't you, Markus? What with all that space, the courts would be huge, twice regulation size if you wanted.' Stalwick took a seat on the cot, somehow knowing that he should avoid the small table and maps set up in the centre of the floor. 'And speaking of chainball, you know that squad from Timmon's old platoon, the one with that big fellow from Wellham Ridge and that kind-of nice-looking woman from the Blackstones? Anyway, anyway, they've challenged the third squad, the one from Brand Krug's company – where is Brand, anyway? But they've challenged the third squad to a chainball game tonight, with archers around the

Common, of course, but it ought to be fun, don't you think? Markus? Maybe we should all go together. You, me and Sharr, when we get off duty, we can find some food and then head down to the Common. I know I could do with a chainball match, especially a muddy one. We could even stop by the boarding house and see if Gita wants to come with us. She might like a break, too. I mean, she works so hard, all the time. She's like you and Sharr, Markus. She's a tough one, and I'm going to miss her when she's gone, but maybe she'll like a chainball game as well. What do you think, Markus? Sharr? What do you think?'

Sharr held the tent flaps open; Len Hernesto slipped inside.

'Stalwick,' Markus said.

'Chainball,' he went on, 'we never played much around here. Did you, Sharr? You'd think in a place this size, we'd have—'

'Stalwick!' Markus shouted.

'What?' Stalwick said, 'what's the matter, Markus?'

'Sharr and I are going to speak with Len. We need you to step outside and stand the post, just for a bit. All right?'

'Take a bow and quiver with you,' Sharr added, 'just in case someone approaches through those trees to the north.'

'Sure, I mean, I can do that. Sure.' He pulled his hood up and stepped outside.

The silence that followed was welcome, even to the harbour-master's assistant, who had been in the tent for just a moment. Outside, the wind had picked up and the freezing rain was a noisy fugue on the walls.

'Len,' Sharr said finally. 'Thank you for coming. This is Markus Fillin, one of our lieutenants.'

'Markus,' Len nodded. He was a full two heads shorter than Sharr and at least fifty Twinmoons older. Clad in an all-weather cloak that dragged on the mud behind him, he had the wind-worn look of a life-long sailor. His grey hair was close-cropped and his beard trimmed. Despite being shorter than his old friend, Len weighed nearly as much as Sharr, evidence that he had given up hauling nets for the relative comfort of the harbourmaster's office, through his forearms were still heavily muscled and his hands remained as strong as ever.

'Welcome, sir.' Markus hung Len's cloak near the fire then offered the older man a chair. 'Can I get you a goblet of wine?'

'Please,' Len said, settling himself, after several tries, on a small camp chair. He glanced at a map Markus had set out earlier that morning.

Sharr joined him. 'I understand you couldn't talk last night, but I hope you can stay the aven. I've got a number of questions – we've got to come up with a plan to fortify the town, feed the populace, house the army – such as we are – and make a decision about where to strike next. Orindale seems an unlikely target – they've got a full infantry division – and Malakasia is out of the question, but if we can reclaim parts of the Central Plains, dig in around some of the ranches and farms, we can hold the East and the Merchants' Highway until spring, oversee the planting, protect the winter stores.'

Len spoke, his voice the raspy burr of a long-time smoker. 'Sharr, you wouldn't have believed it. I was here, and I still don't believe it. No one knew anything. They just commandeered every ketch, catboat – anything that would float, in fact – loaded up a brigade of scared and cold soldiers and set sail for the North Sea. Don't worry, though. Your old bucket is still on her mooring; I think trawlers made them nervous: too many nets and lines. It was rutting madness!' He paused to cough, sighed, and said, 'I've been here a long time. You and I have known each other, what, a hundred and fifty Twinmoons? Two hundred? Anyway, I've had the opportunity to develop some lucrative relationships with Prince Malagon's officers, some of the captains, even a few of the brigade commanders, and I tell you, Sharr, no one knew anything. The order came in from Wellham Ridge, if you can believe it, that little shit-splat in the Blackstones, and the ships were loaded and on their way within a few days. It was madness, pure madness.' He threw up his hands. 'Where could they be going?'

'I was hoping you'd answer that for us,' Sharr laughed.

'I wish I could.' Len Hernesto looked like a man overmatched by the challenges ahead. He breathed heavily, despite the fact that he was sitting, warm and dry, beside Stalwick's fire.

'How is traffic along the Highway?' Markus asked.

'Fine, fine,' Len said. 'They took care of the roads, even the farm roads, running back and forth across the Plains in a spiderweb. It was their rutting food as well, I guess.'

'And the stores?'

'Of that, I'm not certain. They emptied most of the waterfront warehouses onto the vessels that picked them up. None of us have ventured into the barracks buildings here or here.' He pointed to two places on the map. 'They left several stables full of good horses, but they're gone already. Thieves were bold enough to sneak the animals out, but no one's gone inside the barracks proper, not that I know of yet. So there might be food, clothing, maybe bits of useful junk in there. It's certainly a more comfortable place for you to sleep than how you are.'

'Too risky,' Sharr said, shaking his head, 'at least for now. Gita won't let us anywhere near those barracks, not to sleep in, anyway.'

'I suppose she's right,' Len agreed. 'That's all you need, to get in there all snug and warm, and then have a regiment of irritable stormtroopers arrive unexpectedly.'

'Still, we could get in and out, pillage whatever they left behind. Gods know we'll need the food,' Markus said.

'That you will,' Len said. 'And we need to get the commercial fishermen out again. A Moon's haul off the banks will feed this town for some time. Bloody tragic, the way everything they brought in – *you* brought in, Sharr – had to go to those wet-nosed motherhumpers. Lords, but I won't miss them.' He spat a mouthful of viscous phlegm between his boots.

'Hold on,' Sharr held up a finger, 'say that again.'

'What?' Len looked puzzled then said, 'They're a bunch of clods, you know it, Sharr. They're a worthless drain on the land, a waste of food, wine and warm places to sleep. The lot of them aren't worth one Capehill baby, naked at birth!'

'Yes, yes, that, but after that—' Sharr cut himself off, then shouted, 'Stalwick! Get in here!'

Sharr and Markus slogged through the mud and sleet, trying to run and shouting for help at every turn. Stalwick, his assorted weaponry clattering like a skeleton, followed as closely as he could.

Len Hernesto, his days of sprinting well behind him, remained in the little tent, standing the post.

'Where is she?' Markus yelled above the wind and rain.

'The boarding house,' Sharr wheezed, 'go ahead of me. Take Argile Road towards the town centre. I'll be right behind you.'

Markus, younger and faster, lowered his head and sprinted for Gita Kamrec's apartments. He hadn't known Stalwick long enough to experience his strange propensity to foretell the future in unpredictable snippets, but he trusted Sharr: something Stalwick had said that morning had Sharr convinced that Gita was in danger.

Splashing round the last corner, Markus waved to the sentry beside the doors at Gita's boarding house. 'Inside!' he tried to shout, sucking in breaths through clenched teeth, 'get upstairs, now!'

'Lieutenant? What's wrong?'

The guard wore an eye-patch; Markus had seen him in Gita's

shadow for the past Twinmoon, but didn't know his name. 'Upstairs!' he repeated.

Eye-Patch stayed at his post but drew a pair of hunting knives regardless. He wore a bow slung across his back and had a quick-access quiver full of goose-feathered arrows on his belt. 'No one's gone inside all morning, sir,' he said.

Markus skidded, fell in the muddy road and rolled to his feet. 'Listen, I don't—'

'Barrold!' Sharr called, stumbling round the corner, mud-splattered and leading a handful of partisans, none of whom looked like they had any idea why they had been rallied like this. Behind the winded posse, Stalwick staggered, one hand pressing against his side as he gasped.

'Barrold!' Sharr shouted again, 'go!' He panted, then gave up and pointed towards the second floor.

Eye-Patch, Barrold Dayne, who had lost his left eye to Steven Taylor in the caverns below the Medera River, turned suddenly and kicked the boarding house door nearly off its hinges.

'Go,' Sharr panted to Markus, following him inside.

Barrold was already on the upper landing, already inside Gita's apartment, and already shouting for help.

'Rutters,' Markus cursed and bound up the stairs three at a time.

There was a shout, a crash, then silence.

Sharr's vision blurred, he saw swirling spots of yellow and white and knew he was about to pass out. The room spun, then lurched back into place. He sucked in a breath, another, then dropped his sword, shrugged out of his cloak and doubled over, his hands on his knees.

He heard the others; they were all right. The danger, for the moment, had passed, but with adrenalin addling his thoughts, he was glad there was no one here to fight.

'Help him up,' Gita said, then gave a string of orders to the crowd gathered in the corridor.

'Whoa there, old man,' Markus said, holding him beneath one arm.

Something clanged and banged outside the chamber and they heard shouting. 'Let me through,' a familiar voice said, 'I'm with them, I tell you, I'm with them. I need to get in there.'

Sharr half walked and half staggered to a chair, found a mug pressed into his hand and swallowed a few mouthfuls of water. That was better. He coughed hard and felt all manner of stickiness come loose in his chest. 'More, please,' he gasped, and passed the mug to Markus, who passed it to Stalwick, who had managed to get past the guards at the door to take up station next to his friends.

'Get him a beer,' Markus said.

'But I just got here, Markus,' Stalwick explained. 'I just got up the stairs and through that throng, and what's happening in here? Is everyone all right? Did I miss something, and who is that?' Stalwick pointed behind the table where an overturned chair, a map of southern Gorsk and a broken breakfast tray half-hid the inert body of a maid.

Sharr wiped his face on his sleeve, felt his heart slow and managed a smile: Stalwick had been right.

'Just get him a beer, Stalwick. Move it.' Markus shoved him towards the corridor.

The room came back into focus. 'It's all right,' Sharr said, unwilling to stand yet. 'I'm all right. Give me a moment; that's more running than I've done since before you were born, Markus.'

Barrold slapped him hard on the back. 'Better you than me, sir!'

'Go easy on me, Barrold,' Sharr waved up at him in mock surrender. 'I'm still spinning down here.'

Gita pulled a chair up beside him. 'How'd you know?'

'It was Stalwick,' Markus said. 'He said something this morning. Sharr caught it. I don't even remem—'

'He said he would miss you when you were gone,' Sharr said, nodding thanks as Stalwick handed him the froth-topped mug. He drank half of it in one swallow, then handed the mug to Gita who finished it in similar fashion.

'Miss me?'

'It just came out of him,' Sharr explained. 'You know how he gets, rambling on about gardening and boils and pest control and his great-aunt Gaye from Southport? No offence, Stalwick.'

'That's all right, Sharr. I do go on sometimes. I mean, not all the time, and well, my aunt's name isn't Gaye, it's Mavene, and she's not really a great-aunt, more a cousin, although we all call her Aunt Mavene, and she's not really from Southport, she's from a little village not far from here really, but you know, if you were just using that as an example, well, then, I understand what you're—'

'Stalwick.' Gita raised a finger at him. 'Please.'

'Sorry, ma'am, sorry. Sharr, sorry.'

'Anyway,' Sharr went on, 'when he said it, I knew we had to get over here in a hurry.' He nodded towards the body in the corner, 'but it looks like you had things in hand.' Outside, the sleet had stopped; the street was silent. Drops from the roof above plunked an irregular rhythm on the wooden sill.

Gita gave the tired fisherman an uncharacteristic hug, then opened the windows, reaching on tiptoe to get the higher latch. She looked more like the partisans' grandmother than their leader.

'What happened, ma'am?' Barrold picked up the chair, the map and what remained of Gita's breakfast. He turned the body over with his foot. The woman was younger than Sharr, but not young. She was dressed as a maid, but it was impossible to know if she was merely a terrorist, sympathetic to Malakasian rule, or one of the occupation soldiers who had remained behind when the rest of them disappeared across the North Sea.

'She brought a knife with my breakfast,' Gita said calmly. 'It was a mistake.'

'A knife, ma'am?' Markus asked. 'Don't they always bring a knife with your breakfast?'

'I was having eggs and booacore.'

'Well, you don't need a knife for those things, ma'am,' Stalwick broke in to state the obvious. 'What needs cutting, really? I mean, what would you cut with a knife? It isn't as though she brought you a loaf of old bread or anything.'

Sharr tested his legs and went to close the windows. 'It's cold.'

'You all right?' Gita asked.

'Fine, fine.' Sharr checked the street in either direction. 'Just too rutting old for this business.' The temperature had dropped again, and the sleet would freeze by the dinner aven, coating the town in ice. It would be a cold night for chainball.

'Don't talk to me about old, my friend.' Gita smiled. 'Anyway, if this one was Malakasian military, we have to be alert. Who knows what the others might be up to? How many did you say they had left?' She ignored the body as she circled the table, shuffling through maps until she found one of Capehill.

'There was a squad, maybe a handful more,' Sharr said, 'so fifteen, perhaps twenty soldiers.'

'So we assume they're in civilian clothes, hiding here somewhere amongst us.' Gita bent over the map, her nose nearly touching the parchment.

'That's troublesome,' Markus said.

'And there's no way to smoke them out,' Barrold added.

'Unless we round up the locals. You know them, Sharr. Pull two or

362

three soldiers from each platoon, no more than ten from a company. Spread them out; blanket the town. See if anyone's heard anything, seen anything. Find these motherwhoring pukes and bring me one of them alive.'

'Very good, ma'am,' Markus said.

'And Sharr—' Gita tugged her dagger loose from the treacherous maid's chest with a grunt, 'stay on your friend Hernesto. I want as much information as possible on the condition of the roads, the surrounding farms, the winter stores, the slaughterhouses, all of it.' When he nodded agreement, she turned to Barrold and asked, 'Any new additions overnight?'

'Most of one platoon from the Central Plains, and almost a full company from Gorsk,' he said.

'Anyone from Rona?'

'No, ma'am.'

'Bloody Sallax.' Gita frowned. 'And no word from Gilmour and the others either. When's the Twinmoon, anyway?'

'Maybe another day or two.' Sharr checked again out the window, looking north.

'We're going to lose sleep over these leftover soldiers, boys. This isn't good. Sharr, you'd better be right about Hernesto, because if he's dirty, I'm going to eat his heart.' Ignoring the map now, the grey-haired little woman prowled back and forth on bare feet, twirling her bloody dagger absentmindedly. 'We have what . . . a thousand?'

'Just over a thousand, ma'am,' Barrold said.

'Just over a thousand soldiers to feed, clothe and house this Twin-moon. I want to know that we're hauling nets and booacore traps, that we're running carts and wagons out to every farm with a storage cellar or a grain bin, that we're contracting with every tailor, smith—rutters, even any schoolchild who can sharpen a blade or sew on a whoring button, understand?'

'Yes, ma'am,' they echoed in unison.

'This corner of Eldarn is the closest thing we've had to freedom since before your great-grandmothers were in nappies – even yours, Sharr! – and I don't want us making a bloody mess of it. If an armoured division is riding north along the Merchants' Highway, I want to know. If a Malakasian sympathiser is putting chickenshit in the water supply, I want to know. If a local whore is selling information to a Malakasian spy, I want her gutted and served up with greenroot and pepperweed. I want every able-bodied farmer, merchant, sailor, fisherman, bartender, gutter-digger, fruit-picker and teacher armed and ready to defend this town, or to march on my orders. History will *not* recall that we had this opportunity and buggered it up; I don't care how many knife-wielding scullery whores they send in here to stick holes in me.' Gita stood toe-to-toe with Markus Fillin. She was a full head shorter than the Falkan farmer, but Sharr wouldn't have wanted to bet on who would win in a bar fight, especially hand-to-hand.

'Yes, ma'am,' Markus said. Sharr nodded, and ushered Stalwick towards the door.

'And find me these terrorists! Our hold on this town remains in jeopardy until we do.'

Markus saw the first fire before dawn.

Sharr was sleeping. They had been up much of the night, organising the search teams. By the middlenight aven, Markus had questioned hundreds of locals and dispatched pairs of their people to investigate nearly as many reports of suspicious strangers, unknown vagrants or potential terrorists. The people of Capehill either had no idea where twenty Malakasian warriors could have secreted themselves, or they knew exactly where to find the terrorists and were happy to lead Markus and his team to the hideouts. Naturally, each of these forays beneath the coastal town's damp underbelly yielded nothing, and Markus, falling asleep on his feet, dismissed the search deployment for a few avens' sleep.

But now he had the chance, Markus couldn't sleep. He had met Sharr back at the boarding house – they had taken the room next to Gita's, with Stalwick and Barrold in the chamber across the corridor. The big fisherman, exhausted after his heroic sprint across the town, had collapsed in his cloak and boots. He snored loudly for a few moments, then rolled onto his back, his mouth lolling open. Sharr owned an apartment near the waterfront; his wife and two sons were there, but he preferred to spend the night near Gita, on hand should another clandestine plot unfold before dawn.

Markus stirred the coals in their small fireplace, added a few bits of wood and some dried-out corn cobs Stalwick had hauled from the bin in the canning cellar, and warmed his hands. Someone shouted outside: a warning or a cry for help. Markus shuffled to the window, more out of curiosity than concern.

'Who's yelling at this aven?' he asked of no one.

A shadow, dark and quick, hustled towards the town centre. Another followed. There was a second shout, louder this time, from the direction of Argile Street, the downtown business area.

'What's this?' Markus whispered, his breath fogging the blurry pane.

Then he heard the cry again, this time from three or four streets over. *Fire!*

Someone moved in Gita's room. There was a thud, some footsteps, and then the tired creak of her window hinges, complaining in the cold.

The first orange and yellow tendrils danced in the predawn haze. A plume of thin smoke rose above the merchant district, trailing in the light breeze.

'What's wrong?' Sharr asked, without moving.

'Nothing,' Markus said. 'Go back to sleep. One of the alehouses is on fire . . . I think. I'm not sure if it's the Cask and Cork, the one we were in the other night, or the building right next door. It's hard to see from this far away.'

'Next door?' Sharr sat up and rubbed his eyes. 'Which side?' He yawned.

'Um, to the east,' Markus said. The noise outside grew as more locals and a few of Gita's Resistance soldiers hurried to fight the blaze.

'East? That's the fish market.' Sharr poured a goblet of water from the bedside pitcher. He swallowed and said, 'That's odd.'

'What's odd?'

'What's to burn at the fish market?'

Markus shrugged. 'Probably some drunk kicked a brazier over. You want to go help?'

'No.' Sharr fell back into the blankets. 'The locals can handle it. We've got to be up and on our way before the—'

'Wait,' Markus said suddenly, 'oh no, Sharr, this isn't good!'

The first fire was joined by another as the old occupation barracks near the town livery went up in flames. The sound of horses whinnying wildly joined the cries for help as smoke billowed through one of the corrals. From the window, Markus watched as stable hands ran here and there, herding the animals to safety. Then another fire, still just a flicker of colour against the whitening dawn, glowed near the waterfront. It diffused into another and then another; flames burned rooftops across the town, making Capehill look like a monstrous pyre at a holiday festival.

'That's the harbourmaster's office,' Sharr said quietly. 'And *that*—' he pointed south, 'is an assay office. There's a mining equipment shop, a glassworks, and a grain and feed store on that block.'

'Whoring Pragans.' Markus tallied the devastation as he looked across the false dawn rising over Capehill. 'That's six – no, *seven* fires we can see from here. What's happening?'

'It's them.' Sharr was up and on his way across to Stalwick's room when Gita appeared, fully dressed, in the corridor.

'You've seen outside?' she said.

'Yes,' Sharr replied. 'I want to look up north. There are more offices, some critical supply businesses there.'

'I think we've answered any lingering question about the soldiers they left behind.'

'Strike quickly. Burn what you can, and fade back into the populace,' Markus summed up. 'A cunning tactic.'

Before Sharr could knock, Barrold opened the door. He wasn't wearing his eye-patch and Markus winced at the sight of the ragged, hollow socket.

'There's ten, maybe twelve fires burning out here.' He didn't seem surprised to find the rest of them gathered, fully dressed, in the hallway.

Sharr nodded. 'It was probably all planned, or if it wasn't, they decided to move after the attempt on Gita's life failed.'

'They're using slow fuses, I'd bet,' Barrold added, 'rolled tobacco leaves will burn slowly before igniting whatever tinder they're using. It gives them time to get away.'

'On to the next target,' Markus said. 'We'll be three streets behind them all day.'

Stalwick emerged from behind Barrold. Still groggy, he didn't say anything.

'Mother of an open-sored slut!' Gita kicked at the wall, shouted an unintelligible curse, then regained her composure. 'Stalwick, go get the others, all the company commanders, even the ones from Gorsk. I want them downstairs in the front room before my tecan gets cold. Sharr, you've got to think. What else will they hit? Come up with five or six likely places that aren't in flames yet, and let's dispatch platoons – no, squads – to those locations. Be ready to brief the others when they arrive. Stalwick?'

'Yes, ma'am?'

'What are you still doing here?'

'Sorry, ma'am.' Stalwick hurried for the stairs, tightening his cloak. 'I'll just ... well, I'll just go.'

Markus smirked. 'Good show, Stalwick. Hurry back.'

'They're trying to hurt us from within,' Sharr said. 'They're a handful of soldiers, not enough to fight us. So they're attacking our food, horses, supplies, even the water won't be safe.'

'We need to catch one of these motherless bastards!' Gita was fuming. 'We'll dunk him in the harbour until he talks, make him eat broken glass!'

'I don't understand why they abandoned the town,' Barrold said. 'Why give up Capehill, flee around the Gorsk Peninsula, and then leave a squad of spies to terrorise us? What do they have to gain by making our Twinmoon here miserable? Do they really think we'll just sit around and starve, that we won't boil water or buy grain on the Central Plain? Why are they doing this?'

'I'll tell you why,' a strange voice said and someone clomped up the wooden staircase. He had the road-weary look of one who'd competed a forced march, and the soiled cloak and tattered boots to prove it. In the candlelight, his face was drawn and tired and angry. Markus knew he had seen this man before, but couldn't place him until Gita jumped up and screamed in delight.

'Brand! Thank the gods!' She ran to the stranger and threw her arms around him.

Capehill burned all day, the flames reaching skyward as vast swathes of the city, both business and residential property, were reduced to ash. Resistance squads worked with local citizens to fight the fires, but the old wooden structures, many with thatched or wooden-shingled roofs, ignited and burned so quickly that little was salvaged. Sparks blew into neighbouring homes and whole blocks were quickly lost in a fiery haemorrhage.

By midday, it was impossible to know which burning buildings were the terrorists' targets and which were collateral damage. The partisans gave up trying to predict what might burn next and directed their attention to saving what they could of the waterfront businesses, fishing boats and warehouses. Sharr ordered two apartments near the centre of the wharf torn down: the weatherbeaten wood would go up like tinder, putting the pier, the packing warehouse and the waterfront stables at risk. As the fires crept south, the burgeoning heat a harbinger of death, Sharr's soldiers fixed lines to support beams and crossbraces, chopped through key trusses and, once everything was in place, on Sharr's call, collapsed two two-storey buildings into splinter, which they then hauled away, leaving behind a breach for the fire slowly consuming the Capehill waterfront.

Sharr stole a moment to see his family safely onto his trawler, then sent them to a mooring buoy in the harbour until the conflagration was under control. His wife and sons wanted to stay and help, but Sharr had his way, arguing that they were doing their part by saving his boat, nets and traps.

By the dinner aven, most of the burning had been contained or left to consume itself. Capehill was a roadmap of hastily dug trenches and fire lines. Ponderous clouds of acrid smoke swirled over the harbour like a rogue storm. Three strangers, caught outside a textile shop, had been beaten and hanged by angry Falkans bent on revenge. With thirty-one dead, hundreds burned and nearly seventy homes and businesses lost, the people of Capehill found that their reputation for hospitality was wearing thin. No one knew if the three men dangling from a linden tree on what remained of the town green were actually Malakasians in disguise – it was too late to interrogate them – but their dangling bodies were a stark message to the Falkan leaders: life in Capehill has not improved. Gita and her Falkan Resistance soldiers would not be welcome much longer.

At the boarding house, Gita gave orders for half the companies to assist with damage control and clean-up, while the other half broke for an evening meal. They were to switch at the middlenight aven, and then resume their previous assignments, patrolling the town. The search for the Malakasians was broken off.

Sharr watched Gita climb the stairs. She had been dealt a damaging blow by a handful of Malakasians. She, like the rest of them, stank of smoke and burned pitch, and she had a blistering burn on one hand and a bloody gash across her forearm. She permitted Barrold to clean and bind her wounds while she prepared to address the officers. Sharr collapsed into a chair beside Markus; he was glad to see the young man had survived the day.

'Lose anyone?' Markus whispered.

'No,' Sharr said, 'thank the gods. You?'

'Two women from Orindale.' He swept a greasy lock away from his face, then bound his hair with a piece of leather. 'They insisted on going into one of the houses, said they heard someone yelling. I didn't hear anything.' He frowned. 'The upper floor collapsed. I heard them scream once, but then there was nothing.'

'Anyone else go inside?'

'I wouldn't let them,' Markus said. 'I figured we'd lost two already. I don't think their squadmates are very happy with me.'

'They should be thanking you.' Sharr gave his friend's wrist a reassuring squeeze. 'You probably saved their lives.'

Markus, still despondent, didn't answer.

Gita stood near the fireplace in the corner. She thanked Barrold, gave her wrist bandage a final inspection, then turned to those crowded into the room. 'Markus,' she started, 'thank your people for me. I appreciate them securing this street.' To the others, she explained, 'Markus Fillin's squads have been redeployed at either end of this block. We've had to move the sick and the injured from the building we've been using as a hospital to the upper floors of the chandler's across the street. We now have— how many crammed in there, Barrold?'

'Eighty-six, ma'am.' Her personal guard had burns of his own, along both arms and on one side of his face, just below his eye-patch, but he seemed adept at ignoring pain.

'Eighty-six injured today?'

'There were twenty-two already down with illnesses or injuries, ma'am,' he clarified. 'We had sixty-four seriously injured today.'

'And ...'

'And eight lost.'

'Eight, gods rut a whore!' Gita gripped the table with white knuckles. 'And thirty-some-odd locals. Demonshit, that's almost forty people, in one whoring day! Gods keep us!'

'Yes, ma'am.' Barrold looked down at his boots. The rest of the room was silent.

After a moment, Gita leaned over the table and sifted through a collection of maps scattered across it. She found what she was searching for, then looked up again at her officers. 'Thank you all ... for today,' she said quietly. 'Thank you.'

A few of the officers mumbled, 'Yes, ma'am.' Sharr forced a smile.

'All right.' Gita almost visibly shrugged off her grief. 'We've some information I want everyone to hear. Brand is back – he's come from Wellham Ridge – and he's been able to throw some light on why this irritating band of thugs was left behind when our Malakasian friends sailed off.'

Markus asked, 'You mean they aren't here to burn the town to the ground?'

'Ostensibly, yes, but actually, no.' Brand joined Gita by the fireplace. 'They were left here to distract us.'

'Well, they were effective,' Sharr said. 'But distract us from what?'

'From a merchant carrack, a big mother, running up the coast as we speak.'

Sharr sat up. 'A ship? Why? Headed where?'

'Pellia, and then on to Welstar Palace,' Brand said. 'They're hauling something, some kind of milled bark, treated lumber, maybe; I'm not certain exactly what. They loaded it during the last Moon, off the Ronan Peninsula, out beyond the Forbidden Forest near Estrad Village. It's a cargo that Mark Jenkins will do anything to see safely into the Welstar Palace military encampment, some critical ingredient in his recipe for devastation.'

'Who's Mark Jenkins?' asked one of the Gorsk commanders.

'Essentially, he's the acting prince of Eldarn, as powerful as – *more* powerful – than Malagon,' Brand replied.

'And how do you know these things, Brand?' Markus asked. 'And where's Kellin Mora?'

'As many of you are aware, I travelled south as part of an escort for Gilmour Stow and Steven Taylor, the sorcerers trying to retrieve a Larion artefact lost from Sandcliff Palace nearly a thousand Twin-moons ago.'

Sharr surreptitiously let his gaze wander around the table; Brand's tale was, so far, being met with little visible scepticism.

'Steven and Gilmour were able to excavate the artefact, but we lost it shortly thereafter to Mark Jenkins, who, we assume, is transporting it to Welstar Palace.'

'Along with this shipment of milled bark and leaves,' Gita finished.

'Yes . . .' He paused as someone knocked on the door, which opened to admit a young woman, a maid.

'Food, ma'am?' she asked. 'It's a good hearty stew, and the bread's fresh.'

'Thank you, yes,' Gita said, 'and let's have some jugs of beer too, please.'

'Um, how many, ma'am?' She took a cursory head-count.

'Just keep the jugs full until Sharr over there is checking me for a heartbeat,' Gita laughed.

'Very good, ma'am,' the maid said, and disappeared into the corridor.

Gita returned to business. 'Go on, Brand.'

'Kellin Mora remained behind. She's offering what protection she can to Gilmour and Steven. They also have Garec Haile, the great bowman from Rona. When I left them, they were boarding a barge for Orindale.'

'Garec worries me,' Gita said. 'When I last saw him in Traver's Notch, he seemed hesitant, as if he'd lost his edge.'

'He had,' Brand said. 'He cost me half a squad outside Wellham

Ridge, when he wouldn't fire on the advancing enemy, a platoon of them.'

'Son of a whore—' Gita began.

'But two days later, he single-handedly wiped out a squad of armoured cavalry.'

'Great gods of the Northern Forest,' Markus whispered, 'he must be a monster.'

'Actually,' Sharr said, 'he's a nice kid. You'd never know it to talk with him, but he could blind you at two hundred paces.'

Food and beer arrived, and the partisans tucked in like starving refugees. Four beers and three bowls of stew later, Sharr felt fatigue creeping up on him: it had been nearly two days since he had slept. From the head of the table, Brand, sitting now, continued his briefing between mouthfuls.

'How did you learn about the shipment?' a woman from one of the border towns in Gorsk asked.

'Outside Wellham Ridge, less than a day after I left Kellin and the others, I killed two soldiers on patrol. One of the uniforms fit me, so I rode hard across the plains, changing into my own clothing after dark to keep the locals from hanging me from the nearest tree. Wearing the uniform during daylight hours meant I was able to keep up the illusion that I was carrying dispatches.'

'Alone?'

'I wove a convincing story of injured horses and squadmates following close behind. I never stayed attached to a unit for more than half an aven or so, and I never spoke more than a few words to any of the officers. So information was relatively easy to collect. I don't believe I was ever in any real danger; everyone was hustling off somewhere: forced marches, battalions under orders to reach Orindale or Estrad Village. It wasn't until I had ridden far enough to the northeast – and found a country trail to the Merchants' Highway – that I learned of the carrack and the northbound shipment. That was five days ago, just before I left the last Malakasian company and rode for Capehill.'

'There were Malakasian soldiers on the Merchants' Highway five days ago?' Sharr asked.

'Yes, and heading south,' Brand said. 'They were bound for Rona, planning to rendezvous with General Oaklen and then ride for Orindale. It seems the order to abandon Capehill was not wholeheartedly embraced by all officers.'

'It doesn't make sense to me, either,' Gita said. 'Why give up a port town?'

'Because they're being recalled to Welstar Palace,' Brand said, 'by Mark Jenkins.'

'The one who needs this tree bark shipment?' Markus asked.

'Yes.'

'So he needs an army, one larger than the army already stationed at Welstar Palace, as well as a carrack full of magic tree bark to go along with it?'

'Why come this way?' Barrold asked.

'If they're heading for Pellia in a carrack, this is the only way,' Sharr answered. 'They're too late for the Twinmoon, even the secondary tides. They'd never make the run up the Ravenian Sea in time. Going around the archipelago is the only passage deep enough for a ship that size.'

'There's more,' Brand interrupted. 'Again, I can't be certain, and I didn't see for myself, but on two separate occasions I heard that much of Orindale had been destroyed. And if what Gilmour told me is true, I would bet ten Twinmoons of my life that it was Mark Jenkins using the Larion spell table.'

Gita emptied a jug into her tankard, then gestured for Sharr to pass her another. 'Orindale in ruins. Our families and friends lost in the wreckage,' she murmured.

'Rumour also has it that much of the merchant fleet was destroyed,' Brand added.

'And the occupation army recalled to Malakasia, except for Oaklen, who doesn't take orders from anyone in the Eastlands. So he's marching to Orindale, rallying every last footsore grunt he can find between Estrad and the northern Blackstones.' Gita stared into her tankard for a few moments. No one in the room interrupted her thoughts; some took the opportunity to light their pipes and the small room filled quickly with the heady aroma of Falkan tobacco. It was a welcome change from the stench of ashes and soot.

Gita shook her head slightly. Still staring into her beer, she whispered to herself, 'Oaklen riding for Orindale. The capital in ruins. Milled bark. A merchant carrack . . .' Her voice trailed off.

Sharr watched her, waiting for the inevitable order.

Brand asked, 'Sharr, is there a place north of here where this band of terrorists might pilot a launch into deep water?'

'You think they're getting picked up?' he answered without taking his eyes off Gita.

'I do,' Brand said. 'They're either finished here, or they have another day or two of surprises waiting for us, but they'll run, and that boat is their ticket home. Especially if those three hanging across town *are* spies. The others won't linger here much longer.'

'There's no way for them to know if their comrades talked,' Markus added.

'Exactly,' Brand finished his beer. 'So what do you think? Is there someplace they might have stashed a boat or two? Some point from which they can run like rutting madmen for a deep water pick-up?'

Sharr didn't answer.

Gita stood up. 'All of you!'

The room went silent.

'All of you, tonight, pass the word: I want us packed and ready to ride in three days. I'll need mounted dispatchers, one from each company, here by dawn. We have to get word to anyone still on their way up here that we have taken eastern Falkan ... or, rather, it was handed to us. There's nothing left for us to do in Capehill. We can rally the rest of the Resistance on the way. I want two riders from every squad assigned directly to me as a special mounted platoon. There's no telling how many farms and ranches we'll pass on the way. I want everyone to know that Capehill is free, that the port here is open, and that trade has been re-established, minus Prince Malagon's take from every single load and transaction. We need food and supplies running into this town on a schedule as predictable as the tides. Every farmer on the plains has a winter stash somewhere, something the occupation army doesn't know about. We'll have them load up their wagons; let them know they'll be well paid, but they're needed up here, now.'

'Where are we going, ma'am?' Markus asked.

'We're going to Orindale,' Gita said, 'but you're not coming, Markus.'

'Orindale?' Sharr raised an eyebrow. 'Ma'am, there's an entire division of soldiers stationed at Orindale, not to mention the Seron.'

'Not to hear Brand tell it,' Gita said, 'not any more.'

'It's true,' Brand said. 'Word across the Central Plain is that they were all taken, loaded onto ships; every Malakasian navy vessel afloat on the Ravenian Sea is making for the Northern Archipelago and the Northeast Channel.'

'And no officer resisted?' Sharr looked askance at Gita.

'Like I said, Mark Jenkins is a powerful and dangerous man.'

Gita paced alongside the table, back and forth, talking aloud to the floor. 'That has to be why Oaklen is recalling the Ronan occupation forces. There's no one minding the store. The old fart must have shat his leggings when he heard those ships sailed north—'

'Or when he read the dispatch ordering him home to Pellia,' Brand added.

'So what?' Sharr pressed. 'We'll ride to Orindale, securing shipping and farming agreements along the way? And then what? We battle General Oaklen and whomever he has left in the Eastlands?'

'If the people of Orindale haven't already done it for us, Sharr, yes we do,' Gita said. 'But, like Markus, you're not coming.'

'Why not?' Markus asked.

She stopped pacing. 'Because you, Sharr and Brand have another assignment.'

Despite his growing weariness, Sharr Becklen stood straight. 'What assignment, ma'am?'

'You're to sink that carrack,' she said determinedly, the light of battle in her eyes.

KEDGING OFF

'Do you think Mark is in Pellia yet?' Brexan asked Gilmour. Through the wispy fog they could see the coastal forests of Malakasia, the tall trees standing silent sentry. At slack tide, the winds had died and an eerie silence crept over the narrow channel Captain Ford and his remaining crewmembers were charting through the archipelago. With nothing but a few stripes of breakwater between them and the shoreline, Brexan worried that hard aground on a muddy shoal, the *Morning Star* – looking more like a shipwreck than a seaworthy vessel – would be reported by a passing military patrol or a fishing trawler.

As if reading her mind, the captain ordered the Malakasian colours run up the halyard; that ruse might buy them a few avens. Eventually, though, someone would wonder what a brig-sloop was doing working its way through the sandbars, atolls and mud flats off the northeast coast.

The deck canted to starboard. Gilmour hung onto the rail in an effort to maintain his balance. 'No,' he said, 'Mark had a few days' head start, but we were able to come up the coast fast and I don't believe he'll be much further than the initial tacks through the Northeast Channel.'

'So we may reach Pellia before he does?'

Watching the process the captain called kedging off, Gilmour shrugged. 'That depends on how long we spend dragging ourselves through these shallows.'

Brexan agreed. 'It doesn't look like the quickest route, does it?'

'We need to be a bit luckier than we were this morning,' he said.

'That's not very heartening.' Brexan had been on deck when the brig-sloop ran aground. She was sure it hadn't been Captain Ford's fault – the *Morning Star* had been tacking towards a narrow channel between an island and a jumble of rocks Marrin had spotted from aloft. There had appeared to be enough draft for the brig-sloop to pass, even with the receding tide, but just as the captain was bringing the bow about, the topgallants – they were the only sheets he would permit Marrin to set – had caught a vagrant gust from the southeast. Under normal conditions, it would have been nothing, but arriving when it did, just as they were tacking northeast, the rogue breeze had shoved the *Morning Star* just far enough for her bow to catch in the shallows.

An aven later, the tide was out, the rocks Marrin had seen were above the surface and the narrow passage between them and the island was looking a hair's-breadth too thin for the brig-sloop. Once off the sandbar, Captain Ford would have only one chance to thread the needle.

Brexan watched as Garec and Marrin rowed the ship's launch into deeper water, looking comically like a crew in search of a ship as they sat on either side of the *Morning Star*'s anchor. The great metal claw had been lowered gingerly from the cathead and now rested against the bench. It dragged a length of hawser from the capstan to the channel between the island and the rock formation. 'I wonder why he doesn't wait for the tide to come back in,' Brexan mused.

Gilmour pointed towards the shore; though there was not a building to be seen, it was still risky being within hailing distance of Malakasia, especially while immobile. 'I don't think Captain Ford likes having his ship stuck in the mud, Brexan,' he said, 'and I don't know if he needs more water than we have now to work his way through that little passage.'

'It does look skinny, doesn't it?'

'I believe that's why Garec and Marrin are out there.'

Brexan and Gilmour were been whispering. It seemed an appropriate morning for whispering. Both jumped when Marrin, almost out of sight in the grey fog, called in for instructions.

'Captain,' Marrin said, surprisingly loud, 'there's plenty of draft, but I'm worried about whether she'll fit.'

'She'll fit.' Ford's voice was low but resonant; Brexan wondered how far it would carry in the fog. She was reminded of the bells she had heard from the porch at the Topgallant Inn and flashed back to Jacrys Marseth, dipped in blood, trailing blood, but still ringing that whoring bell.

'We'll row through,' Marrin called back. 'We have enough line, and if I can find a decent handful of rocks on the other side, we'll pull her through with the capstan.'

'My thoughts exactly,' Captain Ford said dryly.

'You are the commanding officer, after all,' Marrin teased from inside the burgeoning fogbank.

'Ha!' Ford said, 'and generally the last one to give the orders around here.'

'Yes sir!' Marrin, now completely lost from view, shouted. 'You just keep the old girl on a strict diet while the Ronan killer and I snake through this little stream you've discovered.'

'Good enough,' Ford said. 'We are thinking thin thoughts.'

'Captain Ford?' Garec called, 'once we get the anchor set, I can drown him if you like.'

'Nothing would please me more,' Ford replied with a laugh.

To Brexan his good humour seemed forced, another mask he fashioned while above decks to keep his crew in good spirits. He, like the rest of them, was mourning the loss of three crew to the shapeshifting tan-bak. Losing Kanthil, Sera – *had it eaten her? Or just cast her over the side?* – and finding what was left of Tubbs had caused something inside the captain to come loose. Now sneaking along the coast like this, dousing the lanterns and running the blockade all smacked of retribution, something owed to the crew. While giving Tubbs his rites, Captain Ford told Brexan his crew believed in him because they knew that he was a man motivated by just two things: paying them well and seeing them safely home. This voyage had violated an edict he and his crew – *his family* – had agreed upon Twinmoons earlier. It was the reason so many of them shipped with him season after season: *they do it together, and they go home together.* Chasing a pocketful of easy silver, Ford had gone against his own core values – and he had lost friends as a result.

Reaching Pellia now, even if he had to get out and push the old ship through the shallows, was the only way he could earn himself a measure of redemption.

'Got it,' Marrin shouted.

'What's he done?' Brexan asked.

'He's found a place where he and Garec can lodge that anchor. With that done, and the rest of us manning the capstan like all the gods of the Northern Forest are whipping our backsides, hopefully, the ship will pull itself right through.'

'Kedging off?'

'Kedging off.'

'That seems pretty risky in a ship this size,' Brexan said.

'Again, my dear, I leave that to Captain Ford; he seems capable.'

'Yes, he does,' Brexan mused, watching Ford lean over the rail, straining to see through the fog. She imagined that Versen might have grown to look and act similarly one day. Brexan couldn't allow herself to get personally involved with Doren Ford. Regardless of how obvious it had become that he might welcome a relationship, however ephemeral, she fought the urge to cross the deck and wrap her arms around him, to feel his muscled body against hers. Becoming intimate with him would be too much like making love with a shadowy, older version of Versen. It wouldn't be fair to the captain to use him to recapture what she had lost.

After a moment, Captain Ford called, 'Come back and wait near those rocks. If anything is going to get us, it'll be that bunch, and we can't see them as clearly as we could half an aven ago.'

'Blame Garec,' Marrin replied, 'he rows too bloody slow.'

'It wasn't my idea to row over here with an anchor *in* the boat!' Garec said. 'I'm not much of a sailor, but I've been around the water enough to know that anchors are supposed to go *outside* the boat.'

'That's a good tip,' he called back. 'Now shut yourselves up and hustle back to those rocks. I want to be out of here and on our way as soon as possible.'

'Ah, Captain?' Marrin's voice was ethereal through the fog; it came from everywhere at once.

Ford shook his head. 'What now, Marrin?'

'Have you noticed the fog, sir?'

'Three hundred Twinmoons I've been at sea, Marrin. Of course I've noticed the rutting fog!'

'Well, sir, how are you planning on getting underway in this fog? There's rocks and shoals and mud and shit out here, not to mention the islands. There's *hundreds* of those lying about. We're bound to run into something. Not that this morning was your fault, but sir, there's a lot out here to hit; this place needs a clean-up, and I mean in a raging hurry.'

'We'll be fine making way through the fog,' he said.

'Again, begging your pardon, sir, but how?'

'You and Garec are going to guide us,' he said calmly.

Neither answered, but from their silence it was apparent that they weren't looking forward to spending the day rowing blind, especially with the *Morning Star* in tow.

Kellin and Steven emerged from below and joined Captain Ford at the rail, looking for Garec.

'Can you see them?' Kellin asked.

'Not right now,' he answered, 'but if you follow that length of

378

anchor line into the fog, you can get a fix on them. They're out behind those rocks.'

'Is this dangerous?'

He shook his head. 'Not much. We won't get far, but the bit we navigate before high tide will be slow enough that if we should run aground again, it won't be too bad.'

'We won't sink?'

The captain laughed. 'There's no place to sink, Kellin. On tip-toe you could just about walk to Pellia from here. I thank the gods that you all drink so much. If we had even an extra few crates of beer on board, we'd have to toss them over the side for fear of being too heavy.'

Kellin smiled in return. 'That would be a tragic waste.'

'Anyway, once we get a bit of water coming north again, we'll be able to make better time, but for now, this journey is going to get a touch tedious.' Garec and Marrin appeared through the gloom. 'Ah, there they are,' the captain said, then hailing them, called, 'There's fine. We'll heave her off. Marrin, watch that line. Shout for your mother if it breaks off or pulls free. I don't want us floating around up here.'

'Very good, sir. I'm sure my mother will be happy to help.'

Kellin laughed, then waved to Garec. 'Good morning.'

'Well, hello.' Garec blew her a kiss. 'What's a nice Falkan girl like you doing in a shithole like this?'

Kellin said, 'I understand it's an excellent place to meet eligible young men.'

Marrin interrupted, 'So they told you I was here? Stand fast, my dear: as soon as I'm through rescuing Captain Ford's broken-down old barge I'll be back to sweep you thoroughly off your feet.'

Captain Ford said, 'Garec . . .'

'Now's fine with me, sir,' Garec shouted back.

'Go right ahead – but one thing: you realise with him gone, you'll become my first mate.' He winced, regretting the joke the moment the words left his mouth. No one said anything. Tubbs and Sera's loss was still too close, too raw for this degree of levity. The time for joking had passed, at least for now. After a moment, he announced, 'To the capstan; let's get her out of here.'

Everyone moved at once, happy to have something to do. Brexan joined Ford at the rail. 'Captain,' she started, 'I want to—'

'No,' he cut her off, 'please, just help me at the capstan. We'll be through this channel in a moment. It's going to be a long day.'

'Of course,' she said. As she helped to take up the slack in the anchor-line, Brexan was able to see the way the capstan worked. With six wooden levers rigged at right angles from one another, they all pushed and rotated the great spindle, reeling in the hawser Garec and Marrin had dragged through the channel. Once taut, the capstan fought back, grinding to a halt as the full weight of the *Morning Star* came to bear on the anchor line.

'Great rutters,' Kellin said, 'but this ship didn't look that heavy!'

'With your nose buried in the mud, you'd be hard to extract as well,' Captain Ford said. 'Keep at it, though. She'll come loose.' He grunted encouragement.

'Use your legs,' Gilmour instructed, straining as well. 'Get your backs into it.'

The company pushed and heaved, pressing against the unwieldy capstan with all their might. Even wiry young Pel hurried from the quarterdeck to help break the muddy seal.

'I want you at the helm, Pel,' the captain ordered, his face flushed and sweaty.

'I'm doing no good there, Captain,' Pel said. It was about the only thing Brexan had heard him say since their departure from Orindale. The quiet young man, when not swabbing the brig-sloop from bow to stern, was generally to be found in the rigging, checking cleats, mending frayed ratlines and keeping a wary eye out for the navy. The last encounter had scared him to within a few breaths of the Northern Forest, and simply watching Steven pith the tan-bak had started the Pragan seaman quaking all over again. Talking only to the captain, and keeping his head down, the shy youngster said, 'I'll be back as soon as we get her loose, but let me help.'

The anchor line was taut, as tight as the small group of determined travellers could manage. Brexan waited for something to snap, or for the anchor to pull free from its place in the rocks behind the fog. With only wood, hemp and muscle in the equation, something had to give; the strain was too great.

Finally, groaning in protest, the *Morning Star* moved, just a slight shift to starboard at first. Brexan felt the capstan spin, taking in a bit of line as the deck righted itself.

'One more like that should do it,' the captain encouraged. 'Pel, get back to the helm, now.'

As quickly as he had arrived, the youngster was gone.

Captain Ford called after him, 'Bring the keel to starboard, just enough to get our backside clear, but as soon as she breaks off, get her back to port. I don't want us off the mud and onto those rocks, understand?'

'Aye aye, Captain,' Pel shouted over his shoulder.

'Marrin!' he cried.

'Captain?' The reply came from somewhere over the side.

'Get ready!' On his mark, everyone redoubled their efforts. 'Here we come!'

With that, the hull slipped free, the capstan spun easily, unexpectedly, and both Steven and Kellin fell to their knees, cursing.

The captain was gone, calling, 'Keep taking up the slack, not too fast now, just keep it coming in steady. Then pawl that and wait for me amidships.' From the rail, he checked their heading, then ordered, 'Pel, back to port now, back to port.'

The *Morning Star* bobbed in the channel, turning to take in her anchor line and waiting for a northerly breeze. With another half-aven of slack water, they would have ample time to get through the narrow passage and reset the anchor before another sudden gust threatened to leave them in the mud or push them onto the rocks.

Taking the helm, Captain Ford watched as his crew of seamen and partisans reeled in the anchor line, then guided the brig-sloop carefully through the channel, beyond the island and into deeper, if still fogbound, water.

When the *Morning Star* passed the rocks, Marrin called, 'I didn't think you could do it, Captain, but she's clear.'

Smiling, he said, 'I told you we were thinking thin thoughts!'

Steven said, 'That's more work than I expected to do today.'

'You and me both, cousin,' Gilmour agreed, 'but I don't think we're finished yet.'

'Grand.' Kellin wiped her forehead on her tunic sleeve. 'Don't you two know anything that might help us speed this process up a bit?'

'Nothing we can risk right now,' Steven said. 'With any luck, Mark is honed in on the magic keeping that ... whatever it was—'

'Tan-bak,' Gilmour supplied.

'Keeping that tan-bak alive out there somewhere. We're in enough danger simply from the fact that he might stumble across the mystical energy coming from the far portal and the spell book down in the cabin.'

Brexan said, 'I thought that with Carpello's shipments running north, Mark wouldn't notice the difference between a ship loaded with that Ronan tree bark and one with your Larion toys.'

'We have to hope not,' Gilmour said, 'but judging from our trip thus far, we haven't been very lucky at keeping ourselves invisible. I made a mistake the day we encountered that naval cruiser. I don't know if that's why Mark sent the tan-bak, but I'm unwilling to risk using magic again until we are closer to Pellia. Once there, I'm betting we can use a bit of sorcery and Mark won't be any wiser.'

'Because it will ... what? Mix with the other magic already in Pellia?'

'Correct,' Gilmour said, 'if even one of those shipments is moored in the harbour – and with the tides and the traffic in the Northeast Channel, we have to hope that at least one of them was delayed – my magic shouldn't make much noise at all.'

'But he detected enough powerful magic to decide to destroy that other ship and then send the tan-bak for us,' Brexan said hesitantly. 'Won't he do that again?'

'I don't think so,' Gilmour replied. 'When the Malakasian sorcerer was having at us from his ship, his spells were noisy, like pebbles dropped into a dead-calm mill pond. When I cast the spell protecting Steven, it was a bigger pebble, like a small stone.'

'And Mark felt the difference,' Kellin said.

'He did. But the schooner I discovered from Wellham Ridge was radiating so much energy, I believe I could be hammering away with everything I have and Mark wouldn't be able to tell the difference.'

Brexan untied her cloak and draped it over the forward hatch. 'So a shipment is like a big rock in your mill pond.'

'A boulder,' Gilmour agreed. 'Once we get near Pellia, if we're lucky, Mark will have no idea that we're still alive, still after him.'

'And then what?' Kellin looked at him expectantly.

'By then, it won't matter. If we can't sneak into the city, we'll have to go in the front door, and that will mean using everything in our arsenal.'

Kellin recalled their battle in Meyers' Vale, and for the first time all Twinmoon, the idea that she was travelling with two deadly sorcerers was comforting.

Brexan broke the silence. 'Tell me about that book, Gilmour. What's it say? What's in there?'

The familiar look of uncertainty passed across Gilmour's face. He checked on Garec and Marrin's progress, then said, 'A very long time ago in Gorsk, a man named Lessek—'

'*The* Lessek?' Brexan interrupted, 'as in all the stories we heard when we were young?'

'That's him.' Gilmour rooted in his tunic for a pipe and, unable to

382

find one, looked suddenly like a two-thousand-Twinmoon-old man who didn't know what to do with his hands. Giving up, he went on, 'Lessek used an exceedingly small bit of . . . well, call it magic, coupled with his knowledge to create spells. At first, they were nothing terribly impressive, so I understand – this was Ages and Eras before I was born – but he learned to move air around a room, to wilt a flower, to get water to freeze, carnival tricks, really, but over time, he continued his research and generated a long list of spells. He would investigate the nature of something, study it, interact with it, pick it apart – sometimes even tear it apart, and then use aspects of his previous spellwork to create a bigger and more powerful incantation.'

'Common phrase spells?' Steven asked.

'Exactly,' Gilmour replied, 'spells with parts of various incantations in common so as to harness exponential power, layered magic.'

'Good gods,' Kellin whispered.

'When you think about it, there were few greater discoveries in the history of Eldarn. It's the innovation that made magic such a dominant force in our cultural history. You two have never been to Steven's world, where there's little history of magical innovation, so the culture there is based on religion, common social values and traditions, the family, and democratic and economic ideals. Magic has played almost no role at all in defining who they are; actually, the extent of its thread through the fabric of Steven's cultural history is as entertainment, and it appears in a handful of religious stories. But here, Lessek's contributions to Eldarni history, as a researcher and a scholar, are just that: he made magic one of the building blocks of Eldarni culture. It is a stone in the foundation of who we are.'

Brexan said, 'So before Lessek, there was no magic?'

'Oh, there was plenty—' Gilmour gestured as if the seeds of cultural mysticism were all around them, 'but its purpose had not yet come into focus. It was potential energy, freely floating, essentially useless until Lessek channelled it together.'

'So the book is a listing of his spells?' Brexan jumped ahead.

'Actually, no,' Gilmour said. 'You see, what Lessek did was more than generate an array of spells. By bringing magic to the forefront of Eldarni social development, he started a rock rolling down a mountain. There was no way to stop it; people saw what magic could offer, the role it could play in their lives: in education and medicine, in warfare and yes, even entertainment. Over time, they embraced the notion that magic would be going on around them all the time. It went from something people feared to something they accepted, and a few of them discovered that with training, they could wield it.'

'The Larion Senators,' Kellin said.

'Right,' Steven broke in, 'recognising that there were people amongst them who could perform magic – everyday people, neighbours and friends – would have made it easier for anyone to accept magic and its widening impact.'

'Yes and no,' Gilmour said. 'Like anything difficult to understand, magic had its naysayers, and a sad number of sorcerers were outcasts, ostracised by their communities.'

'But I'd wager they were all there, lined up and waiting for their due, when it came time to heal the sick, to bring in a bumper crop or to revolutionise the shipping industry,' Steven added.

Gilmour shrugged. 'People will be people.'

'Nice to know nothing's really different.'

'You sound like Mark.'

'Go on, Gilmour,' Brexan said, 'you still haven't told us about the spells in the book.'

'Right, sorry, the book.' Gilmour waved to Garec through the fog, then said, 'The book is a spell book, but at the same time, it's more than a spell book.'

'Great, that's helpful. Thanks, Gilmour. Anyone know what's for breakfast?' Brexan grinned. 'I hope you're going to elaborate a bit for us.'

'If you'll give me a chance,' he said, smiling himself. 'There are spells in that volume that are evident, while others are hidden, though implied, just waiting for the right reader to come along and take them for his or her use. It is a comprehensive look at the nature of magic and mysticism, but it doesn't read like a normal book. Granted, the pages are filled with Lessek's handwriting, but it's what lies between the pages and within the pages that makes this particular book so powerful.'

'I still don't understand,' Kellin said. 'So the book carries more than just the words on the pages?'

'Oh, great gods, yes. That book is the gateway to worlds and worlds of information on magic and mystical energy. You see, Lessek's work didn't end with the general acceptance of magic as a fundamental tenet in Eldarni culture. Instead, he went on researching, studying, experimenting and improving his ability to tap into the magics of our world, and of worlds beyond the Fold, as evidenced by our new friends from Colorado.'

'Stop it; I'm blushing,' Steven teased.

'With Lessek's leadership, the Larion Senate was able to find, tap and retrieve magic from planes of existence, memory, emotion, good and evil that we can barely imagine. It was a boom that so changed Eldarn there was no going back. The Larion Senate, a group of mystics, many of whom had been thrown out of their communities, were suddenly the world's teachers and leaders. They had to be; no one else could understand, never mind manipulate, that power.'

'It sounds like things were taking a turn for the worse,' Kellin said.

'They would have, if Lessek hadn't invented a safe means by which to tap into the reservoir of power the Larion Senate had accumulated. With that done, tension and fear in the five lands eased, and Eldarn breathed a sigh of relief.'

'That was the spell table?' Brexan asked.

'Exactly,' Steven said. 'It was an elaborate . . . safe deposit box, for lack of a better term.'

'So the book tells how to operate the table?' Brexan said.

'I wish it were that easy,' Gilmour replied. 'No, the book outlines magic's place in Eldarni culture. It uses Lessek's spells coupled with aspects of Eldarni history, social innovation, creativity and a variety of other common values and cultural cornerstones to describe the very nature of the magic Lessek and the Larion Senate were able to amass in the spell table.'

'So, the good and the bad,' Kellin said, looking for Garec herself.

'More than that,' Gilmour said. 'It describes the possible and the impossible, the nebulous regions between the real and the unreal, the future and the past, the truth as concrete, hard and fast and the truth as malleable, uncertain and out of reach. The book is legendary for sometimes showing what a sorcerer *wants* to know and other times what a sorcerer *needs* to know. There have even been times – although I can't say for certain if this truly happened – when the book showed a sorcerer something false and led the poor sod astray.'

'Just to be funny? It makes jokes?' Brexan was confused.

'Because understanding what is true, real and necessary is often enhanced by one's ability to recognise something unreal, something untrue. Success can only be recognised as the opposite side of failure; without knowing failures and lies, one cannot appreciate successes and truths. The book understands that, and we, even we sorcerers, cannot dictate how magic and knowledge interact. It is a relationship that they form and that they foster. Our lot as the Larion Senate was to try and understand it well enough to tap its power in service to Eldarn.'

'And you did,' Kellin said.

'For a long time, yes.' Gilmour sighed. 'But now, a sorcerer with all the knowledge that I have, with all the experience that I have, and with all the conviction that I have, plans to open the table and use it against Eldarn.'

'Will it stand for that?'

'I don't think it cares.' Gilmour pursed his lips. 'That may be the reason Lessek wanted us to understand magic on a comprehensive level. It wasn't enough to be able to work a few spells and help a few people. We were harnessing an energy source, a power unlike anything we had ever seen, certainly more than most of us could comprehend. Our strongest and most promising practitioner, an old friend of mine named Nerak, pushed too far, and it swallowed him in an instant. It is the energy of life, death, creation and destruction; it is raw emotion and raw power.'

'Can you read the book?' Kellin asked.

Gilmour sighed again. 'To be honest, I haven't tried in about a Twinmoon.'

'Why not?'

'Well, the last couple of times I opened it, Nerak knew, and he used my wide-eyed innocence against me.' Gilmour searched for the right words, then said simply, 'It hurt . . . a lot.'

'Wide-eyed innocence?' Brexan said.

'Yes, actually.' Gilmour was amused. 'For a two-thousand-Twinmoon-old grettan, I have relatively limited experience with magic on this level. Granted, I spent hundreds of Twinmoons hiding all over the Eastlands, generating and experimenting with common-phrase magic, but before our battle on the *Prince Marek*, I'd only seen the book a few times in my life. Nerak had it at Welstar Palace. Any other copies, if there are other copies, were either hidden there or destroyed.'

'How about you, Steven?' Kellin asked. 'Can you read it?'

Steven chuckled. 'I'm able to open the pages and look through it, but much of what it says seems like gibberish to me. I can't understand it at all.'

'But you can touch it; you can flip through it, look at the writing, feel the pages, and nothing leaps out to cripple you, pull at your beard or slap you stupid?'

'The first time I touched the book was on the *Prince Marek*, the night I went back for Lessek's key. I had just begun to tap the power Nerak sublimated into Kantu's old walking stick—'

'That hickory staff?' Kellin interrupted.

'Yes, the one from the glen, but I hadn't come to grips with the suggestion that there might be magic inside me, that I might be one of those rare few who – Twinmoons ago – would have been driven out of my town or shipped off to Sandcliff Palace to join the Larion Senate. When I touched the book that night, it tried to take me.'

'Take you?' Brexan recoiled.

'Engulf me, swallow me whole, I don't know, drag me into oblivion, just for fun. It was phenomenal power; I felt it through my fingertips, everything all at once, everything Gilmour just described, the essence of the book, not just what's written on its pages.'

'So it reached out to you with something true, something false, some joke, what?' Brexan asked.

'I think it reached out to him with everything about itself, about magic,' Gilmour tried to clarify. 'The book understood Steven's potential, long before Steven did, and whether it was communicating with him or trying to purloin his power for itself, the book definitely embraced him with more than just the words written on the pages.' He grinned. 'From one perspective, it was quite an honour for Steven.'

'To be absorbed into the comprehensive essence of magic?' Kellin said. 'No thanks; I'm full.'

Brexan laughed. 'So why can you read it now?'

'I hit a speed bump,' Steven said. 'Lessek's key taught me, by kicking me solidly in the backside, several times, how to recognise the key elements in any magical equation.'

'Equation?'

He shrugged. 'I'm a mathematician; it makes sense to me that way. I was in the garbage dump near my home, preparing myself to spend the next ten Twinmoons digging through rotten meat and broken glass, when the key taught me how to separate what's important from what's not, essentially.'

'What happened?'

'The less important parts blurred together.' He frowned. 'I guess I did it ... I *do* it to them.'

'Do what?'

'Blur them, take them out of the equation so the key variables can come into focus, and then manipulate them based on my knowledge and whatever magic happens to come bursting out of me at the time.' He raised an eyebrow at Gilmour, who smiled and nodded. 'Anyway, after that day, I was able to flip through the book. It was as if on our second meeting, the book recognised that I had grown a good deal in my understanding of my own magic.'

'But you still can't read it,' Brexan persisted.

'Not really, no.'

'And Gilmour, you haven't felt comfortable opening it.'

'The last time I opened it, the book spewed forth a coil of other-worldly serpents armed with a poison so toxic that I had to abandon my former body and go in search of a new host.' He posed comically, then said, 'But to answer your question, no, I haven't been thrilled about opening it again.'

'So do we consider it an asset?' Brexan went on, 'if no one can use it to help us?'

'No one can use it against us, either,' Steven pointed out.

'I suppose that's true,' Brexan said.

'And who knows?' Gilmour added, 'between now and the end of this struggle, it may become necessary to use the book's information again.'

'Information,' Brexan mused.

'Exactly,' Gilmour said, 'more information than power. Granted, it's a monstrously powerful tome, but its purpose is educational.'

From beneath the bow, Marrin called, 'Steven, Kellin, anyone!'

Steven hugged the bowsprit, leaned over and said, 'Since you're going out, I'll take a tube of mint toothpaste.'

Marrin frowned. 'Rutting foreigners!'

Garec grinned. 'They move in and just ruin the village.'

'What do you need?' Steven asked.

'I need a pot of tecan and a burning brazier,' Garec said. 'It's gods-rutting freezing down here.'

'Please tell Captain Ford to leave the anchor in place for now,' Marrin said. 'We'll row over there, around the west side of that big island. It shouldn't take us long to get there and back, but I want you to know where we're going in case this fog gets any worse when the tide starts moving again.'

'Shouldn't it blow north?'

'It probably will, but I want him to know where we've gone in case it doesn't. And don't worry, Garec has a lovely singing voice. If it gets thick, we'll give you a holler.'

'Oh, I understand,' Steven said. 'You don't want us moving from here—'

'Because there might not be enough draft around that island, because you might run aground again between here and there, because

I don't want to lose you in the fog, but mostly because I don't want you losing *us* in the fog.'

Garec smirked. 'The last sounds you hear are your own bones breaking.'

'Got it.' Steven tallied their orders. 'Don't get lost, don't run aground, but most of all, don't run over the little boat with the big boat.'

'Very good,' Marrin smiled. 'We'll make a sailor of you yet. Could you pass that along to our fearless leader?'

'Right away,' Steven started aft.

At the capstan, Brexan asked, 'When Prince Malagon, Nerak, came to Orindale, was he heading for Sandcliff Palace?'

'I thought he was,' Gilmour said, 'because I thought that's where he would go to operate the spell table.'

'But he had actually come to Orindale, because he was going into the Blackstone foothills to retrieve the spell table?'

'It was his understanding that Steven and I were making way for Orindale, hoping to secure a transport to Malakasia, or at least Praga, to search for Hannah Sorenson. Nerak acted under the assumption that with a military blockade on the town, we would either be captured, killed or forced to wait on the outskirts, while he searched for us, killed us and took the keystone. His spies and minions had failed to collect it for him, so Nerak decided to come and get it himself.'

'But you didn't have it, because Steven and Mark had forgotten it back in Colorado?'

'Overlooked it.'

'Rutting whores.'

'My sentiments exactly, my dear.'

'But his plan was to have the key, get the table and open the Fold from the Blackstone foothills?'

'Or at least have the key to experiment with the table on his way back to Pellia.'

'Which is essentially what Mark is doing right now.'

'Essentially.'

'So why did Nerak bring the book with him?'

A moment of silence passed between them. Brexan pulled her hood up and flinched as beads of icy condensation trickled beneath her hair and down the back of her neck.

Finally, Gilmour said, 'I don't know why. Perhaps Nerak was studying the spells, trying to round out his understanding of magic. Perhaps the book had shown him something he believed he would need in order to open the Fold—'

'Or,' Kellin interrupted, 'the book showed him something he believed he would need *after* he opened the Fold.'

Silenced by that possibility, Gilmour recoiled from his memory of the spell book's opening folio. *The Ash Dream,* he thought. *What in all Eldarn is the Ash Dream? Something Mark needs to open the Fold? Something we need to close it for ever? Or maybe Kellin's right and he needs it after his master's arrival.* Staring down at a nebulous cloud of chilly fog as it billowed about his legs, Gilmour said, 'You may be right. The book might have shown Nerak something he would need after he opened the Fold and ushered in an Age of unbridled pain, torture and suffering.'

Kellin blanched, looking as though she was about to retch. 'Oh,' she said. 'In that case, we'll just have to get to Mark before he has a chance to ... to do ... that.'

'That's why we're here, freezing, in this godsforsaken archipelago.'

Brexan looked aft. Most of the Pragan brig-sloop was lost from view; the parts she could see – a few ratlines, the mainmast, a hatch and a stretch of starboard gunwale – looked like bits of a derelict ghost ship. 'Gilmour, are you confident that Nerak actually read the book? Was he able to understand it, to glean anything from it?'

'I don't know,' he replied. 'From what Steven said, Nerak was not nearly as powerful as his legend would have us believe, but it was my experience that he had a good deal more power and knowledge, at least in a mystical arena, than anyone I had ever known.'

'More than you?'

'Oh, certainly more than I ever did.'

'More than Steven?'

Gilmour tried to hide a half-smile. It didn't work. 'No, not more than Steven.'

Brexan smiled herself and glanced aft again. 'Would Nerak have been able to help us now?'

'What's that?'

'If Steven had kept him here, kept him alive somehow, do you think Nerak would have been able to help us close the Fold?' Seeing Gilmour hesitate, Brexan tried to clarify her thoughts. 'From what Steven and Kellin said, right in the moments before he was cast into oblivion, Nerak was different: beaten, submissive, I don't know, maybe less homicidal and power-hungry.'

Gilmour nodded, obviously contemplating his former colleague's demeanour that day in the glen. 'That's true, Brexan, but Steven had made an effort to be compassionate. He gave Nerak the hickory staff. I thought he was insane to do it; we all did. But he gave Nerak the chance to save himself, and instead Nerak used the staff to strike out at him. With the staff, he might have saved himself, banished the evil holding him prisoner, even been restored to his former position of grace and respect. But he ignored Steven's mercy, and that more than anything was what killed him.'

'Was Nerak evil before the terrible essence emerged from the Fold to take him prisoner? How long before his fall did he try to kill you, or to kill the other one ... what's his name ... Kantu?'

Gilmour frowned. 'I don't know exactly, but there was some time before Sandcliff fell that I feared Nerak. I always worried when Kantu, Pikan or I travelled through the far portal. I felt anxious that he was using our absence as an opportunity to develop spells that would kill us or perhaps trap us on the other side of the Fold for ever.'

'So no, then,' Brexan said.

'No, what?'

'No, Nerak probably wouldn't have helped us banish this evil essence and seal off the Fold.'

'No,' Gilmour shook his head, 'most likely not.'

Brexan felt the cold seep inside her cloak. 'I'll get us some tecan,' she said, shivering.

'That would be nice,' Gilmour said, glad for the change of topic. 'Biggest mugs you can find.'

Warmed by the morning brew and empowered by the truths Brexan and Kellin had forced him to examine while kedging the *Morning Star* off the Malakasian shoal, Gilmour Stow of Estrad excused himself from the chilly partisans still watching the fogbank for Garec and Marrin and tiptoed into the companionway leading to his berth, and the leatherbound book of Lessek's writings. Gilmour rarely felt old, but this morning, despite living inside the youngest host he had purloined in nearly a thousand Twinmoons, his body was stiff, cramped, feeling as if it might disintegrate without warning. His shoulders were sore; his lower back ached. One knee was inflamed, while the other had stiffened with the dampness and fog. His fingers felt swollen, clumsy and arthritic, and his eyes were a beat slow, managing to focus on what he had been seeing a step or two after it had fallen behind him. Being two thousand Twinmoons old was not normally physically gruelling – if it was, Gilmour would have been worn to the bone, dead several times over. Instead, it was an intellectual distance run, a tiresome and wearying adventure, and this morning, with his shortcomings and challenges neatly outlined by the curious freedom fighters, Gilmour felt the *emotional* exhaustion in every muscle and bone in his body.

It was a symptom of his fatigue; he knew that, and he knew that a few avens' sleep would have him back in fighting form. But he hadn't been able to rest; he wanted to finish just one last thing before retiring for the day. Then, he would sleep until the dinner aven, resting like the dead. *Or the very nearly dead, anyway*, he thought with a wry smile.

But first, he had to read that book, despite his aches and pains. It hadn't been the actual book lashing out at him; first it had been Nerak, then Mark. The book hadn't done it ... *I hope not, anyway*. There was no reason to fear the writings. He had explained that to Brexan just moments earlier: the book wasn't power per se; the book was knowledge, understanding, and whether or not it told him anything useful this morning, Gilmour didn't care. It wasn't useful information he required; it was confidence. His conversation with the freedom fighters had kindled a tiny bundle of hope, just a faint glow, wrapped in the protective layers he invariably applied whenever hope was all he had. But this morning, Gilmour wanted more; he wanted to feel that hope burgeon into a comforting blaze, something to keep him warm for the few days it would take Captain Doren Ford and his skeleton crew to see them into Pellia.

'Just read the damned book,' he murmured to himself. 'What can happen? Mark won't notice; we're too close already, and he's following the tan-bak. Even I can feel the tan-bak when I search for her. She's like a bloody beacon in a storm out there. He won't bother looking here; we're nowhere near the Northeast Channel, essentially invisible, so there's no excuse. Just read the whoring thing, and then go to bed.'

Crunch.

His tired eyes had overlooked it, brought it into focus a moment too late for his mind to care, but when his foot came down on it, Gilmour stopped to see what he had stepped on.

It was an insect – a roach? A beetle, maybe? He scraped up what he could, but he hadn't been the first to step on it.

It's just a bug, old man. Leave it, and go get your reading done.

But something was wrong. Gilmour felt the warmth leave his body, that quiet glimmer of hope fading. He absentmindedly tugged at one of his earlobes and then felt around inside his ear, tentatively, as if afraid of what he might discover.

The spell book forgotten, his fatigue ignored yet again, Gilmour tucked the insect's remains inside his tunic and went back on deck.

Alen and Milla walked along the riverfront quay, heading for the Hunter's Glade, a quiet café that served a cheap midday meal and whose proprietor, a childless woman named Gisella, fawned on the little sorceress as if Milla was a member of her own family. Alen had found the café one evening while seeking information about barge traffic along the Welstar River. When Gisella discovered that Alen had a little girl, she insisted he bring Milla around. 'Children eat free for the Twinmoon,' she had said, brushing clouds of flour from her apron. 'My sister has three boys, three! Can you imagine the noise when that lot comes for dinner? Rutters!'

Alen had felt a pang of sorrow for Gisella, who seemed a pleasant enough woman; he was sorry she'd not been able to have children, and he promised to return with Milla.

Now, Milla's hand securely clasped in his, he felt some of his own trepidation rub off; perhaps it wouldn't be so bad to work with the child prodigy over the next two hundred Twinmoons.

'Are we going to Gisella's?' Milla skipped beside him, careful to avoid icy patches.

'I thought you might want to go back there,' Alen smiled.

'She's fun, and I like those biscuits, the warm ones. They're so big.'

'Big as your head!' Alen pretended to struggle beneath the weight of a giant pastry.

'Can we bring one back for Hoyt?'

'Of course.'

'Is he going to die?' Milla twirled a length of ribbon around her finger.

'No, Pepperweed. He's going to be just fine.' Alen tried to sound convincing.

'But there's a new hole in his shoulder,' the little girl said sadly. 'One of those soldiers stuck him with a sword.'

'That's almost all better, sweetie. The querlis is fixing that hole right up.'

'But not the other one,' she was quick to point out.

'I know, Pepperweed.'

'Do you think Gilmour will be able to help him?'

'That's a funny thing to ask.'

'Because he's almost here,' Milla said.

'How do you know? Can you sense him out there?' Alen knelt beside her, ignoring the damp seeping through his leggings.

'You know how we felt that big crash from Falkan a while ago?' Milla whispered as if sharing a secret. 'It's like that, only a lot quieter.'

'It must be.' He looked around, thinking perhaps his former colleague might be coming up the quay to join them. 'I can't feel him at all.'

'Well, it's hard, because he's really quiet, but I know where to find him, because I held him that time outside the room.'

'Like you did with me and Hoyt in the wagons?'

'I had to with you and Hoyt, because those Seron things were coming so fast, and you two were dreaming about fireplaces and pretty girls.' Milla snorted with laughter. 'But, yes, just like that.'

'Any idea where he is, Pepperweed?' Alen aligned his finger with hers and Milla wrapped them both in the ribbon.

'A little bit that way.' She pointed southeast, across the inlet and along the coast.

'Are you sure?' Alen asked, 'because if he's coming by sea, he would have to come from that way.' He pointed northeast, where deep water met a wall of atolls and shallow islands in the Northern Archipelago. 'Everyone coming on the water this Twinmoon has to come that way.'

'Nope.' Milla shook her head, her scribbled curls jouncing. 'Not Gilmour. He's coming from over there, around that piece of ground sticking out in the water.'

'All right, Pepperweed, we'll watch for him from that way. And to answer your question: yes, I hope that Gilmour can help Hoyt, or help me help Hoyt get better.'

They walked for a while in silence. Milla stopped to consider, then hopped over a coil of mooring hawser some docker had left along the wharf. Beside them, the Welstar River was a steely grey ribbon.

'Nice jump,' Alen said, retaking her hand, 'but be careful. You don't want to fall in.'

'I know,' Milla shivered. 'It's so cold it made my head hurt, and my skin was like it didn't feel anything.'

'Numb.'

'Numb,' Milla echoed. 'So I had to warm it up, or I would have been too scared to swim.'

'I hear you did a good job swimming.'

Milla beamed. 'I swam the scramble, just like Hannah showed me, but she calls it the dog-paddle, or something like that. I did have to hurt that one man, though – I didn't want to, but he was going to stab Hoyt, and maybe Hannah, too. So I made him stop.' Her lip started to tremble.

Alen picked her up and, holding her close, whispered, 'Don't you worry about it, Pepperweed, not for one more day. Those men were going to take you back to Welstar Palace.'

'Back to Rabeth and the others?' She looked cross. 'But I don't want to go back there. I want to go home to Mama and to find Resta with Hoyt.'

'Resta?'

'You know: Resta the Wonderdog, who writes his name and sings songs.'

'Yes, of course, how could I have forgotten?'

A pair of barges laden with tarpaulin-covered crates moved slowly towards Welstar Palace. Milla waved at one of the sailors. 'You don't think those other soldiers are going to come and find me?'

'Not after what you did to them.'

'That was Hoyt's idea,' Milla said. 'I didn't know if I could do it, but Hannah helped me to come up with a good story, and I just told it to those men, the ones with the hurt legs, and they thought it was true.'

'And Erynn too, right?'

'She was even easier,' Milla said. 'I just make her think that Karel had taken me away because he was mad at her for being in love with Hoyt.'

'That's silly, isn't it?' Alen blew into his cupped hands; Milla mimicked him, warming her fingers.

'Hoyt's too old, anyway.'

'I'm sure he'll be glad you think that way, Pepperweed.'

She giggled. 'Hoyt's silly.'

'That *is* an interesting trick you did, though. I wish I knew how to do that one,' Alen said. 'Did Nerak teach you that one: helping people to remember things the wrong way?'

'No.' Milla wiped her nose on her cloak. 'It was Hoyt. He told me to try it, and so I did. It was hard at first, because those other soldiers were shouting. So it was hard to think about how to do it.'

'I'm impressed,' Alen said, 'but Milla, please don't try that one on me or the others, all right?'

'All right.' Milla didn't seem to care. 'Are we there yet? I'm cold.'

While the Hunter's Glade did indeed have enormous biscuits, some the size of a child's head, Milla's favourite thing about visiting Gisella were her dogs. The lonely café owner had two, a big old wolf-like creature, and a small, feisty creature with a mass of tight curls, a fiery temper and a soft spot for children. As soon as they arrived at the café, Milla rushed over to the dogs and the three of them rolled and wrestled until, exhausted, she joined Alen at their small table near the fireplace. After devouring whatever delicacy Gisella had prepared for her, Milla donned her cloak, kissed the barmaid on the nose and climb into Alen's arms for the journey back to the Wayfarer. After most visits, Milla was asleep before they rounded the first corner.

This aven, the little girl didn't sleep. 'Alen?' she asked, a tiny voice in the twilight air.

'What is it, Pepperweed?'

'I sent those dogs to the wagons, too.'

'I know you did, Pepperweed.'

'Was that a wrong thing to do?'

'You saved me and Hoyt,' he said, 'so no, I don't think it was wrong.'

'But some of those soldiers—'

'They were all fine.' Alen stopped her with the lie he and Hoyt had prepared. 'Hoyt and I were watching while we sneaked away, and when the dogs left, all those soldiers were fine.' She had been so upset at killing the Malakasian sergeant; knowing she had wiped out an entire platoon of Seron warriors would be too much for Milla to handle right now. He changed the subject, saying, 'Can I ask you something?'

'What?'

'How do you do it? How do you get those dogs inside our dreams? Hannah, Hoyt, and I all dreamed about dogs – the same dog, from Southport, the one you sent after Hannah when she came across the Fold. How did you get the dog to follow your orders, and how did you get the same dog to fit so perfectly into our dreams?'

'It's the way those ashes work.' Milla didn't lift her head from his shoulder.

'The ashes?'

'The ash dream,' she yawned into his ear.

'What is that, Pepperweed?' He was getting more confused, not less.

'The dream you get from the trees.'

Ashes, Alen thought, *ashes – yes, there were ashes in the fire grate in Durham, and Hannah mentioned ashes from her father's cigarettes. Hoyt remembered me smoking, although I never did, and Churn smelled the ashes of his family's burning homestead. The ash dream? Dreams of ashes? It doesn't make sense.*

He asked, 'So why did we all dream about ashes, Pepperweed?'

'You dream about your life. I put in the dog for fun. It isn't hard to do.'

'So where do the ashes come from?'

'From whoever wants you to know about ashes. She must be putting the ashes in there.'

'She?'

'Or he. I don't know.'

'So the ash dream is a dream about ashes?' Alen couldn't hide his confusion.

Milla giggled, snuggling closer to ward off the cold. 'No, crazy. The ash dream is the dream that comes from the trees. The ashes are in your dream, because someone put them there.'

'Like your dog.'

'Yup.'

'Because he ... or she ... wanted me to think about ashes?'

'Wanted you to know the name of the dream, probably.'

He propped her a bit higher on his hip. 'Go to sleep now, Milla. I'll wake you when we get back to the Wayfarer.'

'All right,' she yawned. 'Did you remember Hoyt's biscuit?'

'And one for Hannah,' Alen said, feeling her breath tickle his neck.

'That's good,' she whispered and drifted off.

Plodding through the Pellia twilight, Alen analysed what he knew, trying to uncover something salient they had overlooked. *So the ash dream is how someone, Nerak probably, referred to the hypnotic state one experiences in the Forest of Ghosts. Milla sent the dog to follow us, then worked him into our dreams, probably without Nerak knowing, or he would have been rutting furious with her for tipping us off. So why the ashes? Was that you, Fantus? What are you trying to tell me? I know it's the tree bark, but why? What's the point of shipping it here?*

He was still thinking it all through when he arrived back at the Wayfarer Inn. Morgan and Illia Kestral, both working behind the bar, waved to him genially, deeply thankful that they had saved Erynn from Karel, the crazed young soldier, who had kidnapped their daughter and Milla before killing himself. *If you only knew*, Alen thought.

He gestured to Milla and then the stairs: *I'll be right down, just need to take her up.*

'You need a beer?' Morgan whispered.

'Please,' Alen whispered back. An aven or two alone might help him stumble on something he had missed.

INVISIBLE SENTRIES

At Gilmour's call, Steven shouted, 'On my way!' and left Kellin and Garec chatting amiably. Brexan went off to find Captain Ford on the quarterdeck.

Passage along the Malakasian coast had been tiresome. The captain and crew of the *Morning Star* had pushed, pulled, dragged and kedged the little brig-sloop over and through all manner of hazards. Miraculously, the ship remained seaworthy, despite her battered appearance, and finally she rode a high tide through the last of the islands to join an armada of small fishing vessels, trawlers and booacore boats, mostly, working the coastline south of the capital. Steven prayed they had shaved enough time off the Northeast Channel to reach Pellia before Mark and the hijacked frigates.

'What is it?' he asked, catching his breath.

Gilmour pointed. 'See that rocky point on the horizon with the pines running almost out to the end? If my memory and Captain Ford's charts are correct, that's the last slip of land separating us from the Welstar River inlet—'

'And Pellia.'

'And Pellia,' Gilmour agreed. 'If you look northeast, about as far out as you can on the horizon . . .' He pointed again.

Steven sighted along his forearm but couldn't see anything. 'Sorry, but most of us don't sharpen our eyesight with Larion magic.'

'Trust me,' Gilmour said, 'it's there.'

'What's there? A ship?'

'Topsails, anyway. If it was a ship, we'd be in trouble. For now, it's just her sails; she hasn't come hull-up yet. When she does, her lookouts will spot us.'

Steven understood. 'So it's time to get hidden.' He paused, then admitted, 'I don't think that I can hide us well enough to cross the inlet and make way into the harbour unseen. This is an awfully big boat to make disappear. And anyway, you know as well as I do that my cloaking spells don't really make us invisible; they just help people overlook us.'

'I understand,' Gilmour assured him, 'and I also understand that there are a lot of people in Pellia, and many of them will see us approach. What I want you to concentrate on is keeping us camouflaged while we sail inside the blockade. Once we've passed that, anyone on shore will assume we've been cleared to moor.'

'And that's the closest ship, way out there?'

'For now, yes, but when we round this point, there will be a number of smaller boats, shallow-drafting boats, working the inlet. Those are my main concern.'

'Why aren't they on this side of the point?'

'Because no one of any threat or consequence could possibly get a large ship through here. No invading army approaches in a skiff.' Gilmour smiled. 'We were lucky to find Captain Ford.'

'Lucky doesn't cover it! We've Brexan to thank for that one.'

'The blockade captains in the inlet will be working upriver, inspecting barges as they approach from the south. They'll also be downriver, at least glancing at the barges moving north. Those are the ships we'll need to be concerned with, because anything coming off the pier or from a mooring line in the harbour will already have cleared customs and so they won't get more than a cursory look.'

'So the downriver blockade ships are our biggest threat?'

'For the next aven or so, yes.'

'Got it,' Steven said. 'All right, give me a moment, and I'll see if I can get this right.'

'I can probably help if you need it.'

'Really?' Steven was surprised. 'So there's a schooner in the harbour?'

'Full to bursting, unless these old bones are reading the weather wrong.'

'What is it?'

'Carpello's tree bark, I suppose.'

'How did you live in Estrad Village all those Twinmoons and never feel it, especially if there was an entire forest of it growing just across the river?'

'It must somehow become active when it's processed, and I never bothered to check. That forest had been closed for so long; it never crossed my mind it might have been for a reason other than just because he could,' Gilmour said. 'Either way, it's awfully noisy around here, so I can help if you need me.'

'I might. I've been a bit distracted these past few days.' Steven looked for a place to settle in and call up the cloaking spell that had served them so well outside Traver's Notch. He sat in the bow, ducked below the gunwales.

'Distracted by what?'

'By whatever this is that I have in my pocket, this bug you gave me.' He withdrew the remains of what looked like the unlikely offspring of a beetle and a poisonous spider.

'You haven't felt any of them on board, have you?'

'No,' Steven said, 'but let me remind you that I'm no good at all this feeling and detecting that you and Mark and Nerak and Kantu and just about everyone else, including my old Aunt Ethel, can do. You tell me there's a schooner filled with mystical tree bark just around the bend, and I can't feel anything. You tell me to search for a netherworldly insect here to kill us all, and all I want to do is screech like a schoolgirl and climb the rigging to the crow's nest until the exterminator comes and sprays the whole place down with DDT. So yeah, I've been a bit distracted.'

Gilmour checked the horizon, making certain the blockade ship was still hull-down. He crouched beside Steven, and said, 'I don't want you to worry about the insects. I haven't felt any, and it's been days now, so it must have been just this one. If there are others, they're dead too – crushed, frozen, whatever. Right now, you need to concentrate on helping us hide. Can you do that?'

Steven shrugged. 'Sure, just give me a moment.'

'And remember,' Gilmour interrupted, 'you *have* shown an enormous potential to detect all manner of mystical energy, but for you it doesn't happen—'

'Until everything gets blurry,' Steven said to himself. 'When the air gets thick, and everything else turns to melted wax, that's when I can do it.'

Gilmour backed away, whispering, 'That's right. Take your time.'

From the bow, Steven had an unencumbered view of the *Morning Star*. He blinked, let his vision blur and then drew everything back into focus. Concentrating on his mother's old blanket, the ugly one from the 1970s with the big circular knitting that made the whole thing look as though it had been shot by a 12-gauge, Steven inhaled through his nose, felt the cold bite his sinuses and let himself drift back in time. Winters in Colorado. The cold chilled your sinuses there; they nearly froze shut some mornings. Those were the worst headaches, frozen-from-the-inside-out headaches. Every morning,

Steven would amble down the hall, into the living room and curl up on the sofa beneath that old blanket. Most mornings, school mornings, his time there was brief; he had to get dressed, finish homework, catch the bus, sinuses frozen or not. But Saturdays and Sundays were days for lingering beneath the covers, the old wool rubbing against his skin, capturing the heat despite the clumsy, holey stitching. Some mornings he would get lucky and there would be a film on television, some great old epic with John Wayne or Errol Flynn. Stretching out on that couch – not unlike the *Morning Star*, stretching aft, her rigging taut with northerly wind – Steven could fit his whole body under the blanket; he had to be careful not to push his feet through the hole near the far end. Who had done that? His sister? The dog? He couldn't remember. But what a place to hide, warm, safe and nearly invisible as Charlton Heston wrestled freakish-looking monkeys or James Mason battled a giant squid with a steak knife.

'That's it, Steven,' he heard someone say. 'That should do it; excellent work, your best yet, my boy.'

Steven let himself wander, not hurrying, back to the cold foredeck of the Pragan brig-sloop he and his friends had shanghaied into carrying them this far. When he opened his eyes, he wasn't surprised to find that much of the ship – her masts, cordage, sheets and rigging – were a blurry backdrop of brown and white.

'Can he keep it going?' Garec had joined them. His voice sounded as though it was coming from a closed room somewhere down a long hall.

'He's never had any trouble before,' Gilmour, also distant, replied, 'although this is a bigger spell.'

Then he saw something. A bump. *What had Gilmour called them? Ripples on a mill pond?* Moving aft, from port to starboard, somewhere below decks, it was there for just a second: a wrinkle in the paraffin. It moved, and then flattened out again.

'What's that?' Steven heard himself ask.

Gilmour answered, 'I said this is a bigger spell than last time, but you seem to have called it up nicely. Look at those trawlers near the shore, none of them are giving us a second glance.'

'Not that.' Steven stood on shaky legs. Stumbling, he let his vision blur again, then brought the waxy backdrop into focus. He watched for the wrinkle.

'Are you all right?' Garec asked, grabbing him beneath the arm.

'I'm fine.' Steven shrugged him off. 'What was that, though?'

'We didn't see anything,' Gilmour said. 'What do you see?'

Steven reached aft. The air, malleable and thick, felt good in his hands, as it had at the landfill. He waited, watching, reaching out with his senses and hoping to find it again.

It didn't come back.

'Steven?'

He shook his head to clear it. 'I'm all right, I'm fine.' Back amongst them now, he looked around and asked, 'How'd I do?'

'Top marks, my boy,' Gilmour said, 'seamless.'

'Good.' Steven grinned. 'That one's getting easier. I mean, I don't want to hide the Tampa Bay Buccaneers or anything, but that was easier than the first time.'

'We should tell Captain Ford,' Garec said suddenly.

'Right,' Steven agreed. 'Regardless of how well this cover is working, he should hug that point, as close in as he dares, so we get a decent view of the northern part of the Welstar inlet while staying relatively hidden ourselves. Once we round the point, if we can tack south into the river, I think we'll make it across. When we round those rocks, I'll strengthen the spell a bit, and that'll hopefully be enough to keep us out of sight.'

'How is he?' Alen poked his head through the door. He kept Milla in the corridor, shielding her from whatever bad news Hannah might have this morning.

'He had a tough night,' she said. 'His shoulder's infected, and it's spreading. The querlis isn't worth a scoop of dogshit and I don't know what else to do for him.' Hannah's own shoulders slumped; her lip quivered, and she sniffed hard. She had been crying in frustration on and off throughout the night. Now, knowing Milla was listening, she tried to hold herself together. 'This voodoo bullshit that passes for medicine isn't going to save him, Alen. He needs antibiotics; an injection would be best, but pills will work, albeit a bit slower.'

'I don't know what any of that means. I'm sorry.' Alen stepped inside; Milla followed, then crossed to take Hoyt's hand. She had tiny violets in her hair.

Hoyt woke at her touch. 'Hi, Pepperweed,' he whispered. He was pale and wan, damp with cold sweat and too weak to lift his head.

'You look bad,' Milla said.

'I feel like a handful of cold throw-up,' he murmured, forcing a smile, 'but you look nice today. Where'd you get such pretty flowers this Twinmoon?'

'Erynn's mama gave them to me,' Milla said proudly. 'She heard what a great job I did swimming the scramble.'

'It was great swimming, like a professional.' Hoyt ran a hand through her curls. 'Pepperweed, old Hoyt is going to sleep for a while. Will you bring me some lunch later?'

'What do you want?'

'Grilled grettan, a whole one.'

The little girl giggled. 'All right, I'll try, but I don't think he'll fit in here.'

'We'll move Hannah's bed outside.'

Hannah interrupted, ushering Milla into the hall, 'maybe we'll just bring him some soup,' she said. 'Sleep well, Hoyt.'

Out in the corridor, Hannah whispered, 'Alen, I need you to tell me how these far portals work.'

'Hannah, that's ridiculous. You don't know—'

'Alen!'

'We have no idea when they're coming; it could be too late.'

'You have any other suggestions?' She held Milla's hand as if it were sculpted from eggshells, but her face was grim, her jaw set.

Alen sighed. 'No, I don't. But I reiterate: we don't have any idea how or when they'll arrive. They could be—'

'They're coming soon,' Milla said. 'It won't be long now.'

Alen was sceptical. 'Pepperweed, I know you've done some remarkable things, but boats just don't come from that direction. They can't get through.'

'Gilmour's coming,' Milla said simply. 'He'll be here soon.'

Hannah said, 'Steven and I can go through together. We'll step across the Fold and be back in an hour and Hoyt will be on his feet in a day, two at the most. But I need to know how the portals work. I want to travel to a specific place, not find myself dumped on some glacier in the Andes.'

'It's more complicated than that,' Alen said. 'Come on; we need more querlis. We can talk while we go.'

'What's wrong?'

'Nothing,' Alen said. 'I have some ideas about those shipments, the bark and leaves from the forest of ghosts.'

'Really?' Hannah checked the corridor again and lowered her voice.

'I think so,' he said, 'but like you, I need Fantus.'

'Can't you call him, you know, like you did before?'

Alen shook his head. 'No, this will take too long; neither of us can keep up the connection that long.'

'Here's hoping they arrive soon then,' she said nervously. 'We've a lot riding on them.'

'They'll be here,' Milla said again, taking hold of a hand each and swinging her feet off the floor.

Hannah smiled and swung her higher. 'I hope you're right, Pepperweed.'

Steven crept beneath the main hatch, through the port companionway. The hold, below the quarterdeck and Captain Ford's cabin, was a dark, musty hollow. He sent up a flare and then another, twin orbs he brightened with a thought.

The hold was noisy with the creaking rudder chain, the slap of the waves against the hull, the incessant sloshing of the bilge somewhere beneath his feet and the groaning of ratlines against pins between braces in the bulkhead, Steven attuned his eyes to the shadows; his ears would do him little good on this hunting trip.

In the aft corner, starboard behind the mainmast, there were several hogsheads, filled, he guessed, with drinking water, capped and lashed to one another and then to the bulkhead to keep them from tipping or rolling about in heavy seas. In the opposite corner there were wooden boxes, likewise stacked and lashed to the beam supports. Finally, beneath the hatch, tucked under the stairs, was a dwindling stack of wood for the galley oven, purchased in Orindale before the *Morning Star* set sail for the Northern Archipelago.

Apart from these, the main hold was empty.

Halfway to the barrels, the magic crept up on him. Most of the lines, pulleys and braces blurred, but overall, the hold remained in focus, the grain of the planks easy to see. 'So you're in here somewhere,' Steven said, 'but where?'

Even without the noise, Steven would not have heard the tanbak's tiny sentry coming for him. He was focusing his attention on the shadowy places, the dark nooks and cracks between and behind the hogsheads; he hadn't expected the spider-beetle to come from above.

There was a place on the mainmast – where it passed through the upper deck – around which was coiled a length of hawser, maybe where Marrin or Sera had at one time tied off the last bit of line after securing a large cargo. A small ship like the *Morning Star* often hauled as much as her crew could stuff into the comparatively little storage area; it wasn't uncommon to use the mast as an extra brace. Here, the forgotten rope had provided an ideal hiding place for the tanbak's little hunter, which had waited, uncertain which of the crew to take, recognising, after sensing the defeat of its mistress, that there were powerful sorcerers on board.

And one was in the hold with it right now.

As Steven passed the mainmast, actually dragging a hand over its rough surface, the creature dropped, but missed his head. The spiderbeetle grasped the material of his cloak and started climbing.

Steven felt more of the hold blur together, but the barrels, the boxes and the firewood remained in focus. 'This isn't right,' he murmured. 'Something's different; something's wrong.' He thought about shouting for the others. Between them, there were plenty of eyes for watching and especially feet for stomping ... but he didn't. He recalled the wrinkle – *the ripple on a mill pond* – that had moved down here. It had actually shifted his perspective, like light through a turning prism, and there had been nothing Steven could do about it. Whatever was down here was powerful.

The spider-beetle climbed up Steven's cloak and over the hillock of the hood and slipped into the space between the coarse fabric and the curiously smooth, unnatural texture of the coat beneath it. The magician's neck, and especially his ears, were close now.

The barrels blurred, then the boxes and Steven turned on his heel. 'I was right; it's in the firewood,' he said aloud. The glowing orbs floated silently forward to hover over the stack of logs and the tangle of dry branches used for kindling, but a step towards them and even they began to melt. Steven looked at the floor, the mast, the bulkheads, the forward stairs, all of it; everything was blurring into the backdrop. He looked down at the deck beneath his boots ... everything – except *himself*.

He barely had time to shout before the creature struck, biting him on his neck and then scurrying for his left ear. 'Fuck!' he screamed, 'it's already on me – fuck—!'

When the spider-beetle bit him, Steven's fireballs flared out and the hold was plunged into darkness.

Gilmour was on the quarterdeck with Captain Ford when they heard Steven shout from below. Gilmour dived towards the main hatch; the captain hesitated just long enough to shout at Marrin, 'Take the helm; hold her steady!' Then, drawing the knife he used to fillet fish, he followed Gilmour into the darkness.

Steven swatted at the spider-beetle and missed. The insect, almost supernaturally fast and still on the attack, bit him again, this time on the back of his hand. The wound was fiery-hot, like a snakebite, a deep puncture flooded with venom. As a reflex, he threw his hands up, slapping at his neck. He shouted for Gilmour then groaned; his vision was blurring for real now, the mainmast shifting and splitting itself twice and then three times as the poison worked its way through his bloodstream. The deck canted to port, too far – *That can't be a wave; I'm losing it. I'm losing it!* – dumping Steven in a heap. Before landing on his shoulder, he made one last flailing attempt to brush the determined insect off his neck. But he didn't find it tucked inside his hood, where it was waiting for him to lose consciousness. When he fell, the spider-beetle emerged and skittered across the Gore-tex collar of Howard's old ski jacket. It paused just long enough to send a primitive message to its companion. Then it started for Steven's ear.

Gilmour leaped down the stairs, slamming into the bulkhead as he heard Steven shout and then fall. Crying out a spell, he cast a handful of brilliant fire orbs into the darkness. Captain Ford slowed to keep from running blind into one of the braces; he blinked to acclimatise his vision, then cursed when he ran into Gilmour at the end of the corridor.

'Rutting horsecocks,' he shouted, 'I do wish you would give a bit of warning before you just ignite all the fires of—'

Gilmour wasn't listening. 'No, no, no,' he muttered, 'this didn't happen. This did *not* happen!' He shouted something Ford couldn't understand and a howling blast of wind tore through the main hold, rammed the starboard bulkhead and threatened to roll the *Morning Star* to the scuppers.

'What in all Eldarn is—?' the captain began.

'There!' Gilmour cried, 'do you see it? There, against the wall!'

'What am I looking for?' He held his fillet-knife ready to slash at anything that might have sneaked on board or stowed away in his cargo hold.

'Against the wall. Go! It's stunned. Kill it, Captain – but don't get bitten!' Gilmour knelt beside Steven, mumbling furiously. He looked disconcertingly like a father arriving a moment too late to save his son.

Ford noticed Steven for the first time, but, still blinking, turned his attention back to the starboard bulkhead. 'What am I—?'

Then he saw it: a tiny long-legged beetle, or maybe a mutant spider, black, with some kind of coloured markings along its chitinous back. 'That?' Ford started towards it, saying, 'This little thing? I was expecting another of those Fold monsters that killed Sera and Tubbs. I get worse than this outside my house.'

Gilmour looked up long enough to say, 'Rutting whores, Doren, *be careful*! Crush it quickly, before it recovers or gets away.'

'All right, all right, I'll step on the bug – but I don't think this thing could have knocked Steven so—'

Finding its legs, the tan-bak's hunter sprang from the dusty floor to grip a seam in Captain Ford's tunic, just beneath his neck.

'Motherless dryhumping—!' He danced like a man on fire, swatting and slapping at himself, tearing at his cloak, whining something incoherent. The spider-beetle lost its grip and, scurrying like spilled quicksilver, it dashed for the pile of firewood, but this time, Captain Ford was too quick and pounced on the nefarious intruder, stamping on it again and again until the bug looked like a bit of spilled tar.

'Good,' Gilmour said quietly. 'You got it.'

Sweating and shaking now, he knelt for a moment, his head in his hands, then tried to stand up. His hands were trembling as adrenalin rushed through his system; he couldn't stay still. 'What was that?' he asked.

Gilmour ignored him and concentrated on his fallen comrade. 'Come on Steven,' he begged, rubbing his hands, which glowed a soft red in the harsh glare of the false Larion suns. 'Come on, my boy.'

'Did it bite him?'

'At least twice.' Gilmour didn't look up.

'Is he—?'

'Not yet.'

'What can I—?'

'Nothing yet.' Gilmour examined Steven's injured hand. With two fingers, he pinched the bite puncture, then massaged along Steven's forearm with his free hand until a thin stream of blood flowed from the wound and pooled on the dusty wooden floor.

The bloodletting went on for while, long enough for Ford to calm down a little. 'How much do you have to flush out?' he asked.

'I don't know.' Gilmour remained focused on what he was doing.

'Can you do that to his neck?'

'I'll try, but I'm afraid it may be too late for that. I can drain the venom this way, but a bite in the neck—' Gilmour grimaced, 'that's already circulated too deep.'

He let Steven's arm rest beside the puddle and turned his attention to the swollen, purplish marks in the young man's throat.

A wave, different from the swells that had been rolling beneath the brig-sloop all day, tossed the *Morning Star* off her heading. Her bow came down with a splash, noisy in the hold despite the background racket. Ford frowned and muttered, 'Marrin.'

BRANAG'S WOLFHOUND

It was dark almost everywhere, except for a few points of light that were almost blinding. Steven squinted, putting a hand over his brow to see across the parking lot – an absurd gesture after dark, he had to admit. *It's headlights, high beams*, he thought finally. *Those are cars on the highway.* A moment later, a van, a motorcycle and a family SUV passed by on their way into Golden. To the east, Denver glowed like a massive prairie fire, but he was too far into the hills to hear anything more than the occasional truck passing along Interstate 70. Downshifting on the last precarious slope before running out over nearly a thousand miles of flat nothingness, the trucks sometimes sounded like their engines would explode from the effort of slowing through the final downhill turns outside the suburbs. He could smell their brakes, even from here.

He was at the diner in Golden; they had the best pie in the Western hemisphere. It didn't matter what kind; they were all the best. But the lights were out; the place was closed. Even the neon, which usually burned all night, had gone dark. Steven wondered if perhaps the city had run out of electricity.

It smelled good, too: clear mountain air with just a hint of pollution. Eldarn always smelled so clean, so free from pollutants and exhaust. He loved the smell of home; it was the scent of fallibility and progress all wrapped together in one heady aroma.

Hannah was here. She had met him to say good night. *I wish I could see you, just for a minute, just to say good night properly.* Steven had driven down the canyon, anticipation tightening in his chest. He saw her now, leaning against the hood of her car, sipping from a Styrofoam cup. She must have arrived before the diner closed, before the city went black.

It had been too long since he had seen her, too long since they had spoken together. What would he say? What would she think of him, exhausted, thin and careworn, and full of some unexplained mystical legacy? Would it be the same, two twentysomethings dating, thinking about love, careers, marriage, and hoping for the future? He held his breath and crossed the parking lot.

'Hello, Steven,' she said.

'I've been ... I've— Hannah, I've been looking ...' he stammered.

'I know. I've been looking for you too.'

'How did you get here?' he asked.

'It doesn't matter,' she smiled. Even in the dark he could see those tiny lines pulling at the corners of her eyes. *Good Christ, but she's beautiful.* He fought off a wave of dizziness and reached for her.

Hannah boosted herself up on the hood of the car and took him into her arms.

Steven ran his hands across her back and down to the waist of her jeans. She wore the same blue sweatshirt she had worn the last time he had seen her here, but she too was thinner. He could feel her ribs pressing out through the soft cotton weave. 'What happened to you?' he said.

'Never mind.' She slipped a hand through his hair and pulled his face into the nape of her neck.

Steven inhaled. Lilacs. *This has to be the only place left in the world where I can smell lilacs.* The dizziness returned, this time getting the better of him, and his knees threatened to give way. He let her go, pressed his palms on the hood – it was still warm – and held himself up.

Hannah kissed him, soft at first, then harder, ardent, fierce, and he locked his knees, propping himself up so he could hold her, feel her move around him. She was squeezing his hips between her thighs, rubbing herself against him; he could feel heat rising from the engine. It was warmer than the night air in the foothills.

Pushing him back a little, not far, Hannah slipped the blue sweatshirt over her head and unfastened her bra. Steven tugged at it, all at once wanting it gone, out of the way; it caught on one shoulder, just for a second, then slipped free.

'Help me with my jeans,' she whispered.

He fumbled for the button while Hannah reclined, arching her back over the warm steel bed, luxuriating in the heat.

Her jeans were hard to unfasten. Steven struggled to stay focused; his own jeans were ready to burst. Pressing his bulging erection against the car, he tugged until Hannah's buttons came open and she lifted her hips far enough for him to slide the jeans down to mid-thigh, not far enough, but Steven couldn't wait. Yellow and red flares were bursting in the space behind his eyes, blinding him, and he blinked, let go for an agonising moment to rub his head.

'What's the matter?' Hannah whispered, her silky hair splayed across the hood of her car. 'Get up here with me.'

Steven swallowed. His throat was dry. Pressing himself harder against the car, he finally worked his own jeans open, slid the zipper down and tugged to get free. Struck by the hilarity of losing a wrestling match to a pair of pants in a public parking lot, Steven started to laugh. Hannah joined him, reaching a hand down and spreading her fingers across her lower abdomen.

Like an artist's rendition of the Rule of Three, Hannah's jeans were pulled open and askew across her lower thighs, her panties, cream-coloured and rolled over, a tangle of netting, and milky skin, dark hair and that glorious musty aroma that mingled with the smell of oil and exhaust, the smells of fallibility and home.

'I'm gonna come,' he said thickly. 'I'm not even gonna make it up there.'

'Yes, you will.' She touched herself, briefly, before sliding her panties and jeans over her knees. They fell to the ground at Steven's feet.

A dog padded around the front of Hannah's car, stopped to look at them and then continued on. It was a big dog, like a wolf, and Steven yelped when he saw it. 'Jesus whoring Christ,' he cried, 'did you see that?' He let go of her thighs and watched the dog wander towards the far end of the parking lot, as if giving them a minute alone.

'What?' Hannah tried unsuccessfully to cover herself with her hands. She sat up, propped up on one elbow and strained to see. 'Is someone there?'

'No,' Steven said, calming, 'no, it was just a dog, someone's lost dog, some big mutt out wandering around. It's gone now.'

'Well, good.' Hannah ran her fingernails across his hips and down beneath his boxers. 'Let's get you out of these.'

He kissed her. 'Yes, let's do that.'

Steven moved his hips, letting his own jeans fall into a heap beside Hannah's, then pulled down on his boxers. He was ready to burst; he just hoped he wouldn't explode all over the side of her car. That'd be all he needed: to embarrass himself *and* have to find an all-night carwash in Golden.

The first of the spider-beetles crawled from the waistband of his boxers and, scurrying up his stomach, they fanned out on either side of his navel, like scouts for an invasion force.

'What the hell?' he shouted, and that was the cue for the others to come, all at once. Hundreds of beetles crawled, leaped or skittered down his thighs, up and around his erection, beneath his scrotum and between his legs. They were all over his stomach now, inside his navel and crawling under his sweater, digging for his chest and neck.

'What is this? Jesus, help me! Hannah, what is this?'

Sitting naked, one hand splayed across her lower stomach, Hannah said, 'You have to wake up, Steven. Wake up!'

'What?' He couldn't hear her. Terror paralysed him as he felt the swarm – not stinging yet, still deploying – crawling over his body.

'Wake up!' Hannah insisted.

He screamed, losing himself to panic, swatting at hundreds of mutant spider-beetles, nightmare insects with hairy, spindly legs and coloured constellations dotting their tiny thoraxes. Steven's mind ran away from him, left him stranded, half-naked with a hard-on in a parking lot, screaming as a regiment of tiny demon sentries explored every inch of his pallid flesh.

His hand was bleeding, as if something had bitten it, puncturing a vein. The blood ran in a stream, not pumping, like it would from an artery, but rather, pouring out, like water through a hose. Then his neck bled, and it was worse. Trying to brush away legions of bugs, Steven swathed himself in blood, spreading it over his body like a balm, but nothing did any good.

The dog, still watching from the far side of the lot, trotted around the car and bit Steven just above his left ankle. The pain was astonishing, a white-hot needle of agony, but it shocked Steven awake. 'Ah! Jesus Christ, help me!' he screamed before falling backwards to the pavement.

'Ah! Jesus Christ, help me!' Steven screamed, rolling over before slipping back into a stupor.

'I'm losing him,' Gilmour muttered. 'This isn't good.' The *Morning Star* took another wave badly, crashing hard into the trough.

'Marrin,' Captain Ford whispered, 'what in the names of the Northern Gods are you doing up there?'

Gilmour looked up at him. 'Go; it's all right. There's nothing you can do for him. Send Garec down, or Kellin or Brexan – I need some water and some bedding, anything to make him more comfortable. But you see to the ship.'

'The spell you mentioned, the one keeping us ...'

'Out of their attention?'

'Yes, that one.' He made certain to step on the spider-beetle at least once more. 'Will it keep going? Or did our plans just go exceedingly wrong?'

'We should be fine,' Gilmour said. He didn't want to sound insecure, not this close to Pellia. *Get them going, and they'll go on for ever, like the Twinmoon.* He cradled Steven's head in his lap. 'It'll be all right, Captain.'

Steven had rolled in the puddle of his own blood, and now looked as though he had been dipped in crimson paint. Captain Ford backed against the bulkhead, sidling towards the stairs through the main hatch. 'Good luck,' he said softly, heartfelt.

'It'll be all right, Captain,' the Larion Senator muttered, wiping Steven's face.

Captain Ford nearly crashed through the handrail as the *Morning Star* lurched over a wave. As he fought to keep his balance, he shouted, 'Marrin! Will you rutting well watch where you're going!' He reached daylight, and stopped short. Marrin was at the helm, as ordered, but there was something very definitely wrong. Garec, the partisan killer, had an arrow drawn full, aimed right at his first mate.

Garec was shouting, 'Correct our course, Marrin, *now!*'

Confused, Captain Ford started to reach for Garec, then he checked their heading. The *Morning Star* was bearing down on a Malakasian fishing trawler, the biggest one they could see working the shallows. It looked horribly like Marrin meant to ram them.

'What are you ...' He was stunned. Should he tackle Garec and try to disarm him? Or mount the quarterdeck and slap some sense into his first mate?

Garec shouted again, 'Correct our heading, Marrin! Do it now!'

Steven was running. It was the day of the half-marathon, his favourite day of the year, and he, Hannah and Mark had joined the four thousand other runners to do the thirteen-mile course from Georgetown, down the canyon, to Idaho Springs. Each summer, he tried to improve on his previous time. Despite the altitude – the Georgetown starting line was almost 9,000 feet above sea level – after a two-mile loop through Georgetown, the rest of the course was little more than eleven miles of downhill running, making this one of the easiest half-marathons on Steven's dance card. All he did was get to the initial slope, point himself downhill and let go. Gravity did most of the work. The only drawback was the sun. Running east down the canyon, there was nothing between the runners and the morning sun rising over the prairie east of Denver, and it was a merciless running partner. Every year, it seemed, Steven managed to run beside some fool who had forgotten sunglasses, some complainer determined to ruin the race by bitching about it all the way down the hill.

This year, it was his turn.

'I can't believe I forgot the goddamned things,' he muttered, looking down to avoid being blinded. 'This is no kind of view to have, eleven miles of macadam. Christ.'

He had left Mark back about a mile. His friend was an accomplished swimmer, but he was no competitive runner. He didn't enjoy long races like Steven did, but came along for the workout, and the view – not the spectacular natural beauty of the canyon; rather, the appreciation of the number of healthy, trim, female backsides that filled the course.

'There's never a bad one,' he always said, 'it's a goddamned summer camp for great tail. Follow one for a while, get bored with it and pick another. Sometimes she's up ahead a bit; other times, I slow down and let her pass. It's worth all the training, all those miles and all that pain just to be able to jog along behind this crop of perfectly formed women. There's not an excess ounce of fat for thirteen miles.'

'What about your own?' Steven asked. 'Do you imagine any of those women – or men, for that matter – are out there jogging along behind you, taking in your caboose? How does that make you feel, Mr Politically Incorrect?'

'Goddamned great!' Mark didn't hesitate. 'Let 'em look – if they enjoy the view, hey, it's a party! If we all find someone to follow out there, it'll be a raving hootenanny!'

Thinking about Mark and his voyeuristic urges made Steven speed up. Ahead, a hundred yards or so, he thought he caught sight of Hannah; she'd left him and Mark at mile eight, determined to cut time off her personal best. Steven dropped his hands, squinted into the sun and ran to catch up.

He couldn't. A quarter-mile further on, she was still a hundred yards out. 'Yikes, Hannah, but you are motoring today,' he panted.

She was running alone. With her hair pulled into a ponytail and looped through the one-size-fits-all band on the back of her baseball cap, Hannah looked like ten thousand women Steven had followed along dozens of courses over the past five years. Even from this distance, running hard and sucking wind, Steven loved the look of her: the way her clothes fit, the way her hair bobbed up and down, the delicate taper of her tanned legs. Wearing a cropped T-shirt that just brushed the waistband of her shorts, Hannah was an unreachable mirage in the distance, lost periodically in the glare. When he could find her without squinting, Steven did stare, watching her run, wanting to feel her press against him as she slept. He was getting horny; *that* had never happened during a race before.

'Get your head on straight, dipshit. Pay attention to what you're doing,' he chided himself. 'Catch up to her if you're that hot and bothered.' He dropped his hands, lowered his shoulders a bit and speeded up. He would be near death at the finish line, blind and dehydrated, but he wanted to catch her. Panting, he cursed the sun for rising and cursed himself for forgetting his glasses. 'When you're running, run,' he said, and thought that notion felt somehow familiar, like an old blanket he might have thrown over himself, over his friends and their ship.

'Ship? What are you thinking, dipshit? Let's go, move it! What ship? You're getting delusional! Drink some water.'

Hannah ran on, the balls of her feet barely touching the broken yellow line, but Steven slowly closed the distance, passing people, lots of them, *hundreds* of runners, all plodding along at the same pace.

Mile ten.

'I can't keep this up,' he gasped, and moved to the side of the road. At least there he could use the bit of shade from the ponderosas to clear his vision. 'She's too fast,' he told himself.

At mile eleven, he saw the dog, someone's wolfhound, broken free from its owner. Loping along at an easy jog, the dog ran beside him, uninterested in the other runners, apparently unwilling to leave the struggling bank administrator behind.

'What do you want?' Steven asked, coughing up a bit of phlegm. 'A dog biscuit? A bone or something? Why don't you drop back a stretch so my horny roommate can check out your tuckus?' The dog ignored him. 'Nah,' Steven said, waving a hand dismissively at the animal, 'you're not his type.' He passed two runners, chatting about something he couldn't hear, then three singletons, and finally a husband and wife couple wearing matching gear. All the while, the dog kept pace.

'You see that woman up there?' he said. 'She's the one in the hat with the tan legs? No, of course you don't. Well, regardless, I'm trying to catch her, but I can't seem to do it. She's running too hard, and I'm just not up for it today. So why don't you run up there and get her to slow down a bit. Bite her leg for me, will you? Go on. Head up there and look all cute, and maybe she'll stop to pet you. What do you think?'

The dog cocked an eye at him, then turned back to the downhill course.

Mile twelve.

'All right, time to kick,' Steven muttered. 'You ready? Although I don't know how much kick I have left.' He scoped out a path to Hannah, a spot about a quarter-mile along where he would overtake her. He could sprint that far; he knew it. Once there, he would rely on whatever reserves of strength he had to finish the race. 'I'll take her hand and she can drag me to the line,' he told the wolfhound. He wiped his blinded eyes on the tail of his T-shirt, nodded to the dog and said, 'Let's go.'

Running a quarter-mile *fartlek* this far into a half-marathon was like squeezing orange juice out of week-old peel, but to Steven's pleasant surprise, it was working. He knew he would pay at the finish line, for his legs, lungs and lower back were operating on some kind of biological overdraft programme. The moment he stopped running, he would collapse, roll over in that puddle of blood staining the deck and maybe pass out. There were paramedics at the finish line, however. *They'll get an IV in me, hydrate me and make sure I don't die. I can't die, not today*, he thought; he was running too hard to speak. *If I die, they'll take the blanket off. They'll see us. All of them. I can't die.*

He caught up to her, slowing to appreciate the narrow pear shape of her bottom, tucked just above the stitched hem of the tiny running shorts he hoped she had chosen just to drive him mad. Steven inhaled several times before coming alongside.

'Hi—' All he could manage on the shot-glass of breath he had sucked in; anything polysyllabic would have taken his legs out from under him.

In black and white now, an old photo, Hannah smiled. She wasn't panting, or sweating; she wasn't about to collapse or to require medical attention. She wasn't even wearing sunglasses, but she didn't seem to mind the harsh morning light. Instead, as she ran along, less than a half mile from the finish line, she said, 'You have to wake up, Steven!'

The spider-beetle crawled from her ear and skittered on jointed, hairy legs across her cheek. It paused against the perfect tan backdrop of her face, pale grey in the photograph, then crawled with surprising speed over her lip and into her mouth.

Steven stumbled and fell, tumbling over the macadam. He felt his knees and elbows tear open and start bleeding. His chin struck the pavement, scraping itself bare, as did one shoulder and a hip.

Hannah ran on, oblivious.

Steven felt blood seeping from the back of his hand and his neck, not from his cuts and grazes. It pooled in a black puddle around him and he mopped the street with his T-shirt. He looked as though he had been doused with a bucket of heavy syrup.

Too hot, too tired, too dehydrated and too battered to get up, Steven lay in the street, the legions of runners he had passed stepping over or around him as they made for the finish line, most of them awkward, moving in jerky stops like figures in a silent movie. The dog stayed with him, sitting on its haunches, until it finally padded across the road and bit him on the wrist.

Light and colour returned. 'Ow, fucking shit! What did you do that for, you bastard?' he shouted.

The voice rang in his head. Unlike Nerak's, which had boomed from everywhere at once, this was small, plaintive. *Wake up, Steven.*

Things went runny, gelled and shifted, some fading while others shone stark and bold; runners drifted across Stanley Avenue towards Clear Creek. Steven was lying beneath a pair of oak trees that had grown beside the road. They blocked the sun, allowing only flickers of dappled yellow to reach him. Blinking, he sat up and surveyed the damage to his wrist. It wasn't bad. *Everything hurts, though. My arms, legs, lungs, back, knees, chin; fuck, even my eyes hurt, for Christ's sake.*

Wake up, Steven.

Dogs can't talk.

I know that, silly.

Just let me rest. Leave me alone for a second and let me rest.

The boat's going to crash.

What boat? What . . . ? The blanket. You mean the blanket? The boat under the blanket?

Wake up, Steven.

THE INLET

'Come about, Marrin,' Captain Ford said, calmly, sensibly. Garec had been shouting. 'Make your course zero-six-zero. You can see it. We have to round that point.'

Marrin had lashed himself to the helm. He was armed with a battle-axe and a short dagger and waved them wildly when anyone moved towards him. He was lost in the throes of whatever madness had found him on the brig-sloop's quarterdeck. They were closing fast on the Malakasian trawler now.

Garec hadn't lowered his bow, though he had no wish to kill Marrin.

'Wait, Garec, just a moment,' Captain Ford whispered.

'We don't have much time, sir.'

'You think I can't see that?' He reached for a pin near the base of the mainmast and braced himself as the *Morning Star* pitched and bumped over the swells, running into the shore. They would run aground; the water was deep enough to round the point, but if they rammed the trawler, Steven's cloaking spell would be shattered. If they survived the impact, they'd be limping into Pellia, completely exposed.

'Marrin,' he tried again, 'if you ram that ship, it's a tag hanging for all of us. You realise that, don't you?'

The first mate stared somewhere beyond the Malakasian shoreline, and mumbled, nothing the others could understand. It didn't look like he even heard them.

'Let me take him,' Garec said. 'I won't kill him.'

'Not yet. Kellin?'

'I'm here.' Her voice came from somewhere behind him. He didn't turn to look.

'Get below; see if you can help Gilmour.' Warily he moved a few steps closer.

Marrin mumbled louder and tightened the bit of hemp holding him to the brig-sloop's wheel.

Captain Ford stopped. They were close to the trawler; he could hear voices hailing from across the shallows. The breakwater, a few hundred paces offshore, roared a background warning. *Grand*, Ford thought. *Even if we miss the boat, we'll be caught on the mud. We'll never make this tack, not now.* Without taking his eyes off Marrin, he said, 'Brexan?'

'Right behind you.'

'Garec?'

'I'm getting impatient, Captain.'

'Pel?'

No response.

'Pel!' Captain Ford shouted, 'Where are you?'

'Haven't seen him, sir,' Garec said quietly.

'All right, all right, gods rut us all. We'll do it alone.'

'What's that?'

'You two.' He took another step. The quarterdeck was only two paces away now. 'Prepare to come about, wear hard to starboard. Understand?'

'Yes, sir,' Garec and Brexan answered in unison.

'Pel?' he tried again, but no one answered. They were out of time. He had to retake the helm. He didn't want to risk having Garec shoot and possibly kill his first mate, but he also didn't believe that wounding Marrin would do them any good. Marrin looked as though he could be struck senseless by a lightning bolt and would still never release his grip.

'All right you two ... get ready.'

When a hand reached up to grip the stern rail behind Marrin, Captain Ford gasped. For a moment he thought it was another tanbak, come to avenge the one Steven had dealt with, but when he saw the frayed tunic sleeves, the skinny wrists and the pale skin, Ford knew he had found Pel Wandrell.

Gods keep him a thousand Twinmoons, he thought. *The crazy bastard climbed out my cabin window. Good thinking, Pel! Top marks!*

Pel looked terrified, but he never hesitated. He slipped silently over the rail, making eye contact with his captain: he needed a distraction.

Captain Ford understood, and started at Marrin, saying, 'You know we'll never make this tack, not with only three of us hauling these lines, we'll never wear in time, not coming about in this wind.'

Pel sneaked behind Marrin, staying low, and as the captain continued to address the first mate, he leaped on Marrin's back, wrapping one slim arm around his friend's throat while grabbing at the dagger with the other. He was tiny in comparison to the muscular first mate, and for a moment he looked like a child getting a piggy-back from an older brother. He hung on grimly as the captain ran up, his filleting knife already drawn, but Marrin managed to shrug Pel off his shoulders and free his dagger hand. He raised the short blade to stab his shipmate—

'No!' Ford cried, too late. He took two running steps towards the helm, then dived, but he was in midair when what he was seeing finally registered. The first arrow passed clean through Marrin's wrist, and the dagger had clanked to the deck, useless, just as Pel, expecting to feel the cold blade slicing through his flesh, released his death grip about Marrin's throat and fell backwards towards the stern rail. A second shaft, fired at an impossibly short interval behind the first, passed through Marrin's opposite hand, tearing it from the helm, and the possessed or delusional first mate fell back against the ropes holding him up.

Captain Ford pushed himself to his feet and sliced the ropes, then brought the rudder chain as far as he could to starboard, screaming, 'Come about, my darling, come about, old girl!'

Marrin, transfixed by the arrow through his hand, tumbled down beside Pel as Garec and Brexan followed the captain's orders, hauling in slack lines as fast as they could. Slowly, painstakingly, the *Morning Star* began to turn.

'Pel,' Ford shouted, 'Pel, gods love you, son, but you did it! You did it!'

The boy rolled from Marrin's bloody body and sprang to his feet. Mumbling incoherently, and visibly trembling, the young seaman hugged himself as if to be sure he was still intact.

'Pel,' Ford ordered, wanting to stop shock setting in, 'get over here and keep us hard to starboard. We'll miss the trawler, thank all the gods of the Northern Forest, but we're still in trouble with that mud reef. You see those breakers, Pel? Pel!'

'Captain?' Pel whispered, still not quite sure what had happened.

'Pel! To me!' he ordered again.

'What—? Right, yes, sorry, Captain . . .' His voice trailed off.

Captain Ford wrapped an arm around the boy's shoulders, pulled him close, steadying him for a moment, then, calmly, he said, 'All I need you to do, Pel, is keep us on this tack. Just take the helm. I've got to haul in the foresheets, or we're rutting screwed. You understand me?'

'Aye, aye, Captain. I won't let you down, sir. I can—'

The spider-beetle crawled up Pel's cloak and scampered across Captain Ford's wrist.

'Great whoring rutters, Pel, look out! Get back, son! Get back!' He shoved the sailor, too hard, sending him tumbling across the quarterdeck until he rolled to a stop against a rain barrel lashed to the port gunwale.

Letting go the helm, Ford shook his arm frantically, trying to shake the bug loose before it bit him and left him as senseless as Steven. He wasn't a sorcerer; maybe even one puncture would kill him. He stumbled and tripped over Marrin's legs, landing hard on his back.

'Where is the gods-rutting thing?' He was vulnerable, flat on his back like this. 'Get up,' he growled, 'don't wait for it.' He yanked off his cloak and pulled his tunic off over his head, then got up on his knees, scanning the deck for the tan-bak's persistent little sentry. He brushed his hands down his leggings again, then, in a panic, ran his hands through his hair until it was a tousled mess.

'What's the matter with you?' Garec shouted. 'Can't you feel the keel is righting? Take the rutting helm!'

He was oblivious to Garec's warning, concentrating on the deadly little spider-beetle. There it was, skittering across the planks, heading for Pel.

'Watch out!' Captain Ford cried, leaped towards the insect, stomped down hard, missed and stomped again, until he had to catch his breath. As he stood still, doubled over and panting, he realised what Garec had been screaming, and ran back to the helm.

'What was that?' Pel was beginning to think his captain had been infected by whatever had taken Marrin. 'All that for a spider, sir?' His voice wavered a little still.

Captain Ford tried to ignore the fact that he was navigating half-naked – in the winter Twinmoon – and less than an aven from Pellia. He peered across the bow, ignoring the shouts and jeers of the Malakasian fisherman – too close – off the port rail and searched for the mud reef. It was impossible for them to clear, not without a miracle wind from the southwest.

'A wind?' he muttered to himself, then, 'Pel!'

The frightened sailor steadied himself on the rail. 'I know, Captain, haul in the foresheets and make it qui—'

'No, forget them; get below and get Gilmour, tell him to get up here *right now*, and I do mean right this very moment. The survival of this ship – and us – depends up on it. Do you understand?'

422

'Aye, aye, Captain.' Pel rushed for the main hatch.

'We need a gale,' Ford muttered. He looked over at Marrin, who sprawled on the deck, looking deathly pale. His wrist was still bleeding, and Garec's second arrow still protruded from his left hand. A tiny trickle of blood seeped from his left ear.

The trawler crew were screaming curses at him. Ford, naked from the waist up and looking like a madman, waved and blew a kiss to the furious Malakasians. 'Don't you see I have other problems right now?' he shouted. 'I'd love to stay and talk, but I really have to go. I'm running my ship aground, and then I have to get to my hanging; I'd hate to be late. It was lovely to see you, though!'

'He's going to be screaming about us all the way back to Pellia,' Garec pointed out. He looped a length of rope around a pin. It was a tangled mess, but it held.

'There's nothing we can do about it now.'

'I can take them,' Garec said. 'I'd rather not, but I can do it. We can't have them telling the whole city how a rogue sloop nearly sent them to the bottom.'

'We'll worry about it *if* we're still afloat in the next half-aven, but for now, get forward – that foremain is doing us no good. You need to shorten the line and tie it off tight.'

'But there's no wind—'

'And *this* bloody wind is running us aground! Don't argue, Garec, just do it!'

Gilmour appeared from below, looked at Marrin, still in a heap, bleeding, and asked, 'What happened up here?'

'The wind,' Captain Ford cut across him, 'the one you used to blow that thing off Steven's neck – can you do that again? I mean right now.' He pointed at the sails he needed filled.

Gilmour sized up the situation and started incanting the spell, hurrying between the foremast and the main, blowing the sheets full, while Garec and Brexan manned the lines.

The *Morning Star* took her time coming about.

The captain leaned on the helm, his teeth clenched, and watched the sheets fill, empty and fill again as Gilmour blasted away at them. He listened to the roar of the breakwater just beneath the bow and whispered, 'Come on, old girl, come on around. You don't want to bite that mud; you don't want to leave us out here. Come on, my darling girl . . .'

The brig-sloop struck, throwing Garec and Brexan to the deck.

Gilmour kept his feet, still hurling massive gusts into the sails, determined to bring the *Morning Star* about . . .

Captain Ford cursed like a trooper, but never let go of the rudder. 'Hit it again,' he begged, 'aft just a bit, hit it again, my darling, come on, now old girl . . .'

The *Morning Star* obliged, hauling her backside around and bouncing and glancing off the mud reef. The water was just deep enough for the little ship's shallow hull to clear the bottom and make the tack, however bumpy. The captain spared a grin for Garec, for every time he tried to stand, the brig-sloop glanced off the reef, sending him rolling for the starboard rail again and again.

'Pel, get below, see if we're taking on water.' He turned to the sorcerer and said, 'Give us a few more gusts, if you can, please – I'd like to overtake that fishing trawler before he has a chance to alert the entire Malakasian navy.'

Gilmour interrupted his spell-weaving long enough to reply, 'Aye, aye, Captain!'

'And Gilmour, what news of Steven?'

'He'll live—' Gilmour looked nervous, 'but I'm not certain how long he'll be out. I've drained a great deal of blood, so I imagine he'll be weak and disoriented for some time when we finally get him back.'

'Are we still . . .'

'Yes, the spell should keep us well hidden, as long as Steven doesn't die.'

Pel appeared from below and reported, 'One futtock cracked, sir, in the bow, just above the bilge. Probably caused by the initial impact.'

'Then forget it,' Captain Ford said decisively. 'We need you up here. If we make it to port alive, we'll patch it when the tide turns, but right now we're running empty, and I don't care if we take on some water – it won't slow us much more than a bit of extra ballast. We've nearly flown up here this Moon. Dragging our backsides will make honest sailors out of us again.'

'Aye, aye, sir.'

'Now, see to those foresails, on my mark . . .'

Between then, they got the *Morning Star* into position and as she caught the northerly wind – the real wind – she glided towards the inlet with ease. Content with both heading and speed, Ford handed the wheel to Pel and turned to Brexan.

'Time to deal with Marrin,' he said soberly.

*

Marrin lay unconscious in the captain's cabin, breathing in shallow gasps. The spider-beetle's venom had polluted his blood. No one knew when it had burrowed inside his ear canal – it might have been in there for days, ever since the tan-bak killed Sera and Tubbs – but the poison had travelled too far. Gilmour watched the patient and tried to make sure Marrin's vital systems continued to function, though he had no idea what he would do were one to shut down.

The others searched the ship for more spider-beetles, but if there were more of the insect hunters on board, they were well hidden.

Now Pel, Garec, Brexan and Kellin emerged on deck; no one wanted to miss Ford navigating the Welstar River.

When they passed the trawler, the Malakasian fishermen barely gave the graceful brig-sloop a second glance. Brexan said, 'It does look like Steven's cloaking spell is still working.'

'And it might save our lives.' Captain Ford agreed. 'It's as if they see us but don't realise they're seeing us.'

'Look, that man – the captain maybe – he's looking straight through us.'

'Let's hope it works on the whole city.'

The brig-sloop came around the final point, hugging the shore, towards a rocky, windswept jetty, brushed green with a narrow strip of pine forest. Beyond, the Welstar River spread out before them, at least five times as wide as the Medera River in Orindale and looking more like a great lake.

No one spoke at first; they all worried that the slightest sound would bring the full attention of the Malakasian capital down on their little ship.

'Well, there it is,' Captain Ford said at last, 'a veritable highway of bad news for us.'

'You can do it,' Brexan said, full of admiration for his skill that morning.

'Hold your breath,' he warned, 'here we go.'

Gilmour's estimation of Malakasian strength looked to be quite accurate. They could see several patrol boats, flanked by two heavily armoured schooners that were plying the deeper water between the city and a strip of sand on the east bank near the jetty. Two barges passed off the *Morning Star's* bow, one headed north towards a big galleon moored near the main wharf and another tacking south towards the naval schooners and customs boats.

'Well, that certainly cuts off any escape route upriver,' Ford murmured.

'But they don't seem to see us,' Brexan said.

'Or if they do, maybe they're mistaking us for a fishing boat, one of the locals working the shallows. There was a whole fleet of them down there this morning.'

'As big as we are?'

'Steven's your friend, you tell me: is he strong enough to make us look like a fishing boat? I, for one, hope so.'

'What about when we get downriver? And look out for those barges!'

'Brexan, would you just let me steer the ship? I've been doing this for a long time; I'm not going to ram a barge.' He focused his gaze north and, despite all that had happened, stifled a laugh.

Brexan said, 'It looked like you were heading straight into that one – this is frightening enough without you showing off!'

'Showing off?' He scowled. 'We can't be more than half an aven from certain death, and you accuse me of showing off?'

'Well . . .'

'Well, what?'

'Well, how often do you have attractive young women here watching your every move?' she said teasingly, easing the tension.

'All the rutting time,' he shot back, 'and let me remind you that with your Seron-crooked smile, you may not be the most attractive visitor this quarterdeck has ever seen.' He altered their heading slightly, bearing away from the schooners.

'Oh, really? You think so?'

'Oh, really, yes,' he grinned, 'our Tubbs attracted all sorts of fine-looking women, I can assure you!'

'Tubbs?' Brexan burst out laughing, then covered her face when she noticed Garec and Kellin, both deadly serious, looking at her. She caught her breath and asked, 'So what about north of us? Why aren't there more boats down there?'

'I don't—' He broke off mid-sentence and stared.

'What is it?'

'I think it's the reason our Malakasian friends don't have additional patrols working the stretch of water from the wharf to the centre of the river.' He pointed.

'I don't see any . . . Oh.'

The shipmates instinctively moved together as they spotted the three massive frigates emerging like ghost ships over the horizon, dwarfing their escorts, a little fleet of cutters and schooners. There was no mistaking the frigates, which had obviously come through the Northeast Channel and were now making way – with haste, it appeared – towards the Pellia waterfront.

'That's him,' Captain Ford said. 'The downriver patrols have gone out with the harbourmaster. I'll bet it's not every day ships like that come in, let alone three at a time.'

Brexan was beaming. 'Then we made it. We did it. We're here ahead of him. Granted, it may only be by a few avens, but we did it.' She hugged him, briefly but with genuine affection.

Ford gave her a half-hearted embrace in return.

'What's the matter?' she asked, puzzled.

'Now we need Steven.'

PELLIA

Jacrys bunched the blankets beneath his chin and watched as the sun rose over Pellia Harbour and a massive frigate made her way slowly towards a deep-water pier not far from the spy's waterfront safe house. Two others remained moored on the inlet, and a convoy of flat-bottomed barges were waiting to transfer passengers and cargo ashore. Captain Thadrake, still in uniform, dozed in a chair near the smouldering fire.

'Thadrake!' Jacrys wheezed, coughing a constellation of crimson droplets onto the bedding.

'Sir?' Thadrake roused himself, adjusting his tunic as he said, 'Sorry, sir; I must have drifted off.'

'Of course you drifted off, Captain. It's not yet dawn and all of Malakasia is sleeping.'

'What can I get you, sir? Some cheese? Or there's a bit of fruit—Oh, no, that's right; you eat only bread and tecan for breakfast. I'll run down and fetch us a fresh loaf and a couple of warm flagons. I'll need a bit of copper, though. I spent a bit too much on last night's dinner.'

He was halfway to the door when Jacrys found the strength to call him back. 'None of that, Captain, but come here, if you please,' he asked.

Thadrake dragged his chair over beside the cot Jacrys had chosen as his deathbed. 'What is it, sir?'

'Those ships, the frigates, how long have they been here?'

'They arrived yesterday.' He sliced a piece of cheese from the remains of the block standing on the little table and nibbled at one corner, then pointed. 'Those two there have been offloading what looks to be a division of soldiers, I don't know which corps, but I can find out when I go down for breakfast. They appear to be en route for Welstar Palace, just like the other vessels that have been running upriver since we arrived, sir. These frigates are too big to get to the military encampment so they've commandeered anything that floats – every available barge, schooner, even rowboats. I can't think why Prince Malagon would need another division at the palace, but they're here.'

'It seems he's still alive then,' Jacrys muttered.

'Yes, sir.' Thadrake paused. 'There were rumours all over Orindale that he had died, or disappeared, maybe been taken prisoner, but from the looks of these curious troop movements the prince is very much alive and well and most likely back home.'

'Perhaps,' Jacrys said, holding a bloodstained cloth near his mouth.

'Anyway,' Thadrake went on, 'this frigate coming in must be hauling something other than just troops, because she's about to tie up – maybe, if she's come up from the south, from Praga, maybe it's General Hollis. Who knows? And if they're from the east, Falkan or Rona, well, it could be anyone. I didn't hear anything about Prince Malagon calling General Oaklen home, but I've been out of touch.'

Jacrys ignored him, continuing to stare out the window as the wooden giant eased its way alongside the pier. Finally, he whispered, 'Captain, I need you to do me a favour.'

'Of course, sir.' Thadrake stood.

'Take the money we have left, along with whatever you can find amongst my personal effects ... I would like you to locate my father—'

'Should I bring him here, sir?'

'Don't interrupt, Captain!' Jacrys spasmed and started coughing. He rammed the stained kerchief into his mouth and bit down, breathing through his nose, until the shaking stopped. When he removed the cloth, soaked through with blood and phlegm, he repeated, 'Find my father, give him the money and let him know where he can find me. Keep enough – a silver piece or two – to get yourself back to General Oaklen. Sell the fennaroot, keep whatever you get – consider it a bonus for a job well done.'

When he was sure Jacrys had finished, he asked, 'Sir, it may take me several days to locate your father. What if—?'

'I don't care,' the spy whispered. 'I don't anticipate any meaningful reunion. I want my father, because I want him to give me my rites. He'll know how and where.' He paused for a while, then added, 'Consider yourself dismissed, Captain. I wish you well.'

It took just a few moments to gather together Jacrys' scant belongings. 'Anything else before I go, sir?' he asked, feeling rather strange about leaving, even though it was a direct order from a superior officer.

'Please.' The word felt strange on Jacrys' tongue. 'Stoke up the fire, and pour me a goblet of that wine we had last night, fill it up right to the brim.'

Thadrake picked the chunks of wood most likely to burn longest, then passed Jacrys his wine. The dying man cradled the goblet with both hands and watched the frigate, which had tied up at the pier, where it was immediately set upon by a team of stevedores rolling a block-and-tackle crane amidships. A twin-masted ketch, a quick, shallow boat, came alongside and lashed on to the starboard rail. Opening their shallow hold, her crew waited for whatever cargo they were to haul upriver. 'Must be someone special,' Jacrys muttered, but Captain Thadrake was already gone.

'Where are you going so early?' Alen appeared in the open doorway across the hall.

Hannah whirled. 'Jesus! You scared me.' She rested a hand against the wall and willed her heart to stop beating so fast.

'Can't sleep?' Alen asked quietly.

'Did you see those ships that came in yesterday?' Hannah whispered. 'One of them has finished offloading soldiers and now it's heading in to the wharf. I want to go down there and see what's happening.' She didn't want to wake Hoyt or Milla. 'The tide's about to turn; so unless they're planning to stay all day, they'll only be here until they can start upriver. That gives us about half an aven.'

'Hold on a moment,' he said, 'and I'll come along.'

'You don't have to; I'll be fine. I just want to—' She looked at him, her eyes narrowed. 'Alen, what are you doing awake? It isn't like you to be up this early.'

'Something's happening,' he said, fussing with his clothes, 'but I'm not sure what it is.'

'Steven?' Hannah tried to ignore the sudden lurch in her stomach.

'It's something – or some*one*, I should say. It's not like the bark shipments. This is different.'

'Then let's go. Bring Milla in here with Hoyt; we'll be back before either of them wakes up.'

'How is he?' Alen whispered once they'd tucked Milla into Hannah's bed.

'He needs antibiotics, penicillin or something – this voodoo horse-shit isn't working.'

'But he'll sleep for now?' Alen looked worried.

'Yes, deeply, and the querlis poultices keep his fever down, at least for a while, anyway.'

'Very well,' Alen said. 'Lead the way.'

'This is a big gamble,' Captain Ford said, 'and I don't like it.' He followed Brexan and Garec through the twisting maze of Pellia's side-streets; Gilmour trailed behind.

'I agree,' Garec said, 'but I don't think it's one we can avoid.' He kept a look-out for morning patrols.

'We need to find a healer, now,' the captain said for the third or fourth time.

'I understand that,' Garec replied, also for the third or fourth time, 'and we will.' He carried his bow and quivers wrapped in a length of sailcloth, draped over his shoulder, effectively camouflaging the weapons.

'Out here, on the wharf? Come on, Garec, you know as well as I that—'

Garec stopped and took Ford's arm, allowing Brexan to push on to the next corner alone. She checked the cross-street then motioned the others forward.

'Captain, right now, they're both resting,' Garec said, 'and they're both as comfortable as we can make them. Pel and Kellin are with them, and they will stay there until we get back. We watched those frigates closely last night, all night, and none of us saw them unloading cargo; it was all soldiers. Now one of them is making its way to the pier and we have to assume that's Mark, and we have to assume he has the table with him. We'll find someplace to sit for a while; I'll buy you breakfast. We'll wait a bit, and we'll watch. If he has the table, we'll hit him with whatever we can, try to knock him off balance while we steal it, break it, drop it to the bottom of the harbour; I don't know quite what, but we have to try something – and right now, we have to do it alone.'

'Without Steven.'

'You've seen Steven,' Garec said, trying not to sound as exasperated as he was. 'He's in no shape to help us. And from what I understand, if the table is closed, Mark isn't nearly as powerful.'

'So what exactly do we do? I don't like confrontations on dry land, Garec; they make me nervous. Why don't we bring the *Morning Star* around the marina? She's no good to us over there; we can take Mark out as soon as he shows his face; you can hit him from two hundred paces and Gilmour can blast that table to shards.'

'Unfortunately for your plan, I think we need the table intact,' Gilmour said quietly. 'And as much as I would like us to find a healer and hurry back to the ship, we must first find out what Mark is doing. If he ties up at the pier and makes no move to unload the table, then yes, we need to hit him – who knows what he might do this close to Welstar Palace? He flooded Orindale just to stop us; he might destroy all of Pellia in his attempts to stop us pursuing him upriver. But I don't think that'll be the case; I'm betting the next round that he's bringing it to shore. It's heavy, so maybe he needs a crane. Maybe he doesn't want to risk an accident in the water. He's obviously in a hurry and dropping the table overboard would delay him here for a few days, maybe a Moon.'

Pale and sweaty, Gilmour looked like a man on a head-on collision course with Fate. Losing Steven had been an unanticipated blow, and Captain Ford worried that the Larion Senator would soon see the rest of his strategy begin to unravel as well. He checked that his knife was loose in its sheath and joined the others as they hurried after Brexan.

'How much further?' he asked when she was within earshot.

'Not far,' Brexan said quietly. 'A few more blocks, and we'll be back on the river. It's still early, but the wharf's going to be busy in just a little while.'

'That's fine with me,' Garec said. 'It's a lot easier to get lost in a crowd, and we all know the way back to the *Morning Star*. So if things come apart, don't wait around, just get back to the ship, as quickly and as quietly as possible.'

Ford had paid to moor the brig-sloop in a small marina just south of the city wharf. They had been lucky crossing the Welstar River, for most of the Malakasian capital had turned its attention north to Mark's mini-fleet. With the help of Steven's camouflage spell, the *Morning Star* had passed through the barge traffic with little more than a wave from the flat-bottomed river-runners. But now, not sure what the four of them could do against the might of the Larion spell table, Captain Ford wished they had remained onboard; at least there they could escape. His little brig-sloop would easily outrun the prince's barge fleet and be quickly out of reach of the deep-keeled frigates.

'It's cold,' he grumbled aloud.

Garec looked around. 'I said I'll buy you breakfast, just as soon as we get in sight of that fat wooden bitch. I'll find you a nice tavern and buy you anything you want.'

'I want a healer for Marrin,' he complained.

'Soon enough, Captain,' Garec said.

As if reading their minds, Brexan stopped behind a shipwright's workshop. 'There it is,' she said.

'Excellent work, my dear,' Gilmour said, moving past her into the road running along the top of the wharf. Here, the city was wide awake, with dockers and stevedores bustling about and customs officers and shipping merchants reviewing manifests and inventory lists. A group of beggars huddled around a small fire someone had kindled on the cobblestones, and a trio of drunken sailors sang, off-colour and out of tune, as they stumbled towards their waiting ship. As the sun rose behind them, it lit up the Falkan frigate, even larger than they had imagined, which creaked and groaned alongside the deepwater pier. A team of workers rolled a wooden block-and-tackle crane out to greet her the moment she was made fast.

'Look at that,' Captain Ford muttered, 'there's a ketch coming up to starboard. Rutting whores, I should have thought of that.'

'Of what?' Garec whispered. He had been distracted by a Malakasian officer approaching through the early morning mist that hung over the slowly brightening docks. 'Did you think we could sail up and have them load the table straight into the *Morning Star*? That's an interesting thought, my friend, but I'm afraid there are quite enough innovative ways to die out here today without going looking for any others.'

'No, but the ketch answers Gilmour's question.'

'How's that?' Brexan, noticing the officer now, moved into the crowd gathering to watch the great ship take shape in the rising sun. She slouched under her cloak, trying to become invisible.

'What's with her?' Ford whispered, then turned to the officer and said, 'Good morning, Captain. Impressive sight, isn't she?'

The Malakasian, a young man, looked around the wharf, then whispered, 'You lot interested in a bit of fennaroot?'

'Root?' Captain Ford said, surprised. 'Thank you, Captain, but no. We don't get paid until *our* captain signs the manifest; so for now, fennaroot is a bit out of our price range. We were looking for a decent place to get some breakfast, however.'

Thadrake frowned. 'Can't help, I'm afraid,' he said curtly, and moved off without giving them another glance.

Garec watched him go. 'Well, he seemed nice, didn't he? You can come back now, Brexan.'

'You all right?' the captain asked her.

'I know him,' Brexan whispered. 'He was the officer leading the searches in Orindale. I don't know what he's doing up here.'

'Who cares?' Garec grimaced. 'He's a sour one, anyway. I hope his wife beats him up for wearing her underclothes!'

Captain Ford laughed for the first time all morning. 'So are we planning to just stand here all day or can we get some food now?'

'You were telling us how that little ship there—'

'The ketch.'

'Whatever,' Brexan said, 'the ketch, then: so how does that answer Gilmour's question?'

'We may actually be too late.'

'How's that?' Garec asked. 'That crane's only just rolling in, so they can't have offloaded the table yet.'

'Right, but we're at about low tide, and I'm surprised the captain of that beast dared to bring her in here at all.'

Gilmour said, 'I'm quite sure Mark is making all the decisions aboard that ship, Captain Ford.'

'All right, so that makes sense, then. With the tide about to turn, he'll probably move that table onto that little twin-master and ride the incoming water halfway to Welstar Palace.'

'What?' Garec blanched. 'So we need to move now! I have to find a place to make a shot, someplace out of sight from the frontage—'

'No,' Gilmour cut him off, 'we're all right. They're not going to move it yet.' He had taken a few steps towards the pier and was staring into the frigate's rigging, where sailors moved to and fro, as confident aloft as they were on the ground.

'How do you know?' Brexan asked.

'Because Mark knows I'm here.'

'Oh rutters – what do we do? He could be opening the table right now. We've got to get out of here, get back to the *Morning Star*—' Captain Ford was ready to run; the others looked willing to join him.

'No,' Gilmour said again, 'we have some time.'

'How do you know?'

'Because he's looking for Steven.'

'So ... what then?' Garec said.

Gilmour broke from his trance. Grinning, he said, 'Garec, I think you promised the good captain some breakfast.'

Captain Ford, suddenly pale, muttered, 'I'm not sure I'm hungry, thanks.'

'He's here,' Redrick whispered. 'I can smell him, Blackford. I can smell his stench from across the city, but how they survived the tanbak, I haven't a clue.'

'Yes, sir,' Blackford replied, unwilling to say anything else, in case it might cost him his life.

'He's over there somewhere, on the wharf, probably watching us right now . . . okay, this is fucking odd: I can't get a whiff—' Redrick squinted as the sun crested the rooftops, blinding him. 'Ah, no matter. He'll show himself. It's just a matter of time, and he'll come. He has to.'

'Yes, sir,' Blackford repeated, 'and in the meantime, sir, is there anything I can do?'

Redrick hesitated, as if considering his options, then said, 'Yes, Captain Blackford, I would like the cargo in my cabin prepared for transfer right away. A river-runner will be coming alongside in a few moments. Make certain they lash themselves amidships. When they're prepared, and the crane is secure, lash on to the crate; then find me. Do *not* move it without me, Blackford. I want to be ready to sail with the incoming tide. That gives both of us about half an aven. Understand?'

'Yes, sir.' The weary officer shook with equal parts fear and cold and exhaustion.

'Until then, I'm going to do a bit of hunting.' Redrick paused to shout orders to the men preparing the block-and-tackle to transfer the spell table for its journey upriver. Blackford stood on the quarterdeck long enough to see Redrick meander down the gangplank. Then, literally quaking, he summoned what remained of his courage and hurried towards the main cabin. 'I've got to find that stone,' he whispered to the gods of the Northern Forest. 'Please, please let it be in there.'

'Which one is he?' Brexan asked, sipping a welcome mug of hot tecan.

'It's impossible to say.' Gilmour peered through the tavern windows. They had got lucky and found a café open early for the dock workers. 'The whole pier is reverberating with Larion magic, and that means the table is still there, somewhere on that ship. But right now I can't pinpoint Mark, other than to know for certain that he's here, very close now.'

'That's not terribly comforting,' Garec said. 'What if he opens the table?'

'He won't.' Gilmour seemed more confident now that he'd had a moment to think. 'He'll be too afraid to open it until he knows exactly where Steven is – that's Nerak's fear, a Twinmoon later, and still echoing like a fart in a canyon.'

'Nice.' Brexan frowned.

'But true,' Gilmour said. 'Mark didn't know anything about magic, but Nerak did, and Nerak died terrified of Steven Taylor. Thank the gods the creature inhabiting Mark Jenkins had a taste of that insecurity, or we'd all be dead already.'

'Why the fear?'

'He knows we're here, but he can't find Steven,' Gilmour explained. 'If he can't find Steven, he risks Steven crashing down on him the moment he opens the table.'

Captain Ford dipped a crust of bread into his goblet. 'So what will he do?'

Gilmour shook his head. 'I don't know. Wait? Search?'

'Bury the whole city under an avalanche of fire?' Garec added.

'Perhaps,' Gilmour conceded, then dug about in his robes for a pipe.

'Gods, I wish you could feel this,' Alen said.

'What's that? Magic? No thanks.' Hannah tore off a piece of warm bread and wrapped it about a sausage.

'It's everywhere.' Alen appeared to have developed a nervous tic. He ignored his breakfast and checked the wharf. 'It's like Sandcliff used to be, energy all over the place; I can feel it on my skin like summer wind.'

'Whose energy is it?'

'I don't know, but it's enormous, more powerful than me or Fantus, or even Milla.'

'Could it be another shipment of bark? That's an awfully big ship. If even one of the holds was full, it might resonate—'

'No,' Alen interrupted, rubbing his arms against the chill. 'This is like . . .'

'Alen?' Hannah spoke with her mouth full. 'You all right?'

'I wish I had contacted Fantus again.'

'So what should we do?'

'We should wait. It won't be long.'

*

Redrick slipped behind the workers nailing wooden braces into the wharf. The block-and-tackle crane towered overhead as they lashed it to the braces and let out a length of heavy rope, then they hefted crude stone counterweights from a trolley, two men to each stone. They stacked them on each corner and checked the stability, tugging hard on the main line – then waved to the sailors waiting near the quarterdeck.

That'll keep them for a while anyway, Redrick thought as he ducked between the harbourmaster's office and a boarding house. At the frontage road, still out of sight, he sent a seeking spell through the waterfront, but it yielded nothing helpful: there was too much magic around, too many waves of noisy power emanating from the spell table and the keystone, from Fantus and Steven. They were here, nearby, but lost in the miasma, impossible to locate.

Perhaps a bit closer, Redrick thought, and slunk along the road, back towards the deep-water pier. He kept the seeking spell alive, searching the crowds, the side streets, the buildings.

Then Gilmour was there, stepping from a dockside tavern.

But no Steven.

'They're about finished securing that crane.' Garec was sweating. 'We should go.'

'Another moment, please; have another drink.' Gilmour didn't look at him, but stared across the *Bellan's* decks, watching and feeling for signs of Mark. It was a daunting task, locating anything in the mystical fog.

'Why didn't the table give off this kind of power when we found it in Meyers' Vale?' Garec asked. 'I don't remember you being this overwhelmed by it down there.'

'Because this is more than the table,' Gilmour said, 'this is me, Mark, the table, and ... someone else.'

'Kantu?' Brexan asked.

'Maybe.'

'Who else could it be?' Garec swilled the last of his tecan.

Gilmour whispered, almost to himself, 'That little girl, Milla.'

Before the others could respond, Gilmour was bustling towards the door. He tossed a few copper Mareks to the barman and forced a smile. 'Lovely breakfast, my friend. What's on for midday?'

'Fish stew.' The Malakasian was drying tankards with a cloth. He caught the Mareks and stashed them in his apron.

'Shrimp, booacore and jemma?'

'Of course. With potatoes, pepperweed and leeks.'

'Nice and spicy; excellent,' Gilmour said. 'We'll be back.'

The barman shrugged, unimpressed. 'Whatever.'

The others hurried after him; Brexan cried, 'Wait, Gilmour.'

'Did that fellow just say booacore and jemma?' Alen craned his head to see over the bar. 'Delicious. I could do without the leeks, though. They always give me gas.'

Hannah stood. 'I don't know about booacore,' she said, 'but that woman just called that short guy "Gilmour".'

'What? Where?' Alen leapt to his feet.

'There, going out the alley door, that woman. She just called that little stout one "Gilmour". I heard her from here.'

Alen moved towards the window. 'No, it can't be. He's too ...'

'Young?' Hannah laughed. 'Call me crazy, but have you looked in a mirror recently? You look pretty good for a man three hundred years old.'

Alen was only half listening. He brushed his fingers over the goosebumps that had risen on his forearm.

'What is it?' Hannah asked. He looked as if he'd seen a ghost.

'You can't feel it,' he said, 'but the air in here just changed, as if it was sucked out into the street.'

'So what does that mean?'

He looked out of the window and peered down the alley. 'It means you're absolutely right: that's my old friend, Fantus.'

Jacrys finished the wine, tilting the goblet far enough to catch the last drops on his tongue. He let it slip from his fingers and it shattered on the floor.

'Rotten vintage,' he wheezed, 'but if that's the last thing I taste, I suppose it's better than nothing.' He propped himself on a pillow and looked over the wharf. 'Though it would have been nice to have one more Falkan—'

Jacrys' voice faltered; his skin tingled with pins and needles. When he finally remembered to breathe, the noisy rasp that filled the room with the wet sound of death unexpectedly unnerved him.

But I'm not dying. Not yet.

Through sheer force of will he rose from the cot – his deathbed – and drew Thadrake's knife from the block of cheese, then staggered towards the stairs.

It's not her, you dumb rutter. Get back into bed. You can't get down there; you'll die in the stairwell.

But Jacrys ignored his own advice. It *was* her, just below his window, emerging from the tavern beneath his own room. She had probably been enjoying breakfast with her friends. The one with the roll of sailcloth looked like the bowman, Garec Haile, still alive despite taking an arrow in the lungs that night in Orindale.

Get back into bed, he told himself sternly, *you're hallucinating. This is it; this is the end – of course you'd see her at the end. And Garec's dead; you know that, you killed him yourself.*

At the top of the stairs, the former spy, white, wide-eyed with pain and looking like a man possessed, clenched his teeth over the blade and braced his hands against the narrow walls. Blood soaked his tunic in a scarlet bib as he sucked in tortured breaths through his teeth. His lungs felt heavy, like waterlogged bags of sand in his chest. He took a step, then another. Pain lanced through his hips; his leg muscles twitched. Another step.

I'm coming for you, Brexan. I'll be down in just a moment.

Redrick sneaked into a doorway. 'It's him, the short one, sonofabitch,' he muttered. 'I've gotta get back to the table. I never should have boxed the damned thing up. I should have known, should have felt them coming, worthless frigging tan-bak. Shit!'

He peeked from his hiding place. Gilmour was still there, searching the crowds, hustling back and forth along the wharf, obviously panicked about something. His little partisan friends scurried after him.

'What are you looking for, Gilmour?' he asked. 'What do you think you know? And where is Steven?' Redrick watched another moment then stepped onto the road. The table wouldn't help him; Blackford probably had the crate so tangled in crane lines, it would take all day to reach it. 'All right, fine. Better this way, with the surprise element, than from the *Bellan*. He expects me up there.'

Blackford spun around. *Someone's coming!* He took an interminable moment to search the captain's cabin for a hiding place, then gave up – it was no use, the creature haunting Redrick Shen would find him in a heartbeat. He had to lie, and make it look convincing. The crate was his only option.

He moved quickly behind the wooden box and pretended to check the top and sides, as if ensuring the box wouldn't fall open during transfer. *Make it look good. You've got to make this look good.*

There was a soft knock at the cabin door. Blackford snapped to and shouted, 'Who is it?'

'Captain Blackford, sir, it's Kem. The crane's ready, sir. I have the lines here.'

Blackford exhaled quietly in relief and bade him enter; Kem came in, followed by three sailors, each dragging a length of hawser.

Kem looked the box over for a few moments, then announced, 'We'll have to turn it on its side, sir,' he said.

Blackford's heart thudded. 'That's fine,' he said. He considered slipping over the rail, disappearing into the Pellia streets and making for home – he could be there in less than a Moon.

'How'd he— uh, she— Well, you know, how'd it get it in here in the first place?' Kem asked, brushing a callused palm over the rough slats of the packing crate.

Remembering himself, Blackford shook his head.' That's not your concern. Just get it onto the deck and wait there for me.'

Run, fool. Redrick's gone. You'll be home in less than a Moon.

'Yes sir,' Kem said smartly, then turned on the others and shouted, 'Right you lot, let's get this motherless whore turned over.'

Blackford ignored them and was pushing past the crate, making for the companionway, when he saw the chest of drawers. It was fashioned from some ebony-coloured wood from southern Rona, and tucked discreetly away in a recessed area beneath the berth.

That's it, Blackford thought, a leap of excitement making his heart beat faster. *Unless he has it with him, that's where it'll be.*

Kem and the sailors worked behind him, quickly and efficiently, desperate to avoid damaging the stone table – given the probable punishment for damaging it, Blackford could understand why. However, he wasn't about to search the chest until he had the cabin to himself. The sailors wanted to see Redrick – the monster possessing him – leave the *Bellan*, for ever, but Blackford knew scared men would say anything to save their own lives. If they caught him searching the captain's cabin, they'd squeal on him in a heartbeat.

Despite the cold, the men were sweating.

'Kem, go and fetch another two men to help you,' Caption Blackford ordered. 'You three, get above decks and have that dough-headed horsecock of a crane operator slacken the hawsers. Now!'

'But sir,' Kem began, 'we've got—'

'Now!' Blackford shouted again.

'Yes, sir,' they said in unison. At least they had shared accountability should the table fall and crack.

The moment the cabin was empty, Blackford knelt to rifle through the chest. It didn't take long. The stone, a hand-sized lump of grey rock wrapped in a bit of cloth was nestled at the back of the top drawer. He pocketed it, carefully closed the drawer and hurried above decks.

Home in less than a Moon, he thought, *but not without this rock.* He crossed the main deck and made his way towards the gangplank. Kem, two additional sailors in tow, spotted him and called, 'Should we carry on with the crate, Captain?'

Without slowing, Blackford nodded and said, 'Yes, please—I mean, yes, at once! I'm off to fetch Redrick. We'll be back in a moment.'

Home in less than a Moon. Blackford reached the pier, turned along the wharf and didn't look back, even after the explosions echoed across the harbour.

'Gilmour, what are you doing?' Brexan asked.

'Milla, the girl I told you about, the one with Kantu?' He searched the crowd, looking for children. 'I think she's here somewhere. I can feel her.'

Garec, still shouldering his disguised weapons, felt like he was looking pretty suspicious, hurrying back and forth with a rolled length of sailcloth over his shoulder. 'What does she look like?' he asked.

'I don't know,' Gilmour said, 'like a little girl, maybe forty, fifty Twinmoons, not much more.'

'That shouldn't be too difficult,' Garec said. 'How many little—'

'Fantus!' someone shouted from the tavern, 'Fantus, get down!'

Gilmour turned to see a strange young man waving frantically and charging into the road. The stranger was obscured for an instant while a cart laden with headless jemmafish passed between them. When the explosion shattered the morning, the cart flipped end over end, spilling its cargo and splintering on the cobblestones.

With the instant's warning, Gilmour shouted something unintelligible to his friends and dived for the gutter, but it wasn't enough. Mark's spell struck him solidly, casting him up and through the thin wooden walls of a workers' hut. He fell through the stove, burning his back and arms, and crashed into the block-and-tackle crane next to the Falkan frigate.

Garec couldn't make out what the stranger had shouted, but he watched as Gilmour wheeled, shouted as well, then threw himself face-first onto the street.

Acting on instinct, Garec tightened his grip on the sailcloth roll and grasped a fistful of Brexan's sleeve. He heaved himself backwards, hauling Brexan with him, and slammed into Captain Ford. The three of them tumbled into the street beside the tavern as the dockside windows burst outwards in a cloud of flying glass. Several shards ripped through Garec's tunic, tearing open his back.

The street was unforgiving; Garec felt more skin scrape from his hip. Beside him, Ford cursed, and rolled over with a moan.

Brexan lay still, unnervingly silent.

'See to her!' Garec shouted, slipping an arm through one of his quivers, but the captain didn't move. 'Captain Ford!' Garec kicked him hard in the lower leg.

'What? What was that? Garec, what was that?' Shaking, obviously in shock, he covered his face with his hands.

'See to Brexan,' Garec repeated and strung his bow. 'I'll be back.' He watched long enough to see the seaman push himself onto all fours. *Good enough*, he thought, trying not to worry that he'd seen no sign of life from Brexan. There'd be time for that later.

He hesitated at the corner, ignoring the screams of the injured, the headless jemmafish strewn about and the crunch of broken glass beneath his boots. He felt blood trickling down his back and soaking into his clothes. His side ached and his hip blazed where he had scraped it raw. *Not much time*, he thought. *The waterfront guards will be here in two breaths.* There was another explosion, this one further away, somewhere east of the tavern, but like the blood, the fish, the screams and the broken glass, the *Bringer of Death* ignored it. He'd have one shot, maybe two, before Mark Jenkins found and killed him.

'The whoreson was in the tavern the whole time,' he murmured.

Jacrys was a few steps from the tiny foyer when the first explosion rocked the tavern and his upstairs safehouse. Without a banister, his tenuous grip on the cracked wooden walls failed and he tumbled to the lower floor. As the last step creaked beneath his weight, Jacrys took stock of his broken body. His chin dripped blood and a collarbone was broken – painful but not alarming; he needed only one good arm for what he was about to do. One ankle had been wrenched and he recognised the unpleasant tingling sensation that meant he'd torn ligaments. This too was inconvenient, but no real deterrent. The biggest problem was that something had finally broken – irreparably this time – inside his lung. He realised it was filling with blood, and quickly too; he'd drown soon.

So there was precious little time left. Jacrys fumbled for Thadrake's knife, set his jaw and pushed himself to his feet with a groan, screaming involuntarily when the broken ends of his collarbone rubbed together, and again when his ankle thunked against the wall. The sound was horrific, a penultimate death-rattle.

He barely registered the second explosion, nor did he hear the cries of the injured. With blood smeared over his face and bubbling on his lips, Jacrys Marseth staggered into the street.

Alen – *Kantu* – had been outside the tavern for just a moment when he felt the seeking spell. He didn't know why Fantus had failed to detect it, but he would have to act quickly, on faith that he had truly found his old friend. Someone close by was trying to kill him.

He cast a shield to protect himself and Hannah, a spell he hadn't called in over a thousand Twinmoons. Then he screamed, 'Fantus! Fantus, get down!' and pushed Hannah beneath the doorway, hoping the solid construction around the entryway might offer some slight protection. He had an instant's eye contact with Fantus before a wagon loaded with malodorous fish rattled past, then the blast crashed and rolled along the road. There hadn't been time to cast a protection spell over Fantus. His ears ringing, his magic boiling in his blood, Alen sprang to his feet and turned to face their attacker.

It was Nerak, it had to be, and whether he was in the guise of Prince Malagon, Princess Bellan, or a dockside shopkeeper, he didn't care. He had waited half his life for this chance; it was time for vengeance. From the east a muscular South Coaster, a sailor, strode into the carnage, rather than fleeing like most. The sailor stared straight ahead, through the crowds and across the wharf to where Fantus' body lay crumpled against the base of the wooden crane. He didn't turn aside, nor did he appear to flinch, or even to notice Alen at all.

Nine hundred Twinmoons he has his slaves searching for me, and now I'm fifteen paces away and he doesn't know it?

He glanced at Hannah. She was obviously shaken, but unhurt. Brushing bits of glass from her tunic, she looked up at him and shook her head.

I wish you could feel this . . . It's like Sandcliff used to be. The energy is all over the place.

Whose energy is it?

I don't know, but it's enormous, more powerful than me or Fantus, or even Milla.

Alen was shocked into stillness for a moment: nine hundred Twin-moons, and now Nerak didn't wish to face him. It didn't make sense. Then, watching Hannah pull herself up using the door frame, he realised what Fantus had screamed before diving to the cobblestones.

'It's not Nerak,' he whispered.

'What?' Hannah said, her ears still ringing. 'I can't hear you.'

'It's not him.' He pointed discreetly at the Ronan sailor, then clasped his hands together while his mind spiralled, almost out of control. 'What are we doing here?' he asked finally. Larion magic swirled around him. He revelled in it for a moment, allowing it to float him effortlessly back countless Twinmoons, to Sandcliff and to Pikan and his friends. He had been waiting half his life for a chance to kill his old colleague, and in an instant, he had lost it. He could still sense vestiges of Nerak, a faint scent, occasional traces of magic employed in recent Twinmoons, but Fantus had been right: whoever that was, it wasn't Nerak.

'What are we doing here?' he said again, still watching the South Coaster push through the crowd. 'What is that thing?'

'It's them, Alen,' Hannah said, 'your friends – they're here! That's Fantus over there; you said so yourself . . . Alen, help them, now!'

He looked around, then said, 'You're right; Hannah, please, get back inside!' He raised his palms to the sky, feeling his magic marshal itself for battle. Once he was certain the dark-skinned sailor was preoccupied with Fantus, and when the crowds around the Ronan sailor were thinnest, he released an incendiary spell that sent a second shock wave blazing across the pier.

The magic caught Redrick Shen unawares and he crashed through the front window of the Malakasian customs house. Alen started across the road, watching the wreckage and waiting for the South Coaster to reappear. With another spell at his fingertips, he ignored the warning sensation tickling the hairs on the back of his neck. It was nothing; he was just upset. There was nothing to be—

'Mark Jenkins!'

Alen heard the shout, louder and more intense than the here-and-there cries of the injured, but he paid it no attention, preferring instead to watch and wait for the thing inside the customs house. It wouldn't be long; it would be back. Perhaps if he pulled the whole building down, perhaps that might—

Arrow!

He let go the magic before turning around; Garec's first shot glanced up and over his shoulder, striking an invisible Larion barrier.

'You there!' he shouted—

Another arrow; rutters, but this boy is fast!

With a flick of his wrist, he set Garec's second shaft afire, side-stepped it and watched as it embedded itself in the wall of the building behind him.

'Stop shooting at me!' he cried, but another arrow was already on the way. He deflected this one too, then called a spell to stun the bowman, who had appeared out of a side street next to the tavern. The spell hit the archer in the chest, knocking him to the ground amidst a mess of fish and broken glass and wooden splinters.

When Alen started back toward the customs house, the creature was gone.

Thunk. The lights came on, not as before; these weren't swamp lights, orange twilights and red dawns coloured by marsh gases and fog. Rather, these were noisy, overhead lights, the kind one would find in a cafeteria or a warehouse. They came on with an audible *thunk* as the breaker switched. And they didn't brighten the room all of a sudden, like bathroom lights or lights on a stage; they took some time to warm up, and afterwards, the entire swamp would be bathed in the cold, harsh glare of shopping-mall white.

'What the hell is this?' Mark asked, still hugging the column, still watching for the crippled coral snake. 'What now?'

There was no answer.

'Hey,' Mark shouted across the basin and up through the tangled forest on the other side of the Gloriette, 'hey, dickhead, what's going on?'

Again, nothing.

As the marble coping, the marble columns and the narrow arched bridge came into focus, their haunted shadows banished, Mark realised something else: apart from the humming lights, there was no noise; there were no swampy smells. No insects buzzed and nipped at his face; no birds screamed, no frogs belched, nothing moved about in the brush. It was as if he had suddenly found himself on an elaborate sound stage, and all the dials labelled 'Swamp Effects' had been turned to zero.

'Hey, stinky!' he tried again. 'You still up there?'

The warehouse lights brightened the forest enough for him to see where someone had been working. The view, obscured thus far by vines, clouds of fog and shadows, was now relatively clear, and Mark couldn't spot anyone moving on the side of the hill.

'Must've gone out, got hungry,' he murmured.

But the real lights, the natural lights that he had been trying to reach, those were still on.

Mark gnawed on his lower lip, took a last look around, and said, 'Screw it. Let's go.' If the person on the hill, the one responsible for summoning all those gruesome and disfigured creatures, was truly gone, even for a minute or two, it gave Mark the chance to be there when he got back. 'Then I can kick your head in for you, motherfucker,' he murmured as he sneaked along the coping towards the next column in the row.

He was across the bridge and partially up the slope before the warehouse lights went out with a second noisy *thunk*. A few seconds later, the swamp sprang back to life. Insects buzzed, and nibbled at his ears. The humidity went up as the perpetually fading twilight returned, and Mark could hear animals – snakes, rodents and small birds – moving amongst the branches.

Did you miss me?

Mark was huddled in the folding roots of a banyan tree; he kept silent.

Oh Mark, my friend, where are you?

He couldn't see anything from his hiding place, but he could hear someone shuffling around. Whoever it was had found his way back inside the swamp, or the Fold, or wherever this place was.

I'm sorry, old friend, but I was– what's the phrase? – out of it for a while. I ran into your companions, and we had a bit of a disagreement, but everything's fine now.

No, it's not, Mark thought. *You're moving around too much. Something's wrong. Did Steven beat the shit out of you? Got some nasty bruises, have you?* He had to bite his lip to keep from answering.

Don't feel like chatting? I'll see if anyone down there can find you for me.

Mark searched for the coral snake. It would be coming; it could smell him, taste him, whatever it does with that nasty little tongue. He'd have to move soon.

Just a few seconds, Mark thought, *just give me a few seconds to figure out what's going on, and I'll come to you, dickhead. I'll be right there.*

'Blackford!' Redrick screamed as he stalked up the gangplank, and when he failed to appear, the enraged Ronan shouted for Kem. 'Is that thing ready to ship?' He pointed at the crate, trussed up with double and triple safety ropes, just in case.

'Yes, sir, ah, Redrick, sir. Sorry,' Kem stammered. 'It's all secured and ready to go, sir.'

'Load it onto the ketch and do it quick, but if you so much as scratch the planks on that crate, I'll gut the lot of you; understand?'

'Yes, sir,' Kem said, trying not to let the monster see how much he was shaking. His companions nodded agreement. 'Sir, if you don't mind, sir, but are you all right? I mean, we all heard the commotion over that way; it nearly knocked the whole crane down on us, sir.'

'Don't waste my fucking time!' Redrick cried, and stormed off, still screaming for Captain Blackford.

'All right, boys, you heard him,' Kem said. 'Let's get this done right, and we might just live to see tomorrow.' Despite the intricate system of double-block pulleys and winches, the crate was heavy; two of his mates hurried to help him as he manned the main line.

'Haul her away lightly, boys,' Kem sang out, 'just up over the side, and then we'll ease her down gently. That's the way.' They guided the crate over the starboard rail and slowly let the main line relax back through the pulleys. The crate descended into the ketch's hold. Kem watched the little boat's first mate, waited for the correct hand signal, then said, 'And . . . that does it, quick and easy. Nice job, boys. First round's on—'

Kem was thrown to the deck; his assistants were tossed over the side. One fell onto the rail of the ketch; shocked onlookers heard bones snap before he slipped between the two vessels and sank beneath the deep-water pier. The other crashed into the ketch's hold, striking the edge of the crate they had just transferred with such care. By the angle of his head, it looked like his neck was broken cleanly.

The blast had been close, on deck somewhere, and when Kem came to a moment later and saw Redrick Shen bursting from the aft companionway, leaving the door in pieces and planks in the quarterdeck splintered and jutting upwards up like so many broken teeth, he recognised the cause.

'Blackford!' Redrick shouted, 'where's my fucking stone, Blackford?'

Kem tried to feign unconsciousness, figuring it might save his life, but he was too late; his movement had been noticed.

Redrick bounded across the deck, crouched down and asked, 'Did you transfer my cargo?'

'We did, sir,' Kem whispered. 'It's safely aboard the ketch.'

'Excellent. Join them, and have their captain set sail for Welstar Palace immediately. I will catch up to you before the midday aven.

Remain within hailing distance of the west bank. Understand?'

'Yes sir.' Kem's head felt as though it had cracked. He raised his hand to check his scalp for blood, but stopped when he saw Redrick's face.

'Now!' Redrick said; his voice alone was enough to terrify the veteran seaman. 'Where is Captain Blackford?'

Garec crawled towards Captain Ford. 'Is she all right?'

'She's a bit banged about, but she'll live. How about you?'

'I'm fine,' Garec lied. His head was ringing. 'We need to get out of here. I'm going for Gilmour. You two, get ready to move, and watch for that young-looking prick in the sloppy tunic – that's Mark Jenkins. He clobbered me, could've killed me; I don't know why he didn't.'

'Where's Gilmour?' Brexan asked, rubbing her temples.

'The last I saw him, he had crashed through that hut, over near the pier. Keep my bow; I'll be back.' Garec stood with a groan. 'Be ready to run back to the *Morning Star*.'

'Wait,' Ford said, and pointed towards the wharf. 'Look!'

The wharf and the road that fronted it were filling with Malakasian soldiers, their black and gold finery bright in the early sunlight.

'Whoring rutters!' Garec shouted, 'we'll never reach him now.' He searched the street. 'I should've known better,' he muttered. 'I should've known the bow would be useless – but I've no choice, no rutting choice at all.' He grimaced. 'I've just got to try.'

'Garec, look at that,' the captain interrupted. He was staring at a wooden crate suspended above the *Bellan's* main deck. As they watched, it was hoisted carefully over the rail and down into the hold of the small boat lashed to the frigate. 'Look at the way those sailors are handling that thing; it's got two extra lines for rutting sake, and it's bound up tighter than a whore's purse. You'd think it had *Captain's Mother* stencilled on the side.'

'Then we're too late.' Brexan finally spoke. 'We'll have to follow them upriver. Can we catch that boat?'

'If we don't waste any more time around here,' Ford replied. 'That's a ketch, and they can't get much sail on her at all. If we can get out into the tide, we'll run up on her with no trouble. But Mark will see us coming. There won't be any hiding a brig-sloop under full sail running up his backside.'

There was another explosion, a crushing blast, this time from the *Bellan* herself.

'Whoring mothers!' Brexan shouted, 'what now?' She held fast to the captain's arm as she watched the soldiers along the waterfront deploy. It was clear that no one knew what was happening. Officers and sergeants shouted orders, but were largely ignored. Men helped injured comrades to safety, several choosing to make their own escape at the same time.

Then, through the confusion, they noticed a strange little man with messy hair hurrying towards them. He was carrying a plump young man, an unconscious victim of the morning's battle, over his shoulder, and was followed by a lithe woman with pale skin, high cheekbones and wispy hair.

'That's him, the rutter! And he's got Gilmour,' Garec shouted. 'My bow, Captain, give me my bow!'

'No,' Brexan said, teetering as she stood, 'wait!'

'Stay right where you are!' Garec cried, wrestling the bow from Captain Ford. He nocked an arrow and shouted again, 'I said stop, right now!'

The stranger ignored the warnings and crossed the road to join them in the alley beside the tavern. Glaring at Garec, he said, 'Put that away, you fool! Do you want to spend the rest of what will be a very short life in a Malakasian prison? What *are* you thinking? Didn't Fantus teach you anything?' He pushed past the startled bowman and rested Gilmour gingerly against the tavern wall. 'And I would appreciate it if, next time, you check with me before trying to punch me full of holes. I was quite busy just then, I can assure you.'

Stunned, Garec looked to his friends for an answer, and when they shrugged, he wheeled on the presumptuous stranger. 'Who the—'

'Alen Jasper of Middle Fork.' He prised open one of Gilmour's eyelids and checked the pupil. '*He* knows me as Kantu.'

'Kantu,' Garec whispered, 'then you're—'

The woman kneeling beside Gilmour reached out a hand, just as Steven Taylor had done, all those Twinmoons ago, in the orchard outside Estrad. 'Hannah Sorenson.'

Garec smiled and shook his head in disbelief. 'Hannah Sorenson. I know someone who's been looking for you.'

Gilmour gave a low moan and rocked his head from side to side. Alen, supporting his old colleague, said, 'He'll be all right in a moment. Hide that bloody bow and let's get going.'

'I'm Doren Ford, Captain Ford, and I suggest we get back to my ship.'

'Yes,' the strange little man – *Alen* – agreed. 'For the moment that will be safer than our rooms.'

Hannah, who had been looking terrified a moment earlier, now all but beamed. 'Where is he?'

'On my ship,' Ford answered, 'which is where we all need to be if we're to catch up with that table.'

Alen froze. 'Well, that bloody explains it!'

'What?' Hannah asked.

'The magic around here this morning. It's the spell table, isn't it?'

Garec nodded.

'Where is it?'

'They just finished loading it onto that ketch lying alongside the frigate.'

Hannah blanched, knitting her fingers together nervously. 'We can't let them get it to Welstar Palace, not with that army there, those *things* . . .'

'What things?' Garec asked, then interrupted himself. 'Never mind, you can tell us along the way.'

'Hoyt and Milla!' Hannah said. 'I'll go get them.'

'I'm Brexan Carderic. I'll come with you.' To Garec, she said, 'Do you remember the way back to the *Morning Star*?'

'We do,' he said, 'but—'

'I'm fine,' Brexan assured him. 'I am, really. We'll be along in a moment. When you get back, you'll find plenty of healers in Nardic Street, near the marina where we moored. It was out of the way this morning, but you'll be able to find someone there now.'

'There's no time for that,' Alen said. 'The Larion spell table should never have come within a Moon's travel of Welstar Palace. The fact that it's within shouting distance is a dreadful sign for all of us. As luck would have it, we already have a healer with us.'

Hannah frowned. 'Alen . . .'

'What? You said you can have him on his feet in a day, two at the most.'

She pushed a lock of hair behind her ear. 'I can, but we need the far portals.'

'We've got them,' Garec said, 'well, one anyway.'

'Where's the other?' Hannah asked anxiously.

'Your mother has it.'

'My mother! How in all hells did she get into this?'

'Ask Steven.'

Hannah's brow furrowed. 'I can see we've a lot of catching up to do, but this is fine, better even – she *can* help us.'

'Good then,' Garec said. 'See you two on the ship, and be careful; don't stop until you reach the inn, and then don't stop until you get back to the marina.' He helped Alen get Gilmour shakily to his feet, then led them away from the devastation.

'The only time Steven ever quiets down about you is when he's busy defending the lot of us from some demon or a mad sorcerer with a case of constipation,' Brexan said cheerfully as the two women made their way carefully through the disordered crowds.

'Steven?' Hannah repeated, '*my* Steven? Defending the lot of you? I truly don't understand!'

'We do have a lot to talk about,' Brexan said, 'and actually, I think I'll let him tell you about it.'

'And Mark? Is he here as well?'

Brexan started to nod, then shook her head. 'Yes— No, well, not right now.' She watched the soldiers slowly bringing order back to the wharf. 'Um, you should discuss this with Steven.'

Hannah, not appreciating being put off for no apparent reason, pressed for a proper answer. 'What? Mark's either here or he isn't. I don't – holy shit, look at this guy!'

An injured man, blood pouring down his chest, staggering wildly, appeared behind them, using the tavern wall for support. His head was hanging down, his chin dripped blood, and his obviously expensive tunic front was soaked in crimson nearly to his belt.

Hannah took him round the waist and started, 'Sir, you need to sit down. We can find someone to help you, but please, you've got to sit down.'

Jacrys waited until Hannah had ushered him within arm's reach of Brexan Carderic, then he whispered, 'Thank you.'

To Brexan, Hannah said, 'Help me get him against the wall. We'll set him down gently—'

Emboldened by the knowledge that he was about to die anyway, Jacrys found a vast reservoir of strength and quickness. Shoving Hannah aside with his left arm, he drew Thadrake's knife with his right and, screaming a throaty, gurgling cry, slashed wildly at Brexan.

'No!' Hannah shouted, falling back. She landed hard on her shoulder and struck her head on the cobblestones. The waterfront and pier flickered white to black, like a camera shutter opening for an instant.

Her eyes rolled back, and a nauseous feeling took hold of her all at once. She wrestled with consciousness, knowing that she needed to get to her feet, but she couldn't get up, not yet, not even to help Brexan.

Thankfully, Thadrake's knife had been dulled by a Moon's use as a cooking tool; the gansel meat, jemma and cheese had taken enough of the edge off that the blade tore through her cloak and tunic, but did little more than scratch her chest. She shouted and stumbled backwards, reeling, more a reflex than anything, and suddenly realised who her attacker was.

'You,' she growled at the pale-skinned, gangly stranger with the bloody vestments, 'not you, not again!'

Unable to take another step, Jacrys wheezed in his dying breath through gritted teeth. He slumped against the tavern wall, hatred alone holding him upright. 'Come to me, my dear. I've been dreaming of this,' he whispered.

'That's fine with me,' Brexan said.

The Malakasian lunged at her, tried to stab her again, but Brexan batted Jacrys' hand away and watched the blade skitter across the cobblestones. She took Jacrys' chin in one hand and wrenched it upwards – she wanted him looking her in the eye – and leaned in close, as if to kiss him goodbye.

Jacrys tried to bite her, but Brexan gently pushed him back against the wall, just hard enough to feel a gust of exsanguinous breath, stinking of old cheese and rich wine.

'Lieutenant Bronfio,' she whispered. 'Sallax and Brynne Farro. Versen Bier. This is for them, horsecock.' She balled her fist and leaned close enough to feel the greasy strands of his hair caress her face. 'Oh yes, one more thing: the Larion Senator known as Gilmour is still alive. You did know that, didn't you?'

His eyes widened. Bubbles of blood dripped from his lips.

Brexan, remembering where Sallax had stabbed him, in the lung, just below the heart, punched him hard, slamming her fist into the same place, hoping it would rip open and bleed, drowning the Malakasian spy in his own blood.

She watched for moment, listening until the last of his breath bubbled to silence at the back of his throat, then she helped Hannah to her feet.

Hannah was speechless. Silently, they went to find Hoyt and Milla.

*

Winter in Pellia was, during cold Twinmoons, a mostly dark time. People living in Pellia grew accustomed to prolonged periods of orange dawn and interminable stretches of violet twilight, the reality of winter in Eldarn's northernmost city. Glaring yellow sunshine was a rarity during this Twinmoon, so when it did happen, it was a symbol of hope and renewal, of opportunity and rebirth.

Fleeing the wharf, Captain Blackford felt more alive than he had in Twinmoons, and he didn't hesitate to credit the sun; it had been Twinmoons since he had stopped to appreciate the sun on his face. 'I'm heading home,' he said to no one, not caring if anyone heard. 'My sister's there; it's been a long time since I've seen her.'

He paused to lean against a rail for a moment. He knew he had to get away, but he needed this moment's grace, a respite from who he had become. With the strange stone nestled in his pocket, he felt he had done something significant, and a moment of sun on his face was not too much to ask in return. He had seen the monster – call it Major Tavon or Redrick Shen; it was still a monster – using the artefact, and he knew the stone was critical to working the table. Without it, he thought Redrick was just hauling an elaborate slab of cold granite north to Welstar Palace. Without it, the table was nothing more than a fancy rock.

For once in his short life, Blackford had done something significant, something genuinely good.

'Hello, Captain,' Redrick said, emerging from behind a dockside house. 'I know you weren't trying to escape with my key.'

Blackford felt the blood leave his face. Suddenly cold, and very frightened, he stammered, 'No sir, I— Uh—'

Redrick raised his hands in a gesture that said *calm down, please*. 'Don't be afraid, Captain. Truly, I would not be here if it were not for you.'

'Please, sir, I—'

'Captain Blackford,' Redrick said, his voice all at once harsh, 'do you have any idea what I plan to do with that chunk of stone you have hidden in your pocket?'

Blackford swallowed hard. 'No, sir.'

'I'm going to kill everything, everyone. Do you understand, Captain?'

Blackford felt the world rush away from him, as if it could leave him there alone, leaning against a public mooring post. 'I— Uh, no, I don't understand, sir.'

'What's to understand, Captain?' Redrick said, moving closer, looking as amiable as a chainball partner. 'I have work to do, and you're keeping me from it.'

'But sir,' Blackford started, 'I . . .' He felt his resolve draining away. He wasn't a brave man; stealing the stone had been the most courageous thing he had ever done. But if Redrick asked for it back, Blackford knew he would crumble.

Instead, the monster came in close and placed his hand flat on Blackford's chest. 'What makes you think that you can steal from me, Captain?' he asked.

Blackford tried to respond, but the demon's touch was overwhelming. He tried to back away, but couldn't. 'What are you?' he whispered. 'What is that rock? Why are you doing this? I don't want to die. I don't want you to do this to me, not to me. I—'

'Shhh,' Redrick whispered in return, 'It'll be fine, Captain. Just close your eyes. Do it now.'

Blackford did as he was ordered. There was a gentle press on his chest, and he thought of his sister. She was everything he wished he could be, and tragically, with Redrick Shen's fingertips pressing on his ribcage, everything he would never be. Blackford tried, in the final moments of his life, to picture his sister, to make her as clear in his mind as he could. If he had to die, that wouldn't be so bad; she could be with him.

Redrick held the body long enough to withdraw his fingers from Blackford's chest, then wiped his hand on the dead man's clothes and felt through his pockets for the keystone. He left Captain Blackford draped carelessly over the hitching stanchion, his body aglow in the unexpected winter sunlight.

BOOK IV

The Fold

MALAKASIAN COLOURS

'Pel! Kellin!' Captain Ford shouted, 'prepare to get underway – I want to catch the inbound tide. Garec, you help them – no, wait, you go and find us Malakasian colours, the largest you can track down. Buy them, steal them, I don't care; I want to look like Malakasia's greatest patriot.' He leapt to the deck and started securing hatches.

'Will do,' Garec said, then turned to Kellin. 'This is Alen; we'll explain later. How's Steven? And Marrin?'

'About the same,' Kellin said, 'both feverish, pale, sweating up a rutting ocean, but at least they're sleeping.'

'Brexan's bringing someone who might be able to help.' He tossed his bow to Kellin, then jogged off to find a flag.

'Let me have a look at them,' Alen said, starting towards the aft cabins. 'Are they in here?'

'No,' the captain interrupted, 'not yet. If they're sleeping, they'll be fine for now. I need to see you in my cabin.' He looked at Gilmour. 'You too.'

'Very well,' Alen said, 'lead the way.'

'Pel.' He tossed the boy a line. 'When Brexan returns, have her join us. She's bringing someone who might be injured, so make up a berth.'

'Aye aye, Captain.' It was clear that Pel was nervous. Circumstances had granted him an overnight promotion and discovering that his maiden voyage as the brig-sloop's second-in-command would be along the Welstar River was no comfort. He looked as though he might simply lie down and wait to die.

'Pel, you'll be fine,' the captain added. 'Take a breath; it isn't a very difficult boat to sail.' He smiled. 'Let me know as soon as we're ready to make way.'

Inside his cabin, the Larion sorcerers accepted wine and he took a bottle of beer himself. 'I'll get right to it,' he said, sitting down across from them. 'We are about to sail the most dangerous stretch of water in Eldarn. The fact that we have made it this far and are still alive is staggering enough, but at this point, I need honesty from both of you.'

'What can we tell you?' Gilmour said.

'Will we live through this? Will my ship and my crew survive? Or is this a suicide mission?'

Alen said, 'Captain Ford, that's a difficult thing to answer. If you're wondering whether you'll live through the day—'

'I'm not worried about myself.' He didn't care that he had interrupted one of Eldarn's most powerful men; recent events had made him willing to forego the social niceties. 'I'm worried about what's left of my crew, Marrin and Pel, and Kellin and Brexan, and this new woman too, young Hannah. If you're not certain we'll see the end of this endeavour in one healthy piece, I want to give them the opportunity to stay behind.'

'That's fine,' Gilmour said, 'but won't we need them to crew the *Morning Star*?'

'I'll manage without them if it's necessary to save their lives. You two can help.'

'Well then, if we're being frank, I don't much care for our chances without Steven,' Gilmour admitted.

'The staff wielder?' Alen asked.

Gilmour nodded. 'That's him – though he doesn't need the staff any longer. He gave it to Nerak, and its power drained – at least I believe – *into* Steven himself.'

'Gave it to Nerak? I don't understand.' Alen looked as bemused as he sounded.

'We've such a lot to discuss,' Gilmour sighed. 'This was an act of compassion. Steven handed the staff over so that Nerak might gain critical knowledge and, in turn, sever the bonds holding him fast to the evil that had taken him all those Twinmoons ago. It was a chance for Nerak finally to die in peace. Well, you know him; he didn't take advantage of it. Instead, he tried to use the staff to kill Steven ... so Steven threw him into the Fold.'

'*Steven threw him into the Fold?*' Alen repeated, incredulously. 'So Nerak's dead?'

'Sorry, I should have mentioned that.'

'Then who's—' Alen hesitated. 'The thing – the minion itself?'

'Broke from Nerak at the last moment.' Gilmour swallowed a

mouthful of wine. 'It sensed that Steven was about to send it into the Fold, and it broke away.'

'And later it took Mark Jenkins?'

'Confirming for all of us that for the past nine hundred and eighty-three Twinmoons we have been focusing on the wrong thing.'

Alen was still bewildered. 'So it was never him, the motherless horsecock.'

Gilmour patted his old friend's shoulder. 'Oh it was, and it wasn't – but don't worry about it now. We have more important things to do.'

'Which brings us back to my question.' The captain had been listening carefully, but felt none the wiser.

Alen said, 'Captain Ford, I fully intend to survive this ordeal, as does my friend here. However, if anyone is going to die on this journey, it will be us.'

'And Steven, I'm afraid,' Gilmour added. 'But you're right: we should give the others the option of staying behind with the sick.'

'They won't,' Alen said.

'That's probably true.' Ford poured more wine. 'But for my own sanity, I need to make the offer. I've lost too many good people on this journey. I have too many difficult visits to make when I return to Southport.'

'I'm sorry for that, Captain,' Gilmour said. 'It might be some small comfort to their families to know that they died doing the most important thing any of us will ever do.'

'Would it comfort you?'

'No,' Alen said.

He leaned back in his chair. Sighing, he said, 'This is all a mistake, this whole thing.'

Gilmour got up and started pacing, trying to explain. 'Captain, a Falkan merchant named Carpello Jax has been sending schooners to Welstar Palace, filled to bursting with some kind of bark or bits of tree.'

'Old Carpello,' Captain Ford said, 'Yes, I know him – knew him, I should say. What's your point?'

'The bits come from a forest of enchanted trees near Estrad Village in Rona, planted when Prince Marek took control of Eldarn nearly a thousand Twinmoons ago. The forest is closed to the locals, the trees have grown over time, and Carpello has, over the past hundred Twinmoons or so, begun harvesting the bark, leaves and roots for Prince Malagon, Princess Bellan, our former colleague Nerak, and now Mark Jenkins.'

'He's harvesting the Forest of Ghosts as well,' Alen said.

'Given what we learned from Brexan,' Gilmour continued pacing, 'I can't say that I'm surprised at that either.'

'How does this impact the orders I have to give in the next aven?' The captain was trying to stay focused on the safety of his ship and his crew.

Alen took up the story. 'We believe Nerak was milling the bark into a powder, then using it in a powerful spell that traps soldiers – men and Seron warriors – in an endless, mindless nightmare, scenes from their lives, played over and over again. It's a spell Lessek, the Larion founder, called—'

'The ash dream,' Gilmour interrupted, 'holy whores, it's the ash dream!'

'Nicely done, my friend – you have been paying attention.'

Gilmour was as pale as a sheet. He managed a smile. 'At least I've been awake for the past thousand Twinmoons.'

'And you're no further ahead than I am, so maybe there is something to being well-rested.' Alen grinned back at him.

Captain Ford asked, 'Can we get back to the sorcery bit? The stuff about the trees, please?'

'Right, sorry,' Alen continued, 'so all of us, Hannah included, have experimented with bark from the Forest of Ghosts. Some of us were attacked by the trees, but all of us, even my friend Hoyt – who came through the forest unscathed – were subject to the power of the bark once it was harvested. So the implication is that while some can pass through the Forest of Ghosts freely, no one can escape the power of the bark in its milled form. By experimenting, we were able to determine that the bark is unpredictable. Hoyt was entranced for several avens, happily reliving an enjoyable dinner conversation from his youth, and while ensnared, he took orders and performed basic tasks – and even though he should have been falling-down exhausted, he continued working, without a break, until Hannah and I removed the bark. But that only worked with Hoyt; the rest of us, when we were caught in the forest, were inconsolable, unable to take direction, and certainly unwilling to perform even rudimentary jobs.'

'Hoyt was under the influence of the harvested version?' Gilmour asked.

'Yes,' Alen clarified.

'So harvested and milled, this tree bark makes it so that you can listen to orders but not care about what you're asked to do?'

'Yes,' Alen said, 'but again, that's just the harvested bark. We hadn't milled it, and Hoyt hadn't ingested it in any way – he'd not smoked it, snorted it or eaten it; it was just tied round his neck in a leather pouch.'

Gilmour said, 'And presumably the milled form would be even more destructive.'

'But why?' Ford asked. 'Who needs something like this? Prince Malagon, or whoever it is now, already has everything Eldarn has to offer. What more could he possibly want?'

Gilmour swept his cloak back and sat down opposite the Pragan sailor. 'He is probably preparing himself and his army for the advent of an Era so evil, so rife with terror and hatred, that only such a drugged creature could hope to bear the reality of life in Eldarn.'

'Actually, I think we saw them,' Alen said.

'The Seron? They're in the Eastlands as well. I think Nerak started breeding them again when he knew his crop was ready for harvest.'

'No, worse than Seron. There's an encampment at Welstar Palace packed with hundreds of thousands of soldiers, most of whom were obviously under the power of this spell, potion, whatever it is.'

Ford swallowed dryly and checked his tankard. 'Whoring rutters, and that's where we're heading. I hope we catch Mark before he arrives. If we get moving, there's no reason to think we won't.'

'Were they working?' Gilmour asked, 'following orders? Keeping busy?'

'Some, yes,' Alen replied, 'but most were simply staring across the river. It was a wretched, dismal place, the worst conditions I've ever seen ... ever *imagined*. Boils, pox, infections, broken limbs, severed body parts, bugs and lice – and all of them completely ignored by the officers. The stench of the place was unbearable: rotting flesh, dead but not quite convinced of it yet.'

'So that explains the Estrad variable,' Gilmour guessed aloud. 'If the bark from the Forest of Ghosts sends them reeling back through their lives, only to get ensnared in something hideous – or lovely, maybe – I suppose the bark from Estrad is the leveller.'

'I don't understand.' The captain was feeling nauseous.

'The leveller, a fixative,' Gilmour explained. 'The Forest of Ghosts in Praga is legendary, yet no one has ever heard of the Forbidden Forest near Riverend Palace. And why not?'

'Because there are no stories,' Ford answered the rhetorical question, then blushed.

'Exactly!' Gilmour slapped the table, making Alen spill his wine. 'Granted, not too many people have ever gone that far out on the point. But some of us have – Garec, Versen, Sallax, even I – and we know that there's nothing enchanted about those trees. We have certainly never found ourselves trapped in our past.'

'So he uses the two ingredients together, probably burns them into some kind of ash. They might inhale it, or have it rubbed on their skin, who knows?'

'The ash dream,' Gilmour said. 'Well, that clinches it: I have to read that whoring book.' At Alen's quizzical look, he explained, 'Lessek's spell book – I'm embarrassed to admit that I've had it for nearly two Twinmoons and haven't been able to get past the second folio. I acquired it from Nerak's cabin on the *Prince Marek*, the night he followed Steven through the far portal.'

'I remember that night,' Alen said, 'because it was also the night his hunters stopped searching for me, the night much of the mystical energy in Eldarn quietly ground to a stop.'

'I've been putting it off for Twinmoons,' Gilmour admitted. 'Now we've only got a day or two, and I don't even know if it will do us any good.'

'You should try anyway,' Alen said. 'Once we're underway, we can look it over together.'

Someone knocked, and at the captain's word, Brexan peered around the door, not sure if she should interrupt their discussion.

'Yes, come in, please.' Captain Ford stood up, offering his chair. 'Have a seat.'

'I'm fine standing, thanks,' Brexan said. 'How can I help?'

'You mentioned once that you were stationed at Welstar Palace.' He unfolded a river chart and spread it across the table. 'Can you recall how the encampment was organised?'

Brexan leaned over the table. 'I was stationed somewhere along the river in that valley; I don't think I ever came within half an aven's walk of the palace itself – no one did, except for the Home Guard divisions and the Seron warriors. However, I can tell you that if we're heading up that way, the navy patrols the river and there's a whole legion of barges running back and forth delivering goods. The river's a rutting highway.'

'That could be good for us,' Ford said, his finger following the river on the chart. 'We could try to blend in.'

'It makes it awfully difficult to change direction,' Brexan pointed out. 'If you need to turn tail and run, for example, the shipping is so thick that you'd end up ramming someone before you managed to come about.'

'And I'm certain the encampment will have changed in the Twin-moons since you've been there, my dear,' Alen added.

'How do you mean?' Gilmour said.

'The whole west bank – from the village, up to and beyond the keep – is covered with divisions of soldiers already under the influence of the ash dream. You couldn't walk a dog through there without it ending up on someone's menu. There are probably near to a hundred thousand of those creatures there now, Seron beasts transformed into these vacuous, staring monsters, as if Seron weren't bad enough on their own. The east bank was given over to soldiers too, normal ones – most of the northern corps, I'd guess. I didn't see much of them; we fled during the night. But on our trip down from Treven, we noticed that most of the hillsides sloping down to the river were dotted with tents, fires, stables, corrals, muster tents – everything a massive army would need.'

The captain traced the east bank on his chart. Tapping his finger on the site of the encampment, he said, 'And if Mark Jenkins is still transforming soldiers and Seron with his ash stuff, he might already have given the order to administer it to the divisions on the other side of the river.'

'He might have,' Alen said. 'That's a good point.'

'Ash stuff?' Brexan asked.

Gilmour explained quickly, Alen and Captain Ford chiming in.

Brexan shuddered. 'That's horrific! But how would he make them take the ash? I mean, he can't do it individually, can he? If he had to go person to person it would take all Twinmoon.'

Alen considered this, then said, 'I was masquerading as an officer for a few days while Hannah and the others were locked up and I roamed as much of the place as I could, but the only thing I could see in the monsters' encampments were fires, huge braziers, that kept burning all day and all night, looking as if Nerak had called down a constellation from the skies and left it burning on the ground around the palace.'

'That could be it,' Gilmour said, 'but they might have been just fires.'

'I suppose,' Alen conceded, 'but why? If they're trapped in their own fantasies, if they can't escape their own minds, then they wouldn't even notice the cold, would they? They did have the odd campfire here and there, but these braziers were huge – were they for light? I can't quite see what a creature trapped in an endless nightmare would need fire for – unlikely to be light, warmth or comfort.'

Captain Ford gazed out of the cabin window. The sun glinted off the water, blinding him. 'So you think they're inhaling it as ashes or smoke?' he asked, turning back to the Larion sorcerers.

'It's possible,' Alen said. 'I know I didn't see anyone administering anything to them – honestly, it would have been suicide for anyone to set foot in that encampment, never mind try to get Seron warriors to ingest anything they didn't want to, and that includes anything designed to leave them babbling, ignoring all manner of injuries and diseases and following mindless orders.'

'That's it then,' Gilmour said. 'The evil force that took Nerak and now Mark is using the ash dream to create a massive army of unnatural killers – Seron and men alike – to become his slaves when the essence of all evil is ushered through the Fold and allowed to suck the life from the very land beneath our feet.'

Brexan blanched. 'Rutting dogs, but I hope you're wrong.'

'I hope so too,' Captain Ford agreed.

'Why would Lessek have written such a spell?' Alen asked. 'What could he have hoped to gain with such a creation?'

'We need to read to know why,' Gilmour said, then asked Brexan, 'Is Hannah in with Steven?'

As Brexan nodded, Alen asked, 'Where's Hoyt?'

'Hannah's with Steven and Hoyt's resting up front in Sera's berth,' she said. 'He doesn't look like much of a healer – in fact, he needs a healer more than any of us.'

'He's the best in the Westlands,' Alen assured her, 'and I think Hannah has an idea how to fix him up right away.'

Garec appeared in the companionway, a massive Malakasian flag draped over his shoulder. 'Will this do?'

Captain Ford laughed. 'It's the best news I've had all this Moon, Garec. Would you ask Pel to run it up the mainmast and leave the small flag on the halyard, aft? Then Gilmour, Alen and I need to speak with all of you on deck, Hannah included.' Ford rolled the chart, slipped it inside a wall rack and ushered them into the corridor.

Hannah pulled up a bench and rested her head softly on Steven's chest. His clothes stank of sickness, fever and sweat, and his skin was the colour of turned cream. He didn't respond to her touch, but at least he was breathing evenly. She took some comfort in that. Steven's chest rose and fell in a steady rhythm; he was alive, and that was enough for her – for now, anyway.

'I found you first,' she whispered, surprised she wasn't crying. 'It's been a while, huh?' She needed to fill the silence. 'I've heard some remarkable things about you, things neither of us could ever have imagined, back home. Do you remember home? Do you want to go back, maybe just me and you?' She closed her eyes, content to feel the rhythmic motion of his chest. 'We have some catching up to do, don't we? I can't wait. I've missed you, Steven – even though we barely know each other, I do know that if it hadn't been for you, I wouldn't have made it this far.'

The *Morning Star* rolled gently: the tide was coming in. Hannah heard Captain Ford and the Larion Senators shuffle along the companionway and then up to the main deck. She touched Steven's cheek, and ran her fingers through his matted hair. 'You look good with a beard. Do all sorcerers have them? Is it some kind of regulation? You'll have to shave it off when we get home so I can decide which version of you I'll love more.' His forehead was damp; she wiped it with the cloth Kellin had left ready. 'Hey, do you remember that Mexican place we went for lunch? When you came back to the shop to pick up that china cabinet for your sister. I had fajitas. You ate whatever you could stomach after that eleven-course breakfast you thought I didn't know about. I want to go back there, Steven, just us, and start again. What d'you say? Can we get back there if we both try, or are we too far down this road?'

She wiped his face again and said, 'I have some things I have to do, then I'll be back. We need you and Hoyt, both of you, so I'm going to see if I can help.' She kissed him lightly on the lips. 'I'll be back. Promise me you'll still be here.'

Steven didn't answer.

Hannah joined the others on deck. To Alen and Gilmour, she said, 'How do we know when my mother's opening her portal?'

THE CARRACK

'The *Missing Daughter*?' Markus asked, looking down at the trawler from the pier. 'I don't understand.'

'Danelle and I have two sons.' Sharr tossed a coil of rope beneath the transom. 'I thought it was funny.' As Markus chuckled, he added, 'She didn't.'

Markus laughed again. 'I'm surprised she didn't make you change the name.'

'She wanted me to, but then I told her what it would cost to have it redone, to re-register with the harbourmaster, blah, blah, blah and so on.'

'Not bad, Sharr, quick thinking.' Brand gave him a quick, uncharacteristic smile, then stowed the buckets of pitch he had carried on board.

'She floats,' Sharr shrugged.

The *Missing Daughter* looked like the unholy offspring of a sloop, a barge and a booacore boat. Her broad beam, the starboard winch and a short-armed crane made her a steady vessel kitted out for hauling weighted traps and gill-nets. Her two block-and-tackle outriggers were ideal for dragging nets, or – when the fishing was right – trolling the offshore banks for giant sharks, billfish, even tapen. Above the tiny forward cabin, her mainmast was rigged fore and aft, and had a crow's nest high above, perfect for spotting distant schools of fish on calm days. She had a spanker to keep her steady while hauling nets or traps, and a bowsprit that jutted out so far that she had to be backed into a slip or left moored on a buoy. A number of Capehill's unsuspecting dockers had found themselves knocked into the greasy waters beneath the packing warehouse after being whacked by the *Missing Daughter*'s bowsprit.

'What are those lines?' Markus pointed to ropes running from the bowsprit to the middle and top of the mainmast.

'Haven't done much sailing, have you?' Sharr kicked off his leather boots and tugged on a pair of oiled galoshes.

'I'm a farmer,' Markus protested, 'the closest I've ever come to a boat is a hollowed-out log my brothers once launched on the pond in my uncle's orchard.'

Brand searched for a second pair of waterproof boots. 'How'd that work out for them?'

'It didn't,' Markus said. 'It was seaworthy for just about as much time as it took my brother to shout, "We're going down!" Then they did.'

'That—' Sharr pointed to the lower line '—is standing rigging for the bowsprit sail. You can see it reefed there along the spar.'

'It looks big for a boat this size. You, uh, have anything you need to tell us, Sharr? I mean, does a really long bowsprit make up for shortcomings in other arenas?'

'It's massive; I admit,' Sharr grinned. 'I rigged it myself, in my own image. It's for when I need to be a bit quicker than the other boats working the banks or chasing the big schools. That bow sheet gives me a healthy edge.'

'So then, what's that tall one?' Markus shielded his eyes and squinted towards the top of the mainmast.

'That's a little surprise, something I unveil only when necessary.'

'A second sheet?' Brand held a wrinkled, salt-stained boot against his own sole, checking the size.

'Exactly,' Sharr said. 'But it's more than that, it's almost a spinnaker. I only use it when the wind is just right, or when I have to hustle my aged bones out of harm's way – the Malakasian navy and I don't always see things from the same perspective.'

Brand scoffed. 'This old barrel can outrun a naval cutter?'

'Good rutting lords, no!' Sharr laughed. 'Look at her – she can barely get out of her own way.'

'So why the giant sheet?'

'When the navy arrives, my goal is never to outrun them—' He checked that his sons had belayed both outriggers. 'I just need to be faster than the next trawler on the water.'

'Let the navy busy themselves with the slower deer in the herd.' He handed Brand a great coil of line.

'Something like that,' Sharr said. 'But it won't matter for much longer.'

'Because we're going to win?' Brand asked.

'Because we're going to die.' Sharr ignored the outriggers and fell into a comfortable chair he had fixed to the deck.

'But I thought you said this was a fast boat.' Markus finally summoned enough courage to step on board.

'Left foot first,' Sharr warned, '*left* foot!'

'Why?' Markus said.

'Better luck.'

'You just said we were going to die!'

'Yes, but there's no sense inviting misfortune, is there?'

'Rutting whores!' Markus stepped on board with his left foot. 'Any other absurd superstitions I need to know about?'

'Plenty.' Sharr dug in his pockets for a pipe. 'I'll keep you informed as we go.'

'To die.'

'Yes, to die.'

'What makes you so certain we can't do it?' Brand asked.

'Have you ever seen a merchant carrack? It's a four-masted beast with cabins, two and three cabins, stacked on top of one another, giving her a great swollen arse to windward. We could hide my little boat beneath her mainsail. Merchant carracks are like galleons with allergies. Pragan miners use them to transport quarry stones to Orindale, huge piles of rocks, any one of which would send my little boat to the bottom in a blazing hurry. And if that isn't terrifying enough, she could ram us to splinters without feeling so much as a nudge. Oh, and she'll be fast; on a northerly wind, she'll brush past us as if we were swamped.'

'So unless we're right in her path—' Brand started.

'An unfortunate place to be—' Markus was already turning seasick-green, even though the boat was still lashed safely to the pier.

'We can't catch her?'

'Catch her?' Sharr laughed. 'If we're lucky, she'll think we're Malakasian soldiers fleeing Capehill, and heave to.'

'To pick us up?' Brand considered this new option.

'Yes,' Sharr said, 'they'll reef their sheets and welcome us aboard.'

'Aboard a Malakasian ship, filled with soldiers, possibly Seron warriors, and some kind of evil magical tree bark?' Markus asked.

'Exactly.'

'I like the run-us-down option better.'

'Me too,' Sharr said, 'but – as much as I hate to quote Gita behind her back – you're not coming, and neither is Brand. But I do appreciate you two helping me load these crates.' Sharr avoided eye-contact with Brand Krug. He liked Markus Fillin; the two of them had come from similar backgrounds: hard-working parents, strong role models, but Brand was different, difficult to read. Sharr guessed there was brutality in his past, some ugly experience that made the enigmatic freedom fighter keep people at arm's length.

'And why are we not going along?' Brand muttered.

'Because this is suicide,' Sharr explained. 'There's no point in all of us going out there for no reason. We stand about as much chance of sinking that ship – of even *finding* that ship – as I do of sailing to Pellia and single-handedly sacking Welstar Palace.'

'Are there shipping lanes off-shore?' Brand's voice was barely above a whisper. At Sharr's nod, he went on, 'You know where they are?'

'I've fished here all my life.'

'Then that's where we're going.' He looked deadly serious, and he still hadn't moved.

Sharr looked the quiet warrior in the eyes. 'Have you been on the open ocean, Brand? Do you know anything about sailing? Anything at all? The swells out there block your view of the horizon; there are rollers so high they blot out the view ... nothing you've ever seen at the beach or boating in the harbour can give you any idea what we're going to face out there. And it's cold, chill-your-bones-to-aching cold. If we don't get swamped and drown, we'll try to cut the carrack off. And assuming I can accomplish this nearly impossible navigational feat, we will get rammed and die. Or, even better, they will mistake us for their Malakasian comrades, heave to, take us aboard, and *then* we will die.'

Markus interrupted, asking, 'So any scenario in which we don't die, Sharr?'

'Just one.' He grinned.

'Care to elaborate a bit on our role?'

'You don't have a role.' He jumped back to the pier and lowered another wooden crate onto the deck.

'You haven't convinced me you can sail out there and sink that ship by yourself, Sharr,' Brand said.

'Not by myself, no. He's coming with me.' He gestured towards the dockside, where Stalwick Rees, looking more fragile than ever and lugging a massive canvas bag almost as big as he was, moved hesitantly towards the *Missing Daughter*. They could see his lips moving as he nervously talked to no one.

Brand's scepticism was almost palpable, filling the space between them. 'You can't be serious! He'll sink this tub before you even catch the outgoing tide.'

Sharr wheeled on him. 'You really want to come along, Brand? Well, I don't care, come, then – you, too, Markus, if you're so determined to die. But we're not going anywhere without him.'

'Why?' Markus said, waving encouragingly to Stalwick.

'Because he has special gifts.' Sharr started towards the wharf. He turned to say, 'Make peace with the gods tonight, boys, because the tide turns just before dawn tomorrow. If you're coming, I'll see you here. Right now, I'm off home.'

The *Missing Daughter* sailed with the predawn tide. A frigid bank of fog had swallowed Capehill overnight and a ponderous gloom had settled over the trawler. The northerly winds that had been raking the Falkan coast for days died suddenly after middlenight, leaving the wharf blanketed in a foreboding silence.

Sharr set his main and spanker in a broad reach, but didn't bother with the bowsprit; there wasn't enough wind. He leaned at the helm, watching for the channel marker denoting the last lazy tack to port needed to clear the dogleg that was Capehill Harbour; perhaps then they'd get lucky and catch a bit of breeze. Stalwick and Markus huddled together in the middle of the deck; Brand stood in the stern, watching the fog billow past like a ghostly memory.

'Any tecan?' he asked laconically.

'No,' Stalwick was quick to reply, 'but I can make some, Brand. I can. I'm good at tecan, well, not as good as—'

'Stalwick,' Markus stopped him, 'it's over there, in the canvas bag near the top of that chest.'

'Oh, right, thanks. I'll get it going right away, thanks.' Fumbling, he managed to dislodge the pot and a tin of leaves, struggled to open one of the hogsheads lashed to the mainmast, then finally disappeared to the tiny galley to get the mixture brewing.

'Thanks, Stalwick,' Sharr shouted down to him. 'Goblets in that leather bag on the shelf above your head.'

'All right, Sharr, all right. I'll tell you, I was worried, scared even, to go out on the ocean with you three, but I tell you what; this isn't so bad. I'd rather be able to see something, I would, I'll tell you, but this isn't bad sailing at all.'

Still staring at the wall of white, Brand said mockingly, 'Swells that block my view of the horizon, huh, Sharr?'

'Be careful what you wish for, my friend,' Sharr warned. 'We're not even out of the harbour yet.' Like the rest of them, Sharr was dressed in a cotton undertunic, a boiled wool tunic, a leather vest and a boiled wool cloak, all topped with an oiled leather poncho to help ward off the frigid winds. Sharr worried that one of the others, as green as they were, might slip and fall overboard, especially if ice formed on the deck later that day. Layered vestments made winter fishing bearable, but they were not good for swimming.

'We'll never catch them at this rate,' Markus said, helping Stalwick pour out tecan.

'You've got to remember that if we don't have any wind, they don't have any either,' Sharr reminded them. 'Actually, I'm hoping that carrack passed by last night, with all her sails filled to bursting, so we'll never catch her – if that's the case, we'll make a day of it and I'll teach you how to haul a net.'

'All right,' Markus shivered. 'I'm up for a bit of fishing today.'

'That's not very patriotic of you,' Brand said, checking the throwing knives he wore at his belt.

'Call it self-preservation,' Markus said. 'Here, tecan's ready.'

'Thanks,' he said, then looked up suddenly and said, 'Hey, Captain, look at the fog.' From the south, the sound of crashing waves reached them through the gloom.

'What?' Stalwick cried as he turned a full circle, 'what's it doing?'

'It's moving north,' Markus said. 'We've found a bit of wind.'

'Oh, that's good, right, Sharr? A bit of wind, and we can get going out there, right?'

Sharr tested the wind. He checked the mainsail, let the beam out slightly, then belayed the line. 'Be careful what you wish for, my friends,' he muttered again.

By the dinner aven, there was a stiff wind blowing north and the *Missing Daughter* was running before it like a schooner. Markus, Stalwick and Brand were clinging to lines and belaying pins as if they were the last handholds outside the Northern Forest. The deck was wet, and icing over, but none of the intrepid seamen were willing to move from where they stood, so there was no immediate danger of anyone slipping over the side.

At the helm, Sharr sang off-colour songs, obviously enjoying himself. 'You don't get too many days like this!' he cried above the breeze. 'Look there, that's Raven's Point! Great whoring mothers, but that's got to be a new record, for a fishing boat, anyway.' He looked at the others as the *Missing Daughter* rolled over an enormous swell and buried her bow halfway up the following trough. 'You boys all right?'

'Fine,' Brand managed without letting go of the ratline he had looped about his wrist. 'I'm thinking of spending all my winter Twinmoons on the water once this business is finished.'

'Markus,' Sharr shouted, 'Brand just made a joke – he must be terrified!'

The handsome lieutenant, soaked to the undertunic and shivering hard, said, 'I'm too scared to talk right now. I'd rather my life end in silence.'

Sharr laughed. 'You're not going to die in this, Markus. It's a beautiful clear day!'

'Isn't it a bit ... um ... lumpy?' Stalwick asked miserably.

'A bit,' Sharr acknowledged, 'but the old girl'll hold together, don't you worry.'

'What happens if we don't spot that carrack today?' Markus was doing his best to scan the horizon for sails.

'We'll stay off the wind for the night,' Sharr pointed north, 'then jibe, close haul and creep south again tomorrow morning. It wouldn't be wise to do that before first light, though. And if the wind changes with the tide, which it might well do, we'll come about and enjoy a nice run down the coast.'

'You mean stay out here? All night?' He sounded completely horrified.

'Of course,' Sharr said, laughing. 'We'd not make it home now anyway, not tonight – we're against the wind and the tide.'

'I see.' Markus swallowed hard. 'It's just— Well, to be honest, I never thought we'd be out here after dark.'

'You afraid of the dark, Markus?'

'Out here?' He braced himself as the trawler crested another swell. 'Yes, actually, quite.'

Brand came forward, moving hand-over-hand along the starboard gunwale. He gripped the block-and-tackle crane like a lover and shouted, 'Remember this morning, when I teased you about the wind?'

Sharr grinned. 'Vaguely.'

'Sorry about that.'

'Fetch me a beer from that crate below and we'll call it even.'

'I would,' Brand's teeth were chattering, 'but I'm afraid to let go.'

'Here, then—' Sharr took Brand's hand and placed it on the helm, 'keep us on this course and I'll fetch them myself. Who's for a drink, then?'

No one answered; Brand looked as though he was about to soil his leggings.

'All right, beers all around it is then.' Sharr disappeared into the galley, singing, 'I know a girl and her name is Mippa. I bet you five Mareks she'll give you a gripper!' He returned a moment later and passed ceramic bottles to everyone.

Markus looked askance at his, then gripped the cork with his teeth, pulled it out and spat it over the side. He guzzled as much as he could stomach. Brand saw the moribund pallor fade from his friend's face and decided to follow Markus' lead, chugging nearly the entire bottle.

'Better?' Sharr asked.

'Yes,' Brand nodded enthusiastically, 'surprisingly so!'

'How about you, Stal—?' Sharr froze. 'Oh, rutters.'

Blanched and trembling, Stalwick stared straight ahead, his eyes unfocused. He gripped the beer bottle with one hand, squeezing until it shattered. Ceramic shards sliced into his palm; Stalwick didn't notice.

'Holy mothers!' Markus cried, 'what's wrong with him?'

Stalwick collapsed, kicking and scratching in wild spasms, rolling across the deck until he came to rest in a foetal ball beside the miniature dory they'd lashed down that morning.

'I bet it's—' Brand's feet went out from under him and he landed hard on his back, sliding across the icy deck.

'Help me get him into the cabin,' Sharr ordered. 'Markus, there's a cot folded up against the forward bulkhead, inside the storage cubby – go and get it. Brand, drag him in here. Make sure he's breathing, then unfurl that tarp. It'll keep him a bit warmer. There are blankets in the third cupboard, the one beside the cooking pots.'

Brand crawled back to Stalwick, then half-dragged and half-pushed the unconscious man inside the little cabin. He found the oiled canvas tarp and unlashed it so it covered the doorway, shutting out some of the wind. The enclosed space quickly felt warmer.

'He went like this before,' Sharr said, 'when Gilmour used him to warn us that the Malakasians knew we were coming.'

'Listen closely, in case he says anything.'

Stalwick didn't speak; he just lay on the cot, his mouth hanging open and his eyes askew, staring blindly up at the wooden ceiling.

The three men went back to the helm to confer.

'We've got to go back,' Markus said. 'Who knows what this means?'

'I told you: we can't go back, not yet,' Sharr said. 'Just calm down; we're out here at least until dawn when the tide turns.'

'But—'

'But nothing. Wind and water are against us and it would take more sailing skills than you two have combined to get us about and hauled close for Capehill. So as long as he's breathing, we'll give him a few moments and see if he wakes up. Brand, take the helm. Keep us right on this heading.' He slid the binnacle open and showed him the compass. It was pointing east-northeast. 'I'll net us some fish for dinner, and then we'll have a sailing lesson or two, just in case.'

'But we've got dinner,' Markus said plaintively. 'We've brought plenty to eat.'

'But this'll give us something to do. Come on, Markus, I'll bet you've always secretly wanted to learn how to sail, haven't you?'

An aven later, as darkness fell, the three companions ate their fill of fresh-caught jemma and drank enough beer to numb their uncertainty. They had no idea what had befallen Stalwick; he was an inept soldier, but he was also the only one amongst them with even a copper Marek's worth of mystical power. They all felt the same foreboding chill as they watched Stalwick breathe in shallow gasps, his hands frozen in ungainly claws and his eyes fixed half a world away.

Around middlenight, Sharr tossed Markus a blanket and ordered him to get some sleep. 'Brand and I will take the first watch,' he said. 'You and he can trade in an aven.'

'What about you?' Brand said.

'I'll stay at the helm. The wind is dying a bit. If it drops more before dawn, you can keep us on course for a while and I'll try to sleep, but I don't want you two piloting in the dark. Who knows where we might end up?' He laughed, wryly, trying to lighten the mood a little.

'Fine with me.' Markus ducked beneath the tarp curtain and curled up on the floor next to Stalwick's berth. 'See you in an aven,' he called.

Markus traded places with Brand just before the predawn aven. The wind had fallen off and the *Missing Daughter* made her way through the diminishing swells like a pleasure boat on a summer sea. It was warm inside the cabin, with the tarp curtain still closed. Marcus had removed his oiled poncho and cloak; Brand did the same, wrapped himself in Markus' makeshift bed and was asleep in moments, snoring lightly.

'Where are we?' Markus asked softly.

'Off the northeast coast, moving along the outer banks.'

'No sign of our carrack?'

'Hard to say; the winds are down, the tide's about to start running against us. That's bad for sailing, but good for standing the middle watch. If she's out here and her watchlights are burning, we ought to be able to see her. I haven't checked aft in a while; I don't normally keep that tarp unfurled, but with Stalwick and all, I figured I ought to keep it warm in there.'

'Thanks for that. So what am I looking for?'

'A ship that large will have a number of watchlights on deck: fore, aft and amidships, maybe even a few aloft. Downwind, you might even smell her galley, what they're serving for breakfast. So basically, if you see anything that looks like glowing orbs of fire floating just above the water, that's our whore.' He yawned, stretching his shoulders and back. He had been standing over the binnacle, keeping them on course with the changing tide, but finally he gave up and sat in his captain's chair.

'One luxury, I see,' Markus teased him.

'I'm getting older,' Sharr smiled. 'Can't be standing here all day and night.'

'So where's our bowsprit?'

'I reefed it last aven.'

'Over the water? In the dark? Alone? That was brave of you!'

'Nonsense,' Sharr said, 'there are horses all the way out to the end – that's the lines you stand on. When I was a whelp, I worked on a cutter with a naked bowsprit, not a footrope to be seen. Rutting Pragans, but that tested your courage, especially in the rain and ice. You learned balance in a hurry, no mistake, with one hand on the standing rigging, not to mention how to tie a half-hitch with one hand and the occasional toe.'

'Ever lose anyone?'

'We had a few that got dunked, but after a while we worked out we ought to be wearing safety lines.' He sighed. 'Took some of the adventure out of it.'

'You want some tecan?'

'No, let's wait for first light. You'd have to climb over Brand to get in there, anyway.'

Markus sat down gingerly on a coil of rope near the helm started sniffing the wind, hoping for the scent of Malakasian breakfast: boiled greenroot and cabbage or something similarly disagreeable. From time to time he hauled himself to his feet and peered over the gunwale, but he found nothing.

After a quarter-aven, he rested his forehead on his knees, then gradually gave in to sleep.

Markus woke to Sharr shouting, 'Get up, gods rut you raw, *get up*!'

He was on his feet in an instant, gripping the rail to keep from falling. 'What? What's the matter?' he asked, still a little disoriented. 'Is it the carrack?'

'Stalwick's gone!' Sharr cried, looking about him wildly.

'Gone? What? How can he be—?' He peered into the little cabin. The cot was empty. 'But where—?'

Brand pushed past him and took the helm. 'Go ahead,' he said to Sharr, who rolled and lashed the tarp, opening the cabin to the elements. Dawn whitened the horizon. 'Right, listen,' he ordered, 'when we jibe, we've got to let the main out. We've been on this broad reach, so we don't have to let it far, and for rut's sake, wait until I tell you!'

Markus rubbed his eyes, muttering, 'I don't— What's happening? Where—?'

'Markus!' Sharr cried, making him jump, 'watch me, man. When I shout to Brand, you bring that spanker over. Keep it parallel with the main boom. Understand?'

'But I don't—'

'That rope there, the pin's aft on the port side. Come on, Markus, it's not that big a sheet.' Sharr moved out towards the bowsprit.

Markus hurried over to Brand, saying, 'What are we rutting doing?'

'I think we're turning around,' he said. 'I think that's what jibing is, or coming about or whatever he calls it.' Sharr was halfway out the bowsprit now, already over open water. Rather than being chased by towering swells as they had been the previous day, now the *Missing Daughter* faced ranks of rolling waves, splashing over the bow, threatening to wash Sharr all the way to the Northern Forest.

'But why? How do we know Stalwick is back there?'

Brand pointed at the deck: the dory was gone.

'Unholy rutting mothers!' Markus untied the spanker, keeping the line tight as ordered and watching Sharr for the sign to bring it over the transom. 'Demonshit, what did he do? Where is he, Brand? He can't be out alone in that thing – we've got to find him!'

'He's there.' Brand pointed over the transom.

'Great gods of the Northern Forest.' Markus stood in mute

amazement, looking at the carrack in the distance, running north, perhaps a thousand paces off their stern. She was impossibly tall, and massive, and with her sails filled and billowing, looked more like an unchained sea monster than a ship. Between the two vessels, rolling dangerously in the swells, Stalwick Rees rowed furiously, careening from trough to trough. He was dressed as a Malakasian soldier.

Stunned, Markus let go the spanker line, slashing a bloody gash across his palm as the little sheet ripped free, its miniature yard swinging wide to port.

'Markus!' Sharr screamed from the bowsprit. He plunged beneath another wave, but came up, still loosening the forward sheet and shouting, 'Get that rutting line, Markus! Gods cook your mother's arse, don't let it run out of the tackle; you'll never get it back through. Grab it!'

Markus dived for the spanker yard, caught it and pulled back over the transom, then fell on slippery deck and hit his head. He cursed Stalwick's entire family as he crawled on hands and knees to the transom and tugged the rigging line tight with bloody fingers.

Once it was secure, he called to Brand, 'How did he get away?'

'We were sleeping, you and I were, anyway. I'm not sure what he did to Sharr, used some kind of spell, I guess. I don't know; I thought he was dead.'

Markus watched impotently as Stalwick rowed further and further away.

Sharr unfurled the bowsprit, then hauled on its rig and belayed it. The sail fluttered uselessly as he shouted, 'Get ready!' and made his way to the junction of his spinnaker rig and the spar, where he steadied himself while wrestling with the knots. At last he cried, 'All right, Brand, bring us about! Crank her over!'

At first, nothing happened. But as the *Missing Daughter* turned, Markus felt a light tugging on the rig line in his hand: they were catching the wind.

He watched Stalwick stand precariously astride the bench, waving frantically for the carrack's forward watch. The great ship loomed over the rowboat and it seemed certain that Stalwick would be crushed beneath her hull, no one on board any the wiser to his one-man assault.

'Get out of there, you bloody fool!' he cried.

The carrack furled her topsails, then her mains.

The spanker pulled taut. Markus hauled it parallel with the main beam, watching Brand who was watching Sharr, still aloft, but shouting orders.

Stalwick waved at a sailor, who waved back.

'No,' Markus whispered, 'wait, we're coming.'

A rope ladder was lowered off the port bow. Stalwick reached for it, slipped and fell into his little boat, then took the ladder again with both hands. As he clung there, the rowboat thudded along the carrack's hull, then floated away.

The *Missing Daughter* found the wind and her bow came around slowly. A massive swell rolled over the port beam, knocking Markus to the deck, and the bowsprit filled with a noise like a muffled thunderclap. The old trawler made way, staring down a Malakasian carrack twenty times her size.

Stalwick Rees reached the top of the rope ladder and disappeared over the rail, into Malakasian custody.

Aloft, Sharr was still shouting, 'You've got to feel for it, Brand. Back and forth a bit, feel for the wind and watch the swells, they'll show you!' As the bowsprit caught the wind he screamed, 'That's it! Well done, old man, well done!' And with both hands clasped around a length of hemp, Sharr jumped.

The spinnaker rig spun with a humming sound like the drone on a bellamir as Sharr dropped to the foredeck, landing lightly as his secret sail, a vast billowing sheet, unfurled. It was attached with a clever array of looped lines, so all Sharr needed to do was unlash the uppermost and then leap into the morning. The massive sail was a magnificently stained and patched quilt, but it caught the wind, filled with a noisy snap and dragged the *Missing Daughter* towards the carrack.

'Woo hoo!' Sharr jigged like a madman, 'now we're running, boys! Did you see that?'

'Grand.' Markus frowned. 'So what do we do now?'

'Ram her?' Brand suggested.

'Good gods, no,' Sharr said, 'that tub wouldn't even feel us. We have to get on board, maybe get below. The holding cells will be down several levels. If we can break out, one of us might be able to get to her rudder, maybe disable the fat bitch from the inside.'

'Why do you think he did it?' Brand asked, giving up the helm.

'I think he saw it yesterday,' Sharr said, his cheery mood dissolving.

'Saw it?'

'The future. I think he saw himself doing whatever it is he's doing over there right now.'

'He's in manacles right now,' Brand said, 'or bent over the rail taking a beating.'

'Let's hope not,' Markus said. 'He's no threat.'

'They don't care. They'll see through that uniform he's wearing – where'd he get that, anyway?'

'Guilty,' Sharr said. 'I brought one for each of us, figured we might need them.'

'Should we put them on now?' Markus checked out beyond the spinnaker. They were closing fast on the carrack.

'Too late,' Sharr said, 'they've seen us.'

Brand went below, returning with another brace of throwing knives. 'We'll never get on board with bows, rapiers or swords, but if there's going to be a fight, we might be able to keep one or two of these hidden, at least until we're all on deck together.'

'There're two hundred soldiers and sailors on the ship, Brand.' Sharr looked sceptically at the double-edged blades.

'So what?' Brand shoved two more knives into his own belt, then handed two to Markus. 'So we don't fight at all? We let them—'

'Wait,' Markus cut him off, 'look there. What's that?'

'Pissing demons!' Sharr balanced on the transom and squinted. 'One of her sails is on fire.'

'And there goes another!' Brand pointed high in the carrack's rigging.

'Stalwick,' Markus whispered. The North Sea had been a dirge of muted greys for two days. The unexpected smear of orange, brightening the horizon, had Markus transfixed. 'He glimpsed the future, an image of himself . . .' His voice trailed off.

'Setting that thing on fire?' Brand said, 'killing himself out here?'

'That's why he fell apart on us yesterday, why he—' Markus pointed numbly at the empty cot, still a dishevelled jumble of blankets.

'Well, he's not dead yet,' Sharr said. 'You two, look sharp. I'll get us in close. See if he comes over the side.'

'He looks like them,' Markus said. 'How will we know it's him?'

'If only one gets tossed overboard,' Brand said, 'that'll be our boy.'

With a following sea and southerly wind, the *Missing Daughter* was nearly beneath the carrack's jib boom before Markus smelled the flames. A massive plume of smoke rose from the burning rigging and crested in fire; the great ship was a floating torch now, rising over Sharr's trawler like a second sun. While the rigging blazed out of control, the crew fought to save the masts, spars and yards, anything from which they might hang a spare sheet once the fire was out, but all the cutting, dragging, shouting, running and climbing were for naught as a burning spar broke free and crashed through the main deck into the hold.

Markus hoped the fiery missile had come to rest atop the milled bark and roots being shipped to Pellia.

The mizzenmast toppled backwards with the wind, shattering the helm and clearing the quarterdeck of her officers. The sails, ablaze, lay across the bridge like a burning blanket.

'See that?' Sharr said, 'she's just lost her helm. It's over.'

Markus shook his head. 'Not yet it isn't – look!'

Along the rail, the Malakasians who had been scurrying about like madmen regained a measure of discipline as the order was given to abandon the ship. Working together, teams lowered longboats and cast rope ladders over the side. Those with level heads climbed down; others, overcome with panic, leapt into the frigid seawater. Some never resurfaced; others thrashed about for a moment or two before bobbing passively south with the tide. The screams of those still alive were an unnerving counterpoint to the orders and warnings shouted from above.

'We should pick them up,' Markus said.

'Forget them,' Brand muttered, 'we're watching for Stalwick.'

'We can't just leave them to die.'

'Of course we can – and anyway, it's too dangerous for us to be sculling about beneath that thing. If one of those masts falls on us, we'll be on tonight's menu as well.'

With her masts razed to the decks, the carrack was dead in the water and drifting south. Her hull turned lazily, pushing several longboats out of reach. Sailors still clinging to ratlines jumped for it, hoping to come up within arm's length of someone they knew, someone with a hint of compassion. Markus watched as two officers, their absurd black and gold plumage setting them apart from the others, deliberately kept two seamen from climbing aboard their launch. It wasn't difficult: a few slaps, cold fingers prised away, and the sailors sank silently into the deeps.

'Rutting motherhumpers!' Sharr rooted around in the cabin until he found his longbow. 'Drown the commoners, will you?' He nocked an arrow. 'Bloody cowards, the both of them – Brand! Keep us steady; this won't take but a moment.'

Grinning, Brand said, 'Certainly, Captain. Send them to the Northern Forest early. They can keep a seat warm for the rest of us.'

With two quick shots, Sharr dispatched both officers. 'There,' he said as their bodies slumped into the longboat.

'Feel better?' Markus found the murders a bit ironic given the devastation.

'Yes, actually,' Sharr said. 'There are worse things than war, Markus. Now, if you would, please, strike the bowsprit and the spinnaker. I want to make another pass, see if we can find him.'

Markus clung to the guide rope Sharr had affixed to the bulkhead. With only a toehold on either side of the cabin, moving forward on the *Missing Daughter* was a challenge for an untrained farmer from the Central Plains. With his heels dangling unnervingly over open water, Markus slithered into the bow and unlashed both sails.

As soon as the rig lines were free, Sharr shouted, 'Coming about, boys, keep your heads down.' The main boom swung overhead and the trawler slowed to a crawl. 'Leave those sheets, Markus; just tie them off loose for now. We'll need them when we turn tail and run.'

A dead sailor floated past. Markus could smell the smoke and burning bodies. He made a silent vow to abandon the Resistance, sneak home and focus on the spring planting.

'There!' Brand shouted, pointing up at the great ship's stern rail, 'is that him?'

'Hard to tell.' Sharr coughed on a lungful of smoke. 'Markus, can you see him?'

It was Stalwick: he waved frantically with one arm. When he turned, Markus could see the hilt of a knife embedded in his back; it was difficult to see from this distance, but he thought the wound might still be bleeding. Stalwick clumsily cast one leg over the rail, looking as though he was about to jump.

'No!' Sharr screamed, 'not yet! Stalwick, wait. We're too far out!'

Markus jumped up and down, motioning for Stalwick to wait, but the injured sorcerer, his frail form wracked with sobs, ignored him and dived for the *Missing Daughter*, slamming into the water on his side.

'Demonshit,' Brand said, 'we can't get in that far. That tub's turning on her heels. We might reach him, but we'll lose the wind beneath that bloated arse of hers.'

'Markus?' Sharr said.

As if reading his mind, Markus was already stripped to the waist and kicking off his boots. He hugged the bowsprit with both arms as he crawled along the tapered beam. 'A bit further, Sharr!' he called, 'I see him!'

Sharr poked the *Missing Daughter*'s extended bowsprit as close to the burning carrack as he dared. Overhead, the fiery beast rolled gently, her massive stern turning slowly to windward. 'Now, Markus!' he cried, 'and be quick about it – we'll be off the wind in two shakes of your sister's backside!'

Markus dived in. They could hear him screaming before he surfaced as the freezing water bit with a thousand needle-sharp teeth. He saw one of the Malakasians sinking, feet first, about fifty paces down; the sailor's face was frozen in a macabre cry. It wouldn't take long to die out here.

Stalwick paddled gamely with one arm, still weeping like a child, but kicking hard nonetheless. When Markus reached him, he threw himself on his friend, grasping at anything to stay afloat.

'Come on, you mad bastard.' Markus ground his teeth together. 'Calm down and let me get you home, otherwise you'll drown us both.'

'I'm too c-c-c-c-cold,' Stalwick's own teeth chattered, 'and m-m-m-my leg won't w-w-w-work any more and I can't f-f-f-feel m-m-m-my arm!'

'The bleeding arm?' Markus tried to keep him talking as he towed him towards the trawler. 'That's probably good, you blazing fool; with that knife stuck in you, I bet it hurts like the blazes.'

'I d-d-d-d-don't know.' Stalwick's voice died to a whisper.

'Brand!' Markus shouted, surprised at how his own voice had begun to falter, 'throw us a line. Throw—'

Stalwick was a dead weight now. Markus held him up with one hand and clawed at the icy water with the other. *This is it*, he thought, *we're going down*.

The rope struck him in the face. 'Grab it, Markus!' Brand shouted, standing astride the transom. 'Grab it and hold on!'

With weakening fingers, Markus found the line, wrapped it a few times around his wrist and waited for the North Sea to swallow them whole. Just as he imagined them sliding into the vast emptiness below, he heard the *Missing Daughter*'s sails snap with the wind: the carrack had drifted far enough east. Markus took a breath, held it, then sank, dragging Stalwick with him. They drifted for a few agonising moments in the clear northern seas. The silence was infinite, overwhelming . . . then Markus felt a tug on his wrist as Brand reeled them in with the trawler's winch.

His head broke the surface. Stalwick was still with him, his stringy hair matted over his pallid face. His Malakasian uniform, too large, dragged in the current like a shedding skin. Markus held him fast around his chest, listening as Sharr and Brand's voices grew closer. He could feel nothing from the waist down. He wondered if he would be able to let Stalwick go once they had been dragged back on board.

'Why'd you do it?' he whispered, fearing that Stalwick was already dead.

'I'm g-g-g-g-good with f-f-f-f-fires,' Stalwick said. 'I t-t-t-t-tell you what, M-m-m-m-markus, I am g-g-g-good with f-f-f-fires.'

The Malakasian ship, packed to the gunwales with mysteries harvested in Rona's Forbidden Forest, burned for two avens. When the water finally snuffed out the last flames, the massive skeleton upended and sank noiselessly into the North Sea.

MASSACHUSETTS

'Mom?'

Jennifer Sorenson shrieked, dropping a bowl of breakfast cereal that shattered on the floor. 'Hannah?' she cried, 'my God, Hannah? Is it you, baby?' Ignoring the splattered milk and cornflakes, she threw her arms around her daughter, clinging to Hannah as if she would never let go again.

'Are you all right? Oh my God, I thought you'd never come back. I wanted to believe Steven, but it's been so long. I've been waiting and waiting and I just can't believe you're back.' She was crying, laughing, sobbing, all at once. 'Are you hurt, baby? You're too thin; I can tell that just from holding you. But are you hurt? Is anything broken?'

Hannah found herself a little embarrassed at how nice it was to have her mother clutch her so tightly. She knew she ought to feel guilty; she'd put her through a four-month nightmare, but for a few seconds, it was nice to bask in feelings she hadn't thought about since school. 'Mom—' She gently shrugged out of Jennifer's arms, 'we have to close the portal.'

'I'll get it,' Jennifer said, wiping her face with her bathrobe sleeve. 'I'm an old hand at it now.' She used the cereal spoon she was still clutching to fold the edge of the Larion tapestry back over itself. 'There,' she said, then, unable to contain herself, drew Hannah back into her arms and hugged her close.

'Mom?' Hannah said, 'we have some stuff to do, and we have to hurry.' She paused for a second, inhaling her mother's essence: lavender soap and body lotion, nothing expensive or fancy, but the scent of home, of love, of comfort. 'I only have twelve hours.'

She felt Jennifer tense and they broke apart; the poignant moment had passed.

'No.' Jennifer looked exhausted, worn to the nub. Her hair was more grey than blonde now, and she too had lost weight. 'No, you can't, Hannah, you can't go back. I won't let you. We can open the portal for Steven if you like, and Mark, and anyone who wants to join you, but you're staying with me and we're going home together, today.'

Hannah knew Jennifer would resist; she tried to sidestep the argument. 'We'll talk about it as we go, Mom, but I really do have some stuff to do.'

'Go where?'

She hadn't considered that her mother would be anywhere but Grant Street in Denver. 'Where are we?'

'The Berkshires, outside Pittsfield, Massachusetts.'

'Holy shit, what are you doing all the way out here?'

'Aunt Kay has a cottage on Cape Cod. It's closed up for the winter, but she said I could stay there until she opened the place for spring break. I wasn't planning on needing it too long; I kept expecting you.' Jennifer was crying again. 'Every time I opened this goddamned thing, I expected you to come through it—' She kicked at the tapestry.

'Who's Aunt Kay?' Hannah asked, curious.

'Oh, she's not your real aunt,' Jennifer explained. 'And I don't think you've seen her in – what? Twenty-two years, maybe. She went to college with me about a hundred and forty years ago; we were roommates.' She went to the tiny kitchenette in what Hannah now saw was a cheap motel suite. She couldn't believe her mother had been living like this for months. Jennifer returned with a handful of paper towels and started cleaning up the spilled cereal and shards of pottery. 'Anyway, I called her and told her I needed a place to stay, that I was wrestling with an alcohol problem and wanted to get clear of Denver for a while. She didn't mind.'

Hannah was stunned. Lacking something to do, she knelt beside her mother and helped to mop up soggy cornflakes. 'Why, Mom? Why are you doing this?'

'You don't know?'

'No.'

'Then Steven didn't find you?'

'We found each other yesterday, finally,' Hannah said. 'It's been difficult—' she laughed, a little cynically, 'difficult . . . no, it's been a godforsaken mess, but I'm fine.'

'Then why do you—?'

'Steven is sick,' she said, 'and I'm going back, Mom, tonight at seven. They're waiting for me.'

'What about Nerak?' Jennifer dropped the towels and the jagged bits of cereal bowl into the bin and washed her hands under the faucet. She needed something to do with her hands. 'That's why I'm here, you know, because Steven told me I had to keep moving and that I couldn't go anyplace anyone would think of, or be able to guess. Do you realise how challenging that is? And all the while I've been thinking that Nerak might be following me . . . well, hoping, actually.'

'Hoping?'

'Of course. If he was here following me, he couldn't be there chasing after you.'

'Steven killed him.'

Jennifer nodded grimly. After a moment, she said, 'That's good, I suppose.'

Hannah went to the kitchenette and wrapped her arms around her mother's waist. 'God, I missed you, Mom.'

Jennifer broke down again. 'I missed you, too, baby. This is the worst thing I've ever had to do, and until you have your own children, you'll never be able to understand. And that's why I can't—'

'I have to, Mom, and you have to help me,' Hannah said softly. She felt her stomach knot; it was so unfair of her to ask for this, but she had no choice. 'I need you to help me heal him, and maybe save all of us.'

'Okay, I'll go in your place.' Jennifer didn't hesitate.

Hannah laughed and hugged her mother even more tightly. 'No, Mom, that's not what I meant; I need you to keep going like you're going. I need you to keep opening the portal, every day at seven o'clock, a.m. and p.m. And you can't miss a time.'

'I haven't yet.'

'I'll be back, with Steven, very soon.'

Jennifer stared out of the front window across the pot-holed parking lot. It had snowed overnight, but it was already melting into puddles. It was going to be wet and slushy, not the kind of day she had imagined Hannah coming home to. 'Where are we going?' she asked.

'A drugstore first.' Hannah dug for a handful of cornflakes. 'And an Internet café. Let's start with the café.'

Hoyt sat wrapped in a blanket with his chair wedged into the corner of the cabin so it couldn't fall over. He was shivering with fever and hadn't eaten anything but broth in two days, but still he watched Hannah intently. 'That was a quick trip,' he said, trying to hide how pleased he was to see her back.

'I just needed a few things. The hardest part was convincing my mother to let me come back – I thought for a while she was going to chain me up there and cross over here herself.' Hannah had been gone a full day and night. Hoyt didn't mention how worried he had been – how worried they had *all* been – when she didn't return the first time they opened the portal.

Hannah took a seat beside Steven. 'Any change in him?'

Hoyt frowned and shook his head. 'Sorry.'

'It's a gamble, but I'm hoping this will help.' She withdrew a small glass ampoule with a built-in needle and for what felt like the two-hundredth time in two hours, she checked the label.

'What is it?'

'Anti-venom,' she said in English.

'Anti—?'

'This comes from the most deadly poisonous creatures in our world.' She shook the ampoule and held it up to the light. 'It isn't the best option, but I only had a day at home and I needed something fast.'

'And you're going to give it to Steven?'

'Yup.'

'Through that needle?' Hoyt had read about venous injections in an ancient book on Larion magic and medicine. He had never seen an actual needle up close, however.

'I am,' Hannah said, ripping open a little packet and pulling out a small piece of thin cloth that smelled peculiar. She rubbed a spot on Steven's shoulder clean with the strong-smelling cloth, then snapped off the protective cap of the needle and, holding her breath, injected the fluid. 'There,' she said, and passed the ampoule to Hoyt who turned it over in his hands like a piece of treasure.

'Look at that,' he said. 'How do you know how much to inject?'

'I don't,' Hannah said. 'I figure since these are normally administered in emergency situations, what with the built-in needle, I'd just shoot the whole works in there.'

'How long will it take to fix him up?'

'If it works,' Hannah pulled the tattered blankets up to Steven's chin, 'he should be fine by tomorrow, maybe even tonight.'

'And if it doesn't?'

Hannah paused. 'Well, it might make him sicker – I don't *think* it will kill him, but I guess it could.'

Hoyt saw how difficult it was for Hannah to admit that. She could just as easily have told them that the anti-stuff was harmless. What would anyone in Eldarn know? He huddled deeper in his blankets and said, 'Well then, that took courage, Hannah Sorenson. I'm sure he'll be fine.'

She worried a piece of Steven's tunic between her fingers. 'I hope so,' she whispered.

'So how does this work, anyway?'

Hannah explained, 'As far as I know, in my world these deadly creatures are milked for their venom. Then, using tiny doses, they help horses develop immunity. With that done, they isolate what they need – they're called proteins – in the horses' blood, and then use that to extract and mass-produce the anti-venom for people unfortunate enough to be bitten. The molecules in venom are big and slow, especially through the lymph system. With an injection following soon after a bite, the proteins in the anti-venom can usually counteract the effect of the toxin.'

'I was with you until *proteins*,' Hoyt said, smiling. 'Remember, the medical books I read are already a thousand Twinmoons old.'

'Uh, proteins ... huge, specialised molecules.' Hannah dug in her coat pocket. 'That reminds me—' She tossed him a plastic medicine bottle with a child-safety cap. 'You need to take one of those, with food, every six hours ... every two avens, give or take, until they're all gone.'

Hoyt shook the bottle and tried to read the label. 'What is it? More molecules extracted from horse blood?' He laughed; it didn't make him look any healthier. 'And I thought medicine was more advanced in Colorado.'

'It is,' Hannah said, 'and no, that's not extracted from horse blood. Believe it or not, the molecules in that handful of magic come from mould.'

'Mould?'

'Good old-fashioned mould.'

'No thanks.' Hoyt tossed the bottle back. 'I'll take my chances with the querlis.'

'You have no idea what I went through to get that,' Hannah said sternly, 'so you *will* take one, *with* food, every *two* avens, or I will drag you topside and toss your sick-and-sorry self overboard.'

'All right, all right! I surrender,' Hoyt wrestled with the safety cap. 'Good rutters, how do sick people even get them out of the pissing container?'

Hannah sighed. 'Must I do everything?' She gave him a pill, which he examined for a moment, then began to chew.

'Whoring lords!' he cried, 'it tastes like grettan shit!'

488

'You're not supposed to chew them, you dope.' She passed him a water-skin and he tipped the liquid straight down his throat, swishing water round his mouth to get rid of the taste.

'I hope it's powerful medicine, Hannah, because that's the only one of those I'll be eating.' He tried to squeeze the spilled water from his blankets.

Hannah looked at him like a disappointed schoolmarm. 'In two avens' time I'll help you with the second dose. Christ! Men!' She handed him a chunk of bread. 'Now eat that.'

Footsteps sounded in the companionway followed by a knock on the cabin door. 'Come in!' Hoyt wheezed, 'come in and save me from advanced medicine!'

Alen and Gilmour joined them, looking grave. No one had elected to remain behind in Pellia, despite the captain's impassioned speech.

Hoyt sat up. 'Where are we?'

Alen sat on the edge of Steven's berth. Gilmour remained standing. 'We're about a day south of Pellia. The incoming tide helped, but we lose ground when the tide goes out and the tacks are difficult and time-consuming for a boat this size. Captain Ford is working himself to exhaustion.'

'What did you give him?' Alen reached for the spent ampoule.

'Anti-venom,' Hannah said.

'For a biological toxin?' Alen cocked an eyebrow. 'Steven was attacked by a tan-bak.'

'Gilmour said Steven had disabled the tan-bak, but left it alive,' Hannah explained. 'He also said the insects died when you stepped on them or crushed them. That doesn't sound like a creature armed with a mystical toxin. I just hope the bug that bit Steven is close enough to the arachnid family we use to brew up this serum.'

Gilmour agreed. 'While the tan-bak is a monster, Steven's quick thinking showed us that it is a living, vulnerable monster. And, in Steven's case, the tan-bak's tiny emissary didn't have a chance to burrow inside his brain, like the one that attacked Marrin.'

'The first mate?' Hoyt asked.

'That's the one — Marrin had an insect inside his head for days. I can't begin to speculate what it was doing, maybe incubating in there, but when it saw an opportunity, or when it knew its partner had been found out, it struck.'

'And Marrin died.'

'Last night, I'm afraid,' Gilmour said.

'What are you taking?' Alen pointed at the plastic container.

489

'Mould extract.' Hoyt leaned against the bulkhead. He was exhausted and needed to sleep. 'It tastes like last Twinmoon's booacore.'

'Amoxicillin,' Hannah said. 'It kills bacterial infections. There's almost nothing better in our world. And while it's possible that Seron didn't infect Hoyt with a bacterial infection, at least this medication won't do any damage.'

'How'd you get it?' Gilmour asked.

'My mother and I robbed a pharmacy.'

'A what?' Hoyt said, sitting up again.

'A secure office where our doctors keep our strongest and most dangerous medicines – healing substances.' Hannah put a hand on Steven's chest. She felt the comforting rise and fall of his chest and thought of the Mexican restaurant on South Broadway near her grandfather's store.

'That sounds dangerous.' Gilmour felt Hoyt's forehead. Expecting to sense a wave of Larion power, Hoyt flinched. Gilmour said, 'Just checking your temperature, my boy. Don't worry.'

'Sorry.' Hoyt closed his eyes.

'How'd you manage it?' Alen asked.

'It was a small town,' Hannah said, using English for words that wouldn't translate. 'Mom and I drove by the police station; there were only two officers on duty for the night. We stole a car, my mother dropped me off near the pharmacy and then drove out to the edge of the officers' jurisdiction, way out on the side of a mountain. It was cold, and it had snowed the night before; so the roads were a bit icy, especially that far off the main road. My mother drove her car into a ditch, crumpling the front end against a tree, so it looked like a serious accident to passers-by. Then she lit a length of cloth with her lighter—'

'I have one of those,' Gilmour interrupted. 'Steven brought it back for me from Idaho Springs. Alen, remind me later to show you how it ignites—'

Hannah smiled at him and continued her story. 'Anyway, using a lighter, my mother started the car on fire and then ran off through the snow—'

'Thus drawing the two police officers away from town for what was probably the biggest crime any of them had investigated in fifty Twinmoons,' Alen finished for her.

'She wasn't done yet,' Hannah said. 'You see, by fleeing through the forest, she left a trail—'

Gilmour interrupted, 'That led the police and a barrel of helpful neighbours on a merry chase through the snowy woods—'

'And ended at a quiet car park on the outside of town, where,' Alen said, 'the trail suddenly disappeared.'

'It gave me just enough time to break into the pharmacy, steal the penicillin, which was easy to find, and the red spider anti-venom, which was frigging difficult to find—'

'Not a popular item?' Hoyt asked.

'In Massachusetts in the dead of winter? No, not exactly,' Hannah said. 'Anyway, I'm sure the security tapes show me breaking in and the dispatcher at the police station must have had a heart attack when the alarm went off, but with essentially everyone in town out looking for a crazed, injured car thief, there was no one to come after me, at least for a few moments, anyway.'

'What's a security tape?' Hoyt whispered, still listening but nearly asleep now.

'A permanent image of my face,' Hannah said. 'But I've been listed as missing and assumed dead for more than three Twinmoons now. No one is going to connect a minuscule drugs heist with a cold missing person report two thousand miles away.'

'The perfect crime,' Gilmour grinned.

'All it takes is a criminal mind.' Hannah tapped two fingers on her temple. 'A couple of Larion far portals don't hurt, either.'

'How's your mother?' Gilmour asked.

'She's holding together,' Hannah said. 'Thanks for asking.'

'I'm sure she misses you,' Alen said.

'You'd better believe it!' Hannah smiled.

'I know *I* did.'

Hannah spun round so quickly that she slipped off Steven's berth and landed with an embarrassing thud.

'Steven!' Gilmour shouted, 'you're back!'

Hannah picked herself up and, fighting the almost overwhelming urge to throw herself onto the narrow bunk in public, managed to content herself with merely kneeling on the floor, her face close to Steven's. She whispered, 'Are you okay?'

'I feel pretty dismal, I have to admit,' he said. 'You were running and I couldn't catch you.'

Unsure what he meant, Hannah said, 'I would have slowed down if I'd known.'

'Thanks.' Steven licked his lips; they were dry, near to cracking. 'There was a dog that kept biting me.'

Alen, Gilmour and Hoyt shared a knowing glance.

Hannah ignored the dog reference and kissed him lightly. 'Hi,' she whispered.

'Hi.' He kissed her back. 'Come here often?'

Hannah laughed. 'I understand it's a great place to meet men.'

'I missed you.'

'Well, I didn't miss you.' She pressed her face closer to his, her nose brushing gently against his cheek.

'Pushy boyfriend following you everywhere? Never giving you any space?'

'Something like that,' Hannah said, kissing him again, more urgently this time.

'Ahem,' Gilmour cleared his throat, ruining the moment. 'How are you, Steven? Can you feel . . . you know?'

Steven closed his eyes. 'Yes, it's still there. I don't think it took anything from me.'

'We got to you pretty quickly,' Gilmour said. 'I think we bled enough of it out of you that the effects, while still devastating, weren't fatal.'

'And you have Hannah to thank for her own bit of magic,' Hoyt added.

Steven looked confused, and Hannah made introductions. Hoyt sensed there was something she left out, something more she wanted to say about him or Alen, but he let it go.

'Where are we?' Steven asked finally.

'About a day south of Pellia, on the Welstar River,' Gilmour replied a little hesitantly. He didn't want Steven to worry; the young sorcerer wasn't up to much strain yet, and discovering they were within two days of Welstar Palace might make him try to do too much too soon.

As Gilmour had expected, Steven tried to sit up, but when his head started spinning, he had to be content with lying on his side. He took Hannah's hand and said, 'So, all of you, tell me everything.'

Hours later, their stories told and Steven's questions answered, the partisans received their watch assignments from Captain Ford. While some climbed the wooden steps to the main deck, others, Steven and Hannah included, crawled into cramped berths, wrapped themselves in heavy blankets and tried to steal an uneasy aven's sleep.

Steven dreamed of Idaho Springs and 147 Tenth Street. Mark was there; the friends were sharing a pizza and drinking beer. Lessek's key was locked in a rosewood box and the Larion far portal was rolled up like a map and tucked inside its cylindrical case. Nothing tragic or miraculous had happened yet and the two were simply bachelors enjoying dinner and an October baseball game. Steven had fallen victim to curiosity, but who in their life hadn't? He had finagled access to William Higgins' safe deposit box, had found the missing key and had created an opportunity to investigate, but, thus far, that had been the extent of his crimes. He hadn't killed a squad of Seron warriors. He hadn't raced across the United States, mined to his elbows in the city landfill, or battled an almor, acid clouds, a legion of bone-collectors or an army of wraiths. He was just a bank employee who had been tempted by the unknown and given in.

Then he opened the box.

'What is it?' Mark had asked.

'My best guess,' Steven said, removing the stone, 'is that it's a rock.'

Mark had been unable to control himself. 'No, officer, we left all the cash, but couldn't part with this rock . . .'

It was months later, Twinmoons, when his roommate eventually told him the truth.

Mark closed his fist over the stone. 'You know, I never touched this that night in our house, but when you opened that box, I experienced something strange: a warm sensation, like someone reached into our apartment and draped some old blanket over me . . . I remembered being a kid, out at the beach, Jones Beach, on the island. I was in Eldarn less than five goddamned minutes, losing it, going full-on screwball crazy, and all of a sudden, I got a reprieve.'

Steven had been sitting with him, watching Gilmour wade in the chilly waters of the Falkan fjord. 'What do you mean?'

'I'm pretty sure I'm supposed to be remembering something about some afternoon out at Jones Beach with my family . . . and it's happening right now as I sit here, touching Lessek's key: it's as though I'm there – as if part of my mind is there – reliving that day on the beach.'

Steven sat up, tumbling Hannah out of the berth again. 'Holy shit,' he said, 'holy shit!'

'What is it?' Hannah took him in her arms. 'You're shaking, Steven, please, tell me what's wrong.' She worried it was the anti-venom; she'd heard anti-venom was sometimes more dangerous than the bites it was supposed to cure, causing serum sickness, or bronchospasms requiring adrenalin shots. She'd brought some adrenalin too, just in case—

He had stopped sweating, but his skin remained pale, even in the weak light of the hanging lamp. 'We need Captain Ford,' he said, 'and Gilmour, Alen, Garec ... hell, get everyone. We're making a huge mistake.'

'What mistake, Steven?' Hannah tried to get him to lie back down. 'You're sick. You've had a massive injection of a powerful anti-toxin; you need to rest.'

'Hannah, pay attention, please.' He took her by the shoulders and stared into her eyes. 'Help me to Captain Ford's cabin and then wake the others.'

A DESTINATION CHANGE

Mark rested in the yawning roots of the banyan tree. He could see his keeper's shadow, dancing around the sandy hilltop, just beyond the edge of the swamp. Whoever had been taunting him and keeping him imprisoned here was busy, moving incessantly and mumbling to himself. He hadn't spoken to Mark for a while; it was impossible to know how long – the passage of time meant little here. But Mark couldn't help but wonder if his preoccupied warden was nearing the end of something; he seemed very distracted.

The coral snake had failed to find him. It had passed by twice, slithering near the banyan roots, its crooked tongue lancing in and out of its ruined head. On both sweeps, Mark had frozen, holding his breath and focusing on the flawless azure sky with its promise of cool, dry air and cathartic sunshine. On its second journey up the sandy rise, the snake had moved through the banyan roots; it had slithered within inches of Mark's feet, but still he had remained motionless, careful not even to blink. Now the snake was back inside the swamp, down near the Gloriette and the marble-ringed pool. With his blind sentry chasing some imagined vibration and his host lost in his own problems, Mark took the opportunity to stretch his legs, exorcising the stinging numbness. He sidled quietly around the edge of the banyan, paused for a moment, then, with fists clenched, charged.

The man working around the circular stone table was young, black and dressed in a red sweater, *his* sweater. His back was turned, so Mark couldn't see his face, but he knew as he rushed the distracted warden of this marshy nightmare that he would be fighting himself. And it was a fight, a full-on parking lot brawl, complete with biting, kicking, scratching at eyes and butting heads.

At first, Mark was heartened: surprise had served him well, and he felt sure he was winning. He had never been much for fighting, but he threw himself into the fray with abandon. Between punches and kicks, he even taunted himself, colloquial trash talk he would have been embarrassed to utter under normal circumstances. 'C'mon, motherfucker, I'm wearing myself out beating on you,' he cried.

He landed a hard elbow to his jaw, felt it come loose.

'That all you got, pussy?' Mark shoved his former self into the sand and kicked himself hard in the abdomen.

'Because I can bring on this shit all day.' He kicked himself in the face, feeling his nose crunch under Redrick Shen's boot.

But then, Mark realised that he wasn't winning at all; rather, he, his former self, complete with his favourite red sweater, was toying with him, murmuring Mark's intentions beneath his breath, as if reading the fight from a set of choreographed dance steps. Mark heard his own voice in his head:

Elbow to the face; Mark's head snapped back. *Nicely done.*

Wrestle me down, very good; he kicked himself in the stomach. *Excellent.*

Now, boot me in the snout; Mark shattered his own nose. *Ah, very nice, brutal, truly.*

Mark stepped back, confused.

What? He watched himself wipe his nose on his sleeve, red on red, then stand. *You don't think I know what you're planning? We're in here together, Mark.*

He was panting, struggling to catch his breath. Redrick's body rippled with tough muscle, but the Ronan sailor was in miserable cardiovascular shape. The short engagement had left Mark dizzy. 'I can't let you,' he panted, 'can't let you use the table.' Mark charged again, lowering his shoulder and ploughing forward.

Mark sidestepped the attack. *Sorry, old fellow, but as much fun as that was, I must get back to work. We're nearly home now. Can't you smell it?* He inhaled deeply through his flattened nose as he shoved Mark down the rise towards the marsh. *That's Welstar Palace. I love that smell; the stench of dead things rotting!*

Mark found a broken tree limb and rushed back to the table. 'No!' he screamed, wielding the branch like a mace.

Stop it, Mark. You're embarrassing yourself, me, both of us, for pity's sake. The bloodied warden intercepted him and easily wrenched the limb from Mark's hand. He grasped Mark's head with the other. *Why don't you rest now? I'll wake you shortly, when I need you, my prince. We're on the verge of greatness here today.*

'No—' Mark's vision tunnelled and he slipped to his knees in the sand, soft and dry, and there was beach grass, the sharp stuff that threatened to cut fingers and toes, clumped in green tufts along the dune, just like back home.

The nightmare warden, his face torn and bleeding, returned to the spell table. In one hand he tossed an innocent-looking bit of rock, Lessek's key, as if it were an apple, or a piece of candy. *Not long now,* he said, but his voice was a toneless warble on the periphery of Mark's consciousness. Louder, pervading his last cogent thoughts, were the sounds of something familiar: a low and steady roar, punctuated by the cawing of a gull.

'We're making a mistake,' Steven said again. The others had joined him in the captain's cabin. With all of them – save for Pel and Kellin, who were standing the middle watch – packed inside, there was little room to move. 'Captain Ford, we need to turn around, run downriver and escape into deep water. We're endangering you, your crew and your ship for no reason.'

'Steven, we can't,' Gilmour said. 'Mark will reach Welstar Palace in the next two days. We have to catch him. We can't guess how quickly he'll open the Fold once he arrives at the encampment, but we have to assume it'll be right away.'

'It doesn't matter,' Steven said. 'We're not going to fight him there.'

'We have to,' Alen said. 'There's no other way. We're in a race for our lives, for the very existence of Eldarn.'

'True,' Steven said, 'but it isn't Eldarn that he wants; it's Earth: my home, Mark's home.'

Everyone jammed into Doren Ford's modest quarters fell silent. Only the rattle of the rigging and the faint ping of the bridge bell interrupted the steady sound of the wind and the waves. Eventually, Gilmour asked, 'How do you know this?'

'Brexan,' Steven said, 'you mentioned it, last Moon: what is Prince Malagon doing with two hundred thousand troops or more at Welstar Palace? Why have the occupation forces been called back? Gilmour and I saw it in Falkan; Hannah and Alen witnessed it just yesterday: troops filing onto barges and heading upriver. Why?'

Brexan, sitting cross-legged on the floor, said, 'It was Versen who first asked that question. I've been trying to figure it out for a couple of Twinmoons now, but I still don't know why.'

'We thought they might be slaves, a workforce, for when evil ushers its master from the Fold and into Eldarn. The world will come apart; the only survivors will be those unfortunate enough to be slaves to famine and pestilence.' Steven was glad he had taken one of the captain's chairs. His legs were weak; he could feel his adrenalin waning. 'But that's not it. They're not slaves; they're an invasion force. Eldarn isn't evil's goal. Eldarn is a stepping stone, a preparatory step for my world.'

'How can you be certain?' Hoyt was still wrapped in his blanket, but his fever had obviously broken. He nibbled at a chunk of bread.

'Why did Nerak never go to Idaho Springs and take back the keystone?'

Alen said, 'Because with the stone here, he was at greater risk.'

'From whom?' Steven said. 'He always knew when Gilmour was practising magic, and from what I understand of your experiences, Alen, he had teams of magicians watching for you day and night. Who was here to threaten him?'

'No one,' Garec whispered. 'Rutters, but I think you've got a point, Steven.'

'Why was the keystone in my bank all those Twinmoons? Was it because Nerak was protecting it? Was it because he planned to come back and retrieve it? Or was it because he expected that eventually someone would find it and bring it back to Eldarn? Could it have been bait?'

'Stop now, Steven,' Gilmour interrupted. 'He didn't ensure its safety in that bank, because he expected someone would eventually find it. It's a bank, for whore's sake; it was a safe place, a perfect set-up. You're trying too hard.'

'I might be,' Steven agreed, 'but think about it: what would Nerak have to do when he arrived back at the bank a thousand Twinmoons later?'

'Kill someone,' Brexan said, motioning for Hoyt to toss her some bread. 'Right? Just to get the box thing open.'

'Not *kill* someone,' Steven corrected her, 'but *take* someone, and what does Nerak gain when he takes someone?'

'A head full of knowledge,' Garec said.

'Exactly,' Hannah joined in, understanding now, 'a head full of updated knowledge about our home, Earth and everything we know about Earth, its people, its culture, its history, its strengths and vulnerabilities ...' Her voice trailed off mid-list. 'Jesus, Steven, you might be right.'

'An invasion force?' Gilmour said, 'but why not just open the Fold from Eldarn and invite evil to sweep across Earth as well? What need is there for an invasion force?'

'Because maybe Earth isn't the last stop on the line.' Steven shrugged. 'But I'd bet dollars to doughnuts it's because evil wants souls there, too, and two hundred thousand, even three hundred thousand, while impressive numbers, just aren't enough to take our planet.'

'But they could hold a significant corner of it,' Hannah said, 'and probably for a long time.'

'If they choose the right corner,' Steven said, 'and bring the right agents along with them.'

'Good rutters, the ash dream,' Alen said to no one in particular.

'The bark, those roots and leaves,' Steven said. 'What could an army of two hundred thousand do if they were to arrive suddenly inside our borders, armed with that bark? Even if each of them had only a pouch or two? What damage could they do?'

'They could enslave entire cities,' Garec said, 'take whole regions, and without spilling any blood.'

'Mother of Christ,' Hannah whispered. 'They could turn us against ourselves, too, shut down the power, cut off critical food and water resources, *anything*.'

'So what do we do?' Hoyt shifted so he could rest against Captain Ford's sea chest.

'We wait for them on the other side,' Steven said simply.

'For two hundred thousand of them?' Garec swallowed dryly. 'I'm good, Steven, but that's madness.'

'Not if we know where they're coming through.' Steven wished he could stand up, but dared not try. He was sweating again and his muscles ached where the anti-venom was flushing out the foreign toxins.

'All of them in one place?' Alen said. 'That would be counter-productive; it's a big world. A few of them here and there would be infinitely more effective.'

'That's true, Alen,' Steven said, 'they won't all come through in the same place, but if we know where the first wave is crossing, we can be there. Mark will be there with the spell table; you can bet on it. We simply cross over, meet him and the initial forces, however many they are, and seal the Fold for ever with the spell table inside. In doing so, we take the head off the snake here in Eldarn. Everyone wins.'

'You make it sound awfully easy.' Brexan wanted to believe him, but she couldn't banish the scepticism from her voice. 'What will you do with the two hundred thousand warriors?'

Steven looked at Gilmour and sighed. 'I'm afraid that many of them will perish inside the void. There's no other way.'

This piece of information didn't appear to upset the former soldier. 'What about the ones still in the encampment?'

'We'll have to cross that bridge when we come to it, Brexan,' Alen said.

'If they're near the spell table when we strike out at Mark and his initial forces, they'll be lost with the others.'

'How do you know that?' Captain Ford asked. He was the only one who looked remotely comfortable, sitting behind his desk.

Steven grimaced. 'Because we're going to tell them to enter the Fold and remain there for ever.'

'Can you do that?' Garec asked.

Again, Steven looked at Gilmour. 'Can we? She sent us all the same dog, didn't she?'

Hoyt whispered, 'Whoring rutters, it's Milla.'

Gilmour looked around for something to drink. With nothing at hand, he licked his lips and nodded. 'I don't know. I just ... don't know.'

'What's the book say?' Steven pressed.

Alen interjected, 'It says that we can do it: you certainly, Fantus; maybe even I can. The challenge is figuring out how to make it work on thousands simultaneously.'

'That's it, then.' Garec finally understood. 'That's why Nerak had the book with him on the *Prince Marek*. He was learning how to give directions to all of these soldiers at once.'

'To a large group at least, yes. It's called the ash dream and, if I'm guessing correctly, Gilmour, it was a teaching tool, wasn't it? Learn from your own past? Learn emotional and physical self-control, self-image, self-esteem, and all of it stemming from self-knowledge ... because all magic is about knowledge, my friend.' He was speaking only to Gilmour now. 'And what's more important knowledge than self-knowledge? What better research arena than one's own past – and not the boring stuff, hell no. Lessek planned it right: get the highs and the lows. But you were never supposed to go in solo, were you?'

'Very old.' Gilmour didn't look at them. 'It's very old magic, Steven, Lessek's personal writings. We can't pretend to know what he was thinking.'

'But you do,' Steven said. 'You have to believe it, Gilmour, because you have to teach me, and we have all of about two days to get it exactly right.'

'Wait a moment,' Captain Ford interrupted, 'how do you know

where they're going, Steven? What if you guess wrong?'

'Actually, Captain, that's the one piece of this whole nightmarish puzzle that I'm confident I have figured correctly.'

'So where are they going to strike first?' Hannah said, taking his hand.

'Jones Beach, New York.'

Her eyes widened. 'Jesus, that's only thirty miles from New York City.'

'Worse,' Steven added, 'it's only ten miles from Kennedy Airport. Imagine if even one of those soldiers managed to get on an international flight. It would be easy with a pouch of ashes. We'd never know where they had gone. London, Moscow, Beijing, São Paulo – anywhere in the world, in just a few hours.'

'And the military would never bomb that area, no matter how many soldiers came ashore,' Hannah said. 'It's too densely populated.'

'And damned near impossible to evacuate,' Steven said. 'Jones Beach is perfect, and Mark knows it. Especially in winter, that stretch of land is about the only barren piece of real estate within a hundred miles of Manhattan or Kennedy Airport. It's like another planet out there, and just across the causeway, *ka-blam!* Civilisation, access, knowledge, souls, power, all of it a half-hour walk from the end of the Earth.'

Hoyt looked at Alen and whispered, 'What's a mile?'

'About fifteen hundred paces.'

'And an hour?'

'About half an aven.'

'Thanks. I'm caught up.' He tore another piece of bread from the loaf and tossed it to Garec.

The Ronan smiled despite his obvious terror and asked, 'So what do we do now? How do we kill him? Do we have to wait until the table is open, or can we get him from the other side?'

'Great question, Garec,' Steven said, turning to Captain Ford. 'We turn and run, as fast as we can, into the North Sea. Can we get through the blockade and into the Northeast Channel?'

Captain Ford nodded. 'It isn't difficult leaving, not nearly as tricky as coming in.'

'Then that's what you do,' Steven went on, 'all of you, you all sail for Orindale. Try to find Gita Kamrec; tell her that we've won. Help her establish a people's government in Falkan – it's got the strongest economy; it's the best place to start. We'll be back when we can to help you.'

'Tell her we've won?' Garec looked askance at him.

'If you're alive when you reach Orindale and the world hasn't folded up or gone to pieces, yes, you can assume that we've won.'

'But Garec comes with us,' Gilmour said simply. It wasn't a question and Steven decided not to argue with him about it – not yet.

Garec turned around to look his old mentor in the face, then smiled. He didn't look forward to telling Kellin, though.

'What are you all going to do?' Captain Ford asked.

'First, we bring this boat about and get the blazes out of here.'

Captain Ford looked to Gilmour, who nodded grimly. 'All right, then,' the captain said as he started towards the companionway. 'If you'll excuse me, we're coming about.' He disappeared into the corridor and they heard him shouting before he reached the main deck, 'Pel! Do you want a salary raise?'

'Aye, Captain!' came the distant reply.

'Then wear this motherwhoring tub about! Into the wind; let's go! Kellin!'

'Captain!' Her voice was even further away.

'Get down here and learn something! Bloody hurry!'

'Aye, aye, Captain!'

Garec laughed and shook his head. Steven motioned Gilmour to Captain Ford's empty chair and said, 'Hannah, where's your mother tonight?'

'Cape Cod.'

'Good.' Now he did stand up; he wanted to feel the magic rouse itself to help him. 'You go back at seven. Get the portal from her and drive like holy hell to Jones Beach, or someplace nearby. Alen, Gilmour and I have a bit of work to do with the spell book, but we'll come through ... when should we open it?'

'Cape Cod to Long Island? I don't know enough about the East Coast to even hazard a guess—'

'I think there's a ferry from Buzzard's Bay,' Steven broke in. 'Take that; it'll save time, but you'll need to open the portal by the following day, let's say five o'clock, regardless of where you are. That gives you twenty-two hours to get your mother, get the portal and get to Long Island.'

'It should be plenty of time.'

The *Morning Star* turned into the wind. To Steven it felt like the nautical equivalent of running into a wall. He sat back down, his knuckles white on the chair.

Hannah braced herself against the bulkhead. 'Even if it takes me all day to talk her into it, we can make the Island in a few hours.'

'I don't know. Your mother can be awfully persuasive,' Steven recalled getting the hell beaten out of him. She wasn't someone he would ever underestimate again. 'Either way, there or not, open the portal at five o'clock, twenty-two hours after you step through. We'll come through at five past five.'

'Steven, you haven't answered my question,' Garec said. 'How are we going to do this? How do we "take the head off the snake"? Can we attack Mark from the other side before he brings this army of killers through to wipe us all out or, worse, invites a wave of fury and death to mow us down where we stand?'

'I don't know,' Steven said, truthfully.

Alen sighed, clearly unconvinced.

Steven said, 'We've known since my return to South Carolina that Nerak could detect the far portals when they were opened. He followed me through to Charleston Harbour, despite the fact that he should have been tossed anywhere on Earth. Why is that?' Steven didn't wait for an answer. 'He chased me across the country, racing me to Lessek's key, and all the while Garec, Mark and Gilmour were opening their portal every twelve hours. Why didn't he come back, take their portal and simply wait around for me to return? I would have been a sitting duck.

'When I returned, I started paging through Lessek's spell book; Nerak could have used that to return to Eldarn. Eventually, he did. Why did he linger in Colorado? We know he pursued Jennifer Sorenson, Hannah's mother. Why? If he didn't need the portal, why did Nerak follow Jennifer into the mountains? Was it for fun? Did he want the portal, even though he could have returned without it? What was he doing hanging around over there?' Steven tried to answer his own questions. 'Nerak knew we had Lessek's key and that we were about to waste our time running for Sandcliff Palace. With us heading in the wrong direction, there was no need to rush back. We were no threat without the table and he assumed we had no idea where the table was; so he waited—'

'And he learned,' Gilmour interjected. 'He took souls, how many we can't begin to guess, but he probably took new souls every few avens: workers, teachers, doctors, anyone who might help him develop an accurate and comprehensive knowledge of Earth.' He looked at Alen. 'He was filling his own head with a thousand Twin-moons of missing information.'

'And deciding how and where to take your world,' Brexan finished Gilmour's thoughts.

'Taking Mark Jenkins clinches it,' Garec said. 'He's been going on and on about that rutting beach since he arrived. He claims it was Lessek showing him that he's some kind of heir: the prince of Eldarn.'

'The prince of all worlds,' Hoyt said to himself.

'So, Garec, to answer your question, finally,' Steven chuckled, 'I don't know if we can hit Mark before he opens the spell table. If we try, he'll know, because our only resources across the Fold are the far portals and he'll know when we've opened them. However, if we wait to strike until Mark has opened the table—'

'We run the risk of him first inviting this evil essence into Eldarn.'

'He won't,' Steven said. 'He'll be preoccupied with the Fold itself. Moving that many people is a big job, even for the world's most powerful magician. There are only so many ways to do it and if he wants to shift a sizeable force to Jones Beach, Mark will have to rend a significant window for them to cross.'

'They're not going in single file,' Hannah said.

'I'd have to pee about every half-aven,' Hoyt laughed at his own joke.

'While Mark's opening the door, or widening the door, I should say, that's when he'll be vulnerable . . . well, relatively. And, yes, that's when we'll hit him from the other side.'

'So he'll know we're there?' Garec asked. 'He'll know we crossed?'

'Maybe,' Gilmour said, 'if he detected Hannah's little field trip yesterday, he might think we're moving back and forth. If Hannah goes through at seven o'clock and opens the portal for us the following day, Mark may believe one of us is ferrying supplies or weapons.'

'It can't hurt to hope,' Brexan said.

'What time is it now?' Gilmour asked.

Garec checked Steven's old watch. 'Four and forty minutes.'

Hannah suddenly looked nervous. 'All right,' she said, 'I have two hours. I'm going to try and get some sleep.'

'We all should,' Alen said, moving towards the door. 'Tomorrow's going to be a busy day.'

'You're a master at understatement, my friend,' Hoyt said, passing what remained of his bread to Brexan.

'Thanks,' she said as she followed him into the companionway. 'Are you going back?' Brexan whispered.

'Back to Falkan? To Orindale?' Hoyt said.

'Yes.'

Alen slowed to listen; he didn't look back.

Hoyt pressed against the wall, allowing Steven and Hannah to pass. He watched them disappear together into Marrin Stonnel's old cabin. *Turn and look at me, Hannah. Just once. Look at me once, and I'll follow you wherever you're off to.* When the door closed, Hoyt sighed and said, 'Yes, I think I am. You?'

Alen's shoulders slumped and he made his way through the darkened companionway to the stairs in the main hold. *Good*, he thought to himself. *That's good.* Alen never heard Brexan's reply.

Garec waited for Gilmour on the main deck. The breeze was numbingly cold, but it was welcome after the closeness of the captain's cabin. The discussion hadn't taken long, but the Ronan archer was weary, and he could sense that the exhaustion in his bones was not about to let up. He waved to Kellin, gestured that he would be right there and then listened for Gilmour on the stairs.

When Gilmour arrived, he was smiling. 'I wondered where I would run into you.'

'You promised to tell me.' Garec kept his voice down. It was unnecessary on the brig-sloop's deck, but he felt the need to whisper, regardless. 'First, it was at Seer's Peak, when you said you were sure Lessek would want to communicate with me. Then it was in Wellham Ridge, when—'

'When I said that one day I would tell you the truth; yes, I remember.' He pulled a pipe from his tunic and as he put it to his mouth the tobacco apparently already packed tightly in the bowl started smouldering. 'I did promise, didn't I?'

'And since I've just agreed to follow you into another world, a world of *pizza* and *barefoot coffee* and *turkey* and *bullshit*, I think now might be a good time.'

'I want you there with us because I am worried that Mark's analysis of his lineage might be accurate.'

'Mark?' Garec hadn't expected this. 'You mean all that nonsense about being Rona's prince, Eldarn's king?'

'Exactly,' Gilmour said, 'and since so few things we've experienced or encountered in the past several Twinmoons appear to be co-incidental—'

'There haven't been many; I admit.'

'Then I think you may be the one who can save Mark ... or who *will* save Mark, I suppose, if Mark can be saved.'

'Me? How?'

'Again, this is only an old man's speculation, but I believe your great-great-grandfather would have wanted you there, to follow in his footsteps as the king's protector.'

'Hold just a moment, Gilmour.' Garec held up his hands. 'Are you saying that you knew my great-great-grandfather?'

'No,' Gilmour frowned. 'I knew your great-great-grandmother. Her name was Etrina Lippman, and she came from Capehill.'

'Right, right,' Garec yawned. 'My mother mentioned her; they used to call her Ettie or Etta or something.'

'Etrina Lippman of Capehill, Garec. Does that name sound at all familiar to you?'

'Only if you hearken all the way back to my childhood and those early days on the farm with—' he stopped himself. 'Wait . . . Etrina Lippman. I have heard that name. It was—'

'In Tenner Wynne's letter.' Gilmour pulled the faded parchment from his tunic. It had been wet so many times now that the ink was a blurry smear.

'Pissing demons.' Garec exhaled through pursed lips. 'Not me, too. I don't want that. I don't want anything to do with that. That's all—'

'Don't worry. You heard Steven: if he has anything to do with it, Eldarn's new government will be a *democracy*, probably a *republic*, once we get the schools organised and the printing presses up and working and the populace better informed and . . . oh, rutters, but there's lots to do, assuming, of course, that we're all still here in two days.' He turned to lean on the port rail. The river was a black highway in both directions. Barges, shallow drafting schooners, ketches and catboats plied the waters, their watchlights lit and flickering in the middlenight breeze.

Garec looked out over northern Malakasia. There was a tremor in his voice, in part from the cold, but more from the catastrophic news that he was next in line to rule Falkan. 'You use those words, *demo-thing* and *repub-whatever*. Gilmour, I don't even know what they mean.'

'Trust me, Garec, I am not interested in you as a potential monarch of Falkan. I think it would be a profound waste of an otherwise productive and compassionate person. However, I *am* interested in your great-great-grandfather's legacy. He was the king's protector and, like it or not, essentially nothing of what we have encountered, done, seen or accomplished in the past three Twinmoons seems to be by chance.'

'Some grand plan,' Garec muttered. 'It's a perfect tangle to me.

We've barely known if we were up or down, ahead or behind. How can you suggest that this is all part of some intricately woven tapestry?'

'We can't take the risk. We need you there.' Gilmour watched the waves lap and splash along the waterline. 'You've always thought of yourself as the *Bringer of Death*. It was wrong of Sallax and Versen to give you that nickname, because you have a real gift, Garec, you are a real virtuoso with a bow. Like it or not, I believe that's your grandfather's legacy.'

'And a great deal of practising,' Garec said. 'Give me *some* credit. I put in the avens at the yard.'

'True, but think of your dream, that vision from Lessek on Seer's Peak.'

'To be honest, I was hoping you wouldn't bring that up,' Garec admitted. 'It was Rona. I watched Prince Tenner's attempt to continue the Grayslip family line and then I watched as the Forbidden Forest, the hills around Riverend, dried to dust and died.'

'Rona's protector,' Gilmour whispered, 'not the *Bringer of Death*.'

'I won't rule,' Garec insisted. 'It isn't in me. I'm no leader; I'm a worker. I'll do anything, but I won't rule.'

'You think I see that as a character flaw?' Gilmour grinned. 'It may actually be a sign of great wisdom and self-knowledge that you wish to avoid your birthright. But, given our experiences along this merry trail thus far, I need you with us at Jones Beach. You know Steven; he'll be looking for any opportunity to save Mark. It will be his weakness and there's nothing we can do about it, except to convince him that you'll be watching for a chance too.'

'Very well, then.' Garec looked for Kellin; she was still in the bow, wrapped in a cloak and bouncing on her toes to keep warm. 'I'd better go and talk to her.'

'Good luck with that.'

'Thanks,' he said as he started forward, then paused. 'Wait, one other thing – Gilmour, how did you know Ettie?'

'Tenner Wynne never arrived in Capehill. We assume he died the night Riverend burned. That left your great-great-grandmother pregnant and alone, an embarrassing situation for her. She was the daughter of an important import–export merchant from Capehill and rumours about her condition, and how she came to be in that condition, were all over northern Falkan—'

'Where you happened to be wandering, lost and plenty dishevelled—'

'After failing to defeat Nerak at Sandcliff, yes.'

'How'd you meet her?'

'She was a rich woman with no husband and a burgeoning stomach.' Gilmour smirked at the memories. 'But she lost no social standing, suffered no humiliation and never went into hiding. I introduced myself to her and we became friends; I about pissed myself when I read her name in Prince Tenner's notes. But looking back on it now, it makes sense. She held her head high, knowing her child was special.'

'Well, that was certainly— how does it go? Naked pastry-chef luck?'

The old sorcerer laughed out loud and hugged Garec. 'Good night, my boy.'

'Good night, Gilmour.'

He watched Garec move beyond the foremast, then whispered, 'I'm proud of you, Garec. I truly am. If I'd ever had a son—' Gilmour wiped his eyes. 'Well, that's just silly, isn't it?'

EIGHT AVENS

Dawn found the *Morning Star* running north, with Captain Ford at the helm and clearly in his element. He was deeply relieved to be putting distance between his ship and the Welstar docks. Shouting orders to his weary crewman, he gazed downriver, plotting how to reach the Pellia headlands by the midday aven. The morning was cold and steely; the sun barely rose behind low clouds.

'Pel!' he ordered, 'haul those mains in tighter; I want to squeeze this crosswind while it lasts.'

'Aye aye, Captain!'

'Then you and Kellin get some rest. Send Garec and Brexan up to take your place, and Hoyt if he's feeling up to it.'

'Sir, don't you think—?'

'Pel! Tubbs, Kanthil, Marrin and Sera are on their way to the Northern Forest—' he smiled sadly as memories crowded his mind, '—are you honestly going to take over as the one dough-headed horsecock on this boat who insists on questioning my every order?'

'Captain?' Pel snapped to false attention, saluting smartly but comically. '*Everyone* questioned your orders, Captain.'

'Get out of my sight, Pel,' he laughed. 'You too, Kellin. Get some sleep.'

The Falkan woman, clearly not as amused by the sailor's antics, nodded as she disappeared below.

'Garec will have his hands full with that one,' the captain murmured to himself. 'She doesn't look happy, nope, not happy at all.' He hummed a jaunty shanty, at odds with the grey day, and basked in the moment, alone on the deck of his beloved old ship and heading for open water. The Welstar River was still crowded, but no one gave the little brig-sloop with her oversized colours a second glance.

When Pel's replacements appeared, he motioned Garec into the bow and gestured for Hoyt and Brexan to join him at the helm.

'Good morning, Captain,' Hoyt said. 'Did you sleep?'

'Not yet, son. I find it's easier to go with no sleep than to have just a bit.'

'I hear you on that,' Hoyt agreed. 'I feel like I've been run over by a laden wagon.'

'You may feel bad, but I'm pleased to see you actually look a bit better.'

'Those pill-things Hannah brought back for me are working wonders,' Hoyt said, 'especially since I don't have to taste them. My shoulder's dried up, the swelling's gone down and I even feel like eating again. I can walk around a bit too – it's astonishing medication.'

Brexan broke in with a small frown, saying, 'You should still be taking it easy. Why don't you go back and lie down for a while? I can handle this.'

'No, no, I'm fine,' he protested, 'and it feels good to be out here. It's a nice morning to be up and about.'

'That it is,' the captain agreed, then, changing the subject, said, 'I don't need much help up here this morning. We're all shipshape and running fine, and I know I won't be able to sleep until Pellia's no longer in sight. But I do want to talk with you about your plans. I need to get back to Southport before too long. We'll make for Orindale now and I'll take on cargo; it's a captain's market there in the wake of Mark's devastation last Twinmoon.' He paused to watch Garec, in the bow. He'd unslung one of his quivers and was methodically checking fletching and tips, running his fingers down the shafts to check they were all still straight and true. He turned back to Hoyt and Brexan. 'You both know I've lost most of my crew, and so I'm inviting you two to stay on with me, as long as you like. I'm going to be a busy man while Orindale's shipping companies are rebuilding. I'll try to confine my runs to Orindale and Southport – that shouldn't be too difficult to do – so you won't have to worry about going too far from home, either of you.'

Brexan put a hand on his arm to stop him. 'Captain – Doren – thank you. That's a wonderful offer, it really is ... but I've got to get back to Nedra and the Topgallant. She's not getting any younger, and I felt like what I was doing there was– well, something special.'

He looked puzzled. 'And this isn't? Brexan, you're out here saving Eldarn—'

'I suppose, in a way; I made a tiny contribution – but this is different; you can't be a hero every day. There has to be something else, something good, and steady ...'

'Something good and steady? That's why I'm here—' he gestured around the quarterdeck. 'You've just described the reason I sail this little boat back and forth across the Ravenian Sea.'

Brexan said, 'I can see that ... but I've got to find my own peace. It's been a long journey; I've come a long way ...' Her voice tailed off for a moment, then she went on, 'I managed – quite unexpectedly – to kill the man who started me on this road, but you know, when I finally watched him die, I realised I was missing Nedra and the comforting predictability of the boarding house – where, come to think of it, I've got a four-hundred Twinmoon party to reschedule.' She laughed. 'Gods, just think of all that food to cook!'

'That's a curious thing for a soldier-turned-partisan to say.' Hoyt pulled his cloak tight around him and turned away from the wind.

'Who knows?' Brexan said, 'maybe I'm getting old. But I thank you, Captain, for your offer.'

'So you won't go looking for this woman, Gita Kamrec?' Captain Ford asked, still hopeful that the lure of adventure would change Brexan's mind.

'Maybe, if she arrives in Orindale,' Brexan said, 'but to be honest, I spent a Twinmoon looking for Resistance forces in the Eastlands and I couldn't find anyone.' She chuckled. 'Some spy, huh?'

'How about you, Hoyt?' he asked.

'Me?' Hoyt sighed. 'I don't know. I think if they all come back from Jones Beach, or wherever it is they're going, I might accompany them to Sandcliff.'

'In Gorsk?' Brexan hadn't expected this.

'I have quite a collection of textbooks,' Hoyt said, 'medical treatises, most of them old, verging on ancient, but they're about all we have left in Eldarn – outside the library Alen discovered beneath Welstar Palace, of course.' He pulled the spent ampoule out of his tunic pocket. A few drops of anti-venom still clung to the glass. 'Look at it,' he said. 'Hannah was able to steal this from a village healer's shop, a village large enough to require only two guards. That's a small place – and yet look at the technology.'

'So you're going to teach? To conduct medical research?' Brexan asked.

'If Steven and the others succeed in closing the Fold, I'm hoping that perhaps they might find a way to preserve the integrity of the far portals. With those operating, who knows what a healer might bring back? If they'll have me, I'll do anything they want – sweep, dig latrines, whatever – if only we can get a medical university started there in Gorsk.'

'So you're heading for Southport,' Captain Ford said.

'First stop, yes; I have my things to pick up, and a cache of books stored outside the city.'

'And then?' Brexan asked.

'If I can, hitch a ride back to Orindale and wait for Alen and Gilmour to return.'

'I know just the place, good food and comfortable beds guaranteed,' Brexan said with a grin.

'That sounds just right,' Hoyt said. His face dropped as he thought of Churn and Branag, and all they had sacrificed.

Captain Ford cursed under his breath and grumbled, 'All right, I understand ... but I rutting hate signing on a new crew. You never know what you're going to get – drunks, root addicts, shiftless losers ...'

'Maybe you'll get lucky,' Hoyt said, 'after all, I guess there'll be no shortage of out-of-work seamen in Orindale these days.'

'They're probably all drunk and freezing to death out behind the southern warehouses,' he muttered.

'You'll find the right people, I'm sure of it,' Brexan said firmly, then turned to Hoyt, who was hunched over, his hood pulled over his head, looking like a man two hundred Twinmoons his senior. 'And *you* need to get back to bed,' she said, even more firmly.

'It is mercilessly cold out here,' he said defensively.

'Go on, back to bed with you, *Doctor* Navarro – but I do hope when you have your own medical practice or your own classroom you're not this lazy,' Captain Ford teased.

'Only when I can get away with it, Captain,' Hoyt said, smiling himself. 'And like Brexan, I thank you for your offer, but I—'

'Now, don't kill my hopes entirely.' He adjusted their course slightly. 'It's still a long way to Orindale; you might change your mind, so I'm leaving the offer open.'

'And now I think I'll take your suggestion and return to my berth.' Hoyt held the handrail and shakily negotiated the quarterdeck ladder to get below.

Brexan looked out across the grey sea. 'How far to Pellia?'

'About an aven. It's another half-aven into deep water and then half an aven after that to see us through the blockade.'

'What will you tell them? Why are you running empty?'

'I heard about the destruction of the merchant fleet in Orindale; it's worth the journey to secure long-term shipping contracts. Any Malakasian captain with a shallow-running ship would be insane *not* to go. Whether they search us or not will depend on the seas. If it's blowing, they might wave us through. We're obviously not hauling anything big, like refugees or troops, or heavy crates of weapons. Fennaroot is well out of season, and I don't know if they'll board in heavy seas just to track down an illegal shipment of tobacco or wine. Who cares? It isn't a very big boat; so how much could we really be running? As it is, we're practically skipping over the surface, so I'm hoping they'll wave us right through.'

'And if they don't?' Brexan's face showed her anxiety. 'We're a large crew for such a small ship, aren't we? And Hannah and Alen said the Home Guard are looking for Milla. If the wrong officer gets a look at her, we could be in—'

'Then our friends will just have to disappear through their tapestry portal a few avens early, won't they.'

'But that could leave them anywhere in their world, many days' travel from this Jones Beach.' She sounded increasingly worried.

Captain Ford frowned. 'Short of reefing sail and waiting – which is even more dangerous, because then we'd be practically begging them to board us – we have to keep going. We have to look like we're keeping to a normal routine.'

Brexan stared aimlessly into the steel-grey clouds, saying nothing.

After a while, Captain Ford threw up his hands. 'All right, all right. Were you just going to stand there all morning?'

Brexan laughed. 'I just wanted you to see things my way. Sometimes keeping my mouth shut is the best strategy.'

He reached for her and she backed away a step, then blushed when all he did was turn her wrist to stare at Mark's watch. 'How do you read this thing?'

'I don't know.'

'Give it to me.' He stepped back from the helm. 'Keep us on this course. Don't make eye contact with any of the schooner crew, but you can wave or smile at the bargemen. We don't want to look like we're up to no good, but then again, we are up to no good, so we don't want— Oh, rutters, you know what I mean.' He jumped to the main deck and disappeared below.

Captain Ford knocked, then opened Marrin's cabin door to find Steven, Gilmour and Alen huddled over a thick leatherbound book. *There's another item that will have us all hanged*, he thought. *I'm glad I didn't see that before*. Milla was sleeping in Steven's berth and Hannah was gone.

'—like an infection,' Alen said, finishing a thought.

'For lack of a better term, yes,' Gilmour said. 'It was a way to teach the novices, but you're right too: in its most basic form, it's like an infection.'

Steven waved Ford inside and asked, 'What news, Captain?'

He held out Mark's watch. 'I need to know how to read this.'

Steven chuckled. 'We can't be more than an aven from Pellia, we've got a full fleet of Malakasian navy ships and a regiment of Home Guard searching for our little friend here, and there are a myriad other ways for us to die in the next day, and you'd like a lesson in telling time? And pointless time at that, I might add; you know that thing is essentially worthless here in Eldarn?'

'We have a problem.' He held out the watch.

'Shit,' Steven said, his smile melting away, 'I was joking . . .'

'We'll make Pellia in an aven,' he began as Alen closed the ancient book. 'It's another half-aven, maybe more if we lose this wind, to the blockade, and once there, we might wait in line for half an aven, and take another half-aven before they wave us through to the Northeast Channel.'

'But . . .' Gilmour said.

'But we may get boarded, especially if the wind dies down.'

'Shit and shit and shit,' Steven said. 'You're right: this is a problem. I didn't think of this last night, Captain. I'm sorry.'

'If they see Milla, we're sunk – perhaps literally,' the captain said, 'and if they get even a whiff of that thing—' he pointed at the book, 'then we're as good as hanged.'

'And we can't go through the portal early,' Alen said, 'because with my bloody luck, we'd step out onto an Irish potato farm.'

'Exactly – whatever an eyerish potato farm is. So I need to know how to read this, and how much time we have to wait until you all can get off my boat.' He held out the watch.

'What time is it?' Steven checked his own wrist. 'Ten fifty-five. Hannah's been gone four hours; that's almost two avens.' He mumbled to himself for a few moments, then said, 'Eighteen divided by two point five is seven point two – so, to be safe, figure about eight avens.'

'Good rutting lords,' Captain Ford cried, inadvertently waking Milla, 'that's a long time!'

'How can we help?' Gilmour asked.

'You can stay out of sight,' he said. 'We'll moor in the harbour, not the marina where we were; that's too dangerous.'

'Right,' Alen said, 'you're right: we left too quickly on the heels of that mess along the waterfront. They'll be watching for us.'

'I can get a two-aven mooring to resupply. The harbourmaster won't give us a second glance. But if we wait around too long, or we sail back and forth across the inlet too many times—'

'They'll alert the navy,' Gilmour finished for him. 'Very well, Captain. We'll remain below.'

'Three avens from now will be just past low tide,' Captain Ford thought aloud, 'and we can break off the mooring and pretend we're making repairs. The incoming tide will haul us back upriver and at the right moment, we'll put on sail and run for the blockade. You can disappear before we get there.'

'An excellent plan,' Alen said.

'Until it all falls apart,' Captain Ford said glumly.

Steven showed him how to read Mark's watch. 'It will have to reach five o'clock – that rune there – *twice* before we leave. Understand?'

'Got it, I think,' he said after a few more moments studying the round face. 'Right now you're welcome to come up on deck, for about another aven or so, then I'll need you below.' He turned to Milla and managed a smile. 'Especially you, my darling.'

She rubbed her eyes and yawned.

'Thank you, Captain,' Gilmour said again as the tired seaman slipped back into the corridor, already shouting for Pel.

'I'll need it for about two avens,' Captain Ford told the Pellia harbourmaster. 'We're heading in for supplies; we'll be back before the tide changes. I'm leaving two crewmen on board to mind her.' Brexan sat in the brig-sloop's miniature launch, gripping the oars hard to keep her hands from shaking.

'It's fifteen Mareks for two avens,' said the harbourmaster, a thin, reedy man with pale, pockmarked skin and a receding hairline. He stood in the bow of a single-masted ketch while his assistant, a boy of perhaps a hundred and twenty Twinmoons, minded the tiller. Both were wrapped in heavy cloaks which had the Whitward family crest embroidered in gold across the back.

'Let's make it twenty-five Mareks,' he handed the harbourmaster a fistful of coins, 'and you keep an eye on her for me, huh?' He winked. 'We've a long journey ahead of us and I don't want to see anything scraping her.'

'It *is* rather busy today, isn't it?' The scrawny official sniffed noisily. 'All on the heels of that disturbance yesterday morning – Lords, but that was trouble.'

'Those frigates involved?' He nodded towards the bulky Falkan vessels moored side-by-side in the deeper water.

'That's none of your concern, Captain . . .' He fished for the name, but Captain Ford shook his head gently.

'That's none of *your* concern, my friend,' he murmured.

Unperturbed, the harbourmaster pocketed Captain Ford's gratuity. 'We'll see you off in two avens, Captain.'

'Thank you,' he said, winked again and took his seat beside Brexan, who started rowing towards one of the public piers. 'That wasn't so bad,' he whispered. He checked to make sure the harbourmaster was no longer watching them, then asked, 'What time is it?'

Brexan glanced at her watch. 'It's just before the second rune. So fifteen more revolutions—'

'*Hours*,' he said, 'I think they're called *hours*.'

'So fifteen more *hours*,' she repeated obediently.

'So, what's on our shopping list?'

Brexan took a folded piece of parchment from her tunic and he took over the oars while she read aloud, 'Pel wants a woman—'

'A likely story,' the captain snorted. 'Pel wouldn't know what to do with one if she fell from the sky.' He realised what he was saying and blushed.

Unfazed, Brexan went on, 'Hoyt wants ten boxes of tecan, fifteen roast gansels, two hundred crates of Falkan wine, a block of mild cheese, a new set of silk leggings and a log large enough to carve a full-sized woman. A naked, full-sized woman, obviously.'

'Oh. So is that all?'

'Oh no,' Brexan laughed. 'Kellin would like you to kill the man who invented women's underclothes. She also requests a side of beef, twelve barrels of Pragan beer, a more comfortable place to sleep, peace in our time, a slightly smaller backside and a way to keep her berth as warm as summer in Estrad Village.'

'All sounds simple enough. And you?'

'Oh, I'm fine,' Brexan said. 'Maybe a couple of flagons of decent wine, but otherwise, I'll be all right.'

'Good. That's a lot to track down in two avens, so we'd better cut all this pointless chatter and get rowing.' With that he redoubled his efforts and they made speedily for the wharf.

Steven, Alen and Gilmour watched from inside Captain Ford's cabin. Lessek's spell book lay closed on the table. Milla, squatting on a small rug, played a game with a bundle of sticks she'd found. One – she had turned it a lustrous shade of pink – scurried here and there around the floor while the others pursued it, their twig arms grasping blindly for the oddly coloured fugitive. Milla squealed with delight every time her bright pink heroine escaped almost certain death at the hands of the woodland posse.

'Mooring here buys us five hours,' Steven said. 'It's almost two o'clock now, so we can sit tight until seven o'clock.'

'And then we need to find some way to linger inconspicuously on the river for another ten hours,' Alen said. They had been awake for most of the night, an uncommon feat for Alen Jasper, who was looking longingly at the captain's comfortable berth.

'Where does that put Hannah?' Gilmour asked, watching the twigs chasing one of their own around the cabin.

'Assuming her mother didn't offer too much resistance, Hannah should be well on her way to Long Island by now. She has plenty of spare time, in case she runs into anything unforeseen: a flat tyre, a car accident—'

'A tan-bak,' Alen added.

'I hope not,' Steven said. 'I hope that by now Mark is so focused on getting the table ashore, sorting out his officers and getting that army ready to move that he won't be paying any attention to us opening the portals.'

'Or reading Lessek's spell book all night,' Gilmour said.

'But we had to do that,' Steven said nervously.

'Do you think he's there yet?' Gilmour asked.

Alen shrugged. 'Even if he is, Steven's right, he has at least a few avens' preparation before he opens the table. That place is a terrific mess and no matter how brutal he is, it will still take some time before they're ready to move.'

'Do you think he can do it?' Steven asked.

'The ash dream spell?' Gilmour said. 'I'm sure he can, else why would Nerak have been putting all these wheels into motion?'

'Because he believed Lessek's key had come back to Eldarn,' Alen said. He crossed to the captain's berth and sat on the down-filled mattress.

'True,' Gilmour conceded the point, 'but coming to Falkan himself, in that great horrible ship of his, to retrieve the spell table on his own—'

'You're right,' Steven said, 'he was ready; the key was just the final variable in the equation. He had the portal; he could have gone and retrieved the key any time. He either waited for someone to bring it to him – complete with a brain-sized filing cabinet filled with knowledge of Earth – or he would have gone to get it himself, probably right after excavating the table from the river.'

'Prince Nerak could go inside the dreams,' Milla interrupted them as she watched her twigs race about. 'He's the one who showed me how to do it. He said it was a hard spell, but I didn't have to try too hard. There were other things that were a lot harder. Making ice, that was really hard for me.'

'Ice?' Alen gave up the fight and lay down on the bed. 'Ice was one of the first spells we learned as kids. You should have been able to do that one easily, Pepperweed.'

'I don't know why,' Milla said, 'but every time I tried to make ice, the water just bubbled and turned funny colours.' She turned away from her sticks and they all fell dead in mid-stride.

Gilmour said, 'So you know that Nerak was able to go inside the dreams, Pepperweed, because he showed you how to do it with Branag's dog?'

'I could have gone in other ways,' the little girl explained carefully, 'but I liked that puppy and he was so nice when I asked him to follow Hannah.' She waved at the pile of sticks and cried, 'Get up! Let's go again!' The sticks complied, leaping up straight and dashing wildly about again.

Steven watched out of the window as Captain Ford and Brexan tied up at one of the piers. He asked, 'Milla, when I was dreaming, it wasn't the ash dream. I was sick because the tan-bak's bug had bitten me, but you still managed to get inside my nightmares. How did you do that?'

'Oh, I can get inside lots of dreams,' Milla said. 'Once you can do it, the dreams are all about the same. The ash dream is a little easier, because no one can make you leave.'

The three men shared a worried look. 'What do you mean, Pepperweed?' Steven pressed.

'In the ash dream, the person is living the dream, instead of just watching it happen.'

'But I was living those dreams too,' Steven asked, 'wasn't I?'

'It's not the same,' Milla explained. 'If you wanted to, you could have made me leave, or changed the puppy into something else, something that you picked from your own mind, but in the ash dream, you can't do that.'

'Jesus,' Steven whispered, then asked, 'Could you hear me when we were running? I remember talking to you – well, to the puppy –

while I was running that race with all those people.'

Milla giggled. 'Of course I could hear you, silly. I was there with you.'

'But if I wanted to, I could have made you into something else? An iced doughnut, or a flying pig?'

Milla burst out laughing; her animated sticks did a collective leap and some of the driest ones shattered when they crashed down. 'A flying pig?' she giggled. 'That's funny. I've never seen one of them.'

'But I could have, right? And that would have pushed you out of my dream?'

'Yes,' she said, bored with her stick races now. She looked at Steven. 'How did you find me, Milla?' he asked.

'What do you mean?' She stood up and walked across to the little desk they were grouped around.

'I wasn't in the ash dream,' Steven said. 'I was sick and dreaming, but it wasn't the ash dream. What made you come looking for me?'

'I found you by mistake,' Milla said, then asked, 'is there anything to drink? I'm thirsty.'

'Just a moment, Pepperweed,' Alen said, 'and we'll get you a drink. But tell us how you found Steven when he was sick.'

She pouted endearingly and said impatiently, 'I was looking for Gilmour. Hannah and Hoyt and you wanted to know when he was going to get to the inn, so I was searching for him. I talked to him that time and I knew what he felt like, even from pretty far away. I'm good at that—'

'Not like the ice,' Steven teased.

'No,' Milla smiled back, her momentary irritation forgotten, 'I can't do ice. But I was looking for Gilmour that day but I found the other magic.'

'My magic?' Steven said.

'No, I can't find you, ever,' Milla said. 'It was the magic from those bugs. I hadn't felt them before, but that morning, they were really loud.'

'Loud?'

'Easy to hear,' Milla tried to explain. 'There were two of them, right?'

'Right,' Gilmour said.

'And one that had died,' Milla went on. 'They were looking for that one right before they bit Steven and hurt that other man ...'

'Marrin,' Gilmour added, then asked the question all three of them were thinking. 'Pepperweed, could you get inside Mark Jenkins' dreams? Or maybe show one of us how to do it?'

'Yup,' she said, 'but only if he goes to sleep.'

'Shit,' Steven said. 'I hadn't thought of that.'

'That's a bad word!' Milla was indignant. 'Hannah told me that even though she's not at home, she shouldn't say that word.'

Steven raised his hands in surrender. 'She's right. Sorry.'

'Could you show us? Me?' Alen asked.

'You want to learn how?' Milla asked.

'I read that book last night,' Alen said, 'and I think I know how to do it, but Mark would be one of the hardest people to follow. So I want to learn how to do it like you do, as a puppy, or maybe a kitten or even a little mouse on the floor.'

'A mouse!' Milla shrieked excitedly, 'yes, let's be a mouse if you want to!'

'I do, Pepperweed.' Alen clapped his hands. 'Now, how do I know if Mark is sleeping?'

'I'll show you,' Milla said, 'but can we get a drink first?'

'Of course, a drink.' He took her hand and led her from the cabin, saying, 'We'll see if Hoyt or Kellin have something nice to drink.'

When they were gone, Steven asked, 'Have you ever heard of any of this?'

'It wasn't my bailiwick,' Gilmour said. 'I'm sure Nerak and Pikan would have been involved in this sort of work, but my department was more concerned with education than magic. I had access to Lessek's scroll library, as did Kantu, but last night was the first time either of us had ever read through these writings.' He flipped absently through the spell book. 'There's so much more here than just the ash dream, but there must be a reason why Lessek organised this book around this particular spell.'

'I can't make most of it out,' Steven admitted, 'but if you think about how textbooks are organised, there's generally a key theme around which the rest of the chapter is written and every time you learn something new, a bit of extra information is added, like building a wall.'

'And they all relate to the main topic, the cornerstone idea.'

'So do you think the ash dream was the key concept around which Lessek organised his work? Did his research spring from this one place, from the ability to see inside the minds of others as they slept?' Steven was disappointed. He had developed a feeling about the Larion founder, and this theory didn't live up to his idea of Lessek as a powerful yet compassionate magician and teacher.

'I don't know,' Gilmour said, 'but from what I know of Lessek and his work, if he did see the ash dream as a cornerstone construct of Larion magic, we have only seen it from the most narrow of perspectives.'

'This dirty, wrong-feeling perspective that an otherwise intrusive and voyeuristic spell could be so important?'

'Unless it was used for teaching, like you suggested last night,' Gilmour said.

'Unless that, I guess.' Steven wasn't convinced. They hadn't delved deeply enough; something was missing; it was seventeen minutes past two in New York and he prayed they would decipher it all in time.

THE RUN SOUTH

'Cast off that mooring line,' shouted Captain Ford. It was ten past eight by Mark's old watch and the *Morning Star* was still lashed to the two-aven buoy in Pellia Harbour. They had overstayed their welcome by an hour – he credited his generous bribe for that – but now time was running out. 'Pel!' he cried again, 'don't you see him coming? Cast it off now! I don't want to be answering any more questions.'

In the fading twilight they could see the harbourmaster's ketch approaching, slowly but inexorably making its way through the maze of boats moored off the wharf.

'Aye aye, Captain,' Pel shouted as he hurried to untie the brig-sloop. He waved a cheery thanks to the harbourmaster and called, 'See you next time through!'

The Malakasian official gave a half-hearted salute and watched as the incoming tide carried the *Morning Star* upriver a ways. He considered something, then dug in his tunic for a tempine. 'Come about, Jon,' he finally ordered, peeling the fruit. 'One more time around and then it's home for both of us.'

'Yes, sir,' the boy replied, still looking at the brig-sloop. 'Funny the way they're just drifting, isn't it?'

The harbourmaster chewed contentedly; another day was over. 'They saw us coming, Jon, that's all; he didn't want to pay extra for going overtime. They're drifting because they probably weren't ready to get under way just yet.'

'Yes, sir. Strange that he's already setting topsails, though.'

'What's that?' The harbourmaster turned to watch the brig-sloop set her tops and topmains. The ship was running upriver, showing no sign of tacking beyond the headlands. 'But he said he had a long journey ahead of him.'

'I heard him, too,' the boy said, 'but I don't know how long a journey a boat that big can make along this river, maybe just up beyond the palace and back, and what's that? A couple of days for them? Rutters! Look at them go! That's a fast ship!'

The harbourmaster wasn't listening. The captain, if he even *was* their captain, had been lying. 'Jon, run us in to the wharf, now – hurry on with you!'

By one twenty-five the navy ship had tacked east and was running up on the *Morning Star*. She was visible only by her watchlights; probably a schooner with enough sheets on her to overtake a typhoon. The tide had run in, carrying the brig-sloop upriver for the past two avens, but as slack water approached, the winds slowed and the current pushed back against Captain Ford's best efforts to run a beeline south from Pellia.

'What time is it?' he called from the quarterdeck.

'It's about one-thirty,' Steven shouted back, 'less than two avens before we can disappear.'

'That's too much time,' he replied, checking their stern. The schooner was bearing down on them and within an aven, it would be within hailing distance, and at that point, there would be nothing he could do. For now, he could play dumb, claim that he had no idea the navy was after him – why would they be? He paged through viable excuses in his head: just running with the tide while he made repairs, testing a new rudder, breaking in a new crew; just about any excuse would free them, because they were doing nothing wrong, nor hauling anything illegal – apart from partisan sorcerers, a Welstar Palace fugitive and an outlaw text from Prince Malagon's personal library, of course. With Steven and the others gone, however, it would be a different story: they could board him, search his ship, interrogate the crew and all he need to do was tell them, *come on, make yourselves at home; we're just testing this new rudder before we head for Orindale.*

'Two avens,' he muttered to himself. 'How, by all the gods of the Northern Forest, do we avoid being boarded for two avens?'

Pel climbed to the quarterdeck and reported, 'That's all the sheet we can get on her, Captain.'

'Nice job, Pel,' he said generously. 'How long until slack tide?'

'Half an aven, maybe less,' the young sailor said, looking cold and weak with exhaustion. None of them had slept much over the past two days, but while the others were huddled together below, devising a plan to seal the Fold for ever, Pel had been up on deck, out in the wind and weather, keeping the *Morning Star* on course.

'Half an aven,' Captain Ford echoed, 'good. That's what I was thinking.'

'We're going to lose this tailwind, though,' he added. 'When the tide turns, the wind'll change. This is no front blowing us south.'

'I know, I know, but he'll lose the wind, too.'

Less than half an aven later, the southern tidal flow slowed to a trickle, and with it went the *Morning Star*'s tailwind. Slack tide: on the coast it would have meant half an aven of dead water, but here, the Welstar River took over. Captain Ford was talking to himself as he considered the limp sheets and the following naval patrol. 'One chance. That's it. We have to turn east and run back north beyond the city, but we can't look like we're running, son of a raving whore!'

Still at the helm, he was glad to see Steven appear on deck. 'Our list of excuses remains good,' Captain Ford said. 'We're putting her through her paces before heading for the Northeast Channel. Why'd we turn and run downriver? Why not? We needed a bit of time and the tide was coming in, right? When we hit slack water, we turned and headed for the open sea. Simple, believable . . . and yet still likely to have me hanged and my boat pressed into the Malakasian navy.'

Now that it was the middle of the night, Steven could safely be on deck. 'You're fine,' he said. 'With us gone, you've got nothing to hide; just don't do anything that looks suspicious.'

'Easier said than done, my friend,' Captain Ford replied. He felt the brig-sloop turning slowly beneath his boots. He checked the schooner, cursed the river and shouted, 'Pel! Kellin! Garec! We're coming about, let's go! Let's go! I want to make a hard left.'

'Sir, the barges!' Pel's voice rang out.

'You think I don't see them?' The captain wiped his face on his cloak. 'Come about, on my order!' He left the helm to Steven and crossed to the port rail, listening through the darkness for the armada of massive barges plying the river. The broad, flat-bottomed vessels were loaded with crates, lumber, even quarried stone. Passing between them at night was just about the most insane decision he could make. But given the circumstances, it might give them time to escape. The sailors tailing might be interested in the brig-sloop, perhaps even angry with her apparently oblivious captain, but he doubted they would risk death to investigate a boat that had, thus far, done essentially nothing wrong. His mood was turning sour; he retook the helm.

'Captain, this is what I meant by doing something suspicious,' Steven pointed out. 'I'm just wondering what happens if one of those barges runs into us by accident while we're cutting across traffic like a drunken teenager. I've been hoping for a chance to use a bit of magic before I get to Jones Beach, but turning away a five-hundred-ton barge loaded with masonry is more test than I need.'

'If you don't mind, I need to concentrate.' Captain Ford watched upriver, timing the barge traffic, counting the watchlights and estimating the distances between them.

Alen and Gilmour emerged and Steven jumped down to join them, leaving the quarterdeck to the captain.

'What's happening?' Gilmour asked. 'We can see the navy boat's still following.'

'We're taking steps to avoid them now,' Steven said and gestured towards the centre of the river. 'I think the idea is that if we can reach the east bank, we can run north through the city, with the river and the tide at our backs—'

'And the schooner won't follow us—' Gilmour said.

'Because he'd have to be out of his mind,' Alen finished.

'That about sums it up.' Steven watched Pel and Kellin hurry amidships. Garec, who had picked up some rudimentary sailing skills, thanks largely to Kellin, helped where he could. Hoyt and Milla were asleep in the forward cabin, quite unaware that they might soon be swimming to shore.

Brexan, looking bleary-eyed, clomped up to them and asked, 'What's all the rutting shouting?'

'Oh, nothing much,' Garec said cheerfully, 'but since you're up, would you mind giving a hand over here?' He was wrestling with a line affixed, through a system of pulleys, to the main spar.

Brexan traced the line to its terminus, high in the rigging. 'What by all the gods in the Northern Forest are you doing?' she cried, suddenly wide awake.

'Crossing the road,' Garec said, chuckling nervously.

Alen moved to the gunwale, watching as a veritable fleet of big-boned vessels cruised north. To Steven, he said diffidently, 'Do you think you could . . .'

'I have no idea,' Steven read his mind. 'It would be like moving a mountain.'

'A moving mountain,' Gilmour added.

'What time is it, anyway?' Alen squinted at Steven's wrist in the torchlight.

'About twenty to three. We need another hour and a half.'

'If we live through the next five minutes.'

*

Captain Ford waited, feeling the *Morning Star* drift lazily towards the centre of the river. He watched, holding his breath, as a barge passed by like a floating island. From this distance he could see the crew, lined up on the port rail, staring at the madmen on the tiny sloop. Some were shouting, waving him off, or gesturing wildly with storm lanterns. Others stood in mute amazement as the *Morning Star* bobbed in the barge's wake like a child's toy. As the great vessel slipped past, averting catastrophe by just a few paces, the silence was broken as her captain, in a towering rage, shrieked insults across the bow. 'Rutting demonpissing horsecock! Are you mad? Trying to get yourself killed, you whoring motherhumper? If I see you in Pellia, I'll rip your miserable head from your shoulders, I swear I will!'

Captain Ford ignored him, pulling the brig-sloop around and shouting himself, 'Now, Pel, Kellin, Garec, come about! Haul, gods rut you raw, haul away!'

With Kellin and Pel on the foremast, Garec and Brexan on the main, the partisan crew bent low with the effort of turning the brig-sloop in a hard tack straight across the river. Steven, Gilmour and Alen leaped to join them, glad to have something to do, to distract themselves from the next barge in line, another flat-bottomed monster loaded to the gunwales. Already they could hear their crew shouting and cursing, trying to turn their own ship to avoid the maniac in the way.

'We're not going to make it,' Garec grunted, heaving at the main yard. 'Even if we get her turned, there's no wind. We're already drifting downriver.'

Steven let go the line and Garec stumbled, almost falling. He grappled with the rope as it slid across the planks. 'A bit of warning next time!' he shouted as Steven ran for the quarterdeck, mouthing apologies as he went.

'What? You have other plans?' The bowman tried digging his toes into the deck, clawing for any purchase on the icy wood.

'We need wind!' Steven cried.

'Steven, no!' Captain Ford shouted, suddenly realising what he meant to do, 'wait! You'll rip their arms off!'

'What?' Steven shouted, 'why?'

'Garec, Pel!' Captain Ford cried, 'belay those lines – *now*!'

'But we're not all the way over!' Pel shouted.

'Do it now! Both of you!'

Garec scrambled to obey and the main yard spun until the line went taut. He glanced up, saw the barge bearing down on them, her watchlights glowing like the eyes of a river demon, and screamed, 'Now, Steven, now!'

Captain Ford had stood at the helm when Gilmour had filled the brig-sloop's sails with hurricane-force wind and together, they had saved the ship, bouncing her off the mud reef. It had astounded him that anyone could be so powerful as to harness the very wind to his bidding.

But when Steven Taylor raised his hands to the main sheet, Captain Ford felt as though the *Morning Star* was about to spring from the water and take flight.

The wind was deafening, the howling roar of a winter gale. The sails filled, and all but the topmain – which ripped down the middle – held fast. The rigging was pulled so taut that the lines looked to be frozen solid. Captain Ford felt his ship heave forward, as if she had been thrown across the river. The force of the blast was overwhelming and he shouted as he nearly fell backwards from the helm. He held on, pulling hard to keep the rudder to port. Garec, Brexan, Kellin and Pel all tumbled to the deck; Brexan slid across and fell down the forward hatch, cursing Steven's mother all the way.

Alen gripped as many lines as he could while Gilmour braced himself against the mainmast. He was shouting something, but Captain Ford couldn't make it out over the wind; he was too busy trying to keep on course.

Finally, he turned and watched as the barge passed within a hair's breadth of them.

Then it was over. The little brig-sloop had passed through the shipping lanes and was turning north for Pellia with the river current. The naval schooner, her sails hanging limp in the light of her watchlights, drifted lazily backwards along the west bank. For the moment, the *Morning Star* and her crew were safe.

As the raised poop deck of the second barge passed, Captain Ford heard her captain shouting for his head.

'Sorry,' he called back, raising a deferential hand. 'Sorry about that!'

The hoots, hollers and insults continued as the hulking vessel passed out of sight. Captain Ford corrected their course, feeling the seaward current beneath his feet. 'We did it,' he whispered, exhaling a long, cathartic sigh.

Steven bounded up to him. 'You all right, Captain?'

Captain Ford laughed hoarsely. 'Remind me never to do that again.'

'Me either.' Steven clapped him on the shoulder. 'That was some fine sailing.'

'Nonsense.' The captain was sweating in the cold night air, 'all I did was to crank her over and hold on for dear life.'

'History will one day recall your greatness and poise under pressure,' Steven teased.

'I think I pissed myself,' he said.

'Don't feel bad about that; Garec did too.'

Still lying where he had fallen, Garec cried, 'And I'm not ashamed to admit it, either!'

Gilmour laughed and helped him up.

'Captain,' Garec said, 'permission to help myself to your personal store of beer?'

'Permission granted,' Captain Ford said, 'but save eleven or twelve for me, if you please.'

'Done – rutting whores—' he stopped. 'What time is it, anyway?' He peered at his wrist in the firelight. 'Three and ten minutes. Is that enough time for a beer?'

'Enough for one,' Steven said, 'a quick one.'

'I'll join you,' Alen said. 'I could use a bracer as well.'

The naval schooner, having tacked arduously along the west bank, didn't catch up with the *Morning Star* until well after dawn. As he passed the Pellia headlands, Doren Ford was exhausted, but he was also excited at the prospect of sailing safely through the blockade and running northeast along the west edge of the archipelago. Another morning of rare winter sunshine lit the North Sea like an undulating carpet of precious gemstones.

When the schooner captain gave the order to heave to, Captain Ford complied without hesitation. He ordered the brig-sloop's sails reefed and even had Pel toss lines to Prince Malagon's marines as their launch came alongside.

After explaining to the officer leading the boarding party that he had no idea the brig-sloop had been shadowed upriver, Captain Ford encouraged the Malakasians to search his vessel, jib to bilge.

They found nothing illegal: no contraband, no political insurgents or partisans, no outlaw books, not even a sliver of fennaroot.

When asked where he was bound, Captain Ford explained that he had heard of some great storm that had apparently crippled the shipping industry in Falkan, and he was heading south along the Ravenian Sea, running empty in hopes of securing long-term shipping contracts from Orindale to Landry, or even Pellia, if the wind and tides were right.

The lieutenant nodded and started over the rail, then paused and asked, 'Why'd you make that tack last night?'

'Which tack?' Captain Ford played dumb. He was so tired; he hoped the muscles in his face were sagging enough to make him look like the dough-head he'd been called.

'Which tack? That suicidal tack across the river,' the lieutenant said. 'Why try that tack with almost no wind and at slack tide?'

Captain Ford gestured towards his crew: Hoyt (who had slept through it all), Pel, Kellin and Brexan stood sipping tecan and nibbling at breakfast. 'Signed on a couple of new hands last Moon,' he said. 'They've been struggling a bit with the chain of command, so I thought I'd put the fear of the Northern Forest in them before we set out into deep water.'

The lieutenant, clearly amused, asked, 'Did it work?'

'We'll see, my young friend. We will certainly see.'

'Good voyage to you, Captain.'

'Thank you, sir, and the same to you.' He untied the launch and watched as the boarding party heaved away at their oars. Less than half-way back to the schooner, the lieutenant raised a blue pennant and his captain, watching from the quarterdeck, ordered the same pennant run up the schooner's halyard. The *Morning Star* was free to go.

'Set sail for Orindale, Captain?' Hoyt asked, handing Captain Ford a mug of something that smelled suspiciously like beer.

'To Orindale.' Captain Ford took a big mouthful and swallowed, then shouted for his first mate.

JONES BEACH STATE PARK

Steven and Gilmour walked south along the Meadowbrook Parkway, a ten-mile stretch of highway connecting Jones Beach and civilisation. With their backs to Long Island, they could have been on any desolate road in South Dakota or eastern Montana, not twenty minutes from the most densely populated region of the country. Jones Beach in winter was windswept, barren and cold. Only the heartiest of joggers, cyclists and fishermen, and the occasional bundled-up nature photographer, ventured into the park before spring officially arrived in April.

Thinking ahead, Hannah and Jennifer Sorenson had provided hats, gloves and scarves, and a tiny pink snowsuit for Milla, complete with a matching bobble-hat and a pair of pink mittens. The trunk was packed with blankets and a small kerosene heater. They all believed Mark would send a force across the Fold – even if it turned out to be just a small exploratory group first of all – but though they were sure about the location, no one had any idea when it would happen.

The others were crammed inside Jennifer's car, trying to keep warm. Garec insisted on sitting in the front; he was like a child, wanting to press all the buttons, twist the knobs and play with the electric door locks. He marvelled at the automobile, insisting that Jennifer drive back and forth along Ocean Parkway until he understood the basics of steering and shifting gears. He had shouted for her to stop when the car reached fifty miles an hour, and was a little embarrassed when Hannah told him fifty was comparatively slow. Now, with Milla in his lap, the two fiddled with the vents and listened to music, wondering where the smokeless fires were burning and how the car managed to generate such heat on such a frigid day.

When the first jet took off from Kennedy, banked over Jamaica Bay and whined noisily towards Boston, Garec burst from the car, bow at the ready. 'Get down, you two! Get down!' he shouted.

'What is it?' Steven turned on his heel, anxiously searching the dunes.

'I don't know what it is!' He aimed at the jet, a mile up now and climbing.

'Whoa, whoa, Garec.' Steven took him by the wrist. 'Don't waste your arrows, my friend. It's perfectly safe. We travel long distances in those.'

'Up there?'

'Up there.'

Garec said, 'I want to go home. I've seen enough.'

Gilmour smiled. 'You haven't seen anything yet.'

'I'm not sure I'm feeling well,' he said. 'And what's this language we're all speaking all of a sudden? It feels funny on my tongue.'

'It's called English, and it feels funny on all our tongues. Don't fight it.' Steven took the arrow. 'We have to get rid of these, though.' He helped Garec out of his quivers and took the Ronan's bow. 'We might be off the beaten path, but if a park ranger happens to patrol out here, you'll be in handcuffs before lunch. Let's put these away.'

'I don't like being here without my bow,' Garec said to Gilmour, trying to hide the fear that was almost paralysing him now.

'We'll keep it close by,' Gilmour promised as he ushered him back to the car.

They drove together to the Central Mall, where a stone tower in the middle of a roundabout overlooked closed concession stands, a restaurant and public toilets. A wooden boardwalk flanked the beach for about a mile in either direction, with concrete steps leading down to the sand at regular intervals. Behind the boardwalk, vacant car parks were interspersed with rolling dunes.

Further along the beach, the outdoor amphitheatre was silent, awaiting another summer of concerts and night-time shows.

'Come on,' Steven said, 'I'll show you the beach. Mark always says you can barely find a place to sit out here when the weather's nice.'

'But not today,' Hannah shivered. 'We have the whole place to ourselves.'

'For now,' Alen muttered, smoothing gloves over stiff fingers. 'Who knows how many will show up later?'

The beach stretched ten miles east from Point Lookout, across the bay from Rockaway. The Central Mall was about five miles from the point, near the centre of the park. An elderly beachcomber, looking almost swamped in a big padded parka, wandered around.

'Maybe she's looking for seashells,' Steven said, and waved from the bathhouse, but she ignored him. 'Right,' he said to himself, 'now, I forgot where we were.'

Jennifer asked, 'How will we know if this is the right place, or even the right day?'

'Good question,' Garec said, 'and this is a long beach, Steven, so how can we be sure Mark will choose this spot?'

'A couple of reasons,' Steven said, ticking them off on his gloved fingers. 'First, Mark always talked about being a kid out here, playing with his sister, doing the regular beach stuff with his family, but every time he described those outings, he always talked about his father taking him up the beach to buy ice cream. Now, I know that isn't much to go on, but I can't see any other place out here for a kid to get ice cream. So I'm guessing the Jenkins family used to stake out their family plot somewhere nearby.'

'Sure,' Jennifer said, 'that makes sense: two kids, restrooms right up the beach, why not? How else will you know?'

Steven replied, 'We'll know when, because I think the magic will tell us when. It always has so far, and I've no reason to think it'll fail now. So I think aspects of this place will begin to fade slightly, to become blurry around the edges, and then I'll know for sure.'

'Because that's what's happened before,' Jennifer said.

'Well, yes and no,' Steven said, 'and I'm sorry to be so vague, but here, today, I'm betting on yes.'

'Fingers crossed,' Hannah said.

'However,' Steven went on, 'I'd prefer it if you and Hannah left us now. Go back to the island and find a room, and assuming we're all right tonight, I'll call you and you can come and get us. There's no reason for you two to stay.'

Jennifer nodded. 'I agree,' she said, clearly happy to get away. 'I mean, I would stay if I thought we could do anything, but you're talking about things I don't even begin to understand. And you don't need Hannah for this bit, do you?'

'That's right,' Alen said, 'the rest of us may be called upon today, but you two have nothing to gain by being out here. You should go.'

Hannah, seeing a fight coming, just shook her head.

'But Hannah—' Jennifer began.

'No, Mom,' Hannah explained. 'I want to be here – I *need* to be here. Who knows what might happen? Everything could be lost just because we weren't here—'

'What can we do? Tell me honestly, and I'll stay with you.' Jennifer looked to Steven for support.

'I don't know,' Hannah said. 'I honestly don't – but that's why I think we need to stay. And come to think of it, how on earth will you manage to keep warm out here all day? You'll freeze to death in this wind. You need the car.'

'We'll be fine,' Steven said. 'We can break the lock on the res-taurant, or that concession stand. Once we're out of the wind, it'll be warm enough – we've got the kerosene heater, or we can build a fire.'

'And what if Mark doesn't arrive today?'

'We'll stay until he does.' Steven was adamant. 'There's got to be a payphone somewhere around here, so if it looks like we're going to be camped out here for a few days, I'll call your mother's cell phone and you can ferry out food and more blankets, but we're staying. This is the place; I'm sure of it.'

Hannah sighed. 'All right,' she said, 'but take these, in case you get bored later.' She took some sheets of folded paper from her back pocket and handed them to him. 'I'll explain it all tonight.'

'What's this?' Steven asked.

'A little surprise for you,' Hannah said. 'I had my suspicions when I first met Gilmour and Garec. This clinches it.'

Confused, Steven tucked the pages into his jacket and took Hannah in his arms and whispered, 'Please, go now. I just want you safe. Soon this'll all be a distant memory.'

'Promise?' Hannah said.

'I do.'

'Well, when it is, I want to go someplace and get naked.'

'As long as it isn't in Eldarn, I'm right there with you.'

As she kissed him, Steven felt the tension leave his shoulders; his legs threatened to buckle. The wind off the water brushed the hairs on the back of his neck and he would have been content to stand there all morning, feeling her body pressing up against his.

Garec shattered the moment when he asked suddenly, 'Where's Milla?'

Alen said, 'She's right—'

'Shit!' Jennifer pushed past the others on the boardwalk and ran to a little pile of clothes: the pink snowsuit topped with the little girl's matching hat and mittens. 'Milla!' she screamed, panicked.

'There she is.' Garec pointed down the beach at the distant figure making for the water.

'Holy Christ,' Hannah said, running for the steps, but Alen was already ahead of her, bounding wildly across the sand. Steven, Gilmour and Garec followed.

Steven cast off his own jacket as Milla dived into the surf.

The gull was still cawing when Mark woke, the side of his face dusted with a layer of white sand. He blinked his eyes into focus and searched as far as he could see without moving. At the edge of his peripheral vision, the ancient stone tripod supporting the Larion spell table stood unattended. The hilltop was quiet.

Nearby, Mark spotted the branch he had used to kill himself – his former self. It was within reach and, with a fluid motion, he rolled over until he could reach it, grabbed it and rose to a wary crouch. He checked out the side of the dune he had been unable to see, but still there was nothing.

'Where are you, shithead?' he whispered, following the slope into the marsh and around the confused tangle of banyan roots where he had hidden from the coral snake.

He was alone.

Standing over the table, Mark hacked impotently at it with the branch until, sweating and frustrated, he gave up and tossed the battered limb back into the swamp. Then he tried to tip the table over, hoping to stand it upright and roll it downhill. He thought perhaps it would crash through the brush and sink in the enchanted pool, where it would be guarded for ever by tumour-ridden tadpoles and sentient diamond-headed serpents. But it was too heavy; Mark couldn't get it to budge.

He leaned on the table edge and considered his options. He couldn't stand by while evil used the table to open the Fold and bring about the end of Eldarn, nor could he defeat himself. Lessek's key was missing, and it would take days to excavate enough of the hillside to shove the granite artefact into the swamp – and even then, there was no guarantee it would shatter, or sink forever out of sight. He would have to go back to the marsh, maybe use one of the banyan roots to dig up and then drag loads of slick mud and rotting leaves, enough to grease the hillside, making the slope slippery—

'Mark?' a voice called from somewhere behind him.

He leaped to one side and crouched down, expecting another fight, then he heard the strange voice again.

'Mark, is that you?' The voice was gentle, non-threatening. It appeared to be coming from the opposite side of the dune, the side he had forgotten, the side leading out to the azure sky and freedom. 'Mark? Mark Jenkins?'

'Who's there?' he asked softly, inching his way across the hilltop.

'Who is that?' When he stood, Mark could see down the other side, to the beach.

His father, young and lean, wearing his old bathing suit and carrying a beer can, was looking up at him.

'Dad?' Mark slipped in the loose sand and tumbled to the base of the hill. Embarrassed, he regained his feet and shook the sand off himself. 'Dad?'

'Mark? Where have you been?' His father leaned over to help him up. 'Your mother and I have been looking for you for an hour. She's convinced you drowned out there somewhere.'

'What?' Confused, Mark hugged his father like he had as a five-year-old, throwing his arms around the older man and clinging as if it was the last time they would ever see one another.

'Whoa, whoa, sport,' Arlen Jenkins said as he hugged him back, 'you've only been missing a little while, but your mom is upset. You know how she always tells you not to wander off. There's too many people out here, Mark, too many strangers.'

'Too many—' Mark looked beyond the dune. Thousands of people were on the beach. Hundreds of beach umbrellas dotted the strand, a flowing garden of vibrant flowers. The North Atlantic heaved and rolled, its waves crashing in the throaty roar Mark had heard before falling asleep. 'Jesus, it's Jones Beach,' he whispered.

'Of course it's Jones Beach, crazy person. Where else would we be today? You didn't hit your head or anything, did you, son?'

'Not here,' Mark stammered, 'it can't ... no, this can't be it.'

'You all right? You need some water or something?' His father took him around the shoulders. The feeling was reminiscent of every comforting thing he had ever known in his life.

'Wait, Dad.' Mark looked between the sand dune and his father. 'I need your help with something. Come here, it's not far. Come with me, quickly.'

'All right, but it'll be both our butts if we miss lunch.' Arlen seemed simultaneously amused and concerned at his son's antics, but he followed Mark up the dune regardless.

'It's just up here, Dad,' Mark said. 'We need to shove this stone—' The table was gone.

Out of breath, Arlen pulled himself up beside his son. 'What is it, sport? Pirates? Cowboys? Not the New York Yankees!'

'No, Dad, it's— It's nothing, sorry.' He checked the sandy hilltop, then crossed to the marsh side and looked down into the tangle of brush and rotting foliage. *Maybe I pushed it hard enough*, he thought. *Maybe it was sliding a bit and I didn't notice.*

But the marsh had disappeared as well, no humid maw of foetid organic decay, no swamp filled with coral snakes, banyan trees, or mutant tadpoles, just the scrub pine and scraggly brush that lined the boardwalks of Jones Beach State Park.

He was home.

Behind the sea of beach umbrellas, blankets, sunbathers and children digging in the sand with a rainbow array of plastic toys, the roads were crowded with big sedans and slat-sided station wagons. It was the height of summer in New York. Beyond the stone tower in the middle of the roundabout several big trucks turned in to the amphitheatre. There was a concert tonight.

For a few seconds everything was frozen in a sun-baked tableau. Only the breeze moved, brushing sand from his clothes and hair. Beside him, his father was young and strong, a fit, healthy thirty-year-old, the Arlen Jenkins Mark knew only from glimpses of black-and-white memories. Now, with his father's arm around him and the sea breeze caressing his tired limbs, Mark felt the tension, the anxieties and fears, the anger and especially the hopelessness of the past several months begin, slowly, to seep away. He started searching the beach in front of the Central Mall, looking for his family's yellow umbrella. It was eight feet across, difficult to miss, even on a crowded beach. His mother would be there, and his sister, and, presumably, a four- or five-year-old version of himself, another Long Island kid digging for China.

'Can we go back?' he asked himself.

'Of course,' his father answered, 'getting down off this thing's going to be a lot easier than climbing up. But you go first.' He ushered Mark towards the windward side of the dune. 'I think your mom's got tuna in the cooler. I do love a tuna sandwich with a cold beer.'

'I know,' Mark said, checking once more for the missing table. It should have been there; it couldn't have disappeared in the two minutes that he was away. Something was wrong, but being home had eased his sense of foreboding until there was just a faint trace of discomfort.

'Come on, Mark,' his father said, sliding through the sand, heels first, his beer can in one hand, 'and after lunch, we'll go and find some ice cream.'

Mark followed, entranced by the gentle grip of déjà vu. As he passed, people talked, radios clamoured, children shrieked, he even heard a dog barking; the summer fugue clouded Mark's senses and dragged him further from his marsh prison and the Larion spell table.

Gerrold Peterson, his high-school German teacher, sat in a collapsible nylon-web chair reading a dog-eared Günter Grass novel. He looked old, even here, in whatever year this was: 1981 or 1982. He wore the same buttoned-down short-sleeved shirt he had worn every Friday of every week of every year that Mark had attended Massapequa Heights High School. He lifted his pointed sunscreen-smeared snout far enough over the edge of his book to frown and say, '*Wie ist die Suppe heute, Herr Jenkins?*'

Mark didn't answer. Hurrying to keep up with his father, he caught sight of Jody Calloway, looking as she had when Mark had known her in high school. Jody, trapped in the taut young body of a fifteen-year-old, was in a bikini and playing volleyball with some friends. Mark thought he would slip past her unnoticed, but Jody tossed the ball to him, smiled an alluring grin and waved him over. She was every bit as sexy as Mark remembered, as buxom as a woman, yet still as thin as she had been as an adolescent. He was nearly twice her age, but he toyed with the idea of taking Jody up on the offer; if this *was* a hallucination, the sex would be sandy, perverse and exciting, a far cry from the clumsy fumble they had shared behind the columns in the Schönbrunn Gloriette.

'Of course, that's a felony,' Mark told himself. He rolled the ball back and waved. *Maybe next time*, he thought. Jody's body, like Herr Peterson's old shirt, would remain unchanged in his memory for ever.

'You'd better move along,' a familiar voice warned from nearby. 'That girl is too young for you now, soldier.'

'Who's that?' Mark searched the beach. His father was disappearing into the throng; there wasn't time to waste.

'I'm over here.' The reply came from several places at once.

'Brynne?' he said, hesitantly, 'Brynne, where are you?' He turned a tight circle, praying one of the beachgoers would transform into the attractive knife-wielder.

'I'm here.' She was behind him now, closer to the water.

Mark took a last look at his father and ran for the surf. 'Brynne!' he shouted, ignoring the irritated sunbathers. 'Brynne! Where are you? Please, Brynne, wait!'

'I'm here, near the waves.'

'I can't find you!' Mark jogged into the foam. 'Brynne?'

A young girl in a bright yellow bathing suit kept pace with him. She couldn't have been more than four or five years old. She had a head of rowdy curls that blew hither and yon in the breeze. 'Do you want to watch me swim?' she called as she splashed into the breakers.

'What? Who?' He was only half-listening.

'Who? You, silly,' she cried and ducked beneath a rolling wave. When she popped up, she brushed the hair from her face and said, 'I can do the scramble!'

Mark moved along, still searching the myriad faces for Brynne. 'That's nice, dear,' he said, 'but you shouldn't talk to strangers. This is Long Island. Where's your mother?'

'Watch this!' she shrieked, paddling excitedly towards Galway, but fifty yards out, she ducked beneath the surface, then emerged again and turned back towards the beach. She made a halfhearted attempt to stay calm, paddling and kicking tenaciously, then disappeared again.

'Hey!' Mark stopped. 'Hey, kid! Hey!' He ran a few steps up the beach, pointing and calling, 'Anybody know that little girl? Anyone? Out there, in the yellow!' A few sunbathers heard him, lifting their heads and looking around, but no one replied, and no one went in after the girl.

'Ah, shit,' Mark spat. 'Shit and shit. I don't have time for this.' He kept an eye on her while shrugging Redrick's tunic over his head. She was in the throes of a panic attack now, clearly drowning in the undertow. 'Brynne,' he called into the crowd, 'stay here. I'll be right back.'

He sprinted into the waves, diving over incoming breakers and towards the struggling child.

Milla ran until the waves reached her waist. She dived beneath an incoming breaker, holding her breath and paddling furiously for deeper water. The ocean here was icy and rough and her body felt like it was being stung with a thousand prickly needles. When she finally went numb, it was worse, because then it was nearly impossible to get her arms and legs to keep going. She was cold and scared and she sank twice before giving up and casting a spell to warm the water. She knew she shouldn't use magic here; they'd all told her she mustn't, but it was too cold to go on otherwise. Beyond the breakers a man struggled, drowning, flailing and shouting for help.

'Look at me, Hannah,' Milla said, but she wasn't sure anyone could hear. 'I'm doing the doggy-scramble.' Her tangled curls matted on her head in twisting coils; she kicked her way towards the drowning man.

'Hold on,' Milla shouted to him, 'I'm coming.' The water was still rough, but at least it was warm now. Alen and Hannah followed, swimming through cold waves, trying frantically to catch up. Milla didn't wait for them. So far, none of the others seemed to realise she was swimming out to greet them.

Steven pulled up just short of the waves. It was happening, now. The sand and surf blurred, melting into a bluish-beige canvas. 'Shit, this is it,' he shouted. Alen and Hannah were already in the water. Milla was paddling out past the breakers; why, Steven had no idea, but he needed them all back. This wasn't how it was supposed to happen, not with three of them in the water, for Christ's sake. What the hell was going on?

The elderly beachcomber appeared suddenly, tugging gently at his sleeve. 'It's time, Steven Taylor,' she said. 'Are you ready?'

'What?' He nearly lost his footing in the wet sand. 'Who are you? How do you—? Mrs Winter?'

'Hello, Steven. I've been waiting for you to get back.'

'What? Mrs W? You can't be here; this isn't right. What are you doing here?' Despite the waxy backdrop that had been Jones Beach State Park, Mrs Winter, the woman who owned the pastry shop next to the First National Bank of Idaho Springs, was standing there, in sharp focus and looking at him expectantly. 'I don't understand,' was all he could manage to say.

'I'm here to see you through this,' she said. 'Now, pay attention.' She gestured with a bony finger, out past the place Milla was determinedly swimming towards.

'What am I supposed to do?' he asked, bemused.

'Exactly what you came here to do, Steven.' Mrs W spoke as if the answer was obvious. 'Close the Fold. You can do it.'

Knee-deep in roiling grey surf, Garec shouted over the wind, 'There! Steven, Gilmour, look!'

A muscular black man rose from the water until he was chest-deep. Apparently oblivious to the cold, he studied the length of sand. He didn't look like he was treading water to stay in place; it was more like he was sitting on something, a pedestal, maybe, or a submerged bench. His arms hung calmly at his sides; he was obviously waiting for something.

As Steven felt the magic rise, he tried to remember everything Gilmour and Alen had taught him about the ash dream. The sea blurred beyond recognition; but Milla's tiny form, still swimming, remained. She paddled towards the newcomer, shouting to him and reaching out, but all the while, the man – Mark Jenkins, presumably – ignored her.

In a moment, Steven understood why.

Three rips, the ones he had come to expect, formed in the paraffin backdrop, just as they had in Idaho Springs, and again in the glen when he had faced Nerak. The irregular edges were like ragged tears in cloth. The ocean rolled and broke, lapping steadily at the beach, until it encountered one of the tears. Then it simply ceased to be.

Inside the first of the jagged rips, Steven saw what could only be Welstar Palace. Stark and forbidding, sitting atop a short rise above the river, the great keep stood sentinel over a massive military encampment. Alen and Hannah's descriptions had not done the place justice. Steven was glad he had never reached it. Thousands of shadowy figures stood in patient formation, division after division, all awaiting their lord's summons.

Inside the second rip, Steven saw what he expected: a mirror image of the state park, complete with him, Gilmour, Jennifer and Garec. The Ronan bowman was running up the beach, his feet kicking up sand as he hurried towards the Central Mall. Through the Fold and from over his shoulder, Steven heard Gilmour shout in stereo, 'Garec, wait!'

'I need my bow!' came the disembodied reply.

'There's no time! Come back!'

Steven didn't know whether Garec heeded Gilmour's call because he was distracted by what he saw through the third tear. It stood to reason that one opening in the Fold would show one's origins, while the second would reveal a destination, an adjoining room a world away. However, nothing had prepared Steven for what was behind the third. It showed Mark, standing over the spell table, calling forth all manner of dangerous-looking magics, swirling amalgams of creativity and destruction. Leaning into his work, Mark's arms disappeared to the elbow, buried in Ages of accumulated mysticism and knowledge. When he drew them forth, the power of the Larion Senate spilled over the sides in dazzling waves of energy.

Mark was on a sandy hilltop, like a dune, flanked by a forested vale so thick with tangled trees and underbrush that it was impossible to see within, even by the light of scores of braziers emitting clouds of treacherous black smoke.

That's it! Steven thought. *That's how he poisons them. It's the smoke.*

The tears, suspended above the breakwater, moved together and melded into one amoebic laceration, now a gaping hole in the fabric of the world. While Steven watched, the rip moved backwards, coming to rest on the water and swallowing the muscular black man.

'Do it, Steven,' Mrs Winter said, 'before it's too late.' She was still at his side and Steven wondered for a moment why he hadn't seen her when he peered back at himself through the Fold. Was she truly there? Was she some figment of his imagination, a phantom born of his fear and anxiety?

'Do what?' he asked. 'I don't know how to get inside the dreams. I'm not ready.'

'Don't you worry about their dreams,' she said. 'Fantus is taking care of that. You close the Fold. You know how. You could *paint the damned thing yellow* if you wanted.'

Who is this woman?

He decided to start with the black man on the submerged pedestal. Perhaps blasting him into submission might throw off-balance whatever it was Mark had planned.

But the man was gone. And so was Milla. When Steven checked back, he saw Alen swimming clumsily to where the little girl had been; he disappeared into the vacant rip in the mystical canvas. He tried to shout, but Alen had already vanished. Jennifer waded into the surf and started pulling on Hannah's arm, dragging her daughter back to the beach. It looked like Hannah had given up; perhaps she had seen Milla sink beneath the surface, or even disappear inside the Fold. He could see she was shivering and sobbing, inconsolable. Her mother held her tightly across the shoulders as the freezing waves continued to lash at them from behind.

What's happening? Steven thought. *This is mayhem. I don't even know where to start.*

'Think, Steven,' Mrs Winter said, as calmly as ever, '*think*. You know how to do this, but you must act quickly.'

The place where the conjoined tears fell was changing, no longer waxy-blue and beige; now the area was grey, mottled with dabs of black, dark blue and forest green. But it wasn't the colour change that worried him, nor the fact that the rips had joined one another and now spread out like some sorcerer's blanket – *my mother's old coverlet*. What worried Steven was how rapidly the area was growing, and why. In only a few seconds, the hole had stretched nearly the length of the boardwalk. He could smell it now: dank with decay and death, and sweet, like gangrene, a magic tunnel to pestilence and who knew what monsters and atrocities.

The stone-faced black man had disappeared, but as the Fold tore ever wider along the Long Island coast, there remained a disturbance where he had been: a figure, like a man, but formed of sea spray, foam, and some of Mark's dangerous black smoke still stood there, nearly invisible, but there, nonetheless.

It's him, Steven thought, *that's who's directing all this. He opened the Fold, and I stood by and watched it happen.*

The first regiments appeared in a line beyond the break, an inhuman wave, twenty thousand-strong and spread out, shoulder-to-shoulder, over several hundred yards. Their faces bore a mixture of pleasure and pain, of awareness and blissful ignorance. Some could clearly understand what they were doing, where they were and why they had been transported to another world, while others could scarcely recognise even that they were chest-deep in the sea. Some were covered with open sores, or had obviously broken bones and dislocations, even amputations. There was clear evidence of rampant infection, bacterial and viral, but the invasion force ignored all of it. There were some who hooted, chuckled or even roared with laughter; they were trapped somewhere in their lives where life had been hilarious. Others wailed, sobbed or screamed in anger.

But though different memories had them ensnared, they all trod through the breakers, this wall of indefatigable warriors, following the same orders: deliver the milled bark; enslave the populace and await the master's arrival. A second rank followed the first and before the front line had reached the beach, a third emerged from the depths.

Gilmour was sitting cross-legged in the sand, his eyes closed in concentration. He didn't see the first of the warriors as they splashed up the beach.

For Mark, there was nothing like swimming, nothing that made such intense physical demands of him. While he was a New York state champion on the surface – the butterfly, the crawl, the backstroke – he lived for those days when he could dive into the inhospitable waters off the Long Island coast. He had grown up training in a pool, but he and his friends learned early that the real test came *after* their competitive meets, when they would gather on this very beach to discover who was truly the island's strongest swimmer. The race, from Point Lookout across the bay to Rockaway and back, was the unsaddling of many swimmers; Mark had seen too many brazen students, some foolishly emboldened by alcohol, setting out boldly, only to find themselves giving up the fight and being hauled into the trailing rescue boat for the ultimate *row of shame*.

Today, as he made for the drowning girl, Mark anticipated his body's responses, his muscle memory reminding him why he so loved these waters... But nothing happened. Instead of the sleek, economic gestures he expected, Mark found himself kicking and thrashing clumsily: Redrick Shen had obviously not been a swimmer. *Christ, I just hope I don't drown*, he thought. *This guy's times in the 200 metres would be shit. I'll be fish food inside an hour.*

On the surface, he sucked in a massive breath and found the little girl, twenty yards out and in serious trouble, flailing and slapping at the water. A wave broke over her head and Mark watched her go down mid-scream. *Damn it, that's not good*, he thought, *she got a mouthful on that one.* The current was dragging her along, so he picked a point to her left, where he guessed she would be after the next wave. *She must be scared shitless – she'll never get in the water again. Frigging parents' fault, wherever the hell they are.*

The wave passed and the girl sank. When she didn't resurface, Mark dived after her. *Hang on, kiddo. I'll be there in five seconds.*

Below, the ocean was peaceful. The child's yellow bathing suit was easy to spot in the summer sun. She was drifting listlessly towards Jamaica Bay, no longer struggling, her arms and legs moving with the current, her hair a mass of stringy curls. Mark reached for her, snagging her wrist, and hauled her towards the surface, all the time praying that he could keep both of them afloat long enough to start her breathing again.

Less than five feet from safety, he felt something grip him about the chest, as if he had been taken from below. He thought he'd been grasped by a tentacled creature bent on crushing him beneath a rock, tenderising him for dinner. Iron bands squeezed until his ribs felt ready to snap. He tried to break free, but his hands simply slid uselessly across Redrick's muscular chest and abdomen.

He was being pulled towards the bottom.

What in Christ's name—? Mark, in his own body, would have fought the panic; panic meant exhaustion and death, and all good swimmers understood that there was no panic quite as terrifying as drowning. But trapped inside Redrick Shen, Mark realised he was lost. The Ronan sailor couldn't hold his breath and he couldn't kick free, and still the bands around his chest constricted as he sank towards the sandy bottom. When panic struck, Mark was helpless against it; he grasped at anything, the little girl included, as he fought for the surface. Finally his hands closed around something, her ankle, and he tugged, willing to climb her like a lifeline if it meant escape from the deadly ocean.

To Mark's horror, the girl looked down at him; eyes wide and curls bedraggled. She was smiling.

Gilmour wanted to help Jennifer as she dragged Hannah up the beach. The water had numbed his feet through his boots; he couldn't imagine how cold Hannah was. He assumed that Milla and Kantu had both drowned – he hadn't seen Milla sink, but he had watched in horror as his old colleague, still swimming after the little girl, simply disappeared. One moment he was there and, with the next wave, Kantu was gone. Now Hannah lay on the beach sobbing, her mother's and Steven's coats draped over her shivering body. To Garec, Gilmour shouted, 'See to her; I'll watch for that South Coaster to come back. I can't figure where he's gone.'

Garec pulled off his own cloak and added it to the layers covering Hannah.

Gilmour, staring at the sea and hoping for Alen and Milla to reappear, saw the elderly beachcomber come up beside Steven. The two were talking, but he couldn't make out what they were saying. He took a couple of tentative steps towards them, still watching the ocean as it hammered ceaselessly at the beach ... then the soldiers arrived.

They came through the shallows and foam, moving with the steady rhythm of a fugue. There were too many to attack with fire or explosions, and Gilmour knew he would be alone if he sneaked inside their collective nightmare. He sat in the sand, felt the cold caress of the ocean and closed his eyes. If only he had read Lessek's spell book earlier; if only he had made the connection between the ash dream and Lessek's other seminal works. If only he had returned to Sandcliff Palace, retrieved the spell book and kept it from Nerak all those Twinmoons ago. *If only, if only, if only . . .*

Gilmour narrowed his thoughts to a point and felt in the wintry air for the legions of warriors closing down on him. He could smell their breath, and the stink of their injuries and infections. *Here we go*, he thought, and slipped inside their memories. It wasn't as difficult as he had expected, but once inside, Gilmour knew he would not succeed in time.

Steven retreated up the beach. Mrs Winter tagged along. To his right, Garec and Jennifer were half-carrying, half-dragging Hannah away from the macabre warriors emerging from the water.

He screamed as Gilmour was swallowed up, his body trampled and torn to pieces by the few soldiers who paused long enough to pay the old magician any heed. The sea foam about their ankles bubbled crimson, staining the sand.

'No! Jesus Christ, no!' Steven fell to his knees. He cast a wild blast into the forward ranks, devastating the creatures nearest Gilmour's remains. Their shattered bodies flew up and out, like organic shrapnel, into the ranks behind. The amphibious landing slowed for a second or two, then resumed as before.

'What is magic, Steven?' Mrs Winter prompted. 'Remember what Fantus taught you.'

'Do you not see them?' Steven cried. 'Can you not see that I'm busy?' He blasted another spell into the soldiers closing on Garec and Hannah, which bought them a few seconds to escape.

'This is not the answer.' Mrs Winter was calm, as complacent as ever, an old woman who swept the step in front of her shop every morning. 'Think about the clock. Why did Fantus have you restart that clock? And I'm sorry, but I can't give you the answer; I simply cannot. You must decipher this yourself.'

'What?'

'The clock.'

The clock. It was a test. Restart time in Eldarn. Why? Why restart time? Because time and the ability to keep time are essential for any culture to evolve. Appointments need to be kept, timelines established, calendars drafted and adopted. They continued their retreat up the beach. *Could Gilmour have done it? No. He didn't have the magic. What is magic? Magic is power and knowledge. He didn't have the knowledge to start the clock. Magic is useless without knowledge – that's the fundamental premise of the Larion Brotherhood.*

'He didn't have the knowledge,' Steven said aloud.

'Correct, what knowledge? *We can paint the damned thing yellow.* Well, Steven, it's time: get painting.' Mrs Winter zipped her parka up tight, as if the chill along the beach might kill her long before the legions of homicidal warriors got to her.

'It was magic, compassion and maths,' Steven said. 'Maths – all right, I get it – but *what* maths? This isn't a maths problem ...'

'Oh yes it is,' she said.

'But I don't see—' Steven stopped his backwards withdrawal. *What's here? What am I missing? There are soldiers, thousands and thousands of soldiers. They're in ranks, but they aren't straight. It's a mess.*

No straight lines. They came though a hole. What hole? The Fold. How deep is it? Do I fill it? The tears, those rips, that's where the hole came from. They're irregular, nothing predictable or even. An irregular hole, constantly changing shape. It's a half-mile long and three hundred feet across. And how deep? How deep is the Fold? How far is it to Eldarn? It approaches infinity. A half-mile by three hundred feet – but fluctuating – by a number approaching infinity. Fuck this. Fuck this!

Garec and Jennifer were shouting something. Hannah, still wrapped in three coats, was running towards him. Milla and Alen were gone. Gilmour was dead, torn to pieces. And Mrs Winter, the old woman he had nearly trampled as he hurried home for Lessek's key, was here on Jones Beach, prompting him as calmly and reassuringly as a tutor.

A half-mile by three hundred feet, by a number approaching infinity. But it's all in motion; it's a frigging amoeba, impossible to measure; impossible to capture. It isn't a circle; it's a hole, a messy hole. But what? What do I do with it? I can't kill all these people, these— these whatever they are. It was maths, magic and compassion. I can't kill . . . Nerak deserved compassion. It was the hickory staff. Nerak needed a chance; he'd been taken against his will. Compassion was the answer. This is the Fold. This is evil. This is different. Maths, magic and knowledge. Not compassion.

'Not compassion,' he said to Mrs Winter.

'Not this time, no.'

'I was wrong,' Steven said, 'it isn't about compassion. That was for Nerak; the staff's magic, that's how I defeated Nerak.'

'But this is about knowledge.' Mrs Winter took his hand. 'What have you learned? What knowledge have you gained?'

'Magic is about knowledge.'

'And of compassion?'

'It is more powerful; *I* am *most* powerful when I—'

'But not now,' she interrupted.

'We bury these fuckers alive. It's evil; they get nothing from me, from us.'

'Maths, magic and knowledge, Steven.' She squeezed his hand. 'Get painting.'

Mark Jenkins' invasion forces were five ranks deep and nearly half a mile across. Steven estimated their numbers at more than fifty thousand – positively overwhelming, far too many to battle head-on. The jagged tear in the Fold, the origin, the destination and the Larion spell table, had expanded like bacteria mutating in a petri dish. The breakwater south of Jones Beach State Park had all but disappeared, opening into a foul-smelling void that bridged the gap between Steven Taylor and the military encampment outside Welstar Palace. *It's why he ordered them all back to Malakasia,* Steven thought. *He needed as many as he could bring to bear against us. This is the occupation force, cruelly deformed, that held Eldarn hostage for generations. A half-mile by three hundred feet, by a number approaching infinity and growing.*

'Let me up,' Hannah cried, pushing Garec and her mother back.

'Can you run?' Jennifer asked frantically. 'Honey, we need to run!'

'What's that?' Hannah pointed into the breakwater, behind the last row of soldiers wading to shore.

Garec squinted, then stood up suddenly. 'Whoring rutters, it's Milla!'

'What's she doing?' Jennifer asked. 'Is that someone with her? Alen?'

'We have to go!' Hannah shrugged out of the layers. 'We have to reach her.'

'Through them?' Jennifer wrestled her towards the boardwalk. 'We have to save ourselves – there're twenty thousand of those things between us and them.'

Hannah wasn't listening. 'Steven,' she muttered, trying to break free, 'not yet, Steven! Don't do it yet! Milla's out there!' Twisting away, she ran to Steven and the old woman with him.

Garec cursed. 'I'll go after them.'

'Are you out of your mind?' Jennifer shook. Creatures from her worst nightmares – no, even more horrific than that; she could never have dreamed such monstrosities – had emerged from the North Atlantic and were trudging up the beach.

'Maybe I can go around them,' Garec murmured to himself.

'They stretch for half a mile on either side, you raging idiot – you'll get yourself killed.'

Garec grimaced, lowered his shoulders and, unarmed, charged the forward ranks. He managed to bully his way through the first line of dazed killers. The second, however, did not part for him; Garec screamed when they dragged him to the sand.

'Steven,' Hannah cried, 'you have to wait. Milla's out there. She's alive.'

'What?' Steven hoped he'd misunderstood. 'What are you talking about? They're fifty feet away – we can't wait.'

'Look.' She pointed into the breakwater. Someone else was there; Steven guessed it was Alen, but the Larion sorcerer wasn't swimming well: he'd been injured somehow.

'It's all right,' he said, 'she's outside the ranks, outside the Fold. I don't think she'll be hurt.'

Mrs Winter nodded. 'That's right. Well done.'

Steven went on, 'We'll get her in just a moment.'

'What if she can't wait a moment?' Hannah pleaded.

'Then, like us, she'll be dead.' He closed his eyes. Someone nearby was screaming, an unnerving shriek for help. It was a man's voice, but Steven didn't bother to look up. He couldn't afford the distraction now. Milla was paddling towards shore, so he had to finish this quickly or the little girl might swim directly into the Fold. The being of spray and sea foam that Steven had seen orchestrating the invasion was still there, suspended above the very place where the black man, the one oblivious to the cold, had disappeared.

A half-mile by three hundred feet, by a number approaching infinity. Those are the dimensions, but the frigging thing isn't regular. It's all over the place and moving, for fuck's sake. Magic is knowledge and there is no compassion, not today. Today is maths and magic. Christ, it's cold out here. Knowledge and magic equal power, powers of magic, powers of math, powers of dimensions. Holy shit. Holy shit, that's it. Give it limits, what, zero and infinity. No, not infinity. Zero and half a mile, zero and three hundred feet. Yes, length and width, as a function. F of X between zero and half a mile, zero and three hundred feet. F of X minus G of X; all of it times the derivative as depth approaches infinity and fuck you very much.

The numbers lined up in his head, his own ranks of disciplined soldiers. The magic responded like a wellspring, surging from the depths of his consciousness, not a wild blast or a frantic spell to save his life, but a concerted, organised attack, perfectly formed for the threat at hand.

He remembered everything:

Gilmour on horseback in the Ronan meadow: *The Fold is the space between everything that is known and unknown. It is the absence of perception and therefore the absence of reality. Nothing exists there except evil, because the original architects of our universe could not avoid creating it.*

With Gilmour on Seer's Peak: *I was angry with myself, because anyone incapable of mercy is the most evil enemy we can face. That night, I became that person.*

With Gilmour, Garec and Mark beside the Falkan fjord: *We need to know what Lessek knew. He found it, called it a pinprick in the universe . . . he knew how to get to it, how to arrive at that place where he could reach out and grab it – like the air at the city dump. It was no different than it had ever been, but I held it in my hands, pressed against it and moved it around.*

With Gilmour before battling Nerak: *That's exactly right . . . sometimes what's real does change; other times, well, it's just an illusion. That's what separates us from carnival magicians.*

And finally, with Gilmour after their escape from the rogue tidal wave on the Medera River: *Where do you think new spells come from? Why do you think we spent all that time in your world, collected all those books? Why would we have sponsored research and medical teams from Sandcliff Palace for all those Twinmoons? Those spells weren't constructed because their incantations were similar; the incantations were derived because their etiologies, their origins and impacts, overlapped: they had common effects because they were based on overlapping fields of knowledge or research.*

'I can do it,' Steven said without opening his eyes. 'I can see it all, just like Gilmour said; it's a view from above. I can, Mrs W. We're going to be—'

Gnarled hands, impossibly strong, took him by the upper arm, the wrist, the neck, his coat lapels. There were fingers on his thighs, between his legs and around his ankles. Someone grasped at his face; another took a handful of his hair and all at once, all together, they pulled, digging in with cracked yellow fingernails, ripping through his clothes and tearing his skin—

Steven opened his eyes and screamed, his spell forgotten.

Mrs Winter was under attack. She had waited, giving Steven as much time as possible to work out his spell, but it had taken too long. She didn't wish to intervene, wasn't even sure if she would be permitted to, but circumstances gave her no choice. When the first of the rotting warriors grabbed for her, the old woman raised one hand, palm out and released a blast that incinerated a dozen of them and ignited even the wet clothing of another score as they slogged up the beach. One by one, she touched the creatures attacking Steven; it didn't take much, a push here, a gentle tug there until they released him, backed away a pace or two and collapsed, dead.

There were more coming, however, far too many for her to deflect with old parlour tricks or heavy-handed blasts. She had given Steven a moment to gather his thoughts, but the young magician was still on the verge of panic; his eyes were wide and his skin as pale as new parchment.

'Do it now,' she said, taking his face in her hands and forcing him to look into her eyes. 'There is no more time, my friend.'

Behind her, Hannah had fled up the beach and was screaming. Her mother rushed to drag her to safety, but still the young woman wouldn't be budged.

Below, the warriors that had been beating Garec to death stopped suddenly, leaving the Ronan archer lying senseless in the sand. Mrs Winter didn't know why they had let him go, but she could do nothing for him – she had to remain with Steven.

Then the sand at her feet was moving, tumbling over itself in waves, like thin corrugations in the beach, curling and rolling towards the water. Mrs Winter looked with surprise along the narrow ribbon that was Jones Beach, along the rows of Malakasian warriors, and everywhere she saw the same thing: narrow stretches of sand, rolling in perfect waves towards the water.

'What's this then?' she said and turned back to Steven. He was standing straight, some colour back in his face, ignoring the blood dripping from half a dozen deep cuts. He stared over the invading army, his eyes locked on a nearly translucent figure of a man formed of sea foam and smoke and floating above the water, just outside the grim cleft still spewing forth monsters. A veritable hum of resonant energy came from Steven, and the soldiers, oblivious to their surroundings thus far, stopped in their sandy tracks. All along the forward ranks, the grim-faced killers pulled up and waited, all of them watching Steven.

From somewhere deep within the Fold, something howled, the cry of a furious god, of evil rousing itself to claim them all. Steven stood his ground.

'Good gods, then, you've got them!' Mrs Winter cried and hurried to drag Garec's body further up the beach. She was able to elbow her way through the throng to reach him; none of the warriors appeared to notice her at all.

Hannah and Jennifer Sorenson waited near the concrete steps to the Central Mall, neither of them screaming any longer. Like the invading army, they stood transfixed by Steven Taylor.

F of X minus G of X; all of it multiplied by the derivative as the depth approaches infinity. Set limits, from zero to three hundred feet and from zero to half a mile, maybe more now, but no matter. Steven imagined the sand and the water awakening to help him. Depthless sand and black water, as deep as the Fold itself – *as depth approaches infinity*.

He shouted, nothing that made sense, just a primal scream, when he realised it was working. The sand was rolling back, setting limits – *from zero to three hundred feet* – while the water bubbled up in an irregular line, the outline of a ragged hole, just a tear – *from zero to half a mile*. The sand corrugations met the water and the circle was complete. All Steven had to do was to fill it – *F of X minus G of X, times the derivative. Now, fill the hole.*

'As depth approaches infinity.' Steven looked at Mrs Winter and smiled. His muscles were locked; his hair blew about his face, but his eyes were bright with understanding. He could see it all, scrawled across Professor Linnen's blackboard at the University of Denver. He had to understand the Fold: *the absence of perception and the absence of reality, a place where only evil can exist, where even light, love or energy cannot escape.* He understood magic's subtleties: *it's most powerful when we appreciate the fundamental tenets of what we are trying to change, to save, even to destroy.* He knew himself: *a magician whose strength comes from compassion*, but Steven had also gained knowledge about his foe: *it's an enemy from inside the Fold, like the tan-bak, an entity powerful enough to be the Fold's overlord. It deserves no mercy, no compassion.*

'Bury these fuckers alive,' he said again, and raised his arms. The sand and water complied, rolling furiously down the beach, churning the seas to a boil.

The soldiers on the beach were taken by the ankles and dragged towards the breakers. Those unfortunate enough to be in the water, even knee-deep, were swallowed by the waves. 'As depth approaches infinity!' Steven shouted, stepping forward and slugging one of the invaders hard across the jaw. The soldier fell backwards and was absorbed by the beach, gone in a moment.

A handful of the warriors recognised what was happening; they tried to fight back, wrenching at their ankles, attempting to swim as the ocean yawned to engulf them whole. The cries they emitted when they realised they were falling into oblivion were horrific, like the screams of terrified children. It unnerved Steven to hear them. Enraged, he focused his anger on the creature of sea foam and spray and smoke, now dancing wildly on the water, flailing and pushing its hapless soldiers back into the fray.

'It's you,' Steven said, pointing at evil's emissary, 'you're the one. You killed my friends. You killed my roommate, my best friend. You may not die, but I'm going to take you apart.' He punctuated his promise with flicks of his wrist—

'—piece—'

The spray and sea foam creature wailed as part of it was torn away, scattered by the ocean breeze.

'—by—'

Another cry as more of the figure broke apart.

'—piece—'

Steven breathed deep, summoning reserves of energy he could never have imagined, power unlike anything he had wielded, even in his battle with Nerak. 'Now—' He reached for the creature again, taking a few strides down the strand to get closer. The translucent figure was in a panic; its army was being swallowed by the very ground it had hoped to conquer, and it itself was being slashed and broken into harmless spores by the raging magician coming at it through the shallows. It swirled and spun and searched for an escape, but the only place to hide was inside the Fold, which was rapidly sealing itself. It couldn't retreat across the water; the maniacal sorcerer would surely follow it, and to flee onto land would be inviting destruction. Instead, it hurried back and forth along the line of dead and dying warriors. Some shrieked and reached for it, their fingers passing harmlessly through its smoky limbs.

'Now,' Steven said again, 'it is time for you to go.' He gestured towards the figure and it burst apart, the sea foam and spray dissipating, falling harmlessly like rain, while wisps of smoke blew inland across the dunes.

The beach swallowed the last of the soldiers. Some still reached skywards through the sand, hoping for a lifeline, while others simply sank away, still chuckling at whatever had been so funny countless Twinmoons earlier. Those swallowed by the sea did more than drown; they were lost inside the Fold, carried into the void by the chilly waters of the North Atlantic. And as the ragged hole closed for ever, Steven caught a final glimpse of Welstar Palace, where mayhem raged as thousands of soldiers disappeared headlong into the muddy banks of the Welstar River. With them sank the smoothly polished granite spell table, still half-encased in its wooden packing crate.

Jones Beach was empty. Only the waves and the breeze muffled the sounds of a little girl, doggedly paddling through the surf and dragging something along with her.

Garec Haile, the *Bringer of Death*, sat up, helped by Hannah and

Jennifer Sorenson. He was confounded; he had cheated death by the slimmest of margins, but how, he had no idea. He couldn't begin to guess why the soldiers tearing him apart had stopped so suddenly.

When he saw Milla, he forgot how much his head ached or how his arm felt as if it had been broken in a dozen places. He ran down the beach, splashed through the shallow waves and dived into the deeper water. It was cripplingly cold, but Garec welcomed the numbness.

Mrs Winter wandered down the strand and knelt where Gilmour's body had fallen; she was visibly upset as she touched the ground gingerly with one hand. Nothing was left but a crimson stain that would fade with the next tide; the broken limbs and torn flesh had all been swallowed up with the Malakasian divisions.

Steven was dumbstruck at what he had done. Now he wanted to comfort Mrs Winter. He wanted to help Garec, to be with Hannah and Jennifer as they carried Milla to warmth and safety, but he stood rooted in place, his boots half-buried in the sand. He recalled an autumn day, a decade earlier, when he had awakened with a paralysing hangover after a fraternity party and some barman's atrocity called *Hapsburg Piss*, an unappetising concoction made from hazelnut liqueur and plum schnapps. He had thought about skipping class and staying in bed until the coffee was hot and the opiates had quieted the ruthless, thudding pain in his head. But he hadn't; instead, Steven had rolled out of bed, dragged his listless self into the maths building and sat through one of Professor Linnen's lectures on functions and the area under the curve. Now, ten years later, he thought back to the countless undergraduates, and all the times they had complained that they would never need calculus in the real world, and Steven Taylor laughed to himself.

Hannah broke his reverie with a shriek; she stood frozen, her hands clasped together as Garec, staggering from the surf, waved wildly at him further down the beach, while Jennifer sat numbly in the foamy splash of the breakers. They each, in turn, shouted something he couldn't hear. Then Garec cupped his hands over his mouth and bellowed, 'It's Mark!'

Steven stood in stunned silence, staring mutely as Garec helped a muscular black man to his feet. It didn't look like Mark, but when he grinned and waved, Steven knew his roommate was back.

The sounds and smells of the ocean, the feel of the sand and the chill on the breeze, all of it came back to Steven in a rush. It was fundamentally human, and real, an affirmation of everything he had been trying to do since the first time he picked up the hickory staff, that long-ago night in Rona. His stomach roiled painfully; his knees gave way and Steven started to cry.

PEACHES AND TEA

'I didn't see Alen go down,' Garec said, huddling close to the kerosene heater. They were gathered around a Formica table in the sunny dining room of the Windward Restaurant in the Central Mall. A soda machine, unplugged, stood in one corner beside a red and yellow popcorn wagon and a portable ice cream cart with two flat tyres. Bright pictures of sundry deep-fried food adorned the wall behind the service counter in a fifteen-foot cholesterol frieze.

The kitchen was closed for the season and thankfully, no one, not even a security guard, had turned up for work that morning. From the pantry, Mrs Winter had pillaged some big cans of peaches, some warm cola and a few bottles of water. Those with a stomach for food ate from paper plates with the plastic spoons Steven had found behind the register. Jennifer brewed a pot of tea on a gas stove in the kitchen.

'He must have given in to the cold,' Garec said. 'He looked to be swimming strongly when he went out after—' He stopped himself. Milla was upset enough that Alen hadn't come ashore; there was nothing to be gained by belabouring it now.

'It wasn't the cold,' Steven said, 'it was the Fold. He didn't see it – *couldn't* see it.'

'He swam right in,' Milla sniffed. 'I didn't want anyone to follow me. That's why I ran off when you all were talking.'

'How did you know where Mark would be, Pepperweed?' Hannah asked. 'We still don't know what happened out there.'

'He was dreaming about it,' Milla said. 'Gilmour and Alen asked if I could get into Mark's dreams and I told them—'

'Only if he went to sleep,' Steven finished for her.

'That's right.' Mark Jenkins, trapped in the body of Redrick Shen, the burly seaman from Rona's South Coast, had torn down a rack of heavy curtains and had wrapped one around himself as he sat shivering beside Garec. 'I— *it* hadn't slept since we left the glen. I never imagined I could go to sleep, until it told me to.'

'And you dreamed of the beach?' Steven was reeling from the loss of both Gilmour and Alen. He hadn't known Alen – Kantu – well, but that made little difference: two of Eldarn's greatest heroes had perished that morning.

'I did,' Mark said, 'the same dream of the same day, here at the beach when I was a kid. My parents used to erect a yellow umbrella, about a hundred feet from where you dragged me ashore. I saw Milla in the water. She was drowning, so I went in after her.'

'And I went in after you,' Milla said. 'The other man, the one that was keeping you, he didn't know I was coming.'

'How is that, Pepperweed?'

'Because I went into the water in Mark's dream.'

'But I watched you do it,' Garec said, trying to understand the little girl's paradox. 'We all did. Hannah followed you into the waves.'

'Yes, but the one holding Mark wasn't here.'

'Where was he— where was *it*, Pepperweed?' Hannah, still confused, cocked an eyebrow at Mark.

'It was between here and there, in the Fold, working with all the magic in that table,' she said, pushing a piece of peach halfway around her plate, trying to scoop it up.

Mark handed his cup to Hannah and asked for a refill; he was glad to see her safe. To Milla, he said, 'So when I was going in to save you, you were actually coming in to save me?'

'I needed you to get into the water,' Milla said, as if that explained everything.

'Because that's where you knew the creature would open the Fold?' Hannah asked.

'And because I am an excellent swimmer, silly. Didn't you see me doing the scramble?' She giggled and ate the wayward peach, Alen temporarily forgotten.

'It was the ash dream,' Steven said. 'Who would have guessed that of all of us, she would be the only one who could manage it?'

'Prince Nerak taught me,' she said proudly.

Steven looked at the plate of peaches Jennifer was offering him and set them aside. It would be a while before he was ready to eat. 'You were our true hero today, Pepperweed,' he said softly.

'I wouldn't go as far as to say that,' Mrs Winter whispered, peering at him over the top of her glasses. She wore them low on her nose, like a schoolmarm in an old daguerreotype. He had watched her attack the invaders. Steven didn't believe she needed glasses at all.

'Did you see what happened to Gilmour?' Garec asked.

556

Steven wrestled back another bout of tears and nodded. 'He just sat there. I don't know why.'

'Overwhelmed maybe?' Hannah suggested. 'Did he give up? Maybe sacrificed himself to slow them down?'

'Perhaps,' Steven said, uncomforted.

'I wouldn't go as far as to say that either,' Mrs Winter said. 'He was probably trying to break into their dreams, to slow them, or stop them entirely. He might even have been successful, or partially successful, anyway.'

'How can you say that?' Hannah asked. 'What are you even doing here? Who are you, anyway?' She too was still in shock.

Steven interrupted to say, 'Her name is Alfrieda Winter. She owns the shop next to the bank in Idaho Springs, and I will bet you a year of your life to a bacon sandwich that her middle initial is "L".'

'You've never been stupid, Steven,' Alfrieda Winter replied, 'and I've known you a long time, haven't I?'

'Holy shit, it's Lessek!' Mark stood, spilling his tea over the curtain he was wrapped in. 'It's you; you're Lessek, aren't you?'

'I am, Mark, and I've been watching you and Steven for most of your lives.'

'Why? How?' Hannah couldn't cope with this; she looked from face to face, trying to understand.

'I was forced to leave Eldarn a long time ago,' Mrs Winter – *Lessek* – began. 'I did a terrible thing, inadvertently, but a terrible thing nevertheless. I've been here ever since.'

'That virus,' Steven guessed.

'The worst Twinmoon of my life,' the old woman replied. 'Thousands died in Eldarn. My team and I planned to come back, to find a cure, a herb, something to stop the devastation, but I was sick myself, and I wasn't able to keep them from conspiring against me. I escaped to Rome, and then to the Holy Land, where I had friends and colleagues, but without my writings and the spell table, I was unable to control the Fold. Harbach, a power-hungry businessman, and Gaorg, my own brother, ran me out one night, ushering a whole new Era of politics and corruption into the fledgling Larion Senate. I spent thousands of Twinmoons here, decades and decades, watching, listening and hoping to find a way home, when, one day about a hundred and thirty-five years ago—'

'Your own keystone came to you,' Mark said.

'It was as if a bomb detonated half a world away and I felt the aftershock. I was living in a corner of Africa at the time, a place from where I discovered I could communicate with the most powerful of the magicians from the Larion Senate.'

'At Seer's Peak,' Steven said.

'That's right.'

'But Larion Senators had been coming here for generations,' Hannah said, her brow furrowed. 'Why didn't you go back with one of them?'

'That was several Eras later, over an Age had passed, and I was settled here by that time, Hannah,' Mrs Winter replied softly, obviously leaving something unsaid. 'I made a point to help Larion sorcerers when I could, guiding them, leading them to powerful sources of energy, information, research and knowledge. I was an outstanding resource for the Larion Brotherhood, but—'

'You never revealed yourself to them?' Jennifer asked.

'No.' She sipped her tea. 'I was more useful here, even to Nerak – *especially* to Nerak, I should say. He was an astonishing talent from very early on.'

'And then your keystone arrived,' Steven said.

'And things began to unravel in Eldarn. I would have tried to go home then, but Larion journeys across the Fold came to an abrupt halt. Apart from Seer's Peak, there was little opportunity for communication—'

'Except for images,' Steven said.

'And dreams,' Mark added. 'My dreams, the dream of this very beach. How did you do it? My head hurts just thinking about it.' Mark tallied points on his fingers. 'I dream of Jones Beach and my dad. You plant the dream in my head, convincing me that I'm Eldarn's heir. I am taken by the evil minion ruling Eldarn and we end up here, invading my home on this very beach. It doesn't add up.'

'Actually,' she peered over her glasses, 'it adds up perfectly. Lessek's key had been drawing members of your family to Colorado for generations.'

'Those pictures,' Steven said, 'the ones in the hallway at your parents' house . . .'

'That trip,' Mark agreed, 'and my dad's favourite photos.'

The Larion founder laughed. 'You're catching on, boys. You remembered Jones Beach, a day in your childhood when you and your father enjoyed each other's company. I used the ash dream to comfort you that night, but no, I never imagined that you would one day invade Earth from this beach.'

'It was in my head,' Mark said, swirling tea in his cup. 'The evil that took me just found it in there.'

'It and all your analyses and conclusions about yourself as Eldarn's heir,' Steven said.

'My goal was only to comfort you, Mark, to comfort you and to send you a message about your father; that was all. With you in Eldarn so unexpectedly, I had to act quickly, or else risk having you travel through Rona unaware of who you truly were. You chose the memory: the day, the beach, the time, all of it, probably because you happened to arrive on the beach outside Estrad when you fell across the Fold.'

'After we'd been drinking beer at Owen's Pub,' Mark added. 'My dad used to drink all day when we were at the beach.'

Hannah chuckled. 'An important parallel.'

Mark went to the windows. The sun was high overhead now, but a cold wind continued to sweep the beach, kicking up the sand along the boardwalk. 'So I have a vision of my dad, because you used the ash dream, but I picked the beach memory, serendipitously, most likely because I was on a beach outside Estrad. So far so good?'

'Keep at it,' Steven urged.

'You continued to send me dreams and memories of my dad and Jones Beach and when I was taken, I had spent so much time thinking about this place that the minion controlling the Malakasian military decided this would be the perfect place to invade.'

'True, but there were other reasons as well,' Steven said. 'When Nerak was in Colorado, ostensibly tracking down Jennifer, we assume he took numerous people.'

'Gaining knowledge of Earth,' Hannah said. 'Taking you, the minion had everything it had learned from Nerak, plus what it gained inside your mind: knowledge of Kennedy Airport, Manhattan, the millions of people here, so many things. If it had taken me instead, this invasion force might have emerged up near Alamosa Pass, or maybe out on the prairie east of Denver.'

'So here we are,' Garec said, 'living your dream, Mark.'

'How did you get into my head?' Mark asked. 'I never came near any of that bark, or the ashes, or any of those shipments. How did you do it?'

'The same way as Milla,' Mrs Winter said. 'The ash dream was the cornerstone of so many things I had planned to do for the Larion Senate. What a teaching strategy: imagine giving an apprentice a view of themselves, devoid of all the polish and subtle adjustments we apply to convince ourselves that our experiences are more special or important than they truly are. Imagine the learning, the emotional discipline—'

'And the knowledge,' Steven interrupted.

'Most importantly, the knowledge,' the older woman agreed, 'because our most powerful magic hinges on knowledge.'

'And my dream of the Air Force Academy and the almor?'

'Again, you started the ball rolling yourself,' Mrs Winter said. 'I just interjected a key element.'

'My *prince*,' Garec said.

'That's right.' She turned to him. 'It was important for you to know who you were, Mark, certainly before you arrived here this morning. Just as it was important for Fantus to recognise his role as that of a teacher, and Kantu to understand his role as surrogate parent to Milla. The only way we could have turned back the evil that tried to take over our worlds today was for each of us to understand ourselves at our most fundamental level, to understand that we each have an important calling in Eldarn's future. Garec, the king's protector and sovereign of Falkan—'

Steven spat a mouthful of tea on the floor. 'What the Hell—?'

'Don't ask.' Garec shook his head.

Mrs Winter ignored them. 'Mark, the Ronan prince—'

Steven wiped his mouth, then finished Lessek's thought, 'And Milla, the heir apparent to the Larion Senate, the prodigy.'

'Not just Milla,' Hannah said.

'Certainly not.' Mrs Winter smiled and finally removed her glasses.

'What?' Steven asked, 'what am I missing?'

'In your pocket,' Hannah said. 'You were willing to believe that Mark was drawn to Idaho Springs by the power of Lessek's key, but you never bothered to wonder about yourself.' She took a seat beside her mother; they huddled together under a blanket. 'After hearing of your exploits from Brexan and Gilmour, I put two and two together.'

'Two and two?' Steven said. 'Where'd the other two come from?'

'From Alen.'

'Alen?' Steven unfolded the sheets of paper Hannah had given him that morning. They were printed out from an Internet café, somewhere in western Massachusetts. Across the bottom of each page was a common footer: a web domain. 'What is this?' Steven said, turning the first page over several times, trying to make sense of an ornate grid filled with unfamiliar names.

'It's from a genealogical website, a database,' Jennifer said. 'Look at it closely. What do you see?'

'It looks like a printout of a family line, originating somewhere in northern England a couple of centuries ago.'

'Look at the generations spanning the middle page there.' Hannah pointed at the second sheaf. 'The stuff between 1846 and 1881 . . .'

'There's a family, Wakefield, from Bradford who married into the Kirtland family from Durham. They had four children, three boys and one girl, who in turn went on to have, two, three, five, holy shit, *eleven* grandchildren. It was a rutting brood – but so what?'

'So look again,' Hannah said, winking at Mark and adding, 'He's as thick as a bag of broken bricks sometimes.'

'Tell me about it,' Mark groaned.

'Um, all right,' Steven reread the page. 'Whatshername from Bradford marries Kirtland from Durham and they have four, oh, wait, no, five! They have five kids and the last one – that's the one I missed. Hold on.' Mark reached for the pages and Steven relinquished all but the one charting the family line through the mid-1800s. 'She doesn't belong here. Who is she?' He looked pointedly at Hannah. 'The woman who married Thomas Robert Taylor of London in 1892 and moved to America, New Jersey and then to Ohio, before dying at the age of 87 in Denver, Colorado. Who was that woman? My great-grandmother, Margaret Rena Kirtland Taylor?'

'Yes, she was your great-grandmother,' Hannah explained. 'Her name was Reia, not Rena. She was the daughter of Alen Jasper and Pikan Tettarak, the offspring of two Larion sorcerers, and the direct source of your power.'

'Holy shit!' Mark yelled, ripping the key page from his friend's hand.

Steven didn't seem to notice; instead he stared at Hannah, blinking, looking dumbfounded. 'It— No, I can't . . . It came from the staff; it had to!'

'No, it didn't,' Garec said. 'Mark and I have been trying to tell you since the fjord, since Traver's Notch. The magic didn't come from the staff; the staff just brought it to life. It was there all along. I knew it the night we spent in the cavern beneath the river.'

'Cold beer and oil changes for $26.99,' Mark said. 'We were seeing across the Fold.'

'Just like you did today.' Mrs Winter took his hand. 'Milla is not the only heir to the Larion Brotherhood, Steven, you are as well. You will both bring leadership and knowledge to the Larion Senate: Milla is a prodigious talent, certainly, but *you* are the Senate's legacy.'

'Old magic,' Steven said, 'that's what Gilmour called these abilities, nonverbal spells and such.'

'Yes, he did.' Mrs Winter smiled.

'Did he know?'

'The clock.'

'Sonofabitch.' Steven didn't fight the tears this time. Slipping to his knees, he cried out, 'And I buried him. I buried him inside the Fold. I—'

'No, you didn't,' said Mrs Winter, 'he was inside their minds, inside their dreams when it happened. Fantus knew what he was doing.'

'How do you know that?'

'There's your proof.' She pointed at Garec.

'Me?' Garec looked around at the others. 'What did I do?'

'You *didn't* die this morning. Why is that?'

Garec rubbed stiffness from his arm. 'They were killing me. I figured it was over; I was heading for the Northern Forest, or whatever might pass for the Northern Forest around here, but I had to try and reach Milla. I don't know why they stopped; they just left me alone.' His face was a roadmap of cuts and bruises. He thought of Kellin, sailing somewhere along the Northern Archipelago, and wanted badly, right at that moment, to go home.

'The ash dream,' Steven whispered, pulling himself together. 'So he did get in.'

Mrs Winter nodded.

'And all this time, he doubted himself,' Mark said.

Steven took back Hannah's printout. 'So Alen Jasper, Kantu, was my great-great-grandfather?'

'He was.' Hannah crossed to hug him. 'And Pikan Tettarak, the woman he loved more than anyone else in these past five generations, was your great-great-grandmother.'

'Did Alen know?' Steven asked. It felt good to have Hannah against him, feeling the warmth of her, the shape of her, there, still alive, still with him.

'No,' Hannah whispered. 'I'm sorry. I just never thought that he would be gone and he was so preoccupied with caring for—'

'It's all right.' Steven hid his face in the crook of her neck. 'It's all right.' He flashed back to southern Falkan. *We are the Larion Senators.*

'Mrs Winter?' Mark ladled out another scoop of peaches. 'When Steven and I fell across the Fold, the far portal was left open in our house, with your keystone there on the desk. I fell through on a

Thursday night; Steven joined me on what would have been early Friday morning—'

'I didn't fall through until Friday evening,' Hannah added.

'So why did you just leave it there, opened like that? Why didn't you come up to the house and close the portal? Why didn't you take the keystone?' Mark stood. Steven looked up at him; Redrick Shen was noticeably taller than Mark had been.

'I was monitoring the portal,' she replied. 'I knew where the keystone was, but I didn't know if you had accidentally fallen into the portal, or if you had been invited into Eldarn by Fantus or Kantu, perhaps even by Nerak. I didn't close the portal, because if I had and you returned suddenly, you might have found yourself swimming home from the Aleutians.'

'Oh shit, that's right,' Steven said.

'And I didn't want to take the keystone, because if Fantus or Kantu *had* brought you across the Fold, I wanted the key available to them.'

'And if Nerak happened to come through for it, unannounced?'

'I would have known,' she said, donning her glasses again, as if out of habit. 'I actually went to the bank that morning, ostensibly to cash a cheque. Myrna and Howard were working the window and neither of them seemed to know that you had taken anything from the safe. So I didn't imagine there was any cause for concern. I didn't expect anyone would be going into your house; everyone assumed you were climbing Decatur Peak together. Howard breaking in that afternoon came as a complete surprise to me. I rushed over when I saw the flames, but I wasn't permitted anywhere near the fire.'

'Hold on,' Mark interrupted, '*Howard* burned down our house?'

'Didn't you know?'

'No,' Steven said, 'we had no idea. At first I thought it was Nerak, then I guessed maybe it was just a fluke, one of those things.'

'It was Howard Griffin,' she said. 'He apparently left the stove on in your kitchen.'

'I am going to beat the shit out of him,' Mark muttered.

'Friend of yours?' Garec elbowed him in the ribs.

'An abscess in my rectum,' Mark said. 'Howard is Steven's boss.'

'Disgusting, but I am proud to say that I know what all those words mean, in English. Fancy trick, this cross-Fold travel.'

'Mrs—' Steven started, then, 'Sorry, Lessek, why didn't you know if we had fallen through or if Gilmour had come over and invited us back?'

'The portal wasn't opened until late at night. I had been asleep, so I couldn't determine if anyone had come through before Mark disappeared, and you were hanging around so long afterward, I thought perhaps you and he had coordinated something with Fantus or Kantu on the other side.'

'I was a bit nervous before that first crossing,' Steven admitted, blushing at the memory.

'And when they came and hauled away the remains of your house, I tracked the portal and the key and I let them go.'

'To the dump?' Mark was incredulous. 'Why?'

'Why not? It was a damned-near perfect hiding spot: outside of town, buried in the mountains. Who would've thought to go looking for them up there?'

'But the portal was closed!' Steven shouted. 'I nearly drowned coming back, landing in the ocean off South Carolina, and then I had to race across the country with Nerak crawling up my backside the entire trip. I found the house razed to the ground, and then I had to dig around up there, through that mountain of ice and frozen diapers and rotting food and shit until I found the stone and the portal. Why?'

'I had to assume the worst,' Mrs Winter explained calmly. 'You hadn't returned, so protecting the key meant allowing the portal to close. I am afraid, boys, that the keystone and the Eldarni family lines are more important even than the two of you.'

'But aren't *we* the Eldarni family lines?' Mark said. 'Isn't he the incarnation of the Larion Senate? Am I not some errant Ronan prince?'

'You are,' she said, 'but the line doesn't end with you two. You were, sadly, more expendable than my keystone.'

'Your sister.' Steven pointed at Mark.

'*Your* sister,' Mark said.

'Like I said, you're catching on, boys. Losing you two was tragic; oh, I worried about you for weeks, but I couldn't leave the portal open for ever. When the trucks came and hauled the debris up the canyon, I was actually glad: it meant I didn't have to find another relatively permanent storage place for it. And knowing I couldn't get it back into the safe, I let it go up the mountain.'

'How did you get here?' Jennifer had been trying to stay abreast of the conversation. 'We didn't know until yesterday that we had to be here at the beach. How is it that you're here, all the way from Colorado, so quickly?'

'I was following you,' Mrs Winter replied. She considered another go at the peaches, then decided against it. 'When Nerak arrived and nearly destroyed Idaho Springs, I delayed him long enough for Steven to sneak away towards Denver. It wasn't much, a few fire trucks, a handful of police officers in the street, just enough to allow Steven to disappear.'

'Why didn't you kill him?' Hannah asked.

'I'm not strong enough for that, my dear,' Mrs Winter said, 'not here. It's been a long time. I have been able to develop an interesting perspective on Eldarn and the goings-on there, but that's taken me centuries to do. To kill Nerak, I would have had to open the Fold and I couldn't do that without the spell table. When Steven fled with the keystone, I was more nervous than I've been in hundreds of years. I had to assume that with Nerak pursuing him, Steven was working with Fantus and Kantu. However, I couldn't be absolutely certain, not until David Johnson died.'

'Who's David Johnson?' Garec asked of anyone who might know.

'A— Well, he would have been a friend of mine,' Jennifer said, 'from Silverthorn. Nerak killed him, and a woman who worked at his store, right in front of me. It was horrible, terrifying— but how did you know?'

'I read about it in the paper,' Mrs Winter said. 'I knew Nerak was there and I knew that you had the portal. Steven had given it to you, and when you didn't turn it over to Nerak, I knew you and Steven were working on the right side of the fence.' To Steven, she said, 'I'm sorry I didn't say anything to you that morning in Idaho Springs, but I couldn't. I didn't know what had happened since you had left. You could have been rushing home to retrieve the key for Nerak.'

'But you didn't try to stop me when I went to the landfill.' Steven was nonplussed.

'Of course not.' Mrs Winter sighed, a little frustrated at trying to explain herself. 'By that time, Nerak was in the bank killing people and leaving dead bodies all over town, the odious motherfucker.' She paused. 'Poor Myrna; she was just a kid. I couldn't get to the landfill before you, so I had to trust that you were working with Fantus or Kantu. That was one of the more nerve-wracking days of my long, long life.'

'And you couldn't save Myrna?' Mark asked sadly.

Mrs Winter shook her head. 'Nerak would have torn me to pieces. I'm surprised he didn't sense my presence in town when he arrived. He probably thought it was the keystone, or maybe the portal.'

'But you're *Lessek*,' Garec said. 'We were told stories about you from the time we were kids. It was the stuff of great legends. You were the Larion Senate founder, the most powerful sorcerer of all time. You didn't have enough strength to save those people?'

'I had the ash dream,' Mrs Winter said simply. 'It was the primary building block for most of the common-phrase spells I researched and wrote during my Twinmoons at Sandcliff. It was my strength as a researcher and a teacher, the means for me to send messages to Kantu or Fantus, to lead Regona Carvic away from Riverend Palace the night Nerak killed Danmark and Danae. She ended up in Vienna, if memory serves.'

Mark perked up. 'Vienna?'

'Yes. Why?'

'Sorry, go on.' He ran a hand through Milla's curls.

She did. 'The ash dream was the way I made suggestions to Mark about his family, how I charted the evolution of your partisan struggle in Eldarn, even the way I encouraged those fire-fighters to block the on ramp to I-70 when Nerak was chasing Steven towards Denver. But that's it. Oh, I can still dole out a significant blast; I was pleased with my efforts on the beach this morning, but my strength as a sorcerer, a magician capable of levelling a mountain, or whatever legends you might have heard about me in your youth, Garec, was founded on the spell table. I didn't have the spell table, hadn't seen it in nearly a hundred generations, so no, I didn't have the power to subdue Nerak.'

'So the ash dream, this key element in your abilities, is just the power of suggestion?' Garec craned his neck, looking for more tea, but found the pot empty.

'Oh no, the ash dream is the power of knowledge, the one common denominator in any spell. The more one can understand and manipulate perceptions around a body of knowledge, the more flexible and effective his or her spells can grow. If I could have brought one thing with me from Eldarn, well, all right, two, technically, I would have brought my keystone and that book.' Mrs Winter gestured towards the leatherbound tome, wrinkled from so many dunkings in the past three Twinmoons.

'And you followed me, followed the portal, instead of going back with the keystone,' Jennifer added. 'That's why you were already here this morning.'

'I did,' Mrs Winter shrugged. 'I followed you, because—'

'Because you can't go back,' Steven guessed, 'can you?'

'No, Steven, I can't. My ... my so-called *friends* and colleagues arranged that in the wake of my disappearance, sometime around the beginning of the second Age, almost five Eras ago.' She removed her glasses again and ran bony fingers over the lines etched in her face.

A heavy silence fell over the sunlit dining room. Two joggers, bundled up against the cold, passed by on the hard-packed sand near the waterline; neither noticed that the restaurant doors had been forced open. Beyond them, the North Atlantic, glittering gold in the sun, rolled with the tide, unconcerned that it had swallowed an army less than an hour earlier.

Garec, intrigued by the bright colours of the jackets and footwear, watched the joggers disappear into the distance. The world around him slowed, even time seemed to grow weary, trudging along to a soft dirge. They were done. They had won. He ought to feel better about it, but now all he wanted was to go home, to find Kellin and to sleep for a Twinmoon. He hadn't felt safe for much of his life, not until this moment. He honestly hadn't expected it, and now he was afraid even to consider what might lie ahead. How would he handle the realisation of everything he and his friends had ever worked to accomplish? The notion of success, hard-fought and harder-won, unnerved him. Garec decided he would go home and he would sleep. Then he would lock his bow and quivers away and ride for the Blackstones and Renna. The thought of his fiery little mare comforted him and he turned from the windows to ask, 'What do we do now?'

At first, no one answered. The challenges they had met stood taller than those that now lay before them. Saving Eldarn – saving Earth – had seemed so unlikely a battle to win: none of them had ever thought they would live this long. Now, faced with the task of rebuilding Eldarn, of starting over again a thousand Twinmoons later, the breadth of the work ahead was staggering.

Mark, the history teacher, started on their list. 'Education, public health, decent food supplies, shelter, clean water, working farms, shipping, roads, industry, a reliable judiciary, a set of reasonable laws – formative, not summative, not now, no way – and a representative government, right from the start. It might seem like it would be easier to start off with a monarchy and then switch over after a while, but that's not the way to rebuild. They have to own it; there have to be some common values, simple – and I do mean *dirt*-simple – things the people of Eldarn can agree upon; we're talking about a people with basic literacy, not the crew who spent the past fifty Twinmoons under Gilmour's tutelage, but the rest of the population. That's where you start a true grass-roots effort. Holy shit, it'll take lifetimes to get that place put back together. I don't ... I can't even get it all straight in my head. It's too big a problem to even conceptualise without getting dizzy.'

'Was there any beer in that fridge?' Steven whispered to Hannah. 'He works better after a beer or two.'

'I'm sure the school board would be interested to know that little factoid, and no, there isn't any beer back there. You're home now; you can't be drinking beer at ten o'clock in the morning.' She slugged him playfully in the arm.

Mark ignored them. 'And the Larion Senate, the independent states of Gorsk, Praga, Rona and Falkan, even Malakasia. There'll be civil wars, border disputes. The shipping industry will probably come near to collapse before it rights itself again. People will starve. There's no army to speak of, no one to police the populace. Jesus, it's going to be a mess.'

'What about Gita?' Steven said. 'She can probably help.'

'Yes, her, certainly, we'll need to find her,' Mark said. 'Man, this'll take weeks.'

'Weeks,' Hannah said, 'that's not so bad. They can hold together for a few weeks.'

'I mean weeks just to get it all written down, just to get the problems outlined and the resources listed. That'll take weeks. We'll all be old people with see-through skin and brittle bones before Eldarn gets to the stage where people are living healthy, productive, *free* lives.'

'Oh,' Hannah said. 'Sorry, I misunderstood.'

'Mark—' Steven sat next to Mrs Winter, 'Mark, is this truly what you want to do? Are you suggesting that you're ready to go back, to take up the mantle of some leadership position you never asked for?'

'Look at me, Steven. My own family aren't going to recognise me. And what about you? Do you think there's a place in this world for a sorcerer? You'll be grossly misunderstood, or exploited; you'll either be dead or locked up inside a year: prison, maybe, or some psych hospital.'

'You've been through a great deal, Mark,' Garec said. 'Perhaps you ought to take some time before you commit countless Twinmoons of your life to Eldarni cultural reconstruction.'

'It has to start somewhere,' Mark murmured, not to anyone in particular.

Steven said, 'But we've only been home for a couple of hours. We came a long way to get here; can't we just enjoy this for a while? You can take a break: a month or six or whatever, get used to your new

'... self.' Steven avoided looking at Mrs Winter. He hadn't expected to feel selfish, but he couldn't deny the sensation suffusing through him at the moment. His desire to protect Mark was equalled by his need for a few days' of normalcy, some fried food and maybe a real mattress. He knew *he* would be returning to Eldarn if the opportunity arose, but bringing Mark along hadn't crossed his mind, not since he'd been taken in Meyers' Vale. Trying hard not to sound condescending, Steven added, 'This is supposed to be where you ride into the sunset, cousin. I hadn't thought about what we would do after today, but I promise it didn't involve dragging you, or Hannah, back to Eldarn. That's one mistake I prefer to make just once in a lifetime.'

'It isn't your choice to make,' Hannah said quietly.

'Hannah!' Jennifer jumped up, looking startled and indignant.

'Sorry, Mom, but if they're going back, I'm going with them.'

Hannah's mother glared at Steven; she would always blame him.

Garec interrupted, asking Mrs Winter how the Larion Senate could possibly rebuild without the spell table.

'That's a great question, Garec.' The others postponed their disagreement to listen in. 'You see, we don't need the spell table to reconvene the Larion Brotherhood. All we need is Steven, Milla and that book.' Again, she gestured to the leatherbound volume Gilmour had carried across half of Eldarn. 'I was able, in my youth, to capture the essence of magical powers from different places, and all of it I channelled into the spell table. However, while doing so, I studied the magic of Eldarn, the lifeblood of our world, the energies and forces that ran through the very ground beneath our feet.'

'Weren't they in the spell table, too?' Garec asked. 'Would they have been lost when Steven broke it all to bits this morning?'

'Steven?' Mrs Winter raised her eyebrows. 'Would you do the honours, please?' She tossed the empty peach can towards the high dining room ceiling. Steven reached with one hand, captured the can in mid-flight and guided it gently back to the tabletop. There, the can crumpled itself into a compact silver ball and floated in a high arc, across the room, to land in a corner trashcan.

'Nice shot, buddy,' Mark said.

'It was,' Steven said, 'but that wasn't me.'

Mark held a hand out to Milla, who, uncertain what to do, simply stared at it.

'It's called a high-five, sweetie,' Mark whispered. 'Just give it a good whack.'

'All right,' Milla cried and wound herself up for a resonant slap.

'So you see, Garec,' Mrs Winter went on, 'the magic of Eldarn is alive and well. Granted, the spell table is lost, but with my writings and the purity of Steven and Milla's skills, I have great hopes for the next generation of Eldarn's Larion Senate.'

'All right, then,' Mark said, clearing the table, 'let's go.'

'Go where?' Jennifer said.

'To my parents' house,' he replied. 'They're about half an hour from here. We can stay there as long as we need to get our bearings and then, if that portal still works, we can go back, round up the key players and get busy. I don't envy us the task ahead, but screw it, we were able to come this far.'

'You think your parents will recognise you?' Jennifer asked. 'If they're anything like me, they've never given up hope, but seeing you like this, do you think they'll call the police and have you dragged off the lawn?'

'I'm trusting Steven and Milla to convince them,' Mark said.

'Very well,' Steven said, wrapping an arm around Hannah's waist. 'If we don't help them, who will?'

EPILOGUE

Crossroads

LINDEN TREES

Barrold Dayne adjusted his eye-patch and guided his horse along the line of partisans, resting now beside the thawing Falkan roadway. Spring was not yet in the air, but he could feel the frozen ground softening beneath his mount: it would be muddy going before they reached Orindale.

He felt good for the first time since leaving Capehill.

He spotted a lieutenant, a woman from Gorsk, giving curt orders to her platoon as they prepared a hasty meal by the roadside. Two soldiers, each laden with multiple leather skins, scrambled through a fallow field towards an irrigation pond a few hundred paces away, while others sifted through packs, cut strips of dried meat and sniffed dubiously at ageing blocks of cheese.

Seeing Barrold, the lieutenant asked, 'We going to be here long?'

'Probably overnight,' Barrold replied. 'We'll wait for the order from Gita, but I'm betting there's no need to rush.'

'What's up there?' She nodded toward the forward ranks. The Falkan Resistance had grown to nearly three thousand, not an army, but still one of the largest fighting forces mustered in the Eldarni Eastlands in generations.

'Get your crew settled, then take a ride up to that crossroads. You'll see.' Barrold didn't know if General Oaklen's infantry still held Rona or Orindale or southern Falkan; there had been no credible intelligence since Brand Krug's arrival. But the way the locals described it, the Malakasian exodus had been as swift as it had been unexpected. 'Where is she?' he asked.

'Back a bit, still trying to convince that group of farmhands they're needed here.'

'We could use them.'

'So could that farm; the bloody thing's bigger than any ten patches of greenroot we've got growing up in Gorsk, I can tell you.'

Barrold gave the woman a rare, tight-lipped smile, then urged his horse towards the tail-end of the partisan ranks.

Gita Kamrec had dismounted and was looking up into the faces of eight or nine young farmhands, mostly school-age boys, from the look of them. A few had worn canvas packs hefted over their shoulders, ready to march, and at least two carried field tools, the closest they could come to weaponry, Barrold guessed.

Gita, looking every bit this group's grandmother, was entreating them to return to their homes. '—And I really appreciate your sense of duty, boy, I do, and I am going to use you – just in a different way. Boys, *someone*'s got to feed us, and that *someone* is you – all of you. You're too important, all of you, to be running off to war with the spring Twinmoons only days away. Too important, and I don't want to hear another word about it. You get yourselves home. You listen to your planting bosses and your farm foremen. Feeding the people of Capehill is your job, and gods rut us all, I'll be back through this way, and I'll want to see that you're breaking your backs at it. Understand?'

A few of them offered a muffled *Yes, ma'am*, clearly disappointed.

Barrold smothered a laugh, then cleared his throat loudly to signal his presence.

Gita climbed into the saddle and turned to the boys again. 'I'm not joking, boys: we really do appreciate the offer, but you're needed far more where you are. So thank you again.' She watched the would-be soldiers shuffle dejectedly towards a large farmhouse at the far end of a field that looked big enough to feed a nation all by itself.

To Barrold, she said, 'What is it? And why are we making camp? There's still a half-aven of decent light left.'

'You need to see this, ma'am,' he said, and spurred his horse back through the ranks, Gita hard on his heels.

The naked linden trees at the crossroads were stark black against the setting sun, their skeletal branches an unanticipated break in the monotonous Falkan plain. They lined a dirt road leading away from the Merchants' Highway. Gita followed Barrold to the intersection, then reined in and shielded her eyes against the sun.

'Unholy mothers,' she whispered.

Hanging from every tree, for as far as Gita could see, were Malak-asian soldiers, officers, mostly. They dangled like macabre ornaments, sometimes two and three to a branch, all with makeshift signs around their necks spelling out their crimes against the Eldarni people. It was a massive tag hanging, that very same punishment the occupation army had used to keep Falkan's populace subdued for five generations.

The dead soldiers' naturally pale skin, bereft now of blood as well, matched the dusty beige hue of their ragged uniforms.

Some of the tags were misspelled; others looked to have been written in blood. Some had been nailed into the dead men's chests. Gita read a few of them:

Lieutenant, murderer.

Captain, rapist.

Corporal, thief.

Captain, killed my son.

Major, burned homes.

Lieutenant, rapist, murderer.

Gita sighed. 'Well, this answers six or seven of my nine hundred and thirteen questions.'

'What do you suppose happened?'

'I guess their men deserted, most likely, realised that they were over here alone.'

'And that's a long way from home, especially if you're all by your lonesome,' Barrold laughed. 'Good for them.'

'What I don't understand is how it happened – I mean, where are we? What's here? Who did this? Do you see another Resistance army out here anywhere? We're in the middle of nowhere; there's nothing but fallow fields and these few trees for as far as I can see.'

'Maybe they're up from Rona, or maybe it's Sallax's forces, following Oaklen up the Merchants' Highway.'

'Too many maybes,' Gita said. 'Well, regardless, I think the road to Orindale is going to be an interesting one, my friend. I'm sorry Sallax isn't here to see this.'

'This is his kind of entertainment.'

Gita took a last look at the corpses and said, 'Have them cut down. No rites. Just burn the bodies, over there in that field. I want us on our way again with the dawn aven.'

Barrold rode for the Falkan ranks, while Gita stared west into the fading twilight.

$6.3 MILLION

After his parents had finally stopped hugging him and gone to get some sleep, Mark joined Hannah and Steven on the porch. It had taken most of the afternoon to convince his mother and father that their son was actually living inside the body of a young sailor from another place and time. He had answered all their questions, esoteric facts that only Mark would know, but it was Milla, levitating and then rotating – gently – the family cat that finally convinced them something uncommon and wonderful was happening in their front room. The sight of their son, returned to them but not as he had been, ignited smouldering fires of protection deep inside Mr and Mrs Jenkins. They had wept openly, without embarrassment, desperately clinging to him, as if trying to keep him safe from whatever horrors might be lurking in the suburban streets outside. Like Jennifer Sorenson, they refused to entertain any discussion that involved his return to Eldarn and after a while, Mark let the conversation drop, content to address it with them in private, after they had had a few days to get used to his return.

Now Mark pulled on his coat and, after checking several times beneath a porch chair, leant against the railing.

Steven asked, 'You lose something?'

'No,' Mark checked the chair again, 'just looking for snakes.'

Hannah laughed. 'Snakes? Are you kidding? It's freezing out here.'

'I know. I just think ... well, I'm going to be a bit gun-shy around snakes for a while, a few decades, maybe.'

'Anything we can do?' Steven asked.

'Nope,' Mark replied, 'just shout if you see anything poisonous slithering up behind me.'

'Done,' Hannah said. 'I'll take the first watch.'

Mark stared across the sleepy island neighbourhood. 'How did we get here?' he whispered.

Hannah took his arm. 'For starters, Steven robbed the bank. After that, it was all an unstoppable rollercoaster ride for me.'

'Hey,' Steven defended himself, 'I was always going to put that stuff back. It was just a little curiosity.'

'Any way we can get our hands on the money?' Mark huffed out a wintry cloud over the driveway. 'Old whatshisname's, Haggerty's?'

'Higgins,' Steven said. 'William Higgins, and if I'm not mistaken, I damned his soul to eternity inside the Fold, so I think we probably ought to leave his money alone.'

'How much was he worth?' Hannah asked.

'Six point three million dollars,' Steven said.

'Holy cats. He did well, didn't he?'

'It was Nerak,' Steven said. 'He opened the account with silver he stole from hard-working miners, William Higgins included, in Oro City – Leadville.'

'We could do a lot with that money, Steven,' Mark said. 'It would get us rolling in Eldarn. There's a lot we could bring through the portals with six million and change.'

'We don't need money,' Steven muttered, 'we need to be able to bring Lessek back with us. We need Gilmour or Alen. Gilmour would be better, because Alen was in hiding for so long. Gilmour knows more about Eldarn and Eldarni culture than anyone – sorry, he *knew* more about it.'

'It doesn't make sense,' Mark said, 'him and Alen living all that time and then dying five minutes apart.'

Steven whispered, 'Get them going and they'll go on for ever, like the Twinmoons, or the fountains at Sandcliff.'

'What's that?'

'Just something Gilmour used to say.' He shrugged. 'It was time, I guess. Lessek let them go; he let a very old spell spin itself out ... or maybe it was me.'

Hannah kissed him lightly. 'You can't blame yourself for Gilmour. No one could have done what you did today. You heard Lessek; everything had to be perfect. Everything had its place and yours was there, standing down that creature, the minion trying to open the Fold. The rest of us would have been swept away in its wake. You knew where it was coming and you knew what to do. Gilmour would have been proud of you.'

'He was,' Mark added, 'I'm sure of it.'

'We need him,' Steven said. 'We need his knowledge; we're lost, just groping about in the dark without him. We don't know the people, except for Gita. We don't know the cities, the industries, the

...chers, the business owners, the merchants. We're starting off, what, ten, maybe even twenty years behind without him.'

'But we have to do it,' Mark said to the empty yard. 'It will be the defining achievement of our lives.'

'Unless we get the shit kicked out of us,' Hannah said.

'Unless that, of course.' Mark chuckled. 'And I think there's a good chance of that happening, probably more than once. Hey, do either of you want anything before I go to bed? I'm pretty tired. Except for those few minutes this morning, I don't think I've really slept in two months.'

'Nothing for me,' Hannah said. Steven didn't answer.

'What about you, Stevo?'

'Look at that,' Steven whispered to himself.

'At what?' Hannah said, sliding under his arm.

'Down the block, just over there, behind those elms.' He pointed. Hannah and Mark followed his gaze towards the dimly lit sidewalk.

'Sonofabitch,' he whispered.

An elderly man made his way hurriedly towards them. He was tall and gangly, dressed in a worn overcoat buckled at the waist. His balding pate reflected the streetlights like polished marble.

'Who? That old dude?' Mark said. 'He'd better get inside; he'll freeze out here tonight dressed like that.'

'Do you recognise him?' Steven asked urgently. 'Is he somebody who lives on this block?'

Mark squinted. 'Christ, but this sailor's eyesight was shit.' He leaned over the porch rail. 'Nope, don't know him.'

'I do,' Steven said, smiling. He pulled Hannah close and kissed her hard, then laughed. 'My friends,' Steven said into the night, 'things are looking up.'

'What are you up to, sailor?' Hannah asked, moving even closer to him. 'Things are not up yet,' she whispered, sliding her hips forward, 'but there's definite potential.'

'Slut,' Steven teased. He looked longingly at her and felt his very soul lighten as he shouted towards the street, 'Things are looking up! Aren't they?'

The old man leaped the fence and started up the driveway. 'I must learn to operate one of these automobiles. It's gods-rutting cold here,' he grumbled.

THE END